Sojourn at Dusk

Eve Ottenberg

Plain View Press
http://plainviewpress.net

3800 N. Lamar, Suite 730-260
Austin, TX 78756

ISBN: 978-1-935514-63-3
Library of Congress Control Number: 2012950153

Cover art: Photograph by Lon Casler Bixby with permission
         http://www.lcbphotography.com/
Cover design by Pam Knight

Disclaimer: All characters in this book are fictitious, and any resemblance to real persons, living or dead, is coincidental.

For Nicholas, Madeleine and Jasmine

"And even if you found yourself in some prison, whose walls let in none of the world's sounds – wouldn't you still have your childhood, that jewel beyond all price, that treasure house of memories? Turn your attention to it. Try to raise up the sunken feelings of this enormous past; your personality will grow stronger, your solitude will expand and become a place where you can live in the twilight, where the noise of other people passes by, far in the distance."

– Rainer Maria Rilke, Letters to a Young Poet

Contents

I

Mid-Century

In 1950, when Eileen Meer was a baby, her father, Lester, an ardent communist who worked for the Port Authority of New York, narrowly escaped arrest by detectives who had, among other incontrovertible evidence, photographs of him at a meeting with certain members of the longshoreman's union, known Reds. Lester lit out for Mexico and then more exotic parts farther south in Latin America, leaving his wife, Annabelle, a lithe young beauty from South Carolina, somewhat stranded in their attractive, two-story, New Rochelle home. He sent money; she worked, baby Eileen was packed off to the Lichter's down the quiet, shady street. Lily Lichter was Annabelle's closest friend from Charleston, and in fact it had been Lily's enthusiastic description of her comfortable and bosky neighborhood that had enticed the unlucky couple to quit their twelfth-story, rent-controlled aerie, amid the towers of Manhattan, and move there in the first place. The baby girl retained no early childhood memories of her father. Instead she remembered tall, dark-haired Morris Lichter, gentle, funny and full of ridiculous jokes and even magic tricks; an unlikely advertising executive who loved to shower sweets upon children. In the two years that Lily watched the baby girl along with her own growing family, Eileen eagerly awaited Morris' evening return home and the lollipops that invariably accompanied him. She liked green best and would scoot around the front patio, dodging the brightly colored butterfly chairs with the other girls, Naomi and Coralie, Daphne still an infant indoors, all three slurping happily. Then mommy would stroll tiredly up the walk, perspiring in the summer heat, but still a nattily attired local government employee, and give her a hug. She always stayed for a cocktail with her friends before transporting her daughter back to a home whose emptiness since the rather dynamic Lester's disappearance she had sought to decrease by taking in two, unfortunately rather drab, female roommates. This, along with checks from her parents, helped pay the mortgage. Money was tight, but the young wife was smart—smart enough to keep up with her payments, smart enough to outwit the gumshoes who dogged her in the hopes of snaring her husband. She determined not to let that happen, and it never did.

From Mexico, the peregrinating revolutionary moved on to Colombia, then Ecuador. He spoke Spanish fluently, and indeed Catalan, since his mother hailed from Barcelona, and he found work through the party. He was utterly committed to communist revolution, an ambition in which his wife had never shared, though certainly did not disapprove of. He settled at last in Lima, with work and a large apartment in the "gringo's quarter," living under the assumed name of Leon Rathman, and spoke to his spouse at a pay telephone every month. Eileen knew none of this until years later, when it all took on a rather legendary significance for her. But as a child, her father was as insubstantial as a ghost, and it was only when someone in junior high called her a "pinko" that she realized he could still be made to be a part of her life. She never missed him, because she had never known him. Harried, distracted, but superbly organized Annabelle was her world, her tall, light-haired mother, giving to gazing abstractly, with a touch of melancholy, out the window during meals, along with the Lichters, who to young Eileen seemed to symbolize life itself; and of course, who could forget the Lichters' ever fantastically multiplying menagerie of pets? Also there were yearly hegiras to South Carolina and her grandparents, a tall, elegant, silver-haired matched pair, who vociferously kept after their mysteriously stubborn daughter to divorce and remarry. But Annabelle let it be known that although she hesitated to relocate to the mountains and coast of Lima—which her spouse rarely described to her, focused as he was on the city's pullulating slums—she would never abandon her husband, no matter what strange path destiny planted his feet upon and that only the grave could cleave their entwined hearts.

From New Rochelle, they moved to a smaller house, shaded by a magnificent Elm, in Summit, New Jersey, where the little girl attended kindergarten. Her mother snagged a job in the county government, and they rented out the third bedroom in their somewhat cramped, two-story house to a secretary, who commuted to her job at a legal publishing firm in Newark. Annabelle Meer had made a little money from the move, so the constant worry about funds decreased. Trees lined their street, birds sang in the branches, neighbors in this bedroom suburb of Manhattan were friendly, and teenage babysitters plentiful. One such, Michelle, picked the kindergartener up after school every day and watched her for a pittance, all afternoon until six pm. Eileen played out back, rescuing earthworms stranded after a rain on the little concrete path through the blossoming bushes or picking azaleas to put in a vase inside. Once, climbing the dogwood tree, she found a brown, twiggy robin's nest with little blue eggs inside. She did not touch them, because she knew that then the mother would abandon them, and perhaps fly off to Lima to work for the communist party like her father. However, she checked on them regularly, to make sure they received proper care and celebrated when the hairy, pinkish babies hatched.

One afternoon, the sitter marched out back with an ice cream sandwich for her. "There's a man at the front door, asking about your father. I think he's a policeman. He wants to talk to you."

"I don't remember my father," the little girl told the detective, who smelled cloyingly of aftershave.

"But you would know if he called the house."

"I don't know. But I don't think he ever has," something impalpable but definite prompted her to omit mention of the times she sat in the Chevy, while her mother stood in a pay telephone booth, talking.

"We believe he is in Venezuela."

"Where's that?"

The man sighed in exasperation. "Do any men ever call the house?"

The little girl shook her head solemnly.

"Next time I come by, you tell me if they do. It's our little secret."

She glanced at the tall, conventionally handsome and neatly dressed detective, who smelled so annoyingly artificial. She did not want secrets with him, because something whispered that he was not a friend, but that something also told her she had better agree. So she did, and blessedly, he left.

"A man came about Daddy," she told her mother that evening, as they ate their spaghetti and meatballs in the dining nook, a red plastic booth, in the kitchen. Annabelle stopped eating, her fork raised with the noodles dangling sloppily off it. Fear flashed in her ordinarily even blue eyes.

"I didn't tell him anything," the little girl went on. "He was icky. He smelled like sharp perfume, and he wanted to keep secrets with me. I don't even know him. I'm not going to keep secrets with him about you and Daddy."

As they sat in the booth by the window, the shadows seemed suddenly to lengthen and dusk to grow darker and the abyss that separated the members of their family widened and deepened. The child longed to reach across it to her absent parent, but could think of no way to do so.

"You did the right thing," Mrs. Meer said. "Be sure to let me know if he ever comes here again—him or anyone like him. And do what you did today. Don't tell them anything."

They ate their spaghetti in silence, the gloom thickened and entombed the house in a lonely quiet that filled their minds with absences and abandonments. "Do you think we'll ever see Daddy again?" the child asked.

"I don't know," her mother replied, with a glance at her more forlorn than Eileen had hitherto observed.

The last few weeks before kindergarten, the little girl's dark brown hair, which she inherited from her father, who got it from his Spanish mother, had finally grown long enough for Annabelle to braid into two pigtails. Eileen loved this; at last her thick hair no longer coated and clung to the back of her neck, so damp and sweaty in the late August New Jersey heat. Every morning she would perch on a footstool in the bright, sunny living room, while her mother leaned forward from the armchair and deftly braided her hair. Then, in her shorts, cotton sleeveless shirt, socks and Keds, she would race outside to commence her morning activity—riding her red bicycle with the training wheels back and forth on the sun and shade-dappled street beneath the huge Elm in front of the house. In the afternoon, the sitter languidly supervised, while the mother was at work. Sometimes Michelle, on her own bicycle would lead a tour of the neighborhood. Down the block, the McCormack kids often had a lemonade stand, in anticipation of which, Eileen dunned her mother for nickels and dimes. Then she and the sitter would stand in the shade of a maple, balancing their bikes, guzzling lemonade beside the flimsy card table, eyeing the glass pitcher with its pale yellow liquid that glistened like the elixir of eternal life and demanding free refills. Johnny McCormack, aged ten, usually capitulated, though he made it clear to his younger neighbor that this was only due to the presence of a teenager. Had she come alone, Eileen was quite sure she would have had to pay for seconds. She could not wait to be fifteen like her sitter and have people defer to her.

Once or twice she and Michelle bicycled so far they came to the train tracks that stretched away seemingly to nowhere, in their strangely desolate silence that proclaimed, amid shimmering waves of heat, their disuse, as if they were the particular haunt of no one; yet another time they reached the dusty highway, but they generally steered away from such, staying in the more peopled shade of the little, tree-lined streets, with their hedges, well trimmed lawns and perfectly weeded flower beds. Occasionally, a dog would chase them, but as soon as ever-responsible Michelle recognized her charge's deathly fear of these animals, she kept stones in her shorts pockets, which she would pitch at the offending canine. She always hit the mutt on the nose, and it always backed off, whimpering. If not in the wider world, which claimed people for inexplicable reasons, exiled them to countries distant beyond imagining and concealed those, blood-bound, from each other, in an ever-expanding realm of shadow, the little girl nonetheless felt very safe with her sitter.

Mid-afternoons in summer, the northern New Jersey heat lay oppressively on the town, steamy, humid, like a hot, damp blanket smothering anything that moved. The five-year-old passed this time of day in her sitter's basement rec room, watching TV, eating Oreos and drinking milk. Sometimes Mrs. McCleod, willowy but with a touch of the athletic, like her daughter, would join them, admonishing them to keep their feet off the polished coffee table and their cookie crumbs off the carpet. It was too infernally hot to garden, she would complain, and she did not want to mend or cook, so she would lounge for an hour with the two girls in the underground cool, chatting about movie stars, before returning to her chores. The youngsters pushed the panting cats off their laps. It was too hot.

Depending on the weather, Eileen either walked or rode the bus to kindergarten. On foot, she accompanied a noisy troop of other local children, the McCormacks, Willoughbys and her sitter's much younger brother. They would trek along leafy lanes, carrying their books and supplies in little satchels, comparing notes on the exaggerated savageries of their teachers. Eileen loved her teacher, Miss Alones, and especially circle time in the morning. Miss Alones wore full skirts, cinched at the waist, and her beautiful, light brown hair up in a French twist, while her eyes sometimes glimmered at Eileen, like windows into a hidden world of wisdom and wonder. What was that strange, occasional glimmer, that aliveness, that irrefutable trace of a light and a power from somewhere else? Whatever it was, the child instinctively loved it and indeed her heart leapt, whenever she observed it. Miss Alones taught them their alphabet, which Eileen was surprised to see many students did not know—all the letter sounds, how to count to one hundred, and counting by fives, tens and twos. But mostly Miss Alones opened the door to a world of human goodness, a fragile haven where all was secure and accounted for and none vanished, none changed, none walked out the door into absence and unknowing and darkness.

Once or twice in the sitter's absence, Annabelle left work early to fetch her daughter and bring her to the library, where Eileen dawdled in the children's section, perusing books and magazines, while her mother completed office paperwork in the quieter reading room. Unbeknownst to Annabelle, her daughter was perfectly well aware that her mother checked on her regularly.

Two or three other, somewhat older children passed the late afternoon in this gaily cluttered library section, waiting for a harried parent to get off work, and Eileen knew them all. They attended the same public elementary school and agreed that Miss Alones was the best teacher, not like Mrs.

Bluestone in the second grade, who told anyone in the class who did not believe in God to please stand up. The poor idiots who did so soon found themselves with markedly lower grades. Miss Alones would never do anything like that. She did not interrogate, but was, instead, all mildness and gentleness and tolerance, whose being nonetheless seemed to tremble on the edge of something else, something full of splendor and mystery that she transmitted to her little flock, a gift for them, for their entire lives. She treated all her students equally, fairly and as if each was endowed with a unique and inestimable worth. After a few weeks she brought in her favorite book—the paintings of John James Audubon—and showed the timeless pictures of birds to the marveling students. Doves, sparrows, every kind of finch—ordinary and exotic birds filled the pages, which impressed their perfectly colored images so indelibly upon the children's minds that years later they could still easily be recalled, and indeed years later Eileen thought she encountered her favorite, the blue jay, incarnate, straight from the pages of that unforgettable book, when it crashed into a picture window of a friend's country house in winter, fell bleeding into the snow, but then, a half an hour later, by some miracle restored, raised its head and flew off.

For Halloween she dressed up as a bride, wearing a white, lacy costume that came in a box with a cellophane panel. You could look through and see the white dress, but most captivating was the gaudy, glittering, rhinestone necklace. Years after the costume had vanished, she retained that necklace, which never forfeited its luster, and when she finally lost it, considered it a bad omen. Anyway, appareled as a bride, her fake diamonds sparkling gloriously, she participated in the Halloween parade out onto the junior high playing field and up into the bleachers, where they all belted out "The Star Spangled Banner," sat and listened to the principal mumble patriotic platitudes into a screeching microphone, then paraded around again to show off their finery to an appreciative audience of parents.

In winter she rode the school bus. But even then, waiting at the top of the hill on January mornings in the drizzling sleet, her bare legs shivered under her skirt, her numb fingers clutched her little umbrella, and her toes buried under socks inside her galoshes had lost all sensation. She stamped the ground to warm her feet.

"I bet it's not like this where Daddy is," she lamented.

"Probably not, though he says it's very cool in the evenings."

"I want to go to the Andes."

"Shh. Here come the Willoughbys."

"I want to talk about him."

"Not now, but later. I promise."

Somehow later never came, even though the solitary wife was sorely tempted to chuck it all, take her daughter, vanish into the crumbling cities of South America and reunite with her husband; a step from which, however, she knew there would be no return. Lester did not wish her to make an irrevocable decision. On this he was adamant, and since there existed also the distinct possibility that he might defect outright to the Soviet Union, she hesitated. She was quite aware of global political realities in the early 1950s and had absolutely no desire to live in Russia. Peru, perhaps. But the next move was a step too far for her, and one which, for her husband, she regarded as an act of insanity, though she held her tongue and let him pile his specious reasons, one atop the other, into what he called an irrefutable mountain of truth. To her it was the garish rubble of chaos, of their destroyed family life and of her daughter's prospects for normalcy. So she did not discuss her absent spouse. It was too painful.

That spring the little girl met her prodigal parent over the phone. It was a warm and humid June twilight, with pale, hopeless, celestial streaks of sunlight scarcely illuminating the earth any better than the drowsy fireflies against the encroaching darkness, when they set out in their Chevrolet for Newark. Annabelle did not drive directly there, but followed back roads, until they reached a gray, ugly little city, settling like a squat goblin into advancing night, and drove about ten blocks from the train station. They parked on a side-street, exiting the car to traverse cracked, crooked pavement speckled with dog turds and litter. As they opened the door of a glass phone booth, the telephone rang. It was Lester. The tearful woman spoke to her husband, before handing the receiver to her child.

"Daddy, daddy," the little girl cried. "What are you like?"

Periodically they would visit their good friends, the Lichters. If they went just for a Saturday or a Sunday, they would sojourn over in their black 1949 Chevrolet sedan, but if they planned to visit for the night, they took the train Saturday morning into Manhattan, and then splurged on a taxi to Grand Central—or, if Annabelle felt financially pinched, they took the subway. From there they trained out to Westchester, where Lily gathered them up in her white and yellow 1953 Ford. Eileen loved everything about these excursions, from the springy cushions on the commuter trains, to the fake fabric on the subway seats, but best was the roar and throng of Grand Central terminal itself. Holding her mother's hand, as they waited in line for tickets, the child would survey the vast, airy, sun-filled atrium with milling hordes, in awe at the numbers of humanity and wondering where all these important people were going.

"Probably Saturday shopping in Manhattan," her mother explained and, since they had time, bought her a chocolate ice cream cone.

"But men don't shop. And there are lots of men in suits."

"Where did you get the idea men don't shop?"

"I just know it," slurp, slurp on the ice cream cone.

"They shop. There are even stores that are just for men, like Brooks Brothers," Annabelle drawled in her South Carolina accent that, though modified, had not vanished.

"Did they shop in Charleston?"

"Of course. That and play golf at the country clubs were 'bout all they did."

"Did Daddy shop when you met him at college?"

Her mother nodded.

"There's an older kid at my school, a friend of Tommy McCormack's in the fourth grade, who said my Dad's a Red."

"That's right."

"You're not worried about it?"

"I guess if I had been, you wouldn't be here, sweetie."

The ice cream cone was in the molten phase, so the child had to lick it quickly, before the drips got on her hands and made them sticky, but, too late, she was a mess, so they had to go to the ladies room to wash up. As they left, her mother tipped the woman who stood by the door, dark and silent and worn and as motionless as a ancient, black marble statue, and Eileen asked why.

"She keeps the bathroom clean," her mother explained.

"Is that fun?"

"Not very."

They ambled over to the gate and boarded their train. Tunnels, apartment buildings, a long dead space without much in it, all these rushed by, and soon they were speeding through trees, parks, past attractive suburban homes.

"This is prettier than New Jersey," the little girl commented.

"Everything is," her parent sourly replied.

Her old friend met them at the station with her three little girls. The boys had stayed home with Morris. Coralie, the oldest girl, and Eileen could play for hours; they climbed the maple and cherry trees out back, rode bikes, dressed the dolls in the basement rec room and pulled each other up the driveway in a battered red wagon. Sometimes Naomi, with the strangely exotic eyes, eyes almost like Miss Alone's, eyes that glimmered out at you with some unexpected intelligence—sometimes she joined them, but she was only three and a half and could not be included in everything. Daphne was a baby, still in diapers.

Crawling between the gray stones of the back wall and the bushes to a secret hiding place, Eileen blurted out that she wanted her father.

"But he can't come home," Coralie said matter-of-factly, as they settled into their hidden cranny. "He'll go to jail."

"Maybe not. Mommy says maybe not."

"I don't understand what he did wrong to begin with. Mom explained it, but it doesn't make sense."

"He doesn't believe in the American way," Eileen parroted something she had heard from an older child. "He's not a good American."

"Can they put you in jail for that?"

"I guess so."

"How do you think they know?"

"What?"

"If you're a good American?" Coralie's forehead furrowed in worry. "I don't want to go to jail."

Eileen dug in the dirt, collecting chips of mica. "I guess we'll find out," she said at length.

Naomi Lichter always remained acutely conscious that her birth in 1950 coincided with the exact mid-point of the twentieth century. Not that it had some occult meaning for her, nor that she was superstitious. Indeed, unlike many other members of her generation, she never succumbed to the allure of astrology, the I Ching, or any Eastern religious sect, regarding these interests partly as hocus pocus and partly as dangerous distractions from the earth-shaking forces that had riven her era, starting in her teenage years, between old and young, right and left, war and peace. She believed in the mass political movements of the 1960s and 1970s and saw her birth and those of her friends mid-century as most fortuitous, allowing them to ride a tidal wave of revolution into the future. Even as a child, growing up in New Rochelle, she considered her birth year special, just as she knew that the decade that followed was a paradise of affluence and innocence—a false paradise, she later said, a world of illusion, but saying so did not mesh well with her memories, with the particular reality she had experienced and could not, despite her words, deny. For she recalled her childhood in the 1950s as a time of unparalleled comfort, safety and wonder at the world and nature, a wonder constantly rewarded by many small unforgettable experiences, such as the time, on her fifth birthday, when she rode her bicycle along the flagstone path, bordered by red and purple petunias, which led to the protective embrace of her house, and said aloud "I am five today," to which the gracefully swooping and blooming branches of the cherry tree on the front lawn swayed over her, in clouds of pink and white, dappling her in light and shadow and the presence of she knew not what, a something or someone who had more than noted her words. Or there were the rains, the delicate, fragrant downpours of the Westchester suburbs that she and her younger sister celebrated sitting in the little space between the screen door and the front door, with their small blankets, talking and breathing in the indescribably splendid smell of wet plants, damp earth and water traversing flower-perfumed air. She could, later, call it an era of repression, of false security marred by many, many flaws, social and political, but she could never deny the reality of her memories, of their existence, objective, almost separate from her, alive.

In addition to the six noisy Lichter children with their rather overtaxed mother from South Carolina and often befuddled father, who commuted to an advertising job in Manhattan, there was a mammoth menagerie of pets: two dogs, two cats, several kittens, a guinea pig, two rabbits in a hutch, mice in a cage, a terrarium with turtles and salamanders, and frequently dying fish. In moments of exasperation at the children who did not take care of these pets, Lily Lichter would threaten to let all the animals loose in the wooded and, the children were convinced, haunted lot that bordered their property—an announcement invariably greeted with howls of alarm from the seven-year-old down to the baby in diapers, who hollered because all his brothers and sisters were doing so. Naomi first became aware of this possibility of losing her precious cat at the age of three and would clutch Honeybunch so tightly that the feline would screech and claw. She liked animals better than people, she told her mother, because they did not take your toys away, like the oldest, Tommy, who snatched away her dolls, blocks, Honeybunch, food, and candy, without any provocation. Sometimes she thought she hated Tommy, and when his younger brother, Louis, punched him in the nose and made him bleed, she clapped her baby hands so gleefully in such evident delight that she was sent to her room for being "a horrid little girl."

That, however, was the only punishment she could recollect from childhood. Neither her mother nor father ever laid a hand on her, though they did raise their voices. The children basically tumbled around the big Tudor house, with its large yards, front and back, maples and cherry trees, azalea, hydrangea and forsythia bushes and the dark tangle of trees, vines and undergrowth next door, under Lily's watchful eye. When they did notice their mother standing alertly at the front window, they might wonder what she was staring at: it never occurred to them that it was her children. Once when a man stopped a car to talk to Naomi, she was amazed at how quickly her mother appeared at her side. The man instantly drove off.

They were not allowed in the green copse next-door alone, only in groups. It was a large tract, slated for subdivisions, but somehow had not yet been developed, whose denizens included ghouls and zombies, often descried lurking in the shadows and which also contained a gully with a stream full of glimmering frogs, salamanders and little fish. Tommy said they were minnows and tried to catch them in a blue plastic bucket. He was going to make her eat them, he threatened, to which Naomi merely stuck out her tongue and taunted "try and make me." Vines hung from trees, on which the children swung over the silvery little stream, screaming "Tarzan!" The boys peed so proudly in the woods that the girls took to squatting in the underbrush, instead of running home to the bathroom, which occasioned frequent astonished comments from their mother about the presence of leaves and other flora in their underwear.

Once the three little sisters pretended they were lost in this deep forest, impossible of course, as they knew every square foot of it, but they had detected ghosts, goblins and wolves, like *Peter and the Wolf*, and witches, like *Hansel and Gretel*. So they shouted "Hello! Hello! Tommy, Louis where are you? We're lost, and a witch turned Daphne into a rabbit." Whereupon the two older boys appeared, one armed with an amateur slingshot and demanding to know the whereabouts of his foe, the witch, and the other giving Daphne sidelong glances and muttering, "Some rabbit." At length, the sweltering August heat led to the abandonment of these fascinating supernatural adversaries and sent them running back in a sweaty mass to the cool house, with lemonade, cookies and cartoons on TV in the even cooler, wood-paneled basement. Sometimes when the boys weren't there, they watched American Bandstand and danced along. The Lichters' basement was the most popular dance studio in the neighborhood for little girls under the age of eight.

Up the street the Sloanes had a popular dance cellar as well. Naomi and Samantha Sloane spent hours there gyrating to popular music before racing out back to crawl through the dirt down the secret passage along the stone wall separating the Sloane's property from the Solito's. The two girls spent hours in this hideaway, staining their grimy fingers purple, while eating cherries from the tree overhanging the wall and collecting snails for Sam's brother. "Snails in a pail," they called it. These hours were supposed to be spent practicing the recorder, which musical instrument both had taken up at age five and which required weekly lessons a few blocks away with their teacher, Mrs. Kaplan, and several other little girls, to practice their ditties in the stucco house, cool and shaded, with most curtains drawn and lights dimmed. They were laboring over "Row, row, row your boat," and supposedly Naomi visited the Sloane's to practice with her friend. However, they played hooky instead—they danced, explored, compared bellybuttons, dressed dolls, drew and then, one fateful day, decided to ride tricycles down the steep street to the Lichter's. They tore down the hill far too fast, and Naomi lost control and had no time even to fear, as she saw her alarmed mother running out of the house, just before her trike tipped and she banged her head on the curb.

She awoke in the comfort of her parents' room, on a little divan, an ice pack on her head, with her brothers and sisters watching "Captain Kangaroo" on television.

"Thank God she's conscious again," she heard her mother's voice.

Morris Lichter approached tentatively, as if wondering whether she recognized him.

"You've been out a few hours," he said. "Does your head hurt?"

"No."

"Follow my finger." His raised index finger moved from left to right before her face. "Is it blurry?"

"No. Of course not," the girl was annoyed. "I want to watch Captain Kangaroo."

"Stay where you are. The doctor said to take it easy. We'll bring you a burger right here, if you're hungry."

"From now on, you practice your recorder in *this* house," her mother ordered, exiting to the kitchen. "You're too big for a tricycle anyway, and you know it."

Then she remembered what had happened. "Hey," she hollered to her departing father, "I got knocked out. I got a bump. Will I get over it?"

"You may, I won't" he said and followed his wife downstairs.

She realized she could have died. With her would have vanished her earliest memories—of sitting in the high chair of the supermarket cart, as her mother pushed it through the produce section, the oranges, pears, apples, which she reached out for eagerly but unsuccessfully, or of toddling up the Sloane's driveway with some other three year olds, eating pears whose juice cooled them on that hot summer afternoon even as it dribbled down her hands, wrists and arms—these and others so important to her would have disappeared forever if she had perished. The thought made her sit up, and though dizzy, she called to her older sister: "Hey remember the day we ate pears in the Sloane's driveway and got all wet and sticky?"

"Uh-hunh."

"Don't forget."

"Why not?" Coralie asked, not turning away from Captain Kangaroo.

"Because it's important. We did it. We should remember."

Later that summer before kindergarten, the Jacksons up the street, at the top of another hill, had cousins stay with them from North Carolina. Naomi permitted herself, like Sam, to be bossed around by the oldest girl, Mimi, who was nine. Mimi organized bicycle and tricycle races, first on their street, then down hills, any street on any hill she could find, the steeper the better. Naomi found this girl's wild abandon fearsome, while she herself, still mindful of her recent fall, felt the tricycle shimmy under her at unaccustomed speeds with a new trepidation.

"Chicken," Mimi called to the others when they balked at a dangerously high incline. But the five year olds would not budge and retreated instead to hunt magical creatures in the woods. Word came later from Coralie, who ran, puffing and sweating to where they swooped on vines, pretending to fly like fairies, but rather out of character and most indelicately hollering their lungs out, that Mimi, roaring down the hill on a trike with no hands, had fallen off, knocked out a tooth and gotten all scratched up and bruised. There was lots of blood. Maybe even she had gone to the hospital.

"The hopsital," repeated four-year-old Daphne, clinging to her sister's hand.

"No stupid, You say hos-pi-tal."

"Hopsital."

After that, they never saw Mimi again. She was not allowed to play on the street, and shortly after her accident, her family returned to the South.

"I wonder which tooth," Naomi would always say when the subject came up.

"It was a big one in front. And they gave her a gold replacement," Sam would regularly prevaricate.

"How do you know?"

"I saw."

"Did not."

"Did too."

This conversation was repeated more times than anybody cared to count, especially adults, from whom it elicited groans of "no, no, not this again," and frequently in front of an older girl, Jeanine, charged with constant supervision of her retarded younger brother, Melvin.

"You sound like Mel," she would say. "The same thing, over and over."

"Mel doesn't talk," Naomi corrected.

"You just haven't heard him. But he loves to repeat himself."

"Say 'gold tooth,' Melvin," Sam commanded. But the little boy just looked at her out of slightly slanted, mild blue eyes and said nothing. They stood in an empty, weedy, trash-strewn lot, where the grass grew over their heads. Jeanine whacked it with a stick. "I'm clearing the land to build my castle," she explained. "I'm a witch, and this will be my fortress. From here I'll command all the lands around me, as far as I can see. You three are my slaves."

"What do you want us to do?" the two little girls chanted.

"Go pick those white flowers and put them in this cauldron," she held out a pink plastic beach pail to the girls. "We are going to make a powerful potion that will put everyone in New Rochelle to sleep." This servitude to the witch Jeanine lasted throughout the summer.

In the depths of a broiling July, the Lichter children got a new sitter, a slightly squat, rather muscular, teenage girl from up the street, who arrived at dusk and, after the parents had departed, invited friends over to lounge in the butterfly chairs on the front patio and smoke cigarettes. Naomi, spying from her second story bedroom window, saw girls and boys kissing, inhaled the not totally displeasing odor of cigarettes and watched the visitors drink beer. The thick, moist blanket of heat and humidity that lay over the neighborhood at twilight did not seem to bother the teenagers who laughed, shouted and cavorted in the deep shadows on the front lawn. Soon it grew dark. Fireflies came out, the lonely longing of their hopeful little lights illuminating nothing. Silence spread from house to house, but not to the Lichter's, where the hubbub continued far into the night.

"How was Mary Beth?" Lily inquired the next morning.

One daughter shrugged.

"They were kissing," the baby enlightened her mother.

"Who?"

"The boys and the girls. And smoking."

A sharp light entered the mother's eyes. "Where?"

"On the front patio."

Lily stepped out and glanced around. She quickly discovered cigarette butts and two beer bottles in the bushes. "I'm calling her mother," she said, removing her finds to the trash. That was the last time that teenager babysat for them.

"Tattletale," she called Naomi once when they passed on the street.

"It wasn't me," Naomi apologized. "I didn't say anything."

The teenager tossed her brown hair dismissively and climbed onto the handlebars of her boyfriend's bike, before he pedaled them away.

The next sitter was an O'Brien girl, one of the older of their eleven children who had not become a nun. Molly did not smoke, drink or invite boys over. She played board games with the children or made peanut butter and jelly sandwiches with potato chips on the side, gave them ginger ale to drink and settled with them into their parents' large, darkened bedroom to watch TV. After a few weeks of this, Lily complained of ants. Nobody could fathom this mystery. Eventually, however, a child left a telltale sandwich crust on his parent' bed, and that one crust, which somehow escaped Molly's eagle eye when cleaning up, led to the exposure of the vast quantities of evening snacks consumed in the Lichter's bedroom. "It's a wonder we don't have ants the size of trucks," their mother exclaimed.

"Oh but we do," Coralie enlightened her. "Last night Molly saw one as thick as her finger. It walked straight from the TV onto her plate of chips."

The sitter was forbidden to feed the children anywhere outside the kitchen, however, a food/bug crisis soon developed there as well. At first the mother considered the sitter perhaps responsible again, but soon learned the truth behind this invasive pest enigma: every summer evening, when the children lurched in, panting and sweaty from street kickball, always unwillingly, always with loud laments, sometimes even screaming in protest, they were forced to eat their entire dinner, including the vegetables, before returning to the game. If they did not dine quickly, the match could of course end before they made it back. However, Naomi loathed vegetables and soon found herself missing many a game. Then one night the situation became simply intolerable: her mother placed on the Formica kitchen table a serving dish of what at first appeared to be dark brown slabs of an indeterminate meat, but was soon revealed by its disgusting aroma to be liver. Liver! The meat was, in the girl's view, unspeakable, nauseating, and beside it stood a steaming bowl of string beans, also abominable. Her speedy return to kickball was doomed, a game for which her child's heart beat in fierce competition, and, to make matters worse, her team had been winning. Measures had to be taken at once. So, while her father excused himself to the bathroom and her mother's back was turned, Naomi grabbed the revoltingly slimy liver off her plate and stuffed it down the back of the booth in which she sat. The she swiftly snatched her scalding string beans and did the same, so quickly she did not even get burned. She was doodling around with her mashed potatoes, when her parents noticed that she had nearly cleaned her plate. Amid their congratulations, she was permitted to return to kickball.

And so it went for several weeks. At the first opportunity, the young girl would dispose of her vegetables and organ meat and flounce back to kickball. It was a wonderful arrangement, except for the telltale ants, which began to swarm up the side of the booth, straight toward Naomi's seat. Observing this dauntingly large and determined formic squad one night, while his daughter frolicked outside, Morris lifted the seat cushion, peered into the bottom of the booth and discerned an ant-covered mound of rotting food. The guilty child was summoned, scolded, banned from kickball for the rest of the week, and her place was moved from the booth to a chair.

Morris Lichter worked hard. He rose at five-thirty am, in time to catch the seven fifteen train that clattered to Manhattan. He handled many accounts for many corporations, rushed around to meetings, was on the phone, took executives to lunch, approved ad campaigns and never had a free minute. He did not like his job; he had wanted to be a journalist. But what with the war, fighting in Europe and starting a career later than he had expected, and then Lily and all their children, his youthful dreams seemed so unfeasible that he deferred them. Then at some point, he understood that unlike the tree of life, the desire was not to come. They would never be realized. He imagined that maybe when he retired, he would write a novel.

He had instantly warmed to his wife's friend Annabelle, but considered Lester Meer off his rocker. He disagreed with him politically, always arguing for a liberal Democratic, New Deal approach to important governmental matters, and was not surprised one bit when this ferocious advocate of revolution was unmasked as a card-carrying member of the communist party.

"It fits. It just fits," he explained to his wife, who wondered at his extreme lack of shock that Lester was on the lam. "He has such a venomous hatred for corporations and the people in them—colluders with fascism, he once called them and said they'd destroy us all."

"Well, at least he knows what he believes in."

Morris snorted in derision. "He's following a pipe dream. The workers' paradise! It's a workers' hell over there in Russia. I notice he didn't head there, but went to Mexico instead."

"He may yet."

"That'll be the day. He may be out of his mind, but I observe his sense of self-preservation works just fine, so well, in fact, that he was ready for this, had arrangements already made and left his wife and friends to do the talking to the police."

"Don't blame him—"

"Why not? He deserves it."

"For being practical."

"Practical?! Hmmph! If he was practical, he never would have joined the party to begin with."

"Now you're contradicting yourself."

"So what? At least I'm not a fugitive in Central America," Morris lit a cigar. "And I don't intend to become one either. You tell that friend of yours, Annabelle, that if she's a party member too, she's not welcome here anymore. I've got enough headaches without the police thinking I'm sheltering a pack of Reds."

They sat on the patio, drinking martinis and smoking. Lily was pregnant, and though the doctor had told her cigarettes were good for the baby, she smoked less than usual, because somehow she had lost her taste for them. Maybe it was the pregnancy. Maybe it was the anticipation of the upcoming battle with her mother over why she would not baptize yet another infant, a prospect of maternal censure that made her smoke less, eat less, drink less and generally withdraw into her shell.

"My husband is Jewish," she had already explained more times than she cared to remember. "I'm not going to offend him."

"You know very well, Lily, that your husband is a rank atheist. He doesn't give a hoot about religion. Now you baptize that baby in a good Episcopalian church."

"Mother's not letting up," she informed Morris.

"Then baptize the baby."

"And let her win? Never. Who knows what it would be next."

"Baptizing me, I should imagine."

"Bingo."

"Then tell her none of our brats get baptized."

"I have, hundreds of times."

"Maybe you could make a tape recording and send it to her. Then whenever she has the urge to nag you about baptism, she could listen to it."

Thomas and Louis wandered out. "Tommy, get Naomi out of the petunias," Lily instructed. "She's crawling right through them."

Waving the baby's favorite rattle in front of her nose, clever Tommy lured her out of the blossoms and back onto the flagstone path.

"Yuck, martinis," Louis said, pointing at his father's glistening glass.

"When you get older, you'll appreciate them," puff, puff on the cigar.

"And smoke! P-u smoke!" The little boy waved both hands in disgust.

"Now I suppose I'll have to put out the cigar," Morris grumbled. His wife stubbed out her cigarette in the ashtray.

Angela, the cleaning lady, who occasionally doubled as a baby sitter, opened the screen door. "You kids get in here," she ordered. "It's bath time."

"Shucks. I'm not dirty," Tommy said, holding up grime-streaked hands and arms for inspection.

"Vamoose," Morris growled. Quickly the two boys tumbled back into the house. Angela picked up the baby, slung her on her hip and carried her also inside.

"Peace and quiet," Lily breathed.

"For the next forty five minutes," Morris said sourly, "until I take Angela to the train."

"You know, there ought to be something we could do for Annabelle."

"Avoid her, maybe?"

"After all, she's my best friend from when I was so little in Charleston. I would hate to be separated from her."

"Uh-oh."

"There must be something, something we could do…"

"She's not moving in."

"No?"

"Absolutely not," Morris puffed emphatically. "To be married to a fruitcake like Lester—and now he's a certified fruitcake—she must have a few screws loose herself. I say that without reservation, much as I myself like Annabelle—and you know very well that I do—but clearly a few toys got lost in the attic."

"Oh, several. But she's a kind, open, dear person, and we go way back."

"Back is okay. It's forward I'm worried about."

"There's that bedroom in the basement."

"Absolutely not," Morris fumed again. "Don't think for one minute that I am going to capitulate to this harebrained scheme."

"Maybe then I could watch Eileen for her, while she's at work. She said she had to get a job."

"Watching Eileen I can live with, especially since I won't be here. I'll be at the office."

"Then it's settled."

"No one moves into the basement. We're agreed. How about another martini for your exhausted, overworked spouse?"

Very pregnant Lily lumbered out of the butterfly chair and went in to the sideboard in the dining room where they kept their liquor. When she returned, they resumed the topic of Lester and his wild doings. "Can you imagine," Morris asked, "risking your family and home for a few meetings with communists and some cheap talk about revolution?"

"Who knows what they discussed?"

"I didn't tell you, I got a call today from someone who said he was a friend of Lester's, wanted to meet with me. I replied, what made him so sure I would meet with a friend of Lester's, or for that matter wanted to have anything to do with Lester or his associates?" Some furious puffing on the cigar ensued. "It was either one of his communist pals or a bit of police entrapment. Either way, I want nothing to do with it."

"Entrapment!"

"Yes, we're going to have to be on the lookout for that. So will everyone who had anything to do with him."

"Lester sure made a mess."

Morris nodded and gulped his martini. "They're investigating the whole Port Authority because of this. They say it's crawling with communists."

"Well then, Lester got out just in time."

"I just wonder how long it's been going on."

"Annabelle broke down and told me—since before the war."

"Sheesh. He's got some commitment; after all, most of his ilk took one look at the Stalin/Hitler pact and abandoned ship."

"I think that was a little before Lester's time."

"Even worse then; what was he doing joining after something like that?"

They drank in silence as the fireflies came out, floating luminously through the gloaming. "How will he live?" Lily asked quietly after a while.

Morris shrugged. "The party will take care of him, keep him busy and get him a job. Why should I care how he lives? He endangered all of us. We'll have to be looking over our shoulders for police setups for the rest of our lives, thanks to him, while he's busy signing up members in Mexico, organizing factories and peasants and sleeping with beautiful revolutionaries."

"Poor Annabelle."

"Well, she should have thought about this before she married him, because as you say, she knew about his beliefs."

"But you think he'll be unfaithful."

"Sorry," puff, puff, "that was just loose talk, and so was my carping about her, because seriously, you're right—we should help out. Call her tonight and volunteer to watch her kid while she works, that is, if it's not too much for you."

"What's one more? And she's just Coralie's age."

When Morris arrived at work a few days later, in the bright, elegant lobby of his Madison Avenue skyscraper, he found that a federal agent awaited him, a husky government employee of nondescript bureaucratic appearance, whom Morris distinctly did not want in his office; so they decamped to a local coffee shop. Agent Blench was respectful but persistent.

"So you never knew he was a communist?"

"I knew he was a wild-eyed revolutionary, yes, but that he had gone so far as to join the party? Frankly it never crossed my mind."

"He never tried to recruit you?"

"He would have known better than that."

Agent Blench picked the advertising man's brain for over an hour for details about Lester's other friends and associates, about whether Lester had ever exhibited any facility at anything resembling bomb making, or whether he had ever mentioned anyone in the longshoreman's union, and, lastly and quite repetitively, whom did he discuss in local government? Unfortunately for Mr. Blench, Morris knew little about his neighbor's contacts, travels, history, war wounds or toilet training, and had he, would have been reluctant to share it, due to the resentment he felt at being suspected and grilled. He did let slip a few words about an associate Lester sometimes visited in Brooklyn, but could provide no name or address.

"Perhaps Mrs. Meer will know."

"There's an idea. Why don't you try her?"

"She's not particularly cooperative. What do you think about the possibility that she's in this too?"

"Annabelle?" Morris' eyebrows shot up. "She's harmless, just a sweet Southern beauty from a well-to-do family in Charleston. She loves her husband, but she hasn't lost her marbles. I doubt she'd have joined."

"We'll see about that."

"I'm sure you will. Now if you'll excuse me, Agent Blench, I have an advertising campaign for a household cleaner corporation that I have to attend to."

Blench exhibited no signs of readiness to depart, but instead removed a photograph from a manila envelope and passed it to Morris, inquiring, "did you ever see him in the company of this man?"

Morris hesitated, because he had. The hesitation was a little too obvious.

"I see that you have."

Morris frowned. "Maybe."

"This is very serious, Mr. Lichter. That man works for the Soviet government at the UN."

"Oh brother, Lester's really in this up to his eyeballs."

"I would say so. How often did you see them together?"

"Once, I think. But I'm not sure it was that bald hefty fellow. It could have been another."

"He's pretty distinctive with that scar on his cheek, wouldn't you say?"

"It's probably the same one," Morris conceded.

"Would you be able to swear to that?"

"No," Morris ran his fingers through his dark, somewhat overgrown crew cut. "And I hope I won't be asked to. Annabelle Meer is a personal friend of my wife's. Her husband may be an idiot—"

"Or a traitor."

"He may be Benedict Arnold reincarnate for all I know, but I don't like the idea of standing up in a courtroom against one of my wife's childhood friends."

Blench eyed him coolly. "Then let's hope it doesn't come to that."

As he returned to the imposing skyscraper that housed his office, Morris tried to picture Lester in Mexico City. In his mind's eye he saw the tall, lean form of his acquaintance, his thick, prematurely gray hair, his sharp, dark-eyed glance, his aquiline beak of a nose and his sturdy hands. Morris had never been to Mexico City, so he had a rather abstract idea of that. Dusty— he had heard the streets were dusty and there was lots of poverty, visible even in the swank neighborhoods. Lester would have a spacious apartment somewhere, because he somehow always managed to snag very agreeable living accommodations, as was attested by his pre-New Rochelle domicile in Manhattan, which had rather overawed Morris with its unexpected and understated magnificence, and he would be in the company of party members most of the time, or fellow travelers, whom he would not have to harangue about the need to destroy the capitalist system. Well, he sure had his beliefs, Lester did. Morris felt like an imbecile for never having figured it out. But he had to give Lester credit for the perspicacity of never confiding in him. That was smart. Morris might very well have turned him in; then again, he might not have. The revolutionary must have detected this ambivalence and instinctively chosen the safer course of silence, just as Morris had detected Lester's keenly vigilant sense of self-preservation, hints of which shot off like telltale sparks from his secret life, then flamed fully into view when disaster struck. "It's a good thing he's got that, too," the advertising man said to himself, as he hurried down the carpeted hall to his secretary's desk. "He's going to need it."

Back in the leafy suburbs, Lily prepared to take in Eileen. She had Angela fetch the extra crib from the basement, and then she dusted it, washed it and again directed Angela, who set it out on the front lawn in the bright, crisp sunshine, to dry. It was a heavy, partly collapsible wooden affair, painted white, and cleaning it tired her, in her late stage of pregnancy. The two women put the children down for naps, and the mother took one herself. When they arose, the crib was dry.

Harried Annabelle soon arrived with a hefty batch of cotton diapers, safety pins, creams, extra clothes, toys and, of course, Eileen. Since she already worked part-time, she had obtained a full-time position easily, as the first winds of catastrophe, when Lester had phoned her from the airport, en route to Mexico, whipped through the flimsy routines of her married life. She desperately needed someone to look after her baby.

"You're a life saver," she told her childhood friend.

"It's no big deal," her friend replied. "One more doesn't make much difference. The whole house is just one gigantic nursery."

"I hope Morris doesn't mind."

"He only wishes we could do more, as do I."

The abandoned wife wrung her hands. "If only I had some word from Lester."

Lily glanced at her curiously. "Isn't that kind of dangerous, for both of you?"

Annabelle's eyes shifted away from her friend's pale, pretty face. "We have to be very careful," she murmured.

"On second thought, please don't tell me about it," Lily laughed. "You never know who might come asking."

"Agent Blench, that's who. He's in charge of Lester's case, and a very cold fish he is. At least he hasn't arrested me."

After the forlorn wife dropped off the baby gear, she took her daughter to a department store for an extra high chair to keep at the Lichter's. As she strolled along vast aisles of merchandise, she had the vague sense of being disembodied and of being nowhere in particular and of not mattering very much, and this alienated mood seemed to spring as much from her new and dreadful circumstances as from the gaudily empty crowd of products filling the emporium, in which her baby daughter clamored for one thing after another, finally clutching the yellow high chair with the plastic seat, decorated with teddy bears holding balloons. Since Eileen would not let go, her mother, in her strangely dreamy and weary state, purchased this item, then drove them to an ice cream stand and paid for a peppermint cone, which they shared on the big front seat of the Chevrolet. Holding the cone out to her daughter, she had to remember to admonish her to hurry up and lick, the drips were going to get on the car. The baby crunched happily on the sugar cone all the way back to the Lichter's, then ran her tongue over her fingers and palms, while her mother drove like an automaton. By then it was almost seven in the evening, high summer twilight, and Morris was home. "I met a friend of yours today," he grunted, hoisting the box with the highchair out of the back seat. "A charming fellow, federal agent Blench."

"Oh Morris, I'm so sorry," she contritely replied, her miserable mood deepening.

"Well, he's a cold fish, if ever there was one. And I don't think he believed a word I said," the ad man went on, as they walked up the flagstone path, amid luminously floating fireflies. He carried the highchair in the box, she the child, who was nodding off.

"He thinks you're a communist?" She asked, wondering, not for the first time, if everyone she knew was now destined to become entangled in the morass of suspicion and accusation created by her husband's flight.

"He sees them everywhere, probably under his bed, where he sleeps with his hand on a gun."

"I gather you didn't like him," she opened the screen door for him, and they entered the cool, shadowed house.

"He offended me with his presumed guilty until proven innocent attitude. Will you stay for highballs?"

"That's what I love about you, Morris. You just sweep the unimportant stuff right away and get down to what matters. Let me just lay Eileen down upstairs in one of the kids' beds."

Lily emerged from the dining room with two drinks. "There's a third on the sideboard," she said, but her husband did not answer. He was looking up the stairs into the shadows, where Annabelle had gone. "She'll be lucky if they don't arrest her," he commented. "And think what this'll do to that poor child, Eileen."

No one else, however, was ever bothered by the investigation, which appeared to peter out. Lily watched Eileen along with her own children for a few years, and then the Meers economized and at the same time escaped a domicile haunted by memories of the absent Lester, by transplanting to New Jersey. Years passed, and Morris labored on, putting in long hours at the advertising agency, until Naomi was ten, when management changed. He maneuvered well enough to keep his good position, but was so much less appreciated that office rumors became rife that his fat salary and many perks were a cost-cutting target. His days seemed numbered.

"Come move to Philadelphia and work for us," said bluff, open and slightly tipsy Ron Swurl of All American Amalgamated, over lunch one bright, spring afternoon. All American was an immense holding company that owned many diversified corporations, and Swurl, despite the eyebrows raised by his heavy drinking on his long lunch hours, was a very senior manager. "I know Philly might seem like step down for a Manhattanite like yourself, but heading up our public relations operation, you'll make at least as much as here, and the cost of living there is lower. You've done a swell job for us, and I've sung your praises to everyone."

"So you'll match my salary."

"The offer stands."

"Where does one live in Philly?"

"In Center City or the suburbs, out by Ambler or on the Main Line. One of the VPs at All American commutes from Bucks County; beautiful place, that area. You could do a lot worse."

"An old friend of ours, Annabelle Meer moved there a recently, got a wonderful job as an administrator at Drexel University."

"That's a good school, Drexel. I'm hoping my son, also Ron Swurl—but we don't use that junior and senior nonsense—I'm hoping he can pull himself together and go to college there—in engineering."

The ad man leaned back, pushing away his plate, red with the remains of his steak. They were at the 21 Club, Swurl's favorite haunt, because a gossip columnist had once spotted him there and put his name in the paper. After that the out-of-town executive insisted on 21 every time he set foot in New York.

"When would you want me to start?" Morris asked.

"Right away," came the expansive reply, coupled by a hearty pat on the back. "Tomorrow if you want. You can start commuting to Philly, take your time to sell that Westchester mansion of yours."

"I'm giving you a tentative yes, but of course I have to discuss it with Lily."

"Discuss it with whomever, Eisenhower himself, just so you make sure to do it," Swurl beamed, polishing off his Manhattan with a rather undignified slurp, and then brushing back his sparse, light brown hair over his bald spot with his fingertips. Though only medium height, he managed to seem taller and heftier than he was. Morris could never figure it out, but every time he encountered this man, he was surprised to note that they were almost the same size, and whenever Morris saw him striding over the links in Westchester, whistling with joy at his excellent golf game, he was always startled that Ron wasn't much larger. There was something giant about the man's spirit that made one expect a more than average physical size, something big and commanding that made his fellow managers feel that he did not merely represent the corporation, he embodied All American Amalgamated. And yet, in many ways, he was a petty snob, Morris had observed, and he was sloppy about things, like his drinking. The man certainly had his contradictions, and his home life was a scandal.

Ron Swurl supplemented his loud and ostentatious wife with one permanent and many transient girlfriends. Even his six children knew about his infidelities, because they could not help but overhear the knock-down, drag-out parental fights on the subject. The oldest, a sensitive young woman, had quickly married to flee the quarrels that echoed through the enormous domicile. Some of the children were what only could be labeled disturbed as a result of this contentious atmosphere, particularly Ron Swurl (junior), who, at age fourteen, was under the care of a child psychiatrist, Dr. Shapinsky. Aggressive and hostile, though not violent, this boy only seemed at ease when playing sports, and he excelled at a multitude, for which, lucky for him, the family had ample resources, including an Olympic-size swimming pool, built expressly for his regular natation. Young Ron had a terrible mouth, which emitted a continuous stream of nasty remarks, and punishment did not shut him up. He was particularly brutish to girls.

With Morris, as with all his professional associates, however, the paterfamilias managed to conceal much of this pathology. He had his mansion, his stables, his acres, his money, his stocks, bonds, his summer homes, his yacht, his priceless knick knack collection, which included some Fabergé eggs, and he had All American Amalgamated at his disposal. Summers, he, his wife and friends boated up to Bar Harbor from Newport, Rhode Island, and the children were packed off to staggeringly expensive camps. They had been raised largely by a series of European nannies, and so did not miss their parents overmuch on these extended maritime excursions. These feelings were reciprocated. Ron did not miss them at all.

Morris Lichter had been startled to discern as much from a few casual and callous remarks. He thought it odd for a man to have so disassociated his heart from his offspring, a sign of some great, hidden deficiency that he could not name. He himself could not imagine passing a single day without what he lovingly referred to as "my passel of brats," and as for cheating on Lily—such adulterous notions had never strayed across his mind. He was as utterly enamored of his wife as he had been the day he met her at the University of Wisconsin, when he had fallen in love once and forever. She, of course, knew this and could have led him around by the nose, but did not, since her feelings matched his. Their marriage was as close to perfect as either could imagine.

So it was with some astonishment that he found himself shivering in the glacial tension between Mr. and Mrs. Swurl at a swank and crowded cocktail party at their mammoth residence. "Why do they live together, if they hate each other so much?" He wondered, almost out loud as he accepted a highball from Verna Swurl and marveled at her dangerously long and pointed red nails, the enormous diamond on one of her elegant fingers, the perfectly blonde hair, the little hat with the netting that she had just begun to remove and her designer gown. No question she was a knockout, and from the few sharp words he heard from her directed at her spouse, she obviously regularly attempted to knock him out in their verbal bouts as well. She appeared to have the tenacity of many, long simmering grievances. "Oh yes your highness," she responded to one of his requests, and later, "Who could refuse such high-handed commands, almighty prince?" But her verbal barbs just slid off him, as if his unruffled good humor and profound indifference oiled him against the useless scratching of her plaintive affronts. He just continued genially leading the conversation wherever he pleased, and if she caviled too nastily, he either ignored it altogether or grabbed Morris by the elbow and laughed, "did you hear something? I heard something, but I don't know what it was. Sounded like a crow cawing." Verna tossed her honey blonde tresses in exaggerated disgust.

The ad man could not imagine such a marriage. If Lily spoke to him with such routine if futile intent to wound, he had no idea what he would do. It would be the end of everything. No wonder Ron Swurl drank—but was that cause or effect? After all, the executive's drinking led him to chase floozies, the undoubted source of his wife's sharp, black bitterness. Maybe it was some sense of responsibility, some guilt or shame at having caused such a marital calamity that prevented him from abandoning her. Or maybe it was the thought of the alimony.

Morris had just ridden down by train after work that Thursday, his attention meandering over the drab, twilit New Jersey scenery, rushing by in a blur of shadow and gloom, and planned to sleep at the Swurls, visit the office with his host in the morning, then dine with Annabelle, before returning home late Friday. He drank his alcohol and surveyed Ron's impressive collection of priceless gewgaws, housed mainly in his study. "Aren't there supposed to be books in a study?" Morris wondered, "hence its name?" But clearly his benefactor was no reader, not stupid by any means—no not one iota of stupidity in that brain aside from the weakness for booze—but just not literary. His intelligence did not seek out the written word, was not contemplative, pensive, musing, but was instead directed toward action, people, the outdoors, and, like Morris, money. He sank into a large, dark, leather, wing-backed armchair, picked up the phone receiver beside it and dialed his wife.

"Well I met Mrs. Swurl," he said, "and heard her tongue, which she clearly wishes was as sharp as a razor, the better to cause grievous injury."

"Then you stay out of reach, Morris Lichter. Speaking of tongues, your progeny are all running around screaming like a bunch of Banshees."

"Nice to know I'm raising a fine, sensible brood. Some of them do have homework, I presume."

"They lie about it."

"That's what we need: a lie detector in our house. We can hook Tommy up to the polygraph and ask him what he did in school each day and then what his homework is."

"Say hi to Annabelle."

"I love you."

"Who do you love?" Ron demanded, entering the large, shaded study.

"My wife," Morris replied, hanging up the phone.

"Now I know you're bonkers. You come to a wonderful party, all bright with gorgeous women like the lights on Broadway and spend time on the phone with your *wife*? Quick, lemme get you another drink, and we'll forget all about this."

The next day, after a night in a vast, opulent and impersonal guest room, Morris met the senior staff of All American Amalgamated in their gleaming skyscraper offices not far from City Hall in Center City. It was a huge operation, with an equally large public relations department, which, he was told, he would have the authority to expand. A number of freshly minted college graduates worked there, while many young women, also college educated, held secretarial positions. This discrepancy brought to his mind, with a jolt, his three girls, whom he fully expected to go to college, and the probability that their precious education would be squandered taking dictation and serving coffee to haughty male bosses, who at best scarcely noticed their existence and at worst pestered them with unwanted advances. He squirmed at this sudden, horrid and unbidden image of an adult Naomi servile and underpaid, and then angrily determined that he would find a way to prevent it.

They planned to give him an enormous corner office furnished with lavish modernity and with a view, north and east, of the ornate City Hall, crowned with the statue of William Penn. He liked that. He pictured standing there, holding Naomi's hand, and pointing out important landmarks and promising to show her others not visible from that perch: the art museum, the zoo and the Franklin Institute. The money was better at All American than at his New York job, which was, anyway, no longer certain. As Morris saw it, he had no choice but to accept.

Annabelle's hair had turned gray, and she had gained some weight. Worry lines stretched from her nose to the corners of her mouth, and, Morris noted, she had taken to biting her nails. She was still attractive, but had something of the unfocused forlorn about her, detectable in the conversations that occasionally wandered off, hung in the air and dissolved in weary inattention, or in the periodic gray glances out the window, as if her gaze sought someone whose absence rendered her life empty and meaningless. Her daughter, at thirteen, was a raven-haired beauty, with an aquiline nose and dark sloe eyes, who reminded him somehow of Naomi, and whose melodious voice trilled through the Meer's narrow townhouse on Pine Street like the music of life, in counterpoint to her mother's fading despair. Their dwelling was a little shabby, full of books and not too far from Rittenhouse Square, where, they told him, they went in good weather to sit, read and chat with acquaintances. He strolled through the high, airy rooms, pausing to glance at the floor-to-ceiling bookcases crammed with classics and thought of the hours Lily and the children would doubtless spend here, because he had decided to purchase a house in Center City, not too far away, on Delancey Street—a still, quiet enclave with trim little townhouses, balconies covered with lush green creepers and garages. He had wandered through it on his way to Annabelle's and said to himself, "yes, this neighborhood is perfect for us."

"But I really don't know how long we'll be here," his old friend said, standing in the shaded, high-ceilinged study off the living room, where the whoosh and honks of traffic were somehow muffled and distant. "You see, Lester—"

"I don't want to hear about Lester."

"But it's all over—the investigation, the charges. He could probably come home, but he's afraid to. Instead we may have to move to Latin America."

"From a purely selfish perspective, that would be a disappointment. We were counting on you as our guide to Philadelphia, our expert."

"Any move won't happen soon. Over Christmas we're going down there, to see him and look into schools for Eileen—she's fluent in Spanish you know. He desperately wants us to relocate there. We saw him in Quito two years ago, before he moved to Peru. It was wonderful."

"Were you followed?"

"Not at all. That seems to be a thing of the past. Outside the United States he's fine. He only might, *might* have problems if he returned. He's just the same—same Lester, except now his hair's completely gray, and he's rather gaunt. He took us all over the city. It's up in the mountains, you know. Some of the poverty is awful. He works with a group that provides services to the poorest of the poor—"

"A communist front no doubt."

She looked hurt. "Don't say that. It sounds so cynical."

"Pardon a little cynicism about the man who didn't hesitate to leave us all in the lurch, you included. You might have gone to jail."

"I didn't because he was careful, prepared for trouble and determined not to implicate his family or friends," she corrected, then lowered her voice. "Eileen disagrees with me about leaving, but I'm not sure about moving to Peru. It would be so final. And then there's her education."

"That's exactly what I wanted to inquire about. Is there a coffee shop nearby?"

They strolled out into the unseasonably cool breeze of twilight, through the dying crepuscular din of city life that inexplicably made Morris think of Rome in the late empire, crumbling and insecure, ceding immense civilized tracts to invaders daily, the women barren, the cold breath of the Dark Ages already at everyone's shoulders, and then past Panama Street, past the lovely shadow-tossed square to a little place on Walnut Street, beautified with occasional stately trees, whose long, graceful trunks faintly reflected shop lights, while their high branches moved in the strange music of oncoming evening zephyrs. The late Roman Empire ceased to haunt him. Morris concentrated on the matters at hand, learning, over coffee, that Eileen went to a private school in town, which was, in Annabelle's opinion, the best education locally available. For high school, there were two selective public schools. "Even if I do move to Peru," she concluded, "I would want my daughter to stay here to finish her education."

Without even a moment of practical consideration, Morris invited Eileen to live with them. "I'm an idiot," he thought, qualifying that this invitation depended on his wife and whether she could handle another child. But the way Annabelle lit up at this offer convinced him that this unplanned, heedless semi-adoption was now a fait accompli. "Oh thank you, thank you," she cried, splashing her coffee all over the saucer, as she shakily settled it down. "You have no idea what it has been like, being separated from the man I love all these years."

Yes, he did have an idea; he could see it in her gray hair, lined face, sad glance and generally altered appearance. "Does he still talk about moving to Russia?" He asked.

"No. Besides, he says he has put down roots in Lima."

"It certainly has been a long time," Morris mused, gazing out the plate glass window at the darkened streets and treetops, swaying in the night wind. "Will you take the name Mrs. Leon Rathman?"

She gave a brittle little smile. "I don't know."

"I always wondered why he picked a Jewish name."

"A tribute perhaps," Annabelle replied, "to the many famous Jewish revolutionaries."

"As if they deserved a tribute," Morris grumbled. "They're more like skeletons in the cultural closet."

"Admit it, Morris, you enjoyed those political discussions with Lester. You thought his passion was admirable."

"I thought his cookies were cracked. And I could never figure out how you put up with that ranting, raving and grandstanding."

"He was actually quiet about his views, quiet but forceful."

The ad man ran a hand through his crew cut and proclaimed this assessment the understatement of the century.

They talked as the last light of day failed, then paid and ambled along darker, distinctly cooler streets. Morris still had an hour until his train, so he escorted his old friend home, thinking how long he had known her, and how his wife had known her even longer and recognizing suddenly how much this bond of friendship meant to him, that it was for such things and the persistent consciousness of such things that he lived, and how these bonds were but pale reflections of that fierce unbreakable blood-bond to his wife and children, yes, he mused, his life was all about other people and even if he were suddenly deprived of them all, their memory would fill, overflow his solitude and that even now, at times when he found himself alone, he really wasn't, because of these heartfelt connections to other people and the knowledge of their goodness and his link to it, that was forever.

Before she could even unlock the door, however, it swung open and there stood Eileen Meer, pale, brunette, with sorrowful eyes. "You were away so long, I started to worry."

"There's nothing to worry about," her mother replied.

But clearly for the young girl whose father had vanished when she was a baby, there always would be.

Morris taxied to the train station. At Thirtieth Street, he strolled through the high-ceilinged building, bought *The Evening Bulletin* and browsed in bright shop windows. Despite the hour, the place was crowded with men like him, in tan or brown trench coats, women in red, blue, green jackets—a multi-colored mass of people aswirl. He boarded his train, fully intending to read up on news in Philadelphia, but promptly fell asleep and dreamt that he and Lester, now Leon Rathman, were on the run in Argentina, dashing down the busy streets of Buenos Aires with policemen in pursuit. "We have to make the plane to the Soviet Union," Rathman cried, and Morris awoke with a jolt, nearly shouting "No. I'm not going. I hate borscht."

His wife greeted him at the end of the gray flagstone path, standing inside, pushing the screen door open, her face pale and somehow luminous in the evening air, her light brown hair glinting from the hall lamp behind her, baby Anders, four years old, drowsing hotly and damply and cooing in her arms. Morris stopped and thought of Ron and Verna Swurl, of long red nails like talons, of a sarcastic female voice clawing his soul and thanked his luck at having this slender, beautiful woman who loved him and whom he loved. "Lily goes to Philly," he smiled, leaning over to kiss her. "God, how I'll miss this house," he sighed, gazing through the brown dimness at the rooms off to the left, right and forward, then glancing up the stairs, whence came the sound of children merrily clambering about. "We're going to be city people now."

"On the phone you called Center City 'lovely and livable.' You sounded like a real estate agent."

Later, as their children slumbered in shadowed rooms and they settled into their comfortable, double, four-poster bed, Lily said: "So she's been in touch with Lester without any repercussions?"

"I guess J. Edgar Hoover has better things to do with his vast resources than chase down some low level revolutionary in Latin America. He's too busy wiretapping liberal Democrats, here at home. But I should tell you, Annabelle may move down there."

"It's fortunate Eileen speaks Spanish."

"Well, ah, ahem," Morris propped himself up on his elbow and looked down at his wife, palely visible in the gloom. "I kind of offered to, ah, take Eileen in—"

"You what?!"

"So she could finish her education here. But only, only,"

"Morris, have you lost your mind? I have six kids."

"I said only if you think you could do it."

His wife clapped both hands over her eyes. "So now I have to be the bad guy."

"I'll be making so much, we can hire someone full time, to help you."

The children protested this relocation in a murmur of discontent that swelled swiftly into howls of misery and rage, dramatized by copious tears and furious rending of clothes and the air. From Tommy straight down to Anders, they did not want to move, did not want to leave their friends, their schools, their neighborhood, did not want to make new friends, did not like the idea of a new house, certainly detested the thought of living in a city and made perfectly plain their shared belief that their parents had settled on this course of action deliberately and only to torture them. Tommy was fourteen and sweet on Amanda Fein, who lived in Scarsdale and whom he had met at a party. He saw her on weekends. He visited her at her house. They had even sojourned into the city together several times. What was to become of that? Hadn't Morris and Lily considered the devastating effect of a move to Philadelphia upon this earthshaking romance?

"We'll invite her down to stay with us," Lily cajoled.

"She won't come. Who in their right mind wants to go to Philadelphia when they live next to Manhattan? No, if anyone's going any place, it's me—up to Scarsdale, to visit her on weekends. But we could obviate all that by simply not moving in the first place. Philadelphia's a second-rate town."

"It's the fourth biggest city in the nation," Morris corrected, "after Chicago and L.A."

"Yeah and after New York, which is first," Tommy argued. "Why are we moving from first to fourth? Where's the logic in that?"

The youngest, Anders, simply threw himself on the carpet, screamed, kicked and, tears streaming from his green eyes, flailed his arms. Daphne, aged seven, blubbered loudly. Coralie and Louis, dark curls bobbing angrily, argued noisily with their parents. But Naomi maintained her dignity. She did not want to go and said so, confronting her parents with a haughty froideur that bordered on disdain.

"You know, I believe Naomi's giving us the cold shoulder," Morris observed later that night after the circus of protests had been shut down by peremptorily sending every child to bed. "Maybe I should have told the truth: that I'm likely to lose my job here."

"That only would have terrified them. No, saying you have a better offer was a good choice. Children need not know the details of their parents' finances."

The children continued to protest at every step of the move. Morris gave notice, and there were groans; they sold the house in New Rochelle, followed by loud laments; they bought a big, ivy-covered, townhouse on Delancey Street in Philadelphia, which the six young Lichters uniformly deplored; and before Thanksgiving, the family was ensconced in it, amid frequent, unfavorable comparisons to Westchester life. Their new home had four bedrooms and another in the finished basement, so most of the children had to double up, which they did not like. Naomi and Daphne shared a room across from Tommy and Louis on the top floor. Their windows looked out into the orange and red tints of autumn treetops and down on a little brick-lined courtyard, where a fussy, white-haired old man with a big, white, handlebar moustache walked a ridiculously tiny Pekinese on a leash every morning and late afternoon. The seven-year-old called him Merlin, to which Naomi invariably replied that maybe he could employ his wizardry to transport them back to New Rochelle.

Even in the rain, as the drops glimmered on the window glass, they could look down and see lean Merlin's long legs beneath a black umbrella, as he exercised his damp Pekinese. Though loathe to admit it, Naomi liked the new city; but not her school. She loved it when her father took them all out to dinner at the Chuckwagon, getting a pale blue, plastic tray that she filled with delectables that she chose from behind the steamy glass. On occasion she went alone with him to Jaffe's, where they ate delicious, greasy cheese steaks, or they rode to the zoo on a Saturday and fed the elephants peanuts. The green wilds of Fairmount Park and the dark, silent museum at the University of Pennsylvania appealed to her, but best was a stroll through the neighborhood with its locust trees and three-story brick townhouses on a warm evening, or sitting out on the roof that extended to the back from her parents' second story bedroom. There, some months later, in early spring, her mother planted a small vegetable garden—tomatoes and basil in pots, blueberry bushes in big, dark gray buckets, viney squash and zucchini with their broad green leaves in long wooden troughs. Naomi was charged with the watering, Coralie and Lily the weeding, pruning and staking. Over the far edge were the courtyard and Merlin, ambling pensively in the rain.

At school, however, she was the new student and had no friends. By seventh grade, most of the girls wore stockings and makeup, but not Naomi, who therefore associated with two other pariahs, Jane and Christine. Like her, they accepted their status as outcasts without protest, anger or tiny acts of rebellion, but rather submitted to the stringent will of this teenaged female mass like believers to an aloof and harshly rigid god. They were not invited to movies on weekends or parties in the other girls' rec rooms or excursions to the suburban shopping plazas. They were snubbed in the cafeteria, and when a teacher vocally appreciated their answers, snickers broke out like a rash. On a field trip to the Poconos, Naomi awoke in her sleeping bag in the cabin, with toothpaste all over her face. As she rubbed it off and walked to the water spigot, she heard uproarious laughter from the other girls who had pulled this prank and did not even consider it nasty or cruel. Her only two friends had wisely declined this excursion.

On Fridays, her older sister, in her makeup and heels, with her hair curled into a flip, took Naomi to their piano lessons with Mrs. Vandenheim, a Czech-Jewish concentration camp survivor, who lived with her husband and son in a top floor apartment of a gleaming new high-rise. Naomi considered Mrs. Vandenheim the epitome of style, the acme of sartorial panache. Mrs. Vandenheim dressed like Jackie Kennedy and wore big sunglasses like the first lady, though in her case it was because of an eye condition. In her thick, Eastern European accent, she often reminisced about her girlhood in Middle Europe and her dream of emigrating to Israel.

The two girls bounced along in the bus to City Hall and then transferred to another one. On brown, windy autumn days with the leaves swirling on the street corners, Naomi liked to imagine herself in one of the many European cities she had read about, but it never quite worked; even from the picturesque precincts they traversed, the desolation of north Philadelphia was visible, stretching away from City Hall and up behind the art museum, mile after mile of crumbling slums, dangerous, dirty, crime-ridden streets and impoverished residents.

There was a view of it, too, from one of the rooms in Mrs. Vandenheim's swank apartment—a huge map of despair, spreading north as far as the eye could see, under a twilit sky covered with cumulous clouds piled high, shot through with the encroaching black of night, but mostly mauve and magenta, bruised, wounded, like a huge contusion on the heavens. That sky, the misery below, posed such a contrast to the Vandenheim's building, with its blue, plush, hall carpet and its silent, mirror-paneled elevators. Once, leaving, Naomi spotted Suzy Stein, a senior from her school, with her flamboyantly red pageboy and an ostentatious white fur coat. That evening when Morris picked them up, Naomi announced: "I want a coat like Suzy Stein."

"Who's she?"

His daughter pointed.

"Now, that is a Jewish American princess if ever I saw one," Morris commented, and then: "Could you hold off on the coat? Until your wedding? From the look of it, it would cost just about as much, so you could have your pick—big wedding or big coat." But Naomi never forgot that garment, and years later, in tenth grade badgered her mother into purchasing something similar, though less costly, with fake fur.

Her closest friend, a sweet, quiet and rather unattractive girl, Jane Sylvester, whose limp, light hair hung lifelessly to her rounded shoulders, commuted to school from her small house in Upper Darby. Naomi could look at the house from the outside and agree with Coralie that it was little, but somehow, once she got inside, it seemed huge, so vastly spacious that she even lost track of what she did there.

"So how's Jane?" Lily would ask, driving her back home.

"Fine."

"What did you do?"

"Stuff."

"For instance?"

"I don't know. Played with her turtles. I forget."

"You know, Morris," Lily said later, "I hope there's nothing wrong with Naomi."

"She seems fine to me," Morris said, crunching down on a cracker with Brie cheese on it. It was Saturday afternoon, his cheese and cracker time.

"Rather forgetful, I should say."

"Hadn't noticed," crunch, crunch.

"She never remembers what she does at Jane's."

"Maybe it's not worth remembering," more crunches. "Maybe it's so monumentally boring that she can't bear to repeat it, flinches at the very idea."

"She doesn't flinch."

"Just an expression."

"Maybe she needs her head examined."

"Maybe you do."

"Morris! I'm serious. This is the fifth or sixth week in a row: 'nothing, stuff, I can't remember.' That's how she describes her visits."

"Sounds earthshaking to me." The public relations executive cut another slab of Brie and slapped it on a thin white wafer. "Sounds like you might want to let sleeping dogs lie," crunch, crunch.

"What sleeping dogs?"

"Well, once you get her going into the details of these unutterably boring afternoons, the tedium may be lethal. But then it'll be too late and you won't be able to shut her up. You'll have cooked your own goose, like that," and he drew a finger across his neck, as if slitting his throat.

"I think you're mixing verbal and visual metaphors."

"My specialty," crunch, crunch. "I'm an ad man. Remember—me, Morris Lichter, the guy you married, who can mix up any expression in no time flat. Geeze. Maybe you're the one with the memory problem. Maybe Naomi tells you everything and you," he shook an index finger at her, "forget."

"Tosh."

"Tosh?" His eyebrows went up.

"Piffle then."

"What, if I don't like tosh, I get piffle?"

"That's what you're full of—poppycock."

"Sounds like an appetizer."

"You've got an appetizer."

"I want poppycock," crunch, crunch.

"What's poppycock?" Anders demanded, passing through the kitchen.

"Like hamentashen," Morris explained.

"Nonsense," Lily corrected. "It's nonsense."

"Daddy wants to eat nonsense?"

"It wouldn't be the first time," Lily said.

Morris looked at his cracker. "What have you been feeding me? I thought this was Brie."

"It's piffle," his wife snapped. "And now we can't discuss something important,"

"Because I'm here," Anders beamed.

Morris tousled his son's dark, curly hair. "Don't you go anywhere. If you do, then I have to have an important discussion, so boring it'll curl your eyebrows, and I won't be allowed to mix metaphors or mangle clichés, and what'll it all be about? Ennui, that's what."

"What's ennui?" The little boy asked.

"You don't want to know. It's French."

"And you hate the French."

"After their behavior in World War II, I should hope I hate the French. If I didn't, I'm the one who should have his head examined, not Naomi."

"Now you've done it," Lily scowled.

"What's wrong with Naomi's head?"

"I guess I put my foot in it this time," crunch, crunch.

"Looks like a cracker with cheese, to me," Anders said.

"Sometimes, Anders, I get the feeling that you follow much more than we give you credit for," his father continued crunching.

"Naomi's going to a counselor," Anders sang. "Naomi's going to a counselor."

"Shit," Lily breathed.

"Not in front of the children, dear. You watch your mouth."

Then one Saturday when Morris took Naomi and Jane up to Broad Street, where the wind whistled in great gray gusts, to the Horn & Hardart, where they all ate shredded beef and noodles, Jane casually mentioned that she was moving to Washington State.

Naomi finished her food, pondering the dreadful news. Now there would be no one but Christine to talk to at school, and she was not as close to Christine, who teetered on the border between outcast and occasionally acceptable, unlike the other two, utterly beyond the pale. They sat by the plate glass window, watching people in coats, clutching their hats against the wind, bent over as they walked into it toward the bustle of City Hall and Market Street. "I wish we never left New Rochelle," she said to her father, as they left the restaurant and climbed into his Chevrolet station wagon. "I hate it here."

They trekked back to the Lichter's in silence, Naomi thinking, "No more fun, no one to talk to." But even those gloomy ruminations were scarcely articulate. She was simply alone, unhappy, not fitting in and helpless, as if life's most important events, such as having a best friend, were out of her control, just happened to her, were not done by her, and seemed to enter and exit her life without even a hint of her say-so. "I'm a mouse in a society of German Shepherds," she thought.

"My Dad got a job in Seattle," her friend explained, as they looked through fashion magazines up in Naomi's top floor room, which they had to themselves, as Daphne had been banned for the visit's duration. "I don't want to go. I don't know anyone there."

They flipped through the glossy pages morosely, seated on the green carpet with their legs crossed. Outside it had begun to rain. Naomi rose and peered out the water-streaked window. Below, Eileen, Coralie and Lily abandoned their gardening and came in. Farther out, in the courtyard, Merlin, under an umbrella, walked his yappy dog. "Maybe you could live here," she said. "After all, Eileen does. Why not you?"

"My parents," Jane answered. "That's why. Is it true like Mom says that Eileen's father is a Soviet spy, who had to run away and become a fugitive?"

"Not exactly. But boy, is she mad at him. And now she's mad at her mother too, for going away and leaving her with us."

"The world is complicated," Jane observed, smoothing her red and white striped pullover shirt.

"Yes, the world is complicated."

Naomi resumed flipping through the fashion magazines, fully conscious that she looked ungainly and awkward in the pink cotton shirt and tan pants her mother had selected for her. They did not really fit, nothing did. She was too skinny and gangly. She would never resemble a model on the pages before her; such a dream was, she thought, hopeless. She glanced out the window at the gray drizzle, the clouded forms of buildings muffled by the rain and repeated the word in her mind: hopeless—because she had not the faintest idea how to dress, and her mother, always too busy, had no time to attend to it. As a result, in her ill-chosen clothes, she looked like an overgrown nine-year-old, yet she was almost thirteen. She could not seem to wear anything gracefully and as a result was snubbed at school. The same was true of Jane, a misery they had happily shared. But now even that solace vanished. Jane would be gone. She would have to face these heartless cliques alone, but she knew already she would not. She would simply withdraw into herself.

Or, as her mother said, she walked around like someone who had lost everything—bewildered, helpless and stunned.

"Let's not be hyperbolic," Morris replied, gnawing on a drumstick.

"If only I knew what to do. Maybe art lessons?"

Morris paused, the drumstick arrested in mid-air, on its way to his mouth. "The kid's disoriented and wounded, and you think of art lessons?"

"Now look who's hyperbolic. An activity, something she could care about."

"A cat."

"Morris, you're a genius. Ever since Honeybunch got hit by a car, something's been missing, and that's it."

So they sojourned to the ASPCA and selected a little black kitten with a white spot on its throat, which Naomi named Sugar, because he in no way resembled it externally, but had a wildly affectionate disposition.

Up at seven thirty, then downstairs for Rice Krispies, pack up books and papers, cuddle Sugar, then out into the old white station wagon with the wings over the rear lights. All seven children crammed into the car. Only Anders rode back home with Lily.

"Whatever you do this morning," Coralie snapped at Naomi, "don't cling. You have absolutely no reason to come to my locker with me. Yours is at the other end of the building."

So she meandered to her locker, ignoring the girls who ignored her. Christine and Jane waited, bursting with news: Cindy Stein, Suzy's little sister, had invited Christine on an outing that weekend. Tall, blonde, pimply and gawky Christine agonized over what to wear. Since neither of her friends had any good ideas, she hurried off to class to ponder it on her own. The two pariahs made their way to chemistry.

Because Naomi excelled in this difficult subject, other students who would not normally be seen with her, snuck over for help. Later, at lunch or in the hall, they might give her a nod, but refused otherwise to acknowledge her presence. It did not matter. Her mind was elsewhere, specifically on English class, the poetry of Emily Dickinson, more particularly the poem about being nobody, which, like all of her verse, had a simple, solitary elegance, that inspired her to compose poems too. She felt a kinship with Emily Dickinson, unparalleled by her feelings for anyone else, and this led to the strange, solitary and oddly comforting realization that books, not people, were her friends. She began frequenting used book shops and had her father install extra shelves in her room. Despite her mother's admonitions that it was rude, she read at meals and, in fact, anywhere else that she could, between classes, in the car, before bed, in the park. Her mind, her spirit, seemed to merge with the print on the page. She took it all in, she accepted it, just as it so forthrightly and honestly asked to be accepted, merely by being there, waiting to be read. Novels and poems had far more flesh and blood for her than junior high school students. Indeed it was not long before she decided she would be a poet.

"And what will you eat?" Morris demanded when presented with this career ambition.

"Rice Krispies, as usual."

"You won't have enough money for Rice Krispies."

"Then I guess I won't eat them."

So she wrote poetry, submitted it to the school literary magazine, and it was published. This gratified her, though it still won her no friends, now sorely needed, for Jane had moved, and Christine, dazzled at her chances of social success, had become somewhat remote.

Several months after the Lichters moved to Philadelphia, Annabelle flew to Lima. Even thought she only planned a short visit, she closed up the house on Pine Street, locked all the windows, put sheets over the furniture—just in case she extended her stay. Eileen was bundled off to share the basement bedroom with Coralie. She did not want to. She wanted to accompany her mother. But that determined woman would not interrupt her eighth grade daughter's education.

"Did it ever occur to you, I might like to see my father too?" The teenager demanded.

"You will," her mother soothed. "Just not now." They sat in the high-ceilinged, book-lined living room, which had as wintry a look as the bleak January street outside. Out the window could be seen the few passersby hunched into a bitter wind, and the air had the frostbitten, anticipatory look of snow. It was a Saturday, and all errands and activities had been suspended, so that they could spend time together. The girl slurped beef barley soup, and her mother drank a cup of tea. It had been a rather acrimonious tete a tete.

"I still don't understand why we didn't move down there years ago," Eileen argued. "Why now?"

"I'm not moving."

"It sure looks like it."

"I took a temporary leave from work."

"Well, I could take one from school."

"No. Besides, I'll be back before you know it."

"Famous last words, in this family."

At this standoff, each began sipping vigorously, as if to have something to do besides acknowledging in any way the other's presence. The heat hissed and steamed in the radiators, and from the dining room, the grandfather clock, precious heirloom from the family's southern ancestors, chimed eleven.

"One of the reasons," the solitary wife resumed calmly and quietly, "that I am going now is that the pressure if finally off. The government appears to have lost all interest in Lester—"

"That doesn't explain why I can't go with you."

"School."

"Forget that silly school."

"I can't. And I also think it's necessary for me to see him alone; not for long, but Lester and I need some time alone together."

"I hate you," her daughter said, put down the soup and left the room.

As the child predicted, her mother stayed away much longer than anticipated, almost a year.

The father, too, wondered why his wife had not brought their yearning daughter. It emerged later: if by some means they were arrested, Annabelle wanted their child safely out of the picture and ensconced in secure surroundings. Her husband nearly laughed aloud when he heard this, because Leon Rathman had not been bothered by American agents in almost a decade. They considered him as good as dead. And for all the effectiveness of his party organizing, he said, he might as well be. With this failure, he had begun to doubt his commitment and was glad he had not taken matters one step further by defecting to the Soviet Union. At times only the bond to his wife and child had restrained him, and now he was doubly relieved it had. His political uncertainties combined with his love for his family made him shudder at the prospect of his fate, had he relocated to the Stalinist empire. It had been a close call, and one that led him at last to distrust his own judgment, to second guess himself and even, when wakeful in the depths of night, as he gazed wide-eyed at the yellow streak from a street lamp bisecting the ceiling, to wonder if the whole enterprise from joining the party to meeting with Soviet flunkeys had been misbegotten. He had no self-pity and was not inclined to dwell on such futile self-recriminations. What was done was done, and he still harbored the ideology that had somehow led him down such a twisted byway. Still he hesitated to tell his wife his true thoughts: that he could never return home and that it was time for her to bring their daughter to Peru.

From their large apartment in Lima, the Meers could discern the Pacific Ocean, and Annabelle spent much time gazing at the little distant patch of cobalt and wondering if she could dwell in this city permanently. Party meetings and other political obligations occupied her spouse. It was one of the brief periods of civilian rule in Peru's history, but still the communists kept their activity quiet. Leon Rathman had contacts among left-wingers in the military, men with great hostility to the government, which he carefully kept secret from Annabelle—if ever arrested, he did not want to jeopardize her with such dangerous knowledge. So his wife had time to herself, which she passed reading, on various urban explorations or meeting with other expatriate women whose husbands or lovers worked with Lester. Months passed, and though she wrote to Eileen every day, her wounded daughter rarely replied.

That young woman thought she had recovered from her anger at her parents, but the frequent letters churned up feelings that contradicted such a sanguine notion. The postcards picturing the Andes, the city and the shoreline, all seemed to snap, "Look what you've been left out of," like a slap in the face, so much so that she often flipped them over quickly to read the words and never glanced at the image again. Besides, she had better things to think about. Fourteen, she would soon be in ninth grade and had become a startling beauty, whose long, dark hair, pale, oval face and good figure attracted much male attention, while alarming her guardians, Morris and Lily, with apprehensions of adolescent sex and its consequences. By the end of eighth grade, she had a steady boyfriend, who walked her to the Lichters every day after school, with much lingering, sometimes for hours, in leafy, cool Rittenhouse Square. Tall, strong, blond and crazy about her, Jake was given to jealous rages, which, she thought, resembled childhood temper-tantrums, but which rather pleased her. It was nice to be with someone who, unlike her unaccountably indifferent parents, so valued her that absence drove him wild.

"So where's Eileen?" Lily demanded of Coralie. "You've come home without her again."

"And again, and again," the dark-haired, rather thick-set though not unattractive girl huffed. "Why should I care where Eileen is?" She paused and a rather unpleasant, sly smile crept over her face. "Or what boy she's necking with in the park?"

"You have a nasty streak, Coralie Lichter."

"Maybe that's because I'm sick of sharing my bedroom, my family, my life with an ungrateful wretch, who, I should add, is leading Naomi down the primrose path."

"Naomi worships her," Lily commented, thinking that that was part of the problem, because in her oldest daughter's proper order of things, Naomi should worship Coralie, not some interloper, some waif abandoned by her parents, adopted by the Lichters' kindness and thereafter imposing in every way imaginable. Sometimes Lily found her oldest daughter's lack of compassion for their guest very offensive. "And Eileen," the now bristling mother continued, "is brokenhearted over her parents' absence. So you should restrain your harsh words."

"I've heard this lecture before. But I'll tell you, she's an embarrassment and, just like her parents, she'll be nothing but trouble for us." The girl tossed her short, almost black hair, curled into a flip, and reached for a cookie.

"You'll regret that," Lily eyed the treat in her rather pudgy daughter's hand.

"Don't remind me," the teenager bit savagely into the oatmeal cookie and thought bitterly how her lack of self-control would only, once again, redound to her competitor's benefit. She was too plump, the cookie would make her plumper, while Eileen, who did not like sweets, remained slender and lovely. Worse, this unwelcome visitor, who subsisted on her family's charity, heedless of her egregious debt, this unaccountably poised and so unjustifiably self-confident eighth grader had Jake Whitly, the handsomest boy in the ninth grade, madly in love with her. Everybody envied Eileen. Only Coralie had firsthand experience of what an emotional slob she was, how indifferent to life's important little courtesies, how unaware that leaving her shirts on the bedroom floor was an imposition, how oblivious to the repercussions for Coralie of her smoking and making out in public. At times she thought she detested this intruder and urged her parents to write the Meers and remind them of their parental duties. She would always cite the oddity of the situation; indeed the peculiarity of taking in this girl truly affronted her, wounded her in her dearest aspirations for normalcy, acceptance and, yes, respectability, because there was something, after all, not quite acceptable about the Meers, their politics, their trouble with the law, their strange domestic arrangements—and Coralie craved something they didn't seem to give a hoot about, something she could not quite name, but that could easily be called social position. It was bad enough having a clingy outcast of a sister in the sixth grade and questions like, "aren't you poor Naomi Lichter's older sister?" But also to be closely associated with a liability like Eileen Meer sometimes seemed too much to be borne.

"Why can't she just go to Peru?" The teenager irritably demanded, finishing the cookie.

"Shh. She'll hear you."

"She will not. She's busy slobbering over Jake Whitly in Rittenhouse Square, just so the whole world will know I live with the fastest girl in the eighth grade."

"Try not to think quite so much about yourself in these matters—"

"If I don't, who will? You? Not likely. Because if you did, she wouldn't be here in the first place. None of the girls at school want to be associated with her and that rubs off on me."

"But the boys don't mind, and the girls are jealous," Lily retorted, momentarily forgetting her own worries about the dangers of Eileen's alarming beauty.

"They don't like her."

"You could make an effort, you know. She has been through a lot."

Her daughter sighed in exasperation, took another cookie and tromped upstairs. An hour later the young femme fatale fairly danced in.

"Where were you?" Her guardian inquired anxiously, the image her daughter had conjured of ferociously amorous public pawing foremost in her mind. "Coralie got home ages ago."

"I was in the park with Jake. He invited me to the movies Friday night. Can I go?"

Lily wanted to say no, but was perplexed by this poor, deracinated child's evident delight in having found someone, even if it was a teenage boy whose hormones were surging, who loved her and paid slavish attention to her. She had written Annabelle about this romance, requested guidance and received little. "If you go to an early show," she answered tentatively. "I guess it's okay."

In the ensuing months, Coralie's indignation festered, rankled and curdled the small portion of her spirits composed of generosity and cheer. She became snappish with her irritating younger sister, something she feared to do with Eileen, whom she instead cold-shouldered in the ignoble wish that her roommate would be downcast by the chill and thus urge her rightful mother to return. But that did not happen until the fall of their ninth grade year and then under circumstances very different from those envisioned by Coralie and ones that had nothing to do with her and little, in fact, to do with any of the Lichters. Annabelle Meer came home because she had cancer.

She had visited the hospital in Lima, when symptoms appeared. The doctor diagnosed colon cancer and discouraged her from remaining there for treatment, arguing that since she was an American, she should return to the United States. The best cancer care in the world, he assured her, was to be found in the great North American cities.

The airport good-bye was tearful, burdened with bleak premonitions of reunion denied. "If I get very sick," she sobbed, "and can't take care of Eileen—"

"Send her to me," Lester said softly. "We all should have reunited here years ago. What mistakes we've made."

"And if I'm not going to get better—"

"Then come back to me, with Eileen, if you can."

On a dull November day, the sky, gray like iron, threatening rain, Morris and Eileen greeted her at the airport. A cold wind whipped around their coats as they made their way to his rather used station wagon. Electrified by fear at the news of her mother's illness and the looming specter of death, Eileen had forgotten her anger and tried to find the rather paltry comfort in the fact that her mother, though strangely lethargic, looked well, a comfort that could not dispel miserable thoughts of life without her, of the emptiness that would follow her demise, of her unique and irreplaceable mortal worth, hanging by a thread, about to snap. All human life seemed so short and pathetic, its strivings, its wildness, its singularity swept away with the tide of generations, so that in no time an entire, carefully woven human nexus of loves and work and activities, each personal society was no more and was as if indeed it had never been. Through her mother's illness, everything that mattered seemed diminished, transient, almost gone.

"We opened up your house," Morris explained, sliding in behind the wheel, "as soon as we heard you were coming. And Lily made all those medical appointments you requested. She even called the university to say you'd be back at work."

"I doubt that," the traveler replied quietly and with a dozy exhaustion that secretly and separately alarmed the other two.

At her words, her daughter shuddered.

"We're going directly to Pine Street?" Annabelle inquired after a moment.

Morris nodded, then emphatically added: "And you're to take it easy. We hired a woman, Darlene Stubbs from West Philadelphia, to help you. She's a joy—and delighted to have work."

"Oh, but I can't afford it!"

"Yes you can. Eileen and I looked into your insurance through work, and this is covered. In fact everything is, from now till—"

"The end," the invalid finished his phrase, and her daughter shuddered again.

"I was going to say till you get better," Morris corrected.

He parked in front of the Meer's townhouse, tall and bleak in the wan, autumnal light, and Darlene, who had been waiting by the window immediately strode out. A tall, lean, copper-colored woman in her early forties, who had nursing experience, she at once in ways subtle and not so subtle took control of the shocked and disoriented trio. Annabelle was not to unload suitcases. That was not even discussed. Darlene simply handed one suitcase to Morris, another to Eileen and carried the last herself. Then she guided her patient, pale, weary, into the house and then onto the couch, where she lay down. "You better rest, because in exactly two days, Monday morning, I'm taking you up to Hahnemann to see the doctor," Darlene explained. "You can't miss that appointment because you're too tired. The key with this illness is prompt, aggressive treatment."

"You know a lot about it?"

"Oh yes. I worked on a cancer ward five years, saw plenty of what you got. You're very lucky they caught it so early."

"Lucky?" The cancer patient almost laughed.

"Now don't go feeling sorry for yourself. Then you'll just be disappointed when everything works out."

"That's good advice," Morris agreed, seating himself in an armchair across from the couch. He ran his fingers through his short, dark crew cut. "How's Lester?"

"Busy, busy," Annabelle replied. "He sends all his love to you, Eileen, as I told you in the car."

"I mean is he still as…as…"

"Committed?"

Morris nodded.

"No, I don't think so. He seems to have succumbed to a nuclear fatalism. You know, it's all going to end in a firestorm, a nuclear holocaust between the U.S. and the U.S.S.R.—that's what he thinks. He's lost a lot of his optimism."

"He should have come back with you," Eileen spoke bitterly.

"And go to prison?" Her mother asked. "I think not."

Outside the early November wind rattled the panes, tossing leaves and an occasional stray sheet of newspaper high in the air, down the nearly empty street.

"It's 1963," Annabelle mused. "Many years since Hiroshima and Nagasaki. I don't think it will happen again." She paused and sipped from a glass of water Darlene had brought her. "If I…recover—"

"*When* you do," her daughter spoke forcefully, already imitating the bold assurance of the nurse.

Annabelle gave little, weak smile. "Then you and I shall move down there. We should have done so years ago. I let more than a decade go by. I cannot believe it."

When Morris stepped out to the bathroom, Eileen spoke up: "Thank God you're back. Coralie hates me. I was ready to run away."

"But you're close to Naomi."

"She's a little kid."

Annabelle surveyed her daughter appreciatively, noting that she was a fine, young woman now, the image of her mother, but with her father's dark hair and eyes. She was honest and sensitive, but also, despite her efforts to smother it, a certain fury appeared to smolder, indeed recently to have roared, within her. Annabelle sensed that anger might be her undoing.

Back on Delancey Street, Naomi, quiet and miserable, sat at the kitchen counter with her mother. "So Eileen won't be coming back," she remarked.

"Of course you'll see her in school, and she can come visit, if she wants."

"Why would she—for more of Coralie's nasty snobbery?"

"You know, for a seventh grader," Lily smiled, "You pick up a lot."

"Anders is in elementary school. He could pick it up. Anyone could. Coralie meant it to be picked up."

Morris strode in, exuding the casual contentment of one liberated from a more starched office dress code, in his Saturday afternoon jeans and sweater. "Well, they're settled. And that Darlene Stubbs is terrific! What a find!"

"Maybe I could visit?" Naomi asked hopefully.

"Yes, Eileen invited you to spend the night next weekend," Morris replied. "That is, if she isn't out on a date with that Jack fellow."

"Jake," his daughter corrected. "Jake Whitly. Coralie has a mad crush on him."

"Speaking of the little princess—" Morris began.

"She's out shopping with her girlfriends," Lily explained, and all three at once envisioned the same true thing: a gaggle of pampered teenage females, made up, perfumed and fashionably attired, as they gabbled about boys, gossiped viciously about other girls and expertly judged the overpriced merchandise in a glittering department store. The image somewhat nauseated Naomi.

The next weekend, Eileen met her boyfriend and Naomi in Rittenhouse Square, where the trees, skeletally leafless, waved their black branches, like sentries at the outer edge of autumn, signaling against any venture forth into the frigid wind. Although it had been arranged that the younger girl would spend the night at the Meers', that afternoon, Eileen acted as though she did not exist. This, Naomi saw, was no deliberate snub. No, her friend was simply so absorbed in her beau that the rest of the world vanished. They sat, arms entwined on the corner of the park bench with its peeling, dark green paint, and Naomi settled onto the other. They murmured, laughed, nuzzled and knew of nothing besides each other. They could have been anywhere. Naomi would not have been surprised had they begun to undress each other right there, in public. Nor would she have objected, for if they had started to behave thus, it would be, like everything else they did, a natural outcome of their enveloping passion, as if they were in some other realm, with other rules, that they entered when together. To Naomi it seemed, as she sat so long at the far end of the bench, shivering in her thin coat, that she was in a cold, arid waiting room, waiting for her friend to return to her, waiting for her own turn at life.

At last the boy left, in a vaporous trail of romantic absorption, so that by the time they had traversed chilly sidewalks to the Meers' house, Eileen was again a friend like no other. The amorous afflatus had dissolved, and the girls could turn their attention to other matters. Her closet, full of stylish clothes, was open to Naomi, who could wear and keep whatever she wanted. Her frank conversation showed an interest in whatever her guest said. In their profound mutual understanding, either could utter any opinion about anyone, including Jake or her parents, so that by some generational reproduction of the connectedness of souls, their friendship perfectly replicated their mothers'.

They passed their evening in the dim glow of the television, discussing the never-ending and fascinating subject of Jake—how he played the guitar and baseball and went to the Jersey shore in the summer, where, this year, Eileen would join him and his family, if her mother was well. They gossiped about other students and some of Eileen's new friends who attended the selective public schools. They talked about her music—Eileen played the oboe—and she performed several pieces, which her guest genuinely found thrilling. Then they tromped downstairs for dinner with the adults.

"Eileen tells me you're a poet," a rather tired, worn Annabelle addressed the young visitor, as she ladled a beef stew onto noodles for each diner. "Whom do you like?"

"Emily Dickinson."

"Oh my! Her work is so marvelously spare—how hard it would be to emulate! You know, of course, your mother wrote short stories before she got married."

The girl nodded. "And my father wanted to be a journalist."

"A family of writers," Darlene exclaimed and then, holding out her plate to Annabelle, "a few more of those carrots and red potatoes please."

"You put so many in. How *did* you know they're our favorites?"

"You've only been eating them all week—carrots and potato salad, chicken with carrot and potato soup. It's got so I open up the refrigerator and all I see is orange, red and white."

"Naomi's published her poetry in our school's magazine," Eileen reverted to the literary topic.

"Penmanship," Annabelle mused. "Isn't that what the magazine's called?"

The girls confirmed it.

"What an odd name—misleading, don't you think?"

"I agree," Naomi replied, discreetly chewing her beef. "Nobody on staff can figure out where the name came from."

"Then change it," the invalid urged. "Why should you be saddled with 'Penmanship?' It's all wrong." Then after a moment: "So I imagine Morris thinks this plan is impractical?" And when Naomi nodded, she continued: "Morris is a great one for making practical compromises. Oh how I wish a little of that had rubbed off on Lester!"

The girls stared down at their steaming plates, as an awkward silence descended on the little conclave. No outsider was ever sure how to approach the conversational minefield that was Lester—ready to blast any talk into a cloud of sorrow, acrimony or despair—while his daughter at once withdrew into a bleak interior landscape of loss, and his wife hedged each word with the taut awareness of legal ramifications. What if she revealed his address or his alias or his current work? Then she not only endangered him, but also burdened her listener with unwanted and nettlesome knowledge. So he could only be mentioned vaguely, with references to his character or emotions or shortcomings. Darlene, who had grasped this perplexity the very first time Morris alluded to it, adroitly changed the subject to Eileen's music and its derivation from her mother's artistic temperament, which everyone leapt into with evident relief, notable also whenever they escaped the other verboten topic, namely, Annabelle's cancer, even though her prognosis had improved—very early stage and hopefully treatable. So, guests frequently found themselves gingerly skirting the Scylla of exile and the Charybdis of disease, navigated by the competent and ever more assertive Darlene, quite evidently determined that nobody was going to plunge *her* patient into an emotional whirlpool of misery and despair. Such matters could be discussed only when Annabelle was out of the house or sleeping.

"When she says 'I wish he was more practical,' you say there are signs that he is," Darlene hissed, once the cancer patient departed for the bathroom. "And then you change the subject. Don't just stare at your plate. Now you invite your mother to watch *The Umbrellas of Cherbourg* on TV tonight with you. She'll decline, so you don't have to actually watch it, but she'll appreciate the thought."

Decline she immediately did, drifting off into the kitchen for an after-dinner liquor and then standing for some time, gazing through the window at the mid-winter desolation of grays and browns in the tiny, walled-in back yard. "In spring we'll plant flowers in the corner and put out boxes of pansies and impatience," she murmured. "In spring," her nurse asserted, clattering dishes in the sink, "it won't be we, because you won't need me. You'll be on your own again."

"I wonder," the invalid whispered in faint contradiction, as the strange solitude that swathed her from time to time in great remoteness, covered her again. At times like that she seemed one with winter, one even with death. Darlene did not like it a bit, but she said nothing.

The girls could not abide *The Umbrellas of Cherbourg*, so they flipped channels and chatted like magpies about whatever popped into their heads, except, of course, the threats that had loomed earlier, at dinner, namely exile and death. If she so much as sensed one of these towering at the end of a sentence or thought, Eileen cowered away, shivering in terror that her mother would soon die. But Annabelle Meer beat all the odds, until the end of her daughter's senior year. That was when the cancer angrily reawakened, defied the doctors and the return of Darlene and finally, with sudden swift brutality, killed her.

She was buried in South Carolina, and it was Morris, not Lester, who accompanied her daughter to the funeral. By then Eileen, a beatnik-hippie hybrid in beads and sandals, offended the rather more conventional businessman's sense of decorum and of the proprieties of mourning.

"You're going to a funeral ceremony, not a be-in. Didn't you didn't bring a change of clothes, something more formal?" He asked her on the plane, as it bounced along unnervingly in the upper atmosphere.

She shook her head, and her long dark hair swished from side to side.

"Well then, you'll have to shop alone before the funeral, because I am not venturing out in Charleston in the July heat. I have a very clear and unpleasant memory of my last visit here with Lily. I nearly ceased to exist, melted into a puddle with dark hair and horn-rimmed glasses floating in the middle. And that was September. The weather here is atrocious, but so is your apparel. You'll have to shop alone or with one of your aunts. Please," he raised a hand, "do not even attempt to invite me away from an air-conditioner."

"What'll you do in the cemetery?" Eileen asked. It was several days since her mother's death, and she found Morris' complaints wonderfully soothing.

"Die probably."

"Well, that will be very convenient then, won't it? We can bury you there, too." And the tall, grief-stricken teenager almost smiled.

Morris very nearly did suffer heat stroke. For after the coffin had been covered and everyone had left, the grieving teenager insisted on staying, and he could not bear to leave her there alone. At last, after what seemed to him an infernal eternity, she rested her white roses on the grave, turned a tear-stained face to him and said: "I'll come back again, by myself, later."

She declined to sojourn to Peru to see her father. With Morris' help, she sold the house on Pine Street, rented a rather funky apartment in West Philadelphia, whose worn, wooden floors did not quite touch the scuffed moldings, and enrolled in music college. She continued with Jake, who attended Penn, but unwittingly tormented him with her infidelities—

unwittingly, because she believed she concealed them admirably. He saw straight through her, however, and suffered the agonies of a repeatedly shattered heart. His friends called her worthless and advised a rupture. But he demurred, explaining that she was a free spirit, he was not, and if he wanted to keep her, he would have to adapt. What he never elaborated was his certainty that the tragedy of her parents had in some way damaged her, causing her stupid, obtuse faithlessness. This was his final conclusion, reached by a long and tortuous path of miseries, jealousies, and violent fantasies of revenge. However, it was so difficult to abide by this apercu, that by the time she had completed her freshman year, he was, as he put it to his closest friend: "burnt out, through, done with it. We're finished, Eileen and I. I just can't take any more. There's nothing left."

Naomi, too, plunged into the swift currents of the hippie life. Smoking cigarettes, occasionally smoking pot, talking the lingo and passing her afternoons with her Hermann Hesse-quoting boyfriend, she was unrecognizable as the ugly duckling who did not know what to wear, just a few years earlier. Her dark hair hung down to her waist, and her skirts were so short that Morris was apoplectic. She passed her hours after school at her friend Mike Dellico's house, listening to him and the other members of his rock n' roll band at decibel levels that caused frequent threats of the police from the furious neighbors. In their matching purple shirts with Neru collars, with their long bangs falling over their eyes, these musicians' modest goal in life was to be as hip as humanly possible.

"Mike Dellico's cute," Eileen summed up her considered opinion one summer afternoon, as she and Naomi entered the Seven-Eleven on the southwest corner of Rittenhouse Square, "almost as cute as Gilbert Locklane. I think you made the better choice," she concluded in reference to her friend's rather intellectually pretentious paramour. They bought sodas and chips to take to Mike's basement. "Besides," Eileen giggled, "Gilbert goes to Drexel University. That shows he's an upstanding citizen, not an indolent, war protesting, lead guitar playing hippie, who has no idea what to do with his life, like Mike."

"Coralie can't believe I'm Mike's friend."

"I bet she can't. I don't even see why she goes to Penn. Her ambition is to be a housewife."

"I'm never getting married."

"Me neither. It's definitely uncool." With that, the two friends entered the Dellico residence on Lombard Street and found the band making a ferocious, somewhat musical noise in the basement. In that deafening roar, all conversation ceased for several hours, until the next-door neighbor returned from work, pounded on the door, and screamed that he intended to alert local, state and federal authorities, if they did not desist from their barbaric clamor at once.

"She's sleeping with that boyfriend!" Morris hollered at his wife. "He better not come back here, because I may kill him."

"Another scene between you and Gilbert Locklane, and that'll be the end," Lily said calmly. "She'll move in with Eileen or onto some horrible commune and never finish high school. Please try to control yourself."

But Morris could not control himself. At the sight of his daughter's unkempt, smelly, dirty hippie friends, he became so enraged he could scarcely see. "I don't know what's going on with these young people," he would say to his wife, "but it's loathsome."

"They're upset about the war."

"That I can understand. Not bathing and living in the slums is another matter." Morris rued the day his daughter had met her literary amour.

That had occurred two years previously on a late autumn afternoon of weakly dying sunlight, when Mike Dellico and Naomi gallumphed along Twenty First Street, discussing Eric Clapton. Suddenly a rather tall, very muscular, young man in a black T-shirt and jeans, his red curls grazing down past the nape of his neck, emerged from a doorway and hailed Mike. This trio stopped and chatted in the uncommonly mild air, as faint sunbeams sought vainly to brighten the worn, stone steps of a townhouse and the brown, dead petunias in the window box, and Gilbert, upon introduction to Naomi, was visibly stricken. She could not understand why. She had not said anything brilliant or witty or particularly insightful, had, rather, just stood there in the lengthening shadows, muttering agreeable monosyllables. Afterward she heard from Mike that Gilbert was crazy about her. That was fine, and she was willing to accept all his advances, but like the embers of the day they met, crumbling into the ashy sky, her feelings for him commenced more at what one might think of as the tired end of love than at a luminous heart-dawn, and indeed, she never considered him more than a good friend and certainly could not comprehend his operatic passion.

She had passed much of her last two years in high school in Gilbert's company—lounging at a small, cramped book store on Sansom Street, whose ghastly and obese owner had befriended Dellico and his band, or visiting at his family's house on Lombard Street, where they passed hours in the living room, playing chess, a game she did not enjoy and was bad at. But Gilbert was addicted and did not care on whom he inflicted his mania, so long as he had a chess partner. His close friend Nathan Cohen, a somewhat overweight aesthete, homosexual and talented music student with soft, brown, thickly lashed and very sensitive feminine eyes, sometimes relieved the fatigued girlfriend from her chess obligations, and for this she was very grateful. She would sit in a corner, reading *Magister Ludi* or *Demian*, while the two young men brooded on their next move, over by the window, through which wan, dusty light filtered in from the street.

One afternoon, early in her senior year, she and Nathan left their game-addicted friend to contemplate his last, victorious moves on the chessboard. Nathan glanced at her curiously: "You don't love him. Why do you stay with him?"

His words seemed so obvious, she was not even taken aback. "I don't know," she replied. "I don't know why I do anything."

They ambled along Fifteenth Street, dodging dog turds and breathing in great lungs-full of the blue automobile exhaust that encircled the city like a smoke ring and dispersed its smelly self throughout the gray grid of streets. They compounded this insult to their respiratory systems by smoking cigarettes. Nathan inattentively kicked a dirty plastic bottle in front of him, dancing out of his way from left to right now and then not to lose it. "I'm the opposite," he said after a while. "I know every detail of why I do everything so well that life bores me to tears. I suffer from an overdose, a massive overdose of ennui. I would love not to know why I do anything."

"No you wouldn't. You'd feel like a demented imbecile."

"But you're not…" he began.

"So I tell myself."

They paused to sit and smoke on a stone stoop, beneath a withered locust tree. From the tall townhouse, once white, now gray with soot, which rose up behind them, came not a sound. It seemed completely shut up, as if no one had lived there for a hundred years, like some portent of what would become of the homes from which they came, though why it should bring such a thought to her mind, stand as such a stark emblem of abandonment on the road into her future, she could not say.

"I come down this way often," Nathan remarked, "over the years, perhaps a thousand times. I've never seen a soul enter this house or stand on these stairs."

"Then we're christening them."

"They don't seem particularly grateful for the gift of human attention."

"Nothing does."

"My, we're cheerful today."

"You think I should break up with Gilbert."

"I don't and I never said that. It could kill him."

She gazed sternly into her companion's dark, moist eyes, in which, behind his glasses, lurked a furtive friendliness. He inhaled a huge gulp of cigarette smoke. "If you fall in love with someone else, and eventually you will, you'll have to be very careful how you handle Gilbert. He loves you, your family—"

"My family! My father threatened to kill him."

"He loves them anyway. And he wants their approval. He would marry you."

"Oh my goodness!"

"It never occurred to you?"

"Never."

"Well, let it now."

She ran her hand without the cigarette through her long, dark hair. Then she finished smoking and tossed the butt into the litter of the gutter. There it lay, like something understood and abandoned, emitting faint, hopeless wisps of smoke. "I suppose I'd better break it off now," she murmured.

"That strikes me as the wrong conclusion. Kindness and a gradual loosening of the links—that might be better. Gilbert couldn't handle a rupture."

"You're certainly full of insights and advice today."

"It's because I identify with Gilbert. I, too, am utterly and fatally in love, with someone you never met, a drop-out from the music institute, Ronald Swurl; though he's currently doing time in the loony bin."

"Why fatally?"

"Because he's not interested in men. Oh, he'll tolerate my attention, but that's about it."

"Poor Nathan. So you're on Gilbert's side."

He nodded sorrowfully. He looked pale, sad and alone, sitting there aimlessly on the stoop of the empty house, the house of her family's future, of her future, wilting on the steps, like some once sturdy flower that fell out of a bouquet and was forgotten. He was clearly avoiding going home to his big empty apartment across from the quiet, ancient, little church cemetery on Pine Street.

"Mike Dellico has a new girlfriend," she switched the subject. "She's from Lima, and her parents know Eileen's father."

Her companion merely sighed, picked up a crooked stick that lay beside the stoop and poked at the trash behind the little grill next to the stairs. It made a desultory rustling, like wind in fallen leaves, going nowhere.

"It doesn't look like the 'Don't be a litterbug. Keep America beautiful' campaign is working too well on this block," she commented.

"You can't imagine how much garbage would be strewn about here without it," he replied. "Oh, what am I to do?"

"Forget him, like Gilbert should forget me. Neither this Ronald of yours nor I are worth it."

He jammed the stick savagely through the grill. "That's what you think."

In the cooling spirit of that October conversation, which seemed a harbinger of the ever more hibernal state of her heart, Naomi, attempting to douse a fire she never should have allowed to burn in the first place, tried to "loosen the links," but still she and her unloved paramour drifted on, more or less together, spending chill late afternoons in January, lying on his messy bed, talking little, she gazing at the barbells in the corner, he ruminating on his next move in chess against Nathan. Occasionally she would run her index finger through the dust on the windowsill and glance out at the stark, wintry house-fronts across the street, their darkened windows like hollow eyes, staring at nothing. Things were very bad with her parents. Morris had all but disowned her and seemed incapable of addressing her in anything gentler than a shout. She had applied but did not know if she would go to college. There were too many protests, concerts and be-ins to think about school.

One warm Saturday in late April, she and Gilbert rode the creaking old trolley to a Sun Ra concert in Germantown. Everyone was out in their countercultural finery—bright purple tie-dyed, flower bloom T-shirts and manes of hair gleaming everywhere. The concert was cut short by rain, and as she and Gilbert made their way back to Center City, again seated in the drab and nearly empty trolley, she gazed through the window drops at the watery light on the glistening black bark of trees, black of telephone wires and the rain-smudged bricks of the houses, lined up and towering severely over the wet cobblestones and decided that yes, she would attend the University of Illinois, Circle Campus in Chicago and not withdraw, as Gilbert had urged her. She knew he would argue against this.

His intransigence so depressed her that she left early, tromping through the rain with a borrowed umbrella, over to Pine Street, then along, beneath dripping leaves and branches, past trim little houses, some in the Federal style, to the quiet block, where the rain-covered roofs gleamed dully like molten steel in the drizzle. She entered the foyer to ring Nathan's buzzer, but somebody was already there. He was tall with long, yellow hair, dressed in clothes obviously from a thrift store, and sporting little wire-rimmed sunglasses. He was very handsome and observed her pressing the doorbell.

64

"Nathan's not in," he explained. "You must be Naomi. He has great descriptive abilities."

"Who?"

"Nathan. He described you perfectly."

"Well, he didn't describe you."

"Oh," the young man laughed. "I'm nobody. But you can just call me Ron Swurl."

"I remember now. But when he mentioned you, I was sure I'd heard your name before, somewhere else."

"Probably in connection with some mental institution."

"No somewhere…from the past," she mused and watched the rain drip, drip through the glass of the door.

"He's not here. Let's go to Jaffee's for a cheese steak. It seems to be our destiny to wander in the rain."

Ronald Swurl senior and his wife Verna had not endured. Scarcely a year after the Lichters' arrival from New York, their lavish life, with mammoth cocktail parties, whose hordes spilled out of the mansion and teemed on the immense grounds, glasses clinking, their yacht voyages, his scandalous affairs, her rather hypocritical charity work and expensive private schools, summer camps and colleges in the U.S. and in Europe for the children, had titanically crashed to smithereens upon his wildly infatuating encounter with dark-haired and exotic Inez on a vacation in Acapulco. This proud and dazzling young woman descended from a long line of wealthy oligarchs, who topped the totem pole of Mexico's corporate elite, a family that had already casually married into American money more than once. He promptly divorced Verna, wriggled out of as much alimony as he could, gave not another thought to the children, and swept Inez back with him to Houston, where he opened up a new, much ballyhooed headquarters for All American Amalgamated. The Philadelphia office remained a powerhouse, but now, the board had decided, there would be two. All American was heavily invested in Latin American mining, and worrisome winds of change, especially from Peru, had reached the corporation, which thus charged Ronald Swurl with tamping down any Latin American labor problems or talk of nationalization of mining industries, as quickly as possible. Fortunately for him, Inez, from her family's long experience as labor's adversary in Mexico, was able to make wonderfully heartless contributions to this endeavor. Her advocacy of draconian austerity for countries like Peru parroted that of the banking circles that had nourished her mind and inheritance and indeed had been successfully applied for many years, until the left-wing military coup by Juan Alvarado Velasco in 1968 swept away all of All American's holdings.

With her spouse newly married and in Texas, and thanks to the incompetence of her lawyers, Verna Swurl had decamped with her children to a more modest establishment, indeed a row house in Mt. Airy, the front porch of which gave a beautiful view of a cobblestone avenue with tracks. The trolley clattered along these at all hours of the day and night, and the Swurl children rode it happily to school. Verna, less loud now and no longer ostentatious at all, landed a secretarial job. She, too, commuted by trolley. Money was tight, and the financial outlook grim. Only a thin trickle of checks came from "that repulsive beast," as the abandoned wife referred to her ex, who had tied up her claim for half of his fortune in court and looked certain to stalemate her there. Luckily two of her older children, Chester and Marlene, were able to switch from Penn to Temple University, which, as a public college, was relatively cheap. Then Chester committed the ultimate treachery by wangling a high-paying job at the Philadelphia headquarters of All American Amalgamated. Verna telephoned Morris Lichter, whom she knew through her previous contact with the corporation's public relations arm.

"I can't fire him," Morris exclaimed. "He doesn't even work for me! I didn't even know he was employed here."

"He has dropped out of college to work at that horrible company, along with that horrible man I had the misfortune to be married to."

The public relations executive cleared his throat uncomfortably and tried to block an oncoming headache by massaging his temples. This sudden, acrid intimacy with someone he had never particularly cared for baffled him. To end it as quickly as possible, he found himself volunteering to seek out the young miscreant and make the case for resuming his education.

This proved useless. Chester, the perfect image of his bluff, hearty, relentlessly self-advancing father, told him to forget it: he was of age, white, the year was 1961, deep into the modern era, in which a liberal arts education was useless for businessmen.

"Major in business instead. Then come back to the company. You'll make much more money that way."

They sat in Morris' huge, sun-drenched corner office with its opulent yet uncomfortable, hyper-modern furniture.

"I'll make more money while my father's still with All American, as he is now. Who knows how long that will last? I intend to take advantage of it. College can wait. If I really need my BA to advance, I'll enroll for the remaining two years later. I'm in this to make money, you know?" He laughed. "Not to read the classics."

Morris looked across the gleaming expanse of his chrome and glass desk at the young man in the steel and leather sling-back chair opposite him. He wore a stylish suit and, incongruously, a yellow bow tie. He was simply too loud, too big, too smarmily gregarious for this polite accessory. But all the men in Chester's department wore bow ties, so he was certainly not about to buck the trend. Somehow that bow tie made Morris conscious that he disliked this young man, a feeling that had swum silently under the relationship with his father and now emerged from the surface, alive, writhing in the open air and undeniable, as true for the offspring as for the parent. And with this aversion came a distinct and alarming premonition that somehow, in the long run, these Swurls meant trouble for Morris and for all he loved.

He became eager to be rid of the young up and comer, to have him out of the company. But since that was not possible, he suggested a transfer to Houston, where "all the action really is." Chester's light, hazel eyes flashed—whether with ambition or some recognition of his advisor's obscure motive, Morris could not tell. But within the month, the young man had indeed transferred to Texas and, with his father's pull, quickly became a bigwig in the Latin American mining division, abandoning what even he felt were his ridiculous bow ties. Morris was relieved. The unaccountable vatication of danger that had so suddenly electrified him and moved him to subterfuge must have been wrong. It was foolish, really. Now, he told himself, he would never see another Swurl again.

Needless to say, the forsaken wife was bitterly disappointed in the results of Morris' intervention. Though unaware that it was he who had suggested Houston, she could not help but conclude that her meddling had not helped and that Morris was a failure when it came to being useful to her. She never had anything to do with him again, and, with the passage of time, wearing it away like the ocean on a bit of shell, the memory of him faded, was at last utterly effaced and crumbled into nothing, just as hers and indeed those of all the Swurls were swept out of Morris' mind on the gigantic tide of years.

The other Swurl children grew up like nettles in an abandoned garden. Ron junior's memories of the paradise of his youth dissolved into bits and pieces—how he had once excelled at sports and, much earlier, hid behind his mother's glamorous skirts at cocktail parties in a house so big he could and did get lost in it. He remembered genteel therapists in elegant suits and one with a sparkling blue gem on his tie clip, replaced by bored school counselors in tatty jackets without ties. He became angry at these hypocrites, who professed a desire to help him control his rage, but really, he cynically thought, only did so for their fee or paycheck. He drifted like a little tangle of dried leaves through the desert of the public school system—detentions, suspensions, parent conferences—all merely deepened his furious cynicism about what he cursed as "the system." He had no plans for the future, and, with the passage of years, the mid to late 1960s made him even more heedless. He was a hippie who lived on the street, then with other self-styled freaks in an abandoned building on South Street. He could play the oboe. He could compose music. He would be a composer.

At the music institute, he was not held in particularly high regard, but he took to passing afternoons at other local colleges and universities, where the children of the middle class, from well above which he had fallen, exhibited a tendency to fall in love with him. This was flattering. Male, female, he did not care, he basked in their attention and praise of his work. Nathan, with his renowned aestheticism, was a particularly gratifying conquest. They spent many hours together, discussing politics and art, and the plutocrat's discarded son ranted angrily against this, that and the utter turpitude and bankruptcy of middle class values. Indeed he loathed the middle class and did not hesitate to vent this detestation at every opportunity. Nathan, sensing the volcanic churnings of a purely emotional rage behind these tirades, sensed danger and found it thrilling.

In his South Street abode, the rather unfocused artist slept on a mattress in a second floor room. He also had a large desk—after his failure at music, he had decided to become a writer—and a milk crate with his clothes stuffed in at the end of the bed. The room was a shambles, as was the entire, three-story building. The ground floor, an abandoned storefront, contained the dust-covered wreckage of old, unidentifiable machinery, scattered like debris after some catastrophe or the metallic skeletons of weapons abandoned after a war long lost, though two enterprising hippies had begun to make it habitable by clearing out one corner for a bed and an armchair, salvaged from the street. Five others dwelt in the remaining four rooms upstairs. They came and went at odd hours. Sometimes they worked, often they attended peace rallies. They had lived on the street long enough to regard their South Street squatters' haven as a paradise. None of them were drug addicts. That was the only rule in the building—no hard-core drug addicts. Such people would bring the police, and with the police would come evictions.

For Ron, this was the first place since adolescence in the Mt. Airy row-house that he could call home. Often he went to sleep at night with images from the row-house porch—the cobblestones, the trolley, the low, dark porches of the buildings across the way—so vividly before his closed eyes that he thought he was back there, almost the baby of the family, were it not for Howard, who tried to please everybody and whom everybody, even Ron if he was not careful, loved.

Now they had all scattered except Howard and Roz, who still abided with their mother, taking quite seriously her claim that she would die if left alone. Roz worked at a dentists' office and attended classes at a textile college in Germantown, full of foreign students, mostly from Latin America, among them her handsome, black-haired Brazilian boyfriend, who intended to set up textile factories when he returned to Sao Paolo. Ron scorned his sister's bright-eyed plans and "work-you-way-up-the-ladder" attitude, told her it was dreams like that that kept the mass of people passive. She retorted that he was an idiot, who had gone from a stay in the mental hospital to sleeping in doorways and now considered a slum building Shang-ri-la. She didn't think much of his views. Besides, he never helped with their mother, the ruin of whose life by their father he either did not see or did not care to. Why, even selfish, inconstant Chester, who lived a muscular life in Houston, making money, chasing girls and drinking heavily in bars, even he sent money and postcards. But they could go for months without a word from Ron. He seemed to lack even the faintest touch of decency. Could he not imagine how his long spells incommunicado frayed his already edgy mother's nerves? And look at Howard, she would rail, a senior in high school, who drove to his mother's office every afternoon to pick her up, who cleaned the house, did the food shopping and held down a part-time job unloading boxes at a pharmaceutical supply store. Everyone else comprehended the gravity of their mother's precipitous drop in the world, everyone else pitched in and did it cheerfully, never making her feel like a burden—Verna who had sacrificed her entire adult life for her children—everybody, that is, except Ron, who openly grumbled when asked to lend a hand, and whose imbecilically cutting remarks on one visit home had occasioned the pitiful maternal lament, "I guess I'm just a troublesome old bag." The attitude of the children toward their vagabond brother resembled that of guests at a party, who see a boor misbehaving atrociously and maneuver to get him out the door. Let Ron sleep on the street. They could care less.

Except Ron, as he told his friends, was not "buying this version of history." Verna had not devoted her life to her children before the catastrophe; and after it she had let them run loose. They had raised themselves, and when they needed something, one glance into those vacant blue eyes told them they would not get it from her. She did nothing for them. She let them rot. Yet somehow his sisters and brothers had fabricated this other history of her heroism in the face of crushing adversity. They did so, the former mental institution inmate surmised, because it was easier than facing the repulsive truth: their dirty neglected childhoods were straightforwardly the fault of two people—their mother, who lied and said she could not cope, and their supremely selfish father, who abandoned them for a good-looking, rich Mexican woman, who helped propel his faltering career. The Swurls, he said, made him sick. And he said much more, some of it to his drifty friends on the street, then later to his fellow students at the music institute, but most of it to Howard, whom, unbeknownst to the older Swurl children, he phoned once a week, disgorging a load of poison into his ear, which would have sickened anyone else. Howard, with his implacable good humor, was unaffected, unruffled in the least. His brother was ill, he told himself, and regarded everything in a distorted, malign light.

One night, when he had been sleeping in doorways for a particularly long time, the vagabond borderline psychotic tired of this and, restless, with deep, dark circles under his eyes, rode the clattering trolley home through the black blanket of night to find Roz and Reynaldo necking on the front porch. He sat in one of two wicker chairs and watched them paw each other on the glider. Roz's hair, a modified blonde beehive, was a mess, and her skirt was hiked way up. After a moment the unseen visitor whistled lewdly. The lovers straightened up.

"How long have you been here?" Roz demanded.

Her brother ignored her. "It's a warm night. I'd like to sleep on the glider."

"Well it's taken," she snapped, receiving a passionate kiss from her beau. "If you want to sleep inside fine, but bathe first. You smell."

"Thanks sis, for your warm reception."

"Thanks brother, for acting like a peeping Tom."

The ex-mental patient opened the creaky screen door and walked through somnolent, shadowed rooms, until he saw a shaft of yellow light stabbing the gloom on the floor down the hall. Without knocking, he entered to find personable, tired but ever uncomplaining Howard, at work at his desk, deep in his lucubrations on the meaning of *Hamlet*, having finished with those on calculus. The light under the door extended from his little desk lamp. Otherwise, his small room lay in complete darkness.

"Don't give me your lecture on the futility of school, and please don't grab my papers and rip them up like you did last time," Howard said, protectively closing his notebook and holding it close to his chest. He was a big boy, by far the tallest in a family of medium-sized men. With his handsome, even features, thick light brown hair, steady, unsuspecting and unpretentious manner and lively hazel eyes, he exhibited all that was best in the Verna/Ron matchup. Well over six feet and athletically built, he towered genially above everyone else in the family and seemed genuinely sorry that his height irked Chester. Unlike the others, he had accepted his family's misfortune without a word and clearly intended simply to make the best of it. His relentlessly cheerful good humor, optimism and high spirits aggravated his brother Ron beyond words.

"So what's Horatio Alger up to tonight?" His shiftless older brother demanded.

"Acing English and math."

"There's no money left to send you to college. You know that."

"I'll work for two years, while taking classes at community college. Then I'll transfer to Temple. You'll see. It'll all work out."

Ron snorted in derision. "Yeah, like it always does. The way it landed us in this run-down row-house to begin with."

"This house is not so bad. I kind of like it. I have happy childhood memories here. You see, I don't really remember the mansion, so I don't miss it. I guess I was lucky."

"Some people have an odd idea of luck."

"And some people always look on the dark side of things. They shall remain nameless."

Ron smiled in spite of himself. "What are you doing in English?"

"Five tragedies of Shakespeare—*Othello, Hamlet, King Lear, Romeo and Juliet,* and *Julius Caesar.* I'm in the honors class, you know," and the young man beamed with unaffected pride.

"I didn't. And I didn't know they had an honors English class in that pathetic excuse for a high school."

"It's what you make of it."

"It's a pit. You can't make anything of a pit."

Howard sighed. "We never can agree on anything," he marveled, as if there was the least thing remarkable about that.

"Lucky for you. Now that's *real* luck," and Ron cackled.

Howard winced. He had to admit he disliked his brother's cackle. It sounded barely human. There was something feral and frighteningly heartless in it.

"I'm going to be an accountant, you know," Howard asserted, though he did not know why.

Again Ron cackled. "Now that's rich."

"I intend to be."

"Even better. Dream on, little brother, dream on. I bet you want a pretty blonde wife and a brood of little chicks in the rec room too—a rec room in a house on the Main Line, no doubt."

Howard grinned. "I don't need to tell you anything. You've got it all figured out."

"How could you be so…so prosaic?"

"I'm not an artist like you."

Flattered, the deracinated older brother softened and blunted what would otherwise have been a very sharp and nasty dissection of middle class suburban life, of marriage, child rearing and accountancy. Indeed he laid his instruments down, as it were, and did not make a single cut. He only mildly said, "I guess not too many artists can afford Wynnewood."

"Nope. I'll be surrounded by doctors, lawyers, businessmen, housewives driving station wagons and Cadillacs—"

"Sounds nauseating."

"Swimming pools."

"Now I may come visit you for that."

"And lots of little kids playing in the garden and on the swing set—"

"Spare me any further description. My stomach's already churning."

"That's from working as a short order cook in that Greek coffee shop on Eleventh Street."

"I don't do that regularly. I just fill in—enough to keep me fed."

"Don't you have to bathe before you do that?"

"One of the other cooks lets me use his place. He's eager for the time off, so he's happy to get me clean and presentable."

"Not all hippies are dirty," Howard commented blandly, though he did not really know why.

"All the ones I know are."

"Being an artist sure has its sacrifices."

Again Ron basked in the unwonted and—in his brother's case—entirely innocent flattery. Howard was perhaps the only person on earth who found something in Ron to admire. But this, of course, was before the vagabond's creative writing program days at the public university.

"Mom says you can't sleep in any bed here unless you shower first," Howard informed him.

"Thanks for the news, Walter Cronkite," with that Ron headed into the bathroom, stripped and took a long luxuriously hot shower. The bathroom filled with steam, and he greedily inhaled deep, purifying breaths of it. Then he tramped, nude, back into the bedroom he used to share with Howard. There were still two beds, and he flopped down on his.

"Most people wear clothes," Howard remarked, not looking up from the notebook in which he was writing in his clear, even script.

"In case you hadn't noticed, I'm not most people, little brother."

"Well, don't let me disturb you. I'm sure you need your rest."

The prodigal son awoke to a scream. It was Verna, standing in the doorway at seven a.m., gazing at his naked body, sprawled on top of the sheets. "Wear clothes, you barbarian," and she tossed the towel in her hand over him, to make him decent. Considering the amorous gropings and undressing that had transpired on the front porch the previous evening, Ron considered her shock humorous, and either naïve or hypocritical.

"I need money," he mumbled sleepily.

"Get a job."

"I have one. I mean I need money to get to the restaurant."

His mother left and then returned quickly, handing him two dollars from her purse. She looked haggard and old. Her garish hair, which would have been gray but was dyed yellow, and was piled up on her head like a mannequin's wig, contrasted jarringly with the parched lines and wrinkles of her face.

"You should let your hair go its natural color."

"Natural. Everything with you has to be natural. I'd get fired. No businessman wants some old hag typing his letters."

Her son lit a cigarette and offered her one, which she accepted. "I'm thinking of a creative writing program. I might get a scholarship."

"Oh, that's a real practical career move."

"Sarcasm doesn't become you."

"Nothing does. I'm sick of life, sick of work and sick of my children making mistakes."

"Child, singular."

"No, Roz is going to marry that Brazilian, move to Sao Paolo, where he'll cheat on her mercilessly and finally abandon her. You think it's bad being poor here? Try Brazil." Verna exhaled a long stream of blue smoke. "And Marlene is pregnant."

"Again?"

"You'd have thought one abortion was enough. This time she'll marry the jerk. He's an auto mechanic, comes over with black grease under his fingernails. They sit French kissing in the kitchen with him running his black fingernails through her blond hair. I'm sick of it all."

"Come on, I'll ride the trolley with you."

"No, I won't be seen with you in those rags you wear. I might meet someone I know." She left. Howard drove the old Ford to school, and Roz, already in her blue scrubs and white nurse's shoes, bustled around the kitchen, making pancakes.

"I haven't eaten in two days," her periodically homeless brother plaintively hinted.

She eyed him pitilessly, then said, "have a stack," and nearly tossed him a plate with three pancakes on it. "It's not that I mind you sponging," she said, making more pancakes and fixing her hair at the same time, "it's that you're either self-righteous about it or you want us to feel sorry for you. So which is it? You pick."

Ron felt his stomach ache, then heard it growl. He knew if he attempted to climb a high horse in front of Roz, she would snatch the pancakes back. "Have a heart," was all he said and then began bolting his food, the better to finish it all, before the urge to pontificate and declaim against her middle class narrow-mindedness overcame him.

"I do have a heart," she softened and turned to face him, leaning back against the cluttered counter, with her hands pressed white on it, now that she had done fiddling with her hair. "I even think you hippies are right about a lot of things, for instance this horrible war. I think every politician responsible for it should be shot. And the only people who will come out and criticize them are people like you. I just don't like being looked down on for being such a commonplace, pedestrian specimen of the middle class—aspiring to middle class, that is. Forgive me, I'm human."

"You really think that," Ron spoke with his mouth full, and his words muffled, "They should be shot?"

"I think they're war criminals. But that's my personal opinion that I express to you, my brother. Don't you go telling people."

With new respect for her, he chewed the last of his pancakes. He did not give a speech against her, her values or her dreams. Instead he thanked her and, leaving, mulled the apparent contradiction—Roz wanted nothing more than to re-attain the splendor from which her family had fallen, was even ready to leave the country to marry a man who could support her in a more lavish style, a man she possibly did not love, yet she was willing to give a street person like her brother credit for being right about the most important political issue of the day. For Ron that amounted to complexity and depth. And he respected complexity and depth.

Thus musing that people might have more good in them than he generally credited them for and finding himself suddenly and unexpectedly cheered by this glimpse of human goodness and by something irrefutable about that glimpse that filled his heart with blessed hope, he alighted from the trolley at Locust Street and ambled, clean and well fed beneath his rather dirty, thrift shop attire, over to the coffee shop, owned by the vigorous if illiterate Mr. Moustafapoulous and his mixed crew of Greek immigrants and American deadbeats, who ran the place. Amy, the pale, slatternly thirty-five-year-old waitress grunted at him, as he descended the few steps into the eatery. And Richard Moustafapapoulous, nephew of the owner, greeted him at the grill with a shriek of joy: "You here! Now I can take a break!" Nico, the owner, clapped him on the back. "Flip some burgers," he advised in English so accented it sounded like "fleep soma boogas." The vagabond, his soul still illumined by its late vision of human worth, donned his apron and hat and complied.

It was a warm, drizzly day, and every time Ron looked up from cooking eggs, preparing cereal or scarfing down two cheeseburgers on the sly, he saw the damp sidewalk of Locust Street, the silvery, wet telephone wires slithering above and the green of the trolley front, as it clanged through the gentle downpour. Prior to living on the street, he had always loved rain, regarding it as in some obscure way sacred. But many soaking nights in doorsteps had left him with a distaste for it. No, he could no longer romanticize rain. It was the enemy of the roofless hippie just as it had long been for his shabbier forebear, the hobo.

After an hour guzzling black coffee and racing about cleaning, "feexing" things, Nico left the little establishment in his nephew's considerably more lax hands. Indeed the moment Nico's broad back disappeared around the corner of Eleventh Street, Ron and Elijah, the other half of the kitchen help, circled around and cut themselves each a large slice of chocolate cake from the huge confection displayed in a plastic stand on the dully gleaming Formica counter. Richard said nothing. He slouched at the cash register, reading the racing column in *The Philadelphia Daily News*, written, he informed them, by someone whose name matched that of some of the city's most illustrious bigwigs, and wasn't that a fall in the social world? The two kitchen workers retreated to the back to feast in privacy.

Later two very grungy hippies Ron knew well entered searching for him.

"No more sleeping on the street," said Wild Man.

"You look like you slept in the gutter," Ron replied in his surliest manner.

"We're squatting in a building on South Street," said his sidekick, White Man, so named because he was an albino, a condition which, despite his filth, his tattoos and numerous other decorations, was still detectable. "We saved you a room, if you want it."

"I want it."

"Seventeenth and South. We padlocked the place. Meet us there when you get off at four."

"So you're finally going to have a roof over your head," Elijah smiled. Like the true, kind-hearted friend he was, he had kept Ron's homelessness secret from their employers for many months. They had nothing to base it on, but both feared the news might lead to Ron being let go.

"Hey," the erstwhile vagabond sauntered over to Richard. "Big news—I'm living in a building over on Seventeenth Street now."

"You mean you're not sleeping on the street no more?" Richard eyed him coolly. "Cause I saw you one night on Bainbridge, drivin' by. You were snoring your head off."

"You knew?" Ron was astonished that his well-kept secret was no such thing.

"Sure I knew. Nico too. Why you think we came here, to America? We got sick of sleeping outside. I'm glad to hear you did too. Now clean the counter. There's crumbs."

Though abandoned, the building was sound. The squatters repaired the steps, compensated for the lack of water by filling gallon jugs at a nearby restaurant and read by candlelight in the evening. The structure had fireplaces on the second and third floors, so they did not worry about heat in the winter. There were vermin, which they trapped and eliminated, holes in the walls, which they patched and painted, debris in the first floor store-front, which they gradually removed, a kitchen in the back, for which White Man, an accomplished electrician and thief, purloined electricity from a commercial building next door. So they had a refrigerator and an electric range. "Where's the dishwasher?" Ron demanded facetiously. "And I want a washer dryer, too." It was all very well to joke, but in fact the more than half-dozen residents had developed something much akin to pride of ownership, except of course that they did not own. If caught, they could be evicted any time.

"Not bad. Not bad at all," Elijah commented on his one visit to the premises, as Ron and Wild Man showed off their dwelling. Living as he did deep in the heart of the dangerous, dirty, and blasted war-zone that was the North Philadelphia ghetto, Elijah knew whereof he spoke. "I like the paint job." They stood on the decayed steps, next to a psychedelic mural that decorated the stairwell wall. The rest of the house was painted conventionally, trimly, in pastel colors with moldings in beige that were all "beautiful, beautiful," as Elijah put it. Wild Man had highlighted the building's finer points like a realtor, because as he explained, he considered himself a connoisseur of run-down communes, dividing his time, as he did, between "the half-way house," as they called it, and another commune in the shabbier quarters, a district called the Shadow-Lands, of another great but second-rate East Coast city.

One artistic resident had decorated the walls with abstract portraits and landscapes, whose explosions of purples, blues and greens Elijah also praised. One vista in red particularly arrested him, causing him to step back, his chin contemplatively held in both brown hands and to murmur that he would like to meet this painter, whose vision, he remarked in a rare moment of self-revelation, gave him hope for what he otherwise knew to be a sorry and doomed world, an assertion made with such unexpected force from somewhere else, someone else, whose word was so true and final, that it caused White Man to step back, survey him and announce that indeed Elijah was appropriately biblically named. Something glimmered in the older man's eyes, eyes that daily gazed upon the moonscapes of North Philadelphia, upon the ferocious struggle to survive there, in that dreadful place to which its residents had been condemned like prisoners in a war whose winners were scarcely human in their callous indifference to suffering, and those deep brown eyes glimmered with wisdom and life, as he uttered softly, surprisingly, the non sequitur that yes, "Elijah is my name, just as knowledge is to eschew evil and wisdom is to fear the Lord." Then he looked away and it was as if something vanished from them, for when he glanced back, he quietly, blandly said that his only criticisms were the absence of television and that the stairs needed carpeting. Nico Moustafapoulous expressed an interest in seeing Ron's new abode too, with the inquiry, "you got girls?" No, the vagabond shook his head deceitfully, they did not. In truth, however, two women lived at the squatter's commune, hippies from California, one, yclept Mary Magdalene, with a quiet, frightened child, and Ron, despite a marked obtuseness to the wishes of others, especially women, did sense that they would not appreciate Mr. Moustafapoulous' advances.

On cooler currents, the summer of love rolled into fall, when the vagabond-turned-squatter commenced his stint as a creative writing student. Aside from composing lyrical paragraphs and occasional verse, the newly inspired poet learned the utility of his good looks—he always had a smitten girlfriend or two in tow and in no time was leading poor Nathan around by the nose. It was at that young aesthete's abode that Gilbert first met him and pronounced him "not very bright," the most devastating card in Gilbert's deck of criticisms.

"You're right," Nathan sighed, "but he could be an out and out idiot—"

"He is."

"And I'd still love him."

They sat in Nathan's living room, with its churchyard view through leafy treetops, glimmering like some mammoth emerald necklace in the bright, gusty afternoon. Standing at the window and glancing down, Gilbert regarded the tops of the passers'-by heads. He watched Ron's recede along the cracked sidewalks of Pine Street.

"He treats you like you're his dancing bear."

Nathan, rather portly, decided not to take this as a reference to his girth. "If he wants me to perform, I'm happy to oblige."

"He's a sham."

"Really Gilbert. I disagree."

"An imbecile and a fake. Wait and see." This harsh judge then passed from that unpleasant topic to the more felicitous one of the love of his life, Naomi Lichter. Thoughts of her monopolized his every waking moment, and when he slept, he dreamed of her. Her memory distracted him in his college classes and his exercising in the university pool. He could scarcely read his precious Rimbaud, Baudelaire, Celine, Henry Miller, William Burroughs, and as for chess, why he was surely going to lose the current game to Nathan—a dreadful defeat and the first of its kind. The only solution, as he saw it, was to approach love as an intellectual problem.

His companion snorted derisively. "The only solution for you, my boy, is to marry her. Then all your difficulties will vanish. No such solution, however, is available to me."

"You have money, offer to support him in exchange for his…favors," and great glitters of hostility for the person he had just met shone in the depths of Gilbert's blue eyes, "try that and see what happens."

"You think he's a cheap whore."

His friend's eyes glittered again. He gazed out through the wind-tossed branches and the sparkling green of the fluttering leaves and murmured, "soon they'll change color and fall."

"Like they do every year," Nathan snapped. "Stop being poetic and pay attention to what I just did to your queen."

Oddly distracted by the soughing outdoors that seemed suddenly cold and ominous, Gilbert reseated himself at the chessboard by the window and the two players became absorbed in the game and forgot the suddenly iron clouded sky, the cool, autumn wind, the swaying branches, the somber, brown church across the street and the question of whether or not Ron Swurl was a graceful moron or a calculating con artist. All this vanished on the red and black board that stretched between them and the moves of the pieces that resulted that day, for the first time, in Nathan's triumph, accompanied by many unlikely, victorious war-whoops from one accustomed to the subdued self-deprecations of defeat.

Later that evening the two players made their way through the gloom to Mike Dellico's quiet house on Lombard Street, muffled in shadow, only to learn from his pallid and overworked father, leaning out from the darkness beneath the lintel, that he was a few blocks away at a party at Damon Gladly's.

"This should be interesting, with no bathing suit," Gilbert commented, and they struck off in the direction of the Gladly townhouse on Smedly Street, a large abode with a luxurious swimming pool in the basement. "I guess we'll have to skinny dip."

"You may, but like a cat, I abhor water," Nathan replied, lighting a cigarette. "Give me wine, any day."

"Oh I'm sure there will be plenty of that," his friend replied dryly, listening to their lonely footsteps along Pine Street, "and probably an array of mind-altering drugs as well."

He was wrong. There was dancing, and nothing else. But that was sufficient to ruin his evening: he did not dance, but Naomi, who was there, did, with great abandon and with a partner, one Boris Slavonovich, a tall, lean anti-war Vietnam veteran from a Ukrainian neighborhood in another part of town. His long, lank, blond hair swung in one piece in time to the music, as Gilbert dipped into a funk and, at a pause in the ruckus, saw Nathan conversing with his beloved.

"I have advised you repeatedly to let him go slowly," Nathan said, "not torture him. Or, if you can't, then marry him. You could do worse."

"So I'm to break up with him but not see anybody else," Naomi feigned confusion, "or marry him, and of course not see anybody else. What's the difference?"

"Either would be preferable to what you're doing now, which is staying together, while you take up with other men."

"I'm just dancing, Nathan." She waltzed away. "And now I'll dance with Jake Whitly. Eileen won't mind, you'll see."

But Gilbert minded and, at a pause in the music, stalked out. Nathan trailed after him, regaling him with remonstrances.

"Our lives are petty and stupid," Gilbert spoke bitterly, his tall athletic form somewhat bent forward as they passed down dark, deserted streets in the cool night air. "I've lost my heart, soul and mind to a pretty face—"

"And as a result you can't even tell when she's just dancing with a friend."

"Maybe I should enlist."

"Commit suicide before that."

"I'll take it under advisement."

They found themselves strolling in deep shadows under swaying branches along narrow Delancey Street. Up ahead, someone fumbled and clanged with a tin garbage can. They approached, and Morris Lichter, putting out the trash, recognized Gilbert and scowled. "You wouldn't happen to know the whereabouts of my daughter, Naomi?"

"She's at a party at Damon Gladly's," the young man suavely replied, ignoring the scowl. But it deepened at this news.

"Skinny dipping, no doubt," Morris growled.

"Not at all. Dancing, and with everyone but me."

Morris looked rather pleased at this news, but then the scowl crept back. "They'd better not be drinking, or smoking pot. If they are, I'll have the police over there so fast, the Gladlys won't know what hit them."

"No," Gilbert soothed. "The party had more of a political tenor. Lots of anti-war Vietnam veterans and other peaceniks."

Morris brightened; his eyes nearly twinkled behind his horn-rimmed glasses. "Why, that's almost respectable. Not that we should ever dare dream to aspire to such a bourgeois state of affairs."

"Some of us yearn for it," Nathan replied.

"Not you," Morris snapped. "I can't count the number of times I've seen you smoking pot and gyrating around, as Mike Dellico's band roars out music in Rittenhouse Square."

"I long for the upper middle class splendor of my childhood," Nathan intoned.

"Stop making things up, Nathan," Morris snapped again. "You can't pull the wool over my eyes."

"Nathan's in love," Gilbert explained matter-of-factly.

"Oh? What lucky young man is it this week?"

"Something called Ronald Swurl."

Morris gave a start, his eyes flashed with a sudden and unaccountable fury, and the muscles in his suddenly clenched jaw stood out rigidly. Then he crashed the metal lid on the metal trash can with great acoustic effect. "Well, whatever you do," he shouted at Nathan, "Don't bring him around here!" With that, he stalked back into the darkened house and slammed the door.

By the time Naomi encountered Ron in the vestibule of Nathan's building that damp, sunless, spring afternoon, Ron had tired of his attentions, though not, as others had predicted, of his money. So when she broke the silence of their stroll to the restaurant to mention that "Nathan has told me so much about you," he responded with a dismissive hand gesture and the words: "Let's not talk about him. Let's talk about me," he laughed, noting that her upturned face was very pretty and promised in a few years to be quite lovely.

"I have to get out of Philly," he announced later, as they both chomped on their cheese steaks. "It's a back-water. I'm thinking of moving to Boston or San Francisco."

His companion praised Boston, which she visited regularly. It thronged with students, hippies, concerts, rallies and art. He would love this vast temple of the young. She had friends there who could put him up. She herself, however, preferred New York City.

"Not me," the erstwhile vagabond replied, tossing his long blond hair. "I've been there a few times. A place like Manhattan—I'd get eaten alive. New York would kill me." For some reason she could not explain, perhaps the preternaturally clear image that suddenly came to mind of him slouched ragged in some louche East Village doorway, these words contained a truth so undeniable that she hesitated to say: "Not me. It won't eat me alive. I was born there. I come from there. I fit in. After college, that's where I'm going to live, though not permanently."

As their conversation rilled lightly over other topics, it soon dammed up at the coincidence that her father worked for All American Amalgamated. Her companion leaned back, lit a cigarette, exhaled a long, blue stream of smoke and languidly commented: "How odd. Mine does too, but in Houston. He's a horror, a first-class son of a bitch."

Taken aback at these harsh words so devoid of any familial love or respect as to be quite shocking, she fell silent, until, sometime later, overcome by the awkward wordlessness of their mutual link to this firm, she sought to avoid the evident filial fury by inquiring instead about his father's work for the company. "He heads up their mining operations in the Andes, sees to it that the peasants are kept docile by near starvation, frequently lethal working conditions and unmitigated poverty. That's what he does, all for a little copper and zinc and a lot of moolah. I know. I looked into it. I take no money from him."

"Just from Nathan," she blurted out before she realized it.

But, shameless, he was not offended. He simply exhaled another stream of smoke and murmured, "Ah yes, poor Nathan."

Invited to the South Street commune that afternoon, she was treated to the sight reserved for select intimates of watching Ron write. She found she did not like his bombastic compositions, but felt constrained by the good manners of her upbringing hypocritically to utter nothing but praises. Then they found that she had some cash in her brightly colored, woven Mexican bag, so they tromped along to the Theater of the Living Arts to watch *Citizen Kane*, to the "profundities" of which he correctly alerted her. Despite these occasionally accurate judgments, there lurked the suspicion in her mind that his was packed with clichés, platitudes, and things deadeningly ordinary; but then she enjoyed his company and, more important, there was that disturbing business about the Peruvian mine workers. She wondered if her father's money was tainted too, since he worked for the same company, and concluded that it was, but could see no way to avoid taking it. She planned to work part-time in college, just as she had the preceding summer in a restaurant popular with Penn students and the summer before in a clothing store, but if such toil only covered living expenses, tuition eluded her financial reach. She depended on paternal largesse for that, and yet here was her new and knowledgeable acquaintance, informing her that it derived, albeit in part and indirectly in her case, from brutally exploited peasants.

"I've looked into it," she broached the issue with studied casualness at breakfast the next morning, "and it seems All American runs some rather nasty operations in Latin America, treating the locals horribly."

"It pays the bills," Morris said, setting down his coffee cup, but not budging his eyes from the open copy of *The Philadelphia Inquirer* in his other hand.

"Where have you been looking into it?" Her mother wanted to know.

"The public library," the girl lied, and then to add a dollop of truth, "and some of my friends mentioned it. That's what got me curious."

"It's a big, multinational, diversified corporation," her father murmured absent-mindedly, still reading about the upcoming, 1968 election. "It's bound to have some connections that purists would regard as unsavory."

"Wringing every last drop of blood out of Peruvian miners? Working them to the bone like slaves? Do you know how many of them die in those mines?"

"I don't know about that." Morris' glance strayed from the news article to an advertisement for laxatives, which seemed somehow grotesquely out of place. "I thought the company had cut back on many of those operations—too much political unrest, too many communists, union organizers, strikes.

I wouldn't worry about it. Textiles and supplying fast food chains—those seem to be the big things these days."

Somewhat mollified, she finished her Cheerios. "By the way, I'm going to the Democratic national convention in Chicago this summer."

"And your means of locomotion shall be what?" Morris put down the paper and stared at his daughter in sudden bewilderment.

"A veteran I know who's against the war will drive me and Eileen."

"I don't think it's a good idea. There could be riots."

After she left, Morris turned to his wife. "I did not want to come right out and forbid it. That would just have made it irresistible."

"We're going to have to work on this one," Lily replied. "I don't like that idea at all."

That afternoon, practically swimming in the rich, cigarette and marijuana haze that wreathed among the tree trunks and park benches of Rittenhouse Square, Naomi encountered a visibly looped Ron. Ferrying Daphne home, she disliked his mirthful condescension regarding the "two schoolgirls."

"Who is that awful person?" Daphne asked, as they trudged through the warm damp April mist.

"Nathan's boyfriend," her older sister replied, "and the boyfriend of countless college girls too, if rumors are correct."

"He was superior. He was obnoxious."

"He's a street person."

"I could see that."

"I don't understand street people." But she learned to, and quite fast. She learned that they could be brutal, cruel and unreliable, and came to this knowledge in such a way that it blinded her to any compassionate excuses and understanding apologies for what she regarded as horrible behavior. For the next time she saw Ron, they decamped to his commune, where they wound up in bed together. She had not planned it, it happened entirely by accident, but the result was irrevocable: she was utterly in love with him. And then, of course, she did not hear from him. She sought him out after several days, and they made love again. Silence ensued.

"But I don't have a telephone," he carelessly reminded her one afternoon on his front step.

"But you have a dime for a pay phone."

He shrugged, as if this were not worth replying to, and Naomi, who thought she would go insane, just stared at him in disbelief. He offered no excuses, not to her, not to anyone. It was as if no one was worth it. And then a young woman with several telltale canvasses under her arm, clearly an art student—all that was missing was the beret—came up and kissed him. Naomi burst into tears and fled.

After that she found she could not bear Gilbert's presence and, guilt-stricken, avoided Nathan. Others became her constant companions. Weeks passed, then one afternoon, when she had finished her homework, the phone rang, and Daphne entered holding her nose. "It's Ron," she announced rather nasally. He wanted to meet her for food at Nineteenth and Pine, a barren little corner enlivened only by Joe's Pizza.

"You think I'm an animal," he said, gobbling cheese and tomato sauce.

She nodded and nibbled hers.

"I am, but," more gobbling, "so are you."

She put her slice down on the plate. "That's a lie. I treat people I'm intimate with with some decency."

"What about Nathan? Have you treated him with decency?"

She flushed and mumbled that that was different, a betrayal of a friendship, something terrible to be sure, but less atrocious.

They stared at each other across the pizza, until suddenly, for no accountable reason, she started telling him anecdotes, from school, work and home. She began to entertain him. He enjoyed it and dropped their mutual anathematization. "Tell me more about that ridiculous math teacher," he said. And she launched yet another tale. She had no idea whence sprang these many fables or why she narrated them, but they changed everything, endowing her with a sense of safety, as if she had introduced some little bit of civilization into the blasted landscape of their ill-planned affair. "I felt like Scheherazade," she said to herself afterwards, recognizing that in some way her feckless listener frightened her, that she could not make sense of him and that he might, so she rather hysterically thought, just as easily make love to her as cut her throat. He had treated her like garbage and broken her heart, without even thinking. What else might he do or not do? So on those days when he was not busy with another woman, she ended her visits with an anecdote. He would be visibly amused, and she would slip safely away. No one knew of this destructive relationship and, she thought, just as well.

As this deleterious romance continued into the summer, Gilbert, spurned and suspicious, espied them walking one warm afternoon through the hippie carnival of Rittenhouse Square. "Hello, I was unaware you two knew each other," he remarked, stopping before them to light a cigarette.

"It's a recent acquaintance," Naomi quickly put in.

"Nathan will be so pleased," Gilbert spoke to the self-proclaimed poet. "He's so eager for you to know all his friends."

Ron shrugged.

"Silent and mysterious to the end," Gilbert smiled and then, as his rival drifted off after some friends: "but deep?" he asked Naomi. "I doubt it." He paused, calling out, "let's all go over to Nathan's. He's sitting at home alone, pining for you."

"Some other time. I'm staying here," the distractible hippie replied and Naomi watched him turn in the bright sunshine to a group of girls and put his arm around one of them—watched with a pang, which, she noticed, Gilbert observed.

"I'm going home," she announced. "Alone. I need to think." Indeed she did, but no amount of thinking could change the fact that this time with Ron had pulverized her, so that deep down, she would never be the same, that the person she could have been, the woman, the wife she could have been would never now come into being. That woman, that wife, was aborted, and she would have to make do, thence forward, with half measures. "I'm an idiot," she told herself, walking home, oblivious to the glittering, vitreous, sun-filled air, the yellows and reds of flowers in window boxes. "I've fallen in love with a handsome face. There's nothing behind it, just a vacuum of pettiness, pride and self-regard."

"No Gilbert?" Morris, home early, perked up when he saw her. "He was here before, looking for you."

"I saw him. I just didn't want to spend time with him."

Morris clapped his hands together and rubbed them in eager approval. "A wiser decision I couldn't have made myself."

"Oh, it's not wise. It's foolish. But I'm an idiot." She disappeared up the stairs, leaving her rather perplexed parent to scratch his head in the kitchen. She slammed the door to her room and tried to concentrate on *The Brothers Karamazov*, but it was futile. In her largely inarticulate pain, she pictured herself made of stone that periodically cracked from agony, but otherwise remained immobile and dead. The only alive remnant of her was an incongruous longing for winter, above all for snow, lots of it: snowflakes drifting slowly through black, soundless air, silently blanketing the earth, the houses, trees, as it had done for centuries, for eons and would continue to do long after humans were gone.

She decided to talk to Eileen.

"Hi Anna…"

"Belle?" Eileen queried, coming down the front steps of the music institute. "Everyone says I look like my mother. Jake says it's uncanny." She put an arm around her younger friend and recounted her plans to visit her father in Peru now that revolution was coming to that country. She rambled on about the working conditions of miners and the subsistence of farmers, while Naomi gazed inward at mental visions of snowfall.

They ambled down partly renovated Lombard Street then over to Walnut and crossed the bridge into West Philadelphia. Jake pulled up in his Volkswagen Bug and honked. No, they did not want a lift.

"Lester says," for she called her father by his first name, "that the fruits in Latin America are wonderful. I'm introducing myself to the more commonplace ones first. I've been eating mangos and papayas for the past few weeks. By the time I go in September, after the Chicago convention, I'll be a fruitarian."

At last, after wandering well into West Philadelphia, they stopped at the rather shabby tenement where Eileen had lived since her mother's death. She unlocked the door, and they climbed three flights of stairs to her cheery, if roach infested, two bedroom apartment. Sheet music was everywhere, while two oboes stood guard on a battered coffee table.

"Can I live here this summer with you?" Naomi asked abruptly.

"Of course, and it'll be an easy commute to your restaurant here in West Philly."

"Good, I won't have to take the bus. I have to get away from my parents. They're always either prying or screaming at me. And I've decided about next year: I'll take it off, not go to college. Circle campus will delay my entrance until the fall of '69. I'll spend my year on the commune in Northeast, Maryland, where Boris and Damon lived. Mike's moving there this summer. I'll go after the Chicago convention."

Eileen wondered what Gilbert thought of all this.

"All he thinks about is chess with Nathan."

At this mention of their mutual friend, an odd consternation flickered in Eileen's dark eyes—a stricken abasement, one her companion had seen before, in connection with her notorious infidelities. Silence ensued, and the young visitor grimly pondered that look.

"Have you seen Nathan?" The faithless oboist asked casually, turning away.

"Not in ages," Naomi rather guiltily replied. For the truth was, she had avoided her old friend and his wild despair over Ron Swurl.

"Neither have I," Eileen spoke now with her back to her friend, as she gazed out a little window at brightly colored laundry on a line, flapping in the indifferent breeze in the alley. She turned around. "You've probably guessed why."

Her guest admitted that she had no idea.

"It's Ron!" Eileen almost shrieked and collapsed into a red, butterfly chair that matched her red peasant blouse. Tears streamed down her pale face, as she pushed her dark hair out of her eyes. "I've been with him almost six months. No one knows. Not Jake, not Nathan. It would kill Nathan. Oh, he treats me so horribly, as if I'm just trash. You have no idea how destructive it's been."

Naomi straightened up. Outside, through the little window, the multicolored wash rippled in the wind, like flower petals bobbing on a river. The shouts of children rose up from the alley, reminding her of what it was like to be little and consumed with the unconscious joy of being alive. She found herself miserably muttering platitudes. "All you can do is try to find someone else."

"Jake won't do."

"Why not?" Naomi wondered and then found herself equally puzzled by the parallel thought that Gilbert wouldn't do, befuddled by the obvious truth that both were far better people than the idiot who had supplanted them. Again she murmured lamely: "I'm sorry Eileen. I just don't know what you should do."

"Of course not. I'll live. I'll get out of this somehow, but I'll just be…less."

"And so will Nathan and countless others."

"What will become of him?"

"Mister Swurl? Oh, he'll drift out to San Francisco and live in Haight Ashbury and do a little of this and a little of that and, ultimately, die on the street. He's not a monster. He's just deficient. He can't see the good around him, the good that comes to him. Maybe there's just not that much there."

This explanation not only calmed Eileen, but seemed to please her immensely. She stepped into the pathetically tiny and outdated bathroom, where she rinsed her tear-streaked face and asked what her guest would like to do.

"I have to leave, actually. I have an appointment with Dr. Wildinson."

Back on the sidewalk, luckless Naomi walked swiftly to the bus, then rode it down to Center City, her mind a blank. Sitting in the dark, close waiting room, she resolved on silence and absence: she would never tell her friend what had happened and she would never see her erstwhile and heartless lover again. She had found that something was trying to destroy her, and her correct instinct was to flee. She did not falter in her decision even as she left the doctor's office with the news that she was two and a half months pregnant, which made Ron the father. "I will have this child and keep it," she thought, "and he will never know."

On the ill-starred trip to Chicago, before they even reached the sluggish river and industrial bridges of Harrisburg, Boris' beat-up, old, purple Volvo rumbled and wobbled to a stop with its first of three flats. Even as he changed the tire, he could not stop lecturing on the causes and origins of the Vietnam War, the official lies told to cover up the atrocities perpetrated by the U.S. military, how close the situation had come, several times, to becoming nuclear, how there still existed within the senior ranks of the military the intention to use nuclear weapons, how this war proved that the Republic was dead and had been replaced by an empire, and so forth.

"Boris," Eileen remonstrated, standing in her pink, Indian-print dress like some graceful, oversized and unlikely blossom on the roadside, "you can take a break. You don't need to tell us all of this at the speed of sound."

But he could not stop. He devoted every sinew of his being to ending the Vietnam War and had done so from the moment he was shot out of his helicopter and survived. Prior to that catastrophe, he had soured on the war, but as he hovered between life and death in the hospital, his face scarred, his body broken, he underwent a conversion, and swore to the power that let him live that he would never slacken his efforts to end the criminal enterprise in which he had participated. He was a man possessed, and what unleashed torrents of the most furious abuse was the iniquity of the politicians in Washington D. C., responsible for the carnage. Then, after a twenty minute tirade, he would subside, exhausted, and murmur some homage to Gandhi and peaceful nonviolence. Naomi did not believe a word of it. This man, she considered, would throw bombs, if he thought that would end the war.

Meanwhile she silently laid her plans. In Chicago, she would investigate employment, day care, part-time attendance at the college while she worked and arranging to live at the commune on the near North Side where they would stay. Granted it would all be for a year hence, but she would have a nine-month old with her, so nothing could be ad hoc. She did not worry about her time before coming to Chicago. The late stage of her pregnancy, the delivery and the baby's infancy would all occur on the commune in Northeast, Maryland. That part seemed easy. It was the combination of school, work, child-rearing and living in an enormous metropolis that daunted her. So she sat in the back seat, with its worn upholstery, her cheek pressed against the dusty window, the air conditioner chugging noisily, and watched the alternately flat and hilly Pennsylvania scenery flash by in the advancing twilight. They had left late in the day, crawling through swarms of Philadelphia traffic, then zooming along the highway, aiming to spend the first night in Pittsburgh, at the apartment of a friend, also a veteran and war protester. The following morning the foursome intended to drive straight through to Chicago and thus have several days free before the convention, days that the young mother-to-be considered crucial to her plans.

They arrived in Pittsburgh well after nightfall. The sultry summer weather had cooled, so they rolled down the car windows, and in came the acrid smoke of the steel mills. There was other industry too, and a sharp, odiferous blanket of chemicals lay over the hills. They drove up and down, in search of the correct street and, finally locating it and the small house, rang the bell and were ushered up to a third floor apartment. The windows were open to the night, and the same stench of industry wafted in.

"Benzine, I'd say," Boris remarked, after dramatically sniffing the air.

"Oh, we got everything here," Alan Jengo replied. "It keeps the unions busy, filing grievances, and keeps a labor organizer like yours truly busy, backing up the union." Their host had prepared a vegetarian stew, so they sat down in his cramped dining room, crammed with cardboard boxes full of leaflets and flyers, all pertaining to organizing drives, and drank a toast to peaceful revolution.

They inquired about his uncommonly short hair.

"Oh I've got to fit in at the factories and the mills," he answered. "I can't go in with hair down to my shoulders like Boris here and beads, bells and sandals. I'd be out on my ass in no time. I am anyway, but it'd just be quicker. Your average American factory worker, by the way, is not too receptive to anti-war propaganda. Still, I get a few converts every week or two. But I wouldn't get any if I looked like a hippie. Those SDS organizers can look like anything they want. They're mainly in contact with college students and professors. But I've got to look the part of the middle American industrial worker. I do a pretty good job, don't you think?" And he grinned cheerfully.

That night, as she lay on a sleeping bag in the living room, her left leg became numb. This could happen during pregnancy, she had read, so it brought her child's life back into her mind. "There are two of us here, not just one," she thought, conscious of a certain fleshy, abdominal fullness that brought to mind a bud about to bloom, the petals pressing out against enfolding leaves, and was so distinct, so undeniable physically that she asked out loud: "What is it? What do you want?"

"Hunh?" Mumbled Eileen, half asleep and enshrouded in the thick, vague perfume of slumber.

"Just a dream," the mother-to-be replied to her and to the soft sounds of Boris shifting position on the couch.

"I dream," he mumbled drowsily. "I dream about the war."

"That's not it, not it at all," Naomi replied. Then came silence again, to match their dark muffled forms, lit only by some stray beams from a distant street lamp, which touched the gloom despairingly and lost themselves further in. Smoke and cloyingly sweet chemical odors drifted in through the open window, smells of the industrial nightmare that made her murmur again, "that's not it either." She moved her benumbed leg and thought fuzzily, "there's someone alive, *alive* inside of me. That's it, after all."

Well after an orange dawn, they all clambered into the purple Volvo and drove west. Pennsylvania roared past, then the expanses of Ohio, Indiana, and at dusk they entered Gary. Huge smokestacks and factories loomed in the twilight, like the maw, they all rather melodramatically thought, of some monster that fed on men.

"We could stay here," the labor organizer urged. "I have a good friend who's a steel-worker. He'd be delighted to put us up."

But Boris did not like the idea. Monomaniacal in more respects than one, he wanted to finish the drive at a shot, so they sped on through the dusty gloaming to Chicago, which took shape before them even in the dark, as they coasted in on the skyway. In the distance gigantic towers massed against the night, below spread out the silent slums of the South Side. They had arrived.

The two women were startled to find the city so vast, unlike the eastern metropoli. Even in complete shadow, it could be felt to stretch away in all directions, except toward the great, glimmering dark sheen of Lake Michigan to the east, mile after mile of city blocks, slumbering buildings, deserted corners under street lamps, parked cars, rumbling elevated trains and nearly empty buses with their few passengers joined in the little light within. They rode up to the Loop, Alan at the wheel, while Boris snored with his head pressed against the window, and were dazzled by the blaring neon, then kept on to the North Side. Not far from the Body Politic, a landmark they had been alerted to note, they found their friend's commune in a small, three-story house. The visceral rhythms of very loud music emanated from first floor windows, and an upper window glowed bizarrely purple from a lava lamp.

"You said we'd have one room to ourselves," Naomi reproached the now waking Boris. "It looks like there are way too many people for that."

"It's probably just a party," the veteran replied.

And so it was. The visitors located their friends in the sweating throng and were given a back room on the third floor. The two men promptly tossed their bags on a chair and then jogged downstairs to join the crowd. But Naomi shut the door and collapsed, leaning back against it, as the clamor receded and with it the unsettling dizziness of this congregation of what seemed hundreds of strangers. She ran the back of her hand across her pale, perspiring forehead, and then suggested to her friend that they elude the crowd and tramp through the neighborhood.

"The streets are so wide here," Eileen remarked, plucking off strands of hair that clung to her Indian-print dress, "and so deserted at night." They found a little soup restaurant and descended a short stairway to the entrance. Over broccoli and potato soup, Naomi asked the waitress about public transportation to the University of Illinois campus. "It doesn't take long at all," came the reply. "It's a quick commute."

"Planning on living at the commune?" Eileen asked, slurping her mushroom barley soup.

"If I like the people, and they'll have me."

Quiet and dimly lit, the eatery had only a half dozen other customers, mostly couples, and, watching them, Naomi succumbed to a wave of sadness that her child would grow up fatherless and that she herself was alone. "It can't last," she said aloud, and of course her friend wanted to know what.

"This loneliness of mine."

"You could have Gilbert."

And with those words, Naomi suddenly believed that her solitude would last, unbroken, forever.

Over the next few days, she spent much time at the state university campus, ascertaining that her deferred entrance was secure and through the student employment office that she could snag a job at the university—many were available—and locating a suitable day care center nearby. She befriended several communards, receiving assurances that she could live there cheaply. Then she explored the city, occasionally attending confabs with SDS members in Hyde Park, in the Café Saint Juste. There, in the dimness drenched with the aroma of exotic coffees, veterans and students opposed to the war coordinated their efforts. The police, she heard, would likely riot, having prepared thoroughly for the convention, and, as Boris put it, "lots of heads could get cracked." After the second meeting, however, she drifted out of the café and ambled along tree-lined summer streets or browsed in the cool of bookstores, perusing translated classics and settling on Manzoni's *The Betrothed*, which she had never heard of before and was astonished to read that every Italian schoolchild had memorized. At such moments, the ocean of her ignorance spread out before her, vast, churning and liable to drown her any second, something she could never beat back or conquer. The attempt seemed futile. Still, she made her frail little efforts, which, like moth wings thrumming against the deep, made no mark and left her exhausted. "I'll never learn it all," she lamented.

At other times she cast her gaze down the ages of civilization and culture that stretched away like endless dusty stacks in a labyrinthine library and murmured: "It's too tremendous, and I'm too small."

Still, her education had not been negligible. She had read Caesar, Cicero, Vergil and Livy in Latin and in French had read Corneille, Moliere, Racine and some moderns. Otherwise, it had been the standard high school curriculum, which she had sense enough to know needed supplementing with wide reading. Though she did not use the term, at eighteen she was an autodidact. "That's what you are," said Betsy Ein, a University of Chicago student, radical, and ferocious feminist, with whom she had become friendly. "All those books you've read on your own—that's your real education, not high-school math and biology labs." As she spoke, her green eyes looked so very serious that it was almost comical, and Naomi suppressed a smile. "For real," the committed revolutionary insisted, tossing her mane of bright red curls, with mild indignation and remarking that for most women, throughout history, if they wanted education they had taught themselves, mostly just by reading. "Don't snicker. It's what you are, an autodidact."

"What will happen to the autodidact," her interlocutor later wondered, "when the baby arrives?"

The Café Saint Juste meetings continued until the convention, and Naomi regularly drifted out to lounge in dry, dusty deserted parks or by the lake with Betsy. Several times she ventured to Hyde Park at night, but other students warned her of crime. So she passed her evenings in the less questionable precincts of the North Side, where Eileen had decided that she did not much care for Chicago and, to escape her entanglement with Jake and the disaster with Ron, intended to enroll as a music student in San Francisco in the fall. By now she had confided every sordid detail of her ill-fated affair to her younger friend, who bore them stoically and silently, as they slithered across her mental field of vision with their sickening glints of chance and coincidence that invited comparison to her own condition, and this was usually in the tiny soup establishment, where she would stop perusing the local underground newspapers, reading Betsy Ein's book reviews, and glance up to hear yet another installment of what seemed like an endless romantic catastrophe, liable at any time to ensnare her in its ever-widening destruction.

"But you usually have opinions about this sort of thing," Eileen decried the taciturnity of her listener, "and such good advice."

"I think your Ron makes me a dunderhead," Naomi said, idly stirring a mediocre chicken vegetable soup that she could swear she had once tasted from a can.

"You and every other woman in the world."

"Then I will avoid him completely."

Meanwhile the city filled with politicians and protesters.

"We will shut this convention down," Boris announced vehemently one night over dinner at a famous Chicago Greek restaurant, Demos. As the dark haired men danced in the back, clasping each other's arms, as Boris harangued his listeners, his lank hair gleaming gold from the bright overhead lights, as diners at other tables spoke intensely of clashes with the police, consideration of Eileen's predicament—whether or not to purchase a cheap used Volkswagen Bug, gaudily painted with flowers and butterflies—seemed an oasis of the small, the private, the personal, amid the world's exhausting din.

Although she and her friends never got close to the International Amphitheater that housed the visiting Democrats and scarcely even glimpsed the stockyards, they took part in the mid-week pitched battle between demonstrators and police in front of the Conrad Hilton hotel. Pregnant Naomi hung back from the front lines and the fury of the violent, rioting police, but Boris and Alan did not. Both got clobbered over the heads and were dragged, bleeding, to a paddy wagon, crammed with bloody, sweaty yippies and other assorted, wounded radicals. Boris found himself pressed against a Sparticist, still clutching her literature and hollering about overthrowing the elite and battling their bloodthirsty Praetorian guard. Eileen fell and was trampled, but Naomi yanked her to her feet and, in the general rout, they fled. They tried to locate Boris, to no avail. He reappeared at the commune the next morning, still bloody and soot-streaked. At the sight of his red stained T-shirt, Eileen hurried over to support him. "This has gone far enough," she said firmly. "No more rallies for you today, nor for you, my friend," she called back to Alan, staggering in after.

The two protestors collapsed on a ragged maroon couch in the chaos of cluttered books, stacked newspapers and scattered used and unclean crockery that passed for a living room. Naomi retrieved wet dish towels and cleaned their faces. The blood reddened the towels. The dirt was more stubborn, but after much work, they could see that both men had scabbed gashes on their heads.

"There was a pregnant woman next to me," Boris said, wincing as his friend gently palpated his wound. "They clubbed her too. They clubbed everyone in sight. Mayor Daley's finest fascist force—that's what they should call them."

"I threw rocks," Alan added, "but it was futile. They just bounced off the helmets."

"Tonight, when we go back—"

"You won't," Eileen said. "As soon as you're rested, we go to the emergency room."

"The yippies were well organized," Alan continued. "They had good preparation in New York. When the police charged, they dispersed quickly, then regrouped, sometimes behind the police. That way they cut a lot of them off. The cops were scared."

"I didn't notice that stopped them crashing their nightsticks on the yippies' heads though," Boris observed.

Naomi asked a resident for fresh T-shirts.

"You can look in my bureau. I doubt any are what you'd call 'fresh.'"

"Well, not drenched in blood."

He nodded. She entered his room with the green Indian print bedspread covering the mattress on the floor like a stagnant pond, rich with algae and twining water plants. Wind chimes clinked and sang of summer zephyrs in the open window, and incense burned in a clay pot. The bureau stood opposite the bed, every drawer open with a rainbow of apparel hanging out. She rifled around, found two relatively clean T-shirts, just plain white, and put them up to her nose, detecting a slight male odor but nothing else. She then assisted her wounded friends, as they changed their shirts.

A few hours later, they waited in an emergency room, both men complaining of vicious headaches. Neither needed stitches. Both were advised, however, to avoid further contact with nightsticks.

"I've seen about a dozen identical injuries today," the pale, young doctor remarked. "You people sure are taking a beating, and what for?"

"To end an illegal war and shut down the convention of the party that is prosecuting it."

"Oh, I see," the doctor smiled. "So we can have a *Republican* president? Is that what you want?"

"That's not going to happen," Alan snapped.

"Oh? Don't you think a lot of people see these riots on TV and think, 'The Democrats sure have made a mess of things. What we need is an administration that's much tougher and more hard-line?' I would think that's the cumulative effect."

"So you support Daley's orders to his police."

The doctor shook his head. "I'm just saying that you may defeat yourselves. People in this country are sick of violence, sick of riots. There could be a backlash."

"Forget it, doctor," Naomi laughed. "You'll never convince these two."

"Well maybe this prognosis will," the young doctor snapped. "You go back out tonight and get clubbed on the head again? You'll be on your back, in the hospital for weeks. And if you get unlucky enough to get smacked in the same place—I don't even want to predict what could go wrong. So follow you doctor's orders. Go home. Stay in bed for two days. Don't exercise. Don't shout. Take it easy. You're lucky neither one of you has a fractured skull." The doctor had become rather worked up in the course of this harangue, and patches of red and purple now mottled his previously pallid cheeks.

"We will consider your advice," Boris, paler even than the doctor had been, replied.

"You will take it!" The doctor almost shouted. "Or I will keep you here overnight and put stitches in your head, which I'm already half-inclined to do."

"If I need stitches, so be it," the veteran answered stoically. "But I will not spend the night."

"You already have scars, which I take to be war wounds on your head. You cannot subject you skull, no matter how thick it appears, to another beating."

"You may consider me thick-headed, or anything you like, but your original opinion—"

"*Qualified*, uncertain opinion,"

"Was that stitches were unnecessary. So I shall now go home." And Boris rose, the whole, great lanky length of him, unfolding upward out of the little pink plastic chair, as he motioned Alan to follow. Amid plaints such as "perhaps the doc's right, Barry, maybe we should get stitches and stay," Alan was led away on the invisible leash of his companion's frozen fury at all practitioners of medicine.

"People like that are the problem," Boris expatiated once the little quartet had reached the broiling sidewalk. "Every idea is qualified. Every ramification stops them in their tracks. Then, when absolutely immobilized, they resort to insulting others who have resolutely committed themselves to action."

"No speeches, Boris," Eileen insisted with obvious exhaustion, though taking him gently by the arm. "And no more shouting. We're right here. Lower your voice."

In the end, the two injured men stayed home that evening, not by choice, but because Boris, the will power in the duo, fell asleep on the mattress with the green Indian print bedspread and did not awaken until late that night. "Alan," he howled, clutching his head and gasping for a breeze through the open window, whence nothing, however, aside from sultry evening air, not even the melancholy song of the wind chimes, drifted in. "Why didn't you wake me?" He demanded of the miscreant lurking in the doorway.

"You were asleep. I thought I'd let you rest till dawn."

"What time is it?" Boris barked, propping himself up on an elbow and lighting a candle on a milk crate by the mattress.

"Eleven thirty. Naomi and Eileen are still out at that soup place. It must be open all night. But they should be back any minute."

"Did I ask about them? What's the news on TV?"

"More clashes with police. The entire commune's downtown tonight."

Boris socked a fist into a palm. "We've got to get there."

"Why? It's virtually over. Everyone's been arrested or chased away again."

"You don't much like these battles with the police, do you, Alan?"

"I have no problem with that," his friend replied stiffly. "I just thought the doctor had a point, and as you were asleep…"

"The doctor has rocks in his head."

They remained thus a few moments, glaring at each other, two angry shadows whose forms shifted with the candlelight dancing in the gloom. Soon came the music of a high feminine voice on the sidewalk with the counterpoint of Naomi's somewhat deeper, huskier one, a lonely melody on an empty street that suggested the vast night city suddenly vacant, silent, deeply shadowed and deserted. The front door creaked open, then footsteps sounded in the darkened hall.

"So none of us put in an appearance at the protest tonight," the invalid remarked from his mattress and then bitterly: "so much for the Pennsylvania contingent—restaurants and naps. I should have been there, instead I slept the sleep of the dead."

"If you'd gone, you might very well have been dead," trilled a melodious female voice of indeterminate origin in the nocturnal black. "The police rioted again. A lot more heads got bashed, and I doubt yours could have taken another beating."

"That silly doctor just scared you, like Alan here."

"Really Barry, go back to sleep," Naomi soothed. "It's over. Everyone's gone for the night…" but as she uttered these words, a loud snore emanated from the pillows. She approached and blew out the candle. "If only it weren't so beastly hot," she murmured, leaving.

"I guess the communards don't believe in air conditioning," remarked Alan.

"They can't afford it. Tell me, do they have it on the Maryland commune?"

Alan shook his head. "It literally simmers there in the main house until the end of September."

"Oh, this abominable heat!" She repeated, passing down the hall into the dimness of the kitchen, where she ran the cold water in the sink and splashed her face. "Give me snow any day! Snow!"

Eileen Meer settled into the springy blue upholstered seat on her TWA flight from Philadelphia to Miami. Her Eustachian tube shut down uncomfortably, as the plane rose through the air, so she unwrapped a stick of Juicy Fruit and waited for the "No Smoking" sign to go off. The gum helped. Though the plane's rapid rise had impaired her hearing, the steady chewing released some of the auricular pressure. In her flower print peasant frock and beads, with her raven tresses down to her waist and her "Stop the War" button on her chest, she was easily identifiable as a hippie. The man in the business suit next to her suppressed the urge to sniff disapprovingly—after all, she was quite attractive. She turned and gazed out the window at the greens and industrial grays of Pennsylvania and Delaware, vanishing below. Then, when the little red sign blinked off, she lit a Marlboro and pulled her copies of *The Village Voice* and *The Different Drummer* out of her handmade Mexican bag. Undetected by her, the businessman rolled his eyes.

First she perused *The Different Drummer*, to study the various deeds and undertakings of her friends in Philadelphia's underground community. She was pleased to see an article by Jake Whitly on an antiwar protest, and then turned to the arts coverage.

"Vacationing in Florida?" The man next to her inquired, lighting a Marlboro of his own.

"Actually just changing planes. I'm going to Lima, Peru."

"The company I work for has interests in Peru," he said. "Mining."

"The miners are treated abysmally."

"I suppose they are," he paused. "Ever hear of All American Amalgamated?"

The young woman tried to appear distant and uninterested. She wanted to read her newspapers, to catch up on counter-cultural life in New York and Philadelphia. "No," she murmured absent-mindedly, though in fact it seemed remotely familiar.

"We have mining interests throughout Latin America," he smiled at her. "My name's Chester," and he held out a hand and beamed the hearty Swurl smile upon her.

She hesitated, but shook it. "I'm Eileen. Well, I hope the miners in other countries are treated better than those in Peru."

"Peru's pretty shaky right now. It's got a left-wing military about to take over the country. If they nationalize the mines, we stand to lose a lot."

"I bet you do," she replied, eyeing him rather coolly. "What a pity… for you."

"I couldn't care less, frankly. If they want to go communist that's their business. All American just provides my paycheck. I have no particular allegiance to one company or another. But I'll tell you this, in confidence: one threat to their interests in Peru and All American will crush those miners in no time."

She tilted her head and studied him. He was trying to impress her, but she had already decided to pass his confidences on to her father, who she knew very well was advising the Peruvian military. "How?" She asked.

"The combination of a black propaganda campaign against the labor organizers and the sudden withdrawal of all our funds from all the mines. No wages, no unions."

"But when people find out it's your company doing these things, this propaganda—"

"They never will. All American leaves no trace, never a footprint, besides," he winked at her, "we got the full backing of the U.S. Embassy in Lima." He stopped the stewardess and requested a second rum and Coke. Clearly the alcohol had loosened his tongue.

"Where did you say you're going?"

"To our Houston headquarters. That's where we coordinate all our Latin American operations, and if you think we aren't up to our eyeballs in local politics in those countries, think again."

"Oh," she said softly, "I will."

Chester, who had visited the airport bar before the flight and was now visibly tipsy, leaned over, patting her arm. "You should see the way those people live. You wouldn't believe it."

"I guess there's not much they can do about it," she spoke coldly. "They're poor."

"It's disgusting—shanty towns, sewage in the streets. They should just pull themselves up by their bootstraps—"

"Maybe they haven't got any."

"Ha!" He laughed uproariously. "That's a good one." His light blue eyes flickered over her. "How much time did you say you have in Miami?"

"No time," she compressed her lips into a thin brittle little smile. "I have to make my connecting flight right away."

"That's too bad," he slurred. "Miami's a great town."

Their meals came on light green trays—some nondescript triangle of beef, peas and macaroni and cheese. It was no worse than she expected, however, and she chewed thoughtfully. Maybe Chester's remarks could be useful to her father. Maybe he already knew these things. She glanced at her neighbor, who had already polished off his orange macaroni. "Which miners did you say your company will…attack first?"

"In the zinc mines," he loudly replied, waving his fork a little. "Zinc. That's what everything's about in Peru—zinc, zinc and more zinc. Shut down those mines and you've got the country by the—well, I'm not going to offend you."

"Oh," she thought, "but you already have. One crude cliché isn't going to make any difference." She continued eating in silence, then sat back and hoped for no turbulence. She also silently prayed that her neighbor would not open his horrible mouth again.

The plane began its descent, as Chester, sloshing through yet another alcoholic beverage, subsided into inebriated silence and then snores. Turning to study his profile, as her ears began popping, she stubbed out her cigarette and chewed another stick of gum. "There's something familiar about him," she thought, "and All American Amalgamated—where have I heard that?" Morris did not come to mind, because he never referred to the companies for which he worked by the name of the umbrella corporation. So, stumped, she returned to the column by Nat Hentoff in *The Village Voice* that she had started perusing after finishing with *The Different Drummer*. Now at last her seatmate's vaguely nauseating bravado interrupted her no more.

When the plane landed and taxied to the terminal, the sodden corporate climber did not immediately awaken. Therefore the escaping hippie gathered up her brightly colored bag with its folk art designs, stepped over him as gingerly as if he were a dangerous, sleeping bear and congratulated herself on avoiding the inevitable invitation to the bar. By the time he opened the light blue eyes that had so reminded her of someone else, she knew not of whom, she had vanished in the throng. For his part, he gave her not another thought, but turned his rather addled attention instead to exiting the bright and noisy airport and locating the offices of the giant sugar corporation, where he was shortly expected.

Then, about the time Chester alighted from a taxi before a gleaming Miami skyscraper, the young woman was aloft again, aimed at the Southern hemisphere and Peru's Pacific coast. This time her neighbor was more congenial: a well dressed, elderly woman from Lima, whose very poor English afforded Eileen the much prized opportunity to practice her Spanish. Together they stumbled through two languages high above a sapphire Caribbean in an azure sky, unmarred by a single cloud.

It was inky night when she landed in Lima, and her father met her at the airport. Tall, with wiry, iron-gray hair and eyes dark as ponds in a forest, magnified behind his glasses; and what curious creatures seemed to swim in their depths—visible regret at their years of separation, a resolve not to complain about it, a certain pride in his overall, exiled predicament, misery and guilt over his absence at Annabelle's death. Things were simpler for his daughter. Periodically, as they rode back to his apartment through darkened streets, she would say, "but that is the past." Finally he replied, "But of course it is, and it is important. The past is prologue."

"It's over," she replied. "I've put the past behind me."

He exuded a quiet, half-stifled relief that he would not be judged and censured for what he acutely saw as his many failings. "Everything here is on the brink," he responded, leaping metaphorically from the past to the future as he removed his hands from the wheel of the Chevrolet Impala at a stop light and rubbed them together briskly in anticipation of these great things to come. "The military is taking over, and the military is run by leftists."

"That brings me to a curious coincidence," she enunciated slowly. "Is there a company, All American Amalgamated, very heavily invested in zinc mines here?"

"Yes, of course. They're terrible. They exploit the miners mercilessly, who die in droves. That company is in bed with the CIA and pretends to know nothing when labor organizers turn up dead and mutilated in shallow, roadside graves. How did you know of them?"

"A man on the plane. I thought it might be bluster, but I guess he was so drunk, he was telling the truth." She glanced over at her father, whose deep, limpid eyes settled questioningly on her. "He works for that company," she resumed and then reiterated everything Chester had said. As she did, a subtle transformation took place. Mild mannered, retiring Leon Rathman was replaced by the militant Lester Meer, hardened by decades of exile and party discipline. "This is most useful," was all he said, but his manner, his tone, expressed a complete alteration. He was another man, not better or worse, just utterly different. A new personality had emerged.

It was the one his daughter had expected to meet at the airport, not the other, with the dark, liquid eyes inhabited in their depths by strange, conflicting emotions that only revealed themselves with occasional glints, lights suggestive of another, carefully hidden, cavernous interior world. She had expected a party functionary, and her encounter with Chester on the airplane had conspired to bring that person to the fore; her father, with his mixed-up feelings and literary quotes, disappeared. The revolutionary was at the wheel.

This was the man with whom she had come prepared to struggle, the one she had to bend to her will, to convince to give up his cause and come home. She could more easily, perhaps, have convinced that other one, the father, to do this, but would only have encountered resistance from the exiled comrade later. She preferred to attack matters head on, and was emboldened now by the perception that Lester did indeed have another, what she considered "more human," side. But alas for her, the revolutionary was quite human also and thus capable of great obstinacy.

"I knew it would be useful, "she repeated his adjective. "And I was hoping that after that, perhaps the revolution would have got enough use out of you. Why do you have to be an adviser to this left-wing military takeover? They're fine without you. You've been living on the lam for decades. It's time to come home."

"This is my home," he replied simply. "Not the U.S., not the U.S.S.R.," and he turned to flash a smile upon his beautiful daughter. "No more superpowers for me, though it's very kind of you to want me to join you. But what do you suppose would happen to a fugitive communist party member, who returned to the States for his retirement? Would he be allowed to live quietly, privately, in peace? I doubt it."

"The whole atmosphere of the forties and fifties, everything is over. Even Agent Blench—"

"You haven't been talking to him?" Lester sounded alarmed.

"No," She waved a hand in disgust. "No, he died of a massive coronary."

"There are plenty of others to fill his shoes. I knew when I fled in 1950 that this would be permanent. You mother could never accept that. She kept hoping I'd return, while I kept hoping she'd come live here with you. Let's not repeat the past. I don't want to hope that you'll stay and live with your old father, when you have so much waiting for you back in Philadelphia."

"Old? So much? You're wrong about everything."

"Well, let's not quarrel about it, not here in Lima, on the eve of this glorious victory for all that I believe in, all that I've struggled for over the years." The revolutionary, who had receded for a moment into the shadows of paternal love, reemerged, intensity only evident in the white knuckles, as his fingers pressed the wheel.

Lester parked the Impala near his apartment building, which loomed at the edge of a little hill and had small, cramped views of the ocean through the trees and other buildings. Inside, she read the name Rathman in the list of residents. "They all know me as Leon," he smiled at his daughter, leading her to an old elevator in the style of a birdcage. "No one has used the name Lester Meer in nearly two decades. It is a name that has almost vanished from the earth. I say 'almost' because occasionally, to rescue it from oblivion, I say it out loud, to myself. Saying it to you just now was the first time another person's ears had heard it in I don't know how long. Even Annabelle," he said, opening the elevator door at the sixth floor, "even she had trained herself to say Leon Rathman and was so afraid of getting me caught that I believe she never uttered the name Lester Meer—there, I said it again—again after I left New York in 1950." He stood at his apartment entrance and smiled, a smile rendered oddly ghostlike by this account of his legitimate name's disappearance, and his rare, secret summoning of it from the dead.

In his large, dim, high-ceilinged apartment, rooms opened upon rooms, until they vanished in deep shadow, tomb after tomb of secrets that wafted through the darkness like echoes from another world. "As you can see," her father said softly, indicating the spaciousness of his rather gloomy abode, "I have been well provided for."

"But you work for it, too," his daughter protested.

"Both."

He carried her bag into a bedroom and placed it upon a dark, carved wooden chest. "But all this space isn't wasted," he continued, standing by the window and gazing out at the night-city spread below. "I work here and put up so many itinerant organizers that they call it Lima's Red hostel."

"Isn't that rather obvious?" She asked, somewhat alarmed.

"Oh no, it's just among ourselves. To the rest of the world I am just a solitary American with a wide acquaintance, whose friends visit often." And then, as it was very late, he suggested they both retire. "Tomorrow will be a big day, as will, indeed, every day, from now on."

She raised a quizzical eyebrow.

"Because there will be a coup, very soon," he explained, already having turned to go and drifted to the door, and casting his last few words to her over his shoulder, as if they were the merest afterthought and not a bombshell, "I can tell you now, because we're not talking on the telephone and also because everyone knows. October is the month, once again. Socialist victory is finally at hand." And hardened yet again behind the battlements of his ideology, he put the quiet, somewhat confused and bedazzled father he was, to rout.

October was indeed the month. The president was ousted, and a leftist general took his place. The plans of All American Amalgamated and other multinational corporations were thwarted at every turn. The unions gained the upper hand, and contrary to Chester's prediction, the zinc mines remained open. A welcome figure among the new military politicians, Leon Rathman had access to the government's highest echelons. These were his days of triumph, of drafting glorious speeches for the new rulers of Peru and then reiterating their sonorous cadences to his daughter, each night over dinner. The fact that he had had no family to declaim to, except for his wife during her brief stay, had pent up a veritable tidal wave of revolutionary rhetoric. Years of toil, hope, secrecy, rage, came tumbling out over their salads and tortillas, all transmuted in the crucible of recent events into perfect, socialistically correct speeches of which any member of the Politburo could have been proud. Eileen thought she would lose her mind. She felt caged with a fanatic who would not shut up, who even lapsed, from time to time, into calling her "comrade."

"But I'm your daughter," she nearly shrieked, as much at his error as at her own recognition that she could not win the battle for her father's soul, that her wish to "bring him home" was the naïve velleity of a child. How foolish she had been! How ignorant of what it meant to confront someone who was, as her mother had once said, "implacable." She had not believed it. She had allowed herself to hope that the prospect of a life with his daughter could swerve his path back to the United States. She had convinced herself that she could sway her father, change him, that the offer of filial love would prove irresistible. But no, he was absolutely consistent, adamantine. He would never change, not for his wife, not for his child; he would remain as he was, not simply a leftist intellectual, not merely an ideologue, but beyond that, there he was, in the drab inflexible contours of a Soviet agent, still a party functionary; and that came first. At the same time, no one could accuse him of selfishness. Never had he demanded that either wife or daughter move to Lima, as was his right. And he had never complained about their staying away. He understood. He would not inflict his abstract devotion to the workers' paradise upon them. There certainly was that to be said for him.

On the day of her departure, which she had advanced two months in despair of her mission to reclaim him, he left her at the airport ticket counter. There was to be a meeting of representatives of the farmers, who had many unresolved grievances, with the appropriate commissars. Leon Rathman was, appropriately, to preside. He could not be late. He kissed his daughter on the forehead, then gazed into her eyes, bright like stars, not from the strong afternoon sun that beamed in the windows, but from her tears.

"Forgive me," was all he said, and in that instant when the father in him briefly triumphed over the soldier in his endless war, he knew and so did she, that they would never see each other again.

About the time that the remnants of the Meer family were disintegrating, Naomi's pregnancy became visible. Her parents remained ignorant for the moment, however, because she had decamped to the bosky commune in Northeast, Maryland, immediately following the pitched battles with police in Chicago. She informed them that she had deferred her university entrance for a year and that when she did attend, she would do so as a part-time student, working in her free hours. To offer no encouragement in what they regarded as the harebrained scheme of communal life, they let communication lapse. An occasional letter arrived from Lily, warm and chatty, full of tidings about brothers and sisters, but Morris was furious with his wayward second daughter and had told her that he had "washed his hands of her." And this was without knowing she was pregnant. She could only imagine what explosions of paternal rage such news would detonate.

So as the air grew cooler, skinny Naomi's stomach expanded. She had gravely assumed the responsibility of the remains of the rag-tag vegetable garden, upon which everyone depended for much of their food, and in autumn's advancing chill, uneven and premature, like a sudden thatch of gray hair in late youth, she, in her flower print, thrift shop dress, Mike Dellico and Damon Gladly bent among the uneven rows of green dotted with bulbous beige, white and orange squash. They spent long hours weeding, watering and plucking acorn, butternut, summer and spaghetti squash, as well as some elephant zucchini. The pumpkins clearly would be enormous.

"So you mean we can't tell anyone, who has any contact with anyone else in Philly that in a few months you're going to have a baby?" Damon asked, straightening up and surveying the placid, green rolling hills of this corner of Maryland, hills that ultimately sloped down to a tepid and greasy Chesapeake.

She nodded vehemently and explained that she feared her father would refuse to pay her college tuition, if he knew.

"That makes no sense," Mike Dellico argued, pushing up his sweat-drenched, wire-rimmed glasses with dirt-encrusted fingers and leaving large damp brown streaks on his face. "Look at it logically. More than anything, he wants you to go to college. Granted, Illinois isn't Ivy League like your sister Coralie at Penn, but it's college. He's not going to cut off his nose to spite his face."

"He isn't rational about me. There's your error," she corrected, and her eyes flashed at the recollection of her last shouting match with her father. "He's so mad at me, he could kill me. And if he finds out there's a baby coming, he may."

"Well, at least tell us whose it is, if it's not Gilbert's."

"And you can't tell Gilbert."

"Boy, the dad must be a real asshole," Damon remarked.

"Your eloquence quite confounds me," she replied. "I couldn't have put it better myself." She paused, straightened up, placed a hand on her hip and surveyed the long, scraggly, uneven rows of thriving plants. An autumnal breeze ruffled her loose and dreary dress. "You two are the only other people from home here. If word gets back there, I'll be beyond upset and you, whoever spills the beans, will be responsible for ruining not just my life, but the baby's too."

Mike hung his head, his long brown hair glinting in the October sun. Damon scrutinized the bug-infested earth. A fly buzzed in his curly brown mane.

"You know I'd never tell a soul," Mike began.

"Me neither," Damon put in. "But I don't see how it'd ruin the baby's life."

"With no chance at college, I might have to give it up for adoption."

"You'd never do it," Mike insisted. "I know you, never."

"Well, don't put me in a situation where I have to consider it."

"You'd go on welfare first," he continued.

"I may have to as it is. We're already on food stamps." She bent over, and they all resumed weeding.

"So what did this guy do?" Damon asked. "I mean to make him such a jerk. Tell you he didn't care you were having his kid?"

"He doesn't know."

"What?" They both demanded and stood up.

"Naomi, you have to tell him," Mike said.

"I don't and I won't," she replied. "He's loathsome."

"Oh, he cheated on you," Damon said, matter-of-factly.

"He's a cipher."

"No one is," Mike said.

"Then he's no one." She stood up again and dusted the dirt off her hands. "No one."

"No one is no one," Mike growled angrily. "He deserves to know."

"He deserves nothing. How dare you tell me what he deserves? You have no idea what he put me through or how he treated me. He deserves nothing, and that's what he'll get. Now, can you two keep your mouths shut about this?"

"Yes," Mike spoke for them both, "of course we can. But I'm not going to keep my mouth shut about you telling him."

"You'll be wasting your breath."

"So be it."

After that, they all weeded very intently and carefully ignored each other. No one spoke. The green pile of mangled crab grass, clover, and other assorted invasive plants grew higher, as they tossed these unwanted intruders onto it, like fathers, Mike thought bitterly, deemed worthless by angry, judging women, but they saved the wild grape and mint, the burdock and thistle, for they had begun to learn the essentials of foraging. The wicker basket Naomi had brought out for the squash began to fill. Damon picked a pumpkin and stuck it under his Indian shirt.

"What are you doing?" the young mother demanded, anticipating the answer full well.

"I'm having a baby," he laughed, "but you can't tell anyone."

She tossed an acorn squash at the pumpkin under his shirt. Luckily neither vegetable was harmed.

"Hey, that's the next generation you throwing around," Mike said, but still not smiling.

"No, you idiot, it's dinner," she replied, rising and then trundling off to the next squash row.

He followed, concerned now, and complaining: "Now wait a minute, I've never been in your class of idiots before."

"You are now."

"With the morons and the imbeciles too?"

"Yup."

"Your stock really sank today, buddy boy," Damon chuckled.

"So did yours, you retard, Mister 'I'm having a baby,'" she mocked.

"Come on Nay, have a sense of humor," Damon continued, then, on his knees with clasped hands: "Please don't send me down with the retards and the morons. I'll do anything."

"Then you can weed that entire row," she replied, pointing.

"I'll take idiocy any day," Mike replied glumly, still tasting the bitter root of feminine justice and balking, then moving off to a more heavily laden row. "At least it's not back-breaking."

As the afternoon wore on, the pleasant October breezes did little to cool their labors. At last the wicker basket, piled high with the yellows, greens and beiges of the oblongs and circles of squash, they returned to the farmhouse, prepared for squash soup, zucchini quiche and a ratatouille bulked out with summer squash for dinner. But first they lined up for their turns in the shower. Naomi emerged from billowing steam in yet another thrift shop gown, this one with a blue, green and aqua butterfly pattern, lank, dark strands of hair dripping a trail behind her on the floor. As she toweled her hair in the kitchen, standing barefoot on the wooden planks, she watched the two other women and one man preparing the meal.

"Come chop," urged Summer, who sported nothing but a long, elaborate white slip. Meanwhile Rainbow, an ardent cook, with ribbons shimmering in her impossibly long hair, rolled out the pie crust for the quiches. Eleven people dwelt there at that time, though the number varied from month to month, and immense mounds of food had to be assembled each evening. Mornings were simpler. Granola for breakfast was the rather strictly enforced diet. Lunch was on your own. Dinner, however, was the great communal meal, when those who returned from weeding, cleaning, writing novels, painting pictures, following politics on the radio and in the alternative press or centering clay on the potter's wheel, all gathered to discuss their day. No one wanted to miss dinner. It was the time when they showed they were a collective, a group united in their differences and in their flight from normative society. On the screened-in porch at twilight, to the wild, relentless thrum of crickets, crowded at the long picnic table and benches with pots, platters and casseroles of food heaped high, whose aromas mixed with the sweet, sweaty smell of outdoor labor, and the clean, crisp scent of that outdoors itself, they felt very far indeed from the drudgery of nine-to-five work, whooshing, fuel-odored commutes on smooth, polluted superhighways and carking worries about paychecks and bills.

From the dim, yellow kitchen light, whose faint rays died abruptly in the absolute night of the surrounding wilderness, Naomi retired from dishwashing upstairs to her little room in the back, fumbled through the inky dark to the nightstand and lit a candle. The second floor had no electricity, and the two communards who worked part-time in the hamlet of Northeast paid the utilities bills for the rest of the house. It was not a bad arrangement for them: free room and board in exchange for a small monthly payment.

Her room sprang into sudden illumination—the wallpaper with its columns garlanded with multicolored blossoms and leaves, the comfortable single bed with the blue quilt, pillows and reading cushion, the blue and green striped rag rug on the floor, the antique walnut bureau for her thrift shop wardrobe and the tall, completely packed bookcase, with tomes stacked sideways upon others that were standing. She had inherited this tiny refuge from a political activist who had migrated to San Francisco, leaving behind a well-thumbed collection of the works of R. D. Laing, Isaac Deutscher, Louis Fisher, Herbert Marcuse and Abbie Hoffman, all of which she had devoured with the same omnivorous curiosity she brought to Eric Auerbach's *Mimesis* or Benedetto Croce's *Criticism*.

At the foot of her bed stood a white wicker bassinet. One of the men had found it in the attic, washed it and presented it to her, when it became apparent that a child was coming. It had a clean white plastic pad, on top of which lay a small pile of folded pale yellow receiving blankets she had purchased at Sears. Over the bassinet fluttered the thin white curtains with their discreet floral design. She lowered the window by the nightstand, to keep the candle alight. Then she settled onto her reading cushion and opened Curtsius' *European Literature and the Latin Middle Ages*. The curtains swayed on the nocturnal wind, casting gentle shadows over the quilt. From downstairs lilted the melancholy strains of the blues on the record-player. Outside an owl hooted, and darkness spread silently over the encroaching forest. The baby kicked.

The days grew cooler as the weeks flew by, autumn lengthening into the grave of winter, and Mike sojourned back to Philadelphia on his motorcycle. When he returned, Eileen rode behind him.

"Well this is news," she said, greeting her old friend in front of the farmhouse, one bright, blustery November afternoon. She had one hand over her mouth and with the other pointed at Naomi's enlarged midriff.

"Don't ask about the father," Mike grumbled.

"And you're not allowed to tell anyone back home," Damon added.

"The delivery's in December," the young mother said brusquely. "I wondered if you'd be there for me. All the books say it's best to have someone with you. And since it can't be the father or anyone from my family, I thought I'd ask you."

The visitor perched on the edge of the crumbled stone wall that separated the somewhat overgrown front yard from the brown and yellow fields. "Of course," she answered, rather dazed. "Well, yes, I can come down here in December." Later, as she helped Naomi gather the last of the pumpkins—pumpkin seeds, pumpkin pie, pumpkin soup, everyone was sick to death of all these and couldn't wait to start in on their vast basement storage of preserved goods—she expressed her surprise again.

"It was an accident, a mistake, and I'm trying to make the best of it," the young mother replied.

"If that were so, you'd have had an abortion."

"I don't believe in that."

"I think you're getting even with someone, the father. Boy, he must be a heel."

"He doesn't know. Let's forget about him."

Autumn passed, and in mid-November came early snow, awakening Naomi in her little room like the chime of a world transformed. Something, perhaps the difference in the light, she thought, had jolted her out of slumber. Out the window, big, silent flakes drifted down through hushed air. A thick, white, frozen carpet muffled everything—the cars, the wall, the shed, barn, the uneven, hand-planted rows of the vegetable garden. Her heart leapt. She donned her maternity pants, a big sweater and her boots and hurried downstairs. Mike and Damon tossed snowballs at each other in the front yard. A very soft one landed on her face.

"Hey, no aiming at the pregnant lady," she yelled and skipped out into it, throwing her arms wide and tilting her face up at the slowly falling flakes. "There is something divine in this," she thought and stood there for several minutes gazing into the heavens, then at the snow filling the air, concealing the end that was winter, gently hiding the unthinkable from human eyes, lighting on branches, enveloping all, bringing to mind the centuries, the eons in which it had floated thus, down from great altitudes, blanketing everything, time after time, winter after winter, through antiquity, the centuries of the middle ages, the years of the Renaissance, and she thought of all who had noticed it in the past, who had paused in their day to glance at this phenomenon and wonder at it, year after year, for silent ages. She had her place among them, she believed, and, speaking to the bright dimness of the snowy air in a poet's words altered, said, "in its beginning is its end," then turned back to the farmhouse, hoping it would snow all day.

Then, one frozen day in December, two weeks early, her labor began.

"Get the car, Damon, and get me to the hospital," she said.

"But Eileen isn't here," he rather inconsequentially complained.

"Please don't lose your head. Take me to the hospital. Call her from there."

They climbed into his Volkswagen bug and started down the road. She let out a scream.

"You're not going to have the baby in here, are you?" He shouted in a panic.

"Not if you hurry."

The labor lasted throughout the night, and Naomi scarcely noted when her childhood friend arrived to replace Damon, who had risen to the occasion, after his initial quaking, quite admirably.

"Can't you do anything about her pain?" He had asked.

"Yes, general anesthetic and a C-section," the doctor replied. "But she really doesn't need it, so I'd advise against that."

"More Demerol," Naomi yelled.

"We've given you as much as we can," the nurse explained.

"It's not doing a thing! It's useless."

"That's what they all say."

"Then why don't you give me something else?"

"It's the best we've got."

Naomi looked away in disgust.

Outside, on Interstate 95, Eileen drove Jake's Volkswagen through the night, wondering why she had agreed to assist at this birth. "I know nothing about pregnancy, labor, delivery, or babies. I'm supremely unqualified for this task," she thought, peering over the top of the steering wheel into the dark.

"Thank God!" Damon greeted her. "Someone who's qualified to be here."

"Did you read the books I gave you?" the young mother demanded between screams of agony.

"Yes," her friend lied, and then, "I'll take over, Damon. You can go back to the farm or sleep here on the couch in the waiting room."

Later that morning a pink, hairless baby boy appeared in the world. Gazing into his light blue eyes and at his blond eyebrows, Naomi did not see the striking resemblance to his father.

"But Naomi," Eileen cried, "he's the perfect image of Ron Swurl."

"So now you know. Keep it to yourself, please."

"Oh, I'm glad he jilted me."

"We're two of dozens. I got used to that a long time ago." She gazed down at the infant with affection unmarred by the faithlessness of his father, and because she was a hippie, she named him Snow.

It was hot and dusty in the L, as it passed through the northwest side, and Naomi and nine-month-old Snow were in no mood for hugs. Instead they sat disconsolately, him on her lap, his thick blond hair damp with sweat, her arms draped loosely around him, until they exited the train, crowded with the morning rush and caught a bus. It was not air-conditioned. Hot sooty Chicago air blasted in through the partly open windows. Snow whimpered, and his mother tried to sooth him with a limp, no longer cool, damp facecloth. Then, off the bus, she trundled down the blazing sidewalk, baby in one arm, her bag with her books and infant appurtenances in another, until she reached the broad stoop of the brownstone that housed the "Little Feet" daycare. Mrs. Kim, the owner, opened the street level door below the stoop. "Come in, come in. You late. All the other university children are here."

They entered the playroom, and she set her son on the floor. He crawled, scrambled rather, over to the blocks, then sat and began banging them together with loud claps. He glanced up for approval at his mother, who smiled. Shaniqua, an assistant, grabbed another baby under the arms and set him down opposite Snow. They regarded each other seriously for a moment, infant eyes round and contemplative, then began to poke their fingers at each other.

"Here are his diapers for today," Naomi pulled them out of her book bag. "And here's the baby food for lunch and dinner. He had a good breakfast already. Oh, and here's his bottle. You have the formula."

Mrs. Kim collected these items in her arms. "You still breast feed?"

"Not so much. He's getting to like the bottle."

"Bottle good, very good, easier on you."

"Oh the air-conditioning is so nice!" Naomi exclaimed.

"They nap very good in the air-conditioning."

She approached her son and bent over to kiss his golden, downy cheek. "See you later, Snow." He grabbed her around the neck and emitted an extremely loud, desperate, heart-broken wail.

"You mommy come back," Mrs. Kim assured him. "You have her nine months, all to yourself. Now she go to work and school, all to take care of you."

"He quiets down," Shaniqua put in, bright orange earrings jangling above a yellow and black Dashiki, below a large Afro. "Every day, five minutes after you leave, he's totally distracted."

Reassured, the young mother untangled the hot little fingers from around her neck and kissed them. "I love you," she said, then deftly reached into her bag and pulled out the pacifier, which he grabbed and sucked furiously. She stepped away, and after a moment, he resumed poking the other baby. "See you tonight," she said to the staff and tiptoed out of the room. Now she had to hurry. Her English literature class began in twenty minutes, and it was some distance away. She ran down sidewalks, from which the heat shimmered up in waves that soaked her clothes in sweat. "I've got to be able to do this," she said to herself, as she did every day. "It all depends on me. Though I must say, a little help would be nice. But who?" Certainly not her boyfriend, Jack. He loved her son, but so far refused to take any responsibility for him, because his senior year chemistry major was simply too demanding. The people at the commune helped a little, so did the occasional drop-ins from Philadelphia, Mike or Eileen, who both had already visited Chicago. But there was no one on whom she could count. She checked her watch and hurried dazedly through the heat. Certainly not her parents. They did not even know Snow was alive.

II

Vietnam

Gilbert was in a fix. It had started as a funk over his former girlfriend's departure for the Midwest, leading him to drop out of college. This, however, made him vulnerable to the draft. As he scrambled to re-enroll, he was called up. He had a choice: the jail cell of a conscientious objector or a mental health deferment; he quickly decided he was no hero and got a recommendation to a psychiatrist reportedly a wizard at exemptions.

"Your record of course will always show that you're a psycho," Mike Dellico said, lounging on his impressively large, black motorcycle as he unstrapped his helmet. "But hey, it worked for me. I got two years outside of college on the commune, and now I'm going to Boston University. Dr. Sharp is your guy. If he can't keep you out of Nam, no one can."

They strolled down Locust Street, glorious at the height of Indian summer, its many trees brandishing emerald leaves in the sun-filled breeze, and entered a coffee shop on the corner of Twenty First Street. "How'd you get into this pickle, anyway?" Mike wanted to know.

"Naomi being away, I didn't pre-register. Then she left, and I missed the deadlines. Now here it is mid-October, and I'm being drafted. I never thought they could move so damn fast." They ordered burgers and soda.

"This woman I'm friends with up in Boston, Tiwana Allenhurst, they got her husband, some Black Panther or other. He went to Canada, came back, got caught, shipped out to Saigon, then went on patrol up in the country, got ambushed, almost came home in a box. Now there's someone who should have *stayed* in Montreal," Mike bit savagely into his burger.

"Why are you telling me this?" His friend asked angrily. "To kill my appetite?"

"To impress upon you the need for swift and irrevocable action, should your attempt to get a deferment fail."

"But you said Dr. Sharp was unbeatable."

"No one," the draft dodger waved his burger in Gilbert's face, nearly smearing ketchup on his glasses, "is unbeatable. He's just the best. But if I were you, just in case, I'd contact Boris' friends in Montreal."

"Now there's an antiwar fanatic. You see he's even got a Vietnamese girlfriend now, some little chick who was working in a clothes store. They speak Vietnamese together."

"My hat is off to him," Mike said, still snapping vigorously at his burger. "If he can help end this war one day sooner, more power to him."

"What do you hear from Naomi?"

His companion paused, thinking of his recent visit to the commune on the north side of Chicago, of Snow, adorable in his blond, baby, big-eyed dignity, of his own idle trips around the city on the L, the cars full of sunlight as they rattled high through the skyscrapers, his journeys roaring up and down the Dan Ryan Expressway on his motorcycle and on the Eisenhower, the night he babysat for Snow, while Naomi went to the movies with Jack— "my name's Jack Diamond, like the card"—the other men and women drifting in and out of that rather funky dwelling, the September heat blazing down from the sun, up from the sidewalks, from the wide avenues everywhere—he thought of all this and put down his burger. "Forget Naomi. She's got someone new."

"You already told me that."

"She's gone, Gilbert. What about that woman from Temple with the red hair you were going out with?"

"Fane? I still see her from time to time."

"Make it often," Mike said, shifting guiltily at the thought that for well over a year he had withheld the secret of Naomi's motherhood from his friend who so loved her. He was half inclined to tell him now, but his promise prevented him. Instead he doled out advice: "Forget Naomi. She doesn't know what she wants. She's looking for something, over and over, but she doesn't know what it is. So she just goes from man to man, without knowing what she's doing. I don't have a good feeling about her future. Steer clear of her." His conscience thus salved by this dispensation of brotherly advice, advice that would have been the same whether Gilbert knew of Snow's existence or not, Mike exhorted his friend to transfer to B.U. "Once you get your deferment, you should come up and see it. There's more happening in Boston than San Francisco. And students are everywhere. I've said it before—Philly's a backwater."

"Everyone says that."

"Because it's true. Come stay with me in Cambridgeport. You'll never want to leave." As he wrapped his straight brown hair into a ponytail, Mike continued his homilies on weekends in Vermont and western Massachusetts, on the communes in those places, the doings of the hippie community chronicled in a vibrant underground press, the concerts, the happenings, and, what he did not bother to mention, the thrill of tearing around the city to these events on his motorcycle, from Beacon Hill to the Haymarket to Brookline and Somerville, to suburbs like Watertown, along the sparkling Charles River, through busy Harvard Square and out Mass Avenue past MIT. He got himself so worked up, mentally zooming again from one fascinating locale to another, that he referred to it as a paradise on earth.

"It could be, it could be," Gilbert murmured, eating his cheeseburger contemplatively and studying his friend's excited blue eyes behind his wire-rims and his own tattoo of a snake, coiled on his forearm. Perhaps he should transfer. There might very well be a new life for him in Boston. He would forget faithless, love-frittering Naomi, find some new beauty in New England. Who knew what rich romance awaited him, promise of an end to his heart-worn exile? Why should he waste his youth pining? "You only live once," he mumbled.

"Exactly!" Mike exclaimed, and the light brown stubble on his chin, like the highlights of his hair, gleamed assent in the sunbeams that filtered through the plate glass window.

Gilbert pushed his now empty plate forward, over the gray Formica tabletop. The tattooed snake stretched and coiled. Could he have a room in the house that Mike and his friends rented? He could have the basement bedroom, soon to be unoccupied. He suppressed a slight sneer, remembering that musty room, its small, dust-covered window high up, eye level with a sidewalk covered with paper trash and dog turds. But it was not dank, like many cellar rooms, and he had detected no vermin. "Fifty dollars a month?" He repeated. "I'll take it."

"It's a steal," Mike averred. They agreed, however, that this arrangement depended on Gilbert's successful transfer to the university.

Once done eating, they sat a few moments, silently smoking, Mike mentally contemplating the beauties of the Vermont countryside in summer, green and gilt of sleepy, rolling hills, through which boomed the fantastic roar of his motorcycle, Gilbert considering the miseries of a New England winter—gray, wet, slushy and snowy. How he hated snow! He would have preferred a move to Miami, dry all year, no icy, filthy puddles. But Miami was no Mecca for the hip. Boston was. San Francisco was. The East Village was. But San Francisco was too far, and New York repelled him, with its streets at the bottom of skyscraper canyons, like ovens in the summer, everything too expensive, suitable only for the superrich, the high-rises ringing Manhattan like a fortress from which there was no escape. No, Boston was the better choice.

After their cigarettes, Gilbert walked his friend back to his gleaming motorcycle. Mike strapped on his helmet and swung his leg over the bike. He was on his way to the Northeast, to see a musician, and departed, as always, like thunder. Gilbert watched him tear up Locust Street, then merge and vanish in traffic. But long after he lost sight of him, he still heard the motorcycle noisily weaving amongst the cars.

He ambled slowly south, enjoying the clear, warm weather and mentally rehearsing the fibs he would tell the psychiatrist. An elaborate plan gradually emerged in his mind. He inspected it carefully and decided that it would do, was perfect. By the time he reached the front stoop of his parents' house, he was whistling.

He entered the tall townhouse, motes glittering in long, lonely shafts of sunlight, all empty except for the distant sound of his mother vacuuming on the third floor. He walked to the back, into the kitchen, to the phone on the counter, took out the scrap of paper with the number and dialed. A secretary answered. Yes there was an opening. He could see Dr. Sharp tomorrow, Friday, at his home office in Chestnut Hill. He wrote down the address, deciding he would borrow his father's Ford, since he never used it on weekdays anyway.

The next morning the would-be psychiatric case rode out under tree-canopied avenues to Dr. Sharp's Tudor-style home. He rang the bell and soon found himself in a cool, dim vestibule, decorated with garish African masks. He tread over Mexican rugs in one room, Orientals in another, until at last he found himself in the therapist's poorly lit den, all browns, and cluttered, every corner, with pre-Colombian stone heads and covered, every wall, with more African masks and muted Latin American weavings. "This war is a terrible thing, a terrible thing," Dr. Sharp murmured and lit a cigar whose gray smoke wreathed a halo around his long, gray hair. He leaned back in his tall dun armchair and his wily dark eyes glimmered through the shadows like undecipherable signals from the unknown.

"It makes me so anxious," Gilbert responded, "and paranoid."

"How so?"

"I'm convinced people are out to get me. Their doubles are out to get me."

"Their doubles?"

"Yes. Some are good and some are bad, everyone has doubles, triples and quadruples. And since I got my notice, it's just gotten worse. No one is the same. People go out of a room and when they come back in, they're different."

"Listen to that."

"To what?"

"Your word—different."

"I'm afraid, Dr. Sharp, that if I wind up in the military, this will get out of control. I'll go insane."

"No worry there," Dr. Sharp said meditatively, "you already are." He paused to scribble on a pad. "Here is a prescription for Stellazine, and if you come by my office in town on Monday, you may pick up a letter for the draft board. This dreadful war has done enough damage without driving yet another poor psychotic over the edge. You would not believe how many schizophrenics this draft has lured out of the woodwork."

Gilbert could not determine if he was an idiot and serious, or carefully playing his double game. But as Dr. Sharp rose to open the door and let Gilbert out, he smiled, exhaled a thick blue smoke ring and then, so quick that his patient could not be sure he saw it, he seemed to wink. Or did he? The canny dark ocular glimmer like the surface of bottomless wells, revealed nothing, but Gilbert decided to go out on a limb. He gave a thumbs up, something moved again in those inscrutable eyes and not another word was said.

On his ride home, he felt light-hearted. He pulled the car into a small parking area along the East River Drive and strolled on the lawn by the water. The Schuylkill River was choppy, due to the cool, swift breeze, and the little silver waves broke, here and there, into white caps. A couple of lovers lay entwined on a bright orange beach towel, oblivious to the file of ants making off with bits of their untouched sandwiches. University of Pennsylvania rowers competed out in the middle of the water, and occasional gray and white gulls circled, then landed on the gaily painted boathouses. The clean beauty of the scene before him reflected his emotions, the absence at last of the dark, churning anxiety that had kept him awake nights ever since he received his draft notice. All was well now. His fear subsided. The sun lit his face and his soul.

He drove up to the huge art museum, built in the Greek style and overlooking the river. He circled it twice in the car, before parking and walking through the central stone plaza with its view of the tree-lined boulevards below. The fountains on either side of the stairs sprayed visitors and glittered like diamonds. More breeze, more glories of nature and architecture and the end of fear that he might end up dragging his bleeding, bullet-riddled carcass through the mud of some steamy, tropical jungle, half way around the world. "Thank God for Dr. Sharp," he cried aloud.

Unfortunately, the psychiatrist's letter failed to convince the draft board. Perhaps they had received too many from Dr. Sharp; perhaps its wording was phony; perhaps Gilbert's impersonation of a paranoid schizophrenic at his interview fell flat. Whatever the reason, he soon found himself in the undesirable position of having to choose between Montreal and Saigon, exile or war. Inertia and uncertainty got the better of him. It was Saigon and war.

Or, to be more exact, and precisely as he had feared, the jungles well outside the capital's sphere. He was drenched in dirt and sweat. His gear was heavy, and the occasional wounds of his fellow soldiers hideous. He tried to remember his abstract sympathy for the Vietnamese peasantry, but now, when he met villagers, he found himself searching their faces, their dark silent eyes, for some clue as to whether or not they would kill him when his back was turned. He detested his sergeant's constantly repeated maxim that they all were the enemy, but in practice, his reactions confirmed it. The Viet Cong he killed looked very much like the average villagers, whose visages he scrutinized, searching vainly for some common ground, some bit of shared humanity.

"If I get out of this alive," he did not hesitate to tell the other soldiers, "I'm going to join some group for veterans against the war."

"Go Gilbert," would be the reply, or: "Not me. I'm AWOL the first chance I get."

The hatred for the officers in his squad smoldered intensely, at times arcing up in a white heat terrifying to behold in the eyes of men who held guns. He lived in fear that some private would bring down the wrath of the army on them all, by taking matters into his own hands and shooting one of these idiots in the back. Whenever he witnessed that hatred blaze forth, he would unconsciously hold his breath and clench his fingers around whatever weapon was at hand, quite uselessly, for no arms would protect him from the consequences of such murder. But fortunately for him, while such bloody events were not uncommon in other platoons and rumors of them everywhere abounded, they did not occur in his. He bit his lip, bided his time, and noted in rare moments of optimism that he was not dead yet.

Then he found himself outside a village much farther north than he wanted to be and, not surprisingly, ambushed. Crouching behind the wheel of his jeep, covered with mud and blood from a shoulder wound, gazing foggily through the ugly, jagged cracks in the windshield, Gilbert concluded, in a moment when the thunder of death and maiming and hysteria subsided and rationality presented its quiet conclusions, that all was lost. A grenade detonated deafeningly nearby, and, he was out. When he came to, he was in a helicopter with an IV in the one arm that could feel anything and the taste of blood in the back of his mouth. The medic explained that he had multiple wounds.

"Well, I could have told you that. How come I'm not dead?"

"That's a mystery. Everyone else in your squad is, even your sergeant, who put in the call for help. It was goddamn awful."

He subsided into a drug-induced sleep, marred only at the outset by surprise at his immense sorrow that all the soldiers he had known so well no longer existed. He had not thought they meant much to him. But now it seemed as though he had lost something vital, essential to his life, like his home.

His recovery seemed never-ending and filled with vast stretches of boredom. Yet even in this stultifying dullness, if he attended, he could almost feel his body healing itself—wounds resealing after the extraction of bullets, shattered bones re-knitting. For a while—it seemed very long—he was feverish, but even so, still bored, still subliminally aware of his body's tedious, silent struggle back to health. He believed he felt his tissues fighting the infection, ejecting it, defeating it, careful to avoid ambush, unlike his squad; yes, he compared what happened at the cellular level in his limbs, back and stomach to the war in the jungle, except that within him the battle was rational, necessary, good, and, when it was ultimately deemed that he would need no amputations, these forces of reason, goodness and necessity were victorious. He took great satisfaction in that. When his parents visited him in the hospital in Washington D.C., he told them about this internal struggle: "Inch by inch, I'm winning."

"Of course you are, Gilbert," his mother replied and then, aside to his father: "The poor boy's delirious. Can't they give him something to lower his temperature?"

Utterly startling him into recognition of many only subtly visible realities, Fane, the redhead from Temple University, traveled down to Washington by train to visit him. By then he had passed the amputation scare, his fever had dropped and he alternated between reading, daytime television and napping. Deep into *Homage to Catalonia*, one morning he was astonished to see a short, wiry, good-looking girl enter the room, so surprised that he only recognized her by her distinctive hair color, the only one he had ever encountered that exactly matched his own. He had not given her a thought since being drafted and so, was even more amazed that she had worried about him every day. "Now if only it was Naomi," he mused when she told him that—Naomi, whose parents he aspired to please, even though he had alienated Morris, whose house he admired with its undeniable good style and the obvious money that had been lavished on its décor, unlike the clutter and fusty mess of his parents' home, Naomi whose beauty had distracted him from the fact that her thoughts were not of him. But it was not Naomi, it was this other woman, and he decided to pay attention to her, since, he rather portentously told himself, he understood the awfulness of unrequited love.

She stayed with acquaintances in Northwest and visited every day for almost a week. He talked with her for hours, inquired about her classes and friends, and took her hand. But he did not mislead or delude her, as he believed his beloved had him by silence. No, he told her he was in love with Naomi Lichter, who had abandoned him and moved to Chicago, and that it would be a very long time before he could fall in love again.

"Then I will wait," she replied, and the wounded veteran, suppressing a groan, managed a thin smile of encouragement.

"You're leading her on with this elaborate pretense of honesty, in which you omit the key fact—that even absent heartbreak over Naomi, you'd never care for her," Mike chastised him, alarmed to see his friend paying this innocent inamorata in exactly the same dangerously sharp, cheap coin he had received. "Tell her it's hopeless, you're moving to Boston for good, and be done with it. Otherwise you're torturing her, and that's wrong."

"All's fair in love and war," the convalescent murmured.

"Yes, for shitheads, not for decent human beings."

Gilbert did as his friend told him.

When he finally left the hospital, his perennially tired, gray-haired father arrived in the Ford, which was looking ever more used. The trip up I-95 was uneventful, marked mostly by a lengthy paternal monologue upon the president's perfidy. Gilbert's father was a mild mannered, retiring office worker of late middle age, fond of quiet evenings in his armchair with his newspaper and of solitary weekend peregrinations along little known Philadelphia byways, who exhibited nonetheless an utterly incongruous loathing for Nixon, whom he attacked verbally with unwonted vehemence. "It was your generation, with its protests and riots and violence that drove LBJ out of office. And now look what we got! You thought things would get better, but they only got worse. That's the way it always is."

"LBJ could have started withdrawing troops from Vietnam if he wanted to. He didn't."

"He was better than this slimy crook Nixon," Mr. Locklane retorted and then was off ranting again, detailing the president's many crimes.

The brown, scrubby November landscape flew past, even though the highway, mid-afternoon on a weekday, was at capacity. Gilbert anticipated traffic backups, but that only happened once, at the smelly old Baltimore tunnel. There he took the opportunity to eat one of the limp, chicken and cheese on rye sandwiches his mother had packed for them and drank a Coke. "Everyone in my squad was killed," he said, "everyone but me."

"I know. You told us every time we visited."

"I don't remember."

"You were high as a kite, and in no condition to attend that rally."

"What rally?"

"Something in D.C. that that Boris Slovansky, Slovanovich or whatever his name is wanted you to go to."

Gilbert was perturbed. "You should have told me. I'd have gone."

"Not hovering between life and death you wouldn't. You'd have lost yours arms and legs for sure if you'd done stuff like that." They were crossing the big bridge over the Susquehanna, usually sparkling like a vein of diamonds and dotted in summer with gaily colored sailboats, but on that dull, dusty day it merely gleamed greasily at the leaden sky. Gilbert considered his transfer application to Boston University, and the mere thought exhausted him, left him as listless and devoid of any idea about the future as the miserable landscape around him. The urge to sleep overcame him; he wanted a bed, warm and comfortable, for months, but decided the passenger seat would have to do. Soon his father's political diatribe picked up again, only occasionally punctuated by Gilbert's irregular snores. It didn't matter. Terrence Locklane was used to people ignoring his political ideas. He was used to people ignoring him. He talked on.

Arriving at his parents' abode, the young veteran's torpor became so potent, he almost could not exit the car. Terrence's tirade had long since subsided into disgruntled murmurings, as his usual reticence reasserted itself. After he parked, neither one moved for a few moments, conquered by the exhaustion of war wounds, the futility of politics and the ugly day. At length his father mumbled, "We should go in, I think." Gilbert sighed, opened the car door and stumbled out onto the dirty sidewalk, nearly colliding with the blighted locust tree in front of the stoop.

He immediately took to his bed and did not get up for two days, sleeping, dreaming feverishly of damp jungles, torn corpses and the hollow hopeless eyes of village orphans. His mother, who had collected all the necessary recommendations, transcripts and other forms for him, told him that his transfer application had been received. With any luck, he would enroll the following September.

The febrile lethargy finally broke, but a desultory stultification lay upon him for weeks. He did little besides lie in bed or shuffle around the house. More alert now, he seemed to himself more aware of what he had endured. At night he saw himself turning in his seat in the jeep to see the soldier behind him shot in the face. He felt the insects swarming over him again, as he lost consciousness on the ground and all around the mangled bodies of men he had lived with for months. He recalled their anecdotes, their memories of home, their plans for their returns, their profane jokes. These things passed through his mind, ghostlike whispers, and then he would sleep. In those weeks, until Mike visited from Boston, time stalled like a fetid cloud over fields of the dead.

"I found a job for you," Mike announced when he arrived, folding his leather jacket and draping it over the barbells in his friend's room, where the general emptiness and absence of furniture made the mess less noticeable. He stood with his arms akimbo, shaking his head as he surveyed the forlorn surroundings, as if they confirmed some long-held conviction that he had finally decided to act upon, one that involved ejecting his friend forthwith from his wounded and unhealthy miasma.

The still dazed veteran propped himself up on his elbow on the bed. "Go on."

"In a bookstore, near Harvard yard. I got friendly with the manager, explained your situation—unemployed Vietnam vet, against the war, going to college in the fall, will live with us in Cambridgeport—and he said to bring you around, he'll hire you—just like that. So pack up. You have a job and a place to live." Mike bent over, grasped his hand and shook it. "Natalie and I, we needed another roommate anyway. And after that lousy advice I gave you on Dr. Sharp, the least I could do was get you some work." The erstwhile rock musician straightened up, tall and lean in his patched blue jeans and flannel shirt. He picked up his black leather jacket and black motorcycle helmet. "But get up there soon, like in two days. This job won't keep forever."

Gilbert boarded the train to Boston early the next morning in denims with a denim jacket over a sweater and one suitcase, after squinting at a harsh dawn that seemed to set the river aflame. Commuters to Manhattan crammed Thirtieth Street Station, since it was a weekday, and the blear-eyed convalescent found a level of alertness and aggression required that he had not attained in months. But after threading through the swarm, down the escalator, onto the train and into a seat, he exhaled and looked around dazedly. It was all a little disorienting, this sudden competition with travelers for a place on the train, and he needed a moment to collect his thoughts. He opened his copy of *The Different Drummer*, and thought, "soon I'll be reading *The Boston Phoenix*." Then he immersed himself in the depredations of local politicians and the heroic feats of antiwar organizers and did not surface until the train pulled into Trenton, glad that he missed the "Trenton Makes the World Takes" sign, whose contrast between the bold claim and the nearby dilapidated slums, as well as the hint of giving until there was nothing left to give, always depressed him.

Then the New Jersey suburbs rolled by and afterward, outside New York City, what would later be landfill but at that time were still, smelly, scabbed, multicolored mountains of trash. He glanced away in disgust and instead turned to *Ramparts* magazine. Soon, he told himself, the train would enter the tunnel and he would no longer have endless mounds of garbage for scenery. Indeed the train soon sped through this urban detritus and plunged into the dark. By the overhead lights, he read of the efforts of Black Panthers and the speeches of Angela Davis. Thus occupied, Gilbert was carried into Penn Station, where the train disgorged well over three fourths of its passengers.

Creaking and groaning, it later pulled out, heading north. He leaned back, closed his eyes and felt the faint ache of his wounds, the subliminally ever-present memento of Southeast Asia. Even though he was completely healed, this echo of pain lingered like funeral music at a distance, and if he was not careful to ignore these melancholy strains, they tired, weakened and aged him. "I better snap out of it," he said aloud, opening his eyes. He rose and moved to the dining car, a vision of long hair, denim and aviator sunglasses. At the counter, an animated discussion of the war proceeded loudly between the waiter, lurching from Coke cans to sandwiches in plastic wrap, and a large, ruddy man in a business suit, who kept reiterating "the domino effect" like a mantra.

"I've been there," Gilbert put in, leaning on the white Formica counter to steady himself, as the train veered from left to right. "They see us as invaders, pure and simple. Forget dominos. It's just a civil war that we have no business with."

"You're a veteran?" The man asked belligerently.

"Yup, still recovering from my war wounds. We never should have gotten involved in Vietnam."

"Frankly, I'm surprised to hear such defeatist talk from a veteran."

"Then enlist yourself and see what you think."

The businessman shrugged sourly and drank his ginger ale.

Gilbert took a coffee and a small tinfoil bag of peanuts back to his seat. "It's hopeless," he thought. "Ignoramuses like that run the country, vote for Nixon and bomb the Vietnamese peasantry. I give up. I'm not joining any antiwar group. I'm just going to forget it all. It's goddamned hopeless." All through the one-horse towns of the Connecticut coast, he stewed over the idiocy of the American public, politicians and military. Then, mercifully, as the train approached Massachusetts, he dozed off. He dreamt he was smoking pot with Naomi in Fairmount Park, listening to John Coltrane on the radio. It was spring, the emerald lawn spread as far as he could see, beneath weeping willows, maples, oaks and an occasional hemlock. Life was paradise. He awoke with a start, full of longing and with the faint sweet memory of marijuana on the back of his tongue. "She's hopeless too—in love with that moron Ronald Swurl." He had only seen them together twice and had never heard even a whiff of gossip—but those two times his love-sharpened eyes had detected everything. She was crazy about that useless vagabond and did not give any other man a second thought. "Ain't life great," he murmured, turning on his side and staring out at the bleak November countryside, the dark leafless trees scratching the gray sky like skeletons, the occasional small, ugly house with a view of the tracks. "Shit," he muttered. "It's nothing but shit."

He reached his destination late in the day and took the subway from the train station to Central Square. He emerged from underground onto gray, dirty sidewalks, the sky clotted with black telephone wires, slithering in a winter wind, which he bent into, almost limping toward Magazine Street. But less than half way there, a dusty taxi glided by. He hailed it, feeling tired and an unhealed ache in the arm that held the suitcase, and paid the fare to his new domicile, a two-story house, slightly aslant, filled with students and musicians. He was in luck, Mike told him. Instead of the dreary basement, he had a tiny room on the second floor, well lit from its sunny southern exposure, and more important, next to a larger room that contained that floor's sole gas heater. Unlike the residents off the second-story kitchen, he would be toasty in winter. The previous occupant, a young woman who attended a music college and who had moved into Boston proper to be closer to class, had left nothing behind except for a Mexican blanket with black and white geometric designs on the bed. Gilbert could not fathom why she had abandoned this handsome covering, but promptly rolled himself up in it, having obtained a pillow from Mike, laid down on the bed and went to sleep.

He awoke to the clamor though not the odor of breakfast. Mike, his girlfriend and a pretty, blond B. U. graduate student named Ingrid had made a large pot of oatmeal. "Economize, Gilbert, that's what we do around here, economize," Mike said, pointing at the large, dented tin pot. "We buy cheaply, in bulk and with food stamps. That way everyone has plenty to eat. You chip in once a week, and once a month it's your turn to shop." He ladled out a bowl of oats and passed it to his friend. "Sugar's on the table."

The veteran sat down, longing for the smell of hot bacon and eggs, sweetened his cereal, began to eat and inquired about his job at the bookstore.

"Not far from Harvard Square. I'll take you there in a little while," his benefactor replied and then commenced complaining about the bitter cold, especially when travelling around Cambridge by motorcycle.

"I can take you out to B. U. in my Bug," Ingrid volunteered to Mike, "but I'm not returning till this evening."

"Fine, I'll come back by subway."

After this haphazard meal, Mike took the new arrival down to the basement, where old furniture, knick knacks and a host of odds and ends crouched in the shadows like abandoned friendships. The newcomer selected a flimsy dresser, a folding chair, a bookcase, a night-table, a bedside lamp, a stack of hangars for his closet and an old oval hooked rug. They carted these items up two flights of stairs in two trips. When done, the room looked better, more private and personal, except for the bookcase, which stared as emptily as a pauper's pantry at the bedroom door.

"I've got a box of books in my room that I intended to put on the sidewalk," Mike said. "Why don't you take what you want?"

He selected many writings of and commentaries on Karl Marx, Shakespeare's tragedies, a dog-eared dictionary, a collection of stories and essays by Thomas Mann and sundry other classics and added his own few volumes from his suitcase, all of which cheered him with the promise of quiet hours reading in domestic peace. With these worn spines aligned in a row like friends waiting to greet him, the bookcase now appeared less forlorn.

"The bookshop's on Mt. Auburn Street," Mike commented, as they ventured forth into an icy wind.

"It makes my wounds ache," the convalescent replied. "This cold damp will take some getting used to."

"You'll be making this trek five days a week, from what Raoul told me."

"Raoul?"

"He's the owner and manager. He's from Mexico and has published a couple of books. I told him what a voracious reader you are. He only hires bibliophiles. Good thing he hasn't seen that one, lone, little bookcase in your room."

They trudged on in silence, shivering. "Not one of the guys in my squad was into reading," Gilbert said after a while. "Drinking, whoring, cars, but no reading." On that glum note, they arrived at Massachusetts Avenue, where the wind, whipping around a corner, slammed them in the face with a hostile dare to proceed. They did, bent nearly double and miserable.

"Mike Dellico! At last you've brought your friend!" The vigorous, enthusiastic and dark-haired owner greeted them. After introductions and a proud tour of the book-crammed premises, it was resolved that the veteran would help open the store, thus working from eight to four, Monday through Friday. He was encouraged to spend his down time reading. Raoul understood that in September the hours would change to accommodate his course schedule. The new hire was to start the next day.

"That's good," he said, as he and Mike returned to Magazine Street, "because I've got about enough cash to last a week. That's it."

Ingrid waited impatiently on the sidewalk, tapping her foot, beside her red VW Bug. Then she and Mike departed.

The new roommate explored the house. In addition to a storage laundry room, the cellar contained one bedroom inhabited, as far as he could tell, by an utter slob. There was also a basement living room with a sofa bed, clearly in regular use. A large purple and white bedspread with designs he knew were from India covered part of the fake wood paneling, the fabric sagging in limp wrinkles. Brightly colored abstract oil paintings, all yellows and oranges, likely one of the resident's handiwork, decorated the other, warped walls. The half-bathroom had not been cleaned in some time. Toothpaste speckled the sink and the mirror. He was glad he would not have to live down there.

Upstairs he found the living and dining rooms and two bedrooms, one of them Mike and Natalie's with a big, antique brass bed. Someone kept this ground level much cleaner. The wood floors and rugs had been vacuumed, the abstract oil paintings dusted and the bathroom washed. Even the beds were made. He considered the couches and armchairs not half bad, while the two tall bookcases contained neat rows of tomes, alphabetically arranged by author.

On the second floor, the kitchen with its pale yellow walls and white linoleum floor was well kept and bright, but once again, slovenliness had overcome the other bedrooms. Posters of Che Guevara and others celebrating the Venceremos concealed cracked plaster walls in one room. Bookcases did so in the other. Clothing, books, records and the smelly remains of hastily devoured meals littered the poster-filled room. By contrast his own, he noted with a touch of pride, was a paragon of orderliness. He opened his suitcase, stationed on the fold-out chair, and unpacked, pausing now and then to look out his window through the bare black branches of a maple at a bleak sky and then down at the uneven bricks of the sidewalk and the street pitted with potholes. It felt like snow. Even inside with the gas heat on, he could tell that in a few hours the air would be white with whirling flakes. The image reminded him of Naomi, which saddened him. Again he rolled himself up in the Mexican blanket and slept.

Much later, when he awoke, a luminous whiteness and white silence filled the room. Sitting up, he glanced out the window; snow filled the air, the maple branches glistened with a one-inch, white lining. His old friend stood in the doorway with a cup of cocoa, a dusting of snow still visible on the shoulders of his brown leather jacket. Beside him stood a slightly short, attractive African American woman in a dashiki, jeans and boots, with an enormous amount of hair.

"Gilbert, meet Tiwana Allenhurst, writer and political activist."

The veteran yawned, groggily rubbed his eyes, then held out a hand.

"I work with the Panthers and Vietnam vets against the war," she explained. "I do a lot of coordinating, rallies, protests, vigils and other... things." She waved her hand with a vagueness that set off alarms in the back Gilbert's mind, alarms like distant sirens, wailing that those "other things" might be of the sort to get him in trouble with the police. "I'm looking for someone to help me out, with the Nam vets particularly," Tiwana went on. "Mike said that might be you."

"It might," he replied, propped up on an elbow now and surveying her cautiously. "So long as it doesn't interfere with survival. Survival's at the top of my list right now."

She nodded. "Understood. My husband's a Panther out in Chicago. He was tortured by the police. He hasn't been too active since he got out of custody. I guess you could say, he's just healing. Once that's done, we'll see where we go."

"I'm just healing too," the veteran replied. "I haven't been out of the hospital that long. I can still feel my wounds."

"It's gonna be a long war," she said.

"Vietnam?"

"No, *our* war." She turned and walked back toward the kitchen.

"Well, she's honest," Gilbert commented, glancing out at the snow that tricked you into thinking the world was pristine and beautiful.

"No bullshit from Tiwana," his old friend replied.

"I doubt I can do it," Gilbert sighed. "I'm not made of such stern stuff."

"Garbage."

"It's true. Between the war wounds and losing Naomi, frankly, I'm a wreck. I just want to eat, sleep, go to my job and enroll in my courses in the fall. I don't know if I'm ready for a revolution."

"All you have to do is be on the coordinating committee."

"And when we get busted? Then *I* get to get tortured by the cops? No thanks. I've already been through military torture. That was enough."

"Come have some chickpeas and rice. We'll talk it all over."

Despite his forebodings and the mild hostility that his resistance to being dragooned called forth, he liked this emissary from the political underground, who exuded a warmth belied only by the coldness of her gray eyes. She was, she explained, an artist. She had gone to an expensive girls' boarding school and from that and other details, he gathered that she came from a well-to-do, even aristocratic African American family. She was currently at work on a biography of Mohammed Ali and gave poetry readings around Boston. She was transferring to Brandeis, "to follow in Angela Davis' footsteps," she laughed. And she was smart. Her analyses of political issues, her assessments of different figures of the day, currently in the limelight, all exuded a canniness and intelligence that continually surprised him by showing something new, something he had not considered. He found himself sitting back and admiring her, a feeling only occasionally tempered by alarm at that frankly gelid gaze. With someone this brainy leading the way, perhaps it might not lead to disaster; perhaps she was not a wild-eyed, gung-ho radical; perhaps she was a cool-headed, thoughtful, resourceful, clever, principled, exceedingly intelligent radical. She wanted to link two movements, and after listening to her talk for forty-five minutes, he believed that if anyone could bring it about, she was the person. And he might very well *not* get tortured by the police.

But the possibility remained. After all, her husband had had the benefit of her wise counsel and, he thought, look what had happened to him. This was not a good advertisement for her skills at protecting her people. To make matters worse, the confrontations that her political plans would lead to would very quickly become the sort that got people, people like Gilbert, very much in trouble. She was no pacifist. She wanted to engage the enemy. Gilbert figured he knew all about that enemy. He had fought in his war, soldiered in his military. He did not think it likely that a ragtag underground army led by biographers or poets, no matter how smart they were individually, had a chance against such armament.

He was a veteran in every sense of the word: he could assess the struggle, *her* struggle and tell right off who had the upper hand and who was likely to keep it. That was not Tiwana and the Panthers. It was the police and the titanically powerful and corrupt corporate interests they protected. So, warily at first, with humble caution evoked by her swift intelligence, and avoiding that uncomfortably evident, icy, ocular comprehension, he said as much, told her that her side had all the righteousness, all the moral rectitude, all the justice it could possibly have, but that it was a loser. "There is no way you're going to defeat these people," he concluded. "At the first hint of violence, they will crush you and not think twice. This is *the most powerful* empire that has ever existed on the face of the earth, except, perhaps for the Soviet Union. You don't have the money, the people, the arms—there's no way."

"So," she replied calmly, "we should work within the system? This putrid, carrion-feeding monster? Inside that?"

"Be its cancer if you want. I don't know. Didn't Fidel say 'I envy you North Americans, because you live in the heart of the enemy?' Burrow from within. But don't talk to me about a street war. I've fought in the Vietnam war, and I have no desire to be in the crosshairs of American machine guns, tanks or rocket launchers. I can't and I won't. The fight is over for me. I'm out of the ring—fini, kaput, done."

"Let's hope your view is not the prevalent one among the other antiwar veterans."

He shrugged. "I haven't taken any polls. Frankly I was just glad to get out alive. In fact it's a miracle I did, practically an act of God. Somehow I got a second chance. I'm not throwing that away."

Standing behind the cold-eyed revolutionary, Mike made a slicing gesture across his throat. So Gilbert shut up. "He just got out of the hospital," his host hurried to explain, "like your husband." That seemed to soften her.

"I'm sure in a few weeks or months," Mike continued, "he'll feel differently. You don't just plunge from one war into another."

They passed from politics to poetry. Her verse was published by a women's literary collective in Cambridge, located not far from the bookstore where Gilbert would be working. "I read there all the time," she smiled, a facial expression that contrasted starkly with her mirthless gaze. "Perform rather, because there's some singing involved." He promised to attend the next performance, in two weeks, adding rather inconsequentially that he admired the New York School of poetry.

"This is emphatically *not* the New York School," she corrected. "Lots of it's political, and what isn't still touches on a mood that inspires political action."

"What mood?" He was curious.

"Rage."

A momentary silence descended upon the little conclave in the kitchen, heightened somehow by the loud ticking of a large, wind-up clock on the counter. Many plants, hanging from the ceiling, crowding the windowsill, many grains and beans in large glass containers on shelves on the wall, a gleaming silver espresso machine, all the appurtenances and utensils of a well stocked kitchen—everything suggested peace and respite to this tired veteran and to his determination to prevent other people's rage from dragging him away from the quiet, the private, the calm, the domestic. He was going to recover from Vietnam, from Naomi, find a new woman and start over. His ambitions at that moment extended no further. He had no use for rage. But he did not say so. He followed Mike's lead and nodded with deceitful approbation.

"What are you trying to do—get me killed?" He demanded of Mike, after she had departed.

"You may change your views."

"And you might sprout angel wings and strum a harp up to heaven. Change my views! I'm no revolutionary. I'm just licking my wounds and trying to survive. You knew that, yet you dragged this person over here—"

"Ever since I mentioned you, she's been clamoring for a meeting. She's trying to contact as many vets as she can."

"Get them incarcerated or killed is what she's trying to do."

"She doesn't see it that way."

"She needs her head examined."

"She's not stupid, Gilbert."

"She's psycho, thinks she's going to overthrow the government, *this* government! Richard M. Nixon. I don't believe it. I don't believe you subjected me to that."

"Go to her reading."

"And have some FBI informant put my name on a list? No way. I'm avoiding that reading like the plague and frankly, you'd better do the same. That woman means trouble. Don't bring her around here again."

"You really think—"

"I think she's followed, spied upon, tapped. Her husband is a Panther, and was in police custody? You associate with her? You're lucky you haven't been picked up already. I really think! Yes, I really think! Wake up Mike. Where have you been the last few years? You saw what happened at the '68 convention, you read what's happening to all the so-called revolutionary groups. Stop flirting with this crap, if not for yourself, then for Natalie and me."

The tall rock musician frowned, which his generally sunny disposition rarely permitted, so his old friend took it as a sign that his words had hit home. "Finish your last few credits," Gilbert continued. "Get you BA. Play at all the best joints around town with your band. Leave this revolutionary and her street war to those who are suicidal enough to challenge the National Guard. When she transfers to Brandeis in January, let the friendship drop. She can sit at the feet of the great Marcuse, while you go on your merry way. Coordinating committee for antiwar vets and the Panthers—geeze! What were you planning—meetings in this house? So we could get firebombed or arrested in the middle of the night and shot while supposedly resisting arrest?" He paused to fix himself a cup of coffee and let his outrage cool. As it did, a certain pretty face with a long, golden hank of hair that gleamed like sunshine passed before his mind's eye. "By the way," he casually changed the subject, "does Ingrid have someone, a man, or is she free?"

"Is this a lesson in bathos or what?" Mike demanded. "From the terror of the fascist police state to a pretty girl's romantic entanglements in one breath?"

"Oh, she's taken."

"No, she's not friggin' taken. She's a ferocious feminist and doesn't believe in monogamy. She may not believe in men. I wouldn't be surprised to hear her say that we're all figments of a diseased imagination, part of a nightmare from which the women of the world have yet to wake up." He paused to accept the extra cup of coffee his friend offered him. "If I were you, I wouldn't try to touch her with a ten foot pole. She'll bite your head off. She dropped some papers the other day, and when I bent down to pick them up, she lambasted my chivalry for nearly half an hour. You can be damn sure I won't do that again. And she's after Natalie morning, noon and night to join some feminist collective or other and to break the bonds of the, get this, 'patriarchal' relationship she has with me. Is she free! Not free enough. She'll be free enough when she finds her own damn apartment and stops biting the hand she mooches from."

The newcomer was taken aback. "I've never heard you so bitter before, and I thought you said her name's on the lease."

"Unfortunately it is. As for being bitter, I don't like being accused, tried and convicted of things I know nothing about, that probably don't exist and that, if they do, I would seek to correct. She's a harridan. And you think kind, generous Tiwana's trouble! Try Ingrid on a good day. Don't even try to imagine the bad ones."

Ingrid lived on the first floor. Another university student, an undergraduate named Tanya, occupied the room with the books on the second and Jorge, a member of the Young Lords, had the room with the posters. All appeared at seven p.m. in the poorly lit kitchen for dinner. The two hippies who lived in the basement did not. They were in Amherst, smoking as much pot as they could on a commune.

The meal was vegetarian—spinach and feta salad, rice pilaf and a nondescript bean and vegetable stew, accompanied by cheap wine.

"Between pooling our money and the food stamps, each of us gets to eat for a few cents a meal," Tanya explained. Plump and bookish, with lots of curly black hair, she did not attract Gilbert in the least. Her wire-rimmed glasses were loose, which led to many odd and unflattering facial expressions to keep them in place. But dark-eyed, intense Jorge, who ate dinner without removing his brown leather jacket, was clearly enamored. He directed all his remarks and questions to her, hung on her every response and continually offered her more red wine. She was, evidently and self-consciously, an intellectual, a history student, who was soon lecturing on the dialectic, with the Young Lord so rapt that Gilbert half expected him to whip out a pad and start taking notes. It soon became a monologue, punctuated by vague grunts now and then from Ingrid about the patriarchy. Mike and Natalie, inebriated, began to make out.

"Finish chewing before your next kiss please," Ingrid grouched. "It's gross."

"You're just jealous," Natalie, languid though trim and very attractive in a pale, dark-haired way, teased her roommate.

"That'll be the day," the feminist replied, polishing off her wine. "A woman without a man is like a fish without a bicycle."

"Here we go again," Mike muttered.

"And don't expect it to stop any time soon," Ingrid admonished him, waving a bit of onion, speared on her fork, in his face. "Feminism makes new and unique demands on us, though Natalie somehow manages to remain deaf to them."

"I'm in love," that young woman smiled.

"Love," Ingrid snorted. "Don't get me started on the oppression of romance."

"Please," Mike said, "please, we wouldn't dream of it."

"Keep your thoughts on the oppression of romance to yourself," Jorge concurred. "Besides, I think we heard that last night."

"And the night before," Natalie giggled.

"The role of romantic love in the history of the exploitation of women," Tanya mused, "now there's a topic for a dissertation."

"There's a topic for a headache," Mike snapped.

"I agree with Tanya," Ingrid put in.

"Now you've done it," Mike groaned at the historian of oppressive romantic love. "She's going to read us selections from *The Second Sex* any minute."

"You could get out of it, if you just promised to read the book yourself," Ingrid said.

"I tried," he replied. "I wound up contemplating suicide."

"Guilt," Ingrid analyzed.

"An agony of boredom," he corrected.

"Naomi wanted to read *The Second Sex*," Gilbert murmured sadly. "It was on her 'to do' list."

"That and every other pretentious title to come out since the turn of the Twentieth Century," Mike remarked, slurping his wine.

"Sounds like an admirable woman," Ingrid averred.

"Except for her taste in literature," slurp, slurp, "yes."

"Loan it to me," the veteran urged. "I'll read it."

"So then you can write Naomi," more slurping "and impress her with how politically advanced you are."

"You read me like an open book," Gilbert chuckled.

"Just so I don't have to read *The Second Sex* like an open book. I'll be happy to read the cover. Anything more, and I cannot answer for what I may do."

"Such histrionics!" Ingrid exclaimed, tossing her lank, blond tresses back in disgust. "I didn't notice any such reaction when you read *Capital*."

"*Capital* got my attention," Mike poured himself more wine.

"Chauvinist."

"You're barking up the wrong tree. Save your name calling for the real bad guys. I'm on your side. I agree with you. I just don't want to have to read Simone de Beauvoir's version of something I'm already in sync with."

Ingrid rose, with another flash of long golden hair, went downstairs and returned with a tome.

"It's rather large," Gilbert complained.

"She had a lot to say," Ingrid remarked.

"Does she say it well?"

"Not particularly," Mike put in and clapped his friend on the back. "Lucky you: an evening with a sententious French intellectual awaits. Curl up in your bed, snuggle down with Simone de Beauvoir and have a blast. Natalie and I will be imbibing downstairs, if you can tear yourself away or perhaps want to drown your sorrows in booze."

"I hate your philistine routine," Ingrid tossed her rather pert nose haughtily. "It's so phony, tricked out with you fake Francophobia."

Mike rolled his eyes and resumed slurping.

Gilbert rather forlornly opened the book.

"It's not going to impress her," slurp, slurp, "Naomi that is. I doubt her new love, Jack Diamond, ever heard of Simone de Beauvoir. He's a goddamned loon, not a reader. He owns a gun."

The veteran looked up sharply.

"Yup," his old friend went on. "He said he lives in a dangerous Chicago neighborhood, so he bought himself a gun. His friends have guns too. Bunch of cracked pots."

"In East Harlem I owned a gun," Jorge put in. "No cop was gonna take Jorge Ramirez by surprise."

Mike rolled his eyes again. "Jorge Ramirez is damned lucky he never had occasion to use that gun on a cop or he wouldn't be sitting eating rice pilaf at this table right now. He'd be six feet under. Guns! Have all you people gone nuts? Talk to Gilbert. He's handled guns, killed people with them too. He'll tell you about the romance of guns. Bah!"

"You couldn't pay me to own a gun," the spurned lover said. "I can't believe Naomi is in love with a gun nut."

"Believe it, buddy boy. He's got a short fuse too. Put the two together and—well, just hope she isn't around when that happens. Where are you going?"

"To the phone," Gilbert answered, "to call Morris Lichter."

In the corner of the kitchen, Gilbert dialed. "Hello, Mr. Lichter? This is Gilbert."

"Gilbert? Gilbert who?"

"Gilbert and Naomi?"

"Oh, yes. I thought you two broke up."

"We did."

"Oh. So now you want to ask *me* out? I'm sorry, I'm taken."

The young man chuckled. "No, no. It's about her new boyfriend."

"New boyfriend? I didn't know she had one."

"His name is Jack Diamond."

"Like the card."

"Yes, like the card."

"Goody gumdrops. What about him?"

"He's a gun nut."

"Great."

"He owns a gun because he lives in a dangerous Chicago neighborhood."

"Is he a student?"

134

"I believe so. Mr. Lichter, I carried a machine gun in Vietnam. I killed more Viet Cong than I care ever to remember. I think there is something seriously wrong with a college student who's into guns. It really strikes me the wrong, wrong way."

"Tell her, not me. She doesn't listen to a word I say, thanks in large part, I must add, to her relationship with you."

"That was never my intention."

"Well, it was the result. So now we got a gun nut—Diamond. Is he Jewish?"

"How would I know?"

"Because you don't run into too many Jewish gun nuts."

"That's a stereotype and a false one."

"Don't correct me, young man."

"Sorry."

Morris grunted, then was heard shouting. "Lily! Lily! Get over here. Naomi's involved with a gun nut. Gilbert or Norbert or whatever his name is—"

"Gilbert."

"Gilbert called to tell us."

"She doesn't listen to us," Lily said.

"She's very stubborn," Morris said into the phone. "It will be quite difficult, no, next to impossible, to persuade her to leave this guy, because he owns guns. He's not a wacko, is he?"

"Very short-tempered."

"Uh-oh. This sounds like a bad combination."

"I had to use guns against my will, for self-defense in Vietnam," Gilbert continued. "It is my opinion that there is something very wrong with people who want to play with guns."

"Well in Vietnam, you were in a kind of unique situation, I'd venture. You say this Jack Clubs—"

"Jack Diamond."

"Jack Diamonds lives in a dangerous neighborhood. That doesn't sound frivolous. It sounds like self-defense."

"Sounds like a fruitcake."

"That too." Aside Morris sighed to his wife: "She sure can pick 'em. What'd she break up with Norbert for? He seems so rational."

"Gilbert. And you wanted her to break up with him, screamed at her about him for three years until she finally moved out of the house—remember?"

"Oh, yes. That was unpleasant." Into the receiver Morris said: "What do you want me to do? Ground her?"

"Ha!"

"Ha is right, because we're not lookin' at a lot of options here."

"You could withhold tuition."

"Now that is the stupidest thing I ever heard. Punish her for the one and only thing she's doing right? I want her to drop this guy with the guns, not drop out of school. Why don't you go out there yourself and talk some sense into her?"

"No," Gilbert was unequivocal. "I live in Cambridge now. I start a new job tomorrow. Besides, she dropped me."

"She did, hunh?" There was an unmistakable note of satisfaction in Morris' voice. "Well maybe she'll drop Jack Hearts."

"Diamond."

"Before you know it, she'll be through with him."

"And onto somebody else."

"I didn't say that."

"The next guy might own a rocket launcher."

"Very funny."

"Somebody's got to talk to her."

"Not me. I'll have apoplexy. You do it. Telephone her. You can bill the call to me."

"Thanks a lot, Mr. Lichter."

"You're welcome," and there was a click.

Gilbert hung up the phone.

"No luck," Mike Dellico commented.

His friend shook his head. "Mr. Lichter's still basically mad at me."

"That, my friend, is permanent. There's nothing you can do about it. Forget it." Mike went back to gentle necking with Natalie. From where Gilbert stood, they looked like two vines, arms and necks entwined, murmuring to each other, ignored by the other three hunched over the dim table, conversing together in the half dusk, like conspirators or topers from a Daumier painting. In that moment, Gilbert felt oddly at home and at peace and suddenly accepted the fact that the Lichters probably never would like him, never would be impressed by him or his intellectual pretensions and that for Morris he would remain then and forever the louse who had deflowered his daughter. No matter that Gilbert would have married her, no matter any extenuating circumstances. It was settled. He swallowed his disappointment. He loved the Lichters, but they did not love him. They did not even think about him. They never paused in the middle of their days, neither one, to cast their mind over the entity that was Gilbert Locklane and to wonder where he was, what he thought or felt. They, who had meant so much to him, would forget him, for he meant nothing to them. This stood out more clearly before him than anything in the room, over which twilight had settled like the dark shroud of his deceased hopes. He would shed his feeling for them, for their headstrong daughter, would push on to other people and things, but he would never forget the hurt in his heart that the romance had failed, that his situation with her parents had worked out not as he had hoped and that he had had an undeniable role in this outcome.

Jorge shivered in his brown leather jacket, sweater, jeans and boots, as he trudged, hunched over into the sharp, frozen February wind. His cap and scarf did not protect him enough, and his fingers, thrust into his pockets, were numb. It was a gray, icy day. The snow, packed up hard against the curb, had a film of brown and here and there splashes of bright yellow where dogs had urinated, and it stretched, a broken rampart, the length of the slushy street. The sky was a mass of minatory cloud, the sun nowhere to be seen. Massachusetts Avenue was ugly and cold.

"Dogs! Students and their damned dogs," he cursed, as he accidentally stepped on a turd, which was, fortunately for him, frozen solid as a rock. Near the corner of Bay Street, he hurried into a small restaurant that advertised calzones, its picture window steamy, bright and inviting. Tiwana Allenhurst was ensconced at a small table in the back, her afro glistening with little particles of ice, as cold as her wintry eyes.

"So where is he?" The Puerto Rican revolutionary demanded, settling into a delicate cane chair and withdrawing his benumbed fingers from his pockets to warm them with his breath. He huffed vigorously, but they stayed cold.

"Patience, he'll arrive," she answered and sipped her mug of herbal tea.

"I'd like a hot chocolate with extra whipped cream," Jorge told the waitress, a hippie whose curly blond tresses swung down to her waist. "And no hair in it, like the last time."

"Definitely uncool, "she sniffed and rather haughtily removed the menu from his hands.

"Definitely no tip," he said, as he heard her hollering "one hot chocolate, and, get this, No Hair!" in the back.

"Was that necessary?" His companion asked in a tired tone. "She has a living to earn. She doesn't need finicky patrons who withhold tips."

"It was her hair."

"How do you know?"

"It was long, blond and curly. Those Spanish people who work in the back have black hair, like me."

She eyed him critically, the gray of her irises glinting like steel, also picking up the color of her thick, woolly Mexican sweater. "You know, sometimes I think you don't have the temperament for this kind of work."

"What kind of work?"

"Revolution. What kind of revolutionary makes snobbish remarks to waitresses, is so persnickety he considers not tipping someone who depends on tips for her livelihood. Where's your solidarity with the working class?"

"She's a refugee from Newton, one of the most affluent suburbs in Massachusetts."

"How do you know?"

"I asked her."

"And that's another thing, something that offends me as a feminist: you asked her when you were trying to pick her up. She turned you down, and now you're condescending to her and threatening her and complaining about her work in ways that endanger her employment."

"You didn't tell me I was in for a criticism/self-criticism session when you called."

"I hadn't caught your act."

He scowled and blew out a breath in exasperation. But he otherwise kept his mouth shut. His hot chocolate arrived.

"Hairless, as you requested," the waitress rather airily remarked.

He grunted and sipped. "So where's the great man?"

"He's on his way. Keep your sarcasm to yourself. You got a deferment. He got wounded in action." She stirred her tea pensively. "Besides, we have yet to see you deliver any of the Spanish community. He brings a whole movement."

"Any other kindly comparisons you wanna make?"

"You need a shave."

"I need a job, a woman—"

"What about Tanya?"

He thought he detected suppressed mirth at the corners of her mouth. "She's married to her books. She never takes her nose out of them."

"Speaking of that, isn't that the hippie who lives in your basement?" She pointed at a muscular, mustached man with shoulder length brown hair, who had just stepped into the restaurant, reading a volume of *The Prophet Armed*. Jorge turned around. "Hey Alderway," he called. "What's happening?"

The hippie looked up, rubbed the headband across his forehead and made a face of rather elaborate surprise. Jorge gestured him to approach. "That was some bad acid I dropped last weekend," he remarked, sitting down. "I still haven't got my focus back."

"Keep messing around with that dope and you never will," the Young Lord commented.

"What are you, my guidance counselor?" The new arrival put his book down. Reading the title, Tiwana nodded approvingly. He observed this, patted the book and muttered, "great stuff, great stuff."

"I didn't know politics interested you," she said.

"Too much," he replied and then to the waitress, "A coffee with cream, and please, try to keep the hair out of it."

"You go to marches?" Tiwana continued.

"Sure, all of 'em. I'm a foot soldier in the war against the establishment."

Her eyes flashed. "That's how you see yourself?"

"Un-hunh."

"In that case, you're off drugs as of today."

"Hunh? He's my guidance counselor and what are you, my parole officer?"

"You ever been in trouble with the law?"

"I been in my share of paddy wagons."

"After demos?"

"Sure."

She slapped the table angrily. "Jorge, this is exactly what I mean. Here's this guy living right under your nose, in your basement. He could be *useful* for God's sake. You don't even know he exists. We could have drafted him—"

"I'm against the draft."

"I mean for underground activity."

"Oh, I'm all for that," Alderway received his coffee and poked it gingerly with a spoon, looking for hair. Then he glanced up at Tiwana through cannily narrowed eyes. "What do you want me to do?"

"Just stay here. We're meeting someone. It's important. You listen in, get the picture, and afterward I'll tell you how we can use you."

The suddenly sharp eyes swiveled back to the coffee. "Anything to oblige."

"I wouldn't say that if I were you," Jorge muttered.

The trio sat in silence, in the gloomy back of the little restaurant, sipping their beverages and inhaling the aromas of tomato sauce, burgers, melted and in some cases burnt cheese, French fries and other sundry appetizing comestibles. Jorge blew his nose on a Kleenex, noting miserably that his cold had worsened, due, no doubt to his walk through the dreary, windy afternoon. True, his hot chocolate was sans hair, but he was still annoyed at the waitress, who had resisted his blandishments. His thoughts returned to Tanya, but the last time they had made love, she had lectured him afterward on the evils of sexual possessiveness for fifteen minutes. He didn't know if he could go through that again. Besides, she had said things that offended his male pride, remarks that indicated that she had other lovers whom she did not intend to abandon for him. Why were women so explicit about everything these days? And so graphic? What had ever happened to old-fashioned romance? "Feminism," Mike Dellico had told him. "That's what happened." Which put Jorge in a bind, because theoretically he approved of feminism, but the way it translated into practice—the lectures, the scolding, the downright shrewishness—was unbearable. And to have to take a dressing down from Tiwana, someone whom he regarded as brilliant but a cracked pot, that was too much. As if he'd listen to one word from her. Look where all her fine theories had got her husband! She was out of her mind, Jorge thought, no doubt about it. "It'll be a colder day than this in hell before I ask *anybody* from East Harlem to team up with her," he thought. "Let her complain. Either she tells me all about this steering committee or coordinating committee or whatever it is, or she doesn't get any Puerto Ricans. I'm not risking anybody's neck, least of all my own, for her psycho plots."

"Happy thoughts?" Tiwana asked him with a sidelong glance.

"Heavenly," Jorge grunted and slurped his hot chocolate.

Alderway had resumed reading, but strange, suppressed lights danced in his deep, unfathomably deep, dark eyes. Jorge sniffed critically. His roommate could use a bath. Even with a cold, Jorge could detect a musky, pungently sweaty odor that made him think longingly of warm water and soap.

"We got the shower fixed," slurp, slurp on the hot chocolate.

"Great. Did you know that Trotsky—"

"And there was nothing wrong with the bathtub."

"He was a great general."

"Yeah," more slurps, "but did he bathe?"

"I'm trying to read here."

"You should check out the shower at home."

Alderway folded his arms across his chest in annoyance and leaned back, studying his roommate with an inscrutable, dangerously and incongruously intelligent and irritated gaze. "Since when are we so particular about hygiene?"

"I got a sensitive nose."

"Then it should have told you that that pigsty we live in smells like a barnyard, your room included."

Tiwana, obviously irked that this bickering somehow fell far short of the gravitas required by the moment, told them both to shut up. Jorge returned to slurping, Alderway to reading. She shuffled a stack of papers before her on the table.

"What are those," Jorge asked, "minutes of the last Politburo meeting?"

"You are getting on my nerves," she replied.

Alderway glanced up, the sharp level beam of his gaze taking Tiwana in, all too evidently sizing her up. He brushed a few invisible specks off the many fringes of his suede coat, scratched his drooping moustache as if pondering some weighty remark, then lit a cigarette and wisely said nothing.

The door of the eatery opened and in stepped the tall, lean figure of Boris Slavonovich. Snowflakes speckled his long, lank blond hair, and a thin layer of snow lined the shoulders of his black leather jacket, under which could be see the rough weave of a fisherman's sweater. He wore patched jeans and boots. As he removed his leather gloves, he reached up and rubbed the ugly scar that sliced down from his left eye to his jaw. Tiwana rose. He approached the table and shook her extended hand. Introductions proceeded, as he pulled up a chair and quickly ordered a mushroom calzone.

"It's snowing," Boris remarked. "I love it."

"Not me," Jorge slurped. "Give me tropical beaches and palm trees any day."

"It's my Ukrainian blood," the veteran smiled. "I only really feel alive in a blizzard."

"Well, we got a blizzard of things to take care of," Tiwana said.

"There have been some changes," Boris said softly.

Alderway closed his book.

"You've got to cut us some slack," he went on, sipping his water. "My guys are vets. They've done enough killing. Most of them believe in nonviolence."

"Nonviolence!" Tiwana snorted in disdain. Alderway's eyes flickered.

"They will participate in any demonstrations or rallies that your people set up. They'll print and distribute literature," he went on, then glancing down, noted *The Prophet Armed* in Alderway's hand. "Good book," he murmured, then resumed; "But they will not participate in any assaults or killings. They will not commit violence, even against the war criminals in charge of this country. That's final."

She slapped her hand down on her stack of papers, sighed loudly and leaned back, surveying him as if he were a crasher at a wedding. "Nonviolence!" She exclaimed again.

"Gandhi is our model," Boris accepted the plate with his calzone from the waitress. "And I think it's fair to say plenty of your people would go along with us."

"Fair? Perhaps, but not for you to say."

"Well, as you know," chomp, chomp on the calzone, "I just got up here from D.C. The veterans against the war are planning a big rally in two months. If you can put your…your…aversion to nonviolence aside—"

"You mean her bloodthirsty fantasies," Jorge sourly put in.

She gave him a deadly look, and he said no more.

"We might ask you to speak," Boris concluded.

"Well, well, the peaceniks have won out," she rather snidely commented.

"I wish they'd win out in the White House, instead of bombing everything in sight in Vietnam," Boris picked up half of his calzone and bit down savagely. "But seriously, we're not a paramilitary organization."

"No one could mistake you for one."

"And hopefully you aren't either, though I understand you all are riven by factional divisions on this."

"Yup, and you're talking to the wrong faction," she retorted, sipping the last of her tea.

"No," Boris' gemlike blue eyes flashed. "I'm talking to exactly who I aimed to talk to, exactly who *we* aimed for me to talk to. Don't you see that this rhetoric of armed revolution damages us all? It tarnishes us all? Cut it out. Go back into the community, beef up you meals programs in the ghettos, your community centers and free clinics. Stop talking about bombing buildings and stop hoarding machine guns. It's not helping anybody. It's harming you and everyone who wants to be allied with you.

You've already seen how the police react: with murders and torture. Think of your husband."

"I think of him every minute of every day. And in fact when I leave, I'll call him and see what he thinks of you, though I've already got a pretty good idea. Jeremiah will agree with me that we cannot sit idly by and be exterminated. We cannot succumb to a campaign of police brutality and police terror." She put her teacup down, and her eyes were very still and cold. "We have to fight back, and we will."

Jorge sighed. He was not impressed. He had already decided that this Boris Slavonovich was a paragon of clear-headedness and sanity and that he would advise his friends in New York to work with him. Tiwana, as he saw it, was out on a limb. Only the most fanatical of her people were out there with her, and they did not even form a sizeable minority of her group. "I'm with Boris," he announced and guzzled more hot chocolate. "We've got to organize, not revolt. No Puerto Ricans I know are into this kamikaze shit."

Alderway's gaze sparkled strangely over Jorge's face. "Too much acid," Jorge thought, but then this hippie spoke up: "I know I'm not a bigwig in your organization, but Tiwana has a point. You can't just stand by and be wiped out."

The veterans' leader eyed him critically. "Who's being wiped out? Vietnamese peasants, the last time I checked. We don't have time to play cops and robbers back on the home front. We have to hold rallies, sit in at congressmen's offices, organize! Just like Joe Hill said. Not hand the enemy a ready-made script to use against us, that we're a bunch of wild-eyed terrorists ready to throw bombs and shoot up the local chamber of commerce."

"I think this meeting's over," Tiwana said and looked at Alderway: "You stay, please."

Boris scribbled hastily on a scrap of paper. "Here's my number in Brookline. I'll be here another day. I may have meetings, but I'll leave any one of them, should you decide you want to talk further."

She took the paper and gave him a tight, little smile. "That's highly unlikely."

"Hey, I wanna talk further," Jorge said.

"Then walk with me to Central Square," the veteran smiled. The two men left money on the table and walked out into a whirling snowstorm together.

"That was a disaster," Tiwana breathed to herself.

"There will always be setbacks," Alderway said.

"I have to talk to some people in Chicago," she said, donning her red and purple, hand-woven coat that looked more like a cape. "When can I reach you? I always got the impression that you were rarely home, just off floating from one drug party to another."

"Correct. But you can always leave a message for me with Mike or Gilbert. They're the two most reliable people at my house. I'll get it."

Her gaze wandered to the front of the restaurant and fixed on the door. "I'll be in touch soon. I may have something for you to do." She left her money on the table, rose and swept out of the warm little establishment, into the snow.

For several minutes Alderway sat quietly, sipping his coffee. The waitress approached, so he paid the check, then reached in his pocket for a dime. He put it on the table in front of him and stared at it. At last he began to smile. He looked up, checked the entrance—there was no one—then rose, taking the dime, and walked to the black pay telephone at the back of the room. He dialed a number, then said: "Alderway here."

"It's about time," came the little voice through the receiver.

"I'm in."

"With who?"

"The Panthers. The violent, armed wing."

"But you're white. What happened to the Weathermen?"

"That's a problem for New York or Chicago."

"Or SDS?"

"I'm with the Panthers, okay? They won't trust me with state secrets, but they'll let me do errands."

"Do whatever they want. And agitate."

"I already started."

"Encourage them to be as violent as possible. And keep us informed. Don't go out on your own for a while. We don't want any surprises. We don't want any cops getting killed, even undercover slobs like yourself."

"Oh, I'll take good care of yours truly. You can rely on it."

"Who is this Alderway?" Boris asked, as he and his companion from the calzone shop bent into the snow and wind. "Do you trust him?"

"Yeah. He's been living in my house for almost a year. He's a hippie."

"A hippie who encourages armed resistance to the state? Doesn't sound like most hippies I know. Sounds like an agent provocateur."

"No way," Jorge dismissed the notion. "I know the guy. He's basically harmless."

"Still, I'd appreciate it if you kept me, my business, and the doings of the vets out of his earshot."

"Of course, but you're going way overboard. I been telling him about our struggles in East Harlem for months, and nothing bad's come of it. In fact, I told him about a landlord we were dealing with, a real lowlife who evicted old ladies at gunpoint and shot up a cripple's apartment, and something good came of it; he brought us good luck. The son of a bitch landlord got hauled up on tax evasion charges, the building went into receivership, and the city took it over. The city's been a much more civilized landlord. It don't turn off the heat in winter, it keeps the water on, it got rid of the rats, fixes holes in the walls and all the little old Puerto Ricans who live there are in seventh heaven. They never had it so good."

"Hmmph. That could be more than a happy coincidence."

"Don't worry. My lips are sealed."

The wind died, and the snow began to drift down slowly and vertically. "So do you think you could get demonstrators in sizeable numbers to go from New York to the rally in D. C.?" The organizer asked.

Jorge shrugged. "It doesn't hurt to try. Hey this is my turnoff." They stopped and clasped hands.

"Work on Tiwana," Boris said.

"She's a hard case. After what happened to her husband, she has no use for peace of any sort."

"She's going to have to get over that."

"That's easy for you to say. She's the one who got him back from the cops, took him straight to Cook County Hospital. He could barely stand. He's lucky to be alive."

"We all are."

"Say, what?"

The veteran gazed off into the snow. It was night now, and the flakes floated luminously in the black air, like phosphorescence on a dark sea. The cold softness muffled everything, from the pavement to the starless sky, in the quiet lie that life was gentle and had no painful sharpness to it. "That's just my view of life," he tapped the big scar on his cheek, "reinforced by experience." He paused, then spoke softly, "life is the thing, Jorge, the best thing, the chief good, the greatest gift, what everything is really about. Life, and other people."

Boris continued on to the Central Square station, went down into the subway and stood on the platform, crowded with raucous MIT students on their way in town for the evening. He had *The Boston Phoenix* under his arm and opened it to an article on the antiwar movement, then rode into Boston, reading, and switched from the subway to a clattering trolley out to Brookline. Outside, at ground level, the bare trees gleamed with snow, everywhere snow covered bushes, sidewalks, railings, like a carpet of diamonds glittering up at the void. He closed the newspaper and looked out at the broad, snow-covered street. "Alderway," he murmured to himself.

He stepped off the trolley into a soft pad of snow. When he reached the sidewalk, he leaned down and scooped up a small, clean white handful, put it to his mouth and tasted it; it brought forth pictures from his mother's album of the Ukraine, cupolas covered with snow, little wooden cottages with snow on the roofs, the frozen Dnieper in Kiev and a snow-covered path through the woods, pictures that swarmed before him in the night air and now as always elicited the vow, "I will go there before I die." Indeed those were his very words, over and over, in the hospital in Saigon, so that the nurse had asked, "where, Mr. Slavonovich? Where will you go?" He strode on, his tall, lanky figure moving swiftly through the drifting snow, which now and then he tasted by stopping, throwing his head back and opening his mouth. "We come from a wintry country," his grandmother had been wont to tell him in Ukrainian. "You have never been there, but it is your true home."

He turned down a side street, then another and stopped before a trim, three-story house with big bay windows on the second floor. His purple Volvo was parked out front, and he noticed, with some annoyance, that one of the tires was flat. He rang the bell, and the door opened. Alan Jengo's toothy smile and unconventionally short hair greeted him.

"This is way better than Pittsburgh," he enthused. "Too bad I gotta fly back in two days. Boston has so many women! Young women are everywhere." As if on cue, a statuesque blond sidled up to him. "Donna meet Boris. Donna's a cellist. She goes to the Berkeley school of music."

"Hi Donna. Uh, Alan, weren't you supposed to be running a meeting between some vets and union members who were interested in antiwar activity?"

"Oh, that broke up hours ago. I took copious notes, though, just for you. Don't worry, I got everybody's name, address and telephone number. We'll have lots of bodies in Washington."

"Looks like you have been concentrating on the bodies right here."

Donna giggled, and Alan hung his head sheepishly: "Don't draw the wrong conclusion."

"I'm sure I didn't." The veteran entered the living room to greet his host, Jessie Roper, a social worker employed in Roxbury, who vacationed on communes in western Massachusetts and southern Vermont. Boris was eager to visit these places, even in winter, when the communards kept warm by means of wood-burning stoves and many layers of clothes, but he had to return to the nation's capital promptly. With that in mind, he asked Jessie for help changing his flat tire.

They trooped out into the snow, still drifting through night air with the lazy elegance of a socialite in a lamé evening gown. He raised the car with the jack and Jessie, as tall and lanky as his guest, folded up like a fan to squat to change the tire. Yes, Boris, thought, there was something seductive about this snow with its quiet and peace, as if all the rough and tumble of the social world were a lie. He felt the allure of this solitude and silence that would recur each winter and would finally prevail long after humanity had vanished. He found himself contemplating centuries of silence and snow, when his vision was rather sharply punctuated by Jessie's cry of "shit! I dropped it." No, he thought, perhaps it was the reverse, and it was the snow that convinced him of an untruth.

He bent down to help and together they finished changing the tire.

"It's not a two man job, you know," Jessie commented in annoyance.

"I wanted company. The snow, the dark—nature seems so vast tonight, like it's even taken over the city."

"You been smoking that weed?"

"Not at all; just full of strange thoughts."

"Come on. Have those strange thoughts with a little dinner on the side." He led his guest to the kitchen at the back of the house, which had windows overlooking a garden, now a series of shapeless snow-covered lumps. They sat at a small, round, butcher block table, sharing a roast chicken, roasted red potatoes, carrots and cole slaw, drinking beer.

"That was quite a meeting here tonight," the social worker averred, making quick work of a drumstick, meat, gristle and all, then snapped the bone and sucked out the marrow.

"Man, you don't waste a thing," his visitor laughed.

"Too much waste in this society as is. I paid for that chicken. I'm going to make damn sure I eat it all."

"The meeting went well?"

"Un-hunh," chomp, chomp. "There was a real rapport between those custodial workers, I should say shop stewards and organizers, that Alan brought in and your vets. These custodial workers, lots of them live in Roxbury. They're mostly black, their families get counseling from people like me and this type of political action is new to them. Some, one or two, are natural born leaders. You can just see it. And the whole group had lots in common with your guys. Mostly the younger workers are scared to death of getting drafted. They know they're the cannon fodder in this war and that they have no say about it. Gee, if all the meetings you been running these past few days were half as successful as this, you could have the whole East Coast mobilized by April."

"The one I went to tonight was a bust. It wasn't even a meeting, just me and three people, one of whom," he lifted his hand parallel to the table and fluttered it from side to side.

"Shaky? How so?"

"I think he's a police spy. He may have done some good—like getting a criminal landlord in East Harlem busted—"

"East Harlem? I thought you were in Cambridgeport."

"I'm talking about something he heard about and then got the guy busted on tax evasion. Cops and prosecutors do that sort of thing all the time. They get onto some lowlife, can't get him for his crimes, so they send the name on up to the IRS and bingo! The slime's in jail for tax evasion."

"What's his name?"

"The cop? Alderway. He's passing himself off as a hippie. Now he's trying to infiltrate the Panthers. And the Panther I met with didn't have a clue. She has the reputation of being a strategic genius, but for a genius, she sure was slow about sizing this guy up."

"So you brought her up to speed?"

"No. No such opportunity. And she's so enamored of violence, I'm afraid to do so. She might try to have the guy killed."

"Then she's out of her mind." The two men ate thoughtfully, grunting now and then, as if acknowledging some relevant idea.

"I tried to plant the seed in the other guy's mind, Jorge Ramirez from the Young Lords. He said he couldn't believe it, but it's there now, in his brain."

"So you're hoping he'll deal with it, passing the buck to him."

"Look, I don't like these kinds of complications. I work for an antiwar group, and we obey the law. Some of the laws stink, but that's life."

"You better tell this Alderway either he buds out or you'll have to voice your suspicions."

"Shit. For all I know this Tiwana's already got him transporting machine guns across state lines. I could be interfering with a police investigation."

"Then you call up this Jorge, and you don't plant seeds, you make them grow into big, tall, scary, man-eating plants. And you and he figure out what to do. Don't you mention my name."

"He lives in Jorge's house. If Jorge kicked him out, saying he knows he's a police spy—"

"Then maybe this Alderway will get the idea that word already got back to Tiwana, and he'll back off."

"It's the best I can do."

"Don't you mention my name."

"You said that once already."

"Did I say it enough? That's the question."

In the bright, crystal-flashing morning, pounding his gloved hands together to keep them warm, the veterans' leader stepped out onto the snowy sidewalk, inhaled the frozen air quickly, and then made for his car. After cleaning thick snow off the windshield and windows, he started the engine, then drove slowly down unplowed streets until he reached broader avenues, covered with sand. At nine o'clock he parked outside a small establishment not far from Roxbury, turned the key in the ignition and listened to the engine die. He rehearsed his speech. He hoped his words would be strong and true and would expose this enemy and rout him once and for all. Then he stepped out of the car and entered the coffee shop.

Jorge sat in a booth, slurping a hot chocolate. He did not look especially pleased to be there, and looked even less so when he heard what his visitor had to say. "You're the only one who can take care of this," Boris concluded. "Alderway lives with you. He's a cop. You tell him you know, and he has to move out. Thank him for what he did about that landlord. But he has to go, and you don't know if you can keep quiet about it."

"And the next time I see Tiwana?"

"Don't. Avoid her, not just because of this."

"But because of—"

"Because she's nuts." The veteran paused to sip his coffee. "I've got a largely black union of custodial workers ready to team up with us. We don't need, you don't need, these fanatics preaching violence."

"Maybe I disagree."

"You don't."

Jorge sighed. "All right, I don't. I got rid of my gun a long time ago. Don't tell anybody." He slurped his hot chocolate. "So you're telepathic."

"No, I suspected. When you told me the little landlord story, I knew."

"And I always thought he was such a good listener."

"Let's hope you didn't give him too much to listen to."

"He would sit, cross-legged on that filthy mattress of his on the cellar carpet, burning incense. I told him about where I came from, the poor part of San Juan, the tin shacks on the pristine beaches, then the mess and jumble of East Harlem. I confided how it was a Jewish legal aid attorney, Mariah, who enlightened me about social and political reality, radicalized me, how lost I was before I met her, just living in that dump with my parents and brothers and sisters, working odd jobs to pitch in with that astronomical rent." Suddenly he stopped slurping and sat up straight. "Christ, I hope this doesn't get Mariah in trouble. What if—"

"Did she break the law?"

"No."

"Is political discussion against the law?"

"No, but I feel as though somehow I've endangered her, like now her name will be on a list."

"It probably already was." Boris gazed out the window at the snow-covered street. "This is my whole life," he murmured, "this work that I do. There's no pay, my money's running out. When it's gone, I guess I'll just run on air."

His companion nodded sympathetically. "That's why I got me a part-time job at a food co-op in Somerville."

"But it's important," the veteran suddenly swung his level blue-eyed gaze straight at Jorge, who noted again the ugly scar that gashed from cheekbone to jaw and other smaller scars over his face, all bespeaking the wounding of war and the pain and boredom of a long hospital stay. "We can't get tangled up with a police spy. Every day soldiers and villagers die in the mud in Vietnam. Every day more kids get drafted. Every day the lucky ones wind up with this," he tapped his scar and in that moment seemed so human, so injured, so bewildered by the awfulness that had overtaken him, that Jorge had to glance away, out at the street again and at the parked, snow-topped cars. But even so, he was not fast enough to avoid the sudden image in his mind of steel ripping into soft, bleeding facial flesh. "I'll get rid of Alderway," he said, wanting now to escape this ill-concealed pain that reproduced itself with grisly mental pictures so ghastly and vivid that he winced quite noticeably, right there in the restaurant. "Don't worry about it. He will be gone."

Boris sat in the little booth by the bright sunshiny window with its view of glittering whiteness and drank his acrid coffee after his companion had left. He thought of his journey back to Washington, the white fields with occasional yellow patches of grass along the Massachusetts Turnpike, the gleaming towers of Manhattan, the industrial nightmare of Elizabeth, New Jersey and then of his destination—the run-down townhouse in Northwest D.C., their little mimeograph machine in the living room, where he and his friends printed their flyers, his trips to the hospital to talk with wounded veterans. And then the images flitted back to his own time in Vietnam, and as he paid and rose and strode out to his car in the morning that sparkled like an armful of gems, he remembered Sammy, the ten-year-old boy who spoke some English, who had survived the fiery destruction of his village, who attached himself to their unit and to Boris in particular and whose family in Saigon Boris had promised to find.

He turned the key in the ignition, gazed through the window at the whitely heaped streets, at the occasional gaunt tree with its bare snow-covered branches and saw instead the burning hamlet, the dead children piled like broken dolls in front of their huts, heard the gunfire piercing the hush of the jungle as the Vietcong retreated into it and saw the boy for the first time, huddled over the crumpled, blood-stained body of his mother, not screaming, but weeping silently, his eyes gleaming blackly, deep pools of woe that reflected their misery all the way to where Boris crouched as clearly as if the child stood right before him.

"Hey Slavonovich—are you out of your mind?" A buddy called as he sprinted forward, grabbed the boy and dove with him into a ditch.

"He's probably Vietcong," the sergeant said later.

"No sir, no Vietcong," the boy lied, his dark eyes glinting with sorrow and deceit. "Vietcong kill my father." And he was adopted, and Boris, who had an uncanny ability to detect a lie, ignored his intuition, which turned out to be for the best. So what if the boy's family had sheltered the enemy? He would have no such opportunities now, and, Boris saw, it was highly unlikely the child would betray them. He was getting free food, the protection of the American military and, best of all, he had Boris' promise to find his aunt in Saigon.

He eased the car out of the deepest snow and away from the curb. At the red light it skidded, but he turned the Volvo into the skid and the car soon stopped. Carefully he cajoled it out onto a busy thoroughfare, where the sand gave it traction. "Snowflakes are white, cold, beautiful and they dissolve when you touch them," he had told the boy, who had requested the description.

"You will show me snow."

"Me? When?"

"When you take me and my aunt to America."

"Look," Boris crouched down, so as to be on the small, ten-year-old's level. The dark serious eyes studied him. Soot-streaked legs and feet were exposed by the dirty shorts, and his bony arms hung loosely. Even after two weeks of military meals, the boy was still too skinny. "First we have to find your aunt."

"You will, Mr. Boris, I know. You found me."

Not long after, on a break from their patrols, Boris and company were in Saigon. The boy named an address, but no one there had heard of his aunt. "This boy," a middle-aged woman explained in broken English, as she pointed a leathery finger at the photo of Sammy that Boris had extended, "he came here with his mother, one year ago. They wanted to buy antibiotics. That's how he know this address."

"So Sammy," Boris later said quietly as they traversed a hot, crowded street, "there never was any aunt."

"Don't leave me, Mr. Boris."

"I'll do what I can."

But it was not enough. "A squad can't keep a boy as a mascot," his sergeant said. "He goes to the orphanage."

The orphanage was a dismal, ramshackle wooden affair, with leaks, rats and broken steps. The forlorn orphans in sackcloth uniforms milled in the penned in, fly-filled yard, if they were old enough or, if still babies, they stayed in gray moldy cribs upstairs. But they were well fed—three rice-based meals per day and candy treats, courtesy of the U.S. military. They were not kept clean, however, and the whole filthy place reeked. When Boris had to leave the boy in the dirt yard to go speak to the director, Sammy panicked and grabbed his hand. "Don't leave me, Mr. Boris, not here. This is a bad place."

"I'll be right back." An attendant led him down a corridor, the sultry air buzzing with insects, and knocked on a door whose green paint had almost all peeled off. Someone called out, and the attendant opened the door to reveal a man with short gray hair, seated at a large desk with a cross, the South Vietnamese flag and a picture of President Johnson behind him. He spoke English, telling Boris to please sit, which he did, and he began to explain that Sammy's stay was only temporary, that as soon as he finished his tour, he would adopt him.

"Our establishment has not impressed you favorably," he mumbled.

"Frankly, no."

"Mr. Slavonovich, we exist on the charity of the Catholic Church, monies from the government and from the U.S. military. Those are three

152

huge organizations. You would think we would be living in luxury. But the sums from each are paltry," he spoke that last word with particular emphasis, as though proud that this term, which summed up all the orphanage's woes, was part of his English vocabulary. "Paltry," he repeated. "We are keeping these poor children alive. That is the best we can do. That is all we can do. If we didn't, they would starve on the street."

"Just remember: when I'm done my military service, I'm adopting him."

An unexpected firmness came into his mumbling. "But if a family wants him before then, I have to think of the good of the child."

Boris drummed his fingers on the worn wooden arm of his chair. "You'll tell me who they are, though, right?"

"You don't trust that we would find a good placement?"

"I just might want to see, with my own eyes."

He raised his eyes, slanted, unyielding, to him. "I would have to make sure they would accept that."

He sighed, in some exasperation that he would get no concessions from him, and had no leverage. He had to report back to duty within the hour and had been told, in no uncertain terms, that the boy was not to be with him. "I'd like something in writing," he ventured.

"Not if it could negatively affect the welfare of the child. I cannot sign a contract stating that you may remove him from any future placement, should you decide it is inadequate. I cannot do that."

He leaned back and gazed up at the ceiling fan, spinning slowly above his cluttered desk. When he had first set eyes on him, small, mumbling, gray haired, in a shabby western suit, he had not thought he would encounter resistance, no less be stymied by it, and confident in this underestimation he had used no cunning, not even a single tactic and had revealed his whole hand. But now he saw that he was as unyielding as an iron post against the soft, plangent breath of his objections, which were all he had left after his stupid, heedless honesty. He would do things his way, according to his own notions, not Boris', of the welfare of the child. He rose wordlessly, turned and walked out of his office. Already he glimpsed the possibility that after his good-bye, he would never see the child again.

Indeed the boy thought so too. The instant he stepped into the dirt yard, Sammy ran up to him, grabbed his hand and babbled hysterically about not being left there. Boris crouched down, so that their heads were level. "They will feed you here," he said. "And I will be back."

"You will never be back."

"You don't know me."

"I know grown-ups. They go away. They don't come back."

"That's because this is war. But I'm different."

The boy dropped his hand and took a step away. He did not look at the man, but gazed instead, stubbornly, at the barren ground. "Goodbye, Mr. Boris."

"I'll see you again."

"No, good-bye."

Walking away, he never dreamed that the boy was right, that his own certainty of return was so misplaced. But months passed and then there was the fire, blood, broken glass and jagged steel of his helicopter shot down, his friend Ronzell impaled on a metal spike, dying slowly, with screams of agony and Boris trapped, helpless, maydaying into the dead radio. After that came the hospital, the healing of his shattered bones, the surgeries and the drugs. By the time he was able to telephone the orphanage, almost a year had passed, and Sammy, he learned, had run away, scaled the chain link fence and vanished into the hot, damp swirl of a Saigon summer night. He was lost forever. All Boris had was a tattered photograph, worn dull, of the two of them standing, grinning beside a jeep. "Perhaps it's for the best," a friend thoughtlessly remarked.

"No, it's for the worst," He replied in truth.

He returned to Philadelphia, the anger at what had happened to him and to those he had known just beginning to simmer. Perhaps now he was well enough to let it simmer, in any event, he could no longer ignore it; it was there, beneath the surface of things, beneath every word he uttered. He followed war news avidly and protests even more avidly. The moment he heard of Vietnam Veterans Against the War, he walked out of the house and joined. The die was cast, he said. His life's work lay before him. The road into his future was clear.

Like the road he traveled now, as he left Boston behind, crossed 495 and sped west on the Massachusetts Turnpike, that road that Alderway would not obstruct, that the machinations of police and military men could not block. And the snow-covered fields raced by. He sped back toward D.C. with his anger boiling. Once again a police spy had sought to ensnare him and what he believed in. Once again he had foiled the enemy. "Keep coming. I don't care," he said out loud, gripping the steering wheel, staring through the windshield down a great New England highway, seething with thoughts about protest and the antiwar movement and bringing the military/industrial complex to its knees. And the snow-covered fields raced by.

The dome of the statehouse in Hartford glittered before him, late morning. He tore past the little city, bastion of the insurance industry, haven of myriad corporate executives, and onto Interstate 91 South. From there it was not long to the rolling hills and worrisome curves of the Merritt Parkway. It had snowed in Connecticut, too. The branches, laden with their white freight, stooped over the road, which had been well cleared. As he sped under those boughs, he heard Ronzell's screams again, pounded the useless radio, called on God in two languages, lapsed into fevered unconsciousness then awoke again to horror, and gazing through the windshield, seemed to see the Capitol building in Washington D.C. and the White House, engulfed in those screams, and he addressed those proud buildings: "I blame you and you, for the blood and the agony and the wasted lives." He tore into New York State before lunchtime.

On the vast, ugly concrete expanses of the Cross County Expressway, he saw again his homecoming, on crutches and in bandages: the small, two-story house he had lived in all his life in Roxborough, not far from leafy Chestnut Hill, the gentle way his parents, gray-haired but still hale, his father taller than he had remembered, guided him into the living room, onto the overstuffed flower print sofa, telling him not to move, they would take care of everything. He remembered looking around and thinking, "and all the time I was over there, in the steaming jungle, with the blood and mud and bullets, this was here, just the same." The incongruity overcame him and then renewed his sense that this was where all decency was, in modest homes, with small, sun-filled rooms and ordinary people going about their business, not in the high halls of Congress or at the opulent offices of the White House, where war criminals and war racketeers plotted the misery of multitudes.

His grandmother had died in his absence, so his parents now felt free to speak English all the time. As always, framed photographs of the house outside Kiev, of his gaunt grandfather who had died in Stalin's famine in the thirties, of women in scarves and men in warm Ukrainian hats, covered the tables and mantelpiece; but not as many as before. A little at a time, the pictures were being removed, as though it was acceptable, now that grandmother was dead, to forget the past. He wanted to also, particularly Vietnam, but he could not seem to remove the pictures in his mind.

Years faded some of the images. Others stubbornly remained, as vivid as the day they occurred, so vivid that often at night as he drowsed on his parents' living room couch, he seemed to see the shifting net of moonlit leaves above him, to hear the jungle sounds all around and to feel the warmth of a climate inherently alien to him. Those were the neutral memories. The terrible ones could return at any time, night or day and, if during the day, he would stop whatever he was doing for a moment, in a paralysis of memory and woe, waiting for it to pass.

His wounds healed, his scars set. He became that thing revered and ignored, a veteran. He spent his long days filled with emptiness in the company of other veterans. He talked about ending the war. His mother said: "You need a life besides Vietnam."

"Vietnam is my life," he replied, but nevertheless absorbed her humble wisdom. He started seeing women again. For a while he consorted with a hippie he met at a be-in in Fairmount Park, but she was so compulsively unfaithful that he gave it up after a month. Briefly he fell in love with the comely Eileen Meer, and after the Chicago convention, they met a few times in restaurants or at her apartment. She spoke quite frankly with him about her broken heart, given to some idiot named Ronald Swurl, who had crushed it without a second thought.

"He's the father of Naomi's baby, though you can't repeat that to anyone."

"This jerk really gets around," Boris replied angrily.

"He's not a jerk; more like the walking wounded."

"The only men I know that have a right to that name fought in Nam. Tell me he got a deferment."

She nodded.

"It figures," he replied. They sat in a pizza restaurant on the corner of Twelfth and Pine, in the middle of high summer, the streets dusty and sweltering, scarcely tolerable on foot. Big broiling waves of calefaction warped the view, as cars glided by on heat-softened asphalt with their windows rolled shut, occupants at ease in air conditioned splendor. Though cool in the little eatery, sweat from the outdoor warmth still glistened on both diners' foreheads. "Maybe you'll get over this quicker than you think," he ventured.

"I hope. But it just gets worse, not better." They slurped their sodas and chewed their pizza in silence for a moment, he thinking "I would marry this woman, and I probably could have, if it weren't for that imbecile."

They started spending their nights together. By various verbal subterfuges and careful observation of her apartment and schedule, he was able to ascertain that she had no other lovers. This gave him hope, dashed always by her visible melancholy, a large part of which, he understood, stemmed from the loss of her parents, whom she could scarcely discuss without tears. At night, as they lay on her bed, the air conditioner thrumming in the window, there stretched out in all directions urban cement and stone cooling beneath the stars like an oven finally turned off, as he touched her pale body, even then the sadness, the brokenness was palpable.

She recounted how her father, Lester Meer, now Leon Rathman, lived in Peru and was all the family she had in the wide world.

"We could change that," he said.

"Shh," she pressed an index finger to his lips. "Not yet."

There was something not rooted about her. He did not know whether it was Swurl's fault, but chose to think so, because that was easier than accepting her brokenness as something permanent. If it were another man's doing, it could in time be undone. But if she had always drifted, if her unsettledness had begun with her father's exile, then it was part of her character, and he could not see the cure; he could then only see her unmoored, gliding from man to man, city to city. She talked so excitedly about moving to San Francisco that her eyes shone, as if the mere act of traveling elsewhere would solve the question of who she was and what she should do. She did not plan well. Her ideas about how she would live someplace new were vague. "Oh, that'll take care of itself," she said. "I'll get a job." Nights as he lay with her in the cool room in the slums of West Philly, he seemed to see her floating out through the grimy, darkened, deserted streets, tossed like tumbleweed on the wind from town to town, someone with no real purpose, no real home, lost and futureless.

Then one day, walking along the edge of Rittenhouse Square, he saw her from the side, sitting on a bench, entwined with a man with long, flowing brown hair. "Who is that?" he asked a familiar, passing hippie. "Oh, that's Orion. He's from San Francisco, going back in a few days."

"Orion."

"Like the constellation."

"It looks like he'll be taking a woman with him."

The hippie chuckled. "So he says."

"And she?"

"So she says."

He walked on, unsurprised, almost unsaddened. "It was only a question of when," he told himself. She had not the strength to stick with him, but at the first whim, a free ride to the West Coast, she had detached and reattached herself to another man. "This is a great loss," he said, much later, aloud, and with those words, at last, felt it. He did not go to her that night, nor ever again. A month later, he moved to D.C.

He thought of Eileen's sad pallor and beauty as he drove swiftly over the Hudson on the George Washington Bridge. The estuary gleamed dully beneath a smoggy, ominous, iron sky, threatening more snow, which recalled to him that pallor by the faint light of a street lamp, through a window in the darkling, air-conditioned room. "She probably lives in Haight Ashbury still," he thought, "hopefully not on the street." And his car roared into New Jersey, around onto the New Jersey Turnpike where it ran together with Interstate 95, whence he could look out to his left at the gray towers and canyons of Manhattan. Alderway was just a faint half-memory now, no longer a threat.

Before he knew it, he was traversing Elizabeth and instinctively cut off the heat, to stop the car from filling with the industrial stench. "It's amazing they're not all dead of cancer," he thought of the residents, gazing with horrified eyes at the rusting tubes, tanks, ladders, fires, smokestacks and plumes of pollution that coiled and sprawled on either side of the turnpike. The ugliness of it went beyond a defilement of nature; it was a desecration that caused his throat to tighten, assisted in this by the acrid fumes that still somehow managed to seep into the car. He accelerated, thinking, "Not one second, not one instant would I linger here."

Then came the long, snow-patched fields and woods of New Jersey, the boredom and sameness of suburban subdivisions causing him to drowse. So he pulled into a rest stop, got a cup of coffee to go, then sat in the purple Volvo, guzzling.

"Some car," a large, muscular biker in the next space addressed him.

"Some bike."

"Yeah, I love my Harley. You're a veteran? I saw the bumper sticker and the scar."

Boris nodded.

"Me too, and a Hell's Angel."

"Come to the rally against the war in April," he spoke quickly, "in D.C., and bring your friends."

The man smiled a little crookedly. It was more of a leer than a smile, but it was good-natured, and due to a scar, so that the distortion bespoke hard circumstances rather than any wretched lack of fellowship. "Maybe, maybe," he murmured.

"Unless of course you're for this war."

"Only an idiot is for this war."

"And you don't look like one."

"No I ain't," he paused to inhale from his cigarette between broken teeth and his face twisted again slightly into that unintentional mockery. "Maybe, maybe," he murmured again. "You're an organizer?"

"Yep, Vietnam Veterans Against the War."

A look of respect came into the biker's eyes. "Well, well. And your name?"

"Boris Slavonovich."

"Well, well, and a Roosky. I'm Gus Harwood. I may look you up."

"You do that," Boris started the engine. "I'm in the book in D.C. Bring friends, lots of friends."

Harwood grinned, revealing gaps between jagged teeth, where some were missing, and he straightened his black leather jacket. "Maybe," he repeated, flicking his cigarette butt onto the pavement. "Maybe I will, Boris Slavonovich."

He returned to the highway, passing the exits for Camden and Philadelphia and in good time reaching the Delaware Memorial Bridge, the huge oil tanks squatting like repulsive hellions at the entrance, their noxious fumes causing him to gag. Then he was through Delaware, bleak and crowded with traffic, and on into Maryland, with more yellow fields and random white patches of snow. He disliked the scenery around the interstate, this vast dead zone, so he kept his eyes trained on the road unrolling, dark and monotonous, before him. By dinnertime he coasted past the ominous, grim and menacing towers of Baltimore, arrayed like immense prison guards at the entrance of a ramshackle city of decayed slums, buried in deep shadow. "Not long now," he said aloud.

It was dusk, but with the darkness gathering around him, he did not turn on the headlights, no, because there was too much light within him. Why, he thought, he could even see by it at midnight. He smiled, paying his toll, rolling toward the tunnel's mouth, thinking of his destination in Washington and his destiny anywhere. "Not long now," he repeated.

As the veteran sped out of the north, Jorge slouched along wintry pavements back to Cambridgeport. "Why me?" He wondered, sitting in the dim subway. "Why did I have to say I would do it?" He paused to study the other riders, a motley bunch, reading newspapers or gazing emptily about the train, and was conscious that he had no fellow feeling for them, that in fact they looked to him like monsters, creatures utterly alien, whose humanity he doubted. He shook his shoulders and stamped his feet to rid himself of this horrible thought. "It was because of that scar," he resumed his interior monologue, "and him talking about his life and how much this antiwar stuff means. That's what it was. That's why it's me." He exited at Central Square and walked through the hard, glitteringly clear, snow-covered day back home, with the air like cold glass, ready, it seemed, to crack. The brightness everywhere caused him to put on his sunglasses. "I look like a hood," he thought, shivering in his leather jacket. "A hood that's about to get busted." He tramped along Magazine Street to his domicile, fumbled with cold fingers for his key and entered.

He passed through the house, sleep-filled and quiet, to the upstairs kitchen. Gilbert sat at the table, drinking black coffee.

"How important is this Vietnam Veterans Against the War anyway?" Jorge demanded. "You're a vet. You tell me."

Red-haired Gilbert in his red flannel shirt and jeans looked up from his copy of *The Boston Phoenix*, folded it and set it aside. Behind his glasses his bright eyes glimmered with sudden, plunging depth, as he spoke: "Very important, not because they have power, which they don't, but because, in the long run, they'll shape public opinion. But they're important for another reason, a more enduring one, and that is because they are right. They are," he paused to glance out the window at winter, "one of the embodiments of justice."

"What if this group didn't exist?"

Gilbert grunted and was silent for a moment. "Then I would have to go start it up," he said with great finality.

"So we can't do without it?"

"No, we can't." With that and with no further questions, he picked up his newspaper and resumed reading.

Toying with his sunglasses in his hands, Jorge finally set them on the breakfast table. He went to the fridge, poured himself a glass of orange juice, drank and then tromped back downstairs, to the basement. Alderway's snores rumbled loudly from the back room. He moved thither, entered and shut the door. The sleeping man gave a start at the sound and sat up.

"Hey, whoa! What time is it?"

"Time for you to get packing," the Young Lord replied.

Alderway rubbed the sleep out of his eyes, then combed his long brown hair with his fingers. He sat on the mattress on the carpet, looking up at his roommate, now lounging back in a worn, old, wooden swivel chair.

"Packing?" He asked.

Jorge nodded. "I know what you are."

Alderway woke up. A canny gleam came into his eyes. "What am I?"

"You're a police agent."

"Bullshit."

"Yes you are, and you need to take your sneaky, underhanded ways out of this house. These are good people here, not criminals. You have no cause to be investigating us."

"Where did you get this idea?"

"I put it together. There's no use denying it, and if you make a fuss, I'll tell the others."

Alderway surveyed him, the dark hair, the dark eyes, the bad posture, the brown leather jacket, all of him, rocking back in the swivel chair. "Like Tiwana?" He asked at length.

"So it's true," Jorge thought with sudden exhaustion. "All these months, he slept under our roof, ate our food, smoked our dope, made love to the music student. He could have arrested us any time on drug charges, but he didn't. So he must be after something bigger, like Boris says. And he's worried Tiwana knows. So he's setting up the Panthers. That cancels out everything, all the good he did busting that landlord. It means he really is the enemy." Aloud he said, "Like Tiwana."

Alderway stretched, yawned. "I don't suppose it'd slow you down to know that if you do that you'll be interfering with a police investigation."

"It would slow me down some."

"Good," he yawned again, and then looked up sharply. "Don't you forget it."

"Thanks about Rickman."

"Rickman?"

"The landlord in East Harlem."

Alderway chuckled. "A first-class scumbag, that guy. Yeah, well, that was a freebie, on me. You run across any more like him, just give me a holler. We can't have goons shooting up elderly cripples. No we can't." He paused to stroke his drooping moustache. "You wouldn't reconsider evicting me? After all, I could put you on the expense account for tip-offs."

"I'm no snitch," Jorge replied, too tired by the whole unmasking of this insidious fraud even to be offended. "I think you gotta go."

Alderway sighed, but he seemed completely unsurprised by the turn of events. "Well there's this chick I know, down toward Harvard Square—"

"And I don't want to know where you go."

"Yeah, I'll go there," he paused, lit a cigarette and reached for the ashtray on the floor. "You're missing a golden opportunity to come down on the side of the angels."

"I don't see it that way."

"You don't see it right. You people, you 'revolutionaries'" and he raised his fingers to make quote marks, "don't even see that you divide into two groups: the ones who want justice like you and your friend Boris and who are not willing to commit injustice to get it. Then there are the ones who set their faces against the law, and their hearts against the law and decide to break and destroy the law. You don't see the chasm between you and them, because you think that in the end you want the same thing. You don't. They stand for injustice, anarchy, and murder. You and your friend are pacifists. Tiwana isn't. Her friends aren't. And they'll ring you out like a dishrag and throw you away—"

"Don't worry about Tiwana. I know she's nuts. We're not having anything to do with her."

"Good, because you have no idea what's about to come down."

"And I don't want to know. Thank you for not busting us for pot."

Alderway waved a dismissive hand. "I could care less about a few lousy joints. I track down killers, not potheads."

"And you think she's a killer."

"She sure talks like it. But we'll see," he paused to inhale his Lucky Strike. "When do I have to be out by?"

"Tonight, dinnertime. I hate to say it, but the sooner the better."

"A golden opportunity, man."

Jorge shook his head. He was tired; he wanted to go to sleep. The shock that he had lived so long under the same roof as a police spy drained him and made him feel like a fool, a very fatigued fool. And Boris had spotted the truth in less than five minutes. Why hadn't he? Was it because he hadn't been brutally wounded in war? Because he didn't approach social or political justice like a monomaniac? What was wrong with him? How long would he have gone on like a somnambulist, living and wandering among deceitful enemies? How long would this dangerous foe have continued to dwell among them and lay his lousy snares? Once they started, these questions did not stop. But he could not just sit there all day, staring at Alderway in exhausted disbelief, with more questions popping into his mind than out of a toddler's mouth. So he rose, picked his way through the mess and debris of the two inhabited cellar rooms and climbed back upstairs.

"You look sick," Mike Dellico said, on his way out the front door with the trash.

"I think I'm coming down with something."

"What?"

"Life," Jorge growled. "That's gotta be what it is." Upstairs Tanya pounded on her old black typewriter, as he contemplated the dark curls, the slightly plump figure and her pretty profile. "Can you keep the noise down," he finally requested, uninterested, for the first time, by what he saw. "I got a headache."

"It's an article for *The Phoenix* on a local feminist literary collective—wanna read it?"

"I got a headache—didn't you hear me?"

She pouted, which irked him. He was in no literary, political, romantic or sexual mood. He wanted to pull the shades, lie on his bed and not think about how the police spy was going to crucify Tiwana, the police spy he had introduced her to, who represented that same hard, corrupt power that had tortured her husband, who had lived undetected with him for roughly a year, who had required the keen eyes and ears of a veteran, attuned for very survival to discern lies and betrayal, to be unmasked. And as he thought of this poisonous lie that had flourished so long in his basement like some deadly plant that only foragers for truth knew to avoid, he doubted himself utterly, doubted his vision, his intelligence, his solidarity, but never the essential rightness of his beliefs, no, what he doubted was that he was not worthy of what he prized above all, of that justice for downtrodden people, which required alertness and care and the sense to know when he was in the presence of the enemy. Vaguely he considered leaving, returning to New York, to escape this failure. But he knew such a move would amount to little more than flight and besides, would not provide much relief and that from now on, he would not know whom to trust: that was it—this unveiling of Alderway had introduced a new solitariness into his life, one that came of mistrust, whose corrosive effects could already be felt in an insistent desire for solitude. He traversed Tanya's cluttered room without a word, entered his, shut the door, pulled down the shades and threw himself on his bed. He was still wearing his leather jacket when he fell at last and mercifully into a troubled sleep.

*E*arly that afternoon, Alderway wrapped his few, oddly assorted and generally dirty possessions in a stained sheet and cajoled Ingrid into giving him a ride in her VW Bug over to Bay Street.

"I still don't see why you're leaving," Mike said, shuddering at the view out the front door of the hostile face of winter. "That puts us in a fix for next month's rent."

"Oh, I have a friend, coming up from New York for a while," Ingrid put in. "He needs a place to live. He's a weatherman."

Alderway's eyes glittered, and he nearly dropped the sheet.

"Just so he doesn't blow the place up," Mike said sourly. "The last thing we need is a bomb factory in the basement."

"I'll tell him you said so."

"In no uncertain terms. Sheesh, can't we get someone who's not some kind of political fanatic? Just a roommate? A normal hippie, like, like—Alderway. Alderway, man, why do you have to move out?"

"This woman I know, Kay Birn, her roommate split very suddenly. I owe her one, so I gotta help her out." Alderway was thinking quickly, thinking about Ingrid's weatherman. As he stepped into her rather seedy Bug, he very casually and off-handedly asked: "So what's the new roommate's name?"

"Buzz."

"Mike's right. These weathermen can be dangerous."

"I'm not worried about Buzzy," Ingrid turned the key in the ignition and set the heat on high. Then she got the scraper, stepped out and worked on the windshield. Alderway got out to help. "Why not?" He asked.

"Buzzy wants my approval. Before he does anything stupid, he'll ask what I think. I've stopped him from lots of dumb escapades. You can't imagine."

Sweeping the snow away with his arm, Alderway attempted to conceal his interest. "Try me."

"He was going to rob a bank in Manhattan. I told him only a moron would do that, because he'd be so easy to catch. Then he switched to a branch in Scarsdale. I said, on the phone, mind you, 'what's with robbing a bank? Are you just dying to do twenty five years to life? Where are your brains, Buzzy?' So he went into counterfeiting instead. Now he's rolling in dough. But I wouldn't touch it. I said I wasn't interested in his ill-gotten gains."

"So he stopped that too?"

"Nah. I guess I just wasn't persuasive enough. He turned out to have a knack for it. He's a first-rate counterfeiter. He showed me his work. You really can't tell the real from the fake. He says it's an art. I said 'an art for imbeciles.' He said it was a victimless crime. To which I replied, 'yeah, except for the U.S. government and how do you think they're going to feel when they find out?' You know, some people are born with no brains. Bad and brainless, that's Buzzy."

"So aren't you worried he'll be minting money here?"

"In *my* house? He better not try it. Let him set up his stupid little operation somewhere else. If I catch him at it in your room, he'll rue the day he was born," she paused, dusting off gloved hands and then said, confidentially, as if it had never occurred to him, that she had quite a tongue and could be a frightening scold. "A blood-curdling shrew, was how my last lover put it."

Alderway snickered.

"I know it's hard to believe," she went on, as Alderway turned away and rolled his eyes, "but he called me a ball-buster," Ingrid went on in apparent astonishment: "I guess I have a bit of a mouth when I get pissed off. But Buzzy—counterfeiting one hundred dollar bills in *my* house? He better not even think of it."

"So I guess that guarantees he won't be using the house on Magazine Street for his money factory."

"Oh, he'll be doing it somewhere, but not here. That's the last place on earth he'll try, unless he wants to hear from dawn to dusk what a dim-witted, idiotic, imbecilic moron he is. And he doesn't. I've discovered over the years that nitwits don't like being told what they are," she paused and opened the driver's door. Alderway slid into the passenger seat, checking on his possessions in the back. "What do they like?" He asked.

"Going about their incredibly stupid little ways and making lots of trouble for other people. That's what they like." She carefully drove the car down snowy byways toward Bay Street. "I'll miss you," she said simply. "You're the only man in the house who never made a fuss about my feminism. I took it as tacit approval."

"You were correct," he said. "In my experience, women generally have more brains and more idea of what they're doing than men. Look at this Buzzy of yours. No woman would dream of robbing a bank or counterfeiting cash. It's just too stupid and too dangerous. But here he is, ready to jeopardize everyone in the house, and you have to spit fire to get him to stop. A lot of men just have shit for brains. Fewer women. Not that some don't, but fewer."

The car pulled to a stop in front of a nondescript two-story house with gray aluminum siding. "Home sweet home," he murmured.

"You can reconsider."

Alderway looked at her almost sadly. "No I can't. But I could take you to dinner tomorrow night."

She glanced at him with pleased curiosity and pushed her blond hair out of her face with slight self-consciousness. "You are such a mystery. I thought you were always broke, a hippie living on brown rice, and here you're asking me to dinner."

"Hey, I didn't say the Ritz."

"Okay," she laughed, "what time?"

"Seven."

"I'll pick you up here then. And you'll lead the way."

"Coming from you, that *is* a compliment." He gathered up his things and stepped lightly out of the car. He did not return his old key. She forgot, and the police spy did not remind her.

Kay Birn, tall and raw-boned, with a constantly red nose from too much blowing and plain brownish, blondish hair, greeted him in the doorway of the second floor apartment. She was a Radcliffe dropout, who worked in the same bookstore as Gilbert and who summered on a commune in western Massachusetts. Originally from Nebraska, she had the flat though not displeasing accents of that region, as well as its stolid fortitude in the face of adversity, of which she, in her young, orphaned life, had endured her share. She had lived in the Bay Street apartment for two years, first with a lover, with whom she quarreled over his infidelity, then with a roommate who had suddenly departed for the Northwest. She had just advertised in the paper a week ago, and Alderway had said he would keep an ear open. She was surprised to find him moving in himself.

"Things didn't work out at the other place," he explained vaguely.

"Well, they're not going to work out here if you don't buy yourself some amenities, such as a blanket, a pillow, and towels. There's a bed in Leila's old room, she left a bookcase, and the dresser's mine, but you'll have to repair the night-table, and I think the lamp's busted."

Alderway swung his possessions onto the mattress and fiddled with the lamp. "It works," he said after a moment. "It's just a little temperamental." But at Kay's suggestion, he visited a thrift store in Boston, purchasing sheets, blankets, towels, pillows and sundry other necessities. Then he spent the late afternoon sprucing up his room. He would no longer sleep on a mattress on the floor. He had a real bed. He also had the possibility of a female visitor—Ingrid—and had begun to regret the impression his slovenliness at her house must have made upon her. He toiled until twilight, then stopped to gaze approvingly at the red flames of the setting sun. "Come darkness," he murmured, standing at the dusty window. "I'm waiting for you," he said, thinking of matters deep and dangerous and of the darkness within that could match night without.

With the coming of shadows, he called Tiwana, who could not conceal her disappointment with Jorge and Boris.

"Not everyone's cut out for this," he said.

"But you are."

"Me? I'm just a hippie. But I can't see taking annihilation lying down."

"You're right. That's what it is: annihilation. And we won't go down without taking a good number of them with us."

166

"We'll see about that," he thought. "So I'm available," he said aloud, "for what you hinted at before on the phone or whatever you've got that might need a white boy."

She chuckled. "We've got something. Yes we do." She told him about a large purchase of guns from some mobsters in South Boston that no Panther could bring off. They needed someone white and someone soon.

"I'm your man," Alderway smiled, and his teeth gleamed savagely white in the unlit gloom, as he thought with predatory patience of underworld arms traders and violent revolutionaries snared and penned, and the enjoyable concert of his brains and sinews that would bring this about. The hunt was tinged with a barbarism, he knew, a feral taint in the blood that dated from ancient eons when his ancestors dwelt wildly in northern forests. He smiled again and thought to himself, "the call of the wild," and felt its thrill as they arranged to give him a briefcase of cash in three days. He would also have a "bodyguard," which he understood immediately was to guarantee that he did not abscond with the money. The night of this transaction, he would buy, for an "interested party," a huge supply of machine guns. He was not to tell a soul, especially Jorge. "Don't worry," he soothed, "I don't even live there anymore. I'll never see the guy."

It was dark the next night at seven o'clock when Ingrid's small vehicle puttered up before the house on Bay Street. Alderway materialized suddenly from among the shadows.

"My goodness, I didn't even see you," she exclaimed.

"It's a trick of mine," he explained, gliding toward the car, and then sliding into the passenger seat. "Silence and stealth."

"Now that you mention it, I must have observed it subliminally, when you lived with us. Why the silence and stealth?"

"Because you never know what's waiting for you, down the road."

"You sound like a soldier or a fugitive."

He chuckled. "Maybe I am."

"Maybe you're not," she replied and started the engine.

He suggested an establishment not far from Harvard Square, a place with a glass display case in front, filled with quiches and a variety of salads. The food was good and inexpensive, he explained, making no effort to conceal the role that price played in his choice. She appreciated that, considered it sensible and that in some way it made up for her allowing him to pay for them both.

"So you were in Vietnam," she said, settling into her chair. "You never talked about it."

"There's not much to tell," he said, scanning the menu. "I killed a lot of people."

"Men, women and children?"

"Men, women and children," he paused, putting the menu down. "It was horrible. I go to sleep at night to the sound of their screams. Nothing will silence them, not booze, not drugs, not—"

"Women?"

"Not women. I wish I had never gone. I wish I hadn't killed them, and I wish they hadn't killed so many of my buddies. It was all for the pomp and pretense of Washington politics. It makes me sick, if I think about it too long, physically sick. And sometimes it makes me feel like I might snap, like the only thing to do is go out and murder somebody. But then it passes." He picked up the menu again. "I have a hard time living with me. I don't have a lot of choice, so I make the best of it. But things are really damn dark, Ingrid, they really are."

"I never knew that. I always thought you were just a hippie, a child of light."

He put the menu down with some asperity. "There is no light," he said quietly. "No light in the human soul, no light outside of it. The best we can do, if we're really, really lucky, is grope our way along in twilight. But most of us aren't lucky. We're born from darkness, we die into darkness, and for the most part it's darkness in between. Anything else is a fairy tale."

"I guess you would know."

"You got that right."

"One doesn't have to have shot one's way through the jungles of Southeast Asia," Ingrid began after a moment, "to have given deep consideration to matters of hope and despair."

"No, but once you *have* shot your way through, you see how frail and unreasonable hope really is."

"So you have the high ground of morality."

"Not of morality. That's an empty word. But of experience. Here," he said, pointing to the menu, "let's do what all morality is really based on—let's eat."

She laughed and this, to him, seemed auspicious. His words, which had tumbled out in an unintended rush, had not soured her. Rather she seemed to take them as a challenge and to take them with interest. Maybe, he mocked himself, life is not just a solitary journey through a land of darkness. But it was. He knew that firsthand.

"But seriously," she returned to the subject after she had started in on her modest portion of quiche Lorraine and he on his red snapper, "if it's all so dark, what's the point of anything, even going on?"

"We're animals. We try to survive."

"That's what you do?"

"That and crush evil when I see it."

Ingrid laughed. "You sound like a superhero."

"Unfortunately not even an ordinary hero."

"And how do you know what's evil?"

"I know it when I see it. And so do you. There are people who do."

"So maybe there is a little light within."

"Maybe there isn't."

"You are stubborn."

"No, I'm just a student of harsh experience." Quiet descended on the little table, as they ate and sipped red wine. The cutlery glimmered in the dim light, the drinks sparkled, Ingrid's long, golden hair flashed when she moved. From a distance they seemed a perfectly commonplace couple, calm, happy, out on a date. No observer could have detected that Alderway juggled several images in his mind at once: a sadistic lieutenant shooting a Vietnamese villager, a rather young and terrified man, in the chest at point blank range; the crates of darkly lethally gleaming machine guns he would purchase for Tiwana; and a memory of Ingrid in the kitchen at the house on Magazine Street one snow-glittering morning at breakfast, in a diaphanous white nightgown, more like a nymph from ancient Greece than a mid-twentieth century feminist from Chicago. The three images did not clash, there was no dissonance. His mind gazed upon one then the other, then the other, until from the looking he realized that the first two, and others like them, had long prevented him from thinking about the third in any intelligent way. "I could have been in love with her all along," he thought. "It's not just something that happened now." He wanted to consider this further, but the lieutenant and the young man and the crates would not vanish. She interrupted this struggle by remarking that she had not yet seen his new apartment.

"And you aren't *yet* going to."

"Oh," Ingrid smiled, "but I am."

"Well," he thought, "if she insists, who am I to gainsay her?"

Glancing back over the months, he could not say when he had fallen in love with her. But it had been some time ago, perhaps that early morning of the nightgown and snow. Whenever it had been, the feeling had concealed itself well; he had not even needed to summon thoughts like "it's not reciprocated," or "it'll never work," to submerge it back into his subconscious. It had lain there like a treasure buried in the dirt, and now, having unearthed it, he was dazzled by the gemlike quality of emotions he had not expected to experience, above all the sparkling beauty of "she feels the same way." Alderway, deep in the night of his soul, knew that while he had not and never would come across a star, he had found the next best thing, a diamond that shone only for him. A star, he thought, can guide anyone. This, is just for me. And, in his soul, he hid this unexpected love again, strangely fearful that someone might know of it and steal it.

She spent the night and the next two, and then he told her that he had to attend to some insurrectionary business. Of course he did not say what, nor did she ask. She simply took it as one more surprising development connected with him, one among a number. "Maybe we'll get married," he had said that first night, astonishing her, but not as much as her own unpracticed reply, "yes, I'd like that." Whence had that come—she who did not believe in marriage? Indeed everything these days was a fathomless surprise.

At the house on Magazine Street, she had long wondered how he paid his rent, having no visible means of support. Now she asked him.

"I do odd jobs for people," came the reply.

"What odd jobs—drug dealing?"

"No, and I can't tell you now. But I will soon."

Another mystery! "Perhaps you're a CIA agent," she said.

"Nothing that glamorous," he laughed. "You're going to be very disappointed." Or, he feared, worse. How would she react to having taken an undercover policeman under her roof and now into her bed and heart? He could not predict. It might not matter or it might infuriate her. He began to prepare placating paragraphs of explanation, little homilies about it being merely a living, not a calling, just a means of keeping the wolf from the door. Ingrid was practical—that was a virtue he admired in her—and so would see the economic necessity of his work, even if she disapproved of it. And then, he could tell that she regarded him as having many unexpected strengths—for instance that he was so at ease with her feminism, did not regard her as shrill, was willing to let her make decisions and deferred to her vastly more thorough education—which he hoped would outweigh the fact that he had, after all, deceived her.

Alderway began to make plans. He brooded less about Vietnam, the horrors he had witnessed, the atrocities, the mutilated corpses of children, the stark defoliated forests and the village huts burning with screams emanating from within. All of that, the pasture in which his mind usually grazed, ceased to be ever-present. Oh, it was still there, and there most of the time, along with the scarred faces of criminals he had framed, men who spent their days in gray, barred cells and cursed his name—because Alderway was good at his work, he was thorough and closed his cases with convictions and long jail sentences. But now there was this new treasure, which, in those first few days, made him start thoughts with the phrase, "when Ingrid and I live together," or "when I marry Ingrid." And then he would imagine building a house—she could help, if it interested her—in western Massachusetts. She could teach at the state university, and he would change his job. How he would change it was the subject of much speculation on his part. Perhaps he would commute into Boston four days a week, or he would try to get a position in some rural police department—with his years and all his skills, he thought he might be able to impress the yokels and land a good sinecure. He would fix the engine of Ingrid's VW, get it some new tires, and on weekends they would drive into the mountains to hike and fish. He began thinking like this after their first night together. Such notions sprouted spontaneously, like the flowers beneath the feet of the gods that he had read about in mythology. And he did not hesitate to inform her of his ideas, because he felt sure they would appeal to her and she would concur. She did. So he began to plan more, to remember less and to approach a novel state that he could only describe as felicity.

Then the gun deal was postponed. Tiwana called to say that they did not yet have enough cash, and everything had to wait. He was almost relieved, because he had believed that when he made his arrests, word would leak out through the activist community that Alderway was a police spy. He would be identified at once and forever as the enemy, though he did not believe such tarring with a broad brush was correct, because, in fact, he sympathized with many, many of the people he deceived, though not his targets, not in the least. Those he regarded as dangerous criminals. But their friends would see things differently and would curse him. Ingrid would hear it. So he had debated telling her beforehand and had decided, with some trepidation, to do so. Now he could wait—drop hints, but let their love sink some roots first.

"What *are* these odd jobs you do?" She asked. "Everything is so enigmatic."

"It has to be for now. But I swear I'll tell you all of it, before much more time goes by."

"Should I be alarmed? You're not really some weatherman, like Buzz?"

"No, no," he soothed. "There is nothing at all to be alarmed about."

"But you're not what you seem?"

Alderway hesitated.

"That has to be true," she went on. "You appear to be a happy-go-lucky pothead. But that's not the case at all. So I've already penetrated one layer of incorrect seeming. There's more, right? That's it?"

"Patience, patience. It's no big deal."

Tall, lithe and blond, Ingrid was in a PhD program in comparative literature and belonged to a woman's writing collective that published chapbooks under the imprint "Athena." She herself had presented the world with many volumes of poetry, exuding a style of feminism so ferocious that after he had read a few poems, Alderway took to calling her "my Valkyrie." Alternately, he referred to her as "woman warrior." Neither appellation had any effect on Ingrid, whose quick temper and tendency to see injustice and male chauvinism everywhere made her most fearsome to the males of her acquaintance. She was, in short, a terror, and he reveled in it. One afternoon when they encountered Jorge on Mt. Auburn Street, and Ingrid berated her roommate for some passing and thoughtless act of chivalry the night before, Alderway had to chuckle at the fear in the young organizer's eyes.

"When you gonna tell her, man?" Jorge later demanded, encountering him in the little calzone shop.

"Soon enough, but *I'm* going to do it, not you."

"Don't you worry about that," Jorge replied, slipping into the seat opposite him and combing back his thick, dark hair with his fingers. "I would not want to be in the shoes of any guy telling Ingrid her old man is a police spy."

"Shh, keep it down."

"Do you know what she'll *do* to you?"

Alderway chuckled. "What?"

"I can't even begin to imagine. I don't want to imagine. How can you sleep with that castrating female? How can you dare to think for one minute that you're going to tell her what you are and walk away in one piece?"

"I think she'll appreciate it."

"I think you better get your head examined."

"Ingrid's not a monster."

"She's a terrifying virago."

"Good word."

"I wish it was just a word. I have to live under the same roof with her."

"I would too and would like to. But you kicked me out."

"I have to listen to her lectures about male oppressors and women arming themselves to deal with harassment, morning, noon and night, about fighting back against rape, against intimidation, against chivalry, for God's sake. If she drops a book and I pick it up for her, I'm in for holy hell. 'Who do I think she is? Some helpless little girl? She can pick up her own goddamned books' and on and on in the foulest language you can imagine. You have no idea."

"I think I do," Alderway chuckled again and slurped his soda.

"You like it?" Jorge was astonished.

"Yeah," slurp, chuckle. "I like it."

His companion stared.

"I think," slurp, slurp, "that if the world were filled with women like Ingrid, chances are it'd be a much better place. Men would have to improve their behavior. A lot of phony games men and women play would vanish. Yup," slurp, slurp, "the world would be a better place."

"You couldn't pay me to take her out on a date."

"You couldn't pay me not to," and Alderway grinned, his long, white, toothy, predatory grin, which had never struck Jorge quite as carnivorously as it did just then, as if Jorge and all the men like him, who sweet-talked women and deceived them, would make a nice lunch in Alderway's bizarre idea of paradise. He shivered. "You don't make any sense to me."

"But you do to me, and to Ingrid. Besides, I think living with her has done you good."

"It's broken my spirit."

"Maybe that's not such a bad thing, maybe it's an opportunity to learn new and better ways."

"You're kidding right? Have you heard her up on her high horse?"

"Many times."

Jorge rose, shaking his head. "You don't make any sense," he repeated and left.

After a month, Ingrid insisted he move back into the house on Magazine Street. "Besides, Buzz is getting on my nerves," she said.

"How about we just skip your place and move out to Amherst? I'll build us a house."

"Am I allowed to help?" She almost snarled.

"You're expected to," he soothed. "And once you get the hang of it, you can direct. I have an aversion to executive decision making."

She smiled, mollified. They were lying on the bed in his apartment on Bay Street. Cold winter afternoon light filtered through the blinds, highlighting Ingrid's unearthly pallor.

"The White Witch," Alderway murmured.

"Who? What?" Ingrid demanded.

"Did you ever read the children's fantasy series, *The Lion, the Witch and the Wardrobe?*"

"Yes. You think I'm the White Witch? That's a compliment?"

"I always secretly rooted for her."

Ingrid harrumphed. "I'll move out into the snows of western Massachusetts with you, and commute to the university, when you tell me what you do."

"You're so sure I lead a double life?" He grinned toothily, then he became serious, placing a hand in her lovely, long hair. "I'll tell you what I do, on one condition—that after I tell you, we drive out there and look at property. You promise?"

"Of course I promise."

"Well then, guess."

"You're an FBI agent provocateur."

"You're warm."

"You're going to arrest me for advocating the arming of my sisters."

"No, but I may help you get your hands on the weapons."

"An undercover FBI agent who approves?"

"Not FBI. Just a lowly police spy, arranging gun deals for bloodthirsty revolutionaries."

"You could get killed," Ingrid said, clearly thinking very quickly. "That Tiwana, you're after her, aren't you?"

"You're telepathic."

"I'd rather you didn't get killed. And if you try anything on her and those mobsters she deals with—"

"I'll just be buying the guns from them."

"They'll kill you."

Alderway's eyes glimmered with strange, predatory lights. "Maybe not."

"That's kind of a flimsy reassurance on which I base my future, isn't it? You quit this lousy job."

"I may, especially if we move to Amherst, because I can't move back to your place. Jorge knows and kicked me out."

"He had no business doing that. My name's on the lease. What did he think he was doing, protecting little old innocent me from the truth that only a man can take? I'll have to talk to him, oh yes."

"Shh, calm. I promised not to put him in this situation. Don't talk to him. Don't bother. Talk to me. Tell me we're going to use our meager savings to put a down payment on some land in western Massachusetts. Tell me we're going to live there, build a house together and commute to work and school here."

"Not if some mobster shoots you, we won't. Or if someone like Buzz—Oh my God, if Jorge tells Buzz! Think of the network he's plugged into with his funny money. Someone may bomb your apartment."

"So you have no political problems with being involved with a police spy?"

"I didn't say that."

"So you do."

"Yes. But it's a living. I can understand where something as vital as a paycheck's concerned. We just have to find a less objectionable and less dangerous paycheck."

"What if I like it?" Alderway spoke softly. "What if I like sending up bad guys, making sure they go away for twenty years."

Ingrid sat up. "You better not tell me you're going to go buy those guns in the Haymarket because you like it."

Alderway's eyes sparkled. "But I do."

"Because I sympathize with Tiwana's cadre of revolutionaries, number one. And number two, I don't want your body washing up in the Charles River."

"Oh, if it comes to that, I won't be the one washing up. And I can see your point about those revolutionaries, many of whom are quite sympathetic. But then there are those who aren't. And then, even better, there are those shady arms dealers, thugs who deserve exactly what they are going to get from me."

They lay on his bed in the cold wan light that covered them like a thin blanket of snow, Alderway pensively stroking his moustache and thinking that he was made for this woman and Ingrid convinced that his job would get him killed. She began to argue again, but he shushed her, then promised, if they moved to the country, that he would find work in some sleepy, rustic police department. "And spend your day in your cruiser, eating pizza and only stepping out to give speeding tickets? You'll get fat, and I don't believe it anyway," she said.

"Tell me if I do it for you, you're mine forever."

"I don't belong to anyone."

"I was afraid of that."

"But I may make an exception in your case."

The weak, watery light filtered in, filling Alderway with an exhilaration that he had won the only thing that mattered, this wintry maiden whose icy convictions had softened a bit. "My Valkyrie," he murmured again, and they drowsed off into luxurious, late afternoon sleep. Outside, snow drifted luminously down.

Tiwana trudged through the dirty, gray curbside snow to the yellow frame house on Washington Street in Somerville, where she shared a floor with her roommate, formerly Denzel Jackson, now Olushola Nwagami, currently afflicted with a ferocious head cold, bordering on pneumonia. In her hand-woven Mexican bag, she carried his antibiotics, which she had just fetched from the pharmacy, in what had been less an act of mercy than despair—she could not suffer through another night of Olushola hacking, sneezing, moaning and coughing in the next room. She was dizzy from lack of sleep and longed for nothing so much as a nap, once she had dispensed his medicine.

She picked her way carefully over the icy patches of the uneven sidewalk, considering gloomily Shola's remark, before he became sick, that he could no longer chauffeur white revolutionaries to meetings with mobsters, that said criminals nauseated him, their racist remarks infuriated him, and the next time one of them uttered a derogatory comment, he intended to take out his gun and shoot the bigot between the eyes. He did not care that these gangsters provided cheap weaponry and lots of it, he did not give a hoot for Tiwana's twaddle about means and ends or strange bedfellows, he was not concerned about starting a race war, he was going to kill the next bastard who insulted him, so she had better think that over before she ordered him to guard Alderway, when their money came through for the next purchase. No, Shola had not been reasonable. He had been furious, righteously indignant and seething with desire for revenge. Then he got sick—too sick to fulminate against Italian bigotry, the stupidity of gangsters, the ugliness and all around repulsiveness of white, underworld bigwigs and his desire to take a machine gun and in one act of mass murder cleanse the world of about two dozen racist "maggots." Fortunately he had been far too ill for much more of that talk, and his rage had subsided into a rumbling cough. She did not know which was worse, the shouting, cursing and imprecations, or the noisy nocturnal symptoms. She was beginning to see the appeal of living alone, sans any roommate.

Shola was in a foul mood when she arrived. "It took you long enough," he grumbled.

"If you weren't my husband's best friend, I don't think I'd put up with your constant carping," she replied.

"But I am, so you do," he responded, snatching the bottle of antibiotics out of her hand. He read the dosage instructions and swallowed a pill. "That idiot Alderway called. What a pothead! Always looking for dope. As if I peddle marijuana. You might want to think twice about relying on him. He'll be so high when he buys those guns, he might just shoot up the place. And if those bigots make one snotty remark, I might join him. Then you'll have one holy mess on your hands, note I said *your*, because I will be in Canada—you got that? If these sons of bitches provoke me into killing them, I won't be sticking around. And they've already provoked me. I just may kill them for good measure—"

"Enough!" She exclaimed. "No more about the bigotry of mobsters who deserve to die and what a public service you'd be performing. I have a headache."

"Better watch out. You could be catching what I got."

"That's not possible," she growled. "I was born clear-headed."

"Sometimes a man's gotta act."

"Sometimes a man's gotta shut up."

Shola extracted the carton of orange juice from her shopping bag and huffed off to the kitchen. After a moment she followed, intending to commence dinner preparations, but the telephone rang—her husband, Jeremiah, calling to say that his doctor's visit had gone well, that his aunt, with whom he was living on Chicago's South Side, had proclaimed him completely recovered from his beatings. Tiwana sank down onto a chair in relief, not just at the news, but the organized, focused, undamaged tone, one she had wondered if she would ever hear from her husband again. While she had nursed him round the clock when he first left the hospital, she had departed for Boston hugely worried: what if, in some fundamental way, he never recovered? He had been beaten so badly, he almost died. But now, the partial paralysis of his arm and leg had abated, so had his general fogginess. He was clear-headed, healthy and angry. He told her to collect the money and purchase the guns, pronto. She rejoined that funds were scarce. He gave her some names, with the proviso that, no cash forthcoming, he would sojourn to Boston personally to oversee the financing of his latest operation. She should have been overjoyed. But since encountering obstacles, a foreboding had settled in her mind over the whole project, and thence pervaded her entire being, so that whenever she considered

Alderway or machine guns or illegal arms dealers, anxiety crawled around in her stomach like a live animal, and worry trembled loudly in her voice.

"You're not backing out?" He asked, drawn up sharp.

"No, no," she wavered. "I just have a bad feeling about this. Maybe we should be more cautious."

"So far we've done nothing. We can't get more cautious than that."

"Jeremiah? Just come out here to live. Let's do that for a while. Forget all these guns. Come home."

"I am coming home," he stated, rather ominously, she thought. "You'll see."

Suddenly an immense exhaustion crashed over her, the fatigue of nursing him for months, then of waiting for him, while running hither and yon, following his orders to arrange this and that; bone tired, so drained at the end of each frantic day that all she wanted was to lie down and…sleep? Die? Because wasn't that what Jeremiah was saying—that he was so angry, he was ready to die? And how could she tend to that? It was much thornier and more difficult than mere wounds. He was ready for action, furious, fatal action, and she doubted her strength to stop him. He no longer cared for his own safety, that was obvious enough, so she would have to double her caring, do it for two, talk him out of his revenge and do it quickly, but she had no energy for it, only a strange, powerful, unaccommodating desire for sleep. She did not want her husband to perish, was willing to sacrifice her politics to keep him alive, but at that moment did not even have the energy to utter one word in argument. Instead she murmured: "You're just determined to get yourself killed."

"I am a soldier," he replied.

In the silence that followed, her nerve came back and with it the truth: "No, Jeremiah, you are a veteran."

"Some veterans fight again," Shola interjected.

"And again and again?" She demanded. "Forever?"

"Forever," Jeremiah spoke so firmly and loudly that Shola heard his voice in the receiver across the kitchen table.

"Amen," Shola said.

"I don't amen to that," she responded. "There are limits. There is a time to stop, especially if the sacrifice is needless."

"Who says that?" Her husband demanded.

"I do. Our cause is just. It will prevail in the long run."

"Not if we abandon it."

"No one could ever accuse us of that. We have done enough, more than enough. You may be ready to die, you may be so angry, you're ready to kill and be killed, but I say, before I go to sleep, which is what I'm going to do—sleep and forget—I say, it will be a waste."

"And in your view, what wouldn't be?"

"To work for our people, not kill for them."

Shola shook his head in disagreement and left the room.

"What's come over you?" Her husband demanded.

"The truth," she instantly replied, "a clear perception of the truth."

After she hung up the phone, she retreated to the desk in her room, an oasis of light and calm, surrounded by silence and shadow, to work on a paper on the early history of slavery, which began, she asserted, with the enslavement and subsequent near extinction of the indigenous people of Central America, as noted by Las Casas. As this pool of slave labor shrank, the Europeans turned to Africa. She read and wrote, but on some deeper, subterranean level, a dispute progressed between her husband and her old self on one side and on the other a newer, more cautious wife, who had only emerged in recent weeks, as the reality that his recent wounds had not deterred him but had instead terrifyingly confirmed him on his path into certain doom. Her desk faced a window. Outside, snow drifted down, turning the world white and cold and eerily, mournfully calm, as if her husband were already dead. She watched the slow crystals meander through the air, "like me," she thought, "too indirect, not rapid enough, not forceful enough. I must convince him." But even as these words flitted through her brain, she sighed, it was a breath of languor and despair, of the hopelessness of argument, of her husband's irreversible fury and certain death. She wanted reassurance from someone, but the only person she could safely confide in was Shola, utterly opposed to her newfound caution, with no use for her novel desire to preserve life.

It was difficult to square the violent revolutionary her husband had become with the bookish intellectual she had met and married. But even back then, the contours of his future extremism had already been dimly visible: he admired Malcolm X not Martin Luther King, Trotsky, not Gandhi. Incrementalism, gradualism repelled him. Even at their first encounter at a lecture at Columbia and then later over coffee in a bohemian café on the Upper West Side, he had expressed an approval of taking up arms that had only grown over the years, despite setbacks and defeats, into an implacable resolve. She had never dreamed that one day she would oppose it, and on such flimsy grounds—not as incorrect, morally questionable or impractical, but simply that she did not want him to come to harm. He would dismiss such a concern, had done so already, and thus reduced her to a mere, fearful, nagging wife. It was not a role she was familiar or comfortable with. For she had been a firebrand—speaking at rallies, publishing articles, organizing "underground resistance" cells, always calling for action, if not outright revolt. She and her husband had grown in their advocacy of violence together, and now she regarded this scorched and inhospitable terrain they had entered with dread and regret. If only she had hesitated sooner. If only she had considered where his disregard of his own mortality would lead him. She had no particular fear nor care for herself. If the police crashed through her door and shot her that evening, she could accept it with equanimity. It would be no surprise; she had long been prepared for it. But if this happened to her husband—she did not think she could endure the guilt, the missing of him, the remorse and grief, which would become permanent features of her life. They would last until she died and, doubtless, hasten her into an early grave.

She sighed again and tried to return to work, but instead the insistent question of how she had allowed her spouse and herself to fall into their predicament haunted her. With it came the recollection of an old, wry thought, the recognition of the monumental disapproval she would have incurred from her parents, had they been alive. Her father especially would have frozen in horror at her political agitation and her husband's. He had believed in the system, that if you abided by the rules, paid your dues and did not make trouble, things could prosper as they had for him— with an economics professorship at Howard University, a beautiful wife who did not have to work and an elegant house on Jennifer Street in the swanky Northwest section of Washington D.C. She vividly recalled this paterfamilias presiding over formal meals in their large, high-ceilinged dining room, the fan blowing but not dissipating the heavy, steamy July heat, her four brothers kicking each other under the table. Even at the height of summer, her father, who disliked air-conditioning, always sported a suit and tie at meals and shoes so perfectly polished that they reflected the chandelier's lights like mirrors. Tall, hefty, dark and serious, he towered over his slight, lighter, only daughter, who lived in awe of him and fear of his displeasure. He was very stern, not sweet and loving like Mamma, and exuded uncrossable, paternal authority. His say was final, his rules were law, and though liberal enough not to resort to corporal punishment, it was always understood to be a threat. As the only daughter and his "good girl," she was somewhat indulged. But she could only imagine his reaction to her current law-breaking. She was convinced he would have beaten her to within an inch of her life, despite the fact that she was an independent adult. The idea that his "good girl" had become a flaming revolutionary would have enraged him, and while Mamma might in the end have forgiven her child, her father, whom she always addressed as "father," would have cast her out, anathematized her, once and for all.

Yes, she had been his "good girl"—but in those days her name was Charlene Philips, not Tiwana Allenhurst—who had done everything he asked or wanted out of terror and love, much the way one is biblically enjoined to approach God; thus had she approached her father, the tremendous figure that towered over her childhood, the ultimate arbiter, the being who had final say over all matters of any importance that concerned her. At those meals he was especially impressive. She would sit on his right and listen to his words about government or politics or the advancement of his people—her people—with the same awe with which she attended to his silences, punctuated by the soft, muffled sound of chewing. He was an intellectual, a leader, a man consulted by the NAACP, and she would speak of him proudly to her friends, white and black, who all agreed that he was an incomparable personage and who all privately thought that it must be rather frightening to live with such an eminence. Yet he had instilled in her an unshakable respect for the world of the intellect and a belief in progress almost religious in its intensity. She had listened to his speeches at dinner, thinking only of the sweltering heat that made her white Sunday dress stick damply to her back and the sonorous rumblings from the head of the table, unaware that in fact the meaning was sinking in, that the importance of distinguishing absolutely between right and wrong was affirmed for her again and again, as she munched her fried chicken and poked at her beans.

In summer, when she, Tamara and Alana jumped rope on the front walk, she could bring any discussion to a halt with the three magic words "my daddy says." Her friends understood his importance. Why, Alana did not even have a father at home, and would twist her pretty black pigtails with quiet seriousness, as she mulled the words of Dr. Philips, reported carefully by his daughter.

"Mamma says your daddy's a great leader," Alana commented one afternoon at the end of one of Charlene's recitations of her father's oratory, "that there's no telling where he'll end up. Someplace high and important, she says." The three little girls, all eight years old, stopped jumping rope and clustered together in the shade of the dogwood tree. Outside those shadows the sun blistered down fiercely; it was a stifling hot July afternoon, and the city, suffering in this swelter that unfurled in all directions beneath a merciless fireball, was uncharacteristically silent.

"Probably," Charlene said, wiping beads of sweat off her upper lip with the back of her hand.

"I wish I had my daddy at home," Alana said, "even if he isn't important. Why, Mamma says he doesn't even have a job now, but last time I saw him, he said that'd change soon."

Tamara guffawed. "That was a year ago, Lana."

"So!" Alana stuck out her tongue. "That doesn't mean anything. He could have a job, could have one right now. Maybe he's just too busy to come tell us."

Charlene as always made peace between her friends, before firing them up for some new project of hers. "Sure he's got a job, sure. That's why you haven't seen him."

Alana wiped away a tear. "Yeah, that's why."

"Maybe he's a sailor, on a boat in the navy," Charlene went on. "Maybe we should fill the plastic pool out back and swim like sailors."

"Maybe he's in the navy," Alana murmured, casing a sidelong, tentative glance at Tamara.

"Maybe," Tamara conceded, and they trooped along the little path through the azalea bushes to the back.

The blue plastic pool with pink flamingos on the bottom had some water in it already, with a thin scum of grass and dead insects on top. "We're sailors," Charlene shouted, running to the pool and picking up a purple plastic beach bucket. "We gotta bail." Soon they had cleaned out the dirty water, a task that, under the blazing sun, soon coated each of them in sweat. Charlene raced to the back of the house and turned on the hose. Tamara grabbed the end and squirted water on herself, then her two friends. Then Charlene lay down in the pool, her arms stretched out on the sides, as it filled. "This is the life!" She exclaimed. The two other girls kicked in the water, churning it. By now their shorts and shirts were drenched. "My daddy's a sailor," Alana sang out, splashing her little brown feet at a furious pace.

"Charlene Philips!" Mamma called, stepping out the back door. "You know you're supposed to put on your suit in the pool! I have told you that more times than I care to count."

"It was hot, Mamma, and besides Alana's daddy's a sailor."

"Oh how nice," Mrs. Philips ambled over to the pool. "I'm so glad he got a good job. But your mothers are going to scold me, girls, for letting you get soaked in your clothes."

"We'll dry off before they go home," Charlene said and then, grinning, "we've done it before."

Mrs. Philips pretended to look shocked. She was, unlike her husband, a pushover. That was partly why Charlene adored her, that and the fact that she was the kindest, gentlest, most polite and beautiful person Charlene had ever known. She came from a rich family in Georgia, and one of her grandmothers was white. They had always known how to live in style, or so she often told her children, and part of that style was making people feel welcome and at ease, which she did at that moment by placing a pitcher of lemonade on the table under the umbrella. The three little girls splashed out of the water and skipped over for their beverages. "Lemonade, lemonade," Tamara chanted. "My favorite."

They stood by the table, alternately guzzling their drinks and plunging back into the water, beneath an unmarked, perfectly blue sky, their happy cries commingling with the songs of birds braving the blazing heat and Charlene thinking, "I want this. I want it to stay like this forever."

But it did not. Within five years Mamma was dead of a heart attack, and her two oldest brothers were in the military. Her father disapproved. He had wanted them to go to college, to Howard, but they had always been rebellious, and both wanted to see the world. In their absence, with their challenge to his authority forever lingering in the air, he became more tyrannical than ever. Without his wife to soften his ultimatums, he became solely a figure of fear to his daughter, the despot who forbade her to socialize with Alana, who was going "bad," and with Tamara, who had become "wild."

Charlene still snuck out occasionally to have a milk shake at the pharmacy on Connecticut Avenue with her friends, but she had to be very careful.

"Your father's right," Alana said one summer afternoon over chocolate ice cream sodas. "I've been in nothing but trouble for months."

"He may be right," Charlene retorted, "but it's still cruel. I have nobody to talk to. I just sit in that big empty house with him. All I'm allowed to do is read books. No friends, no TV, nothing. I hate it. Oh, I miss Mamma. She made everything all right. She made him bearable. Now everything's just cold and rigid and empty."

They slurped in unison, in miserable contemplation of life without a best friend. "But at least we can still get together sometimes," Charlene said. "I can still get around him a little bit. It's not as if he sees everything." She heard a step behind her, swiveled and found herself staring into the crisp, well-pressed shirtfront and elegant suit of an enraged Dr. Philips.

"You disobedient child," he snapped, reaching over, grasping her arm and pulling her away from the counter stool. "You may be sure this will never happen again. Goodbye, Alana." Charlene's friend meekly and mutely rose and left the pharmacy.

"Home!" Her father boomed, shaking with fury. Charlene bowed her head and trudged wretchedly out of the shop.

That evening her father summoned her to his study and announced that in September she would attend a very expensive, fancy and newly integrated girl's boarding school in New Jersey.

"But daddy—"

"Don't you dare contradict me. We are not equal, you and I. Do you understand that?"

Charlene nodded.

"You have summer reading to do for your new school, and some writing assignments. You will start them tomorrow."

Charlene was not eager to integrate a rich white school. The thought intimidated her. "I won't have any friends," she told Alana over the phone. "And I'll be living in the middle of nowhere, way out in the suburbs."

"Well, the school won't be *all* white. Didn't your daddy say there'd be other colored kids?"

"Maybe one per grade in the high school. And Alana, it's a *boarding* school. I'll be living with these people. I don't want to go. I like D.C. Oh, I wish Mamma was alive. She'd listen to me. She'd talk to him. If she were here, I'd never have to go to this white girls' boarding school." So the summer passed in miserable anticipation of the fall. Sympathy did come from one surprising quarter—her older brother, Joseph, whom she overheard daring to argue with her father about the decision. But then, Joseph was in a position of strength and paternal approval—he would enroll in Howard in the fall, a pre-medicine major. So he could talk back, a little. He called the arrangements for Charlene "cruel."

"Cruel?" Dr. Philips demanded. He and his son stood in the warm, sunny living room, each leaning against Dr. Philip's beloved, leather wing-back armchairs. Charlene hid and overheard in the hall. "The chance of a lifetime and you call it cruel? Why, this is one of the best girls' schools in the country. She'll be able to go to any college she likes, write her own ticket—"

"What if these rich white girls don't like her? And they probably won't. Where's she going to turn? She'll be living there. The staff is white, so are the teachers. Who will she turn to?"

"No one. She doesn't need to turn to anyone. She'll have to learn to stand on her own two feet. It's about time. Her mother pampered her, and her friends here are bad influences. She needs a change, a bracing change."

"I think it's heartless."

"Heartless!"

"Unless she herself volunteers for it, yes, that's exactly what it is."

Dr. Philips drew himself up to his great height, inhaling and expanding his elegant Sunday suit. "Sometimes I don't understand you, Joseph. But I don't need to, to know you're wrong. Now I don't want to hear another word of this nonsense. She goes in September. The matter is closed." With that the tall, impressively sure professor waved his hand rather imperiously, to indicate that his son should leave the room.

"It won't be so bad," Joseph said to her later. "Think, you'll be moving in high society."

"I don't want to move in high society," his younger sister replied. "I don't want to move. I want to stay here and see Alana and Tamara."

"Those girls get in an awful lot of trouble."

"It's not their fault."

"Look, you better finish that English paper before the weekend or daddy will be furious."

So she sighed, returned to work, and before she knew it, she was unpacking her suitcase in a wood-paneled dormitory room that she shared with a white girl from Mississippi.

"Look, I know what you're thinkin,'" Josephine drawled after they had talked briefly. "That you hit bottom in the lottery here and wound up with Scarlett O'Hara for a roommate. But I'm not just a white girl from Mississippi. I'm a white *Jewish* girl from Mississippi. And there's a big difference."

That difference meant, apparently, that Joe did not abandon her in the dining room and that she acknowledged her in the halls. But after the first day, Charlene had befriended all five of the other African American girls, and they stuck together, at meals, sports, everywhere. The older girls talked incessantly about a black leader named Malcolm X, so Charlene read his writings, and her world changed. True, she studied Greek and Latin at a swanky boarding school, but she became a black nationalist, who believed in black power, just like Nadine from Virginia, an older girl with whom she spent most of her time. No small part of the attraction to Nadine and her radical views was the fact that, if ever known, it would enrage her father, would make him rue the day he ever sent her away to a white boarding school.

For the most part, she did not get to know the girls at her school. Standing on the field, in her tunic, holding her hockey stick, Charlene, sweaty and winded, gazed out over the faces and forms of her teammates and realized she was looking at an assembly of strangers. They said hello, exchanged pleasantries, she had even been to one or two of the day students' lavish suburban homes. But they were not friends. She knew none of them well, and, by her senior year, did not want to. She wanted only to escape this false world that had somehow enmired her in a false reality, enroll in college and help foment revolution. She had no use for these proud Anglo-Saxon princesses. Her course lay clear before her. Indeed, that autumn she had visited Columbia, where, at a political science lecture, she had met Jeremiah Allenhurst. They had decided to get married as soon as she graduated and devote themselves to the promulgation of black power. She could scarcely wait for the day. Every minute coddled in her high school bastion of privilege was, for her, a minute wasted. Her future lay in New York.

But then, she was not accepted at Columbia. So she decided to take the year off and live in Harlem with her soon-to-be husband. Over winter break, her father, somewhat oddly enfeebled, had given her his permission to attend Columbia—but that was before her rejection. On another visit, in February, he slurred his words. His health, her brother Joseph informed her, was failing. But this consideration did not mitigate the message she was determined to deliver: marriage to an avowed revolutionary, a year off from school, a move to the very sort of neighborhood that her parents had sought to shield her from all her life. She decided to tell her father over spring break.

At dinner, her first night back, she noticed that Dr. Philips' large hands shook. When she mentioned casually that her friends had taken to calling her Tiwana instead of Charlene, he scarcely noticed. He smiled, mumbled, "nice, very nice," and fumbled with his steak. Joseph rose to cut it for him. Surprised that her name-change had not set off paternal fireworks, she decided to withhold the rest of her news until the next day, when she could speak with him alone and be sure he understood. He was to know all the details of her break with his world, and she intended to be sure she impressed them upon his faltering mind.

The next morning, before she arose, Dr. Philips sat in his favorite, leather wingback armchair in the living room, trying to concentrate on *The Washington Post*'s front page; but the headlines would not come into focus, and the type everywhere seemed to be melting. Worse, he had a bad feeling from his spine into the back of his head, a very bad feeling, as if whole chunks of his brain twitched and disintegrated. There was a darkness to this feeling, and it was spreading. He felt a rigid seizure in his back, in his head. It was seven a.m., and the sun shone brightly, but already for him the room had sunk into shadow. At nine thirty, his daughter entered, facing the back of his favorite chair. She saw his elegantly attired leg and shoe, a corner of the newspaper visible on the edge of his lap. She stopped. She suddenly lost her nerve; she could not face him, but she could not retreat. So she began, all in a rush, to address him without looking into his eyes.

"Father, there are some big changes I have to tell you about. Not just changing my first name to Tiwana. But I met a man, a radical, a black nationalist, named Jeremiah Allenhurst in New York, and I'm going there in June to marry him and live with him in Harlem. I'll take a year off school and then reapply to Columbia. Nothing, absolutely nothing you can say, no matter how critical, nothing can change my mind. I believe there's a revolution coming for black people, and I intend to be part of it." She continued in this vein for quite some time, getting more and more worked up, until, after about fifteen minutes, she was shouting at her father. Still he did not answer. So finally, her frustration and rage overcoming her fear, she swung around in front of him, only to find that for the past quarter of an hour she had been haranguing and yelling at a corpse.

She collapsed into the chair next to his, her hand on his on the armrest. "Dear God," she whispered, then "father, I'm so sorry." She thought she had killed him, and in that instant saw her life transformed by monstrous guilt, which struck her down, all her vitality, strength and commitment, scorched and crippled her like a bolt from a furious god, but later the doctor explained that he must have been dead for over an hour, before she called for her brother Joseph. That news created ambiguity. Her sense of guilt did not vanish, instead it transformed into simple grief. He had been dying, while in her room she had paced from the old, mahogany bureau to the large, framed mirror and alternately fumed or thought with angry triumph of their coming encounter. Perhaps had she cared more for him, she would have understood his growing weakness for the fatal threat it was and would have insisted on medical help, instead of thinking only of her fury and their inevitable clash. As things had transpired, she had no happy final memory of him, only of a dead person incapable of responding to her rage, of the cruelty of that rage, of the blindness it had caused and ultimately, the loss. She told no one the truth. Instead she reported that she had entered the quiet, sunny room and found him slumped peacefully in his favorite chair. Everyone seemed to like this fable. "A good death," her brother called it, as she turned away, frozen in horror at what she considered her weakness and deceit.

Gilbert ran from the hut with the dead, charred children sprawled on the dirt floor, ran until he reached the ditch, jumped in and crouched down, his arms over his head, as explosions boomed all around him. The roar of grenades, machine guns and rocket launchers deafened him. He was separated from his squad, from the men who had killed those children in the hut, and did not know how to find them again or if he even intended to. "Maybe I'll just die here in this ditch," he thought, his teeth chattering in terror. There followed more explosions, more terrified villagers running hither and yon, collapsing as they were killed. Above, a cerulean heaven beamed carelessly and happily down upon the carnage, as if to say "the smoke and smell of blood and burnt flesh in your nostrils means nothing to me. I am the beautiful day, and your pain is not even an insignificant joke. It is nothing." As the lone Viet Cong soldier, machine gun in hand, loomed over him, Gilbert thrashed, missed his weapons and yelled out in terror and despair.

"What's wrong?" Ingrid's sharp voice came from the doorway of his room, where she stood, tall and fearsome. "Why are you yelling?"

He propped himself up on an elbow and, fully awake, explained it was dream about Vietnam.

A glint of interest flashed in her blue eyes. "They occur regularly, I guess." He nodded.

"And there's nothing you can do about them?"

"Drugs."

"You mean if you smoke dope before you go to sleep, they're not so bad."

The veteran nodded again.

"Maybe that's why Alderway's such a pothead."

"It'd take a lot of pot to block out what he went through," Gilbert commented.

"He told you?"

"We were drinking together one night, drinking a lot. He described a commanding officer who ordered atrocities and who was 'accidentally' shot in the back by a soldier who was Alderway's friend. He witnessed this 'accident.' He never said a word. He witnessed the atrocities. He never said a word. Mute agony was how he described his condition in Vietnam. Not over the c.o. If his friend hadn't shot him, Alderway said he would have had to do it. But mute agony in the nine months of serving under a sadist, who could at best be described as a war criminal. It was a fucking nightmare—not to put too fine a point on it."

"No wonder he won't talk about it."

"Yeah, well, he had to get totally wasted and listen to my horror stories first. Then all this came out. Rider was the c.o.'s name, and I won't trouble your sleep for the rest of your life by describing what he did and made his men do."

"Sometime you will tell me," Ingrid stated, after a moment of silence.

"What's Alderway to you?"

"More than you know."

"Oh," the veteran paused, still leaning on his elbow, half under his blankets, his skin oddly yellowish in the weak, late morning light. "Well, you could be getting in over your head."

"What's that supposed to mean?" She demanded, undeterred and annoyed.

"Alderway is a dark soul, who's been through terrible things. Not to be too melodramatic, but, as far as I can tell, he exists in utter darkness, and he wrestles with demons…and he doesn't mind. You might want to think about that."

"I have," she tossed her head defiantly.

"If you're still with him, you haven't enough."

Ingrid glared at him.

"Look, I apologize for the impertinence," he continued. "And I mean that sincerely. I know I'm out of line. What you do is your business. But I have some experience of Vietnam too, like him, and I'm just trying to warn you."

"I think I can take care of myself."

"Yes, but can you take care of him?" Gilbert lit a cigarette, exhaled a long stream of gray smoke. "Can anyone? Why would a person want to? He's killed a lot of people. Taking care of someone, living with someone, who's killed a lot of people, some of them in horrible ways, puts unique demands on a person. You might want to think about that."

"That's the second time you've given me that advice."

"Mention this topic again, and it won't be the last."

"What did he do?" Ingrid asked, determined now to forge ahead, as if, somehow, he had challenged her.

"I don't want to talk about it."

"Why not?" She demanded, walking over, taking a cigarette and, gazing down at him critically, lighting it. In the faint winter sun through dusty window panes, she appeared tall and beautiful and full of the dignity of what she did not know.

"Because it makes me sick," he smoked some more. "Go ask him, if you have to know. Get him good and drunk. He'll tell you." Blue gray smoke filled the room, swirling like a polluted river through beams of wan, whitish light.

"I have to know," she said after a moment.

"Maybe he doesn't look at it that way."

"Too bad," Ingrid replied. "My will is stronger."

"Oh? That's interesting. Just do me a favor: don't mention that I somehow planted this desire in your brain."

"You didn't," she answered, turning back to the doorway. "And I wouldn't call it a desire."

"What then?"

She paused before leaving, tall and blond and unknowing and, in her own right, inscrutable. "An imperative," she said.

He sighed and reached over for the volume of *The Second Sex* that Ingrid had loaned him some time ago. "No," he said aloud. "I can't take it. Not on my day off." He rose, wrapped his warm bathrobe around himself, stepped into his slippers and padded through Tanya's room—she and Jorge lay snoring under the covers—then Jorge's, into the kitchen. The desire to talk to Naomi had come over him. When this happened, sometimes he phoned her, sometimes he phoned someone else. He ladled out some oatmeal into a bowl of dubious cleanliness and deliberated. "She still hasn't ditched Jack Diamond, so I would undoubtedly have to hear about that nutcase," he thought, a consideration that was most unappealing, so his mind wandered to other acquaintances and settled on Eileen, currently living in the Mission district in San Francisco, working as a waitress and taking music classes at the state college. As far as he knew, she had no boyfriend, at least none as obnoxiously offensive as the gun-owning mid-westerner, so he would not have to listen to the romantic yammering of an addled twenty year old. Yes, talking to Eileen was vastly preferable.

Buzz came up from the basement for breakfast, ink all over his fingers.

"Ingrid told me you weren't making any more funny money while you lived here," the veteran snapped.

"I'm not," Buzz replied, guzzling his orange juice and not daring to meet his housemate's eyes in the midst of such a bold-faced lie. "I was doing art."

"Doing art!" Gilbert snapped again.

"Yup," guzzle, guzzle.

"The kind of art federal agents might knock down the door to get a look at?"

"Nope, abstract art." The counterfeiter stared at the floor.

"What kind of an idiot do you take me for?" Gilbert hollered.

190

"An art-loving—?"

"I will turn you in, do you understand? Rather than get busted as an accomplice."

"I'll testify you have nothing to do with it."

"Thanks, but that and twenty five cents won't even get me on the subway. You cut that crap out."

"Who said I'm doing it?"

"I said, okay? I don't know what kind of mindless moron you think Ingrid is, and who knows, maybe you can even pull the wool over her eyes, but forget it with me. If I so much as suspect you're counterfeiting again, I will go to the cops. Do you understand?"

"Sure," more guzzling.

"And I'll go to the bomb squad while I'm at it."

"Why?" Guzzle, guzzle.

"Because I don't trust you in that department either!" Gilbert hollered. "Now get out of my sight, before I get even more pissed and call them now!"

Buzz slunk away, muttering something about petty bourgeois prejudices, eating his granola as he went, having finished the juice.

Grumbling and cursing to himself, Gilbert Locklane glanced out the window at the dirty, white sky, smudged here and there with gray, as if someone had used it to wipe soot off his hands. He dialed Eileen's number. On the tenth ring, she picked up, clearly awakened from a deep sleep. Her hello seemed to travel up from the profound depths of a well, echoing with uncertainty about who or where she was. He apologized for disturbing her but did not volunteer to call back later. Chomping now on a granola bar, he advised her to get some food.

"Some sleep is what I need."

"Well, I need a friend."

"What about Mike Dellico? You live with him."

"He's out with Natalie in some country town," chomp, chomp, "antiquing."

She sounded more alert, as if, with an effort, she had shaken loose from a thick blanket of slumber. "I didn't know he liked antiques."

"Neither did he," more chomps, "till Natalie told him."

There was a pause. "My life's a wreck," Gilbert resumed. "The pay at my job is miserable. I don't start my university classes till the fall, and one of my roommates is a revolutionary slash counterfeiter. I could wind up in jail any day 'cause of this creep."

"Call the cops."

"Ingrid would kick me out. She has a soft spot for this turd. He's an utter loser. He's going to get us all in trouble."

"My three roommates are a bunch of hapless hippies, who spend their days stoned, hanging out in Haight Ashbury. One was so high two nights ago, he just walked into a mugger's arms, lost all his cash and his pot. Now he moans his life is ruined, the idiot. I'll tell you when his life is ruined, when he can't make the rent, that's when, because I'll kick him out and sublet his room to Ronald Swurl."

"I thought you dumped that rat."

"He dumped me."

"I meant forgot about him."

Eileen paused meditatively. "That's not so easy."

"Uh-oh."

"He's not so bad."

"Don't start," chomp, chomp, "I may hang up."

"Is that a promise?"

"What about a female roommate—to keep yourself out of trouble."

"I'm not a teenager who needs supervision."

"Indeed."

"I might want to marry him."

"He might not be interested in marriage. He might not be the type."

"And who's the type?"

"Me, Mike, Jorge."

"The Jorge I met when I visited last year? That condescending, macho Jorge?"

"I predict the first woman he finds who's interested in marriage, he'll get hitched."

"You need to hitch your brain. He looked like a compulsive philanderer."

"That's an unfair aspersion."

"And you, presumably, would marry Naomi?"

"Not anymore. She's too flighty and doesn't know what she wants."

"She seems to want Jack Diamond."

"That loon," a certain bitterness crept into his tone, as he thought of the tall, light-haired young man—and not long-haired—in the photo with Naomi that Mike had shown him. It was easy enough to see what she liked about the man; he was handsome. Gilbert did not believe for a minute that she had any other criterion on which she had based this current attachment.

What he did not like to admit to himself, however, was that she had shown a surprising and uncharacteristic sureness and steadfastness about Jack, or so others had reported. She talked of moving out west with him after graduation and had even picked up some of what Gilbert regarded as his bizarre conservative views, though she had not completely abandoned the radicalism, to which she, uninfluenced, inclined. Indeed, she still studied Russian and talked of participating in an exchange student program with the Soviet Union, though not, he knew, for political reasons, but, first because she regarded the existence of the Soviet Union as a central fact of the twentieth century, indeed of modern civilization, and wanted to go and see it herself, to set her own eyes on its greatness and abjectness, second, because she loved Russian literature, wanted to read it in the original and third, out of a perverse, or was it principled, defiance that refused to allow the USSR's status as an enemy of the US to influence or deter her in any way. The vague perception that she was more complicated than he had known, not merely the lovely girl with intellectual parents he had hoped to impress and that this failure to perceive her nature had in fact resulted in the collapse of their love affair; this dim realization annoyed him, made him eager to banish thoughts of her and of what could have been had he come to this insight sooner.

Disgruntled by this dissatisfying turn of thought, he shifted to the greener conversational pastures of Ingrid's fanatical feminism.

"She refuses to cook," he said, "on the grounds that she will never be chained to the stove, like so many millions of women. When her boyfriend comes here for dinner, he makes chili or chicken cacciatore for her. When she goes there, he cooks too. Now how is that equality? He's chained to the stove instead of her."

"Maybe he likes to cook. Some men do."

Gilbert snorted derisively. "He needs his head examined. We were out at a bar recently and he referred to her as brilliant. The only thing brilliant about her is how she manages to get out of every chore by loading it on some man's shoulders, because she will not be enslaved to women's work. They're some pair. And I only just found out today that they're an item. Before that I thought they merely dated occasionally. But it's serious. This guy needs therapy, lots of it and the sooner the better."

He felt much improved after this outburst, enough to inquire about Jack Diamond.

"He's apparently a tough guy to live with," his friend responded. "He's either aloof or very demanding, and he has some very bizarre beliefs, religious and political. He thinks fascism is coming to America and the way to respond to it is with gun ownership. So he owns several guns. And he uses them for self-defense. He surprised a burglar one night in his apartment and put his handgun to the guy's head. Naomi was frantic, she thought he might blow the criminal's brains out right there. But he just turned him over to the police. He's insisting that she learn how to handle these guns, because he doesn't like the idea of her and…of her being alone in his apartment with no means of self-defense."

"Her and who—you started to say."

"Just a slip. I was distracted."

"Well, I suppose if it's that dangerous," Gilbert grumbled. "He has a point."

"It is. A friend of Naomi's was raped in her apartment and another in her car. That South Side sometimes sounds really scary." She paused to slurp her coffee. "The one who got raped in the apartment had to have an illegal abortion and almost died."

"You're full of uplifting news this morning."

"Hey, *you* called *me*. Not the other way around. And you woke me up, I might add, on a rainy, cold, dreary day, when I could have spent long morning hours curled up cozily in bed."

"It's cold here too, but there's snow everywhere and along the curbs it's all brown, gray or black, from dirt and car exhaust," he sighed. "So she's learning to handle a gun."

"Nope, she won't, she's opposed to it. And you know how stubborn she can be when she gets the idea she's against something. It's just not worth the fight. Jack doesn't know that yet, but he'll find out."

"Maybe they'll break up over it?" Gilbert asked hopefully.

"Not likely. He's making plans for them to live in some cabin in the wilds of Wyoming, away from any decadent Eastern cities. Even Chicago's too civilized for his taste, and frankly, it didn't strike me as all that civilized. The police at the '68 convention were barbarians if ever there were any. And Jack doesn't like the police. He doesn't like criminals either. In fact, he has one very long shitlist. I think I'm on it, because he knows I tried to dissuade Naomi from this Wyoming idea. Sheesh, sometimes life is too complicated."

"Maybe I should visit. This guy doesn't sound too good for her."

"Nah, you don't want to do that," Eileen hastily advised, thinking of baby Snow and the secret of his existence. "Besides, Jack's not too keen on Naomi's exes. Ronald Swurl showed up to stay at the commune where she lives and before she even got home from work, Jack had had a fight with him and punched him out. Ron got on the next bus to the west coast. He never even saw Naomi."

The veteran chuckled. The thought of Ronald's bloody nose did not bother him in the least. "By the way is he Jewish? Mr. Lichter wanted to know."

"Ron? A WASP if ever there was one."

"No, Jack."

"Oh, paternal grandfather, hence the name, Diamond. The rest, I don't know—English, Scot, Scandinavian, some mix like that."

He listened sympathetically as she then described her precarious financial state—barely able to pay the rent each month and living in fear of eviction and homelessness, and even greater fear of the mental disorganization that such prospects seemed to bring on, a state that precluded proper planning and enshrouded her in isolation like a tomb of ice, from which she was scarcely able to see another soul, no less reach out to one. Her father in Peru had remarried, which perhaps explained why the infrequent checks from him had trickled down to nothing. She had managed to purchase a used Ford sedan— "I could always drive to the Southwest, Santa Fe or some such place and if it was too expensive, camp in my car," she explained. When Gilbert observed that she might do better to sell the sedan and keep the money in the bank, she laughed with an unhealthy and vague desperation, remarking that he did not know how little it was worth. He pictured her in her run-down, dingy apartment, lithe, beautiful, dark-haired, chewing on her fingernails as she fretted over the rent. "You're knock-out gorgeous," he said. "Marry some rich guy. Just find one, hold your nose and do it."

"Some people are a little more sentimental about marriage than that," she retorted and returned to dithering nervously about her penury.

"You could always return to Philly, move back in with the Lichters and take up with your old boyfriend at Penn," he rather sardonically suggested.

"You scoff," she said, "but with each passing day that or some part of that looks increasingly appealing."

He wanted to keep the conversation on this topic. He loved hearing her ramble and gossip about Morris and Lily, especially Lily, who had always gone out of her way to make him feel welcome and at home. Regarding Morris, what he sought was some clue, some thread that would lead into the man's good graces, but Morris' character always remained contradictory and thus as vague to him as the smudges on the grimy sky, with no definite shape, suggesting no clear means of impressing his worthiness on his beloved's father, because he could not clearly apprehend his personality. Yes, Morris was a very liberal Democrat, who nonetheless loathed the hippy dippy tone of his era, someone who had once characterized himself in Gilbert's hearing as "one hundred and fifty percent Jewish," yet remained intractably assimilated, who had regarded his Ivy League education (he had transferred to Cornell from Madison) as an entrance to a WASP upper class world from which he intended never to seek an exit, someone with what Gilbert could only think of as social climbing aspirations for his children, aspirations in which, Gilbert sourly reflected, he, Gilbert Locklane, played no part. But as the acrid wave of this nasty thought washed over him, it dissolved some of his preconceptions: he saw the dim outlines of another possible relationship, as faint as the imprint of a shell on wet sand, vanishing with the retreating and approaching water, the role he could have had in Morris' life if he had taken a different approach to his daughter, if, instead of what he regarded as a torrid love affair, he had chastely pursued her as a wife. It seemed old-fashioned and ridiculous, yet he had to admit that had he tried it, he might well have been more than an unpleasant afterthought in Morris Lichter's memory, one which the older man was forgetting as rapidly as he possibly could.

So they mulled over their social world in Philadelphia, fondly recalling this or that character, this or that event, until Eileen mentioned "how angry Morris is at what has happened to Naomi." Of course this referred to his reception of the recent news of his grandson's existence, of which Gilbert knew nothing, as well as the sexual activity it betokened, for which Gilbert was directly responsible. "Certainly he can't want her to marry this Jack Diamond lunatic," the spurned lover put in.

"I think anybody would do, and barring an immediate marriage, vowing to take her place in a nunnery. You have no notion of the paternal fury at her ways. But it's not directed at her. It's directed at whoever she happens to be involved with. If Jack asks her to marry him, it will vanish in an instant—provided, of course, that she accepts. If she doesn't, he will be consigned to the 'not good enough for her' dust heap."

"Where yours truly resides."

"Sadly, Gilbert, yes."

"How can I change that?"

"You can't. Forget it."

"I could go out to Chicago, visit her and propose."

"And get shot by Mr. Diamond? Haven't you heard a word I've been saying? He does not, *not* like her exes, especially ones with plans to lure her away into marriage. Besides is it Naomi you want to marry or her father? I'm confused."

"Oh shut up."

He ended the conversation as Jorge, dark hair sleep-tousled, dark, rather leathery face still slumber-filmed, slouched into the kitchen, inspected the pot on the worn, old, gas stove and groaned, "Oatmeal! Not again! She's tryin' to kill us."

"Be glad she cooks the oatmeal. It's the only thing she cooks."

"I think Ingrid's torturing us for our dependence on her for breakfast."

"We drew lots—remember? The rest of us rotate dinners. Ingrid got lucky. She hates making dinner and got breakfast."

"I think she rigged that drawing."

"Could be. Do you want to be the one to confront her?"

Jorge grumbled something incomprehensible and filled yet another imperfectly clean bowl with oatmeal. "Why not granola? Or pancakes? Boy, I'd really love some pancakes."

"Dream on."

"Hey, why aren't you at work?"

"Morning off. You know she's seeing Alderway."

"Old news," Jorge blew on a hot spoonful. "They're two wacked-out egotists. They deserve each other. He calls her 'my Valkyrie.' Who wants a Valkyrie? I'd settle for an occasional good meal, like I get when Tanya makes one of her casseroles. That Alderway—he fell for Ingrid hook, line and sinker. I wouldn't be surprised if they get married—or" he paused to contemplate the gray day out the dirty window pane, "whatever you do when you sign your life over to a radical feminist. I doubt she'd call it marriage, and in all likelihood he'll probably be the one who'll have to change his name."

He ate with a slow, simmering discontent, his dark eyes glimmering now with resentments that were clearly ready to bubble forth from his lips. His love-dejected housemate was in no mood to hear more of it, no matter how much he agreed.

"Slavonovich called last night."

"Goody, goody gumdrops," Jorge replied. "I'm not moving fast enough for him. You know, sometimes I think I'm ready to retire from the revolution."

"I doubt that. Then you'd have to get a real job, not just that part-time gig at the food co-op." Gilbert fixed himself another bowl of oatmeal. It was, he decided, peculiarly lacking in any taste whatsoever. They ate in silence, bare feet and slippers pressed against the white linoleum floor, badly in need of a sweeping. Food-encrusted dishes overflowed the sink, testimony to the absence of a dishwasher and of women willing to clean up after men. Gilbert guiltlessly noticed his soup bowl from last night's dinner, not even rinsed. "I'll do it after lunch," he thought and carried over his oatmeal bowl to add to the clutter. In a rare moment of domestic concern for his environment, he took a sponge and cleaned the counters.

"Hey, the table could use it too," Jorge urged.

"You do it," He dropped the sponge in front of his roommate and padded over the crumbs, out of the kitchen and back to his room. He dressed in old jeans, a warm pull-over and a thick brown Mexican sweater. Then he laced up his work-boots, pulled his ski-cap over his abundant red hair, got his gloves, donned his leather coat and tromped downstairs to the street. It was a cold, raw, overcast late morning. Everything looked filthy, except the black and silver telephone wires standing out against the ugly gray-white sky, and all, the day, the weather, the moment struck him as particularly hostile to human endeavor. "Try what you will," they chimed in their frozen and ominous magic, like music from another, dreadful world, "none of it will work."

"I feel like a piece of shit," he muttered to himself, as he began trudging along Magazine Street, "a nobody going nowhere for no reason." The afternoon, he decided, was making the case that it was a good day for suicide, but even that seemed to involve too much effort. "It's simpler just to idle on my day off, and go to work the rest of the time." He thought of the bookstore, "The Bibliophile," where he spent so many hours, as a haven, although most of the time there he was bored beyond words. Raoul Umanzor was a very relaxed employer and certainly did not mind his clerk reading behind the cash register, as he waited for customers. But Gilbert had long passed the "entrancement with the novelty of endless hours to read" phase of his employment. An hour or two was fine, six or seven— too much. The alternative—literary/political debates with his boss—was almost as exhausting, though he still liked to hear about the leading literati of Mexico City. In fact, he lured Raoul onto the topic of his enormous, pollution-clogged native metropolis as often as possible and had decided that at the first opportunity he would visit it. "Maybe Naomi and I can honeymoon there," he thought bitterly.

He came up to Massachusetts Avenue, busy and choked with automobile exhaust. Below the grimy, snow-covered pavement, the subway rumbled into Central Square, reminding him suddenly of the subway in Philadelphia, and the trolley that he had taken down to West Philadelphia to visit friends from Penn. Once he had gone with Naomi, and well did he recall the surge of adrenalin when he set eyes on the car full of what he regarded as thugs, following them along dark and dangerous Baltimore Avenue, and his determination to protect her. It filled him with a sense of waste now; what was the point of those years spent with her, when they had come to nothing? And what was the point of finding someone new, as Mike advised, when the same thing could just happen again? Then he would be doubly miserable. No, he told himself, pausing to gaze up at the belligerent sky and to catch again that terrible harmony from somewhere else that he never wanted to visit, no, it was a wretched state of affairs. He would just have to subsist until it improved, that was, unless the prospect of suicide became irresistible.

That prospect became suddenly much more resistible, as a short, pretty woman with many blond curls crossed his path and pushed the door open to a small coffee shop. Automatically, he followed her in. As they stood at the counter, waiting for their coffees to go, he learned that her name was Annie, that she attended Boston College but lived in far away Cambridge, planned to go to medical school, came originally from Ohio and did not have a boyfriend. He elicited all of this information in about two minutes, and then imparted his own. She had a copy of *The Boston Phoenix* under her arm and confided that she loved fiction and reviewed occasionally for it. "That's where I've seen you name!" He ecstatically lied. Evidently thrilled at having met one of her readers, she suggested they sit. They did so. They discussed literature, life— "Ohio's not a bad place to be from, especially when you come from a big German-American family like me"—travel (she too wanted to visit Mexico City) and education. She sympathized with the travails of a veteran who had to postpone college but fully approved of Boston University and appreciated his literary interests, but did not agree that he should therefore major in English. Indeed, within ten minutes, she was advising him on his future career as a lawyer and his undergraduate pre-law major. He was happy to go along with it. In fact, as he gazed into her beautifully sparkling blue eyes, he decided that he would go along with whatever she wanted—smart, attractive, cheerful, why here was the antidote to self-destruction. Mike Dellico was right!

They sat in the steamy, busy little restaurant, a crowd bustling around them, he thinking how just twenty minutes before, this place, with all its life that did not include him, would have depressed and alienated him. But now, he seemed preternaturally aware of all its details and enlivened by them, as those strange, alien strains haunting him so recently outside began to recede. He passed his gloved hands over his ears in an unconscious gesture to banish the threats of that high, hostile melody and glanced around. He liked the way the waiter from the take-out counter shouted orders into the kitchen and then bagged them in a few swift motions. The hippies slurping herbal tea at the next table seemed friendly and good-hearted. The students across from them looked sincerely engrossed in their books. Goodness, he suddenly, wonderfully believed, filled the heart of humanity. Being alive, being human and alive was the acme of all. People were what was worth living for, while the smells of breakfast—eggs, bacon, toast—banished the wretched memory of Ingrid's bland oatmeal and suddenly, "let me buy you a meal," they were feasting on pancakes together, and he was thinking that yes, this was a better world than any other, certainly better than that terrifying one he had begun to glean out alone in the winter.

He steered the conversation to literature in one of its weightiest forms—the Russian classics, which, not surprisingly, constituted Annie's weak spot. They passed many minutes on the works of Dostoyevsky, Tolstoy, Chekhov, Pushkin, Turgenev and Gogol. She would be late for her class and he for a hastily invented and unspecified appointment, but their literary discoveries exhilarated them, most of all they *themselves* exhilarated each other. Suddenly she glanced at her watch and, in a flurry, they prepared to part, but not before he had arranged for them to see a Fellini movie together on Friday night. She loved Fellini—also de Sica, Rosellini, Antonioni, Bunuel and a list of other, serious European film-makers, whom he had not discussed with a woman since Naomi had abandoned him.

He walked her to the Central Square subway entrance. By then they had exchanged phone numbers and were talking like old acquaintances. Neither noticed the bite in the cold damp New England wind, nor did they observe the disgruntled commuters, forced to pick their way around the young couple standing in the subway entrance.

"I'll call you tonight," he promised.

She nodded and her curls glinted gold even in the dull, dirty light.

"And by then I'll have read this week's *Phoenix*, and we can discuss these dissident Russian novelists you rave about."

They continued talking. Neither wanted to part, and when they finally did, both had the distinct impression that something new and irreplaceable had just begun, something that could last a very long time. He whistled all the way back home.

Winter, rarely severe in Washington, D.C., had turned to spring, and before Boris knew it, April was upon him, and he was racing around, putting the finishing touches on his rally preparations. He had plenty of help. Alan Jengo had journeyed in from Pittsburgh, Jessie Roper came down from Boston and Gus Harwood had appeared on the doorstep of Boris' commune near American University, with a veritable army of Hell's Angels, who promptly camped in the first floor and basement living rooms, thus taking over two of the run-down and under-furnished house's four stories. Though leery of them at first, the veteran soon set his doubts aside. They were willing to work. They took his posters and nailed them to trees and telephone poles all over town. They attended meetings and manned telephones. He was delighted. Jessie and Alan were astounded.

"In New England these guys do nothing but roar through the countryside striking terror in the hearts of the locals," Jessie said.

"They'll have their own section at the rally."

"Just so as they don't come armed," the Pittsburgh labor organizer warned, "because then the police will have an excuse to start attacking, tear gassing and shooting us."

One of Boris' housemates, Rebecca Harrison and Gus Harwood fell in love. They were a most unlikely couple—she a senior at George Washington University, and he, well, a major in anarchy in the Hell's Angels league. Boris could not imagine what sort of future this relationship had, but held his tongue, limiting himself to the observation that "I guess you'll be sticking around after the political events."

"Looks like it," Gus smiled and leaned back against the shabby, yellow wallpaper in the dining room and lowered the hammer, with which he had been repairing a bookcase. His brown hair, prematurely streaked with gray was pulled back into a pony tail, and his face, with the dark stubble on his lean cheeks, had a worn look, as if in years on the open road it had suffered too much exposure to the elements, and, the scars suggested, too much violence. His old, black leather jacket lay on the table, and he wore a black T-shirt, which revealed, among other tattoos, a hammer and sickle on his bicep. "You folks could use a member of a motorcycle gang for protection," and he pointed to his handgun, next to his jacket.

"Just don't bring it to the march," the organizer cautioned. "None of that. We're not giving the police any excuses to riot."

"I thought you might not want to give them any chances."

"Excuses, Gus. We don't want them thinking we're armed. If they do, it'll be a slaughter."

Rebecca and Boris had long been close friends. So late one morning, he invited her out for a sandwich at a local deli. As always, the tall, green-eyed, black-haired beauty drew stares, even if she was bony.

"Don't you think this fling has gone far enough?" He asked, as their food arrived at their small, wobbly table.

"It's no fling," she replied, biting into her tuna fish sandwich on whole wheat bread.

"Really? Exactly how is a woman who wants a PhD in public health going to fit a motorcycle gang leader into her future? Tell me what I'm missing here."

"The whole thing—it's called love."

"Oh Becca, please."

"*Some* people aren't cynics about love."

"And some aren't hopeless romantics. How on earth will this work?"

"Very simply. I'll get into a graduate program, who knows where, and he'll relocate with me. Meanwhile we spend the spring and summer here together."

"Along with his entire, gun-toting, black leather clad, motorcycle roaring entourage?"

"No. They go back to where they came from."

"You're sure?"

She nodded, chewing thoughtfully. "You're wrong to regard them as low-lifes."

"I don't. They're just different from you. Note I said you. Not me." He pushed back his long, lank, blond hair and rubbed the scar on his cheek. Some days, for no apparent reason, it hurt. He thought it had to do with the weather. He must have winced, because she looked suddenly concerned. "You should see a doctor. Maybe that didn't heal right or there was nerve damage that could be treated."

"I'm not going back to that VA hospital to get told my wounds are psychosomatic. No thank you," He paused pensively over his BLT. Out of the corner of his eye, he noted the interest with which two well-groomed and rather elegantly attired businessmen regarded his friend. He threw his sandwich onto the plate in disgust. "Christ, Becca, you could have anyone you want, anyone. Why Gus Harwood?"

"This class bias of yours and sudden aspiration for me to rise into what— upper middle or upper class luxury—is really surprising. But, to answer your question, he is a pure soul."

He groaned, glanced over at the next table, noted the discreet attentiveness of its sole, elderly occupant, but did not care if their discussion was overheard.

"Oh yes. He is what he is, no pretense, no lies. He doesn't pull any fast ones. He's like a rock. I'm surprised you didn't notice that."

"I did," he groaned again.

"The Bible says: 'Above all things, keep the heart pure, for it is the starting point of life.' That's what I'm doing, Boris. My heart is pure. And you, of all people, ought to respect that. Gus is no stepping stone for me. He's the destination, the point of it all, the reason for it. He is my destiny."

He bit savagely into the last of his BLT. "It sounds like your mind's made up."

"It's just following my heart."

"And that's true and pure."

"Pure as the driven snow."

"Shit."

"You can curse all you like—"

"I'm responsible for this. I brought him into our house."

"And I am truly grateful."

The level blue gaze of his eyes caught the green one of hers. "And I am truly sorry." Then he looked away and found himself staring into the boundless depths of the old man's eyes, the solitary man at the next table, who had clearly overheard their conversation, whose dark eyes glimmered with a life, even Boris in his discontent could recognize it, from an unseen world, a glimmer, a light and a light darkness that had sprung forth with her words about the heart and her biblical quote and in which there impalpably but undeniably hovered the question, would Boris now desist and accept? And that was not all that was there in those fathomless eyes, it was only a tiny part, there seemed so much more, so much that was utterly past Boris, but in his preoccupation he did not pause to consider this. Only much later, alone, passing over his memory of that meal, did he recall that unforgettable glance from the next table, and in recalling it, identified it as something extraordinary, somehow past the merely human, a vision from another world.

But that afternoon, as they stepped out into the slanting sunlight on Wisconsin Avenue, the buses and cars whooshing by, other thoughts held him: he thought that sunlight seemed so blindingly strong, meeting that other light, equally strong, which shone from within him, illuminating their two divergent ways and casting its bright rays down the years of her path, the light from within, the light from without, blazing over all this so that it stood as clearly before him as the row of brown, dusty low-rise apartment buildings on the corner. He pressed her hand and wished her good luck, with a catch in his voice.

"Hey, it's not like I won't see you at dinner," she smiled and turned to tread that new and separate path away from him. He stepped into a People's pharmacy for relief, slid onto a counter stool and ordered a vanilla ice cream soda. Slowly that too bright light faded. In the kinder shadows, he thought of Becca, Eileen, Sammy, Alan and Gus. He thought of Jessie, Jorge in Boston and Naomi and Snow in Chicago and how that powerful inner light lit their essential goodness and hid their flaws. "It's for my friends, my brothers and sisters," he said aloud of the light, but he could only say it now that he was in the shade, now that he wasn't speechless from it, "for my friends."

In those days, he drove a city bus, but he lingered for a brief while before going to work. He bought a *Washington Star* and perused the headlines about more dead in Vietnam, more protests and more campus unrest.

"Country's coming apart at the seams," said the pimply kid behind the counter, who worked the soda fountain.

"Given all the horrible things we've been doing, it's about time," he replied.

"Now there's a new angle on it."

"How come the draft missed you?"

"Bad foot."

"That foot probably saved your life."

"I think so too. I never thought I'd be grateful for it, but the day the army told me they didn't want no man with a bad foot, I thought how stupid I'd been. This here foot," he bent down and tapped his lower leg, "kept me out of a body bag." He paused to wipe the counter with his rag, and then glanced up at his customer. "Looks like you got tore up pretty bad."

"They didn't think I'd make it. But I did, out of spite. I made myself and God a promise that if I survived I'd come to the capital and work day and night to end this horrible war." He pulled a folded flyer out of his jacket pocket and handed it to the young man: "Add your voice to ours."

"I ain't got no voice, not one anybody wants to hear, anyway."

The veteran scowled. "If I don't see you there, I'll be back here to find out why," he said and left. He hurried through dusty streets to the bus station, surmising from the smell and feel of the air that spring would turn to summer very quickly, perhaps in a matter of weeks, as it sometimes did in Washington. His shift did not end until nine p.m. that evening, and he drove through the hours as he always did, like a traveler in a dream, a dream of the final journey through the night, darker than the city that stretched out before him, that last, unlit sojourn. The passengers got on, their change clinked into the fare bucket, they got off. Some were regulars whom he recognized from the depths of the vatic trance induced by the night, the motion of the bus, the blackness of the road that unfurled before him, most were not. Some neighborhoods summoned him back into alertness and tension, made him nervous, others he scarcely noted, as he coasted on his vision of the end of his light. Such was his mood as he rode down safe, smug, prosperous Wisconsin Avenue toward wealthy Friendship Heights. Nothing ever went wrong here. He had a busload of college students and affluent suburban matrons. He hardly even bothered to look at his passengers.

Perhaps that was why he was unaware of when exactly the ruckus started. But suddenly he heard shouting and then a loud thud, followed by another as two men hit the floor. He pulled the vehicle over, stopped it and turned to see two young Hispanic men pummeling a large African American teenager in the aisle.

"Off the bus!" Boris roared, rising from his seat as he opened the doors. One of the assailants exited, the other, locked in a wrestling hold with the teenager, was cursing loudly, "you sonofabitch! You goddamned sonofabitch!" Without thinking, the veteran approached and struggled to separate them. At last the attacker broke free, cursed in Spanish, glaring at Boris and the other man. He started down the steps, turned to cast his gaze, dark and molten with fury, upon the bus driver and upon his victim. So quickly that none saw it coming, he reached into his leather jacket, withdrew a gun and shot them both. Panic and mayhem ensued. Young women screamed and rushed to the exits, and an older man used his wife's scarf to try to staunch the driver's bleeding shoulder. The teenager lay on the floor, the red abdominal stain on his white shirt spreading outward like a sinister, blossoming rose.

"Help him," Boris groaned, as he lay on the rubber aisle mat, blood pooling beneath him. "He's in much worse shape."

"Did you get a look at him, the shooter?" The older man asked another passenger.

"Yeah," the man replied, "I'll never forget that face."

Police and an ambulance arrived. "I saw the guy who shot them," the man told an officer. "I could pick that face out of a million. He was about twenty, Puerto Rican, I think, with straight black hair slicked back and dark, dark eyes. He's had acne and got a scar on his face." The police removed the witness from the bus to question him further. From the top of the step, Boris could see the man pointing into the night where the youth had fled, with all the speed and stealth of sudden death. A policeman got into his squad car, barked into his radio and then tore off. Other police cars arrived. Bus passengers were detained and interviewed.

After being loaded into the ambulance, Boris heard its siren start to wail and the paramedic say: "you're the lucky one. It didn't hit any major organs or arteries. You're damn lucky."

"What about him?" The veteran glanced at the teenager, lying quiet and motionless on a stretcher. The paramedic's face lengthened. "Not so lucky," he said.

On the ride to the hospital in Northwest a shadow seemed to lengthen over Boris, who, groaning from pain, glanced from time to time from the wounded bus passenger ominously silent to confusing images of injuries in Vietnam, of wounded men on stretchers and on the ground, screaming from gruesome lacerations. The scar on his face throbbed violently, as if it had just been stitched up; his back and legs, where he had been shot, ached again.

"Tell me I'm in America," he said to the medic.

"You're in America," came the reply. "Where else would you be?"

"I could be in a hospital in Saigon."

"Oh, you're a veteran."

"Tell me I'm in D.C."

"You're in D.C."

"And there's no chance I'll be sent back into battle."

"There's no chance."

The veteran, who had raised his head with considerable pain to look at the medic, lowered it again. "This is nothing," he said. "Just one gunshot wound. I've survived worse."

His surgery was so brief that he soon found himself in a semi-private room, watching the evening news about the latest bombings in North Vietnam. He fell asleep breathing imprecations on Richard Nixon.

He awoke to bright sunlight, inexplicably possessed by the memory of the man at the next table in the deli, wondering who he was and how he could be so different from everybody else, and there was a doctor insisting that he skip the upcoming rally. "What happened to me in Vietnam makes this shoulder wound look like a hangnail. I saw more people die in more horrible ways than you can imagine. My best friend died in my arms. Putting an end to this criminal war is not some optional extracurricular activity for me. It is my life. It is the reason I breathe. So don't forbid me to march against it. Nothing short of being completely crippled or dead could keep me away."

"I forbid it," the doctor curtly repeated, turned on his heel and walked out of the room.

"Well that was a real effective approach," remarked Gus Harwood, swaggering over to his bed, all scars, tattoos and long, stringy hair. "I didn't intend to eavesdrop, but I was standing right in the doorway and overheard the whole thing."

"Doctors don't know everything."

"About your body—yeah, they kind of do….I hear you been advising your roommate against me."

"Becca? You bet. You two have nothing in common."

"We're in love and plan to be married."

"That's the biggest mistake either one of you ever made."

Gus grinned. Despite his aviator sunglasses, his eyes visibly sparkled. "That may be, but it'll also be the best mistake we ever made."

The patient harrumphed.

"Look, I saw that photo of that Eileen you got on the mirror in your room, and Becca told me the story. You're the one who made the biggest mistake of your life. She's a hippie for God's sake. Since when do you let jealousy or masculine pride ruin a relationship with a hippie?"

"If you came here to harangue me about her, I'm gonna have to ask you to leave. I'm not a well man."

"But you're well enough to get in a shouting match with the surgeon," the Hell's Angel chuckled, the chains on his black leather jacket clinking merrily. "I called this Eileen and told her what happened. She's on the next bus here from the west coast."

"You did what?" The patient hollered with sudden vigor.

"One good deed deserves another. You tried to come between me and the love of my life, so I thought I'd sic the one you ran away from back on your trail."

Silence ensued.

"Exactly how am I supposed to tolerate life with a woman who can't remain faithful for longer than a week?"

Gus simply smiled.

"I get shot. I'm lying in my hospital bed, and you come here, dragging that faithless female back into my life," the veteran paused. "I guess you sure got even with me."

"You could say that," and, still smiling, the Hell's Angel pulled up a chair, grasped Boris' hand and said: "Brother, you never really told me what happened to you in Nam. I want to know, and somehow, I have the feeling it would do you a world of good to tell me."

The wounded man gazed at him first in surprise, then with a look of new appreciation, but then stared straight at the ever-present image of Ronzell, impaled and dying on the steel spike, and turned his head and said no.

Alderway slouched along Massachusetts Avenue toward Magazine Street through the December snow, thinking that a year had passed and now, at last, Tiwana wanted him to purchase three crates of assault weapons. He was also, in some other part of his mind, back in the jungles of South Vietnam, stalking his c.o., Rider, thinking he was tired of waiting for another soldier to kill the monster and that he would just as soon do it himself. Light snow fell and melted on his face, decorated his dark Fu Manchu moustache, but instead he saw sunbeams through green foliage and the light brown hair of Rider's hated head directly before him. He raised his gun, aimed directly at the back of that head—how many times had he relived this moment? But before he could pull the trigger, there came a shot and the head fell from his sight like the moon into a bed of clouds. He raced forward, ignoring the sharp scrape of impeding branches. His buddy Hollowel, gray, wiry, light-haired, trembling and sweating, stood over the corpse, contemplating it quietly, and then gave the dead man a poke with his mud-spattered toe.

"We'll say it was the Viet Cong," Alderway stated.

"Say what you want. I'm perfectly happy to take credit for killing a murdering sadist."

"But I'm not perfectly happy to see you court-martialed and executed. So keep your mouth shut."

"Should we do to him what he liked to do to them?"

"Nah," Alderway also poked the body with the toe of his boot, as if to make absolutely sure he was dead. "Mutilating corpses was never my idea of a good time."

"It was the mutilating of live people that got to me."

"Yeah, well, he won't be doing much of that anymore."

"The things he made me do, the things I watched him do, when I wasn't busy throwing up, will haunt me till the day I die."

"Me too, but knowing he's dead, somehow that makes it bearable, like that I'll be able to face it and defeat it."

"I don't share your confidence," his weary companion paused glumly, wiping beads of sweat off his upper lip with the back of his mud-streaked hand, "your optimism." Where the moisture had glistened on the blond stubble, a faint stain now gave the impression of an incongruously brown moustache, something odd and out-of-place, like a dead man lying on a bed of vines or a psychopath commanding soldiers.

"Now that's the first time," Alderway replied softly, again nudging the sadist's corpse, this time with his rifle, "anyone's ever called me an optimist."

"I mean in comparison to me. Ever since I started serving under Rider, everything became darkness. I can't find the light anywhere. It's like it went out of the world, like there's no goodness in anything, anywhere. It's all deep, dark night." In six months, Holowell proved the truth of his words, a suicide who had put the muzzle of his gun in his mouth and pulled the trigger. But at that moment, as they stood together in the steaming, brilliantly verdant undergrowth, over the carcass of their detested and murdered commanding officer, there was a conspiratorial camaraderie and, almost, hope—hope that they had rid the world of a terrible evil. Alderway reveled in that grandiose and, as he later saw it, futile hope, perhaps the first time he had ever done so, not least because he shared it with his brave friend Holowell, and it lasted until the latter's death, but not beyond.

"It should have been me that killed him," Alderway said on that day, gazing down at the ugly dead face, and said it again when he and another soldier found Holowell's mangled body. "It should have been me that killed him."

"Who?" The soldier asked.

"Rider."

"Well, we were all bucking for that privilege," the soldier said and threw a jacket over what was left of Holowell's ashen face.

"It was my task. He was hellion, and it was my job to destroy him, but I was too late. And now this," he gestured at his self-destroyed friend. "I'll never be too late again."

"If I were you, I'd hope never to be called on to perform an execution again."

"But you're not me. Rider wasn't the first, and he won't be the last. There are lots of Riders out there. Now that I've really breathed the stench of them, I guess you could say I've found my life's work, I've found my calling." Then he turned and went to notify his commanding officer that his fearless friend had shot his own head off.

Sometimes in Cambridge, as he lay in bed nights before falling asleep, with the spring breeze wafting in the open window or the gas heat roaring in winter, he would see that sad, mangled face again, and think of the horrendous crimes they had witnessed together, and how that witnessing had transformed them, leading one into the grave and himself on an unthinkable sojourn through darkness, with, as he saw it, wickedness all around. What they had seen and been compelled to participate in, even if only passively, negatively, by not being able to stop it, had changed them irrevocably and put normal human life far beyond their reach. His dead friend, or so Alderway thought as he studied the exploded face before his mind's eye on those nights before falling asleep, could not tolerate the loss of normal human life and had decided, Alderway mused, that without it, he would not live at all. But he, on the other hand, succumbed to the transformation, had accepted his fate, the unbroken darkness, solitude and struggle, until Ingrid had appeared, or rather, until he became aware of his feelings for her, and while they did not render his life "normal," they gave him solace, and if not light exactly, then a bit of twilight. And the irony was that she who brought this softness and tenderness into his life had none of that about her; she was all fire and fury, a human tornado—his Valkyrie.

So as he trudged through the lightly falling snow, he thought of her, as he always did, with a mixture of happiness, satisfaction and awe at his luck—luck in finding her and luck in recognizing his own emotions in time to act on them and not, as sometimes happened, a decade hence. The air was very still, like a breath suspended over a grave, the grave that was the past; through that stillness drifted the snow, glittering but not brightly, for the sun was nowhere to be seen, could not even be located in the generally luminous white and gray that was above and seemed also to have descended with the snow and enveloped the streets and buildings with its muffled wintery silence. But although it enveloped, it was also somehow clear and spread its transparent emptiness between the snowflakes, everywhere. "Oh," he exclaimed aloud, "but this is a day for Ingrid!" Then he slid back into brooding about Vietnam and slunk along, oblivious to the strange, pristine beauty of falling snow, as he revisited firefights in mephitic swamps, friends blown to bits by grenades, flame-throwers roasting enemy soldiers alive, jungle villages littered with corpses that sprawled in pools of blood and war crimes generally. His tall, strong form bent forward, hunched into his flannel shirt and leather coat, and he cursed aloud, forgetting Ingrid and where he was, thinking only of war. "It'll never end," he muttered. "Those bastards in Washington are up to their eyeballs in blood, and they'll never let it end."

He turned off the avenue and glanced up at the phone wires wriggling like black and silver eels beneath the gray ice of a frozen pond. He looked at many things, the pale, frame houses, the skeletal, snow-covered trees, the litter in the gutter, but he saw little. His eyes were turned toward the inner darkness and the memories of atrocities that lurked there. He could have been walking through a summer wood or on a tropical beach as easily as the sleet-covered town sidewalk—it would have made no difference to him, he was unaware of his surrounding and certainly unconcerned with the weather. And this attitude, this focus on the inner night was so common with him that sometimes he found himself surprised that he had even dressed properly at all, because he could not recall noting his environment long enough to adapt his attire. He had concluded that he did so automatically, that some very tiny corner of his brain routinely observed the world outside his inky interior and kept him prepared for it. Every time he found an umbrella in his hand on a rainy day, he was grateful for that persistent speck of observation, though he wondered often at the fact that it had not been engulfed by the fury of darkness.

When he arrived at Ingrid's, she took one look at him and said, "Snap out of it. You're on Magazine Street, not the Ho Chi Minh trail." She wore a red and green Japanese bathrobe and sported white slippers. Steam from the spout of the teapot in her hand wreathed around her long, straw-colored hair. She had scarcely glanced at him, as he entered the second floor kitchen. She was too busy. She was making tea.

Or so every detail of her reaction to him suggested. It was as if she would not yield an inch or tolerate for a moment his trancelike state. She had seen it before, and she didn't like it. She wanted him there, with her, at that moment, alert and present, not fixated on some inner struggle or the memory of a battle that had occurred years ago. "I mean it," she snapped again in some irritation, only glancing momentarily at him. "Wake up. You're here with me, Ingrid, in Massachusetts, the woman you plan to marry." She slammed the metal teapot down onto the burner—he still had not come back. "Is this what I have to look forward to when we decamp to the western part of the state?" She demanded.

His gaze swiveled outward and took her in. "I have some bad news," he said.

"Well, I'm glad you have some news and aren't just going to stand there transfixed by your gruesome memories. Welcome to 1970 in the USA, Alderway."

"Remember Tiwana's gun deal?"

"Uh-oh."

"It's this weekend."

"Great. That's just dandy. The mobsters will make mincemeat of you. Instead of a lover and husband, I'll get a corpse."

"Shhh," he put his hand on the back of her neck and ran his fingers through her hair. "Have a little faith in your old man. I've done worse than this before."

"And look at you: a psychological wreck."

"But this will be fun," he replied, his eyes glittering darkly.

"What if I told you Tiwana's a friend, and I'm on the same side as her revolutionary comrades."

"I'm not after her revolutionary comrades."

"So now you're after the mob?"

He nodded and smiled slightly.

"Have you lost your mind? They'll never forget it. They'll never let you—me—live in peace."

"They won't be able to do anything about us. The ones I don't put in jail will be dead."

"A little overconfident, aren't we?"

"Just extrapolating from past experience," and he grinned his toothy, carnivorous grin. "Don't worry. Come Sunday, there will be a dozen newly defunct gangsters no longer befouling the world we live in."

"I forbid it," she nearly shouted.

He laughed and continued laughing.

"If you go out to South Boston or wherever this deal takes place this weekend, you can forget about coming back here afterward. I refuse to live in terror that every time you go out the door, I'm seeing the last of you."

"You're serious?" He seemed truly astonished.

"I am."

Alderway cocked his head, as if sizing her up. "Then I guess I can't do it," he lied.

"Good," she removed the tea kettle and poured more water into her mug. The aroma of cinnamon and rose hips hung in the air between them. "Now tell me about this property near Amherst that you found."

During her infamous oatmeal and her more tolerable cinnamon tea, Jorge entered the kitchen, groggy from sleeping late, in his beige flannel pajama bottoms, and lifted the lid on the pot of cereal. He made a face.

"If you don't like it," she sipped her tea, "you can make yourself something else. You're a big, strong grown-up, perfectly capable of making toast or scrambled eggs."

Jorge frowned. "Are you saying if I was a toddler, you'd make toast for me?"

"If you were a toddler, you wouldn't be here."

His frown deepened. "We have an arrangement here. We rotate preparing breakfast. You're not supposed to make the same thing every day."

"Like the lady said," Alderway mildly remarked, "take it or leave it."

"You people!" Jorge growled, noisily pulling a skillet out of a cabinet.

"Hey, if you're making eggs," Tanya called form the next room, "make some for me too."

Jorge's scowl darkened, but he said nothing. Instead he cracked four eggs in a bowl. "You're lucky Tanya was asleep when you were discussing Tiwana's gun deal," he said quietly.

"Best forget what you overheard," the policeman advised.

"These are Italian and Irish mobsters she buys from," Jorge continued, his voice low. "They'll cut you into little pieces and put you out with the trash."

"He's not doing it, all right?" Ingrid rejoined loudly.

Jorge regarded her skeptically but said nothing. He resumed beating his four eggs with a fork.

"What are you three fighting about?" Tanya loomed groggily in the doorway, her pale, round face still held the calm of sleep and her long, dark, frizzy hair covered her shoulders and the entire top of her white terry cloth bathrobe.

"About who cooks what," Alderway replied. "Perhaps you'd like to relieve Jorge here of the chore of his scrambled eggs."

"No way," she giggled. "Cooking for me is good for him."

Grumbling, Jorge scrambled the eggs, and then he and his lady-love departed to her room to eat them.

Alderway reached across the little table and took his intended's hand. "Look at the snow," he nodded at the window next to the table. Both gazed out at the slowly drifting flakes and the strange, muted luminosity of the air.

"We can still go out to the country," she murmured.

"Of course, it'll be better than ever."

"I like days like this," she said absently.

"I know. You were made for them and they for you."

Her blue eyes sparkled, as she swiveled her gaze from the window to his face. "I have a surprise for you." She reached back to the shelf behind her and brought forth a small, brown-covered tome.

"More of your poems?"

She nodded. "Just published."

His eyes glittered. "Are they as…as…violent as the last ones?"

She tossed her head, and her long hair shone palely in the reflected light of falling snow. "I guess you could say that," she replied, "maybe more so."

Alderway reached over and took the volume, then grinned toothily. "I'll read them with pleasure and, no doubt, admiration." He opened the book, perused a few pages, shut it and glanced across at her. She took his hands again. "Let's drive through the snow to western Massachusetts and look over this 'wooded lot' where you want to build a house. I know nothing about building a house."

"Then I'll teach you."

She nodded, then they rose, went down to her room, and since she had to dress, he could not resist, and some time was spent in love making before they tromped out into the snow, then into the warm, cozy, overheated interior of Ingrid's little red, snow-covered VW Bug that she drove west, into the swirling snow.

A few nights later, a black Saab, sleek because it had been washed that afternoon, pulled up in front of the darkened house on Bay Street, Shola at the wheel. He sat quietly in the car, which blent into the blackness of the street and the night sky, offset by the coldly glittering stars above and the snow along the broken brick sidewalk. All was silent, still; only a rare yellow light shone from a house window. Shola had the heat on, but, still cold, he hunched down into his warm, thick black coat and pulled the black ski cap over his ears. He glanced through the window up into the inky vastness of the heaven, at the stars of the Milky Way, scattered like ice crystals on a black velvet cloth and thought that he might die that night.

"Not without a fight," he said aloud and then tried to soothe himself with the thought that the arms dealers had just as much of an interest in a peaceable transaction as he did. But they were white, and bigots to boot, and he was black, so the odds of an uncomplicated exchange decreased. He glanced over across the barren little unkempt yard, with its low, sagging wire fence, at the shrouded, two-story house. "Step on it, Alderway," he murmured and lit a cigarette.

He rolled the window down a crack; wisps of smoke drifted out and up into the painfully clear, cold air. All was as still and quiet as a graveyard. Not a leaf stirred, and everywhere the snow glittered with bitter, clean brightness.

The house door creaked, then footsteps crunched on snow across the dismal yard. The policeman opened the passenger door and slid into the seat beside him.

"I hope you're discreetly armed," Shola said, without any other greeting.

"O, very discreetly," he replied, and in the gloom Shola could see the brilliant white of his predatory grin.

The car slid out of the parking space and glided up through the gloom towards Massachusetts Avenue. Shola drove in silence, and his passenger sat without speaking in the shadows. The car's heater rattled a bit, and over that noise Alderway finally said: "you wait in the car, while I make the purchase."

"Fine with me," Shola replied. "I'd rather not see their ugly faces, if I can help it."

Eventually they wended their way into Boston and found a back street lined by warehouses. Shola pulled the Saab up to a ramp, stopped it, then reached in back and hauled forth a canvas sack, which he gave to his passenger. "Try not to get killed," he said.

"Oh, I'm good at that," the police spy replied.

He was ushered into a large, dimly lit room, filled with crates, some tables and four scarred and burly men. One drew forth a machine gun from an already opened box and indicated that Alderway could test it on the far wall. At that moment a fifth, hulking thug entered the room. "I know him," the man yelled, "He's an undercover cop!" Two of the arms dealers took aim at their buyer, but he shot them first. They fell and lay in rapidly growing pools of blood that spread and merged beneath them like a fatally expanding, sinister sunset. Two others tried to flee, and Alderway's bullets hit their legs. Crippled, they hit the floor, howling. The last man, the one who had identified him, stood with his hands up, as Shola, alarmed by the gunfire, entered the room with his own hand gun drawn.

"Put it down," Alderway said. "You're under arrest."

Shola shot him and was shot in return. As they slumped over the tables hollering in pain, Shola angrily accused him: "You were after us all along."

"No, after them."

In the distance, the sirens' wail approached.

"You're my witness," Alderway concluded.

"What if I don't wanna be?"

"Too bad. You shot me. Why'd you have to go and shoot me? Now I'll have to kill you if you won't testify." He pointed the machine gun at his erstwhile driver, who gazed back in wonder.

"You are really crazy," Shola began.

"And you're taking the stand."

"All right, all right, point it at that scumbag over there, before he gets away."

By the time the police arrived and radioed for an ambulance, six stretchers were required. Two carried corpses.

"You're an idiot, Alderway," one of the policemen said.

"Yeah," he replied. "My girlfriend's gonna kill me."

"You're an idiot," Ingrid said, as he awoke from surgery in his hospital bed. Wan dawn light streaked into the room, lighting her pale angry face and straw-colored hair.

"But I'm a lucky idiot," he replied.

"Not so lucky. You could have died."

"Lucky," he repeated and reached for her hand. "I have you."

She withdrew hers and scowled at him. "You lied to me."

"Not exactly."

"Exactly," she paused to gaze out the window at the watery light touching the sides of grimy buildings.

"I didn't want to lose you," he said simply.

"Oh, but it's okay for me to lose you. You quit this job, or I'm gone."

"What am I supposed to live on?"

"I'll support you, until you find something else. I'll kick Buzz out. I can't stand him anyway. His compulsive law-breaking gets on my nerves. You can have the room in the basement back, rent free."

A glimmer appeared in Alderway's dark eyes. "If I quit, will you stop postponing marriage and live up to your promise?"

"When?"

"When? Now. Here in the hospital."

"You want to marry me in your hospital bed?"

He nodded. "I won't quit without your word, because I don't believe you really can bring yourself to get married."

Ingrid tossed her head haughtily. "Then one of our vows will be 'no more lies.'"

"No more lies," he agreed, and she took his hand.

"I guess since you're incapacitated, I'll have to buy the ring," she said. "But that's okay. That way I'll be sure to get something I like."

Alderway smiled. "That's my girl."

"Woman," she corrected.

III

Chicago

Jack Diamond emptied another bottle of cheap vodka into the fruit punch vat. He did so methodically, with a serious expression, apparently oblivious to the hippie antics going on around him in the dingy apartment of a fellow chemistry student at Fifty Fourth and University. He had been helping prepare for this Friday night bash all afternoon. He had brought over his LP collection of Chicago blues, Motown and soul. He had purchased the vodka and other spirits. He had accepted a joint from one of the long-haired students, who capered into the under-furnished living room and sampled the punch, then sent the fellow out to Ribs and More Ribs to buy a sufficient supply for the early arrivals. He had even arranged for Snow's babysitter that night. Yes, everything was in order, and he could get utterly blasted.

"Damn," he muttered after tasting the punch. "We need more vodka." He donned his coat and addressed the student hippies lounging on the crippled living room couch and the chairs. "I'm going out. Anyone who drops acid in this punch, I will personally strangle you. Got that?" The little conclave nodded and grumbled assent. "I mean it," he continued. "I will beat the crap out of you. We have plenty of straight guests tonight, including more than one assistant professor. And the head of SDS intends to be organizing, not tripping. So don't get any funny ideas. Or do I need to kick you all out?"

"You can't," one of them replied. "It's Adam's apartment, not yours."

"Adam!" Jack hollered. Said young man appeared, his long hair down to his shoulders, his patched blue jeans a rainbow of contrasting fabrics. "I told these idiots that if they spike this punch with hallucinogens, I'll either kill them or beat them to a bloody pulp. Agreed?"

The host nodded.

"Now I'm going to the liquor store. You guard the punch. If they try anything, throw the bums out."

He pulled on his ski cap and gloves and ventured forth into the bitterly cold January twilight. University Avenue was deserted, the piles of snow between the parked cars covered with a frozen film of dirt and grit. Jack paid close attention to his surroundings—to the doorways and vestibules he passed, the sidewalk before and behind him, because he did not intend to get mugged and carried his gun in his pocket to make sure of it. His friend Ishmael, who, with a grizzled afro and a gun tucked into his belt, was the owner of the liquor store on Fifty Third Street, regaled him with a tale of violence and gore.

"So last night Little Ricky was behind the counter. I was in back. I hear these sons of bitches sticking the place up, two of them. I don't wait," the owner pulled forth his shotgun from under the counter. "I had this with me. At night I keep it with me wherever I go. I just shoot the first one in the throat—bam! His blood spills out all over the counter. I say, 'Die you bastard. Choke in your own blood.' The other one, he don't move. I got the gun on him. He starts hollerin' 'don't kill me, mister.' I say, 'why not?' He has no answer. Little Ricky calls the police. While he's on the phone, the second robber tries to run, see? So I take pity on him and shoot him in the leg. The cops, they'll give me an award: more hold-ups than any liquor store on the entire South Side and more dead robbers. But I tell you Jack, it's bad for business. The customers—they scared I might shoot 'em if they look at me funny, and the thing is, after you been robbed more 'n a few times, it's possible. It's distinctly possible you might shoot the wrong person."

"Well, that's one less cockroach to worry about."

"Two. The other will be up in prison a long time. He's got a record as long as my arm. And you better believe I'll testify against him."

Little Ricky came out of the back, dazzling in an orange dashiki and large afro. "You shoulda heard what he said to the one he shot."

"I told him to choke in his own blood," the furious liquor-store owner repeated. "And he did. He choked on it and died in his own blood right there," Ishmael tapped the counter with the end of his shotgun. "I had to clean it up with ammonia afterwards. What a mess."

"A lot of good it does," Jack remarked, reaching for the vodka in the brown paper bag. "There's a hundred more where he came from."

"And I'm ready for 'em," the man replied. "I killed nearly a dozen so far, I'll be happy to blow the brains out of a few more. It don't bother me. Vermin is what they are. People can't even walk down Fifty Third Street at night. They live in terror. Drug addicts with their guns, gangs with their guns, they scared all the decent people away. I say you gotta fight back. A man's gotta fight back. I don't know what a woman should do—hell, move someplace else."

The young man left the liquor store, thinking of a robber, his throat blasted open, dying in a pool of blood on the counter. On Fifty Third Street the wind smacked him in the face like a boxer who had been waiting to throw his meanest punch. He huddled into his coat, turned up the collar, pulled down his ski cap. His nose and mouth felt frozen, his cheeks like little sheets of ice. "Why do I live in this inhospitable place, as cold as the arctic, filled with murderers and thieves?" He asked himself. By the time he turned left on University, he was dreaming of lying on a tropical beach with Naomi and her son, then he decided maybe her son could stay with a babysitter, and he would lie there only with her. The sidewalk was dark and deserted. He did not like it, so he did what his women friends did in these circumstances—walked down the middle of the street. There were no cars, and besides, the danger of getting run over was much less than that of getting assaulted. The street lamps guided him back to the building with the party.

Inside he spotted the full red mane of curls of Betsy Ein over in a corner; she was conversing animatedly with an intense young black revolutionary, whom he knew by reputation. Her Indian print dress hung to the middle of her calves, revealing high boots, while her companion's jeans, black turtleneck and small wire-rimmed spectacles made him look like a beatnik. After dispensing the vodka into the punch, Jack helped himself to a large cup and ambled over.

"Jack Diamond, meet Jeremiah Allenhurst, of whom everyone in Chicago has heard. We were just discussing guns—of which I usually disapprove. But I think you and Jeremiah have something in common."

"Allenhurst—pleased to meet you. I've heard your name somewhere recently."

"Probably my wife," the quiet, serious revolutionary replied, shaking Jack's hand. "The celebrated gun bust in Boston. She's a witness against the mob."

"Well, that'll certainly make your life more interesting."

"No kidding. I bought another shotgun just today. So what brings you here? You don't look like a hippie."

"I'm not, but," the chemistry student finished his punch, considerably more relaxed and comfortable than when he had left the liquor store, "I share some of the ethos, the ability to detect fascism in all its guises and the aversion to it. I just respond differently. Instead of smoking pot, I load my twenty two."

"You both are out of your minds," Betsy remarked, "and probably headed to jail."

"Already released from there," Jeremiah replied. "The police nearly killed me, as you know. Besides, I seem to recall you taking quite a different line at a political meeting out on Garfield Boulevard just a few months back."

"That was different. What about a more peaceable line of work?" She persisted. "Non-violent community organizer? Intellectual or artist? Jazz musician? Something other than violent revolutionary."

"I don't believe the woman who lives with Shane Richards, the most fanatical Marxist I ever met, is giving me such advice," Jack laughed. Everything had taken on an agreeable fluidity and looseness. The muted lights concealing the apartment's dismal appointments, the crowd, the aroma of ribs from the kitchen mingling with sweat, incense, and perfume from the dancers, all soothed and uplifted him, filled him with delightful, unexpected wishes—a long midnight tramp through the snowbound city, or drinking himself into oblivion, or getting his car and Naomi and driving west, west, beyond the vast, dark apartment blocks, the wide urban periphery of small houses with low wire fences and flat silent avenues, dozy in the gloom, past the suburbs into the flat frozen brown and white stubble of cornfields to gaze up at the glittering constellations, with their hints of inconceivable distances, vastness and eternity. His mind wandered from one vision to the next and settled on alcohol-induced oblivion. Anything else involved exposure to the cold, and above all, he did not want to leave the interior warmth, the union with people swaying in semi-darkness, the music, the fragrance of life, of his friends, girlfriend and people he had yet to meet.

Such commonality was a rare feeling for him. Generally aloof, cool and sardonic, he kept to himself and was given to anatomizing his acquaintances in scientific detachment, after the manner of his chemistry training. There was little that was warm or inviting about him. Rarely did he seem relaxed around others; excepting Snow—with that toddler he was uninhibited and playful, "a different person," his girlfriend had observed. Even with the boy's mother he remained a bit guarded. "You don't give anybody an inch," she complained.

"Why should I?" He invariably replied.

So Jack was not gregarious. He spent much time at his job alone in the anatomy lab, where he was employed tending pale, cold cadavers and passed the long, empty, tedious hours writing letters to his three brothers, Harry, Ethan and Tom. Harry had stayed in Wichita, where they had all grown up, and ran a car dealership—the very same one their father, a car salesman, had abandoned years earlier for the life of a carney and a tramp. This brother supported Janice, their mother, and was known on occasion to seek solace from the dreary windswept loneliness of the Kansas plain in drink. Ethan was in Da Nang. He had shot his way through the jungles of

Vietnam, killing, in his words "more Viet Cong than I can count. And a sorry accomplishment it is." Tom, a hippie, resided on the beach in La Jolla, California, receiving his brothers' many missives and other mail care of a friend, who owned a head shop in San Diego. Jack urged him to find a job, apartment and woman—someone who could stabilize him, keep him off drugs and prevent him from sleeping in the street. The feckless youngest thought this was funny, but appreciated the fraternal solicitude.

His brothers wrote regularly, but Harry the most. "HiyaJack," he would begin every epistle. "So get this, the latest moron I hired goes and sells a Chevy Impala for half, get this, half the price I told him. And the sticker was on the car! You would not believe how many imbeciles there are in this world. And every one of them thinks he can be a car salesman. Kinda like Dad, though not too many are in the same, first-class loser league as him. What a lousy car salesman he was—and you know I don't say that lightly, since it was always me defending him against you. But Jones told me the other day, if Dad hadn't quit and run off, he would have been fired. So it's official. The guy couldn't hold down any job. Remember when he was security at that office building downtown? The night watchman, he called it. The only thing he watched was the TV, while those burglars robbed the place of every valuable and every stick of furniture. It was just one more firing for him, one more job in an endless string of jobs. You'd have thought he could have kept one of them. I don't know how Mom put up with it. Speaking of which, she's not doing too well…" No, Mrs. Diamond was never doing too well. She had been peaky, on and off, ever since she married Sven Diamond, and Jack secretly suspected the marriage as the cause. What, he wondered, could life have been like for the young, frequently pregnant wife of such a pathologically disorganized wastrel? How she had been snookered into this union and why she had remained in it were unsolvable mysteries to him. When, as a young man, he asked her, she waved a pallid hand lethargically and said, "Oh, there was something very attractive about him. In some way he was really charismatic." What that way was, Jack could not begin to imagine. There was nothing even remotely charismatic about the tall but stooped, shuffling, slovenly mess that was the memory of his father. His sparse, straw-colored hair, his red-rimmed eyes, always misty, never focused, with never so much as a glimmer of intelligence in them, the frequent odor of alcohol on his breath, the spittle at the corners of his mouth when he spoke, the jutting Adam's apple, the halting, meandering speech—all composed what he found to be a most repulsive figure, hardly what he thought of as a man. No—what kind of man ran off and left his wife to shift for herself with four boys? That was no man! That wasn't even a mouse. "That," he wrote Harry, "was a low-life, a louse, a selfish idiot."

Yes, he, Harry and Ethan saw more or less eye to eye about old Sven, but all three hesitated to mention their view to Tom, who seemed so ominously to follow in his broken-down father's footsteps. He even shuffled like his luckless progenitor, dragged his feet and lurched sloppily about. Jack found the similarity bone-chilling. The thought that his shiftless parent had managed to replicate his repugnant ways struck him with fear for his hapless baby brother, who, at least, had finished high school. That was more than could be said for his father.

Not that Tom liked or was remotely drawn to their father. No, he was as absolute in his disapproval as the other three, often remarking that the old man had ruined his childhood and that his dissolution had destroyed their mother, who had aged so rapidly after her husband's shambling, desperate departure over a horizon of shattered hopes, abandoned promises and love pulverized into graveyard dust. Her luxuriant light brown hair turned gray, lines appeared on her forehead and stretched from her nose to the corners of her mouth. Her skin became pasty and her body frail. Sometimes, Tom said, he feared the winter Wichita wind would blow her right down the street, she was so slight and birdlike. Though ultimately it was Harry who took responsibility, Tom had been closest to her, and she had doted on him. She always inquired about him: "He's not still living on the street like his father, is he?"

"No Mom," Harry would lie, taking packages of food to the fridge on his twice weekly visit. "He's got a swell place in San Diego," he fabricated. "Lots of sun, fresh air and a view of the beach."

"Well then, let's visit."

"We can't afford to."

"You make good money at your car dealership."

"Not that good. I got you to support, too. Remember? And I send Tom money and then there are my loans to Jack for his tuition. I got too many bills, Ma, to go off gallivanting on some vacation to San Diego."

Then she would commence wheedling. Why couldn't Tom send the money, if he could afford such a swank apartment? Or even Ethan, who had not spent one dime of his military pay. Exasperated, her son, who had looked forward all day to leaving work to visit her, to the chimera that this time it would be different, would make excuses and leave early.

Harry took good care of his mother, partly because he was the oldest and thus regarded it as his responsibility. And then, at twenty six, with no college education, he was, in his view, a wildly successful businessman. After all—his own car dealership! Luck was with him. He had escaped the draft, sold hundreds of cars and worked his way up in record time. He could afford to support the little old lady, prematurely ancient, addled and lonely in her two-story house, whom he would always find in the small living room, in pants and a pullover, her hair up in pink curlers, watching a soap opera and smoking. Sometimes she mixed up the characters from the TV show with people in real life, and the constant, damp wheeze of her smoker's cough brought to his mind hospital beds and hospital halls and the short trip from them to the mortuary. "When Tom gets back," she would begin many a sentence, not noticing that her oldest son invariably winced at this mention of the prodigal's unlikely return. On Jack's occasional visits it was the same: the cramped living quarters, saturated with the odor of cigarette smoke, the same unhealthy, pasty complexion, the watery, wandering eyes that seemed only to ask, "where did everybody go?" and then the inevitable "when Tom gets back…" The second son would glance at Harry, who would put a finger to his lip for silence and then say: "he'll be home before you know it, Ma."

When Jack thought of his mother, this was always how he pictured her: seated before the gray glow of the television in her living room, barely big enough for the couch and two chairs, stale with the tobacco odor, her gray hair up in curlers, and the vacant, glazedly hypnotized look in her dim eyes. It was, to him, as if she had no other life. He could not imagine her driving her rather battered Chevy or pushing a cart down the aisles of a supermarket. Once Harry told him she had visited a branch of the public library, and Jack was surprised to find himself incapable of picturing that small, defeated form perusing a book. She mostly read *The National Enquirer* and other tabloids about celebrities. No, he could not conceive of her reading a book. It would be like trying to imagine his broken father in a suit—impossible.

It had not always been thus. From childhood, Jack recalled a handsome, tall paternal form, with a shock of thick blond hair and his slender, petite and darkly beautiful wife—that is, before she dyed her hair blond. Sven was an outdoorsman. They vacationed in Wisconsin, where he boated, swam and hunted. Perhaps that was why, after the disaster, he took to the wild—sleeping in brown, stubbled fields or between high green corn rows and tramping on the highways during the day. Even as a hobo he loved the solitude of woods, the quiet of a lonely lakeside, the utter isolation of the Rockies. Jumping trains, he would gaze out the door of a cattle car at the deep green beauties of northern forests and, as the wheels slowed, would jump out, literally in the middle of nowhere and ramble for days through uninhabited lands. Unlike many of his wandering brethren, he planned for the future, in that he packed a sack of rice, a water jug, tin bowl and cigarette lighter. Yes, he would say to himself, "I come prepared." In the depths of a Montana winter, he would seek out a town and get himself arrested for vagrancy, because life in a jail cell was warm and well-fed. But the rest of the year, he was on the road, or the rails, sojourning from nowhere to nowhere, aimlessly on the move, without plans and without the slightest thought for his wife and four sons in Wichita. His goal was to forget. And the longer he wandered, the better he stifled the insistent promptings of unwanted remembrance and remorse.

Before these peregrinations, he had been the strong, towering father of Jack's earliest memory, always in the company of his beloved, equally huge and handsome younger brother, Eric. They had been competitors for Janice, but no hard feelings accompanied Sven's success. For a while they worked together at a trucking company, making good enough money for Sven to buy the small frame house for his growing family and brother. Then they left the trucking company and became car salesmen, around which time things began to sour. Eric always drank, but had a system capacious enough to absorb large quantities of alcohol without visible effect; even after much beer and hard liquor, he could still hammer together a table or upholster a chair. He had always made furniture in his spare time, much of it exceptional, which he sold to a list of clients he had developed over the years—individuals, stores and an outlet for local cabinet-makers. In good weather, the three boys and their toddler baby brother crowded onto the back step to watch their uncle work. A cigarette dangling from the corner of his mouth, the taciturn giant sawed, sanded, hammered and polished for hours on end.

He had a hard, angular face, blue eyes that pierced like a laser and large, very white teeth. Like his brother, he had the hale look of one given to much activity—with no noticeable defect to detract from his appearance; all of those were internal. Both had very straight, rather prominent noses, bushy blond eyebrows and stubborn, strong jaws that betokened a tendency to hold grudges for years and to take offense quickly. They usually stared at an interlocutor for a long time before coming forth with a rejoinder, as if weighing the heft of an adversary, which was perhaps a holdover from the boxing and wrestling they had done in high school and continued to do, in the back yard, for years afterward, with the four boys as audience. Eric was bigger, but Sven was faster and cleverer, so the matches dragged on, to the delight of the four young males perched on the back fence, pumping their fists in the air and hollering: "Don't stop! Give it to him!" And other such words of encouragement.

Aside from size, speed and Sven's superior stealth, the only visible differences between them were the young father's slate colored eyes, like flagstones on a dark day after rain, and a certain scarcely noticeable unevenness to his jaw that, though slight, gave an impression of crookedness that contrasted with his brother's massive, balanced angularity. Otherwise they could have been twins, not mere brothers, and in fact were as close as twins, whose characters only imperceptibly diverged. Eric drank, but so did his brother, just more sociably—starting at dinner and on into the evening. The problem was, Eric started taking a flask to work and then his brother had to cover up for him, which he did, affably enough, in the beginning.

In the evenings Eric frequented Wichita's bars, sometimes in his brother's company. He could be seen, as the shadows lengthened, skulking along some dilapidated side street, until he arrived at a little blue blinking neon sign and turned in for his whisky. He was a sullen drunk. Hunched over the bar, poking at the ice cubes in his hard liquor, his hulking form as big as a bear, he would, from time to time, comment acerbically on life or curse softly under his breath. A dark current of misery flowed through his soul and swelled, with enough booze, into a plunging cataract. He never became maudlin, only wretched. "It's a bad joke, a cheap, lousy joke, this life of ours," he remarked one night to the assembled Diamond family, as he returned from his alcoholic roamings. "It don't make me laugh, though," he concluded, lurching unsteadily toward his room in the back, off the kitchen. The golden stubble on his cheeks and chin, suggestive of a laxity about personal hygiene, his unfocussed eyes, the reek of rye whiskey—all seemed to confirm his dour conclusion: "It makes me sick, just plain sick."

Years passed, and the uncle in the back room rose late, fighting off hangovers. At work, Sven had convinced the powers that be that his brother had an incurable, chronic medical condition that prevented his timely arrival. No matter, the manager said, he sold enough cars; though in point of fact, he did not. His brother stealthily steered customers his way, the ones who were sure to buy, and thus inflated his sales numbers.

This steady imbibing was only interrupted by moonlighting as a grave-digger. His brother turned up his nose at this manual labor, but Eric chortled over the good pay and said he did not mind a little grime under his nails. What he failed to mention and perhaps, his nephew thought, could not articulate, was his affinity for the quiet, the endings, the final, fatal frustration of all that would torment people in life, the defiant unlikely persistence of that human life, even among the graves—the boys, the men digging—and the sharp, macabre humor of the laborers that glinted and glanced among the tombs, beneath the deathly hush, like guerrilla warfare. Afternoons off from the car dealership, he would take two of the boys over to the cemetery where they would pass what were, for Jack, the happiest times of his childhood, skipping homework and jumping on tombstones instead, while his uncle and his buddies shoveled pits for soon to be interred coffins. He adored Eric, who always brought Janice a fresh bouquet for the dining room table, straight from the graveyard. Oddly, she never inquired as to its origins, always assuming it came from a florist. "You don't tell your mother," he would admonish the boys, "she won't want flowers offa no grave, so just keep your traps shut and hurry up. Pick me out some white roses." Thrilled, the boys would leapfrog over the headstones in search of blossoms, while their uncle leaned up against a marble memorial and chain-smoked. "I like the graveyard," he said to them. "The dead are real polite. They don't talk back to you. You can say anything you want to them and all they reply with is blessed silence. Now there's something to think about. The peace and quiet of oblivion." He would exhale a dirty brownish cloud of smoke that dissolved in the afternoon air and blent with the yellow and brown of the dying, under-watered grass on the graves. Everywhere the wind rasped its dry breath of nothing in the leaves and the tall man would rasp back at it hoarsely, through the dryness and the nothing, "Go on, I don't care." Occasionally in summer a sprinkler would hydrate the paths, but Eric made a point of shutting them off with the words: "The dead don't like the wet. Bad enough they endure snow and rain. They don't need no goddamn sprinklers. Who in their right mind wants their eternal rest to be damp? Now I ask you." From time to time he would pull his red bandana out of his pocket and dust the top of a tombstone or polish the lettering. "I take good care of these old, dead souls," he would explain.

He befriended the other grave-diggers, and for a while spoke loudly and in an out of kilter manner about unionizing them. They would sit on the shriveled grass, their backs to an old crypt and pass around a bottle, while they played marbles or cards. The sun beams shot through the leaves and branches above, lending their grizzled, light-dappled faces an incongruous peace; for they were anything but peaceful. When not working their two or three jobs, they were rowdy drunks, who sometimes showed up at the back door, stinking of booze and hollering for Eric. Early on, one of them was killed in a knife fight outside a bar in the most run-down district of Wichita. "No one knowed who kilt him," the uncle explained over dinner at the house one night. "But we suspect Eddie," one of the other grave-diggers, "cause he owed him money, and Eddie's real mean about money." This news prompted Janice to ban his companions from the house and yard. Her husband agreed, and thus were the seeds of dissension sown. Somehow the mother's ukase did not extend to preventing the boys from sojourning to the cemetery and there assisting their uncle. In summer they would still play hide and seek behind the headstones or join in when the older men brought out the marbles or listen to tales of other kinds of work, for instance in a hog butchering plant not far out of town. It was when Harry returned home one afternoon, regaling his mother with the gory details of hog slaughter, of animals trapped and bound, shrieking in terror, and men up to their elbows in blood, that she finally prohibited the graveside pow-wows; but the boys never heeded her for an instant, nor did their uncle. He even went so far one fine summer day as to have Jack jump into a grave on top of some pauper's pine coffin to retrieve an unexpectedly fine bouquet that had fallen in. Jack bragged about this escapade at home and at school for days. Though his mother must have heard it, she said nothing.

Their uncle continued to work at the dealership. As a result of his two jobs, he always had money—a few coins to send Jack to the corner store for newspapers and gum, a quarter for Harry to buy him a soda, nickels for Ethan and baby Tom, so they could feel rich. He would sit out on the back step, enjoying the sun on his face, ignoring his sister-in-law's exhortations to clean up the wood shavings and sawdust and admitting, when accused by her, that yes, indeed, he was nothing but a wastrel. "I guess you picked the right brother to marry," he would conclude from time to time.

"I guess I did," she would reply, with a sureness that was mostly bravado, as, in her mind and some alarm, she contemplated the already shambling form of her husband, as he lurched around the house Saturday morning, having slept until eleven.

Then, as she turned away, her brother-in-law's lips would set in a thin, pale line of reconfirmed discontent and he would flick the ash off his cigarette and toy with the buttons on his worn, blue cotton shirt.

"They tried to overcharge me on that lumber I wanted to buy yesterday," he explained one such morning to Harry and Jack. "But they learned their lesson. Nobody overcharges me, me or my brother. I made like I was walking out, and they dropped the price, forty percent. That's called bargaining, boys. Now all I got to do is slap together this dresser for the Harstons, and I come out way ahead. That's cause I got bizness sense," and he tapped his temple at the edge of the shock of thick, straight blond hair, with his nicotine-stained fingers, the cigarette still clenched firmly between them.

One August afternoon, just back from the barber with a clean crew cut that accentuated the razor sharp line of his eyes perpendicular to his straight nose, the uncle, assigned the task of babysitter, took all four boys to a local tavern where they amused themselves at the pool table, while he watched golf on the TV, wedged up in a corner, and downed numerous beers. He had betted on games all winter, spring and summer and lost steadily, so now he cast a critical eye upon the golfers on the luminous screen, suspended in the gloom like phosphorescence on a dark ocean and cursed softly. "That's one game I ain't betting on," he said and gestured at the TV with his glass of beer.

"Bores me to tears, personally," the bartender averred.

"A rich man's game," Eric continued, now slurping his beverage, his eyebrows contracted angrily above his nose. "You gotta have a Lacoste shirt to play that."

"Gotta have more than that," the bartender chuckled.

"Start with a German car."

"Not those rambling old Cadillacs you sell."

"Hey they're new."

"But they ain't Mercedes.'

"Give me a GM engine any day," Eric finished his beer. "Something I know how to fix when it's got trouble. Nobody makes a engine like GM."

"You driving your brother's family up to Wisconsin in that Oldsmobile?"

"Sure. I do it every summer. He and Janice take the Chevy. I take the brats. They're good kids."

"Them kid's trouble."

"Not like some."

"Sure enough. Sven know you bet his Chevy?"

"I'll tell him by and by."

"And you better haul yourself outta town by and by, too."

"Chevy's in my name."

"Name only—he paid for it."

"He'll understand. Another beer. Put it on Sven's tab."

By now Tom was dancing on the pool table.

"Get that brat offa the felt," the bartender pointed at the boy with an empty beer bottle.

Their uncle turned. One angry stare was enough for Tom, who clambered back to the floor.

"See," guzzle, guzzle. "They mind."

"I just hope they ain't dancing on the tombs in the crypts, when you take them out to the graveyard."

"No one's going to sue."

"Don't be too sure. They're getting a reputation. The little graveyard demons, that's what your co-worker Hal calls 'em. Says one of 'em jumped right into an open grave the other day, right on top of a coffin."

"Some flowers fell in."

"Still, you can't have them brats dancing on the dead. It ain't right."

"You're brain ain't right. They're dead, aren't they? What do they know or care?"

"Their relatives might know or care."

"I ain't seen one yet that did," guzzle, guzzle. "All they think about is getting back to business and making a buck. I'm the only one cares for the dead. I bury 'em properly, dust off the cross or the stone and, if I don't need 'em for Janice, I make sure the flowers are set just right. Not one relation ever hung around to help me. I do it from the kindness of my heart."

As his constant betting suggested, Eric was always on the lookout for a get-rich-quick scheme, each more pathetic in its utter lack of imagination than the last—from encyclopedia salesman to correspondence school test grader, each occupation was more notable than the last for the utter improbability that it would make him rich; each was more of a dead end than the last, each gave off a more powerful whiff of poverty and desperation than the last. The wastrel was, as he confided to his bartenders, going nowhere fast, digging a huge pit that he had come to suspect was his own grave, and the less likely it became that he would ever strike it rich—a opposed to being able to show off to his nephews with a few quarters—the more he drank. "He's figured something out," he would say to Harry or Jack when some particularly posh car glided past, its occupants swaddled in expensive attire, "something that escapes me. I keep grabbing at it, but it keeps jumpin' away." This was true enough. He had no head for business and not a crafty bone in his body. He was, in his brother's words, a loser.

Every minute of every day, when not in a bar, the grave-digger, in his thoughtless, clumsy, ill-planned way pursued the dollar. And periodically he was flush. He sold cars, furniture and dug deep in the cemetery. He worked as a security guard in an office building downtown. He drove a cab, a bus. He part-owned an automobile repair shop, until it went bankrupt. He worked for a farmer, way outside town in summer and fall. He bet money on every sporting event conceivable. He delivered newspapers until he could not stand the early rising and gave his route to Harry. He was a short order cook and a terrible one. He labored as a local handyman, assisting neighborhood housewives. But for all this bustle, he had surprisingly little to show for it. He was a man in quicksand, whose frantic efforts to escape only brought him deeper into the bottomless swirl of destitution.

The summer he bet and lost his brother's car, Sven only learned of this profligate transaction on the sweltering, dry, dusty day before the family packed and piled into both vehicles for a week in the riverside Wisconsin cabin. Sven drove the Chevy in a silent fury that his brother was unable to appreciate, being ensconced in the boisterous madness of the Oldsmobile crammed with the four noisy boys. Harry and Ethan played a game that involved identifying the make and model of passing cars at the tops of their lungs, while Jack noisily kept tabs on out-of-state license plates, rapturously singing them out as if they were saints encountered on the way to heaven. Four-year-old Tommy snoozed against the car door, a steady flow of warm drool leaking out the corner of his half open mouth, or, frequently, woke and yelled. It was hot and flat, and there was nothing to look at but cornfields in every direction.

"Corn-fed yokels, that's who we live amongst," their uncle snarled at the countryside. "I'm a city boy, a sophisticated urbanite from Wichita, not one of your rubes from Podunk. This is pathetic." And sputtering through a monologue suffused with resentment, rage and contempt for all bumpkins, he floored the accelerator and sped past the silent, swaying stalks of a nearly tropical greenery, the temperature close to one hundred degrees, the car windows all rolled own, heat blasting in like a furnace, three or four boys whooping and hollering, the only other signs of human life the occasional pickup on the roadside, the farmer standing nearby in his hat and denim overalls, a cigarette at the corner of his mouth, oblivious to the rare highway traffic and to the curses, heaped on his head because of his pickup, cornfields, tractor, barn, the brown grit under his nails, not so very different from a gravedigger's grit, his gray grizzled cheeks and his squint, blithely unaware, which only added to the fury and abuse streaming from the lips, along with cigarette smoke of an outraged Eric Diamond.

Behind him, always keeping pace and always tracked through the rearview mirror, rumbled the Chevy, object of the previous evening's bitter contention.

"You didn't have to bet the damn car, you moron!"

"It's mine to do with as I please."

"I paid you back for it."

"Not with interest."

"Interest!"

"Besides, don't worry about vacation. They ain't gonna come for the car till Friday. By then we'll be fishing in Wisconsin."

"Yeah, and that white trash you pal around with'll burn down the house, if they can't get the car."

"Hmm."

"Didn't think of that, did you, smartass?"

"I'll call 'em and tell 'em we're going out of town, and they can have it in two weeks."

"Then how in God's name am I sposed to get to work?"

"I'll drive you in the Olds."

"Maybe I don't want to carpool with you."

"Then take the bus. One stops at the corner. It ain't far. Or, is that too much walkin' for you?"

"I'll take the Olds—you walk to work, genius."

"I don't like that arrangement."

"Well, you can shove it you know where. You're the one lost the damn car."

Eric had no answer to that, being congenitally incapable of gainsaying the truth. That much could be said for him: he was no liar. Deceit, on the spot, was simply impossible for him, as was its chief wile, a facile tongue, but now, after the dispute, imagination supplied the artifice he had previously lacked, so that, from time to time, he pounded a huge palm against the steering wheel and shouted, "*That's* what I shoulda said!" So he drove along, angry, and every time he pictured himself squeezed between other commuters on the bus to work, he slammed on the accelerator and cursed with the wrath on one who has gambled, lost and determined to blame another.

The days at the cabin stretched out long and tense, as the two brothers drank and quarreled or, alternately, steamed the small abode with the hot, deliberate silence of animosity and unspoken accusation, the most wounding of which, implied in every exchange, in every furious turn of the back, was that Sven somehow fell short in fraternal generosity and love, that he was a crimped and miserly soul, who had lost sight of the big things in life, and in fact his curses, his shrugs all conveyed just that nasty skepticism that maybe those big things really did not matter as much as the price of a car. "You ain't worth that Chevy," his sarcasms and sardonic remarks all implied. As this message seeped deeper into his brother's consciousness, he responded with accusing glares, but more and more a dumb helplessness that had, as its only outlet, booze and the unconsciousness of many alcohol-induced stupors passed sprawled and snoring thunderously, like some immense, drowsing Norse god, on the rickety, wood-framed couch.

Then, unable to endure the sultry atmosphere of sullenness and recrimination, the woman of the household would announce brightly, "I'm going to town." The conglomeration of habitations she mentioned scarcely added up to a hamlet, no less a town, but there was a general store, with penny candy, so some of the boys invariably shouted, "take me, take me," and the group would tromp out to the car, then vanish in a hubbub of anticipation of sweets and artificial optimism about a minor change of scene clearing the air. But it never did. The foul sullenness impregnated the cabin's interior and wafted with them into the store, where its angry portents continued to disease their brains with an unshakable sense of doom. And unshakable yet, of course it was still there when they got back, a simmering alcoholic anger that, as Janice put it, ruined everything.

Halfway through the week, she had departed with Ethan and Harry to escape the acrid bitterness of the two topers, who had long since graduated from beer to bourbon to whisky. Jack sat in a corner, eating salted sunflower seeds and following the adventures of Batman through his comic book collection, alternating occasionally with an issue of *Mad* magazine, from time to time waving his hand before his nose to banish the alcoholic fumes and muttering "phew." Barely able to stand, Eric challenged his brother to canoe with him downriver.

"You can't hold a paddle, no less use it," the other drunk slurred in reply.

"Take me! Take me!" Thus Tommy.

"Now you done it. The kid wants to go." So the two inebriates lurched down to the dock, the baby toddling behind them. Jack followed, comic book and sunflower seeds in hand, regarding them skeptically as they clambered into the canoe and pushed off into the current. He was ten at the time and knew a bad idea when he saw it, which was almost instantaneously, as the boat was swept into the middle of the dark, churning river and pulled downstream, in the shadow of rustling, overhanging trees. The brothers were hollering at each other, until Eric, in front, turned around yelling for the other to "shut the fuck up." Swiveling back, he lost his balance and tipped the canoe. Jack plunged off the end of the dock, stroked for the boat and grabbed the toddler, sputtering and floundering in the cold current.

"Get uncle Eric!" He coughed at his father, as he towed his little brother to shore.

His father swam up alongside and took over the rescue of his baby son without a word about his brother. By the time they reached the dock, the canoe had disappeared around the bend, and there was no sign of Eric, whose straw hat bobbed lazily in some lily pads near shore.

"Well do something!" Jack screamed.

"It's too late. The canoe hit him on the head."

"You saw that, and you didn't grab him?"

"I was none too clear myself. Besides I was looking for Tommy, who can't swim."

"Uncle Eric's too drunk to swim."

"Uncle Eric's dead."

At those words, Jack dove off the dock and swam out to where the canoe had capsized. He plunged deep into the water, his eyes wide open, but did not see his beloved uncle. Surfacing, he heard his father from the dock: "Get out of the current, before you drown."

Three times Jack swam down toward the bottom of the river, kicking desperately deeper, before he realized he was tiring and had better swim back to shore.

"You think you're strong enough to haul him back yourself?" His father, strangely more sober now, asked.

"You didn't even try!" The boy accused. "You just left him there to drown."

"I was looking for Tommy."

"I had Tommy. You saw that, and you still didn't even lift a finger. You let him drown."

"Shut up, Jack." And with those words the tall, drenched drunk, no longer quite so drunk, turned on his heel, left the two boys on the wooden dock, covered with sunflower seeds, and drove off to the nearest town to notify the authorities about the accident. By the time he returned, he really was sober and a changed man, a broken one, who had finally grasped that he was more than partly responsible for his brother's death.

"He was drunk, and he just disappeared," Jack told the police officer and gestured out at the current that gurgled and hurried innocuously, as if it had never killed a man just a few hours before. Wide, dark and careless, overhung with trees on either bank, the river had swallowed up one human being, and, said the officer, "you're lucky all four of you didn't drown."

"That depends on your definition of luck," the furious ten-year-old replied.

The policeman raised an eyebrow but said no more.

After that, there was no controlling Jack. Not that his father would have been able to, had he been unbowed, but he was a shattered man, with a wild, raging ten-year-old boy, witness to his homicidal neglect of his brother and son, a boy who talked back and came and went as he pleased and called him a word new in their household, a word he got out of the thesaurus—a fratricide. When Sven looked the word up in the dictionary, he turned pale and trembled—he always trembled now, but after learning the meaning, he shook more and sought to hide from the accusing, ten-year-old glare that, he had come to believe, transmitted a biblical wrath, the pure, certain and furious knowledge of his guilt, shared by Jack, the witness, and the Lord God who saw his crime through the boy's eyes. He hid from his own son, and drank and deteriorated and became a shambling, blear-eyed husk.

The boy drove him out of the house. He knew his rage terrified his father, and in his rage he was, he understood, in the possession of something bigger than either of them, something he could only describe to himself as "the justice of it," not even sure what that meant, but certain that the spirit that glared through his furious blue eyes at his parent derived from the knowledge that his father had done wrong, terribly, fatally, irrevocably wrong and that he should suffer for it. He was pitiless. It was the scorching, innocent pitilessness of which only children are capable. And the sight of this ferocious, judging, merciless child reduced the man to a trembling, blathering old grisard, scared of his own shadow.

The son showed his father no mercy. The minute a glimmer of it flared in his heart, he recalled his parent, defiantly drunk, turning away from the river and his surely drowning brother, he thought of the days at the graveyard with his uncle and his mates that would never come again, the hilariously macabre bouquets for unsuspecting Janice, plucked from beneath the headstones, the thought of lazy afternoons in the bar, Eric teaching him how to shoot pool, and numerous other memories of longing and loss that smothered any sympathy for his heartless and guilty father, who had taken so much less care of him, had been only too happy to palm his four sons off on his brother as babysitter, who in fact had become, over the years, the real father, the one they felt loved them most.

It took a while for his father actually to quit the premises, though. For almost a year before the carnival came to town, he skulked in rooms where Jack was not, then solved the problem of his relentless son by purchasing a small black and white TV for his bedroom, where he sat, drinking, smoking, eating chips and his wife's fried chicken, as he watched soap operas through the long, dreary days after he was fired by the dealership, by a boss who shook his head and wondered, as everyone who knew Sven did, how he had become such a wretch. In these doldrums of disrepute and languor that soon became sloth, he seemed oblivious to the manner in which the household remained solvent. Janice got a secretarial job, and the two oldest boys had paper routes. Briefly their father operated a forklift, but lost that employment too, claiming the work was beneath him anyway. Even Harry, aged fourteen and his father's staunchest defender, began treating him with discernible contempt: "How were the soaps today, Pop? Didn't wear you out, I hope." One evening over dinner, he announced that he would not be going to college, but, instead, to work right after high school.

"But it was always our dream and yours for you to go to college," his mother lamented.

"Yours maybe, but I don't think Pop's too concerned about it. Anyway, I don't see him earning any money to make it happen."

"But I get a good paycheck."

"That everybody lives on. Nope, I have to work."

Jack regarded his father with a contempt that bordered on hatred. "Well, ain't you gonna say anything?" He demanded.

"Leave him alone," Harry slurped his vegetable soup.

"It's his lazy fault," Jack snapped.

"Leave him alone," Harry glared at his younger brother and then continued as if his father were not even in the room, as if the person seated at the head of the table was a pile of mindless flesh, an utter cipher. "He's gotta live with his conscience, and, in case you hadn't noticed, it's not going too well. So Dad," he turned to the doddering paterfamilias, enunciating his words carefully, as if he were talking to a mental defective, "when you pull yourself together and get work, then I'll think about college."

"Good boy," the decrepit wretch slurped his soup, and it dribbled in a slovenly manner from the corner of his mouth.

His wife's lower lip trembled.

He never pulled himself together. His afternoons before the TV blurred into one another, as he smoked continuously, drank and gorged on junk food. The parental bedroom took on a fetid odor that mixed rather unpleasantly with the stale cigarette smoke and the smell of the large body, rarely bathed, of the wreck whose gaze wandered, as he mumbled incoherently to any interlocutor. And yet his second son, in his boyish rage, did not see these things; no, every time he caught sight of his father, he saw the careless swagger by the riverside, as his uncle sank to a watery death. Where his father was concerned, that moment possessed him. None other existed. He did not recall their relationship prior to that drunken deadly afternoon, and there had been nothing since, except the memory of it, which possessed Sven's son, some said, like the vengeance of the Lord. Everyone saw that Jack could never forgive his father, and they all began to wonder if the day would ever come when he could forgive himself for his contribution to the poor drunk's demise. For they saw what he was blind to: a broken bum whose every exchange with his son took him one step closer to skid row.

For a while he struggled against his miserable fate, but he was like a man accursed. Shortly after the family's return from Wisconsin, Jack and Harry pointedly refusing to ride in the Chevy with their father— "you won't find me in some car he thought was worth more 'n uncle Eric," thus Jack—the father, unable to keep himself presentable enough to sell cars, instead took over his brother's job with the grave-digging crew. Harry went too, but fortunately for his parent, Jack refused—it was doubtful that broken man could have long tolerated his second son's sarcasm on the subject of Sven digging Eric's graves. He did not continue his brother's humorous tradition of stealing bouquets from graves to present to Janice—anything remotely related to laughter had dissolved like sunlight in an evening mist. Instead, he slumped along with the crew in his baggy dungarees and red flannel shirt, frayed at the cuffs, the shovel on his shoulder and lived, as far as the more compassionate eldest son could tell, from moment to moment. The father's life seemed a series of skirmishes against a scatterbrained forgetfulness, whose victories consisted of minute, short-term plans, like bringing his dull and dented lunch box to the cemetery every day. You would think, Harry mused, that the world revolved around that lunch pail and the damp, ham and cheese sandwich it contained, and heaven forbid Janice should forget the chips. After that happened once, occasioning what Harry feared would be a nervous breakdown, his father took to inventorying the contents of the lunch box at dawn, before he left for work. He lived for that lunch box, and for dinner and breakfast. Suddenly, the world revolved around his stomach, with preparations for the slightest pain of hunger drawn up and executed like the battle plans of an idiot general, who suspected enemies lurking everywhere and regarded each successfully chewed and swallowed mouthful as a triumph over some unnamable and relentlessly pursuing evil. Harry could have wept, watching his father eat.

The demented man was the same about "As The World Turns." Harry never forgot that the afternoon this soap opera was cancelled for a golf tournament, his father actually shed tears. "It'll be on tomorrow, Dad. Geeze, get a grip."

"But it was supposed to be on today," the pathetic hulk blubbered. Harry could not stand the sight of such human dilapidation and left the room. When he returned twenty minutes later, his father still sprawled in the overstuffed armchair, but now his head was thrown back, his eyes shut as he snored, his mouth gaping open. A thin line of spittle dripped from his lip over his poorly shaved chin, and the cat, asleep on his lap, had shed fur all over his filthy dungarees. The room was close, nearly stifling, with yet again the stench of a large, unwashed body that mingled with the odor from the many ashtrays stuffed with old cigarette butts. His half eaten bowl of Frosted Flakes still sat on the side table, since breakfast, and the milk in it struck Harry as disgusting, more repulsive than any other detail of the ugly, smelly room. He wanted to take that bowl and fling it against the wall, but, unlike his brother, he pitied his father and knew that such a gesture would only upset and frighten the prematurely aged wreck.

But then, Harry had not seen his father swagger away from the river, his head high and heart hard.

Even Jack, however, had to mute his fury when his father began rambling about Eric as though he were still alive.

"Get the door, Jack—it's uncle Eric knocking. He probably forgot his key," his father said one afternoon. And instead of "it ain't uncle Eric, you let him drown," Jack just stared at his unshaven, wandering-eyed parent, lounging in his filthy armchair and said: "Nobody's there, Dad. You must've imagined something."

"How come you didn't set a place for Eric?" Sven asked querulously that night at dinner.

His wife glanced down at her plate, then looked up at her quavering husband. "Because he's gone, Sven, gone forever."

"Nonsense. Harry, you go get the dishes and set him a place. He'll be ticked when he comes home and sees not only we ate without him, but we didn't even set him a place." By the end of the meal, he seemed to have forgotten about his brother.

But he had not. Two days later, he recounted to the assembled family a conversation he had had with his brother that afternoon, in which Eric had sworn he had won back the Chevy. "He's on a lucky streak at last," the lunatic head of the household said almost brightly. "This could be the turning point for all of us."

Harry and Jack looked at each other.

"Well, it's a turning point, that's for sure," Harry said. "Now we got a ghost in the family."

"You shut your mouth, Harry," his mother said. "Can't you tell your father's not feeling right? Don't make it worse."

"I'm fine," her husband contradicted. "Never better. Now that Eric got the car back, I won't have to drive that mildewed Oldsmobile."

"You haven't driven it in six months," Jack commented. "Last time you went to the cemetery you took the bus. Mom takes the car to the office, remember?"

"Well your mother can quit that job soon," his father continued, before returning to his room and the security of his favorite and quite disgustingly dirty armchair, "now that Eric's doing so well for us."

"Great. Then we can starve for real," thus Jack.

"Hush Jack," his mother whispered. "He's not in his right mind."

"An imbecile could tell that, Ma. But humoring him won't help."

"Since when are you a psychiatrist?"

"Since I saw him let Eric drown. His guilty conscience is eating him alive."

"Listen to you! You're not even a teenager, and you're taking your father's mind apart."

"An idiot could do it. It's that plain what happened. I saw it with my own eyes."

"Things just keep going from bad to worse around here," Harry said. "First Eric dies, then Dad stops working, now he's losing his marbles."

"At least I found a good job," their mother put in optimistically.

"I need to finish school, so I can find one," Harry replied. "That's what we need next."

"Don't you dream of dropping out," she admonished.

"I said finish, not quit."

"You still might go to college."

"And I might sprout wings and fly."

"Stop it."

"Then be reasonable. I can't go to college. This family needs more money and the next in line to make it is me. Jack'll go to college, and he better get ready for that and quit saying 'ain't', cause guys that go to college don't say ain't."

"Maybe I'll work like you," Jack retorted.

"And I'll break your neck if you do. I'm not giving up my future, so everyone else can give up theirs."

"Hush," their mother soothed. "No one's giving up their future. When your father pulls himself together—"

"Not gonna happen," thus Harry, who then stalked out of the room. "I'll be happy to discuss it further with you two, when you come back to the real world," he called from his bedroom.

The paternal hallucinations brought them right back to what Harry had called the real world with a garish lightening flash over their blasted future, littered with abandoned hopes and crushed dreams.

"Eric told me today he's going back to the dealership," the father announced one night at dinner. Harry and Jack exchanged a glance. Janice saw this and in the awareness that her children were witnessing things they shouldn't, momentarily bowed her head. Then she looked up. "Harry, Jack, clear the table. Don't just sit there. Can't you see everybody's eaten? I'll get the desert—peach pie."

"Eric's favorite," Sven said.

"It's not for Eric," she snapped. "It's for us."

"Let's save him a piece."

"Let's not," she retorted and walked into the kitchen, away from the table, cluttered with dirty dishes, string beans in one bowl, mashed potatoes in another and the remains of a pot roast and away from her two oldest sons, contemplating the nightmare future with an insane parent. Alone, she buried her face in her hands.

"You better quit that," Harry said, entering the room, his arms laden with dirty crockery. "Pull yourself together. You know you're all we got left. The kids I know at school in foster care say it's horrible."

"Don't you dare think for a minute—"

"Then don't let it get to you. I've got a feeling we're going to be hearing a lot more about Eric in the days to come. This thing isn't going away. It's getting worse."

Indeed, the next cold wintry afternoon, when he came in from school, a dusting of snow on the shoulders of his coat, Harry heard loud talking from his parents' bedroom. Wondering what his mother was doing home from work so early, he approached the door, pausing with his hand on the knob, to listen. There came only one voice—his father's. He entered the room to see Sven, slovenly, sprawled, engaged in conversation apparently with the bedroom window. He swiveled his head and focused his rheumy eyes on his son. "Don't you come barging in here when Eric and I are having an important discussion about money. Get out!"

The oldest son glanced around the empty room once more, then backed out, muttering, "worse and worse." He went and sat in the cold, down-falling snow on the front step, until he descried Jack's blue, bundled up form and Ethan's, in a gray snowsuit, trundling down the sidewalk toward the house.

"He's insane," he said, as they approached. They stopped before him, quiet-faced and solemn, as they considered his words and seeming to await his permission to enter the house. There was no question to whom he referred: they knew. "He's talking to the empty air. He sees Eric, but uncle Eric—"

"Ain't there," Jack finished. "He's at the bottom of the river. Fish food."

Ethan began to cry, sniffling that he wanted his mother, that he was cold and wanted to enter the house. Harry shook his head and gravely forbade it with the words that burned into the brains of both younger boys: "There's no telling what he might do."

"Maybe we should go to Tommy's sitter's house," Jack suggested.

"No," Harry soberly replied. "Then we'll have to explain why we're there. And that won't do. Nope, we wait till Mom comes home. She'll have to decide what's next."

"But that's almost two hours, and it's really darn cold," Jack protested.

"You got a better idea?"

They sat down, one on either side of Harry, squishing together for warmth. Harry fixed Ethan's scarf, under the snowsuit hood, wrapping it carefully around the lower half of his face, so that all that showed were his cheekbones, eyes and a bit of forehead. "Better?" Harry asked. The younger boy nodded and stamped his boots. Then Jack did too, and soon all three were sitting, stamping their boots on the second step. Then Harry told Ethan the story of the monster that lived in the basement and chased little boys who ventured down there at night and had been known to try to eat them.

"I'm not Tommy," Ethan said. "I'm seven. I don't believe in no cellar monsters."

"Then I dare you to go down there tonight in the dark," Jack sourly put in.

"Knock it off, Jack," Harry said.

Jack turned away and sulked in his own, quiet, angry world.

"The cellar monster tried to eat me," Harry continued.

Ethan's eyes rounded until they looked like blue pennies, shining in astonishment. "What'd you do?"

"I hit it with Dad's hammer, from the work-bench. Hit it right on the nose."

"Why'd that jerk have to go and lose his mind?" Jack muttered furiously. "Bad enough he lays around all day and sponges off Mom. He even takes my paper route money. There ain't nothin' he won't sink to."

"Isn't," Harry corrected.

"Isn't," Jack repeated, raging now. "First he good as kills uncle Eric. I seen it with my own eyes. And he coulda killed Tommy too. Then the creep—"

"Whoa, Jack. Don't talk about Dad like that."

"Then whatever you want to call him loses his job, through his own fault, like he don't got a wife and four boys to support. You're the one always wanted to go to college, not me, and now you're giving that up. Meanwhile, whatever you want to call him makes himself feel better, buys off his guilty conscience by pretending Eric's still alive. And pretty soon the dingbat's mind snaps and he believes it. So now he's hallucinating. I got no pity for him."

"So I see," Harry said. "But you could use some."

"What for?" Jack whirled and faced his brother, his eyes suddenly blazing.

"For him—and for yourself, someday," Harry paused and dusted snow off Jack's shoulders. "Where you think he's gonna be in ten years, Jack?"

"I don't know and I don't care."

"No place good—can you see that?"

"So?"

"And how will you feel about how you treated him then?"

"The same. He doesn't deserve any place good."

"You better lighten up. If not for his sake, for yours."

"So now you're the family guidance counselor, like Miss Hall."

"Guess so."

"Well, she's a moron."

"But I'm not."

Jack merely curled his lip and turned away.

So the oldest told scary stories to the youngest, and the middle continued what would become a lifelong habit of retreating into his own dour ruminations and stewing there morosely.

After half an hour, the front door behind them flew open, and there, looming unsteadily, stood their father. "Did you see him leave?"

"Who, Dad?" Harry asked.

"Your uncle. I had a name to give him at the dealership, a string to pull."

The three boys sat silently, as snow drifted down on their coats and hoods, as silently as sleep with its promise of release from the unbearable.

"Hey, it's winter!" their mad father exclaimed. "And here I thought it was still fall. Why're you sitting out in the cold? Come in."

"We're waiting for Mom," the oldest explained.

"I want to go in," Ethan whimpered.

"Come on, son. I'll fix you some Campbell's soup."

"You?" Jack demanded, then under his breath: "I'll believe that when I see it."

"I got chicken with stars," Sven sang out, like he was in a Christmas chorus and his voice a gift to the world. The little boy rose, but Harry grasped the waist of his snowsuit and pulled him back down to a sitting position on the step. He gazed severely, minatorily into his younger brother's round, sorrowful eyes, yearning for the Campbell's soup in the comforting warmth of his mother's trim little kitchen.

"We'll just wait till Mom gets home," Harry said evenly.

"Suit yourself," their thoughtless parent replied, closing the door on the three boys hunched in the cold and the snow. "Kids are crazy these days."

"You meant fathers, didn't you?" Jack asked harshly, but the door had already shut, so the man thus apostrophized heard nothing.

The barred shadows of the white, paint-chipped, wood fence lengthened across the whitely-blanketed yard, intersecting the crooked ones of the oak tree, as the littlest boy's plaints became louder and more insistent, finally merging into one, relentless high-pitched whine of misery. Of all evenings, that night their mother was late, and when she finally pulled the car in front of the house, exited carrying her bundled-up baby and made her way crunching on snow up the walk, she was too tired to ask why they sat on the step, pale, shivering, lips blue with cold and on their shoulders and hats an inch of the frozen white crystals that their fingers had been too numbly gelid to sweep off . But no matter, Ethan told her: "Daddy's crazy, and Harry won't let us in the house with him."

The corners of her mouth trembled and, for a moment, she faltered, but then strode forward. "Stop this nonsense," she ordered. "It's too darn cold. Get in before you catch your death of pneumonia." Inside, her bleached blonde beehive, somewhat crushed when she removed her winter scarf, fit somehow with her wavering features. She seemed unsure again, as she and they heard the father talking loudly in the bedroom. After a moment of silent listening, she recovered herself. "Harry, Jack, set the table. Ethan, take Tommy into your room, shut the door and play with him. Keep him busy, while I cook dinner."

"What is it tonight, Ma?" The oldest politely asked.

"Tuna casserole and peas and carrots."

Jack frowned.

"I know, I know," she gently tousled his straight, sandy hair, "we just had it recently, and it's not your favorite. But it's economical, and we have to be wise with our money."

"You mean our pennies," Jack said. "So why don't you tell Dad to stop stealing my newspaper money to buy bourbon?"

"Shh. Don't talk about your father like that."

"But it's the truth. He takes my money. I caught him, seen him with my own eyes."

"Seems like you're always catching him, seeing him with your own eyes," Harry remarked.

Janice gazed down at her second son, maternal worry suddenly causing tears to well in her eyes. "That's his burden," she said softly, "to witness his father doing things he shouldn't, a cross he'll have to bear forever."

"Great," thus Jack, with a fury that then expressed itself in the slamming of the plates down on the table as he set it.

"Cut that out," his older brother said quietly. "You'll break one."

"Know what I do? I imagine each one is his lyin', shiftless, good-for-nothing head."

"You better get a hold of yourself, Jack."

"If you're worried about me simmering down before I do my homework, don't."

"I'm worried about the angry, sulking man you're going to grow into."

"Quit it." Jack stopped, with a plate mid-air. "You been after me about this for days. Next thing you know you'll want me to go to church—which you can forget. There ain't no God. I figured that out the afternoon uncle Eric drowned. Wasn't God that rescued Tommy either."

"It was you and Dad, but—"

"Dad came later. I shamed him. He woulda let Tommy sink like uncle Eric if I hadn't been there."

"Maybe God was working through you."

"Maybe He wasn't. Because I'd kind of know if he was, wouldn't I?"

"Maybe He works through you more than you know."

Jack slammed the plate down on the table. Miraculously it did not break.

"Maybe he don't."

"Doesn't."

"And wouldn't He prefer to work through someone like you, who yammers on about Him all the time, than someone like me, who lost my religion?"

"I don't know what He would prefer to do, and neither do you."

"Yeah right. I know I ain't gonna waste my time thinking about your God, who hasn't helped anybody around here much, as far as I can see."

"Stop saying ain't. You picked it up from those grave-diggers."

"And a lot else—like you work and you get paid, if your deadbeat Dad don't steal your money, and God has no part in it. Don't care if you work, if you get your pay or if you starve—cause he don't exist and if he does, he don't care what happens to you, me or any of us. So don't talk to me about church. Besides, I notice you don't go too often anymore either."

A look of pain and worry clouded the oldest's generally clear eyes. "I don't because of you, because I think I see Him working through you and testing you."

"Stop it, Harry."

"I think," Harry spoke very slowly, enunciating each word, as if to make sure his brother did not miss a syllable, "I think it's really important, more than you know, for you to learn to forgive. I think—"

"Forget it. I don't forgive easily, nor do I forget. I know what I saw. Don't you think I'd forget it if I could? I'm not like you. We're different. I didn't believe that Sunday school stuff before that afternoon on the river. And I sure as shootin' don't believe it now. I figured out there was no hereafter when I saw the first dead body at the funeral home where Eric took us; that first dead man, I looked at him and I knew we weren't going anywhere after we die. We're just like the plants and the animals. And that's all I'll say about it. I don't know how many times I have to explain to you that I figured out there's nothing out there, no God, no heaven, no angels, and that I'm not going to be convinced by you or anybody to change my mind."

"You could still forgive him."

"No I couldn't. And I never will."

They set the remainder of the table in silence, placing the stainless steel cutlery carefully, with a precision that betokened some mechanically complex and decisively important operation, as if the machinery of the meal would not commence, not click into gear, if they did not lay each fork and spoon just so. And indeed, moments later, as they all sat down for their tuna casserole, it did not take off, but stalled right there in the middle of the dining room, as their hallucinating father lumbered in to eat, causing all conversation to cease.

Jack glared at him once, then lowered his eyes to his plate. Harry glanced worriedly at his brittly smiling mother, then bowed his head, as if weighed down by the many considerations induced by the demise of the adults in the room and hoping, obscurely, for help from another realm. The two youngest boys ate greedily, like children accustomed to going too long between meals, Ethan because he was in the care of his brothers with only crackers for snacks in the house and Tommy because his sitter did not give snacks and his mother did not pack them for him, out of penury but with the excuse that she did not believe in eating between meals. The father gobbled his noodles and tuna in his new manner—since the return from Wisconsin he bolted his food, as if he secretly believed it was about to be taken from him. Thus he ate more, which showed in his expanding middle. He reached for another helping.

"There's not enough for seconds, if Tommy and Ethan are going to get them too," Jack said, looking not at his father but at his mother. "I thought we were supposed to leave seconds for them, cause they're always so hungry."

The mother stopped chewing; once again every feature on her face suddenly looked fragile and strained, not up to the challenge of replying to her son.

"I saw a box of macaroni and cheese in the cupboard," Harry spoke softly, regarding his plate, having found in his quiet ponderings, perhaps, the answer to his question. "I'll go make it for Tommy and Ethan right now." He rose and went to the kitchen, as his mother followed him with her eyes, in which lurked pain and fear, as though his words and motion were a rebuke to her, an implicit criticism of her motherhood, of her insufficient care for her youngest sons, her fretful, suffering eyes, which failed utterly to discern the relief that her oldest found in his sudden activity. Jack cast her a quietly anguished glance that took all this in. "Maybe you should help him, Ma. You know how clumsy Harry is with a pot of water."

"Yes, yes, you're right Jack," she put her napkin on the table and rose, cowed and exuding her own miserable confirmation and belief that the rebuke of her maternal care was correct.

Jack happened to catch sight of his father, still slobbering over his food in that characteristic headlong rush, and looked away, glowering with blame for the prematurely aging man for all the misfortunes besetting the family. The foursome sat quietly at the table, while Harry and his mother clattered around in the kitchen. Eventually, kicking his legs, the baby whispered gleefully to Ethan: "macaroni!"

To Jack's fury, his father spoke up: "I guess I'll have a taste of that, too."

Jack rose and stomped into the kitchen. "If you let him eat Tommy and Ethan's macaroni and cheese, I will leave home." The other two turned and stared at him in a silence filled with astonishment and foreboding.

"You've never talked like that before, Jack," his mother said.

"You can't leave. We need you." Harry said flatly.

Trapped, Jack writhed for a moment and was then released by his older brother's return to the dining room and quite audible announcement to the overfed father that there was only enough macaroni for the boys.

Briefly after that, for about two months, the head of the household startlingly pulled himself together. In the depths of a frigid February, he returned to the car dealership and recovered his position. Each morning, he could be heard clomping about on the wooden floor of the cold, under-heated house, performing his ablutions before departing for work. He shaved, showered, wore freshly laundered clothes—all things he had abandoned since the summer. He no longer drank. Instead of squandering his paycheck, as his two eldest sons at first feared, he turned it over to his wife, who, anxious now and foreseeing a relapse, banked as much of it as she could, after using the rest to pay off the debt to Tommy's sitter. She went so far as to use some of this new found wealth to pay the woman a month in advance, anticipating hard times, but still thriftily calculating that they might be able to make it to summer, when the older boys could watch him instead of someone she had to pay; and then after that, the baby would be in all-day kindergarten, thus drastically reducing the costs of child-care.

During this period of paternal employment, Jack's fury abated. He avoided his father, but when they did have contact, the strangely alien fire that roared within him and fed on memories of wonderful times with his dead uncle and the last image of the river waters closing over his head, burned lower, not utterly consuming him. He did not attend the county fair with his family in May, where his father met his future employer, obtaining the promise of a job selling toys and trinkets in a booth, if he should ever want it. Instead, that day Jack stayed home alone, did his homework and tried not to recall that it was on warm, gorgeous weekend afternoons such as this that his adored uncle would take him and his brother to the cemetery and entertain them with darkly humorous musing on life, or the absence of it, in the hereafter, as he dug graves. Sprawled on the glider on the back porch, enjoying the warmth of the noon but protected from the blazing sun, the boy dozed off and dreamt he stood at the entrance of Heaven's Gate cemetery, next to the huge, blond and beloved uncle, who made wisecracks about it being the gate to nowhere and nothing, because that was what was in heaven anyway.

"But don't you tell your mother. It'd break her heart. Like lots of people, she's got her hopes pinned on a rosy hereafter. It makes the shit we gotta put up with in this life more bearable. But I think you might as well look the monster in the face and grab him by the shoulders. Shake him as hard as you can. Truth is, we got nothing after we're dead, Jack, nothing. And who's afraid of nothing?" And, just as he had that sunny afternoon a year earlier, now the memory of him, behind the boy's hot, half-wakeful eyelids, brought his hand before the boy's face and rubbed the end of his thumb against the tips of his fingers to signify nothing.

"I don't like nothing," Jack had said.

"Neither do I," his uncle replied. "But I ain't afraid of it. Are you?"

Jack considered. He thought about this void just mentioned and the absence of anything before his first memories around the age of four. No, he averred, he was not afraid of it.

"Then you can live your life a free man," the huge grave-digger rejoiced, clapping him on the shoulder, so that he lurched forward on the gravel path between the headstones, as his uncle laughed, shovel on his shoulder and repeated in a loud, joyous voice: "Free of heaven, free of hell, my boy Jack, he'll do real well." With that he reached in the pocket of his faded dungarees and withdrew a pack of M&Ms, handing it to his nephew. "Here, to celebrate your freedom from that Sunday school hokum." So, sharing chocolates, they proceeded through the graves.

"You don't think maybe we get reborn, like Harry says, and get to do it all over again?" The boy asked tentatively, stopping in the sun-dappled shade of a maple and enjoying the last of the M&Ms.

His uncle shook his head. "What evidence is there for that?" He asked. "Harry just don't like nothing. I've noticed this before. People will go to extraordinary lengths to deny it. Why? It can't hurt you. It's just," Then that gesture again, thumb against finger tips: "nothing. See them dead roses on that grave? They'll decay, and turn to dust, and the wind will blow the dust hither and yon, and the people who put them there will forget them, and eventually those people won't even be able to remember them if they wanted to, 'cause they'll be dust, and it'll be as if those roses never were. Just like it was before they grew on the bush. Is that so terrible? Whole generations of people come and go, just like that, and soon, before you know it, there's not even the faintest memory of them. There's just nothing. Nothing wins in the end, every time."

And then Jack, half-dozing, half-remembering on the glider, saw his uncle's drunken lurch in the kelly-green canoe and saw again the gaily sparkling and indifferent river close over his head. He sat up with a start, sunbeams dancing all around. "Eric!" He shouted at the heap of plywood over by the shed, remnant of his uncle's last furniture-making project, dazzling white in the heat and light. "Eric! I want more than nothing!" But no one replied. So he sank back onto the threadbare cushions and in his mind, his uncle's voice resounded: "You ain't gonna get it."

It rang like a bell, so pure and lifelike that he bolted up and looked around, half-expecting to see the huge, yellow-haired form lurking by the bent corner of the back porch. "Maybe that's what it's like for Dad," he thought, reclining again on the glider. "Maybe the voice is that clear, and then he thinks he sees him, too." This revelation, however, did nothing to mitigate his keen sense of his father's guilt; rather he found it merely curious, a small bit of evidence of the mind's ability to play tricks. "I didn't get it neither," he heard next, amid the crickets' dry chirping in the brown grass, and then leaned forward, poised to attend to any further declamations from the beyond. But none came. Those two were aberrations, he concluded, the product of too much sleep, sultry weather and glider motion in the middle of a warm spring afternoon.

Later, sitting on the front step, bored and waiting for his family, he saw the Oldsmobile cruising down the road, then pulling up before the worn, old wooden fence with its peeling white paint. His father sat at the wheel, like, he incongruously thought, some enormous toad, enveloped in the peculiar aura of satisfaction, ever-present when he drove his old car, an attitude that reminded his son of him in his precious red Chevy. "Him and that damn car," the boy thought bitterly, "worth more to him than his own brother." The three brothers tumbled out the back door, faces smeared with ice cream, candy and sweat, Ethan holding a stick of pink cotton candy and snapping at it with the delighted but purposeful vim of a hungry animal doing tricks. Their mother gracefully stepped out of the front passenger door, her blond beehive high and magnificent. Last came the driver, paterfamilias himself, triumphantly smirking up to Jack and clapping him on the shoulder. "Got a job offer," he announced.

"Stop it, dear," his wife reproached him. "The dealership's better any day, even with the so-called travel."

"Daddy's gonna work at the carnival," thus the baby.

"Daddy needs his head examined," Harry breathed, and Jack glanced at him sharply. The thick, blond hair, the pale face marked with freckles and kindness, and the alertly hopeful blue eyes were the same, yet it was unlike his older brother to mock or belittle either parent; but then he had become so comfortable, too comfortable in Jack's view, in recent months with his father back at his old job that he was bound to rue anything that even remotely threatened it. Why, Harry had even allowed himself to hope again that he might go to college. This Jack knew, because his brother had confided it in him one evening, leaning his long form back against the scratched Formica counter, back into the shadows that filled that part of the kitchen with a safe darkness, in which he could articulate his hopes, entrust them to his younger brother with the words: "If Dad can stay on track like this, I won't have to help Mom support the rest of the family. Then I can do what I want." And of course Jack knew that meant getting his BA in government.

Later he joined his older brother on the glider out back. Harry had his U.S. history textbook open to a section on reconstruction in the South and was taking notes, periodically smoothing down the partially crumpled paper, as it lifted in the fresh, warm May breeze.

"Don't you count on Dad," Jack said, sitting down and giving the glider a push. It creaked the healthy creak of old machinery that will never give out. "If you do, you're making a big mistake."

The other glanced up, his keen cerulean eyes busy with internal calculations. "He's just got to make it a couple of years. We're banking half his paycheck as it is right now. If he gives out around the time I go to college, it doesn't matter. Mom'll have enough to support the rest of you, and I can work my own way through school. It's just a year or two."

"You're too optimistic."

"So you've said ever since he went back to work. But it's been three months, and look at him—almost normal. No more of that loony stuff."

"Except this nonsense about the carnival. I got a feeling he'll run off with them. He wouldn't have mentioned it otherwise."

Something flickered deep down amongst the hopes that always dwelt in those eyes, and in the quiet that followed, he seemed to consider it, finally murmuring, "then we have to stop him." He resumed note-taking, as Jack rocked the glider with his foot. "Uncle Eric—" Jack began.

"Darn it," his brother hissed. "Have you lost your mind? Don't mention him, not here, not in this house, not anywhere Dad could hear. If you can't get over it, well, then just keep it to yourself. We need Dad sane and working, and you talking about this grudge of yours is one certain way to unhinge him." The glider creak creaked, both rocking it now, enjoying the fragrance of flowers borne in by the breeze from the garden next-door.

Occasional, out-of-joint details began to support Jack's premonitions. That very evening his father mentioned the carnival again; two days later, he suggested to Tommy and Ethan that they go back to the fair. This was over dinner. Jack glanced sharply at Harry, who immediately addressed his father, while returning his brother's gaze, as if to say: "This is the line we have to take, and you must back me up."

"No Dad," Harry began, nodding gravely at his brother, "Tommy and Ethan don't need to go back to the fair. Once was enough. It's expensive, and we need to save."

Their father's mouth settled into a wavering line of discontent and unsureness as to how to meet this obstacle to his plans and their ulterior motive.

"Harry's right," his wife put in. "Those rides cost a lot, and the food is overpriced."

"To say nothing of the fact that it's bad," Harry added. "Those were the greasiest fries I ever ate in my life."

"Maybe I'll just go by myself," the father replied querulously, "and have a look around."

"At what?" Jack snapped suddenly. "You already had a look around. You wanna inspect them pigs again? Or watch the Ferris wheel? Or—"

"I got a job offer," his father whined.

"That ain't a job," Jack shouted. "It's a way to go broke. It's brainless, it's," he broke off, silenced by his older brother's level glare.

"Mom, maybe you can take Dad to the fair on Saturday, show him what a lousy deal it would be."

The mother, who had crumpled at her husband's words, just said to him, "Dear, I wish you wouldn't talk like that." The remainder of the meal passed in silence, as the two little boys ate every drop of their spaghetti and meat sauce, while the two older ones stared out the windows at the gray dusk of destitution.

The next weekend, Harry's spirits visibly dampened by his parents' trip to the carnival, he joined his younger brother on the back porch glider. Jack was eating chips.

"I thought he got it. But I was wrong," the older boy started, tossing his sandy hair out of his eyes, in which there flickered not so much unwonted anger as the little flame of a truth realized, one that had cleared the air of fantasies, but also toughened him, against his will.

"Who? The old deadbeat?"

For once Harry did not correct his young brother's parental disrespect. Instead he gazed off into the neighbor's garden, where daffodils bloomed yellow and white.

"You mean," crunch, crunch, "you actually thought he had pulled himself together, realized he had a wife and four kids and some responsibility for them and that he was going to act like a grownup?"

"Yeah," Harry growled. "Something like that."

"What planet are you on?" More crunches. "Here's a guy, let's his own brother drown out of spite over a stupid car, nearly kills his son, quits his job, drinks all day for months, steals his kids' newspaper route money—*my* money—and you think he's suddenly out of the blue reformed?"

"He got his job back," Harry growled again, that little truth, alive in his eyes, still not yielding. "It looked like he was headed in the right direction."

"He's headed to run off with that carnival and leave us in the ditch. That's the direction he's headed in." The two boys rocked lazily on the glider in the warm May breeze, as sounds of their younger brothers, playing and shouting happily in the living room, drifted out the back screen door. They looked almost identical, except that Harry, nearly sixteen, was taller and lankier. In that moment they seemed peaceful, two teenage boys, enjoying a lovely spring afternoon—one would never have guessed that the older was lost in a landscape of misery and gloom, illumined only by a faint, unpalatable truth, while the younger seethed with rage, and that both had their minds fixed on their family's dire prospects once their feckless father gallivanted off on his new adventure.

"I knew it was too good to be true," Harry mumbled at length.

"How's about this? You go to college, and I'll help support Mom, Ethan and Tommy. I ain't—"

"Am not,"

"Am not inarested in college anyhow."

"You'd have to drop out of high school."

"So?"

"I can't have that."

"Well, what're you going to do?"

"You know very well. I'm graduating a year early. After next year I was planning on the state college. But if Dad screws up—"

"You mean when."

Harry ignored this. "Then I'll just get a full-time job."

"Mom'll go to pieces," crunch, crunch, "if he runs off."

"Yeah, I thought of that."

"Not that he'd care."

"It's not that, Jack. He just doesn't seem capable of planning, of envisioning the future. Something, the accident mainly, but something else too, has destroyed him, destroyed his mental world. It's like a bomb went off in his mind, blasted everything, and he's just not capable of thoughtful action anymore."

"There's a lot he don't seem capable of. God help me if I start to try to list it all."

"Yes Jack. God help you."

Two months later, Jack's prediction came true. One sultry July evening, as fireflies drifted and glimmered by the front shrubs, their impassioned little lights fading like lost hopes, the father failed to come home for dinner. The next morning his wife, in a panic and suspecting news of an untimely death, called his employer, who, in some surprise at her ignorance, explained that her husband had essentially been fired (he had frightened customers by talking to someone who was not there) and quit at the same time—thus ruining his chances of ever returning to the dealership—and taken a job with a traveling carnival. His wife's voice died. Harry, observing this, took the receiver from her faltering grasp and had his father's boss repeat the news. Jack's clear blue eyes, taking all this in from his perch on the couch, hardened as his brother hung up the phone, turned and addressed the assembled family: "Dad took that job with the carnival. He won't be back for a while."

"He won't be back never," Jack stated.

With great effort their stricken mother collected her wits. "I can't be late for work," she said. "Not now, not ever again." And she hurried off to the bathroom to apply her makeup.

Sven was neither seen nor heard from until the following April, when, one afternoon, he turned up in his shabby, dusty, brown pants and jacket at the track of his second son's high school. He approached Jack with a cigarette between his teeth. His son merely glared at him with a filial fury that should have scorched him to silence, but did not. But it was an altered fury, altered by the perception of how far, far, far his father had fallen, by the holes in Sven's shoes, the tremor in his hand, the grime under his nails, the dirty shirt soaked in sweat and by a strange little resolve to enlighten him in some small way as to what that fall meant for the rest of the family.

"Hey Jack, how 'bout you loan me your lunch money."

Jack reached into the pocket of his jeans and pulled out a dollar.

"Thanks son, I'll remember that."

"If you knew what I was thinking, you wouldn't," he flailed uselessly, trying to engage the wreck before him in some human interchange, even if it was only verbal sparring.

His father smiled uncomprehendingly, but then, as if conscious that some bit of explanation was due, mumbled: "life on the road's kind of hard."

"So the carnival didn't work out."

"No, no, not that. I'm on leave, kind of. I'll be back at it soon enough."

"Not soon enough for me," Jack flailed again.

"Maybe I'll get my old job back selling cars for a while."

"Maybe you won't. After how you treated them, they don't ever want to catch sight of you again."

"Harry going to college?"

"On what money?" Jack asked and then, seizing his opportunity "what do you think we live on, your four sons and your wife? You think we have college money? We'll be lucky to keep the house."

"Hey, you don't have more'n this dollar, do you?"

The teenager reached into his pocket again and withdrew two quarters. Overhead, in the vast altitudes of a crystal cerulean heaven, little fluffs of cloud, pink, silver and mauve, scudded by in serenity and beautiful indifference to the young man's misery at the derelict before him, and somehow this equanimity of the day, of the sky, in the face of such obvious human suffering made it all worse and filled him with despair. A few students glanced at Jack curiously, the resemblance between father and son effaced by the older man's unshaved cheeks and shabby attire.

"I'd call," the father continued, "but I never seem to have the change."

"Don't bother."

"Well, you give my best to everybody."

"And what would that be?"

"Why, my love, Jack. You give them my love. God bless you all. He's watchin' out for you, I know."

"That would be Harry and Mom, working themselves to the bone, and me with a job at the supermarket, not God."

His father caught that remark, and for a moment there was a glint, a surprisingly intelligent glint in his otherwise misted and befuddled eyes. Then he backed away, fumbling to put Jack's money in his pants pocket and mumbling: "God bless, God bless. Don't you say nothin' against the Lord, Jack. I know you're mad at Him. Don't be. God bless."

"I was mad at you, but you're not even you anymore," Jack said quietly to himself. "God's got nothing to do with it and never did." But his father was already out of earshot.

That night he did not mention his father's visit to the family, nor did he a few days later, when Sven showed up again and, to the boy's impotent fury, wretchedness and shame, beneath that clear and heartless sky, requested and took his lunch money again. Over the next month, his father reappeared four times, begging for the same handout. The last time, Jack scarcely greeted him, simply pulling a dollar out of his pocket and proffering it. "Thanks Jack, you're a life-saver," the old man said, indeed he looked older each time Jack saw him, as though he were gaining age at some wildly accelerated rate. And at their last encounter, he noticed a tooth missing.

"Better see a dentist," he remarked.

"No dentist's getting my money," his father chuckled.

"I guess the dentist is no different from anybody else then."

"Give your mother my love," his father concluded, backing away as he always did in that cowed and frightened manner, which Jack had begun to recognize as characteristic, as too was the secret triumph, with which he regarded the pathetically tiny sum he had cadged.

"I wouldn't dream of it," Jack whispered to himself, picturing the dreadful effect on her of a narration of these recent events. In all of the father's sojourns to the high school, never once did his son invite him to return home, nor—and Jack never knew exactly why but still found it fitting—did he once suggest it or ask.

Jack resisted the idea of college for a long time, fought it whenever the topic came up, fortified himself against this elite enemy that would surely drag him away from a world of memories of sublime summer afternoons, of the smells of sweat and fresh turned earth, of the quiet, of the wind, spreading over headstones like an echo of millennia of wind, marked only rarely by some macabre joke from his towering uncle or his fellow laborers.

But somehow his older brother always got the upper hand, and their disputes would end with him saying: "You're going, and I'm paying, and that's that." Harry started work as an administrative assistant at the dealership long before he graduated; within a year of leaving high school, he was selling cars there. The other salesmen were full of competitive admiration and vocally impressed that the son and nephew of those wastrels, the Diamond brothers, had turned out so neat and sharp. Within three years he was the lead salesman, paying for his younger brother's college and, with his mother, supporting the other two at home. He never smoked, drank only occasionally, kept his affairs with women discreetly to himself. The only visible scar left by his father and uncle was the determination not to marry, ostensibly because he had too many other responsibilities, but in reality, Jack was sure, due to the trauma of the one's death and the other's living death, that deterioration that had rotted his father's ensouled remains like a decayed carcass in the summer sun. There was nothing soft or unfocussed about Harry. He was all business and determination to do exactly as he said, and he achieved his aims, with only two notable failures—failures that puzzled him, but because they involved two other personalities, one of them obviously wounded, could not fairly be laid at his door: Ethan enlisting in the military instead of pursuing his education, and Tommy going straight from high school to becoming a hippie drifter. But all that came later, once Jack was well into his graduate work, and no one except Harry blamed Harry for his youngest brothers' choices.

In considering them, he always wondered that Jack, by far the most ornery, had yet proved the most malleable—after all, Harry had compelled him to go to college by sheer force of will. Yet against Ethan's solitary manliness or Tommy's wild hobo ways, that power of his had shattered like glass against granite. Unlike Jack, they were not stubborn nor given to sullen, unyielding introspection, quite the opposite. The youngest was dandelion fluff, blown on the lightest breeze—one day he was in twelfth grade, the next day, right after graduation, bellbottoms, beads, long hair and tie-dyed T-shirt, he was gone, who knew where. Sporadic collect phone calls from pay telephone booths informed his frantic mother of his life on the road. And Ethan, well, there was just no question of him ever doing anything other than joining the Marines. He was, he said, born to fight. He went his own way, not out of obstinacy, but because it was his nature, he could do nothing else, and nothing, no one, could hold him, not Harry with his will of steel, not his mother's tears and weeping the day he went to the recruiter that he would die in the mud and jungles of Vietnam. Jack, it turned out, was the most like Harry, and grudgingly deferred to the latter's judgment as the eldest, and conceded his stronger will. Against it at first,

Jack went to college, lost his "ain'ts," and then, finding his calling and later, in Naomi, he believed, his wife, stayed on, for it was everything to him. He had no desire to return to Wichita. In his mind it was a desert, and if he could have rescued his mother and brother from it, he would have.

But they could not be rescued. Long years stretched from the father's ill-omened disappearance to Jack's graduate student days, years in which the abandoned wife became infirm and prematurely aged, in which the oldest set his heart against anything other than his responsibilities to his most immediate kin, as if he had dug himself a safe spot in a long war, where, in loyalty only to those few, he resisted, defied and survived the advances of an enemy who's brutality and barbarism he had witnessed in the fates of the men of his family, years in which joy or pleasure were utterly forgotten, in which the wildness and wonder of life came to be regarded as an enemy, and all replaced by mind-numbing routine and retreat from the world, or, as Jack put it, "Harry and Mom just hide in that little box, scurry off to work and scurry back." It was an apt description of his mother, but not his brother, who in truth hid from nothing, but rejected anything fortune might throw at him, who wrote Ethan in Da Nang that as soon as he came back to Wichita, there would be a job waiting for him selling cars—two brothers employed together once again, though of course he did not put it like that and did not care to think of the parallel. But Jack considered it and told Naomi it gave him the willies.

Sven took to waiting outside his wife's office building for a handout from her, until Harry discovered it and bought him off with five hundred dollars. He then moved into a rooming house, where his oldest son took to visiting him, doling out cash gifts. This arrangement lasted for the better part of a year, until the father, footloose and feckless and having drunk his money away, took to the road again, with his sack of rice and few cooking supplies, so that he could survive far from the ministrations of civilization and, more significantly, his worried family. He was not heard from again for years. Apparently, before vanishing, he attempted to apologize for depriving Harry of his prized college education—an attempt which only served to infuriate his generally forgiving oldest son, by exposing the father's superficial regret and callousness, the transformative results of pummeling by that nameless, aforementioned enemy. After that, Harry had fewer concerns and was generally less preoccupied with his father's miserable fate.

Jack, on the other hand, never thought of him. He had pushed his decrepit parent out of his mind and preferred not to be reminded of him. Only when it became inescapably apparent that Tommy was fatally cut in the paternal mold, did he allow himself to consider what had become of the old drifter, and then only in order to see if he could devise some rescue for the youngest. But he was forced to conclude that his brother was doomed. Somehow the tender, wayward child had grown up to be his father, tossed down the road like a piece of paper trash in the wind. The three brothers watched in horror, helpless.

Jack had heard from the young nomad the day of the party. He pictured him ragged and barefoot, in a telephone booth on the La Jolla beach, a warm, gentle breeze blowing, the waves folding gently, not crashing, onto the shore, and the crystalline blue of the Pacific glimmering gemlike to the horizon. Tommy was the image of his dead uncle, huge, hulking and with the same sharp edge to his humor about things people commonly took for granted and the eternities of nothing that envelop the brief flickering of the little human flame—but that was the extent of the resemblance. The rest was all his father—the shambling, the uncertainly, the wifty inability to keep his mind on one thing at a time. But he had not seen his father in over a decade, so he could not be in any way consciously imitating him. No, said Jack, the scientist, "it's genetic."

He gazed into the darkened room filled with the vague motion of the murmurous crowd. "Here I am at a party," he thought, "while my youngest brother is lying on the beach, under the stars, drinking bourbon, unmoored, like his father and uncle, from the bonds of normal life, adrift like a mote in the galaxy, who knows what severed him? Yes, there's a bad gene in our family." He turned to glance at the light that shot at once through the shadowed room from the hall, through the suddenly opened front door.

"Naomi," he called to the lithe young woman bathed in that flood of light, as all considerations of bad genes, dead uncles and vagrant fathers slid from his mind. She glided toward him through the dancing revelers, and as she approached, the image of the defeated young man, the prone form on the nocturnal beach, inebriated, beyond rescue, singing to himself in solitude on the phosphorescently white sand beneath a billion stars in a night sky, began, at last and mercifully but still disquietingly, to recede.

"**D**id I arrive at a bad time?" Betsy Ein inquired, her bright red curls matched by her apple cheeks, rosy from a cool, strong, spring Chicago wind.

Distracted by the question and her arrival, Jack and Naomi fell silent, mid-dispute, as little Snow, reading a book in a corner, glanced up.

"No," the young mother said firmly. "I'm packing to go to the Soviet Union, Jack's packing to take Snow to the wilds of Wyoming, we have to be out by the weekend and I need a place to store some of my stuff—is your house available?"

"Yes, if you don't mind schlepping your gear up to the North Side."

They resumed packing, this time silently. They had been arguing about Naomi's hegira, which her lover opposed. He regarded it as unwise in many ways, not least of which was the separation from her son, whose desperate attachment to his mother Jack observed with some alarm. Perhaps it was the way the seven-year-old retreated into books or the occasional sarcastic remark—too old and bitter for a child—but Jack had come to see a lot of himself in the boy he had also come to regard as his. This two-month sojourn behind the iron curtain could, he feared, damage Snow. He said so, at first gently, then firmly, then with some acrimony. But his girlfriend was stubborn and, besides, had convinced herself that time alone together would benefit those left behind. Soon Jack had resorted to sarcasm.

She had trained herself to disregard her son's physical resemblance to his biological father and to see instead the mannerism and style that he mimicked from Jack. Just then he was reading a children's simplified version of *Robinson Caruso*. "It'll be like a desert island, out in Wyoming, just you and me," the boy addressed the man, who smiled for the first time that morning and tousled the young one's thick, light brown hair. "Keep reading," he replied. "It gets better." The child settled further into the frayed, old, brown armchair, which Jack had rescued from the sidewalk trash two years earlier. Late morning sunbeams bisected the room, illuminating piles of household items, partially packed, in some disarray. Most of all there were books—Jack's chemistry tomes, his girlfriend's classics and Russian language volumes, her son's chapter books and picture books. There were toys, a matchbox car collection, but not much else. Winter clothing spilled out of cardboard boxes, while the calico cat snoozed on a heap of bedding. "I thought we were getting a dog today," the boy said plaintively, without looking up from his book.

"We'll go over to the ASPCA later," the man promised, "once we're done packing. I said we couldn't live in Wyoming without a dog, and I meant it."

"What's the ASPCA?"

"It's where we got Sniffles," Jack jerked his thumb at the drowsing feline. "I believe in rescuing animals."

"So do I," the boy concurred. "Let's rescue two dogs."

"Maybe."

"And another cat."

"We only have a three-bedroom cabin in Tower Oaks Bend," Jack admonished. "There's got to be space for people. And remember Harry's coming out for a visit as soon as we arrive. I doubt he'll stay the whole week with a house packed full of animals."

"Harry's the best," the child averred, unwrapping a lollipop he had discovered in his pants' pocket. "He gave me that fishing rod."

"Which we're going to use this summer in Wyoming," the man turned and glared at the woman, muttering, "too bad you won't be there to participate."

She ignored this.

"How come, Mom," slurp, slurp on the lollipop. "How come you gotta go to Russia?"

"For the language and the literature. So I don't forget everything I've learned. And to see it with my own eyes. I want to set my eyes on it and not forget what I see."

"Just don't forget us," Jack snapped and stalked into the kitchen to pack pots and pans.

Their love affair seemed to have degenerated into disputes and disagreements, ever since Tommy, a year earlier, had drifted into the wide, flat, brown and often deserted streets of Chicago's South Side. He had stayed six months, sleeping on his older brother's couch, drinking and generally causing the place to devolve into squalor. Every morning Jack would stumble sleepily into the living room, only to find the mirror image, the twin of his detested father, the degraded twin of his beloved uncle, snoring with his mouth open, his stubbled chin jutting like the derelict prow of some smashed boat on a rocky beach into the air, sprawled on the black and white, threadbare sofa, a half-empty bourbon bottle on the floor, his heaped and rancidly odiferous clothing next to it. This sight ruined every day, as Jack retreated from it into himself, into sardonic bitterness and anger that became cold waves of sarcasm, crashing over his lover's bewildered head. She could not wait to go to Russia.

Meanwhile Morris Lichter was in a fit. "You mean instead of letting that Jack Diamond marry you and make an honest woman of you, you're flitting off to where? To the Soviet Union? Have you lost your marbles? What if they don't let you leave?"

"It's a large group of American college students," she had explained into the phone. "Of course they'll let us leave."

"They don't let the Jews who live there leave. And you're Jewish. And they're a bunch of anti-Semites. Are you nuts?"

"No, but you're mind is obviously made up—"

"Of course it's made up. I know a lousy idea when I see one."

"It's a UN program."

"Like I give a good goddamn if it's a UN program? I don't care if it's a military program, or an Israeli program, or a Martian program. You're not going, and that's final."

"I'm paying for it myself."

"So just because you earned a little money, you're going to go throw your life away and very likely wind up in some Siberian work camp?"

"To do that to American students would be very bad for their image."

"You think those thugs care about their image? If they decide to lock you up, for any reason under the sun, you can kiss your foot-loose freedom goodbye. Go to France and Italy instead. You studied those languages. I'll pay for it."

"You really don't need to worry."

Morris, apoplectic now, sputtered into the phone: "You're going to the Soviet Union, and I don't need to worry? You think I've got the brain of a gnat? Please, just consider the possibilities."

"I have, and I'm not worried."

"Then there's something very wrong with you."

"I have friends who went last year."

"Goody for them."

"They came back fine. They said it was a once in a lifetime experience."

"They go to a totalitarian country, where you utter a peep against the government and wind up in a labor camp and they enjoyed this?" Hollered her irate parent. "What kind of friends do you have?"

"Russian scholars."

"You couldn't pay me to go to that country."

"Good, because you're not going. I am. It's going to be a learning experience."

"Learning what—how to live under constant surveillance? With that kind of learning, give me ignorance."

"I don't have to, you've already got it."

"You're so pigheaded and foolish, you don't think I have any idea what it'll be like. But you, young lady, are the one who'll be in for a surprise."

"Oh?"

"It'll be a disaster at worst; at best, two months in a dreary, paranoid environment. Take my advice, marry Harry."

"Harry is Jack's brother."

"Well, marry one of them. Don't go. Oh, I should have sent you to a convent school."

"I fail to see how that has any bearing on whether I travel to the Soviet Union."

"When was the last time you heard about nuns touring communist countries?"

"Well, if I was a nun, I couldn't get married."

"I could live with that. At least consider it."

"What?"

"Taking a vow. Join the Catholic Church. It's better than defecting."

"I'm not defecting."

"What about summer in Honolulu—all expenses paid?"

"Really, it will be okay. Besides, the idea of Hawaii makes me sick."

"But Moscow doesn't. What's wrong with you? You need your head examined. Get a shrink. I'll pay for it. Spend the summer in intensive psychotherapy."

Jack sidled up to the receiver. "It's hopeless," he shouted. "She's as stubborn as a mule."

"Well, he got that right," Morris said.

"Maybe *you* should marry Jack."

"I would if it would keep you out of the Soviet Union. Lily," Morris hollered. "I can't take it. She's too stupid and stubborn. You talk to her."

"She won't listen to me," Lily said, but took the phone anyway. "Morris would really rather you went to Paris this summer."

"Paris? I thought it was Honolulu."

"He told me Paris. That's what we discussed."

"Tell him to get his story straight."

"All expenses paid."

"Boy, you two are really flinging the money around today."

"It's his idea. But I agree. Russia doesn't sound wise."

"But you've got to agree it'll improve my Russian language skills."

"So what? I don't care about that."

"Oh," and the conversation ground to an awkward halt.

"I know we haven't had much of a relationship since you went to college," her mother began after a moment.

"We talk on the phone about twice a month. And you paid my tuition."

"Your father was very stubborn."

"So I'm not the only pig-headed one in the family."

"I think if we had had more contact, you wouldn't be doing this."

"No," her daughter sighed. "I really am doing this for Russian literature and the Russian language."

After this warm, family confab, Jack was moodier than ever. Little snide comments popped out now and then to the effect that Naomi was not the best mother she could be. He crowded in and made a show of fixing her son his meals, but Snow was not deceived. He acted then as always as if his life depended on his mother, as it did, and begged her not to go away in the summer. She persuaded him to accept it with beautiful pictures of life in the cabin at Tower Oaks Bend and promises of treats and toys from cold, exotic, far-off Russia. At his eager request, she described what she had learned about the vast, flat, snow-covered steppe, stretching away to meet the horizon, as stupendous as the ocean. She read him bed-time stories about Baba-Yaga, the witch who lived in a hut on chicken legs deep in a birch forest, and, at his request, did so aloud in Russian, a language he could not understand but loved the sound of. She told him that somewhere she had read that Russian was the language of angels, and as she uttered its different diphthongs, he pictured magnificent seraphs, their immense silver wings sweeping through a whitely snow-filled sky. In fact, she read to him in Russian every night, until the small warm form became limp and the blondish, brownish head pressed damply in slumber against her. Then Jack would scoop the sleeping child up, carry him in to his bed, where they would draw up the covers.

"How will I get him asleep when you're away? I don't read Russian."

"Read in Spanish."

By the time Betsy Ein breezed in to help with the packing, the frost between them was palpable. Betsy—a Marxist feminist who, upon graduation from the University of Chicago, took up residence in a women's collective on the North Side, where she barely supported herself writing book reviews for local alternative newspapers and working in a local women's health clinic—sided with Naomi, having convinced herself that this odyssey to the Soviet Union was politically motivated, despite her friend's frequent insistence on the contrary and on the general principal that any assertion of independence by the female half of a couple was to be encouraged. There was plenty of that in her own romantic relationship. The man Betsy cohabitated with, Shane Richards, a college drop-out, who spent his days in a pool hall on Division Street, supported her in these and indeed all of her often shrill, never understated views. He worked evenings at a North Side coffee house/bookstore where he functioned as a general manager. When that failed to cover the bills, he sold small quantities of marijuana at exorbitant prices to students, hippies and other assorted street people and was a familiar figure on the North Side and indeed in Hyde Park, tall, raw-boned, with long, light brown hair, a perennial floppy blue hat and a grin crowded with long, rather sharp teeth that somewhat belied his easy-going, relaxed and slangy air, and hinted at concealed depths of craftiness and connivance, which were, partially, the street smarts of someone who had lived hand to mouth and by his wits for a number of years.

Shane was an honorary member of the women's collective. Only one other man was permitted to live there, and both had had their feminism, political views and attitudes toward household chores thoroughly vetted. In addition to his political purity, Shane appealed to the collective because he was an artist, an abstract expressionist, sometimes conceptualist, sometimes minimalist painter, who spent his days splashing bright blues, greens, oranges, mauves and pinks onto large canvases—but most important, a creative spirit who did not succumb to the petty bourgeois individualism that, the members of the collective all agreed, infected most artists. Shane was a serious political revolutionary, who supported the violent overthrow of the government, the redistribution of all wealth and the end of all imperialist wars. He had some rather unorthodox and lurid ideas about what should be done with the members of the ruling class that he was careful to explain, in gory detail, only to listeners he was sure of. These corporate bigwigs and millionaire CEOs he viscerally loathed, never referring to them as anything other than "America's titled nobility." Posters of Che and Fidel decorated the walls of the room he and Betsy shared, and both belonged to a Marxist study group. Though he lived hand to mouth, somehow he always had money, a fact attributed by his roommates to his vigorous participation in the underground economy.

"I thought you'd be out shooting pool," Betsy remarked, lugging a large, threadbare suitcase through the drab and dimly lit kitchen to their room in the back. Shane lounged at the gray Formica table, stirring a cup of instant coffee and smoking a cigarette, the blue gray smoke of which filtered through the shaft of sunlight that penetrated the gloom from one grimy, back alley window. In that light and smoke, his hair gleamed bluishly, as did his eyes and teeth.

"No money to be made today," the deep vibrato of his voice filled the room. "What's that?" With his cigarette he indicated the tattered piece of luggage.

"Naomi's. We're storing it while she goes to the USSR."

"Vive la revolucion."

"She claims that's got nothing to do with it. It's all literature and language for her. Boy, that Jack Diamond is one ill-tempered, reactionary son of a bitch. I don't know how she puts up with him and his relentless sarcasm directed at anything she does that fails to involve stroking his male ego. I'd have fled or murdered him years ago."

"Jack's not so bad," Shane remarked lightly, placing his cigarette in the little, battered tin ashtray and withdrawing a joint from his shirt pocket. "Pays good money for his pot."

"I don't care if he pays gold bullion. He's a tireless sexist and gun-nut, and the way he talks to her makes me sick. It's abusive."

"Went through somethin' awful in his childhood. Father killed his uncle or some such."

"Should've killed Jack, rid the world of one more egotistical chauvinist, who wakes up on the wrong side of bed and takes it out on some woman. She's got to be out of her mind, putting up with that sardonic, contemptuous, scornful, critical—"

Shane held up a scarred and sinewy hand. "I get the picture." With his other hand, equally marked and muscled, he offered her the joint, whose sweet cloying smoke now drifted through the dimness. Betsy shook her many red curls. "I've got a review to write."

"So Snow stays with Jack," Shane mused, holding his breath after a long inhalation. He exhaled and rested the joint in the ashtray, taking up his cigarette whose blue smoke somehow reflected a similar tint from the pallor of his shaven cheeks. Then, with the cigarette fixed in his mouth below his thick brown moustache, said: "I always liked that little rat."

"Poor thing—thinks Jack's his father, imitates him in every way. Whoever heard of a sarcastic seven year old?"

"The little rat's got a sense of humor. I drove him to his summer camp at the Y once. He said the building looked like a minimum security prison. He was right too, what with the barbed wire above the pool fence. I wouldn't mind having a kid like that around."

His lover's green eyes suddenly opened wide and blazed, her fists clenched and her well-formed body beneath her jeans, T-shirt and vest tightened, as if a current of electric rage had suddenly jolted through it. "I *had* to have that abortion," she growled. "There is no way we could afford a kid."

"Not strictly true, Bets."

"Call me Besty, please."

"Besty." He pushed back his long brown hair, cast her a glittering-eyed reproach. "You know I can get more money if I have to."

"In a pinch, yes. But not day to day, year in, year out. We're too busy living hand to mouth to start raising children. Do you have any idea what it's been like for Naomi? I do, because I remember what it was like being her roommate for two years. Having a baby, a toddler, it's a responsibility that doesn't go away. You can't take a vacation from it or send the kid back wherever he came from when you get tired. No, I can't do it. Besides, last year you worked on an assembly line in Flint; how would you continue that kind of work and the organizing—you were talking about going back to the steel mills in Gary, starting in July."

"That could wait." He had been leaning forward, taut, listening to her. Now he slumped back into the pale, slack torpor that had held him when she first entered the room. "It's your body—"

"Damn straight."

"And you can do what you want with it, and I support you in that. But it wasn't just your baby. It was mine too. So you should know, if the matter ever comes up again, I will provide whatever money is needed, and I will do the child-raising."

"Really? Where? At the pool hall? And where will little Johnny go while you're pouring molten steel in Gary?"

"Don't be so angry," he spoke softly. "You know I always find a way to do what's necessary."

"True enough," she replied, somewhat placated. "But I think you, like any man, have little idea what's involved—"

"Naomi managed it—work, college, raising a boy, all on her own. You know Jack didn't do much beyond the occasional baby-sitting."

"True, true," she repeated, taking the cigarette he had shaken out of the pack of Marlboros and proffered her.

"So you'll consider it."

"We're not trying for a child."

"I never said that. I said *if* there's another mishap."

"Why don't you take Snow for the summer? Get this out of your system."

Shane grinned—it glimmered whitely in the gloaming. "No can do. I got my job in the steel mills just in time for the strike. I start next week."

"This *is* news. When's the strike vote?"

"Soon. Probably right after I start."

"Did Sarkowski get you the job?"

He nodded and resumed smoking his cigarette. The forgotten joint smoldered in the dented ashtray. "He's packing the mill with radicals. Not that he needs to. The workforce there is already a cauldron of activism. They're not just ready to strike, they're ready to take to the streets. But he's leaving nothing to chance, good old Rolo."

"Well, well," she stood in the shadows, a dark form except for the failing light reflected from her eyes, focused motionlessly on his face. "I'll take over your job at the bookstore, run some sort of disclaimer at the bottom of my reviews. We could use the extra cash."

"Always."

"So how will you get to Gary?"

"I'll commute in the Pontiac, of course, like I used to."

"That piece for junk? You'll be lucky to make it to the South Side, one day."

"I have faith in that old car."

She threw back her head, and peals of melodious laughter filled the room, splashed over his head and into his ears, so that soon he was laughing too, and stood up to take her in his arms. Still convulsed with the hilarity of anyone believing in the battered old black Pontiac that rumbled like thunder as Shane tore down Division Street in it, they commenced waltzing in the kitchen shadows.

"Maybe I'll sell a few big pieces to *Vogue* and buy you a BMW," she giggled.

"And maybe I'll die and go to heaven," he chuckled.

"And maybe there is a heaven." At that they nearly collapsed upon each other. He reached over, flipped on the radio, and Chicago blues filled the room. He put his arm around her waist and soon the laughter subsided, and they were clutching each other desperately, dancing closely in the twilight that purled with sounds of traffic, other, distant music and sidewalk conversations, drifting in with the end of the day. From time to time they listened absent-mindedly as they held each other and danced there in the dying light.

They had met in their first year at the University of Chicago, she originally from an affluent Jewish neighborhood in Los Angeles, followed by La Jolla, where her father, a professor and an engineer, worked for a defense contractor, and he from Lubbock, Texas, from a neighborhood that was definitely a walk on the wild side compared to hers, although Shane had spent most of his childhood in his grandfather's trailer, receiving occasional beatings from the old man, a strict disciplinarian and God-fearing Baptist, who was convinced the boy would turn out like his no-good father. While her ex-boyfriends from Southern California headed off to medical and law school, Shane plunged into the revolution, alternately a street person or factory worker, agitating for higher wages and more job security. He did not think of the future in the way her high school friends had— college, professional school, years of high earnings, followed by a secure retirement. Such thoughts apparently never crossed his mind. Except for the one startling aberration—acceptance into and attendance at a top U.S. college—he belonged, as he put it, quoting Mao, swimming in the vast seas of the people, furthering the cause of revolution. He did not plan ahead in the way that future doctors and lawyers did, nor did he intend to live to retirement. Life would be short and furious, the fatal struggle early engaged, already engaged, evident in the calluses on his hands, his scars and sinews, the surprising gray in the stubble on his chin, unfeigned, honest mark everywhere of the mortal human animal who knows what is coming. In the depths of Chicago winters, with snow piled to the window ledges, he would say that it was time to migrate to Mexico.

"And live how?" she would ask.

"Hand to mouth."

"We can do that better here."

So they lived by their wits. More than anything, even more than their passionate politics, their young lives were already marked by the absence of, struggle for and need for money. And then he discovered painting, or, more accurately, selling his paintings. He was a one-man assembly line, mass producing abstract art and selling it with astonishing alacrity. He had a knack for it, knew what people wanted, and the canvasses just poured out of his third floor studio in the Marxist, feminist collective.

"It looks like a Frankenthaler," remarked Rema Roberts, the history graduate student, who lived for a brief while with the only other man permitted in the collective.

"She's my inspiration," he replied absently.

"Really? I thought it was conceptual art these days."

"I'm going back to my roots."

"The roots you put down twenty minutes ago?"

"I started this over a year ago, I'll have you know."

She laughed, her large eyes and strangely attractive, crooked nose reconfiguring into an image of lovely mirth. "They sure sell like hotcakes," she added, after a moment.

He grinned toothily. "Do they ever."

Once Rema poked her pretty head in the doorway and saw him alternately splashing color on a canvass and then gazing at an art magazine, open to a page with a huge color photograph of a painting. "No plagiarizing," she admonished. He turned, tall, long-haired, lupine, his big bones visible in his hands, tattooed arms and shoulders, with the look in his eyes of a wolf caught feasting on a carcass.

"Wouldn't dream of it."

"How much'll you get for that one?" She asked.

"Lot's," he replied, then picked up the magazine and read: "over twenty five hundred dollars. Not bad for a half an hour's work." He chuckled, lowered the journal and resumed painting, humming and singing under his breath: "Before you drift into unconsciousness, I'd like to have another kiss."

"Before, you were singing about your papa," she lit a cigarette and inhaled greedily.

"Oh yes."

"Another no-goodnik, like Jack Diamond's?"

"You got it," he paused to smoke the cigarette that smoldered in a large metal bottle cap, where it had left a liquid brown stain. "Always on the move, my Daddy was, very busy, littering Texas with kids, Oh, and gambling. That was his thing. It's a miracle," he drawled, "I attended college."

Betsy came up. "Shane here was telling me about his father," Rema remarked.

"Really?" His paramour looked mildly surprised, slurping carrot juice through a straw. "It's not his favorite topic."

"How *do* you drink that crap?" he asked.

"It's good for me."

"God help us."

"It'll help you live longer."

"Drinking that, who would want to?"

"Shane, when you're on your death bed," slurp, slurp, "and I'm standing beside you, the picture of health, I will be sure *not* to remind you that the reason is all those gallons of carrot juice I drank—"

"You better not."

"While you smoked cigarettes and guzzled coffee and bourbon."

"Cause if you do, I'll leap up off my deathbed and wring your neck."

"Let me try it," Rema took the offered straw and drank and gagged. "That's awful," she concluded.

"You got that right," thus Shane. "Ladies, I'm too inspired to move at the moment. But all this talk of beverages has awakened my thirst. Would one of you be so kind as to get me a Coca Cola from the fridge?"

The women looked at each other. "Get it yourself," they said in unison.

"I'm not your servant," slurp, slurp.

"Me neither."

"Shit," he flung down the paint brush. "There goes that inspiration."

"Just copy instead," Betsy giggled. "It's what you do best."

The women drifted back to their studies, while he remained at the easel, methodically layering paint onto the canvas. Hours passed, day turned slowly to twilight, as the murmurs of traffic from the dim street below thickened with the shadows at rush hour. The street lamp shot in its hopeless light that stretched across the floor in a long rectangle. Observing it, he realized he was painting nearly in the dark. "No matter," he said to himself, "it might even come out better." Somewhere in the distance church bells chimed seven times. He paused, ambled over to the window and gazed out over the gloom-enfolded rooftops, still visible in the crepuscular glow of the dying day. Down beside the curb stood his battered Pontiac with two neighborhood kids, he noticed, leaning against it. He opened the window. "Get the fuck off of my car," he hollered down three stories. Alarmed, the boys jumped up, looking around to detect the origin of the voice. "Now beat it. Scram!" He yelled again, and they fled, down the side street and around the corner to the busy, traffic-clogged thoroughfare, where the gloaming was thick with honking horns and screeching brakes. "I won't bring my cue tonight," he thought of the bar with the pool tables. "I'll use theirs." Then he drifted back to the canvass, painting absentmindedly, dreaming of the village of Manzanillo in Mexico, on the Pacific Coast, and the stupendous marijuana he had purchased there the previous summer.

He and Besty had ridden a train south from Mexicali through the blistering dessert to Guadalajara. The windows were sealed shut, and the air-conditioning broken, so they spent the trip on the small, scorching, bouncing metal platform between two cars. To their amazement, the other passengers remained in their seats, drenched in sweat and near heat prostration, unwilling to relinquish the privilege of sitting that they had paid for. There was, he suspected, some principle of the impoverished economy here. You bought a seat, so if you stood, you were being cheated. So they sat, exclaiming in wonderment over the heat in the oven-like train cars, their chickens silent in wooden cages with their feathers damp and wilted, their children sprawled next to them, dark eyes glistening, occasionally moaning, but mostly listless, silent and sweat-soaked. Shane and Betsy stood, smoked, watched the desert pass and tried to cool themselves in the furnace blast of wind that rolled off the barren plain that stretched away, tan and empty. Each had only a worn knapsack and the jeans and T-shirts they wore. She also carried a bright red and white woven Mexican bag that served as a purse, vital repository of money, aspirin for her headaches and cigarettes.

It was an inauspicious introduction to the country. After a few hours, Shane, shirtless and perspiring, wished they had stayed in La Jolla with his girlfriend's parents. There they could have luxuriated in the beach, the pool, the air-conditioned splendor of the house and sundry university coffee shops. He was in no mood for anything strenuous, such as enduring the intense solar heat or standing for long periods. Once or twice they attempted to rest in the sauna-like cars, but gave up almost immediately, choking on the stale, burning air. "The city will be better," she had assured him. "All the rooms in our hotel have fans."

"Fans?" He asked. "I'm ready for some refrigeration."

"AC is too expensive. We'll live with the fans."

"I suppose I can tolerate it if they can," he jerked his thumb in the direction of an elderly Mexican, seated in the train car, whose magnificent white moustache and mane glistened with perspiration. He did not complain, nor even loosen his collar, but instead sat stolidly, glaring down the aisle, a look in which accusation and resignation mingled with a grudging acceptance of a human condition that had to put up with such miseries. In this, the old man reminded Shane of his grandfather, of his facial expression when the faucet water came out brown or the toilet would not flush, or when he and his grandson nearly tripped over each other because the tiny trailer was so cramped. "I am a human being," the expression said, "and look what I put up with." Even his grandfather's ferocious creed of sin and retribution could not efface that complaint, that lament of the species that lit his eyes and cast his voice into a minor key whenever he encountered yet another indignity.

The children slumped on the seats, not even curious about the two gringos, who came and sat across from them.

"It is terrible, no?" The elderly man demanded in heavily accented English. "They treat us worse than animals, worse than dead meat. That, at least, they would refrigerate." He expected no response, but fell silent and continued glaring.

"You English is excellent," Shane ventured.

The old man snorted derisively. "I should hope so. Forty years I worked in factories in America, from Texas to Chicago. Always when I come home in the summer, this horrible train trip, in a sealed car, as hot as an oven. They treat me like a bundle of hay. I send my grandchildren to college, but can't even get a window that opens."

The children across the aisle groaned miserably, while their fat mother fanned herself with a newspaper.

"I can't take it," Betsy said. "Let's go back between the cars."

By the time the train started pulling into small, dusty impoverished towns, Shane had seen enough of the desert, he thought, forever. He had never much liked it in Texas, where its sandy desolation had greeted him year in and year out as a confirmation of his fate, until the miracle of his acceptance and scholarship to the University of Chicago. Prior to that, he had not even been sure there would be enough money for the University of Texas at Austin, his top, what he considered at the time most likely, choice, that bohemian enclave beckoning with all the enchantment of a crystal city in the clouds, when viewed from the dry doldrums of his Lubbock trailer park. He had never dismissed the possibility of years in his grandfather's trailer, working at the convenience store, staggering home drunk and then berated by the old man's fierce diatribe on drink and hellfire, delivered at the top of his lungs and followed by equally loud eclats, as he subsided from religious fury into the snores that nightly shook their tiny abode from one end to the other.

Teenage Shane would sit, chastened but still inebriated, at the minute kitchenette table, and ruefully contemplate his barren future. The only thing he knew was that it could not be worse than the past, because now, at least, the old man was too frightened of the boy's size to try to beat him.

Harriston, "Hank" Richards, also known by the sobriquet "Root," which Shane hated, was tall and raw-boned like his sons and grandsons and usually could not keep track of which offspring had fathered Shane. "Bred like rabbits, not people," he could be heard mumbling to himself of his progeny. But he had taken Shane in when he was abandoned, and had set his sights on a true Christian upbringing, much to the chagrin of the boy, who had decided early on that religion was nonsense, turning the other cheek was a way to get trampled and love they neighbor was impossible when they kept lots of guns and pit bulls that roamed and bit freely. "You want me to love Skunk Simsbury, just cause he lives in the trailer next door?" Shane demanded. "He *set* that dog on me."

"Now, now, you don't know that."

"I saw him."

"You will follow the word of the Gospel, of Christ our Lord."

"I will follow my own common sense."

And then whack went the belt across his legs.

By the time he was fifteen, however, that had stopped. One day he defied the old man, who glanced up at the hulking adolescent and lost his nerve. Thereafter Hank kept his belt around his waist, and Shane did as he pleased, which included drinking and smoking pot, but not to the exclusion of his studies. College was the ticket out of the trailer park, and he did not intend to miss that. It was also in high school that Shane began to reveal his radical bent. "I hope those black Panthers blow up Chicago, blow up

New York, blow up L.A." he said one morning, perusing the newspaper over scrambled eggs and buttered toast. "If I was black, I sure would."

"There's something wrong with you."

"Rage."

"Always were a strange kid. Funny in the head. I tried my darndest to keep your feet on the straight and narrow, the path of Christ our Lord—"

"Instead it's Che Guevara and Malcolm X."

"Sinners, hell-bound if ever anybody was."

"I'm not discussing it with you."

"You better get yourself in church, boy."

Shane glowered at the old man over the top of his newspaper and almost told him to shut up.

"You follow these godless communists and before you know it, the police will fill your body with bullets."

"We'll see about that."

The relationship with his grandfather had undergone many changes, beginning with Shane's childhood terror of the belt and weary submission to all the rigors of the old man's church, a period in which Hank, despite his hours as an assistant in the local pharmacy, was an ever-present authority, never to be questioned, only feared, but also ambivalently loved, as the one adult who had rescued Shane from the drunken chaos, the neglect of filth and frequently missed meals and finally the brutal abandonment by his father. He fed the boy, sheltered him, sent him to school and sat with him in the evenings at the little Formica kitchenette table, to help him with his homework. The old man attended parent/teacher conferences and once even took the boy on a three-day vacation to Galveston that shimmered in his mind like a memory of paradise. Without grandpa, Shane had no idea what would have become of him; but living with the old man certainly had its drawbacks. Fortunately the beatings were rare; even so, they damaged the boy's love and sense of gratitude and led him to seek something else to cling to, in his reading of books, newspapers, then, in the school library, magazines. By the time he was fifteen, when Hank was rethinking the wisdom of attempting to discipline him physically, Shane had peeled away what he learned to call the lies of capitalism to gaze directly on the rotten fruit within. He was a Marxist. A Red, Hank called him and was scared out of his wits that someone would find out and do something horrible to the boy. The old man was uncertain whether or not the state could punish Shane for his shocking political views, but he did not intend to find out and so sought at every opportunity to change the boy's mind or at least instill enough healthy fear to get him to keep his mouth shut. These attempts failed miserably. By the late 1960s, the young man had, in Hank's words, "gone completely wild," and travelled to Chicago ready to join SDS.

In spite of his fear, the old pharmacist's assistant found himself listening to the rebel's rants, and while he would never admit to agreeing with a single word, found himself, in odd moments, considering that some of it fit well with what Christ said about the poor. This observation would fire up his sense of religion, and he would urge Shane again to attend church. "What the bible says about a rich man and a camel passing through the eye of a needle, Shane, you would agree with. Listen to what the reverend says."

"Grandpa, I had a decade of that mumbo jumbo. It didn't take. You like it. I don't."

"It's not a matter of liking. It's seeing the truth and the wisdom of the Lord's way."

Shane glanced appreciatively at the gently pleading blue eyes, the grizzled old face that looked even older with the upper denture out for the evening, floating in a glass of water on the tiny table. The old man really did care, genuinely worried about the salvation of his grandson's soul and about protecting him from the consequences of his political views. Shane saw this, but would not deceive his grandfather, no matter how soothing a soft white lie would be. He realized with a little shock that he respected his grandfather too much for that. Running his sinewy fingers through his long brown hair, Shane took a deep breath, then leaned forward, having made up his mind. "Tonight's the night I tell you about *Capital*."

"That thick book of communist trash you been reading?"

"Call it what you like, but listen."

Grumbling, Hank did, but in the end, of course, neither could convert the other.

In his senior year, Shane worked at the local convenience store, spending some of his pin money on pot and cigarettes, but turning the rest over to his grandfather at the end of each week. Friday night often saw them closeted in the small trailer, as Hank reworked the monthly finances, in the glow of the little table lamp, reflected off the plastic and vinyl walls. "You don't need college, Shane. Get yourself a trade. Be a plumber or an auto mechanic. They make good money. That's what I wish I'da done."

Shane glanced keenly at the old man. "You always said you liked clean work, like what you go now."

Hank snorted derisively. "I'd like good money better, even if I had to get dirty. Shane, find yourself a trade!" His knobby, gnarled hands fumbled with the checkbook. "Never enough," he mumbled, wiping the back of his hand across his gray, grizzled cheek. "It's never enough and never has been." He paused, then looked up almost beseechingly "and now finally, when there's two of us earning paychecks, you're going to up and go away to Chicago. What do you need to go to the windy city for? I been there. Lots of poor folk, out of work, living in those wide, flat, barren neighborhoods. Stay here and get yourself some honest work."

"I'll get higher pay with a college degree."

His grandfather waved his hand and shook his head, which, when he stopped, wobbled uncertainly and agedly. "You'll become an intellectual. That's what'll happen to you. Intellectuals don't work. They live off the fat of the land."

Far into the night Shane sat at the convenience store beneath the fluorescent bulb, the empty desolation of Texas enfolding him as he read *Capital*, *Soul on Ice*, or the prison journals of Gramsci or the writings of Isaac Deutscher or *The Wretched of the Earth* or other revolutionary works. He checked *Ramparts*, *The Nation*, and numerous alternative publications out from the public library. He sat and smoked in his little island of light, surrounded by a vast, sultry sea of darkness, and his desire to destroy the capitalist system smoldered in his heart. One night a young man entered, the only customer for hours, pointed a gun at him and demanded the contents of the cash register. "Take it all," Shane said, "like I give a fuck what happens to the WestTex Corporation's profits."

"What's that?"

"The company that owns this store."

"I'm takin' a Slurpee, too."

"Take whatever you want. Just put that thing away," Shane gestured at the gun.

"Hostess cupcakes?"

"Take all that Hostess shit. What are you asking me for? You're the robber."

"Oh."

"But if I may make a suggestion?"

The pale, young, crew-cutted thief, who had the words "ex con" practically tattooed on his forehead, nodded expectantly.

"Skip the hotdogs. They're horrible."

"How 'bout them donuts?"

"The donuts are okay. I eat 'em myself. Here, you want cigarettes too?"

"Marlboros," the criminal called over his shoulder from the Slurpee machine, and then, slouching back over to the counter, "but I need my protein."

"Eat those hot dogs at your own risk."

"What about the beef jerky?"

"Better than those hot dogs. I nearly threw up last time I bit into one of those."

"Please, show some consideration." The robber held out a plastic bag, and Shane unloaded the cash into it, along with a carton of Marlboros. After filching some donuts and the beef jerky, the felon looked satisfied. "What ya readin'?"

"Prison diaries, by a revolutionary."

"Oh yeah. There's lots of revolutionaries in the joint."

"Let's hope they get out and burn this system to the ground."

The young man smiled. "To the revolution!" He said, toasting the cashier with his Slurpee and then strolled back out to his pickup, leaving Shane with his ferocious books and his furious desire for destruction, alone in the dry, quiet, all-surrounding Texas night.

Later, after he reported the crime, he walked out to his grandfather's white Impala, the one he thundered to high school in every day, the roar of its souped-up engine audible for miles around. He tossed his copy of *Capital* onto the passenger seat and guided the car onto the black, flat, empty road. Usually he had the radio blaring, but that night he just let his thoughts roam the quiet like wild animals—surplus labor, surplus value, prison, ex-cons and, in the fall, Chicago colored in his mind by tints from *The Jungle*, which he had just read.

The boy from a Texas trailer arrived in Hyde Park in September, settled into his dorm room and, on his first day, caught sight of the sparkling green eyes and luxurious red curls of a girl from California and lost his heart, once and forever. He asked her out immediately, and found what he had already surmised from various clues, that she too was bent on a revolution that would change political and social relations in the United States forever. A week later she moved into his dorm room, and his roommate moved out. She was wild, but he was wilder, and together they surrendered to the cyclone of the Chicago underground in the late 1960s.

As he gazed at her pale, freckled arms and face, next to him on the little platform between train cars, bound for Guadalajara, Shane saw again that here was the pole around which his life revolved—the compact but somewhat voluptuous figure, the sharp intelligence, the occasionally nasty tongue and the hard-headed practicality, all that had eclipsed even his political fury, though the couple was united in that too.

"Joined at the hip," he grinned down at her, wiping the sweat off his forehead with the back of his hand.

274

"Who, what?"

"Us."

"Oh that," she smiled. "Old news."

They arrived in the city at night and made their way through warm, noisy streets to their little, dilapidated hotel. There was no fan. But the close, stifling oven they had traveled in was gone: it was now merely summer. So they washed up and, though both felt amorous, she thought they should quickly look up their Mexican friends, who lived in a student/worker cooperative. They padded down the carpeted hotel steps that creaked and wobbled and through the decayed lobby and soon found themselves in a nocturnal crowd, where their college Spanish served them well enough to find their bus. They rode with numerous night workers across town, then down wide, dusty avenues to the outskirts, following their directions to a small house with an overgrown garden in front. Betsy knocked on the door and shouted in Spanish, and shortly a medium-height student with a bushy, black moustache let them in to a foyer crammed with books and newspapers. Behind him, they discerned a young woman in jeans, with an embroidered white blouse, sitting in the lamplight at a table. She did not look up from her book. Her black hair fell in a long braid down her back and except for occasionally raising her hand to smoke her cigarette, she seemed perfectly immobile.

"Renita?" Betsy asked. "Renita Montero?"

The young woman glanced up, noticed them for the first time, and her intensely dark eyes glistened with such life, it was as if her entire being were ensouled there. "Our comrades from Chicago," she explained to the young man who had let them enter and who, at these words, visibly relaxed. He gently shut the door. "This way," he spoke softly and gestured down the hall toward the room where the woman with the remarkable eyes waited, smiling.

"You've arrived in time for preparations for our back-to-school student strike," she said in perfect, unaccented English.

"That was the idea," Shane replied.

"Since you have such experience in this area."

"You could say that."

She offered them coffee and biscuits, which they, hot, tired and still a bit grimy from their journey, gladly accepted, all the while exuding a cool self-possession legendary in her circles. She emanated discretion and the restraint of some shy, wild animal lurking in shadow, carefully sizing up the creatures out in the light. She had been described to the two Americans as having a plan for everything, of great care with regard to all possible contingencies, and, on one of these, she started right in: "This is a map of the university buildings," she said, spreading a paper before them. "The police usually mass and charge from here," she tapped the indication of an avenue with her pencil. "But we have to be prepared for them to come from this street also," again she pointed. "How do we get out with minimum injury and arrests, if they do that?" She glanced up, her eyes two dark, alive, molten pools, the only part of her aside from her notably thick, coarse, black hair, that was not average. She was neither tall nor short, thin nor fat, dark nor fair, beautiful nor ugly. Except for those eyes and that braid, she would blend in anywhere, "to swim like a fish in the ocean of the people," she later remarked, to which Shane replied, "don't we all." And she dressed so as to highlight her ordinariness, never to stand out. Her earrings were very simple: small gold hoops. Her only other jewelry was a little woman's watch. She kept her nails clipped short—"like a good communist"—and there was something fine and sinewy about her fingers. She was energetic, but not overwhelmingly so, intelligent but without dazzle, cautious and thorough, but she camouflaged it, and always politically aware. "Welcome sister," she had greeted Betsy, thus conveying her knowledge of her guest's feminism, the feminist collective where she lived and her solidarity with its aims. With every word, this alert, nondescript young woman conveyed volumes.

Betsy felt drawn to her, as to a kindred spirit, with whom the most important things were already mutually understood. She wanted to discuss her work as a midwife and nurse at the women's health clinic on a shabby little byway just off Division Street, to describe the immigrant factory workers and janitors who populated the dreary waiting room with its cheap, orange plastic chairs, the street vendors and domestics, so many of whom came from Mexico. Renita could work at the clinic too—it was exactly the sort of place where she would fit it. Betsy could easily imagine her taking a patient's blood pressure or reading a pregnancy test. Of course, her native Spanish language would help also. Betsy spoke it, but often thought that she missed idioms, drew a blank on critical slang and sometimes stumbled through her sentences. For some reason this sudden fantasy of her new friend working at the health center overcame her, and she could so barely suppress her enthusiasm that she asked if such clinics existed in Guadalajara.

"Sadly very few," the Mexican woman replied. "Ours is, as you know, a very macho culture and very Catholic, too. A clinic that recommended where to get a legal abortion? Such a thing would be unheard of, would have to be very clandestine here. In this regard, we have a long, long way to go, to catch up to you in the U.S."

Everyone was hungry, so this remarkably self-possessed activist and a young man named Fernando from a local machine parts factory brought forth tamales, rice and beans, while she explained that workers from local plants would join the university strike and that the police had threatened to use live ammunition. But Betsy's concentration was elsewhere. She heard the dry rasp of branches and leaves in the night wind through the open back door, and gazed out the window at the vast darkness of Mexico, spread silently all around, its occasional lights twinkling, back to the desert they had traversed in the train, to the passengers and the near heat prostration. The feel of the cramped bus was still noticeable in her arms and legs. And then there was Shane, quiet and vulpine, his long hair greasy from sweat and no showers, his hand on her shoulder, as he sat beside her, now as always, her partner forever. This, she thought accurately, would never change. By some miracle they had found each other. Here in the black night of a hot, poor, southern country, more than ever she felt that they were of the same mind and heart, ready to join in this fight to which they had come as outsiders. She thanked the young woman for the tamales, and thought how the arc of her life had brought her here, to this moment in this place and of all that lay before her and her beloved. Grateful for the delicious food, she ate with a sense of completion and purpose.

That night they did not go back to the hotel, but stayed at the little house, quietly filled with people, on the outskirts of town. Sharing the rumpled but fairly clean bedding under an open second-story window, her only distraction from the mood that had come over her at dinner was their love-making. After that, she lay, gazing up and out at the star-flecked sky, running her fingers through Shane's long, brownish hair, as he murmured about his grandfather in their Texas trailer and decided that that summer she would meet this guardian of his childhood, on their return to Chicago. She wanted to set eyes upon him before he died.

And suddenly a fear that he would die seized her, and she sat bolt up, naked in the night and looked down at the man she loved. "Let's not stay here long," she said. "Let's do our work, and then head back to Lubbock. It's time I met Mr. Richards."

Shane glanced at her curiously, his eyes glimmering in the dark, as they always did, with more thoughts than he would express. "He's not anything like professor Ein out in San Diego, who used to have an impressive job with a defense contractor. No big house, no donations to the anti-defamation league, no published papers."

"It's time I met him."

"He'll demand to know when we're getting married."

"Well—when?"

"Say the word."

"Soon," she said at length, shaking her long, thick, red curls. "It'll require some planning and discussion with the collective. "

He chuckled. "You lead, and they will follow. I always said so."

"Soon," she repeated softly. "We'll do it soon."

The next day they again rode the bus with its open windows and clouds of road dust billowing in, back into the city, checked out of their hotel and then returned to the little house with its nine occupants. The creepers that twined up the front, the several dark cats in the small, dry yard, the mostly drawn shades in the windows, the two full flower boxes on the sills, everything was withdrawn and deliberately unremarkable. How so many people could live so quietly in such close quarters Betsy found quite mysterious. But there it was: the house was always full and silent, as though its occupants kept some secret deathwatch— "for this semi-fascist, capitalist state," Shane replied, when she divulged her thoughts, "That's whose death they're watching."

"You mean praying for."

"Both."

Later that day they walked through gray drizzle with Renita and Fernando past slabs of sooty warehouses and drab little brick homes with sagging lintels and moldy windows, past a small brackish river and a filthy little canal, over which towered a decrepit cinderblock apartment building, its metal balconies festooned with tattered and brightly colored laundry, like ragged flags on decayed, becalmed but still peopled ships. On they went to a machine parts factory, not Fernando's, where they had no difficulty entering, since no one in authority was anywhere visible. They fanned out, each with a stack of leaflets, whose recipients all grasped them with a serious nod of the head and, still in that serious silence of people who have worked long hours and are carefully conserving their energy, began to read.

They leafleted for scarcely twenty minutes, when suddenly a phalanx of armed policeman burst upon the shop floor and began clubbing them. Betsy ran and felt the impact of a truncheon across her back, but it did not stop her. She stumbled but kept on, scattering her leaflets like confetti on the dirt floor, as she fled off the premises and into a little dead wintry wood beside the factory. The trees there seemed not to acknowledge that it was summer, but stood stark and leafless, as a small, neon green, polluted creek gurgled over their roots. She stopped at last, panting and turned to look at the factory. Someone ran toward her. Instinctively she jumped behind a tree, but saw a moment later that it was Renita, her mouth bloody, still carrying her leaflets. She called to her, asking about the others.

"They took them away," the Mexican woman panted, stopping and bending over to catch her breath. "Shane will be okay, because they'll discover that he's an American. But I'm afraid they might beat Fernando to death." She glanced at her guest imploringly, her hugely swollen upper lip as fiery red and purple as a sunset in dense pollution. "You might be able to help. Go to the police station. Say you have a lawyer."

"But I don't."

"I will give you a name."

"What's the likelihood they'll just arrest me?"

The bruised woman cast her gaze to the ashy ground and shrugged. "What is it ever? Anything we do could lead to trouble with the police. Still, it's worth a try. As an American—"

Betsy elongated her back in a stretch, to alleviate the pain of the attack. "All right," she replied, as they began traversing the dull little wood. "I'll try."

She was ashamed to admit it, but her worry about Shane was suddenly overwhelmed by her fear of approaching the police. What if they beat her again? Or just arrested her, throwing her into a tiny, dank, dark, bug-infested cell? As her mind probed these possibilities, she forgot about the two men and so, was shamed again when Renita said: "Did you see you Shane fighting the police? What a hero! What courage!"

"No, I missed it; too busy running away, I guess."

They again traversed the shabby outskirts of the city, past little, tumble-down gray habitations, arrayed like defeated fortresses after the onslaught of a grimly indomitable enemy, back to their modest, quietly overpopulated and still-resistant house, where, the Mexican woman said, they should wait for one of the residents, who had a car, to return. They sat in the small, sunless kitchen, and suddenly Betsy's terror of the police and thoughts only of survival vanished and in their place came a new fright—what if they killed her man? What if he was badly hurt or died from the beating? How would she live without him? As she sat at the tiny, scarred, wooden table, running her fingers nervously through her red curls, she could not keep quiet. "If they're injured, will they get to see a doctor?"

"Fernando no. Shane maybe."

The image of the former, his dark hair, eyes and skin, lying in a pool of blood, passed through her mind, but before she could panic about it, she pictured Shane struggling, outnumbered and beaten, and she leapt up.

"We should have gone back to the factory."

"For what? We couldn't help. Hopefully they ran away like we did."

She paced, frantic now, and as she did she ranted, her words filling the dark little room and reverberating off its walls. Why didn't the man with the car come?

"He was across town, at another job site, leafleting. He'll be back soon."

The front door creaked, then came heavy, irregular steps in the hall and a soft, muffled sound, which, she realized, was someone slumping to the floor. She hurried out to see Shane, bloody and groaning, lying against the wall, and the phrase "where there is life, there is hope" passed through her mind. "Fernando got away," he moaned. "I saw him running." His vest, his collarless shirt, were spattered with red. Renita brought a wet towel, and together the two women cleaned his face and hands, then moved him to the broken, uneven, living room couch. In her relief to find him alive, Betsy forgot the other man and almost forgot to ask what had happened.

"I saw you run," he said to her, then, "Ow, my head. Do we have any aspirin?"

Renita fetched it. He downed the pill with a bottle of soda. "I'm so thirsty," he guzzled. "I was relieved to see you escaped. But then they piled on me, about five. I would have been a goner, for sure, if one of the plant workers hadn't yelled out 'fire!' When they heard that, the cops stampeded out. I went out another way and saw Fernando running. I tried to follow, but I lost him. He was calling your name, Renita, in terror, just plain terror at what might have happened to you." He drank more soda and leaned back, groaning slightly. "Is this what always happens in Mexico when you try to organize?"

"Pretty often," Renita replied, undoing her disheveled braid and brushing her lustrous black hair. "But this happened so fast, I think they knew we were coming," she looked pensive, rebraiding her hair. "How though? How would they know?"

"Because I told the employees at the plant we'd be back today." It was Fernando, who had come in so quietly, no one had noticed. He leaned against the doorway, breathing heavily, his two black eyes just a shade darker than his skin. "I'll never do that again."

"We must ask Luis—he's our contact there—who gets a promotion after today. Then we'll know who is the—"

"Snitch is the word you're looking for," Shane said. "It's slang for informer."

The Mexican woman helped the unsteady new arrival into an armchair. "We will find this, this snitch," Fernando said, "and leave matters with Luis. He will know how to take care of this."

"Won't they just beat the crap out of him?"

"Nothing so obvious. There are other, less dangerous ways to deal with informers."

"I'm only sorry I ran away so fast," Betsy remarked.

"No, no, you did good," her lover reassured her. "You can't imagine my relief as I saw you sprinting out that gate. Then all I had to worry about was me. I had been terrified to think what they might do to you." He ran his fingers through her curls, as though they were a treasure he had almost lost. "You know, maybe you were right—maybe we should return to see my grandfather."

"But there's so much work to do," Renita said.

"Well, Bets?"

His beloved lit a cigarette for him. "Renita's right. I think we should stay longer. Besides, you're here officially, as a union representative."

He wanted to doze, so the two women retreated to the kitchen shadows, where they talked in low voices for an hour, as other members of the household came and went, vanishing as silently and with the same, almost otherworldly, poignant, lost purposiveness of mist in moonlight. Fernando entered, looking for aspirin, then, in a rare display of emotion, kissed Renita passionately, told her in Spanish that he loved her forever and was ready to kill the policeman who had hit her across the mouth and then retired upstairs to rest. The American visitor remarked that she had not known until that moment that they were a couple, whereupon Renita said simply: "He is my husband." Her eyes glowed intently, and she added: "We come from villages in Yucatan. We met at the university, where we became communists."

"I thought before you said socialists."

"Things are different here," her companion replied, "from the way they are in America. We have journeyed as far from this rotten, corrupt system as we can possibly go."

That night, as she lay beside Shane under the open window, stroking his hair and gazing up at the billions of stars, she wondered, who did they think they were, sojourning into Mexico to organize factory workers? The rules were clearly quite different here, and if she might be spared the brunt of official violence because she was a woman, that would not be so for Shane. And what if he got killed? Life would be unlivable, and as she gazed upon this sudden, stark prospect of an existence without him, everything withered and dissolved into ash and shadow and terror for the future. For eventually they would grow old, he would die, and then she would have to make do without his hazel green eyes with the strange lights, the strong hands, long teeth, vulpine air, the laconic speech, the hatred of all forms of oppression that flashed out in unexpected moments. No, she could not do without any of this. They had to return to the United States. It was too dangerous to stay. She said so.

"I knew you were thinking that. You had that look. But Betsy, it was just one beating."

"Next time you could get killed."

"Not likely."

"But possible."

"Lots of things are possible."

She, propped up on her elbow, lay beside him and considered his moonlit face and his boundless certainly that no matter what risk he took, he would survive. She had no such certainty. She saw the dangers that confronted them and clearly toted up the odds against them. These things she regarded not only with fear, but also with what she considered a healthy caution. Thus, during the days of rage in Chicago, she had retired quickly from the scene, after fruitlessly attempting to drag him with her. Even the threat of a break-up had failed to move him, largely because he did not believe it, but saw it as a ploy on her part to protect him. And indeed when he had turned up at the house the next day, beaten and bloody, after a night spent groaning on a park bench, there had been no talk of break-ups. He was right. He had gauged the risk of losing her absolutely correctly. Instead of "never darken my door again," she had instantly washed his cuts, given him aspirin and then loaded him into his Pontiac and driven him to the nearest emergency room. Yes, Shane knew exactly how much he could get away with with her. But she worried that in the application of a similar calculus to the fury of the powers that be, he was considerably more ignorant and would, in the end, find himself maimed or dead.

"You think I'm going to misjudge and blow it," he said, lying on his back in the moonlight, looking up at her face, from which, though obscured by shadow, from the tilt of her head, the intentness of her unshifting gaze and from the way she hung suspended over him, as if by some invisible thread of worry, from all this he could decipher her thoughts. "Don't worry, babe."

"I'm no babe."

"Darlin' then. Don't worry. No meathead cop's gonna kill me."

"One of these days, one of them will judge you for the enemy you are, then—"

"They lump us all together. They're too damn stupid to know which ones are their enemies unto death."

She called this facile, wishful thinking.

He propped himself up on his elbow too and lit two cigarettes, one for her, one for him. "All that matters is us," he said simply.

"Then don't get killed."

He grinned, and his long crooked teeth gleamed like ivory in the moonlight. "Wouldn't dream of it. Now how about we figure out some way to get you or me on that field trip Naomi's taking to the Soviet Union next summer."

"Forget it. It's for Russian language students only. She had a friend who went last year, said the group guide was KGB and several of the student tourists were CIA. But still you get to see the country and speak lots of Russian."

"Doesn't sound like it would suit my purposes."

"Her friend also said they were under constant surveillance, and he wasn't so sure it stopped when they got back home."

"I think I'll just organize in the steel mills instead."

"You do that," she paused to inhale from her cigarette, its ember glowing orange in the dark. "And Shane?"

"Yes?"

"When the police charge you, you run the other way."

"Sure thing."

"Otherwise I will."

"I don't believe that for a minute."

"Try me."

"I already have, four times."

"It's called assaulting a police officer. Are you insane?"

"You know it."

"Your grandfather was right when he told me on the phone I would be a young widow."

"My grandfather talks to Jesus and had a vision of Armageddon coming last summer. He's a nutcase."

"And you're not."

"Nope. I'm just mad as hell."

She could not imagine life without him. While her sisters professed to be mystified as to what she saw in this furious radical and her parents mildly disapproved—what were his plans? His ambitions? Might he go to medical school? If not, how would he support a family?—she could see no other path than the one she shared with him, and if that path wound through a landscape with no visible means of support, she accepted that, because it was their path, the one they chose together. Long ago he had disclosed that he would not be adverse to marriage, but she had demurred, not so much from skepticism about the institution as a worry about what it might do to each of them. She was ashamed to admit that she thought it would make them, somehow, older. Then there had been the surprise of an unintended pregnancy, and his unexpected welcoming of it. She felt that she was always two steps behind him. Only now, in Mexico, on the day when he could have been beaten to death by police who would have thought nothing of it, in a country where such things happened routinely to people like him, did she see that she had caught up, strode right alongside him and was ready to get married and even, perhaps, have a child. Somehow in the sultry moonlight, with a gigantic alien land spread out in all directions from where they lay on their ambiguously clean bedding, she had moved forward to inhabit his frame of mind. Life seemed short, and he was all that mattered, now and forever.

In the morning, Renita found them sleeping soundly under golden waves of sunlight, crashing in through the open window. Gazing at the blue and purple contusion by Shane's eyebrow and recalling Fernando's groans of pain in the night, she did not have the heart to wake them for another day of leafleting.

"Maybe we'll take a little vacation," she thought, and, as if in assent, Shane turned, yawned and wrapped an arm around his partner. Renita tiptoed out.

For six weeks they organized, rode crowded buses down dusty thoroughfares, dined on tortillas, rice and beans, spent mornings tromping through odiferous, cramped working class districts. At one small factory, their efforts succeeded. The new union gained a legal toehold. At the university numerous students professed interest in the planned demonstrations. Shane wanted to stay into September, but she insisted on a pilgrimage to Lubbock and the paterfamilias. So, after a brief vacation on the Pacific coast, they rode the stifling train back to Mexicali and buses thence.

They found old Mr. Richards sitting in a frayed, green lawn chair outside his trailer with his brown mutt Cindy stretched out beside the bare cement front steps, panting in the early morning heat. The old man's thin white hair had an indentation that circled his head, suggesting that he had not long before removed a tight hat. His long bony face and haunting eyes bore a striking resemblance to Shane's, but his lips were pallid and his skin papery and aged. Despite the many liver spots and thick pronounced veins, his sinewy hands showed a similar structure, too. He was smoking a cigarette, drinking a cup of coffee and complaining about a stain he had just got on his seersucker pants. His white shirt was spotless.

"So you're the Jezebel livin' with my Shane in sin. Not that he's without blemish," Mr. Richards began.

"My name's Betsy, not Jezebel."

"You go to church, Betsy?"

"I'm Jewish."

"Then that wouldn't be a relevant question, now would it?"

"I believe you should have asked if she went to temple," Shane put in, slurping on a Coca Cola from a can.

"Jews, atheists, revolutionaries—Shane, you and your kind better come to Jesus, that's all I'll say. Come to Jesus or be damned."

"Nice to see you too, Pop."

"I don't waste no time on small talk."

"So I see," Betsy said.

"I believe in coming to the point."

"Got it," slurp, slurp on the Coke.

"So when you gonna make an honest woman of her and get married?"

"You don't mind that I'm Jewish?"

"I don't care if you're Hindu. You're living in sin with Shane. Now he better do the right thing and get you in front of a preacher. Then we'll think about you converting."

Shane guffawed. "She already did convert, like me, to atheism."

"Better wake up, boy. The day of the Lord's a coming. And he will separate the wheat from the chaff."

"Well, you'll be happy to know even the chaff is considering marriage."

"That's a step in the right direction." The long, lean old man dropped his cigarette in the dust and crushed it out with his well-shined shoe. "Hand me one of them Marlboros, Shane." His grandson did so.

"Hear about your daddy?"

"No, what?"

"In prison, gone from gambling and whoring to outright thievery. He won't be seeing the outside of them walls for quite some time."

"Isn't he a bit old for a life of crime?"

"He's a reprobate. Don't matter how young or old his is. Nothing good ever came of him, except you." He fussed at the stain on his pants.

"Just spot it with detergent next time you wash it," Betsy advised.

"You think that'll work?"

"Always does for me."

"It was nice of you to dress up for us," more slurping.

"Well, I see you didn't bother to return the favor."

"We've been travelling for two days."

"Besides I just come from church—"

"Well, you wouldn't want us to get the mistaken notion that there was anything special about our visit."

"—where I prayed for the both of you." He glowered. He gestured at some folded, equally worn lawn chairs leaning against the side of the trailer. Little threads of green and white plastic hung from the overused straps. "Make yourselves at home."

They opened two chairs and sat facing him in the already blistering sunshine. Cindy rose, came over and gave them each an exploratory sniff.

"In another hour, it'll be too hot to sit out," the old man remarked. "Then we can move in with the air-conditioning. I thought we'd go to the Hot Shoppes for lunch. Their coffee stinks, but it does everywhere. You want a good cup of coffee, you got to make it yourself." He paused to smoke a bit, and then gave a sharp-eyed glance up at the cerulean, cloudless sky. "No rain today."

"No rain ever in Texas in summer," Shane slurped.

"You still aim to overthrow the gummint?"

The young man nodded.

"Her too?" He pointed his cigarette at Betsy.

Shane nodded again.

"Lord help us all." He smoked some more. "How could a lovely young woman like you go in for such nonsense?"

She opened her mouth to reply, but Shane broke in: "That was a rhetorical question."

"Shane hasn't been in his right mind about politics since high school. You'd do well not to listen to him on that subject."

"I think Betsy can make up her own mind about that."

Betsy giggled. She could not help it. There was something unexpectedly humorous about the tension between Shane and his grandfather. It made it quite difficult to take their differences seriously.

"What's funny?" Slurp, slurp.

"You are. Here we came so I could meet Mr. Richards, and already we're rehashing old disagreements about your high school politics."

"Old disagreements? Young lady, you should have been here. Shane and I just about tore each other apart. And they were no mere disagreements.

I was trying to save this poor boy from the certain hellfire that awaits his violent and heathen ways. You see how much I succeeded. Or maybe you're determined to burn forever too?"

"We burn together," Shane said.

"Ignorant, short-sighted and ornery. That's what you are. I hope that—" he pointed his cigarette at Betsy.

"Betsy, that's her name," Shane said.

"Betsy, yes, Betsy, can change some of that." He paused to wipe the sheen of perspiration off his forehead. "Ein, Ein? Is that a Jewish name?"

"Of course it's a Jewish name," slurp, slurp on the soda. "What else would it be—Chinese?"

"I don't know. I'm asking you. It don't sound Jewish."

"And you know what does? Ha!"

"I've been around in my time. I seen the world."

"It means one," Betsy explained. "In German, it's one."

"Like the one true God."

"I wasn't exactly thinking of that."

"I was."

"You always are," more slurps. "You don't think of anything else. It's a goddamned monomania."

"Don't you take the name of the Lord in vain."

"See? It never stops."

"So tell me about Chicago," the old man changed the subject. "Do you ever make it to the commodities exchange?"

Shane stared levelly at his grandfather. "The what?"

"You heard me. I got a tip, a way to make some money."

"You got a tip."

"You heard me."

"From who?"

"Dwight Sewell," the old man sat forward and, with outstretched arm, pointed to his right, "who lives—"

"I know Dwight Sewell. He's one of the raving lunatics with the pit bulls."

"He's not cracked."

"Oh yes he is. My senior year in high school, he charged me with a sawed-off shotgun and two dogs when I came home from work late one night, said he thought I was part of 'an ocean of underground black nationalists, seething through this white Christian nation.' Then he told me Armageddon was just around the corner."

"Not so far off."

"About one hundred and eighty degrees and a few million years at least. So he's got a tip on commodities futures, hunh?"

"Yep."

"Who'd he get it from—Jesus Christ?"

"How'd you guess?"

Shane rolled his eyes. "Since when has J. C. taken an interest in the price of corn?"

"Since about two weeks ago, when he come to Dwight in a divine vision of brilliance, light and glory."

"Shit," Shane said and started loudly crumpling his Coca Cola can. "I won't do it."

"Don't talk back to me, boy. You're investing my money when you get back to Chicago."

"I really don't think this is a good idea," Betsy gently put in.

"Hush. Women don't know nothin' 'bout money."

"Betsy's father is a professor of finance. He's also an engineer."

"I don't need no professor. I got the Lord God almighty telling me how to invest."

"You got a nut who lives in a filthy little trailer with too many dogs, too many guns and too much bourbon, who couldn't find his bottle one night and thinks he saw the king of the universe. Next thing, he'll be telling you what He wore."

The old man nodded sagely and slowly. "He surely did. That's a fact."

Shane put his head in his hands. His long brown hair flopped over his dust-stained arms. "Pop" he said without moving his head. "You hang on to your money. You'll need it. Don't take the advice of some fruitcake who's toys got lost in the attic years ago. The psycho almost shot me."

"He thought you were an emissary of black power."

"Do I look black?" Shane shouted, lifting his head and pointing at it with both hands. "Do I?"

"I believe in visions, Shane. I've had some myself. I've met the Lord—"

"So you've told me, more times than I could count."

"I've talked with Him—"

"Uh-oh."

"And He said—"

"No," Shane jumped forward, his hand outstretched in the "halt" position. "I don't want to hear it again."

"If it's the last thing I do, I got to bring you to Him," Hank paused, mulling things over, rubbing his cleanly shaved chin. "Hmm. Maybe Betsy could help me with that."

"And maybe Betsy could fly to the moon."

"What do you say, young lady?"

"She says in a pig's eye," Shane put in. "I already told you. We're in agreement. We're joined at the hip. What she thinks, I think and vice versa."

Mr. Richards scrutinized her through suddenly narrowed eyes. "You support him in this revolution poppycock?"

She nodded.

"You're against marriage too?"

"No," Betsy shook her head. "Like we said, we're considering it."

"Praise the Lord. Betsy, I'll take you two to the church today."

"There's not going to be any church," Shane put in.

"If you two are to be man and wife in the eyes of the Lord, there darn well better be a church."

"Oh, so now people who get married by a town clerk aren't really married?"

Just then a huge, rotund form, clad in dirty overalls, chewing tobacco and accompanied by a mangy pit bull on a leash, loomed into view.

"Who's getting married?" Dwight Sewell demanded, looking at Shane. "I didn't think you commies went in for that."

"Last time we met, I believe you thought you were disparaging me by calling me a hippie. To what do I owe this change in status?"

"Hunh? Root, he still talks funny."

"Don't you call my grandfather Root."

"That's his name, he don't mind. Right Root?"

Root nodded.

"To what do we owe this concession to civilization?" Shane asked, indicating the leash, on which the ferocious dog was straining.

"Hunh? Root, you translate."

"He wonders about the leash."

"Oh," Dwight grinned to horrible effect, revealing dentition in an advanced state of decay. Not only that, but his tiny, malicious, porcine eyes, virtually disappeared in folds of fat when he smiled, while his little snub nose shone greasily. Dwight spat, without dislodging his tobacco. "One of the neighbors threatened to sue. Diaz. Ought to go back to Mexico where he came from, stupid day laborer."

"Not like you," Shane said, "working for that bill collector."

"Dwight got laid off," Shane's grandfather explained.

"Isn't that a tragedy."

"Make all the snide remarks you want, Shane, but I'm gonna be rich before you know it," Dwight spat and leered again.

"Well, you keep your hands offa my grandfather's money. And his name's Hank, Mr. Richards to you. He doesn't have a lot of money, and what he has, he needs."

Too big for one of the folded lawn chairs, Dwight wheezed his considerable bulk over to the concrete front steps of the old man's trailer and sat down.

"I didn't hear anyone invite him, did you?" Shane demanded of Betsy and his grandfather.

"Be polite, Shane," old Mr. Richards waved a hand in annoyance.

"Yeah boy. Where's your manners?" Dwight asked, yanking on his hideous pit bull's chain. He continued chewing his tobacco, though a horrible, thin, yellow line of spittle dribbled out the corner of his mouth. "Root and I gonna pool our resources and gonna invest up in Chicago."

"Over my dead body."

"Tut, tut, Shane," Root said quietly.

Dwight laughed, spat his wad of tobacco right out onto the ground and spoke: "Nonsense. You gonna invest it for us. I had a vision."

"You had the DTs." Shane pointed at the disgusting lump of sodden tobacco by the doorstep. "And clean up your mess before you leave here today." The dog crapped on the other side of the step. "That too," Shane added.

"Your vision must be mistaken, Mr. Sewell," Betsy spoke up. "Shane has never set foot in the commodities exchange and never would on principle. He thinks those people are sharks, criminal gamblers with the peoples' essentials of life like corn and wheat. And he's right."

Dwight's little slobbery mouth opened into an "oh" of surprise. For the first time since his arrival, he seemed at a loss for words.

"What's this about criminals?" Mr. Richards demanded.

Shane immediately launched an analysis of capitalism, surplus labor, the necessities of life, the parasitic nature of financial speculation and the chicanery by which prices of core commodities were manipulated to the great disadvantage of the vast majority of people.

"Where'd you learn all that?" Dwight demanded, staring at Shane through narrowed eyes.

Root rubbed his chin contemplatively. "I don't like the sound of it. Shane sure makes it sound unsavory. I don't know if I'd want to put my money in something like that. Them speculators sound just like Wall Street sharpies. You told me they was different, Dwight."

"Hallelujah," Shane breathed.

"Since when you got religion, you hippie atheist?" Dwight demanded.

"I'm gonna have to go over it with the reverend," Root continued. "To see what he thinks."

"You know Reverend Peterson's as tight fisted as they come," Dwight complained. "He's sure to advise you against it. He'll see himself as Jeremiah railing against the whore of Jerusalem."

"You got a problem with that?" Root demanded, "'cause I don't. Reverend Peterson's a righteous man of the Lord."

"I'll come with you," Shane put in.

"Me too," Betsy added.

Now it was Root's turn to stare at them through narrowed eyes. "And you'll let him baptize you?" He asked Betsy.

"If he can persuade you not to throw your money away, I might consider it," she said.

"What about marrying the both of you?"

"Maybe the marrying, but skip the baptizing," Shane protectively put in.

Root rubbed his chin. "The Lord works in mysterious ways," he turned to address Dwight. "I believe some good may have come of your visit to me here today."

Dwight spat in disgust. "I wouldn't mention me to Reverend Peterson," he put in.

A light flickered in Shane's eyes. "Why not?" He asked softly.

"That skinflint's got it in for me. Something about mishandlin' church funds, which I never did. But he's as stubborn as a mule when he gets an idea lodged in that creaky old brain of his."

"Creaky old brain!" Old Mr. Richards was shocked. "Dwight, I'll have you know forty five years ago that stubborn, as you call him, old man saved my soul. He brought me to Jesus, he—"

"Looks like Dwight here's afraid he might bring him to the sheriff," Shane chuckled.

Dwight snorted, again in disgust. "I don't have to take nothing from you Shane Richards. You no count—"

"Then don't."

Dwight stood up, yanked again on his dog's leash. "Come on, Lulu. We know where we ain't wanted. I'll be heading back home now."

"You do that," Shane said, "and stay a long time. Don't come back."

"You're lucky I got such a high regard for your grandfather—"

"Now, now," Mr. Richards put in, "no harsh words."

Later that dry, blazing hot day, Shane pulled his grandfather's Chrysler into the parking lot of the McKenzie Flats First Baptist Church. His grandfather sat beside him in the front, Betsy in back. They stepped out onto the recently repaved black top, so overheated it was soft, and then squished across it to the minister's office inside the church building.

After hearing the story of Dwight's vision and the old man's close shave with bankruptcy, the minister straightened his gold-rimmed spectacles, and gazed at Shane with very sharp blue eyes, undimmed by his obvious, white-haired senectitude. "I believe the Lord sent you," he said, "to save Root from this madness—"

"Please don't call him Root."

"That's his name. To save him and protect him from the sharp dealing of that lying, thieving Dwight Sewell, who made off with twenty five hundred dollars from this very church," he paused, cleared his throat, and sat up very erect, fragile with age, yet somehow still exuding strength. He turned his nimbly alert gaze upon Betsy. "Now I gather you have no intention of converting."

She nodded.

"I, for one, am not one of those Christians who awaits the conversion of the Jews. God has his plans, which time will disclose. And I also understand that Shane here has no belief. But Shane was brought up in this church, and we live in the hope that, in his heart, he will one day return to it. So yes, Root, I will marry them and put an end to their sinful, heathen union, and frankly, I think, the sooner the better."

That night Betsy conferred with the rest of the Chicago collective by phone from Hank's trailer. Then she called her parents.

"You're being married in a Baptist church?" Her father asked.

"It will make Mr. Richards very happy."

"It will make me very unhappy," Gregory Ein replied, but then, relenting a bit, "however, your mother and I have hoped for some time that you and Shane would either get married or—"

"Or what?"

He paused in embarrassed silence. "Let's just leave it at that. Of course we'll come. Just tell us the date."

And that was how Betsy Ein, who had attended the Jewish Day School, worked on a kibbutz in Israel in high school, joined the Socialist Workers party, lived in a feminist collective and leafleted for the Sparticists, came to be married in a Baptist church in Lubbock Texas. "Thank you," Shane said as they left the church. "You don't know what this means to my grandfather."

"Mr. Richards? Yes, I believe I do know what this means to him. And I'm glad of it. But don't let him get any ideas about conversion. That's not in the cards. Oh, and I promise never to call him Root."

"I'm sure he'll appreciate it."

"No, he won't. But you will." And they decamped to a reception at a local hotel that the Eins had paid for and drank champagne until they couldn't see straight.

Rema Roberts defined herself by whether or not she was sleeping with a man and who he was. This self-conception was unknown to the other members of the house not far from Division Street, as was the fact that she had set her sights upon Shane Richards. She herself did not know why she had selected him, after all he was newly married, but she found him attractive and never doubted for an instant that her feelings were reciprocated. The fact was, however, that he had never given her a second thought before he married Betsy and, once hitched, scarcely noticed her existence. This surprising development did not go completely unremarked by the would-be interloper, but in time she evolved an intricate interpretation of it, one that involved him not knowing his own true feelings. But he did know them, and when it came to Rema, for the fleeting seconds that he turned his attention to her, he described what he saw to his wife: "She's a cat in heat."

"Oh nonsense," his spouse replied. "She just believes in free love."

Rema paid close attention to Shane's painting, studying each opus carefully and offering helpful suggestions. She especially liked his Frankenthaler knock-offs, though she worried out loud but with careful sensitivity that they rather too much resembled the renowned artist's work. She saw that she could have saved her discretion. If she had said his pictures were outright copies, he would not have cared in the least. The joy for him, she thought, came in the doing and the selling. He admired various artists, and so he imitated them. "The highest form of flattery," he reminded her, after she had delicately hinted at the obvious influence of some modernist master.

To further involve herself in his work, she took to frequenting galleries and reporting back to him what she had observed. To her surprise, this seemed to irk him mildly, but she thought she must be mistaken and so did not abbreviate this new practice.

And then there was transportation, which she was determined to share with him. After all, she had to commute to the South Side for her graduate history classes, while he thundered right by in his old Pontiac on the way to his job in the steel mills. What could be more natural than that he should drop her off in Hyde Park on the way? It reduced her commuting costs and his, since she helped with the gas. If only she could get him off the topic of factory organizing and into the more alluring fields of her summer wardrobe and which skimpy outfits looked best on her. He could not seem to concentrate on that, and the one time she did snag his attention, with her mention of a white bikini, his response was most disappointing: "Betsy has one. You should have seen her on the beach in Manzanillo, down in Mexico. She was dazzling. Yeah, you should definitely wear that to the lake."

After this miserable failure, she stuck to the safer topic of art, about which she actually knew quite a bit, and indeed regarded her knowledge as superior to that of anyone else in her acquaintance. "I especially like this canvass with the brown and the pink," she commented one afternoon in his bright studio, where the sun spilled over the clutter, illuminating it with the timeless and purposive peace of a Vermeer.

"Oh yeah, that one's going to be a winner. Lots of money. I got a buyer lined up already." He grinned toothily. "Gonna take Betsy out to Grocery Diana when I get paid for that."

"Grocery Diana!" his admirer was appalled. "That's no place to celebrate a, a—"

"A killing? It's good enough for us."

"Go someplace fancy."

"I don't like such places. Neither does she."

Mulling these very words, a few weeks later, Rema traipsed into the sparkling light—a light which brought to mind the unique and expensive brightness of priceless gems—of a swanky art gallery on the near North Side. She gazed critically at the sundry works of art, but then gave a little gasp when she descried the brown and pink of Shane's canvass on a far wall. Pleased at the opportunity of remarking to the gallery owner that she knew the artist well, she approached to see how he was identified. Imagine her shock, to discover that the information text on the wall attributed the painting to a famous New York artist. Confused and flustered, she stepped back. "Maybe I was mistaken," she thought. But no, it was the very work she had seen on the easel in his studio. And as the truth began to dawn on her, shock replaced confusion, and after that the certainty that she alone knew Shane's secret. This, she realized, could be useful, perhaps as a wedge between him and his wife. For never once did she consider that the wife could know that her husband's counterfeit picture hung on the wall of a posh, stylish uptown gallery. No, she knew something that Betsy did not, and it could come in handy. She exited the gallery with a little, ugly sense of triumph in her heart.

For all her political correctness, Rema was aware that with regard to men, she lived by the law of the jungle. She also knew that many, many of her acquaintance did the same and would only judge her on results: if she succeeded in ripping this man from his entanglement with his wife, he would be hers and regarded as such—though what she would do with him, she hardly knew. And this ignorance, this uncertainty shamed her a bit, made her contemplate her small feeling of triumph with some embarrassment, with a desire to negate it, to say that it was not what it was. Still, the revelation about the painting had opened her eyes. He was not what he seemed, and a man who engaged in such fraud could surely be induced to cheat on his wife. Never for an instant did she enter into his view of what she had now dubbed "his counterfeiting enterprise." Never for an instant did she suspect that he would not be cowed and beholden to her when unmasked.

But he was not.

"So I rip off the art snobs. Sue me," he said.

Her jaw dropped.

"You could go to jail."

"If you want to put me there," he replied, bristling with hostility. They stood in the strong September light of his studio; he had a paintbrush in hand, which he pointed at her with all the amity of a rocket launcher. He had been working on another masterful forgery. "Capitalists are thieves," he said and resumed painting. "I'm just giving a little payback."

"You're cheating artists."

"Oh and they're a sacred class, right? They're the special ones, to be worshipped and adored? Well, not by me."

Her eyes rounded. "You've been doing this all along, out of, out of," she paused unable to utter the word.

"Hate is the term I believe you're looking for. Yes, out of hate." He turned to look at her, and his eyes glittered. "And I love my hate. Don't you think for a moment, Rema Roberts, that you can take it from me."

But she was not done. She went downstairs to the kitchen, and then crossed into the little bedroom in the back. There, in the shadow of a maple just outside the open window, Betsy sat at her typewriter, tapping out a review, a light sound that fortified the deliberate quiet of the secluded spot. A breeze rustled her papers and blew cigarette ashes from the ashtray like dust across her cluttered desk. Her thick, long, red curls were tied up in back in a high ponytail, and she wore wire-rimmed glasses. Her pale attractive, oval face had an intently abstracted look. For some reason the words, "like an old maid," flitted through Rema's mind.

"I saw Shane's study in brown and pink at the North Star gallery," she began.

"Did you?" his wife absently replied. "How nice."

"It had the label of a well-known New York artist."

Betsy glanced up sharply, a flash of something—anger? dislike? barely suppressed in her sea green eyes— "So?"

"I thought you just might want to know."

"Know what?"

"That your husband is forging masterpieces."

"You thought that somehow I didn't know?"

Again Rema's large, round eyes grew larger and rounded. "You approve."

"I neither approve nor disapprove. He's an adult. It's his business how he makes money, not, I might add, yours."

Her visitor tossed her thick stylishly cut brown hair. "I just happened to see it."

"Indeed."

"Accidents happen."

"So do coincidences. But less often than what we might call deliberate accidents." The wife cast her a green-eyed glare. "I have to finish this review, unless, of course, there's anything else you believe I don't but should know about Shane." The breeze rustled the paper in the typewriter, as if impatiently calling the reviewer back to her work. The intruder backed out of the room.

A day or two later, the art-forger was cleaning his brushes with turpentine in the studio, standing in a flood of brilliant early autumn light, when he happened to glance through the doorway into Rema's room. He could do so, because she had left her door ajar, revealing her floor-length mirror against the wall. And reflected there, lo and behold, was that young woman herself, stark naked, staring straight back at him. She had obviously been changing her clothes quickly and not bothered to shut the door. Or so he instantly assumed. To her disappointed surprise, he therefore averted his eyes. She did not hear him mutter to himself, "she's nothing compared to Betsy," but she did not need to. His refusal to stare appreciatively lodged like a splinter in her pride. That he took not one step in her direction cankered her self-regard long, long after. The next day she sat down and wrote an anonymous letter to the owner of the North Star gallery.

Thereafter she continued to accept his rides to Hyde Park, always inquiring politely about his work, but he never mentioned any trouble regarding his dubious artistic activities. Evidently her attempt to unmask him with the gallery had failed, but she soon forgot about it, having become romantically involved with a famous, married, history and literature professor, Palsy, at the university.

Now, riding in the roaring Pontiac with Shane down the bright October highways, she could not imagine what she had seen in him. He had crooked teeth, long greasy hair, tattoos, scarred hands with grime under the nails and shabby, left-over hippie attire. He never said anything new; always the same rant about corporations, steel workers, strikes, organizing, the owning classes. True, she agreed with all this, but did she have to hear it day in and day out? How could Betsy tolerate it? Yes, he was right, what he believed in was correct, but it was all doomed. Rema had learned this from her famous professor. The left was a dead end, caught up in mindless cant that led nowhere except, ultimately, to Soviet gulags. Feminism was still somehow acceptable, though even with that, she thought she had caught a light, mocking, ironical look in his eyes more than once, as if the very term conjured up the memory of an old, secret joke. She paid close attention to all this, because the professor was renowned for his brilliance; he had told her that the country would swing to the right, that reactionaries would one day soon control the government, probably even after the coming election. Vietnam was over, political activism dying, the counterculture in tatters, and Ford would surely have to placate the conservatives in his party. She and the members of her laughably pathetic little collective had better wake up to the future, or become utterly irrelevant.

She did not like this condescension, but had to admit that in the deepest recesses of her soul, she considered that this luminary's fame gave him a right to his sense of superiority. Still, he could be wrong. She hoped so. Not that she would enjoy seeing events contradict his certainty about an icy, powerful wave of conservatism sweeping the country simply to bring him down a peg—it was more that she feared that wave itself, feared how it would sweep away fragile, contingent arrangements, like the women's collective she lived in and that it would bring out the worst in people. She decided that if Palsy was right, she would borough deep into the safety of academe, get her PhD in history, and then a teaching job. She would publish the necessary papers in the respected journals and thus construct a high, protective wall against the ravages of this reactionary scourge. Resist, fortify, survive, was her modified motto from Hemmingway. She believed that she had lived through a remarkable time, that she heard its dying echo in Shane's early morning speeches in his Pontiac, and her study of history led her to regard with trepidation the periods that followed remarkable times. Yes, the prestigious Palsy might be right. Counterrevolution was afoot. If so, she had to be ready.

Like many women who go from man to man, in some very fundamental way Rema was alone. Not that she wanted to be—far from it. She frequently fell in love and had more than once tried to finagle a marriage out of an affair. Once she had even become pregnant, which she tried to leverage into a wedding. When that had failed, she obtained an abortion abroad, where the procedure was legal, having utterly no interest in children or raising a child, certainly not on her own. The pregnancy had been a means to an end. When that failed, after three months, she "threw in the towel," as she rather cynically put it to Betsy, who could not understand what she saw in the father in the first place. Over time she had come to see herself as perpetually single. There were affairs—after all, she was a woman of remarkable though very irregular beauty, and she knew it. But these liaisons did not dent the shell of solitude that had begun to accrue around her. Somehow, each one only added another layer of aloneness and contributed to a self-conception in which the term "couple" did not figure. So when an internationally acclaimed academic, with whom she was cavorting secretly while his wife believed him to be working in his office, when that luminary told her that what he regarded as her little left-wing world was about to be swept away by tidal forces of reaction, she listened, and deep within evolved a determination to take refuge in the university where she would not be persecuted for her views, which were after all quite sincere though, given her character, somewhat eccentric in their expression.

Early in her college career, she had had a fling with Jack Diamond; now she had befriended Naomi, who considered this quondam romance a thing of the ancient past. So did Rema—on the surface. But underneath, she was surprised to find a feeling that "he's mine," lurking in the layers of pre-consciousness with surprising tenacity. She had long ago given up on Jack, when her shot at getting him to marry her misfired, yet here she was, years later, not exactly envying her friend so much as resenting her; as if Naomi had stolen something Rema had not known she valued. Oddly, as a result of all this, she found it most unpleasant to be around the man she coveted, as if she were continually on the verge of committing an insane faux pas, of blurting out, "but you don't know who you belong to." Most peculiar of all was the fact that truly, she did not want him in the least.

Rema had grown up in Northampton, Massachusetts with her mother, brother and generous alimony and child support from her stockbroker father in Manhattan, who regretted his flitting marriage to a young woman from Westchester, felt sorry that his children had to grow up with no male head of household and had been only too happy to purchase them a refurbished farmhouse in the Berkshires and to set his ex-wife up as a gallery owner in the picturesque little town. In tourist season, she did quite well, he was happy to hear, but unlike many former husbands in his situation, did not use the news to turn scofflaw on his obligations. No, he paid—a lot and regularly, and often hosted Rema and Judge for long weekends in the city. The girl had loved those Saturday mornings, waking in the spacious Park Avenue apartment, with the smell of pancakes and bacon, which her father cooked for them himself, drifting in from the kitchen. She loved it when he took her shopping on the Upper East Side or Fifth Avenue and always sobbed miserably when he drove her and Judge over to her mother's boyfriend's apartment on Central Park West or to her grandparent's sizeable house in Scarsdale late Sunday afternoon. All the good things, the designer clothes, the Tiffany jewelry, the paternal Bentley, the servants, the patisseries, the caviar, all seemed to swirl away, down, down the drain the closer they got to the West Side. She adored her father. He was the smartest, funniest, richest, most handsome man in the world. She wished she lived with him, not her struggling, absent-minded and depleted mother.

Her brother did not share her view, but took instead their mother's side, referring to his father, despite his incontestable generosity, as "that deadbeat." On weekends, in what Shane later called in her hearing "Manhattan, that playground for the rich," Judge preferred the pr man's rambling upper West Side apartment or his grandparents' small mansion to his father's opulent home and could only be dragged thither despite vigorous protests. "But think of all the stuff he's going to get for us," Rema enthused in the back of her mother's black Mercedes, as they approached the city.

"Money isn't everything," Lena Roberts said from behind the wheel.

Her daughter snorted in disbelief. She herself had overheard her jilted mother tell her best friend that she was "taking him for everything I can get." At the time, she had not been shocked. After all, even to a twelve year old it was obvious that raising two children alone could have its difficulties, but nonetheless Rema felt a protective instinct toward her father—he was not a mere bank account, to be emptied as quickly as possible before he found some new romance and forgot about them (although he was a source of constant, costly gewgaws, never to be depreciated.) This contingency, which her mother mentioned often, the girl found quite ridiculous. Her father, Randolph Roberts, would never forget about her, no matter what society lady he fell in love with. The thought was quite impossible. His daughter never felt surer of this than when she lay in bed in *her* room in his apartment on a Saturday morning, sniffing the yummy things he cooked for her himself, without the cook, and contemplating the luxurious day of self-indulgence ahead in Bloomingdale's, Saks and Bergdorf's. At such times she could almost delude herself into thinking that she was the center of her father's world. Forget her? Absurd. That day would never come.

But it did. "Um, this weekend is not so good," Randolph said into the telephone to his fourteen-year-old daughter, stunned and horrified, seated in her mother's fashionably decorated Northampton living room. "Carolyn has me out both evenings, and we're having friends of hers in most of Saturday. Carolyn doesn't think it's a good weekend for kids."

"Told you so," said sixteen-year-old Judge, hulking by on his way to the stairs to change out of his football gear.

"Carolyn? Carolyn?" The slighted child sputtered. "What do I care what Carolyn thinks? I care what you think."

"I agree with Carolyn."

"What? Have you lost your free will? Whatever she thinks, you think?"

"Not exactly," her father almost whined. Yes, Rema had to admit, the words to describe his tone were weaselly whining.

"Then let me and Judge come stay on Friday. We've been planning to come down for over a month."

"What about next month?"

"Count me out," Judge called from the stairs. "I don't intend to be 'tolerated' by that deadbeat and his fashion-plate girlfriend."

"What about this weekend?" the girl insisted. Strangely, at that moment, she thought she detected the fragrance of pancakes and bacon, drifting away.

"Um…"

"I've never heard 'um' from you before. If that's what Carolyn's doing to you, I don't think it's very good."

"Try to understand."

"Oh, I think I do, which is why I'm coming down to visit you this weekend." Although that time and many others she prevailed over the girlfriend, something between her and her father was forever altered, that intimate, "only entre nous," that affectionate known and being known, that almost secret sharing of love and purpose had mostly dissolved, so that now she and her father were estranged and confronted each other across an alien expanse of mutual incomprehension. The inevitable had occurred. She had lost him. And even though Carolyn did not last until Rema went off to college in Chicago, her replacement was worse, far more grasping and conscious of what there was to extract from this Wall Street broker, far more determined to sweep any troublesome children out of her path. And by then, Rema no longer had the will for the fight. The man she would have struggled for, the special father-daughter relationship had vanished long before this particular harridan appeared on the scene. So she capitulated to the extent that she no longer slept at her father's. She told her mother she was going to Manhattan for the weekend, dropped in on her father late Friday, then gallivanted off to the East Village, where she passed the remainder of her visit in her boyfriend's apartment or smoking pot with him at the crowded, grimy and sweaty Fillmore East. Randolph Roberts never even asked where she slept. He hardly seemed to notice.

The lover in the East Village was soon replaced by a graduate student at Columbia University, a member of SDS who participated in the student protests and radicalized her. Even though their affair only lasted through her last year of high school, it altered her forever. She regarded him as the first person in her entire acquaintance who had stumbled on any of life's important truths, all of which, she would argue, had to do with power, money, class and gender. As she lay naked on his bed, smoking cigarettes after making love, they would chat about *Eros and Civilization*, the vast, oppressive capitalist, machine, the failure of the Soviet system to offer a viable alternative, the writings of Marx, the heroics of Che Guevara, the Venceremos and so forth. During these and other conversations, the young woman felt as though a chemical alteration had taken place in her, one that made her see, hear, feel, think and perceive the entire world differently. Nothing was the same. Everything she had known before these conversations was now irrevocably transformed. The injustice around her filled her with rage.

She was quite sure she had unearthed a true and imperishable paradigm that explained once and forever the social world; it was precious, it was accurate, and it could not be gainsaid. She felt like an explorer who has stumbled upon some ageless treasure, a gem, but one that had unique effects upon its discoverer, one that got into the blood in an undeniable and welcome manner, with an enlightenment that enabled her brain to make sense of people and events whose deepest truths, previously, she had not even realized eluded her.

By the time Rema and her mother made the hegira to Chicago in their Ford station-wagon, with the young woman's luggage crammed into the back and pressed hard against the windows, no one in her family could tolerate her incessant political diatribes. Lena compelled her daughter to vow not to mention the Vietnam War, the draft, black power, civil rights, race riots, women's rights, socialism, the capitalist exploitation of Latin America or any subject remotely bordering on one of these on their sojourn along the interstates to the windy city. So instead this child of plutocrats took the opportunity to horrify her trapped parent with descriptions of her associates in New York City, the drug-taking hippies of the East Village and the fire-breathing revolutionaries of Columbia and the Upper West Side. Lena Roberts sat behind the wheel, her lovely, thick, light brown hair up in a French braid with small streaks of gray at the temples, her perfect make-up and stylish blouse and shorts, her blue eyes wide with shock, as she repeated: "But Randolph never told me any of these things. He never mentioned these people. How could he never utter a single word?"

"Randolph stopped noticing anything I did four years ago," Rema replied, tossing back her thick, waist-length hair and lighting a cigarette. "He doesn't give a shit."

"Rema! Don't talk like that. He's your father."

"He's a stranger, the sorriest excuse for a father I could imagine."

"How could he not tell me?" Lena asked again and again, "about these awful people. Not one word."

At a Howard Johnson's in Connecticut, as they waited in a booth for Rema's cheeseburger and Lena's fish-sticks, the mother excused herself, tread over the standard blue carpet to the pay telephone and dialed her ex-husband's work number collect.

"You never told me about Rema's friends," she accused.

"Her friends? What friends? I thought you were on the road to Chicago. She didn't bring any friends along, did she?"

"I should hope not, considering what they sound like. How could you?"

"How could I what?"

"Let her consort with drug addicts and left-wing fanatics."

Randolph sat up straight. His periwinkle eyes focused alertly on the black telephone. "Drug addicts?"

"Yes, on the Lower East Side, riff-raff, people who smoke pot at rock concerts and drop acid at parties."

"She never mentioned that."

"Well she did today. All this time I thought you were taking her to the Metropolitan Museum of Art, she was down at the Fillmore East, stoned out of her mind. How could you?"

"How could I?"

"Yes."

"Me?"

"You."

"What have I got to do with it?"

"Well that evidently was the problem."

"You've lost me."

"Well it's not the first time, and hopefully it won't be the last. I am shocked and appalled."

"So am I. You said leftists?"

"Out and out Marxists."

"Holy cow."

"Wake up, Randolph. Where have you been?"

"Well, you didn't know either."

"She wasn't romping around with them in Northampton."

"How do you know?"

Lena was stumped.

"Do you even know who her friends are in Massachusetts?"

"She never appeared to have any."

"Ha!'

"What ha?"

"She never appeared to have any in New York either."

"That's a lot of baloney, Randolph. She told me, she'd just say she was going out with friends and you never stopped her."

"Oh," caught in an absent-minded lie, the stylish stockbroker squirmed and ran a hand through his handsome, silver hair. "I guess I did."

"How could you?"

"She didn't say they wanted to overthrow the government."

"You never asked."

"I trusted her. She seems so, so reasonable."

"Reasonable? With her tirades against Wall Street and the profit system? That strikes you as reasonable?" Lena paused. A couple at the back booth had turned to eavesdrop. In a lower tone, she continued: "And if she's been smoking pot, Randolph, what then? She could get pregnant."

"Pot does lots of things, but I never heard of it causing pregnancy."

"You know what I mean."

"No, I don't."

"She might have lost her judgment and slept with one of these, these—" Lena waved her hand in exasperation, "these people," she concluded, settling on the word "people" with such percussive emphasis that Randolph moved the phone away from his ear.

"Well of course they're people."

"I mean men."

"Well of course they're men."

"Are you suggesting I thought she was a lesbian?"

"Why did you think that?"

"I never thought that."

"Then why did you say it? Sleeping with men is bad enough. She's only eighteen. Is she on the pill?"

"How would I know?"

"Well you seem to know everything else."

"Only because of the very unusual circumstance of being cooped up with her for nineteen hours in a station wagon."

"Maybe you should have taken the Mercedes."

"Oh, you idiot."

"I just meant that maybe ignorance is preferable. Christ, she could be addicted to drugs and about to give birth to a deformed baby."

"Why deformed?"

"From the drugs."

"Randolph, what you don't know could fill the Grand Canyon."

"Not anymore, and let me tell you, I was a lot happier that way."

"Well, what do we do now?"

"This is the first time in I don't know how long I've heard you use the word 'we' in this manner, in the sense of a shared, mutual interest."

"Well I'm desperate. I suppose I should ask her if she needs an abortion."

"Always jumping to the worst conclusions."

"You're the one who mentioned a deformed fetus."

"Definitely get her an abortion. But maybe you should find out who the father is."

"Who cares about him? After what he's done to our Rema."

"You're sure she's pregnant?"

"No, but it's a logical conclusion."

"We need facts, Lena. What we don't know is vast, tremendous, humongous."

"What we *didn't* know, you mean."

"Yes, but now that we've got a glimpse of it, who knows what else is lurking out there? She could belong to some radical youth organization."

"Oh, what do *you* know about those?"

"Absolutely nothing. I'm a stockbroker for God's sake. I know what I see on the evening news. They took over some building at Columbia. I don't suppose she was involved with that?"

"Up to her eyeballs. I think she was sleeping with one of the organizers."

"So he's the father."

"I think there were others."

"How many?"

"Enough, Randolph," Lena shouted into the phone. "There were enough. She's eighteen and she very well could have been around the block a dozen times at least."

"God in heaven!"

"Well, He's not going to help. You'll have to come up with something better than that."

"Put her on the phone. I'm not going to tolerate this."

"Oh shut up, you nincompoop. She was at it right under your nose, and you were too busy with your Helena ever to notice."

"Now you don't know for sure. You're speculating. You don't have any actual evidence. She didn't *say* she'd been sleeping around, did she?"

"No, but it's certainly probable."

"Let's deal in facts, Lena, facts. What do we know for sure?"

"We know that every Friday and Saturday evening that she was in Manhattan over the last two years, she spent the night, the *entire* night either with drug-taking hippies in the East Village or fanatical anti-war revolutionaries at Columbia. We now know how she became the intolerable, loud-mouthed Marxist Leninist she has become. We know why she dresses so oddly and uses such incomprehensible slang and filthy language. She confessed to smoking pot."

"You pulled it out of her, eh?"

"Does it sound like something I want to know? No, you moron. She volunteered it. She has me trapped behind the wheel, and she's torturing me with the, the—"

"Truth, with the truth. Well at least she's going to college and not to Haight Ashbury or Moscow."

"Don't count on it lasting. Besides, who said anything about Moscow?"

"Just a thought."

"Keep it to yourself. I don't need to try to follow your addle-pated ramblings. I need help here, and I'm not getting it."

"Ahem," Randolph cleared his throat portentously. "I'm going to call Judge at Amherst."

"What for?"

"He'll know exactly what she's been up to. She always told him everything."

"And he hasn't been on speaking terms with you for five years."

"Oh, yes. I forgot about that."

"Well, remember."

"I'll have to find a way to ingratiate myself."

"Good luck."

"And when I do, I'll tell you what I've learned."

"Oh Randolph, how could you?"

"I don't know, but evidently I'm guilty as charged."

Lena hung up the phone and returned to the booth. Her fish sticks were cold and few. "Kind of skimpy with the servings," she remarked.

"I tried some," her daughter explained. "They were mushy. So'd you call Randolph?"

Lena sighed and gazed down at her light pink polished nails, arranged before her on the Formica table top like tiny perfect shells. "I never could keep anything from you. And he's not Randolph. He's your father."

"He's an imbecile."

"That too. Thank God for divorce."

"Well, I won't have to worry about that. When I get married, it'll be for life."

"Don't be too sure," Lena replied sourly, picking at her sorry fish sticks. "Maybe we should have tried to find a decent restaurant."

"Maybe you should have ordered a cheeseburger. Mine was fucking delicious."

Lena put her head in her hands.

At a rest stop in Ohio, Rema announced her intention to live in a commune in Chicago.

"I believe you're required to live in the dorm," Lena replied with some irritation.

"Only the first year. I've been in touch with some friends who are upper classmen, and they've asked me to consider living in their house."

"Wonderful," Lena growled, and aggressively guzzled her iced coffee. "I suppose I'll be financing this?"

"Randolph will, not you."

"Don't be too sure."

"He always does what I tell him."

"Fantastic. Could I have one of your Camels?"

"I thought you quit smoking."

"Not on this trip." Lena lit up, inhaled and exhaled loudly. "Who are these 'friends'?"

"People I knew who had a commune in the Berkshires."

Her mother gagged.

"I used to visit them, Oh, almost every weekend I wasn't in New York."

"You never told me."

"You would have forbidden it."

"Very clever of you."

"I thought so."

"So now they're in Chicago," slurp, slurp on the coffee.

"Yup, and in SDS."

"How delightful. You do plan to attend some classes?"

"Oh that," Rema airily waved a hand. "Schoolwork's always been a breeze for me, as you're well aware."

"Shit."

"What did you say?"

"Shoot. I said shoot."

"You said shit."

"If this keeps up, I'll be drinking and driving, not just muttering curses."

"What? If what keeps up?"

"Nothing, darling. You just go on being your charming self."

Her daughter was true to her word. After a year in a crowded dorm, a year of all-night parties, brief romances, birth control pills, various venereal problems all treated by student health services, much pot, much alcohol, raucous courses in which furious students denounced Plato as a fascist only to be thrown out of classrooms by crusty, irate professors, political speeches on the quads and marches in the Loop, after all this, she moved into a house full of hippies and assorted students and radicals on Blackstone Avenue, from which she thoughtfully sent her mother photographs of herself and her friends, so that Lena could experience her apoplexy in the peace and solitude of her beautifully appointed house in Northampton. That year Rema did not come home over Christmas. Instead she journeyed to the East Village, and over the summer to San Francisco. By then her mother had reconciled to the knowledge that she had utterly lost her daughter, which was somewhat assuaged by a renewed closeness to her son, nearby in graduate school and frequently in touch. Thus it came as something of a shock, well into her daughter's college years, to learn that she lived in a women's collective on the North Side and was eager to have her mother visit.

"What could it possibly mean?" She asked Judge over the phone.

"That you're her mother, and she would like some sort of relationship with you perhaps?"

"She never wanted that before."

"Maybe she grew up."

"Highly unlikely. She probably needs money."

But Rema did not. She wanted her mother to sojourn to Chicago and stay at the collective for a weekend. When Lena assented, Randolph was flabbergasted. "You're not only going to visit that hive of communist iniquity, you're going to sleep there!" He exclaimed.

"Worried one of the young men might take a fancy to me?"

"No. You said it's a women's collective. What *is* a collective, anyway?"

"Beats me. The only collectives I ever heard of were collective farms over in Russia, which were supposed to be hellholes."

"And you're going to sleep in that hellhole. At least book a night at the Ritz, just in case good sense prevails and you can't stand it."

"Since when all this regard for my welfare?"

"Lena, it will offend you," Randolph pronounced with great authority.

"Oh? How would you know?"

"Hippies, drugs, dirt, sex. These are not the sorts of things that create an environment you might favor."

"My, my, so solicitous. Well, if Rema can stand it, I imagine I can. And you can keep your new found concern to yourself. You're just guilty, because it's your fault she lives this way and turned out so badly."

"She's getting a PhD," he wheedled vainly.

"Oh pooh. Half the people getting PhDs are raving radical lunatics these days. She's one of them, and it's your fault, because you didn't keep tabs on her in high school. Judge agrees with me."

"Judge has a poker up his ass."

"Randolph! I am horrified. That's our son you're disparaging in such unseemly gutter language."

"He hasn't talked to me for the better part of a decade, in any language, gutter or otherwise."

"Perhaps he has reasons. Good reasons. Frankly I don't know why I talk to you. I don't know why anyone does."

Her ex-husband sighed. "Because I have lots of money."

"That does help."

"I will pay for you to stay at the Ritz."

"No. You go stew in your guilt. I'm staying at Rema's!"

So Lena Roberts went to the hair salon, had the tint on her honey blond hair spruced up, donned her Yves St. Laurent casual wear and her Chanel jacket in case it was cold mid-May, drove to the airport in Albany and flew out to O'Hare. She traveled business class, ordered a martini and found herself in conversation with a handsome commodities trader, who drank a scotch on the rocks, underestimated her age by at least a decade and was well on his way into her good graces, when he expressed his hearty approval of the Kent State shootings. Lena, who envisioned her daughter lying on a college quadrangle in a pool of blood every time she heard anything related to these events, glared at him in horror. "Those were somebody's children!" She exclaimed.

"That somebody sure did a poor job of raising them."

"No matter. That somebody didn't deserve to have his or her defenseless child gunned down in cold blood." She sipped her beverage savagely. "Hmmph," she thought. "He's not so good-looking after all. There's something crude about his nose. And there's nothing light or fun about his eyes." She placed her martini on the tray and opened her issue of *The New Yorker*.

"Now just exactly what did I do?" The rather bumbling trader wondered, sighed and returned to his *Wall Street Journal*.

Lena rented a car at O'Hare airport and followed her daughter's directions into Chicago and thence to her house on the North Side. Rema sat on the front stoop with two companions and looked completely different from her mother's recollection. Her hair was cropped short, and she now had bangs, which somehow made her large, beautiful eyes look enormous. She wore a miniskirt and a beaded blouse that had clearly come from an antique store, smoked compulsively and glanced every few seconds at the young woman with red curls, sea green eyes and the stunning figure, who sat next to her. Or, she would turn inquiringly to the tall, long-haired and decidedly wily looking young man with a pool stick in a case, who kept his arm around the redhead's waist and paid close attention to her every word.

"Betsy, Shane, my mother Lena Roberts." Everyone shook hands, and an awkward silence promptly ensued.

"Terrible business at Kent State," Lena eventually remarked.

"Wouldn't have been so terrible if the protesters had had their own guns," Shane replied.

"You're suggesting they should have shot at the National Guard?"

"Sure looks like it would have been a good idea."

Rema exhaled a rich, melodious trill of laughter along with a lungful of smoke. "When it comes to any place other than Vietnam, Shane's no pacifist."

"Where are you from, Shane?"

"Trailer park in Lubbock, Texas," came the clipped and almost automatic reply, as if someone had put a coin in a machine and got a recorded message.

"How nice."

"Not really. This house in Chi-town's a thousand times better any day."

The visitor glanced skeptically beyond him at the small, unpretentious three-story structure of brick and aluminum siding. The windows were all open and the sounds of not so faintly sexually suggestive music—the Doors, though Lena would not have recognized the group, never having heard of them—emanated from the second story. "So your parents live in Lubbock," she stated rather flatly.

"I haven't got the vaguest idea where they live. I was raised by my granddaddy, a fierce, teetotaling church-going, bible thumping, dirt poor cracker if ever there was one."

"Oh, I see," Lena weakly replied, somewhat unsettled by the image the young man had so vividly presented and utterly uncertain about how to make further polite chit chat on this subject.

"I haven't asked him about Kent State," Shane continued, "but I know what he'd say: too bad the National Guard didn't mow down the whole rabble of godless, drug-taking, pinko, homosexual hippies."

"Oh dear."

"Yeah, well, at least with him you always know where you stand—kind of like being the target at a shooting range." He paused to light a cigarette from the end of the one he was finishing. "The odd thing was, when I lived there, he was totally on my side, saw his job as a.) trying to convert me and if that failed b.) trying to hide my true nature from the rest of the world, which he assumed looked at things his way. I guess it never occurred to him that there was a whole, vast universe out there of deviants just like yours truly and that like a moth to a flame, I'd gravitate to it in no time."

"Which you did," Betsy grinned and kissed him passionately. "You found me."

Their visitor, embarrassed, looked away.

Noticing her mother's discomfort, Rema, with hitherto uncharacteristic solicitude, reached over and guided her by the elbow into the house. They left the couple, entwined in their white-hot amour and oblivious to the world on the front step, amid the dust, traffic and honking horns of a too warm spring afternoon and ascended the inside stairs to the young woman's room.

"I put fresh sheets on my bed for you," she explained in obvious expectation of praise.

"How thoughtful of you."

"I'll use the sleeping bag on the floor."

At the back of the house, Rema's window was still somehow flooded with late afternoon light that caused the walls, painted a rich yellow, to glow. She had installed a few shelves in the window and covered them with potted plants, whose lush greenery overflowed the sill, sending out verdure in long creepers over the desk and bureau, so alive, so fertile and expanding, that it seemed one room-encircling creature, ready to take over the house. Tall, overflowing book shelves covered the far wall, while posters of Vermeer paintings decorated the space above the bed. There was something so unexpectedly unique about this room to Lena that for a moment she just stared at her daughter. Then she drifted over to the crammed bookshelves and gazed at the title's and authors' names: Huizinga, Burkhardt, Teilhard de Chardin, Remy de Gourment, E.P. Thompson, Durkheim, Weber, Christopher Hill, Hobsbawn, Marx—ah, there was a name that jangled a harsh bell. She withdrew the thick, well-thumbed tome of *Capital* and glanced over at her daughter, who regarded her with an expression of anticipatory curiosity, as if awaiting her mother's verdict on her library.

"I read that my first year at Chicago," she clarified, unbidden. "It's a most amazing book. Though it purports to be economics and history, it reads like a vision of fire, like a late novel of Dickens or Balzac on the corrosive effects of money on character and humanity. It's an astonishing book. It's a vision of the world as hell. I never expected it to be what I found. Read it—you'll be astounded."

Her mother weighed the book in her hands, up and down, judging its heft. "My, my," she said softly. "My, my." She gestured at the other books questioningly.

"Historians mostly," her daughter answered the unspoken query. "But not in the shallow fashion of today. These were and are people, men I should say, who thought deeply about the forces at work in society, the—"

"Men, of course. They're all men."

Rema cocked her head, surprised. "Actually there's one woman, and she's quite modern. Here," she pulled out a book and showed it to her mother. The author's name was Hannah Arendt.

"I've taken classes with her."

"She's famous," Lena replied. "I've read articles by her in …*The New Yorker*, I believe."

Her daughter smiled, but not in the least patronizingly. "Yes and she writes for *The New York Review of Books* and teaches part-time at the New School. She's one of the few women in what many describe as the pantheon of great historians and political theorists. Personally I have no use for such pantheons, set, as they usually are, in stone. They need to be remade, constantly."

Lena thought this over, and then took the book her child handed her. "But I know nothing about totalitarianism," she half-heartedly protested.

"Then read it and learn."

That evening Lena lay in the dark in her daughter's bed and listened to her child's soft steady breath from the floor on the sleeping bag. The room, so full of plants, seemed nocturnally alive. Indeed, sometime after midnight, a cat opened the door with a creak, padded in and curled up on the end of the bed. Feline, plants, people, all crowded in together seemed to participate in one, unified, somnolent Life. The young woman mumbled in her sleep, something about Naomi and Jack. And her mother, listening, found her memory catapulted back many years to that first night in the hospital, when her newborn baby daughter, wrapped in soft, white blankets, lay beside her in a little cradle, snuffling, breathing loudly and uttering occasional, plangent cries. She wondered if, after their long separation, she finally had her daughter back—this radical intellectual, who had become a stranger, who had let a thick sheen of ice form between them, who had never called, never written, who had rebelled against anything that might possibly suggest her parents, this strange, tall beauty with her cropped hair, cigarettes and Trotsky's *History of the Russian Revolution*—Oh, how she had gone on about that book that afternoon—Rema was back! Not that she would come home, she would never do that and Lena did not dare hope for it. But she had remembered her mother. Something had reignited the recollection of her love, and she had summoned Lena, who had not hesitated for a moment. Now as she lay in the dark listening to her daughter murmur in her sleep about people she did not know, she felt that she was back in the maternity ward, reliving that first night, when her life was transformed for the second time, by a baby.

Over mushroom and cheddar cheese omelets, which her daughter cooked for them the next morning, they planned their day. Lena wanted to go on a Chicago architecture tour and also to see Hyde Park. Rema, Betsy and Shane thought she should sightsee in the ghetto. She nixed that, and architecture it was. The couple bowed out—he to the pool hall and she to the small, shadowed back room on the first floor where she typed her reviews. Alone in the kitchen with her daughter, for the first time the older woman really took in her dim surroundings. A poster of Che Guevara in his beret gazed down upon her omelet through the gloom, and the floor, she noted, had not been swept in a while.

"Ever," Rema corrected.

"What is this—dirt as a matter of principle?"

"Actually yes. No one in this collective has time to sweep the kitchen."

Lena glanced up at the cupboards and the many mismatched pieces of crockery behind the dusty panes, at the table itself, made from she knew not what and painted purple, at the Soviet posters with their red Cyrillic captions across from Che, at the withered philodendron in the grimy window and at her daughter, blooming like a rose in a trash heap. "She'll grow out of it," she sighed to herself. "After all, the prodigal has already returned."

That prodigal wanted to take public transportation down to the loop, but her mother insisted on the rented car.

"You'll have no place to park it," her daughter warned.

"Ever hear of a lot?"

"But they're so expensive," Rema tossed her head. "I would never use a lot."

"We differ," her mother replied. "In more than one way. Surprise, surprise." They took the car.

Her daughter had never toured the architecture of Chicago and to her surprise found Sullivan's buildings, which she had previously taken for granted, suddenly arresting. Afterward, however, she insisted on an exploration by car of parts of the rather more dilapidated West and

South Sides. Her mother found the flat blocks of small houses and shabby apartment building, stretching away as far as the eye could see, depressing, but she also appreciated that these precincts did not have the same effect on her daughter. No…something else entirely.

Later they went to a well-known Chicago eatery for dinner. Rema described it as "a fancy pizza joint in the Loop."

"But I detest pizza."

"There are other things on the menu."

"Not burgers, I hope, because I loathe them too."

"You're not going to be able to get a fancy steak or French cuisine, if that's what you want. And it isn't Delmonico's or the 21 Club."

Grumbling, her mother nevertheless assented. They arrived and went downstairs. "Christmas décor in May, how charming," Lena commented.

"If you're going to be unpleasant—"

"No, no. It just slipped out. I'll reserve judgment till I eat my, my—"

"Noodles."

"Noodles."

Over pasta and pizza the young woman reminisced about her previous commune in Hyde Park on Blackstone Avenue and one resident in particular, a hippie named Elaine, who waitressed for money at a local café, a dark-haired, dark-eyed, depressive beauty.

"Depressive?" Lena asked, more to make conversation than anything else.

"She had this idea that everything had gone wrong in her world because of her," her daughter chomped down on her sausage pizza. "And she had some pretty whacked-out delusions about what had gone wrong. Anyway, I said to Betsy that I thought Elaine, for all her brilliance—and she knew seven languages and took the most abstruse philosophy courses—I said I thought Elaine was going to kill herself. I don't know why I said it. It just came from the heart, and the moment I heard myself utter the words, I knew they were true," she paused to lick tomato sauce off her fingers, carefully, thoroughly, one by one. "But I didn't know what to do, you see? You can't just go up to someone and say 'look, I know you're considering suicide, but don't do it.' It's damn presumptuous. Worse, it might look like you think they should be contemplating suicide. It's like suggesting it, in a back-handed way. So I let Betsy tell me I was off the wall, and I tried to forget about it. But meanwhile, Elaine was so depressed she stopped getting out of bed. The guy she lived with would get up, make himself breakfast and go off to his lab, while she'd lie on the sheets, naked half the time except for her long, dark hair, which kind of covered her up. She drank in the evenings, took pills and fell behind in her share of the rent," she paused to drink some of her mother's red wine, glancing almost surreptitiously at her to see if she was still paying attention.

"Then one night I came home, and there at the bottom of the first to second floor flight of steps was Elaine, with her neck broken. At first I didn't realize she was dead. I thought she'd passed out from booze and drugs, so I stood there, hollering at her. Shane heard me and hurried down. When he turned her face, and we saw the eyes open, we knew. Later, on her desk we found a note. I memorized it. It said: 'Somehow it's all my fault. The good I was supposed to do, I couldn't do, and now everything is abandoned. I don't know how I caused this trouble, but I did, and I don't know what opposed me and opposed what was good, but it is too strong, too prevalent, too powerful and too dangerous. Sometimes in the dark depths of my own soul, where I know my failure and my terror, sometimes I think that that powerful, dangerous something rules the world. It comes through people, some people, and is outside of them too. I can feel it. It has battered me to the point where I no longer recognize myself, no longer recognize my own soul. I am nearly destroyed. I cannot prevail against it. And the good in the world is always so weak, and my efforts to help it, which are the only efforts I was ever supposed to make, are always so futile. The little flame of the one enduring truth, a truth about human beings and what is good and right, a flame of which I was a guardian, I don't know where it is or what has become of it and I fear the very worst. So I'm handing myself or what's left of me over to the reaper, the one companion I deserve. I see him waiting for me, not just now, but all the time, at class, in the bookstore, under the trees along the sidewalk—death is there for me, and it's time I faced him. The little I should have done I didn't do, I couldn't do, because I never understood until too late how strong this was that was arrayed against me. I have failed utterly.' When the police came, they said she must have thrown herself down the stairs, head first, her body was broken in so many places." She paused and lit a cigarette. "I just thought you should know this, because she wasn't just a friend—she was my closest friend. And that's why we had to get out of Hyde Park and move up here, and it's why, no matter what I do, I have this sense that truly, I don't understand anybody and that I can't, that in fact no one can, because we're all basically unknowable and hurtling like Elaine into the arms of death."

Lena took her daughter's hand, "poor Elaine."

"Poor Elaine."

"And poor you."

"Poor me."

"You should have told me."

"I decided to wait until I saw you. You see, I knew. I don't know how I knew, but in my heart I knew she would kill herself. And I did nothing."

"You didn't really know."

"The moment I uttered the words, I recognized them as the truth. Just as I recognized Elaine as a corpse when we turned her over." She exhaled a long, blue-gray stream of smoke. "There has been nothing but regret and shame, since it happened."

"And your friends Shane and Betsy?"

"They feel the same way. We can't even talk about it. The last time we did, Shane got utterly ripped and nearly killed himself roaring around the North Side on a friend's motorcycle. It's horrible. It never goes away."

"Is that way you invited me out here?"

"It's a cause, though, as Aristotle would say, neither the sufficient nor the final cause."

"Come again?"

Rema smiled sadly. "It was only partly why."

"Good."

"She's a very complicated person," Lena told her ex-husband over the phone that night from the Ritz, where she had decided, relenting, to spend her last evening in Chicago, "part intellectual, part hippie. And although she's a rabid feminist, I think she wants to get married."

"Who's the lucky guy?"

"Did I say there was one?"

"Uh-oh, it's not a woman, is it?"

"It's no one, you idiot."

"Well, you said—"

"Shut up and listen," Lena paused to light a cigarette. "She's needy."

"This better not be a pitch for money."

"I mean emotionally."

"Oh. Good."

"No, stupid, not good. Needy people make bad decisions. That's why we should try to increase her sense of security. You should send her money, lots of it."

"I knew it."

"You have thousands to spare, so don't try your excuses on me. I know you just bought that Melanie of yours a Jaguar."

"Yes, but I got something in return."

"You are revolting. This is your daughter I'm talking about."

"Who hasn't bothered to write or call in years. It was *you* she invited out there, remember? Not me."

"Randolph Roberts, you send her a check for ten thousand dollars! Do you hear? I want her to have her own car, not have to hitch rides in that noisy, hideous Pontiac that Shane or somebody or other drives."

"Maybe she likes riding around with that Shane or somebody or other."

"Maybe you don't know your ass from your elbow."

"Lena! I'm shocked."

"Oh, come off it. You reduce me to profanity every time we talk. You just conveniently forget."

Incoherent male grumblings emanated from the other end of the line.

"What did you say?"

More grumbling.

"I didn't catch it."

"I'll send her the damn check. But she sure as shooting better write or call to thank me."

"You're in no position to demand anything."

"I'm not?"

"Not after your atrocious behavior."

"My what?"

"It's your fault she turned out like this. She could have been in the society pages, Randolph, where she belonged, but Oh, no. You had to go and screw everything up."

A week later, Betsy came into Rema's sun-drenched yellow room, with the ubiquitous, wild greenery and the serenity exuded by the Vermeer posters, and handed her a thin, white, rectangular envelope, which bore the return name "Randolph Roberts." The recipient waited until her roommate departed, then, filled with curiosity and surprise, opened it with her finger. Out fell a blue check for ten thousand dollars, made out to her. There was a terse, inappropriate note: "Mad money. Love, Dad." It brought to mind her summer days in Haight Ashbury, panhandling on street corners, or fighting off the advances of a driver in California, with whom she had hitched a ride, because she did not have bus fare. This man, her father, had not even paid her tuition after the first year of college. Her mother did that. In four years he had never sent her a cent. "I could have starved and died," she said aloud to the bookcase, teeming with tomes by Brecht, Deutscher, Adorno and Horkheimer. "And he would not even have known." Her first impulse was to tear the check to shreds. But then something canny and compromised crept into her heart. "Take it," this thing said. "Deposit it and be sure to ask for more. There's plenty where that came from." She folded the little blue check and placed it in her wallet. "I hope this doesn't mean I have to take telephone calls from him," she said aloud to the empty air.

Nonetheless her upbringing prevailed, and she wrote a thank you note, which her father was obtuse enough to miss as an opening for a correspondence. Thereafter, every year when her mother came to visit, she stayed at the Ritz, treated her daughter to fancy meals at sundry, expensive Chicago steakhouses and, a week or so later, a generous check would arrive from the careless father. Rema duly deposited it and sent a thank you note. He, just as routinely, failed to respond to what he took to be a formality and indeed was, though like most such, it offered an opportunity which his eyes, with uncaring dimness, failed to perceive. By the time his daughter was well into graduate school, she had many tens of thousands of dollars in the bank.

As the years passed, she all but forgot about the special account she had opened for her father's gifts, and the money just sat there, accruing interest. Her strange and sudden infatuation with Shane came and went, while her affair with the renowned and married academic gained her a certain notoriety, not just in Hyde Park but Chicago generally, as the wife taught at the Art Institute school and was widely liked.

"You could do the honorable thing and break it off," Jack Diamond advised, one morning over coffee in a student eatery.

"The 'honorable' thing," she smiled, making quote marks with her fingers. "How quaint."

"No, you were never big on honor," he asserted, suddenly savage.

"Neither were you, if I recall correctly," and she smiled rather coyly, giving him a melting look. He did not respond. Instead he slurped his black coffee absentmindedly. "But no matter," she continued, almost sourly. "Elaine never knew we were having an affair, never suspected a thing. She killed herself because she was half-way psychotic and afraid she'd become a full-blown lunatic. She never detected a hint of what was really going on."

His level, blue-eyed glare assessed her coldly. "Indeed," he said. "I always thought you were the one who told her."

Rema dropped her cup. It landed in the saucer, spilling a large puddle of coffee with cream over the wooden table top. "You never said…all this time, never a word. She knew?"

He nodded.

"How is this possible?"

He regarded her through narrow, still suspicious eyes. "I guess she wasn't as dumb as you thought."

"You're guessing," his former girlfriend insisted. "You're not sure."

"I'm not? She confronted me the night before she threw herself down the stairs."

Rema fell back against the booth, her mouth a perfect little "oh" of surprise.

"So why'd you tell her?"

"Jack, I didn't. I swear. I never dreamed she knew. And I certainly had no idea it might have pushed her over the edge to, to…suicide. I wouldn't have done that."

"I guess you two were different."

"All this time and you never said anything."

He poured a little cream into his coffee and idly flicked the spoon around. "Yeah, well, if there was a chance you hadn't told her, I didn't want you to feel guilty for destroying three lives."

"Three?"

"Elaine, her mother and—"

"And?"

"Me, Rema. What do you think it did to me?"

"But you have Naomi now, and Snow."

"And a big, deep scar running right though the middle of my heart."

She paused, reflecting, as a dim, mirthless sun began to shed its pale beams over the realm of shadow into which she had plunged with the commencement of this awful tete a tete. "You said her mother, Mrs. Elias?"

"Elaine wasn't the only one who went over the edge. Mrs. Elias, her mother and sole surviving relative always had a few screws loose. Elaine's death drove her nuts, completely. She lives in a facility in Louisville, Kentucky, now. If you want the address," he spoke rather acidly, "I have it memorized, because that's where I send the monthly check."

His companion stared at him.

"I help support her, Rema. It's the least I could do."

She rose, pallid and shaking. "Why are you telling me all this now? After so much time?"

"To prevent history from repeating itself, with you and your illustrious professor."

"It won't," she said and left.

A month later, Jack received a letter from the mental institution wherein Mrs. Elias resided, stating that she had received an anonymous donation of many tens of thousands of dollars, to be used for her support for the rest of her life. Therefore, his contribution would no longer be needed. He stared at the letter for a long time, then glanced over at Naomi, reading to her son in the living room. It meant he was financially sound enough, legally, to adopt the boy, once he and his intended married. He wondered for a moment where this windfall had originated, then decided he did not care, that it was a gift from the heaven he did not believe in.

As for Rema's famous professor, she never saw him again. That afternoon of her conversation with Jack, she went home, typed a letter decrying the cruelty and dangers of adultery and mailed it to Palsy. An unrepentant philanderer, that illustrious intellectual saw fit never to reply and within a few weeks had become romantically involved with yet another student. Betsy reported this bit of news to her at dusk one spring evening, leaning against the doorway, her scarlet curls aglow like fire from the last of the sunset in the windows of Shane's studio.

"I wrote him an angry, loud-mouthed letter," Rema replied, "telling him to stick to his wife."

Her visitor's green eyes glimmered like the sea, as she emitted a peal of laughter. "Him? Oh Rema, he's infamous. It's his fifth wife and undoubtedly his five hundred and fifty-fifth affair. He was probably dumbfounded."

"I hope so," Rema answered sourly, "because eventually when one of those wives finds out, it will destroy her world."

Her visitor's eyes glimmered strangely again and though not with love, with a trace of a sudden, warm sympathy that had never been there before for the one with whom she spoke. "Who put that idea in your mind?"

"I'm going to ignore the unspoken assumption behind that remark," Rema tossed her close-cropped head, "but if you must know, it was Jack, with his dark streak."

"Dark streak? Yes, I guess he does have a dark streak."

"He always sees the worst in people."

"And he saw it in you?"

Rema squirmed and gazed at the flaming curls, the perfect figure, the emerald eyes and seemed to see them once again, rounded in horror, as she gazed down from the top of the stairs on Blackstone Avenue at what only just then, with Shane's words called up to her, "she's dead," had she realized was Elaine Elias' corpse.

"But why would she kill herself?" Betsy had asked immediately, as if the thought that it might have been an accident were too unlikely, too preposterous, given all that was known about that desperate young woman, even to have entered her head. And Shane, caught in the same powerful current of certainty, said: "I don't know why, but she did," while Rema gazed down in dread at her friend and secret rival's long tousled dark hair and glazed, lifeless stare. She saw it all again in her mind, and now she thought, "I did that, and it can never be undone," with a clarity and novelty that belied the many hints of it, the suggestion of it, the vague unformed possibility that had lurked all those years in her excessive grief, her remorse and above all the relentless shame, as though she were soiled forever by some criminal and unspeakable act.

"Yes," Rema replied, looking up at her roommate, aflame in the dying day, "he saw the worst in me."

"Worse than you could imagine," Betsy stated. No, there was no question in her tone.

"I hope so," Rema paused, then almost pleading: "I believe so."

"Then it must be so. Only you can know—"

"Know what?"

"Your motives, I guess. Only you…"

"Only me," she huddled on the end of her bed but did not receive nor expect comfort from her companion.

"After all, it was all about him, mister big-shot writer and academic," Betsy said musingly, "the hot-shot literary lion. You weren't thinking of his wife."

"Are you excusing me?"

"No," her visitor said softly. "I can't. But I'm glad you thought of her, even if it took Jack's dark streak to compel you to."

Rema wanted to say that she wrote the letter more for dead Elaine Elias than for the injured wife, whom she had never met—while it could perhaps be said that she had murdered her friend, with a betrayal quite personal, even intimate and prolonged, whose consequences had now stranded her in that sunless realm, first glimpsed as an expanding, sky-swallowing whorl of shadow borne of Jack's revelations in their harrowing talk.

There came sounds of Shane, tromping up the stairs. He caught sight of his wife and slid an arm around her waspish waist. "You just think about it," Betsy said softly.

"About what?" He asked, glancing curiously from one woman to the other.

"Something else," his wife replied, embracing him as they exited to his studio, limbs locked.

"I fell like something the cat dragged in," Rema whispered to the plants, the books, the posters, the interests, intellectual pursuits and pretensions, the hippie habits so close to old-fashioned vices, which all murmured back:

"You are." That evening and for many thereafter, she skipped the criticism/self-criticism session. Instead she shivered in her room and brooded.

So her dead friend had known. The shock of it still immobilized her, the thought that for so long she had been mistaken in the smugness of her secret. How had she found out? Who had told her? Who could have? As far as Rema had known, only she and Jack were aware that they had resumed their affair, broken off long before. She could not have killed herself over that—could she? She thought back to the last few weeks of her friend's life. She had been losing weight, the delicate beauty looked gaunt, had sunk to about ninety pounds. She remembered Betsy joking at their communal dinners, "eat, eat, you're too thin," but the doomed lovely barely touched their stews, casseroles and ratatouille. Maybe that was it, she thought with a sudden jolt of humor and hope, maybe Elaine hated eggplant, tomatoes and zucchini.

"No," she said aloud to her books, plants and posters, "Elaine hated her life, and a big part of it was Jack and me." If she had hoped that uttering the truth out loud would assuage the guilt that clung to her like damp gauze on a wound, she realized at once that she was wrong. Elaine had known, Elaine had killed herself, and for years the other guilty party had pretended to be cordial but had believed she had deliberately told her, perhaps consciously driving her to suicide. "He must have thought I was a monster," the dazed woman, whose mental sight seemed so alarmingly to be dimming, murmured again and again heard the response of her intimate possessions, her cozy room—"you are."

Then she resolved to think about it logically. Apart from romantic troubles, why had Elaine Elias been so sad, whence her sense of doom and persecution? Was it all a deep, unshakable clinical depression? Why hadn't she got help—ah, but she had. Rema sat up. Yes, she had had a therapist, a Dr. Dark, with an office on Fifty Fifth Street over by Lake Michigan. She decided to phone her the next day.

She slept fitfully that night, but toward dawn got some rest, dreaming that she and her deceased roommate were on the road to San Francisco in Elaine's rickety Saab. They had an animated discussion about feminism, while someone, a shadowy male figure in the back, alternately Jack and then Shane, made occasional comments. They chain-smoked across the prairie, and then stopped in a glass city, where, Rema explained, she had to leave to catch a train. The ambiguous man in the back seat moved up front, and he and Elaine Elias, somehow dead now, drove off, leaving the dreamer alone, in the middle of an unknown metropolis, and suddenly aware that she had no money. She awoke with a start.

She thudded down to the dim little kitchen and telephoned Dr. Dark. A husky female voice answered.

"I'm Rema Roberts, an old friend of your former patient, Elaine Elias."

"Did you say Rema Roberts?" The voice inquired, pausing to inhale from a cigarette.

"Yes, and I'd like to make an appointment."

Silence.

"Are you there?"

"Yes, but I'm not taking any new patients. After that young woman's death, I cut my practice way back. Now I plan eventually to switch into another field altogether."

"I had hoped—"

"I imagine you did."

"For one or two sessions."

"No, I'm sorry."

"Did she blame me?"

"I really cannot discuss anything to do with Miss Elias. It is impossible. Impossible."

"But it was so horrible."

"Yes, and you are not the only one it affected, though I'm surprised you're calling me now. Why now? Why not back then, when everything collapsed and she died?"

"Back then I didn't know I might have been responsible, Dr. Dark."

"Ahh."

"That's all—ahh?"

"Yes, Rema Roberts, I'm afraid that's all." There followed a silence and then a click. The connection was broken.

"So I'll never know," the desolate young woman said aloud, watching clouds of darkness and deserved, she thought, despair swirl over her mental field of vision.

"Was that Elaine's old doctor you were on the phone with?" Shane asked, emerging shirtless and in patched jeans from the shadows of the little room he shared with his wife.

"Yes, I need a therapist."

"Try another one. Her track record ain't too good." And he loped off into the living room in search of his cigarettes.

She suddenly felt feverish, then cold. "Maybe I should eat something," she thought, but had no appetite. Shaking slightly, she telephoned the man she had come to consider her erstwhile ambiguous partner in crime. Naomi answered, her voice melodious and clear, the opposite of Rema's tense, grating rasp.

"What's up?" He demanded.

"You have to tell me everything you know about Elaine and why she killed herself. I never knew until yesterday that I may have been responsible."

"Well, now you know. Get used to it."

"I can't live with this."

"Then don't."

"Thanks, Jack," she snarled.

"What do you want me to say? It didn't matter that we cheated on her? That would be a lie. It did. Maybe it wasn't the sole cause of what she did, but it sure contributed."

"What did she say? What were her words about it?"

"That I was a shithead and you were too. Two sleazes in a pod. Two rats. Two two-timing lice. She was pissed."

"That sounds very sane."

"She could be at times, in fact most of the time. It was only when that black despair came over her that everything suddenly took on some overpoweringly sinister significance. And that's why it would have been better if you and I had never met."

"They say ignorance is bliss," she murmured.

"Yeah, well, you don't deserve bliss and neither do I."

"I broke off the affair with mister world-class academic."

"Well, some good came of our talk the other day."

"That's about all. I haven't been able to sleep or eat."

"Tell me about it," he said and hung up.

"You look sick," Shane commented, smoking and slinking back to his room with Betsy.

"Thinking about Elaine."

He seemed surprised. "Again? You been upset about her a lot lately."

She closed her eyes and saw her friend at the bottom of the stairs, the reddish brown wood—was it cedar?—of the banister, the muted pastels of the floral patterned wall paper, the clutter of books and bicycles in the first floor hall, Elaine in her jeans and T-shirt, lying crumpled on the floor. She saw Jack's eyes blazing cobalt blue retaliation at her over coffee, a flash of lightening from depths of night, spreading that night everywhere. "It's haunting me," she replied.

"Tell me about it," Shane said.

She crawled back into bed. Fortunately that afternoon she had no classes. She managed to read a bit and watered her plants, but she could not eat and when she slept, she only dozed fitfully, hot and uncomfortable, dreaming of life on Blackstone Avenue, of Elaine coming and going to classes, studying Russian, speaking German, waitressing on Fifty-Seventh Street and writing peculiarly eloquent papers for her philosophy classes. And then there were the biblical dreams—Elaine Elias on a dark, windswept road that tore into the sky, masses of black cloud and occasional lightening, the earth shaking, heaven cracking, portents flashing terrifyingly all around, till she cried out in terror in the dream and it subsided, and Elaine Elias was her normal self again. She would wake, hopefully convinced that her friend was still alive, then glance around at the familiar objects in her room and remember that she was dead, had take her life years ago, had doubtless partly blamed Rema for her unendurable misery.

She passed the next few days in a quasi-delirium, eating little, sleeping less and finally begging Shane to get her a bottle of Jack Daniels. He duly retrieved this potation from the local liquor store, and she promptly got herself plastered. With drunkenness, her appetite somewhat returned. Other members of the collective were startled to see her at three or four o'clock in the morning, staggering around the kitchen, cooking scrambled eggs.

"This has got to stop," Betsy said at last deep in the middle of the night. She stood in the entrance to the little kitchen, her famously beautiful figure swathed in a bright red and orange Japanese bathrobe.

Rema, lolling on a rickety wooden chair, slobbering over her eggs, slurred out: "I did something terrible."

"Well, that's obvious," her roommate snapped, yanking another chair out from the table and seating herself opposite. "And it clearly has something to do with Elaine, because you won't stop maundering on about her."

Through the open window, on a warm spring breeze, came a peal of laughter from the sidewalk.

"It's not funny," Rema said. "I had an affair with Jack."

"So? That's news?"

She sat up, startled out of her drunken stupor.

"You think we were blind? Everybody knew that. You went after him like a shark. And Elaine knew it too."

"I just found out."

Betsy glared at her. "You're even stupider than I thought. How could she not know, you idiot? But don't flatter yourself with the thought that you were the sole reason she leapt down the stairs. She had some very strange notions and some even stranger psychic scars. They were deep and not of this world. She'd have been suicidal without you." She paused but continued glaring furiously at her roommate. "Still, I must say, it's about time you started blaming yourself. I thought the day would never come. And you talk about solidarity. Rema, the next time you jump into bed with somebody, make sure he isn't attached first. It would be damned thoughtful of you, and uncharacteristic too, I might add."

Rema stared at her in amazement. "You knew she knew, all this time," she repeated, lost in a dumbfounded stupor, in the retributive but strangely clarifying, if only in rare moments, darkness that had enveloped her mind.

"Everybody knew, you moron, everybody but you. But you conveniently only ever seem to know what suits you, so now you're shocked that we weren't in the dark like you. Well, wake up, dear. You're going to have to live with this for the rest of your life. Take a cue from Jack. Stay sober and accept it."

The young woman lurched through the next few weeks drunk and wretched, oppressed by an excessive, or was it possibly salutary, sense of guilt. In moments of sobriety, she graded papers, but it provided no solace. At first the alcohol did, but after a while its soothing effect wore off, and she realized she did not have enough conviction to make a permanent drunk. Instead of scotch in the morning, she cut back to four or five beers at night, then three, then just a glass of Chianti. Once she visited her dead friend's grave on the West Side. It was a forlorn, flat, anonymous cemetery, suitable, she supposed, for someone with no kin other than a deranged mother in Kentucky. There was not a soul in sight, and she stood long and alone, head bent, reading and rereading the name, Elias, a silent witness in that dismal landscape to a dreadful, individual calamity that had, by some unknown, frightening and powerful means, left many people bereft, even Dr. Dark, bowing their heads and moving forward, into they knew not what. She placed some white roses by the small headstone, stood for awhile, ignoring the light rain, and then departed.

On the bus home, through gray, dreary streets, realizing that spring was almost over and summer would soon arrive, she resolved to finish up her work and then take July and August off. "I did something really low, and now I'm playing the price," she said softly to the rain splashing on the windows, to the other, unknown passengers, huddled in their wet ponchos and raincoats, to the wide, seemingly endless avenue the bus traversed, past little frame houses and big, brown, oblong warehouses, like the life that stretched before her, dull and unchanging, through brief affairs and a loveless adulthood, university papers and academic infighting, through the monotony of work, guilt and solitude, of achievements that meant little and friendships that meant less, from one failure of the heart to another, one emptiness to another, with the sureness and immutability of destiny.

"Where were you?" Betsy asked, as she entered the house, a row of raindrops depending from the brim of her rain hat.

"Putting flowers on Elaine's grave."

"Did that help?"

"Nothing will ever help. But I'm not going to be a drunk, and I sure as shit am not going to be a suicide. So I guess I'll just have to live with it." And she lit a cigarette, then tramped upstairs.

"I think Rema finally grew up," the sharp-tongued and sharper-minded redhead said, glancing at her husband, who had just sidled into the kitchen.

"It's about time," he replied, then, encircling his wife's waist with his arm. "I got a strange call from North Star gallery. Apparently someone wrote them a letter that one of their New York School masterpieces was really a Shane Richards."

"It had to happen sooner or later. Were they upset?"

"Nope," he chuckled. "They just went ahead and sold it for a fortune."

"Be careful who you let into your studio."

"No kidding. I bought me a lock today."

"It's not anyone in the house, Shane!"

"But people have guests. Some of you women have lots of guests. What if Rema had brought her great man over here and he figured out what was up? There would have been no end of trouble, with a self-righteous big shot like him who worships at the altar of high art. No, no, no. Locked it is, and locked it'll stay."

"Rema's not seeing him anymore," his wife mused. "Something tells me she's destined for the single life."

"Could have been us, if we hadn't met."

"There's something cold in her."

"Aloof?"

"No, cold, too cold—I don't know how to put it. But it's there, and it'll get colder as time passes."

Upstairs Rema threw her damp hat on the desk and inspected her African violets on the window shelves. She removed her wet shoes, and gulped the glass of red wine that had sat on her night stand since the previous evening. Raindrops drizzled on the window pane and made everything, the buildings, the houses, gray, smudged, fluid. She could not seem to fix her eyes on any recognizable object outside, but then, she did not really try, for that would mean focusing her mind's eye on something other than the image of a young woman's corpse in a coffin under six feet of dirt and mud in a flat, abandoned cemetery on the West Side of Chicago, on something other than this grave that no one ever visited, that stood with its small, inexpensive headstone, a silent, unobtrusive, easily ignored rebuke to Rema Roberts and the conduct of her life. "God damnit," she said, and lit a new cigarette off her old one.

"Some people wouldn't care," she spoke aloud after a moment. "They would just go on with their lives and figure well, she was a mess, and this was inevitable. But it sticks in my throat, my heart—somewhere I can't get rid of it. And it's not just the loss, the loss of a talented, brilliant young woman and friend, and it's not that my sleeping with Jack drove her to it, because I don't believe that. She'd been through stuff like that before, and she was tough when she needed to be, and flexible. She'd also been through things none of us could imagine, things so beyond our ken…It's that somehow I knew, and if I'd acted on that knowledge I maybe could have stopped it. It's that maybe the reason I didn't act had something to do with my feelings for Jack. Is that really possible? It has to be considered. Was I trying to take him away—yes. And did that make me callous—yes. And, worst of all, she knew. And she handed him to me, but who could ever want anything or anyone obtained like that? Or was it that she didn't care—didn't care what happened to him once she was gone. Or, equally terrible, considering all my guilt, did she just not care what would happen to me? That's far more likely than the thought that she was twisting the knife. She wanted to be dead. That was more important than any person, any relationship, or any cheating friend. And I knew she wanted to be dead, and it just stopped me in my tracks, paralyzed me. Oh, there are so many things I should have done, thought, felt and said. But I was numb, shocked, stopped, as immobile as a statue, while she went ahead, took matters into her own hands and got herself clear out of this intolerable world. Oh, I should have said I hate it too, that life makes me sick too. A little genuine commiseration could have gone a long way—and it would have been genuine. But her wish to be dead overpowered me and even now, it reaches out of her grave and ensnares me at every turn."

After that, this compromised witness to the mysteriously expanding and enveloping effects of what most regarded as merely a personal disaster spent a solitary, loveless stretch completing her PhD in history. She and Jack drifted apart. By the time he was preparing to take Snow to Wyoming in the late 1970s, while his girlfriend studied in the Soviet Union, they had not talked in months. From time to time she regarded Shane and Betsy, immersed in their conjugal felicity, with a distant curiosity and wondered how he had once so captivated her. She applied for positions as an assistant professor on the West Coast, but the one that she obtained was in upper New York State, not far from Northampton.

"Yes Mom," she repeated to a startled and delighted Lena over the phone. "I'm coming home."

IV

Night

Before her trip to the USSR, Naomi spent several weeks in Vienna, having found her way into an apartment with an assortment of other American students and a woman linked to the program sponsoring her trip behind the iron curtain, an apartment that was spacious and comfortable, but that filled her sleep with nightmares and where she thought she was losing her mind, because of a startling inability to convince herself of the unreality of those nightmares. On one occasion the young woman of hitherto imperturbable sanity woke in the dead of night, screaming for help, convinced that she, bound and tumbling, had fallen through the night into another world, while a tall, blond man with blazing eyes of ferocious malice stared through the transom above her bedroom door as she plunged. Indeed after this terrifying experience, the world was utterly transformed, completely other, not as it had been before. Or was it she who was now literally a different woman, a weaker replacement, one who was somehow already utterly broken and enchained by the harsh regime of night whence she had come? She wondered at such thoughts, wondered where her stronger, sounder self had vanished to, how that previous woman would survive this swap and fare in that shadowed prison world, whence she felt she had come. And she wondered if her sanity had been compromised.

After this terrifying schism in the fabric of reality, Leningrad was cold and often dark, full of shabby, aimlessly milling people, thronging the mighty avenues, pale and unhealthy, almost all with either a sharp hungry gleam or the worn-down listlessness of defeat in their eyes. Nevsky Prospect was either dusty in sun or damp in rain—in both it was dreary, vaguely desperate. Some of the friends Naomi made wanted to leave, imparted their few, scrupulously observed rules for survival and begged for stories of life in America, though there were some friends who had no such desire for exile, who had found their quiet niche, made modest lives, kept their thoughts to themselves, and were content. These tended the little gardens of their unobtrusive lives, read their books, exhibited a gentle curiosity about the outside world, guarded their humanity, occasionally noted the excesses of the powers that be with a humorous or even sardonic remark, and did not complain. They evinced no desire to leave, simply because this was the industrial civilization into which they had been born and in which they had grown up, and they knew very well that without it, they would probably have been landless peasants, at the mercy of a cruel, haughty and baronial elite. She lived in a high-ceilinged, wooden, ramshackle dorm room that she shared with many, many bedbugs and five other students, their every comment monitored by the large, ugly, obtrusive microphone perched on the wall like an enormous cockroach. Most alien were the public showers with the large, blond, East German girls, who acted as if the American students did not exist, with a deliberate silence that exceeded mere coldness, crept instead into altitudes of aloofness that were as fearsome to behold as their brief discussions in a German that Naomi all too clearly understood were to hear.

Two weeks into her stay, a ferocious chest infection felled her, made her take to her bed, miss classes, and happily, quit smoking. Several other American students became ill, and two were hospitalized. They returned from this ordeal with tales of medieval medicine, of cupping and other techniques not experienced in the West in many decades. Meanwhile Naomi lay on her bed by the window, unable to sleep in the white nights when twilight extended until one a.m. and dreaming fitfully of hordes of listless people, neither living nor dead, shuffling around, directionless, purposeless, below her window and along the wide, drab boulevards, as far as she could see. In her dreams these crowds had issued forth from brown pyramids under a reddish brown sky and seemed in every detail to proclaim that they were of some necropolis. But they were alive, too, or so it seemed as she tossed in a fever, too hot even to notice the itchy bites of the bedbugs. At that latitude, at that season, it seemed never properly to get dark, and so she never slept well, but was plagued by an extremely mild insomnia.

Once recovered, she and Sonya, a Wellesley student, walked to class, a long ways to and fro, giving Naomi, who had never previously cared to exercise and had always been rather weak and indeed physically lethargic, for the first time in her life, a modicum of strength. The university cafeteria food was ghastly, mostly variations on limp, pale greenishly translucent, overcooked cabbage, but, perhaps due to the unwonted exercise, for the first time in her life, her hunger was not suppressed, and she ate a lot, and miserable though the fare was, it fortified her in some new way, so that the tiredness that had hitherto plagued her limbs vanished. When she attended to it, with her inner eyes and ears, she could almost see and hear a growth and a physical healing, something that was new, something that was entirely of the body.

Shivering in the cool wind, the two young foreigners marveled at the inhumanly gigantic statues that decorated their route over bridges and along wide avenues. They bought pirogies from a street vendor, hoping for something better than their dreadful cafeteria cabbage, boiled in a murky soup, but, biting into hers, Naomi one day found it rotten with gray mold and flung it, in disgust, into the river. She could not get coffee anywhere. But sugar—sugar from Havana—was ubiquitous. So she settled for tea with sugar in little glasses that glimmered like hints of seraphs, hidden in the world, guzzling it at every opportunity.

Her Russian improved, so that soon she dreamt in the language. She read some Dostoyevsky and Tolstoy in the original and practiced the language with her local acquaintances, most of whom wanted to practice their English with her. So she mangled Russian, they mangled English, and somehow they understood each other. Sonya was fluent—child of a Russian emigré—and thus Naomi found it a bit easier to decipher her surroundings than had she been completely on her own. Like all the American students, they quickly ascertained that their Soviet group leader, Tanya, a scrawny, pasty, dyspeptic woman with glasses, lots of rat-like teeth and mousy brown hair, was KGB and that one of the students, a tall young man from the Midwest, was CIA. He was forever detaching himself from their group and wandering off, quickly followed by what had seemed to be the stray Russians always ambling with them. Wherever they went, such individuals would glom onto their group—all assumed by the Americans to be KGB agents—so that by the time they reached their tourist destination, museum, abandoned church or monument, their number would have nearly doubled. But these add-ons always followed the tall young man, exhibiting not the slightest interest in the other students. Sonya and Naomi found that they could tramp all through the gray brown streets of Leningrad for hours, without being followed, bothered or watched.

"Think, wherever that guy goes, he's got a crowd behind him."

"He's an idiot," Sonya replied. "And he obviously thinks the Reds are morons, which is a big mistake." This young woman's frequent, acid remarks made it clear that bitterness toward the Soviet Union had saturated her upbringing. She planned to work as a Russian translator when they returned to the United States and was visibly disturbed by the dilapidation of the Russian Orthodox churches in which she sought to worship. She was no leftist like Naomi, no, not even a liberal, but they shared a love of Russian language, literature and culture.

They made good friends with locals who, though dissatisfied with their government, would shrug and ask "what can you do?" and who had no intention of leaving or defecting. In one friend's Moscow apartment, she noted that instead of hooting at offensively imbecilic TV commercials designed by Madison Avenue, here people hooted at state sponsored propaganda. Nor did her friends bother to read *Pravda*. Few dared to obtain *Samizdat*, getting their information instead by word of mouth. They loved their country but were embarrassed by its ham-handed ideological stupidity and disgusted by the dictatorship.

In Tallinn, however, things were different. The Estonians detested the Russians, who, in turn, shielded their American guests from the locals and local opinion as much as possible. "They killed us, sent us in cattle cars to labor camps," said one young Estonian, who briefly chatted with them in a restaurant, "and they lie to you about who's buried in that cemetery you visited today. Not heroes of the revolution, like they said, but Estonians, nationalists, whom they killed." It was rainy in Tallinn, and the wet cobblestones gleamed darkly at the ignorant Americans, just as the residents glanced at them, before deciding to stay out of trouble and slinking away. In that city there was no question of wandering off on one's own; the westerners had an unsubtle escort from the state's security apparatus wherever they went. At dusk they were herded onto their tour bus and out of the people's republic of Estonia.

Letters from Tower Oaks Bend came regularly. Jack and Snow had settled into their small house, and the soon-to-be adoptive father had begun preparing for his job in the fall as an assistant professor of chemistry at the nearby University of Wyoming. Harry had visited, and the two brothers had gone hunting with Snow, who wept over the deer they shot and refused to eat the venison. Enclosed with each letter came a drawing from her son, mostly of local flora and fauna, but also of the elementary school he had seen, where he would attend third grade in the fall.

"And what will I do?" she had written.

"Enroll at the university for your PhD in comparative literature or write poetry," her boyfriend wrote back. But she dreamt of East Coast cities and journalism, though she did not mention this, partly because she anticipated a monumental fight and partly because she feared that Snow would not accept a separation from the man he regarded as his father. So, supine, she raised no objections to Jack's plans for the three of them, even when he wrote about their impending marriage and his legal adoption of her son.

"It sounds idyllic," Sonya mused. "The mountains of Wyoming."

"It sounds remote and isolated," Naomi replied. "But I don't seem to have a lot of choice."

Thus strangely immobilized, she drifted through Kiev, riding spotless trams, admiring the slate-colored Dnieper, the luxuriant yet trim parks, the old women with their scarves and parcels. The city reminded her somehow of Philadelphia, large yet a sleepy backwater composed of many distinct neighborhoods, in which residents went about their busy, unrecorded lives. She did not want to leave, but soon found herself on a terrifying Aeroflot journey to Yerevan, where Armenians spoke of their slaughter at Turkish hands much earlier in the century and of their solidarity with Soviet Jews. "First they come for the Jews, next it's the Armenians," a student told her and Sonya in fluent Russian. Then they returned to Moscow, white with terror on yet another Aeroflot jet piloted, once again, by two obvious drunks, one of whom offered Sonya his half-empty vodka bottle.

Stepping off the bus at Tower Oaks Bend in early September, the returning traveler scarcely recognized her son, now quite big for his age, while Jack, in a red and black flannel shirt, jeans and work-boots, looked like a lumberman from the Northwest. A warm wind blew in her face, stirring a piney fragrance that made her suddenly alert to the distance between herself and her son and husband-to-be.

"Got that roosky shit out of your system?" Jack asked, as they all clambered into the cab of his red Ford pickup truck.

"No, I'm reading Chekov in Russian."

"Just teasing you," he smiled, and for once there was no edge in his voice. She looked at him curiously, then said: "it was so different there."

He snorted and lit a Lucky Strike. "I'll bet. Totalitarian societies supposedly are a bit different."

"Not just that," she murmured, "the people, the long-suffering Russian people."

"They can stew in their own juice," he snorted again.

"That's my Jack," she snapped, brushing back her long dark hair, "open-minded as always."

"Could you two fight another time?" The little boy demanded. "I'm trying to read this Batman comic." They rode in silence the rest of the way.

The cabin was deep in the woods, off a dirt road. "No problem with too much social life here," she remarked, stepping down from the truck.

"Who needs people anyway?" He grinned at her, his cigarette clamped between his widely visible, bared teeth.

"We planted winter squash for you," her son said, grasping his mother's hand in his small sweaty one and leading her over to a fenced vegetable garden by the side of the house. She began poking at the poorly weeded rows. "You should've picked this lettuce," she remonstrated.

"Put it in late," Jack replied, "real late. Like everything. We wanted it all coming up when you were here."

She glanced up at him, "That was thoughtful."

"So's this. We go to town tomorrow and get hitched."

"I'd like to call my parents."

"I did. They can't come. Going to Europe, got the tickets six months ago."

"We could wait till they return."

"I want to adopt Snow, as his father legally, as soon as possible. It would really help if we got married right away."

"Well, I wanted to get my hair all cut off."

"Then we'll make it a day."

"And honeymoon—where?"

"Right here!" And for emphasis he drove the shovel he had been leaning on straight into the ground. "Why cut your hair?"

She shrugged. "Too much work like this. I want it real short."

He dropped his cigarette and crushed it into the ground. "I always liked it long."

"And I wanted my parents to attend our wedding."

"Nope, it can't wait," and he wrapped his arms around her.

"Don't you two get mushy on me," thus Snow.

"No danger of that," Jack grinned again. "You mom's as huggable as a cactus."

"They're my parents," she frowned.

"And he's going to be my son, legally," he pointed at the boy. "Say what— we'll get married now and have some big ceremony later, in Philly. My mom could come out from Wichita with Harry, Ethan too. And Tommy—"

"I can just see my father's face when he sets eyes on Tommy."

"We'll clean him up first. No one will ever know he's a homeless tramp."

The cabin, three bedrooms—one used as a study—a kitchen, bath, living room, dining room and screened in porch suggested long, lonely afternoons to her, while her husband worked at the university in Laramie and her soon attended school. "I have to get a car," she said immediately, upon surveying her new domicile, quiet, secluded and shadowed with the forest in the back, growing right up to the bedroom window. Though somewhat alarmed by the isolation, she found an unexpected relief in the shade, as if something came to her from it that she had never imagined before, had always associated exclusively with light, and with this strange thought came others, about thinking itself.

"I thought you wanted to stay home and write," came the rather terse and accusing reply.

"I won't live here without a car. I'd be marooned in the forest."

He fetched a campus newspaper with for sale advertisements in the back. "I'll pay for it," he muttered and soon was dialing a listed telephone number. "Yes, what about the Dodge for sale? It's a compact? Good. I'll have to look at the engine. All right, tomorrow."

"I'll pay you back," she said, still musing on the shiftings of light and shadow out the window, as she hoisted her back pack and with the other hand lifting a no longer spiffy suitcase.

"Did you actually see Baba-Yaga?" Her son pestered her.

"No, but I brought you a book," she rummaged through her bags and pulled out a children's book in Russian, with vivid pictures. "A friend gave it to me when she heard I had a little boy."

"Read it to me." So they sat on the edge of the bed, and she read the story of the witch with the hut on chicken legs, very haltingly—first a sentence in Russian, then she translated, then more Russian and so forth.

"I always liked this language," he said. "Teach it to me."

"I found you a car," Jack loomed in the doorway. "So tomorrow we go into town—haircut, car, marriage, not necessarily in that order." In the perfect stillness of that dim, remote room, she put the book down and exclaimed anxiously, "I don't know a soul here."

"Neither do we," said her son.

"Not strictly true," the man corrected. "There are some folks in the bio and chem departments who're quite friendly." He lit another cigarette, offering one to his wife-to-be, who declined with a quietly dismissive gesture. "You quit?"

She nodded.

Impressed, he came over and sat beside them. "We got a TV, but it only gets two stations out here. Still, it's better than nothing. We can keep up with President Ford's latest pratfalls."

"It's so isolated here."

"That's the idea."

"Maybe, for winter, we should think about moving into Laramie."

"It ain't Chicago," Jack grinned. "The biggest thing about that town's the university."

She gave him another worried look and began unpacking. "What happens in a storm?" She asked. "All the lights go out?"

"It's been known to occur."

"Just last week," the little boy added.

"Give it time," Jack soothed. "You'll get to like it here."

"I don't like it here," the boy went on. "I miss my friends from Hyde Park."

The man reached over and tousled his thatch of blond hair. "You do too like it here."

"No I don't. And you hunt. I don't like that. If you thought I was going to eat that rabbit, you're crazy."

"You shot a rabbit?" She was horrified.

"More than one," her son enlightened her. "He goes out with one of his rifles every other day."

"One of his? How many guns do you have in this house, Jack?"

"A few. I have to hunt, and then I need handguns for self-defense."

"Self-defense? Against who—Snow? There's not a soul for miles around."

"I believe when I'm out here in the woods that I'm a magnet for every escaped psycho in the state."

"Baloney."

"Well, maybe that's an exaggeration. But I got you and our boy to defend, so don't even begin to argue. The guns stay right here."

"I'm against this gun owning business."

"So you've said."

"There could be an accident."

"Not likely."

"Harry brought guns too," her son put in.

"What are you, the local cub reporter?" Jack demanded.

"And lots of liquor," Snow added.

The woman glared at the man.

"Now look what you've done," Jack lamented. "I thought we had a deal."

"I forgot," the boy said simply.

"So you've been boozing it up with your brother and then rushing off into the trees to shoot anything that moves," she snapped.

"We never touched the rifles after we had a drink."

"What about the handguns?"

"Nor those."

"Snow, go do your homework."

"I ain't got any."

"Haven't. Where are all these ain'ts coming from?"

"Haven't. School hasn't started yet."

"Then go read a book, in your room."

"Let's not start off on the wrong foot," Jack said.

She glared at him again.

"Harry gave me a toy machine gun," the boy volunteered, then left the room only to reenter with a surprisingly accurate imitation Uzi that made a horrible racket.

"I don't know if you adopting him is such a good idea," Naomi shouted over the noise.

"He needs a father."

"A father, yes, a gun fanatic, no."

"Uh oh," the boy said, lowering his toy machine gun, as Jack bent over to kiss his bride. "It's getting mushy again."

The next day they made the long journey into Laramie, passing, she noted, all of half a dozen inhabited dwellings on the road. She had looked up a salon in the yellow pages, and Jack directed the truck thither, where, to his chagrin, her very long tresses, sheared off, soon lay forlornly on the hardwood floor. "You look different," her son said.

Her intended, disgruntled, uttered not a word, but drove in silence to the home of the owner of the used Dodge. He raised the hood, poked around for forty-five minutes and finally declared it an acceptable vehicle. So for six hundred dollars, Naomi and Snow climbed in the front seat, and then drove behind the truck to the city hall, where a clerk informed them they needed a witness.

"Hey mister," Jack hollered to a passing attorney, and then, having explained the predicament, led the fellow into the appropriate office. In minutes they were married. Afterward the new husband took his small family to celebrate in a nice restaurant not far from campus, where they sat in tides of sunlight that periodically swept the room through large, glittering windows, as the few clouds that sailed through the bright atmosphere passed out of the way of the source of this endless ocean of light.

"So now I'll be your father," he said to the boy.

"You already were," the child replied. "And in case you didn't know, you were mom's husband, too."

"I knew. But I wanted it to be official."

"So it's official," she smiled tentatively, for the first time that day.

"Official and forever," her husband replied, glanced from one to the other, both aglow in the dazzling flood of endless light, rubbed his cleanly shaven cheek and ordered lunch.

❖

By the late 1970s, Mike Dellico, still cohabitating with Natalie, had moved to Manhattan to take a high-paying job in a music studio. They found a large, cheap, very used, second story apartment on Essex Street on the Lower East Side, facing Seward Park, which was frequented by drug addicts, gang members and thieves. Indeed, every Sunday morning at dawn this enclave was the site of a thriving thieves' market, where electronic gear from all over the city could be purchased for a fraction of its original price, from the crooks who had purloined it. They shared this abode with Boris Slavonovich, now a social worker, who toiled in a shabby East Village storefront converted to a social services center, to improve the lives of homeless veterans. The one advantage of their dirty, crime-ridden neighborhood, so Mike joked, was that the Son of Sam, then terrorizing the city with his random murders, appeared uninterested in it.

"Too much competition," Boris said over a dinner of fresh crab salad with dill that Natalie had made after her long day at the office as a graphic designer. The preparation of meals rotated on a weekly basis, and the veteran, always tired after work, happily contemplated the prospect of two entire weeks before he had to worry about cooking.

"That neighborhood in Brooklyn wasn't so wonderful," Mike put in, chewing, "but that didn't stop him from shooting that couple in the parked car." Since they ate early, it was dusk, the last rays of the sun had long since vanished behind the dark buildings across the park, looming like portals to the void, and shouts issued up from the street through the gloaming and the apartment's open window. "It's that Chinese gang again," Mike remarked, loading his plate with seconds. The veteran scowled, rose, left the dining room and approached the living room windows. "Nope," he said, "it's the Puerto Ricans from those high rises. Two of 'em," he spoke still chewing, "got in a fist fight. Uh oh. One pulled out a chain." The other man rose to join him and to inspect this scene of unchecked criminality. "The other's got a razor," Boris went on.

"This is exactly like something I saw in Philly, a decade ago on South Street at three a.m.," Mike spoke, peering over his plate in one hand, down at the street, while with the other hand he continued to lift forkfuls of crab into his mouth. "But those guys were older and heftier. The white guy had the razor, the black guy was whipping his chain around at him, and I was watching from a second story window, just like now."

"Yeah, well, now it's two teenaged Puerto Ricans," the veteran said, chewing and never moving his eyes from the threat of violence below.

"They're just facing off," munch, munch on the crab salad.

"First one that lunges, I'm calling the cops," Boris went on. "These gangs are terrible. You should see what they do when they get their hands on some broken, homeless vet."

"Uh-oh, there goes the chain."

"That does it," Boris put his plate down on the coffee table, strode back into the kitchen and called the police. "No they're not just threatening each other," he said into the receiver. "The guy with the chain just tried to swipe the guy with the razor's head off. No not one car. You better send more. There's at least another ten of them out there. Yes, right outside my goddamn window. And please don't mention I called."

"This is some neighborhood you picked, Mike," Natalie remarked, pouring herself a glass of red wine.

"The price is right. And Jorge recommended it."

"Jorge, who now lives in beautiful, rustic, Concord, Massachusetts? I think he was trying to get us killed. You're lucky, I've decided I'm happy here."

"Well the price is about to get even better," her lover said, returning to the table. "Because we're getting a roommate for one of the two empty bedrooms."

"That other bedroom is not empty," she corrected in mild irritation. "It's my studio."

"Who's the roommate?" The veteran demanded, not leaving the dark window, still gazing down at the snapping hostilities unfolding beneath a crime light.

"Naomi Diamond—I mean Lichter. She and Jack are separating. Irreconcilable blah, blah, blah. She writes lots of book reviews and features for Chicago, Philadelphia and Boston papers. She's going to look for a job here."

"But she has a kid!" The young woman exclaimed.

"Snow's not coming; he refused to leave his father."

"But Jack's not his father."

"He adopted him. And Jack refused to let her take him, went to a judge and everything; said she had no visible means of support."

"Sounds amicable."

"There's nothing amicable about Jack, and there never was. So she's coming here alone and needs a place to live, cheap. I told her we got it. She'll be here tomorrow night."

"Thanks for the notice," his girlfriend grumped.

"She never should have married that guy," the veteran mused. "There goes that chain again. Where are those cops already? Now she'll lose her kid. He'll get custody, say she's an unfit mother, and that'll be that."

"Well don't mention these brilliant apercus to her," Mike chomped on his vegetables. "She's upset enough already."

"Where's she want to work?" Natalie inquired.

"She has an interview at *The Soho News*."

The wail of sirens sliced through the night air, and soon a swirl of flashing red and blue danced on the shadowed living room ceiling from the street below. "They sure took their sweet time," Boris muttered, then, "that's right, cuff 'em all, lousy bunch of vet killing thugs."

"What vets have they killed?" Mike demanded.

"They beat up one of my clients within an inch of his life just last week," he began cursing softly under his breath, as he watched the officers disarm the gang. "Arrest them, arrest those bastards," he muttered, still guiding forkfuls of crab into his mouth, "arrest them all."

Natalie shook back her short, red-hennaed hair. "So that's why you painted that bedroom last week."

"I thought she might come here. I've been following this ugly break-up of theirs for some time. It seems Jack's rather abusive, verbally, that is."

"Surprise, surprise."

"You could've fooled me. I thought the guy was okay, a little weird about guns, a little sarcastic perhaps, but look how he adopted Snow, made himself the kid's father, when way back at first, he didn't have the slightest interest in it. But then he tried to stop her getting that reporting job on the Laramie paper, and once she got it, he wouldn't let up, just harassed her mercilessly that she was ignoring him and her son, that he did all the childcare and she had abandoned them. I was afraid she'd back down and quit."

"But not Naomi," his girlfriend said. "So meantime he set about meticulously documenting his case that she neglected her child. And when she found out and quit, he said 'no visible means of support.'"

"How did you know?"

Before she could answer, the veteran loped over to the dining room table. "Because that's the kind of vengeful son-of-bitch he is," Boris remarked, heaping his plate with more crab and fried zucchini. "He was probably planning to give her the boot all along."

"No, no," Mike clarified, "she left him."

"Good for her," the others said in unison.

"She's lucky," munch, munch on the zucchini, as Boris ambled back to the window, "he didn't blow her head off. Hey they got a paddy-wagon now. They're arresting the whole gang."

"She was worried about that."

"What?" Natalie asked. "The police?"

"The police were involved?" Boris looked surprised.

"No!" Mike protested. "Who said that? She was worried he might shoot her."

"That's just female hysteria," the veteran commented. "That guy's got way too much self-preservation to do a dumb thing like that."

"You yourself just said she was lucky he didn't blow her head off and that he was vengeful," Mike said.

"But not stupid. Hey, they got the chain and the razor—that's evidence. Now all the cops need is a witness that those creeps were using those weapons."

"Not you, I hope, 'cause if so," Mike glanced at him sharply, "you can move out first."

"You're impeding the course of justice."

"I'm impeding the course of gangland retaliation. I have no intention of having my apartment bombed or burned and my girlfriend raped."

Natalie looked up: "That's final, Boris."

He returned to the table. "You're both right, of course."

"Glad we got that straight," thus Mike.

"So where's Naomi now?"

"With her friends Betsy and Shane in Chicago. She flies in tomorrow night."

"That Shane turned into some union organizer," the young woman averred.

"Two steps ahead of the law," Boris replied. "They almost busted him for all those forgeries he painted. Somehow or other he wriggled out of it. The police were on their way to the house, and Betsy painted over all the works in progress. Black, I think."

"Paint it black," Mike hummed.

"She saved his neck," the veteran resumed, "told the cops her husband was depressed, was in his 'dark canvass' phase. Lucky for them both, they believed her. So after that, he kind of threw all his energies into organizing, with astounding results. If I'd known he had that kind of knack back when

I was working against the war, I would have leapt at the chance to use his skills. But who knew? I thought he was just another shifty street person—"

"Who also happened to be a doctrinaire Marxist Leninist," Natalie contrarily added.

"Well, I didn't pay attention to that. I thought it was just talk. Besides, I never went in for that doctrine anyway."

"Just talk!" Mike cried, throwing his fork on his plate with a sharp clatter. "The guy went on about it nonstop, morning till night, every minute he wasn't groping his wife, he was yammering on about the proletarian revolution and deporting all members of the establishment to labor camps. You considered that just talk?"

"He was a little fixated."

"Fixated? I'd say obsessed, obsessed with the violent overthrow of the government. To this day, I'm amazed he didn't defect to the Soviet Union and drag that poor Betsy Ein with him."

"Poor nothing," Natalie put in. "That bitch can take care of herself."

"Watch your language," the veteran corrected. "You're talking about a noted Chicago literary critic, who also, also," he wagged an index finger at her, "is such a committed feminist that she has worked as a midwife at a women's health clinic for almost a decade."

"She told me I didn't know it, but I was a lesbian."

"She has a sharp tongue in her head."

"I think I'd know."

Mike chuckled. "I think I would too."

"Some people are in the closet."

"But they know they're there," Natalie snapped. "And I'm not."

The red and blue lights swirling on the living room ceiling vanished, as the sirens' screech receded. Darkness descended on the little conclave at the table, lit only by an oblong shaft of yellow light that stretched into the room from the kitchen door, standing ajar. "Poor Snow," Mike said simply, after a moment, "he's too little to know what a dreadful mistake he's made."

"He'll find out," Natalie snapped again. "I never did like that Chicago crew, not Jack, not Betsy, not Shane—"

"Not Jeremiah," put in the veteran.

"Pul-ease," she pushed her chair away from the table, "don't get me started on that psychopath."

"You liked Alderway," Boris said softly, slight accusation thrumming behind his words.

344

"At least he doesn't have a nasty, sardonic tongue in his head."

"He better not," Mike laughed, "not around that raging Valkyrie of a wife of his."

"You mean Brunhilde," Natalie chuckled. "No," she went on pensively, "he at least was easy-going, well-mannered—"

"Duplicitous and dangerous," the former anti-war organizer concluded.

"Poor Snow," Mike repeated.

"Enough with poor Snow," Natalie snapped yet again. "We get the picture, but there's not much we can do about it. The person for that job was Naomi, and she failed. The kid's on his own."

"Barely ten years old," Boris mused. "Maybe Jack will turn out to be a good father."

"If he was, he wouldn't have driven the kid's mother away," she spoke sharply. "I have no patience for this sentimental wishful thinking. Good father indeed! The boy's situation is atrocious, but there's nothing anybody can do. So face it and shut up."

"Is that what you intend to tell our new roommate?" Boris asked.

"I intend to avoid the topic assiduously. And I suggest you do the same."

Silence descended on the little group, and except for a man hooting on the corner, probably at a woman, silence emanated up from the street too, a vast incongruous metropolitan silence, filled, in their dining room, with the silence of a boy whose world had just collapsed and who did not know why or how: Yes, Mike thought, that boy would go to bed that night wondering where his mother was, and would already know better than to turn in his inarticulate pain to the man reading the lab reports in the living room as he drank Jack Daniels.

"I bought her a bed," Mike said rather sadly. "And a dresser from the Salvation Army. We had an extra lamp and night table, so I put them in too."

"I know where I can get her a nice rug," Boris added.

"I'll buy some flowers in a vase," Natalie said. "We might as well let her know this is a home if she wants it."

"She wants her son," Mike blurted out, and no one else said a word.

The veteran looked away in sudden anger at this entire course of events and in regret, then rose and strolled over again to the street windows. "I guess we won't have to worry about that gang for a while," he said softly.

"They'll be back on the street tomorrow," Mike said, "with new chains, razors and guns, doing drugs right in that park, where we can see 'em and ambushing every stray member of every other gang that they can. Fortunately, I notice that most of this activity is nocturnal."

"I've never had any trouble, shopping on Essex, or getting home from the East Broadway subway stop," Natalie remarked.

"It's a teeming neighborhood. The gangs are small. They only seem big when they're fighting in front of your window," the veteran mused, his glance sweeping up now from the abandoned sidewalk to the fathomless night and seeming to take in its accustomed lesson, one he often voiced at such moments, about human wickedness and celestial indifference, or, if not that, purposes unknown, and the point that the only thing that mattered was the personal loyalty between individuals who had reason for it, and doing some good as cheerfully as possible.

"Maybe we should move into one of those swanky tenements on Forsythe Street," Mike said, "away from this gang nonsense."

"One of my co-workers lives on Forsythe, and loves it," Boris mused. "The brownstones face the park—so what if the walls are full of holes and the mice are everywhere—"

"Mice?" His friend asked. "Only mice?"

The veteran sighed, "Their larger cousins, too" then, after a pause, "Gus and Rebecca invited me up to Vermont. You know she teaches at the university there. I could use a vacation."

"You could use to have your head examined. The terms 'vacation' and 'Gus Harwood' don't mix," his friend averred. "That biker is a lunatic. He'll have you tearing all over those back roads on some motorcycle—"

"You used to own one."

"I drove sanely. And I wore a helmet, not a bandana. Fat lot of good that'll do you when your head smacks the pavement."

"I'm just sick of gangs, Son of Sam—"

"We're all sick of Son of Sam," Natalie said, "but until they catch him, the papers and the TV news aren't covering anything else."

The next afternoon, as he straightened the documents on his desk before leaving his dreary little East First Street office, the veteran looked up into a pair of alert brown eyes, noted the dark-haired bob, the brown corduroy pants, slim figure and mutedly striped, button down shirt of Naomi Lichter.

"Hey don't you look like a mainstream working girl," he smiled.

"I try to blend in these days."

"No more floor length, Indian print serapes."

"Not for years, Boris. You know that."

They turned their steps toward the wan light of an unseasonably cold afternoon, with a breeze tossing brown leaves, old newspapers and other assorted paper trash up in the air and along the street, like their dreams of a different world, ten years earlier.

She withdrew a startlingly good drawing of horses in a mountain field and held it before him.

"Snow did that?" He was amazed. "That's some talented kid."

"He gets it from his father, I suppose, the biological one, I mean, not that stubborn, cantankerous, cranky misogynist he lives with now."

"Neither one was ever very good."

"I just can't believe I lost him, my own son."

"Well of the two, at least Jack'll keep a roof over his head. That Ron Swurl lives hand to mouth on the streets of San Francisco."

"He still doesn't even know his son exists, not that he'd care."

"You never told him" Boris stated with morose flatness, "to this day."

"And never will."

"Forgive but don't forget."

"No," her eyes flashed angrily. "Don't forgive and don't forget."

"Stubborn as always, but at least you finally told your parents about Snow."

"I'm part of a stiff-necked race," she continued with her previous thought, "you know that."

They walked along the Bowery— "my clients," he smiled self-deprecatingly, while gesturing at the drunks sprawled on the sidewalk, mouths open, shirts open, snores rumbling up into the indifferent air—then traversed a few bleak byways to Christie Street. By now he was carrying her duffle bag, while she kept the pack on her back.

"Let's go over to Forsythe Street. I like it. I dream of living there," he said.

"It looks like a slum to me."

"It's a slum with style."

They crossed the park and ambled along its edge. Here and there men lay sleeping in the bare brown grass, while pigeons cooed mellifluously in the peeling trees.

"Maybe once they were fashionable," she gestured at the brown facades facing the decayed little refuge, "you know, fell on evil days, but still retain traces of their original grandeur."

"My thought exactly, just like certain parts of Northwest and Northeast D.C. or along Girard Avenue in Philly." He paused to light a cigarette. "Speaking of which, how are your folks? Does Morris still work for Amalgamated, one of the most evil corporations ever to pillage the backwaters of Latin America?"

"He doesn't see it that way," she sighed.

"Talk about stiff-necked."

"A year and a half ago, Eileen and I visited, presented him with a folder of articles and clippings about that company's depredations in Peru. He just said, 'where'd you get this? From comrade Meer?' Who, by the way, has done more work than any other soul on the planet to check that corporation's rapacity. I don't care if he's a card-carrying member of the CP."

"He is."

"Well, we knew that years ago, from time immemorial. But yes, sadly, my father still toils and moils for what can only be described as a force of evil. At least I don't take his money."

They paused to rest on a vandalized bench, decorated with black graffiti comprised of strikingly vivid obscenities.

"He's in fifth grade," she murmured, withdrawing a creased photograph of a little boy from her worn, leather pocketbook. Her friend reached over and took the picture. "And finally starting to look like you," he said.

"Very outdoorsy. Of course, living in the woods, he'd have to be. But he hunts now, fishes, can even make nets, knows his wild edible plants, can start a fire without a match, the whole nine yards. Jack taught him all that. I taught him Russian, how to appreciate good books and tend a vegetable garden," she paused as a tear dropped from her cheek onto her clenched hands.

"He'll be fine," her friend murmured softly. "It sounds like he already knows more than I do."

"If I could have tolerated it, I'd have stayed," she went on. "You know that, don't you?"

"Shh. You did what you had to. Sometimes separation is necessary. Look at me—when Eileen moved into my house in Washington, it only took me six months to abandon her."

"You had good reasons, legitimate, text-book reasons—I mean her wanton infidelity."

"Jack's wanton wicked, nasty tongue," her friend spoke abruptly, suddenly angry, "emotional abuse. I've been on the receiving end of his sarcasm and let me tell you, I couldn't put up with it for ten minutes."

Brazen, undeterred by broad daylight, a scruffy gray rat scampered across the stoop of one of the dilapidated brownstones opposite. The new arrival observed it, muttering in wonder, "and you dream, *dream* of living here."

"They have a certain moldy elegance," he gestured at the decayed and listing buildings. "Wait till you see our living room library on Essex Street—a whole huge wall full of books."

"I hope there's room for mine. I shipped five cartons, left five behind—for Snow."

"I'll build you shelves in your room."

"It's big enough?"

He nodded "We got one of the cheapest, roomiest apartments in Manhattan. When's your interview?"

"Tomorrow, with an Ian Donohue, city editor at *The Soho News*."

"I read him all the time. He covers housing, city hall, the courts, the political clubs, city council, the unions, the mobsters, you name it. He's very tough-minded, and somehow he gets stories that otherwise would be completely neglected. I've found his series on local landlords very useful, since some of my clients are their tenants."

"That's what he wants me to cover, housing."

"I've got some legal aid attorneys who can bring you up to speed real fast."

"Thanks Boris," she gazed forlornly at the photograph of her son he had just handed back. "I call him every night you know."

"I should hope so."

"Sometimes I read him a chapter of *The Three Musketeers* over the phone."

"That could get expensive."

"Not *whole* chapters. But at the rate we're going, we should finish, oh, before the millennium."

They rose and picked their way through the litter and dog turds along Forsythe Street, then onto other byways, finally arriving at Seward Park, where her friend, the old hand at this neighborhood, explained that on Sunday at dawn they could visit the thieves' market and purchase a stereo for her very inexpensively. "We just have to make sure we don't get robbed and lose it before we get back in the apartment." Then he unlocked a nondescript, windowless door on Essex Street, and she climbed the stairs to see her new home. "You could open a bookstore," she exclaimed, gazing admiringly at the shelves crammed with tomes in the living room. But the true surprise came with the discovery that her friends had already and very thoughtfully furnished her room. Natalie was there, taping up Mondrian posters that she had left work early to purchase at the Museum of Modern Art gift store. Boris' blue and green Mexican rug, heirloom of a friend leaving town in a hurry, covered a freshly washed wooden floor— "I'll have you know I skipped out of work at lunch today to pick that rug up and get it here."

"And somebody Murphy oiled the floor!" Naomi exclaimed.

"Yours truly," Natalie beamed. "We wouldn't want you to think we live like slobs. Where's you typewriter?"

"In one of the boxes I mailed last week."

Mike wandered in, his brown hair and smudged aviator glasses both in need of cleaning. He asked if she had money, to which she replied by showing him a cashier's check for one thousand dollars, her life's savings, emptied out of her account in Laramie.

"That's it," she said. "I'll open an account with it tomorrow."

"It's my night to cook," Natalie said. "And it's chicken cacciatore with rice."

"Not again," the two men groaned, then Mike said: "I thought we were onto something new with that crab salad last night."

"I love chicken cacciatore," Naomi said.

"She makes it constantly," Mike complained.

"What about chicken marsala?" Boris asked.

"Or chicken parmigana?"

"Or fried chicken?"

"Or roast chicken?"

Natalie crossed her arms over her chest and tapped her foot. "Of course I could make burgers."

"No!" The two men howled.

"What's wrong with burgers?" Naomi was dumbfounded.

"It's the only thing she makes more than chicken cacciatore," Mike said.

"Another burger and I may throw up," Boris put in. "I had one for lunch today and yesterday."

"Then cook for yourselves," Natalie hissed.

"But we have a schedule," Mike started.

"An equitable one," Boris added.

"Such carryings on," Naomi marveled. "Jack and Snow ate everything I gave them, and I'm afraid the repertoire was very limited."

"That's their problem," Mike said.

"We don't want a limited repertoire," Boris elaborated. "We want Indian cuisine, nouvelle cuisine, French cuisine,"

"Then go to cooking school, 'cause otherwise it's chicken cacciatore and burgers, at least when it's my week to cook."

"What do you cook?" Mike interviewed the newcomer hopefully.

"Burgers, stews, goulash, stuffed cabbage,"

The men exchanged skeptical glances.

"Well next week is my week," Mike said, rubbing his hands together eagerly, "and it's going to have a Middle Eastern theme."

"Great," Natalie said, "we're going to drown in tahini."

"Better than chicken drenched in a tomato wine sauce with mushrooms," Mike said.

"I make burritos," Naomi ventured.

"I want burritos, I'll go to Taco Bell on Long Island," Mike complained.

"My goodness," Naomi said.

"You have no idea," Natalie warned, stalking off to the kitchen, "no idea."

Later, after their much-discussed chicken cacciatore, Naomi closeted herself in the kitchen and dialed the number in Tower Oaks Bend.

"But Snow went to bed early," the father said. "He has a cold."

"I want to talk to him."

"Always what you want."

"I think it's a good idea for a mother to talk to her son every day."

"Depends on the mother," he grumbled, but put the receiver down and went to fetch the boy.

"High baby," she began.

"I'm not a baby."

"Of course not. You're almost in the double digits."

"I punched Howard in the nose today," he proudly announced.

"Uh-oh, principal's office."

"Yeah, but not for too long. Howard won't pick on me again."

"You're not hanging out with those rough sixth graders?"

"Just sometimes."

"Sometimes?"

"Like on the bus."

"And they taught you how to punch somebody in the nose?"

"Nope. Daddy did that."

"Great."

"He says if somebody hits me, I hit him right back."

"And Howard hit you."

"He was going to."

"But Daddy said only if somebody hits you."

"Not really. He said if somebody messes with me."

"No, no, Snow. Only if someone actually hits you, and even then—"

"I think Daddy knows more about it than you."

"Oh?"

"'Cause he's a man, and guys know about this stuff. He says if I listen to you, I'll get pussy-whipped."

"Uh-oh," came from Jack, loud and clear in the background.

"Snow! You put him on this instant."

"He overheard me," the father immediately clarified. "I'd never say that to him directly. I was talking to Tommy."

"So now Tommy's there?"

"Hey, if you can spend a week with an art-forging revolutionary and his radical feminist wife, I'm allowed to put my brother up for a few days, especially considering he has no place else to go."

"He's a terrible influence."

"Snow knows. I told him uncle Tommy's a bum and never do what he does. Hey, when are you going to can this independence crap and get back out here?"

The conversation did not end happily.

That evening, as she lay in her bed, a peculiarly specific ache of loneliness, a feeling only know by a mother who has been forcibly separated from a child, an exquisite awareness of the absence of a small person, a physical recollection that her own body had harbored that person alive within it—all this kept her awake and fidgeting miserably into the depths of night. She thought of courts and custody orders and legal papers and then some sudden wind from some unnamable place scattered all that from her mind and the only thing that mattered anywhere was her child and the connection, heart to heart, from her to him and she rose, ready to return to the West, took a step, remembered and stopped. "Damn that Jack Diamond," she cursed, and cursed again groggily, when she rose at eight a.m.

In her corduroys and man-tailored shirt, she entered *The Soho News* storefront, was directed to the editorial offices in the back and thence into a small room, occupied by a muscular, medium height man in his late twenties, whose sharp features and thick Bronx accent seemed utterly at odds with his gentle dark curls. He leafed through her clips, glanced at her resumé, told her that she would be called a senior editor but that in fact what he needed was another city reporter. "I can't do it myself. It's too much, especially the housing beat. In this city it's huge, and no one else besides *The Village Voice* covers it. I need a weekly column from you, one thousand words at least, mostly on housing, and I need it yesterday. Can you do this?"

"If you can help me get started, point me at the right people—"

"Here," he handed her a folder. "Those are all the important clips on housing that have run in this city in the past three years. I need you to cover the housing court. The volume there is tremendous, the judges are petty tyrants and megalomaniacs, who run kangaroo courts, the tenants are treated like second class citizens, and not one reporter from any paper in this city covers those courts. Murray Kempton used to, but he's too busy over with the criminal courts—which I'll expect you to cover as well. But housing first; as much human interest as you want, but keep your facts about evictions, rents and receiverships, absolutely straight. These landlords will sue at the drop of a hat, and they're used to having their way. Here," he began leafing through the folder, "a building over in Hell's Kitchen, the landlord, Foleto, has been evicting tenants at gunpoint, no repairs in eighteen months, no working toilets, rats, vermin, no heat, wants to sell it to a developer who'll tear it down and put up luxury coops. Only problem—it's fully inhabited by low-income Greeks, Hispanics, African Americans, who become homeless the minute they hit the pavement. Talk to the tenants. Query Foleto about their charges. He'll say they're lying, but go look and see for yourself. Dead bodies have turned up in that building. Here, another building in the East Village. The owner's been using gangs to terrorize elderly tenants, wants to evict them, convert to coops and make a financial killing. That's the big thing in Manhattan real estate now—throw out your rent-stabilized or rent-controlled low-income residents, repaint and sell the apartment for a fortune. The incentives are all on the side of abuse; abuse—that's putting it mildly. Some of these owners commit murder, arson, you name it, anything to terrorize the inconvenient tenants and get them out. And I can't do it. I don't have the time. I gotta cover city hall, the criminal courts, the political clubs, the cops, the mob. So you do it. Start today. Every week," he was nearly shouting now, jabbing an index finger ferociously in the air, "I want that housing court in the paper every week!"

Later, as he gave her a tour of the editorial office, and introduced her to reporters, copy editors, editors, typesetters, proofreaders and the production crew, she ventured, "You're from the Bronx, Mr. Donohue?"

"Call me Ian. Yes, Kossuth Avenue, end of the D train, not far from the L on Jerome Avenue, born and raised with my brother in the same, first floor, two-bedroom apartment where my parents still live. City College," he beamed proudly at her, "that's where I went."

"Don't you believe this proletarian saga," a gray-haired, grizzled typesetter put in. "He went to Columbia University journalism school."

"That was after City College. And I went on a scholarship."

"The tornado from da Bronx," the typesetter clucked, peering over his bifocals at Naomi. "So you're the new city reporter from where is it— Laramie, Wyoming?"

"I know I've got a lot to learn about this place,"

"Lady, that's the understatement of the year."

"But I grew up in Philly and went to school in Chicago, so,"

"So that's a little more encouraging."

"Let me do the hiring interview," Ian snapped. "Okay Tapper? Her clips are terrific. She turned Laramie on its head."

"That's not saying much. It probably didn't have a head to turn on, it's so small."

"She also wrote for *The Baltimore Sun*, *The Philadelphia Inquirer* and the Chicago papers—from Wyoming."

"That's better."

"Hey, who runs this place?"

"You do."

Ian grasped her elbow and guided her away. "Here I'll take you out for a coffee and talk about me. But not too long, I've got to get back and file."

He was remarkably voluble and forthcoming. His mother, a school teacher, and father, a transit worker, had both nearly lost their jobs in the 1950s, "due to a previous association with the communist party. Fortunately they were too insignificant to attract much notice. The next near catastrophe was when they almost moved to Coop City. I'd have committed suicide if they did that and told them so. Luckily they backed down, and I got to spend my entire childhood and adolescence in the much maligned, underappreciated but, as only the aficionados know, truly splendiferous Bronx. I know that borough like the back of my hand, even

354

the South Bronx—every neighborhood, every subway stop, the Botanics, even Riverdale. I explored it nonstop for eighteen years. Then I went to City College, and I did the same thing in Manhattan. Queens, Brooklyn and Staten Island I'm a little sketchy on, though I've never yet gotten lost there. But that apartment on Kossuth Avenue, it's not far from Montefiore Hospital, I love that place. And I still go home almost once every week for dinner. My mother always overcooks the meat of course, she's Jewish. My father's Irish. But he's reached the point after thirty years of marriage where he can't even eat a brisket unless it tastes like shoe leather. Sometimes, I have to say, when I'm treating some bigwig source to drinks at Sardis, it just comes over me, that here I am, the little, snot-nosed kid from Kossuth Avenue, with my own city section in Manhattan. The contrast is overwhelming. I always have to have another drink when I think about it, you know, just to celebrate."

Ian lived at that time in the West Village and was utterly immersed in the prosecutions of several drug dealers from Harlem, one from East Harlem. So after he left Naomi at the office, with instructions on how to approach Foleto's buildings, he betook himself to the subway and was soon being jostled and jolted on the clattering Lexington Avenue line north. He exited uptown and strode through the unseasonably warm late autumn air of East Harlem to a small lounge with an irregularly blinking neon sign that said "Beer" and slid into a booth in the back. The bar was dark, and for a moment, his sun-blinded eyes could not discern any details. But as they adapted, he saw his source, in jeans and a black leather jacket approach.

"Jorge Ramirez? We meet at last."

"Yeah, well, I don't like just talkin' over the phone to someone I never met."

"But should you be around here? I mean the story is you live up in Concord, Massachusetts. Witness protection is getting sloppy."

"I'm not in it—yet."

"After you testify against Cortez you damn well better be. He's one vindictive heroin dealer, known for inflicting slow and painful deaths upon his opponents."

"He's vermin, a parasite living off the poverty and misery of my people. He's looking at life—several consecutive sentences, I might add."

"Depends on the judge."

"We got a hangin' judge. Wears a gun in an ankle holster, while he's at the bench, and uses it, too—stopped an armed robbery in progress in his Upper East Side neighborhood."

"Levin?"

"Yup."

"You lucked out."

"It wasn't luck. It was hard work, a lot of string pulling, and frankly, judge shopping. But it was worth it. I read up on this judge. He had a murder conviction in his court, the guy had shot a woman in the head after raping her at gunpoint, multiple times. Levin gave him twenty five to life three times consecutively, said to the newspaper reporter he went home, had a good dinner, went to bed and slept soundly, knowing he had removed a monster from the streets of New York. Then there was the time a defendant, another drug dealer, tried to flee the courtroom. Levin tackled him in the aisle and put his gun to the punk's head. Of course the case had to be moved to another judge after that, but hey, the guy was still convicted."

"But this judge can't protect you, and you wore a wire."

"And I'd wear it again to put this creep away."

"Cortez is mob-connected."

"You don't think I know? I got it on the tape, him bragging about his friends in this family and that family and how they bankrolled him, helped him get his lousy start in the heroin biz. The guy makes me sick. How could a Puerto Rican do what he did to his people, to his barrio? If it was an outsider, one of these Italians—"

"You wouldn't have done it."

"Probably not—ginger ale," he told the languid, dark-haired waitress, "and hey, this time, please keep the flies out of it."

"That was an aberration," she said.

"Aberration—where'd you learn that word? Not here, dropping flies in customer's beverages."

"Don't be a snob. And it was an accident, since you don't like aberration."

"Yeah, well, no flies please."

"It's a good thing you don't have a wife and family," Ian remarked, once the waitress left.

"If I did, I wouldn't be talking to you. So I guess you're the one it's a good thing for."

Ian flipped through his notepad, "now he boasted about murdering this Edward Garcia,"

"Yeah, there's your family man. Cortez slit his throat personally and had his, get this, quote secretary unquote, dump the body in the East River, leaving Garcia's wife and four kids with very little means of support. She works part time as a domestic, but that's the extent of her wealth. It makes me sick to think about it."

"What did this Garcia do?"

"He was a pothead. His boss sells a little pot on the side, and he pilfered a bit."

"For that he got his throat cut?"

"Maybe he pilfered a lot and stole his boss' clients by underselling. But there are ways of settling such matters short of severing a person's carotid artery."

Ian let out a low whistle, as the ginger ale arrived.

"*Sans* fly," the waitress remarked.

"You're Spanish, not French," Jorge riposted.

"And you're a snob," she said, departing.

"No tip for her."

"Now you used to be in the Young Lords," Ian began.

"You can't print that. And no profile, no profile of me now or ever. I thought we had that straight."

"I wouldn't dream of it," the reporter soothed. "I just wondered if it was your old political connections that put you onto this…this situation."

"You mean that this lowlife and his smack-dealing gang were terrorizing my neighborhood? I didn't need a political connection to find out about that. All I had to do was visit one weekend. It's common knowledge, and it's been going on for two years."

"So you essentially went to the DA and volunteered."

"I went to the Feds. This is a joint, state and federal investigation with multiple targets. I explained I'd grown up with some of these, these,"

"Gangsters."

"Gangsters. And they gave me a wire and told me I was going into witness protection. I said that could wait."

"But now you're not so sure."

"They spooked me, showed me pictures of this guy's victims after he got done with them. Those gave me the heebie-jeebies."

"So you said maybe."

Jorge nodded. "What's that black speck in my soda? You see that?"

Ian peered at the drink. "It's not a fly."

"Excuse me," Jorge called, "waitress!"

She slouched over to their booth.

"What's that?" Jorge demanded, pointing at the ginger ale.

"What's what?"

"That black speck."

She picked up the glass to examine it. "Dirt."

"Dirt? You serve your Canada Dry with dirt in it?"

"I'll get you a new one, on the house, big spender."

"It better be on the house."

"Picky, picky," the waitress muttered, removing the offending potation.

"So when do you testify?" Ian asked.

"Tomorrow, so be there."

"Don't worry. And you better tell the feebs you want witness protection—today."

"That's a good idea."

"Thank you," the reporter said, closing his notebook "take my advice, for free—call them after you leave here."

Ian hurried out of the bar to a pay telephone booth and dialed a number.

"Judge Levin's chambers."

"Tell him it's Ian Donohue about the Cortez homicide-heroin case."

"You know I can't talk about a case in progress," the judge growled into the phone.

"I just spoke to Jorge Ramirez."

"You tell that Ramirez to get his ass in witness protection, before the prosecution has one dead witness. And I better not hear you been talking to any other witnesses, and I sure as hell better not read anything they say in that little Soho snooze of yours or you'll find yourself in contempt of court so fast you won't know what hit you."

"Have I not behaved as a model member of the press in your courtroom in the past?"

"This is different. Nothing on the record. These are very evil people. And if you louse it up for some scoop—- and who are you scooping? *The Village Voice?* Don't make me laugh—but if you foul it up, I'll get you on contempt for the way your hair's parted. You got that?"

"I thought I might get an interview or a profile after the case is over and his guilt or innocence is determined."

"Guilt or innocence?" Judge Levin shouted. "We got five dead, mutilated bodies, eye witnesses, confessions on a wire, more heroin from the perpetrator's car than we can keep track of—"

"Alleged perpetrator."

"Are you stupid?"

"Why can't you keep track of it?"

"Some of it disappeared."

"What?"

"You heard me and you can't quote me. But you might want to look into it."

"What kind of corrupt—"

"Did I say corrupt? Did I use the word corruption?"

"I'll have to look into this," the reporter scribbled furiously.

"You might want to look into witness protection as well," Judge Levin said and hung up.

The next morning Ian Donohue made his way by subway to Centre Street, then hurried to the high-ceilinged halls of the criminal court and, more specifically, to the courtroom of the State Supreme Court Justice M. J. Levin. The judge had just slammed his gavel on the desktop, not because the half-empty room was disorderly, but to get the attention of the prosecutor, at whose table there was some hubbub.

"So is he in witness protection or what?" The judge demanded, when the assistant district attorney approached the bench.

"Not yet your honor."

"When's he planning on it—the next life?"

"He has principles."

"At least he has a suit. That'll make a much better impression on the jury than that black leather jacket he wore into my chambers. Where did he think he was—a motorcycle gang convention? And what are these principles?"

"Something about living in East Harlem and working in the community. He used to be a radical, a Young Lord, your honor."

"Well, he's a stupid radical. After today, the next time he shows his face in his beloved community, he's a dead man. Does he realize this?"

"We are making every effort."

"Make more. It's not my job to tell you what to do, but I don't want any dead witnesses turning up in the middle of this trial."

Jorge Ramirez, dapper in a gray suit, spotless white shirt and tie, took the stand. His beautifully polished shoes gleamed brightly, and his dark hair shone from the cream he had used to slick it back.

"I'm looking at a dead man," the judge muttered to his assistant.

"Dead witness," the assistant corrected.

"That's even worse." He leaned over and whispered: "Should I make a speech? Scare the bee-jesus out of these lowlife, drug-dealing killers?"

"I don't think so," the assistant whispered back. "They know you're a hanging judge. That defense attorney's ready to go for a mistrial and change of venue at the drop of a hat. He does *not* repeat *not* want you as judge on this case."

"Then I better behave myself. But if they kill this witness, I cannot be responsible for what I may say or do."

"So, Mr. Ramirez," the prosecutor was saying, "will you repeat what Mr. Cortez said to you regarding the deceased, Edward Garcia?"

"That he had cut him up with a Swiss army knife real bad, then he slit his throat and had the body dumped in the East River."

At the defendant's table, Raoul Cortez, glowering at the witness, made a slicing motion with his index finger across his throat. Judge Levin saw this and slammed down his gavel. "Wake up prosecutor. Let the record show that defendant is threatening the witness."

The assistant district attorney, whose back had been turned to the defendant, looked confused.

"Like so," the judge said and imitated the slicing gesture.

The defense attorney was on his feet, claiming his client had an itch on his Adam's apple.

"No itch!" Mr. Cortez shouted, leapt to his feet, staring furiously at Jorge, and for emphases made the gesture again, even more violently. The jury gasped.

"At least Mr. Cortez is an absolute idiot," Judge Levin murmured to his assistant again. "If this ADA can't get a guilty verdict, he should go into another line of work."

Meanwhile Ian scribbled furiously, noting that the defense attorney was requesting his removal.

"This is a public proceeding," Judge Levin replied evenly. "The press has every right to be here. I cannot help it if your client behaves in a prejudicial manner."

"He had an itch."

"Twice?" Judge Levin demanded.

"Three times," the attorney shouted, as Mr. Cortez did it again.

"Mr. Cortez," the judge asked politely, "do you have an itch?"

"No itch," came the furious reply.

"Will you kindly explain to the court what you mean by this gesture that you have now directed at the witness three times?"

"Everybody knows what I mean."

"Objection," the defense attorney shouted.

"If they don't know, they're morons," Mr. Cortez calmly concluded.

"Well," Judge Levin gave a cold, grim little smile, "that about settles it."

"It is a matter of interpretation," the defense attorney said.

"But not a matter of an itch," the judge replied. "Are we agreed on that?"

"Agreed."

Ian spent the entire day at Raoul Cortez's trial, then returned to *The Soho News*, where he found Tapper holding an uncorrected galley with a look on his face that said "I am very impressed."

"That Lichter lady," he began, "she's making her column out of short items and filed two of them today." Ian snatched the galley out of his hand. "Not bad for a first day," he murmured, after reading the account of the erratic behavior of one of housing court Judge Pepper, who had compelled the litigants in his courtroom to open proceedings that day by singing "The Star Spangled Banner" and then gone on to harangue the members of the tenants' association with his belief that their organization was, in reality, a communist front. He had also displayed personal military memorabilia from his stint in the Korean War, concluding with much finger-wagging at the assembled and aggrieved tenants that he knew Reds when he saw them, and he saw them "right now."

There was also a colorful item on Foleto— "you can fuck off and that's on the record. In fact I *insist* you print it"—and the travails of his tenants in the truly horrendous and dangerously collapsing building in Hell's Kitchen. "She's off to a good start," Tapper remarked, sharp eyes glimmering over reading glasses, as he ran his fingers through his tough, wiry gray hair. "How'd she get onto Pepper? I thought he was our little secret."

"That folder of clips I gave her. *The Village Voice* ran its ten worst landlord series, which included a description of Pepper as 'a psychopath on the bench,' and 'a raving lunatic in robes.' That must have caught her eye."

"The damndest thing is Pepper can't sue," Tapper went on, "because then the *real* truth would come out."

"Truth is stranger than fiction. I say it every time I set foot in the housing court." Then Ian went off in search of his new reporter, congratulated her and suggested she file a few items every day, like the two he had just seen. "Then we'll put it altogether for our weekly deadline, and that'll fill a lot of our city news hole." He returned to his desk and sat typing up his notes well into the night.

Later he walked through shuttered Soho, where the lights twinkled in the windows too high overhead to illumine the deep shadows of the street, then through the more typically residential South Village, across Houston and up Sixth Avenue to a good, simple, cheap eatery, where he ordered a large plate of mussels marinara, which he ate with a beer, catching up on the articles in *The New York Times*, *The Daily News*, and *The New York Post* that he had not had time to read earlier. Then he started in on *The New Yorker*. He had already read the *Voice* cover to cover that week, along with *The Nation*, and several other newspapers and magazines. Finally finished with these periodicals, he ordered a piece of chocolate cake, chatted with the somewhat shaky elderly waiter, and then turned toward Sixth Avenue, teeming at ten p.m. He stopped at a newsstand to enjoy the headlines he had written for the front page of his paper, then ambled on, plying a toothpick, discreetly ogling attractive women, then dismissing the thought that had flitted through his mind upon meeting Naomi— "no, she's got a son and isn't even divorced yet"—thought about visiting his girlfriend but then, swinging left on Christopher Street, decided that no, he was too tired for his fading romance—really all he wanted was another beer, the quiet of his one bedroom apartment on Thirteenth Street and a little, mindless television.

As he approached his small, modern apartment building, he noted a medium height, heavy-set, dark-haired man lounging on the low brick wall by the entrance. He wore jeans, a jacket and a polo shirt and appeared to be waiting for someone, as he smoked his cigarette. "Mr. Donohue," he said, flicking the cigarette out into the gutter as Ian approached.

"Do I know you?"

"Yes and no. I saw you in the courtroom today."

A memory of a heavyset Hispanic man seated behind the defendant passed through the reporter's mind. He stopped and took a step back.

"Esteban Hernandez, that's my name." He did not hold out his hand.

"You're a friend of Mr. Cortez's?"

The man nodded. "He and I would appreciate it if you would forget that little incident with the itch."

"Are you threatening a reporter?" Ian asked, "Because if so, that's page one news."

Esteban looked a little befuddled. "It is?"

The reporter nodded.

"Well this is just a request. I ain't dealt with no reporters before."

"You're dealing with one now. I could put everything you say in a story, or maybe I'll just settle for the anecdote about the itch, which, I should remind you, is already a matter of public record."

"It is?"

"Of course it is," Ian cried. "It happened in open court. The judge noted it. The court reporter wrote it down, and the prosecutor's adding it to his charges."

"That's not what Raoul said."

"Raoul's living in a dream world, where you can threaten a state's witness with murder in the courtroom of the toughest judge in town. This is a hanging judge. Your friend better know that before he even thinks of tampering with witnesses or intimidating reporters."

"Who's intimidating?" The rather muscular thug backed off, gently waving both hands before his chest, where they fluttered with the futility of leaves in a night wind, in a gesture of negation, as if threatening a member of the press was the last thing that would ever cross his rather dim mind.

"He told you to scare me, didn't he?"

"Who?"

"Raoul."

"No, no. Why would he do a stupid thing like that? Raoul, he's the one with the brains."

Ian rolled his eyes.

"He just hoped you would keep in mind that he was rather upset, there being so many charges against him—"

"It's the longest indictment I've ever seen."

"There. That's why he lost it. And then to find out that a friend like Mr. Ramirez was wearing a wire was such a shock. And that he misinterpreted everything Raoul said—well, you can imagine it ain't been no picnic for Raoul."

"Let's hope not."

"And he's rather hot-tempered."

"Infamously."

"Given to saying things and making gestures that might be very incriminating—"

"You got that right."

"But never in a million years would he harm a hair on Mr. Ramirez's head, not a pimple on that ugly little nose, no less slit his throat. Who could imagine such a thing?"

"The judge and the jury."

"Oh Raoul, he has so many problems."

"Like twenty-five to life, several times, consecutively."

"You think? Maybe concurrent."

"Ha!"

"Perhaps I should talk to Judge Levin."

"Perhaps I'm going to put you in my story."

"No, no," again the burly man's hands fluttered before him, as though attached against their will to his massive body and trying to escape. "Raoul only likes to read nice things about himself in the papers. He's very kind to animals, you know. Put that in your story, and say I said so."

"You can count on it."

"Esteban. That's E, S, T, E, B, A, N."

"I can spell."

"Hernandez. But everybody knows how to spell Hernandez." He paused, panting slightly as if from mental effort. "He's very good with babies too. Babies and dogs, they love him. And he always has presents for children."

"A veritable Santa Claus."

"There," the idiot goon beamed at Ian, "you got it." He paused again, as if the effort of his lucubrations required frequent rests. "You see," he resumed stolidly, "there really always are two sides to every story."

The reporter almost burst out laughing, but in view of his visitor's heft, suppressed it. He walked into his building's entranceway, keys in hand.

"Balance," the hopeless heavyweight called after him. "You reporters need balance."

"And you need an IQ," Ian muttered to himself, as he unlocked the door to the lobby. He turned: "Good night, Esteban. Sweet dreams. And tell Raoul I'd love to interview him after the trial, wherever he may be at that time."

"A free man, if we can get a different judge."

"And a model citizen, no doubt."

"Of course."

He rode up the elevator to the third floor, unlocked his door and entered the quiet, shadow-muffled apartment with its view of St. Vincent's hospital across Thirteenth Street. He retrieved a bottle of beer from his fridge, threw himself on the living room couch, where he sprawled, guzzling and gazing at the ceiling, the walls with their large, framed photographs of New York, the carpet, the other chairs, anything other than the thick tome, *The Making of the English Working Class*, that stared up at him from the coffee table with the little yellow slip of paper that marked his progress about half way through. At length his gaze settled on it. "Not tonight, okay?" He addressed the book. Fortunately the telephone rang before the book could respond.

"Hi Ma, how's Dad's hernia?"

"Well it's gone now he had the operation."

"That's what I meant."

"Oh, he's getting around, did a little business with Donny today."

"You tell him to stay away from that bookie."

"How can I? He lives next door, and we run into him every time we go out."

"Chiletti is mob-connected, Mom. I looked into it."

"Oh, nonsense. If he is, it's so low level, it doesn't matter."

"It always matters. That's what you and Dad said about the party, then McCarthy came along and look what happened, you almost lost your jobs. Too low level—that has to be the lamest excuse yet. You tell Donny Chiletti that Dad doesn't need his services. He'll understand. And don't then turn around and invite him to dinner. Besides, he's eating you out of house and home."

"I didn't call for a lecture on Donny. I called to see how you're doing and if you've decided to marry Carol yet."

In the background, Ian heard his father howl: "For God's sake Irma, leave him alone."

"I've decided not to marry Carol."

Despite her hand over the mouthpiece, Ian distinctly heard his mother say, "He's decided *not* to marry Carol. I knew he'd blow it."

"I just had a hernia operation!" His father cried. "I could care less if he marries Cardinal Spellman."

"Carol's a very nice girl."

"He'll find another nice girl."

"Hello! Hello! I'm still here. I can hear every word you say," their son shouted.

"But he's almost thirty, Brendan. I want grandchildren."

"I just had a hernia operation! I don't want grandchildren."

"You're getting yourself upset."

"*You're* getting me upset."

"Can you patch it up?" His mother asked into the phone. "Bring her up to the Bronx for dinner."

"That'll be the last we see of her," Brendan hollered in the background. "Boy, did I marry into the wrong culture, cuisine-wise. Did it ever occur to you, Irma, that maybe the reason Carol broke up with him was that meal with the burnt steak you served her when she came to dinner?"

The hand went back over the mouthpiece. "She didn't break up with him—"

"I would've, after a meal like that."

"He broke up with her. He's been doing this now since college: six months or a year with a girl, then he breaks it off."

"You keep going just like that Ian," his father hollered. "You find yourself someone who can cook."

"And now he says you gotta stop placing bets with Donny."

"Oh well. He can forget that."

"Donny's a mobster," their son shouted.

"Very low level," Irma replied.

"I thought the mafia offended your ideological purity," Ian said.

"Well yes," his mother wavered, then the hand went over the receiver again. "Now he's going on about our political beliefs."

"Well don't get me started on his. The new left! Give me the old left any day."

"That's right, Dad, just crank out the guillotine."

"Now he says you should get out the guillotine."

"Better that than this system of Republican reactionaries running the show and that nincompoop Gerald Ford. Thank God he's gone. Now we've got the cracker peanut king."

"I like Carter," Ian shouted.

"He says he likes Carter."

"He needs his head examined."

"What's this got to do with Carol?" Irma demanded.

"I thought we were done with Carol—history," Brendan replied.

"Invite her up for dinner," Irma shouted into the phone.

"No way. I'm breaking off with her."

"That was so loud I heard it across the room," the father said. "I think Carol's kaput. You better face it, Irma."

"What about Donny's granddaughter? She's twenty, goes to Fordham, beautiful girl—" Irma began.

"I'm not marrying into the mob," the young man paused, placed the receiver in his lap and took a deep breath. Then he picked it up again. "Mother," he began.

"I'm so disappointed."

"I'm not," Brendan shouted, "anything to postpone grandchildren."

"I thought you called to tell me how Dad's recovery is progressing."

"Well, as you can hear, he can still shout."

"Not at the TV, I hope, when the political news comes on."

"Oh yes, that wasn't even interrupted by the operation. He was doing it in the hospital."

"You know, Brezhnev is hardly God's gift to mankind."

"Don't start, Ian. He's an invalid."

"I am not a goddamn invalid," Brendan hollered.

"You would be if you heard what he just said."

"What did he say?"

"I won't repeat it, or the stupid snide implication. For your own good," Irma paused. "As if we support Brezhnev."

"He said what?! Gimme that phone."

"I don't think our phone call has had a soothing effect," Irma said. There came a telltale click: Brendan had picked up the other line.

"I don't think anything soothing has happened in that apartment in thirty years," Ian replied.

"Oh yes it has," Irma said.

"What?" Both men demanded.

"Nixon resigned."

"But he didn't go to jail." Brendan said.

"Nothing in life is perfect," Irma concluded.

*E*ileen sat across the restaurant table from the man with short, light brown hair and hazel eyes, who continued to lecture her intently on reincarnation, the evils of psychiatry, the theories, previous lives and the and the genius of L. Ron Hubbard. A sad look had replaced the initial joy with which she had greeted him.

"I can't talk long," she said. "I *am* a waitress here."

"But there are almost no customers, and nobody even in Berkeley is up for organic food at nine a.m."

"I'm not a scientologist, Larry, and I never will be one," she said firmly.

"That's what I said in the beginning."

"When was that?"

"Oh back in 1971. And here it is 1981 and night has fallen on the counterculture, on political revolution, on all of that. But the church of scientology still goes on."

"Well, I appreciate what you've done for Ron Swurl. Helping him out like that was great. He's been down and out, living on the street, for the longest time."

"How are *you* doing?"

She shrugged, shifting her glance uneasily away from his rather intent gaze. "I have two jobs, this and occasional work in a recording studio. I compose music in my spare time. I had a little performance of one piece at one point."

"When?"

"Three years ago," she paused. "Larry Lawless! You were in Naomi's class, right?"

"Yup. She was my first true love, before that Gilbert creep swept her away. But it worked out. I met Olga, we joined the church and started working for it, spreading the word."

"Don't spread it here please. I could lose my job."

"Actually, I hoped you might speak to Ron for me. I think scientology's perfect for him."

"I don't speak to Ron," a pained, evasive look came into her eyes. "I see him by accident from time to time. He sleeps in a park near here. But I… we…have no communication."

"Oh," her visitor seemed taken aback. "Since you had such an interest in his welfare, I assumed—"

"Don't, don't assume. I just don't want to hear someday that he died on the street."

"You know humanity came here from other planets."

She looked at him a moment. "No, Larry, I didn't know that."

"Here," he withdrew a pamphlet from the little pile of papers he had placed on the table. "Scientology turned my life around, Eileen. No more of this political radicalism nonsense, no more hippie garbage. It explains everything."

"How much does it cost?"

"Oh, I work for the church, and of course I let it take as much of my salary as it needs. I would give them everything."

"Except Olga Anderson."

"Even Olga."

She glanced at him with ill-concealed horror. "Even Olga? That nice young woman I met, whom you married?"

"She'd be the first to agree with me. Eileen, scientology could change your life."

"I don't want to change my life."

He looked skeptical. "I think you do."

"Well, I'd like to make more money."

"It can help with that."

"And I'd like to see my father again."

"Where is he?"

"In Lima, Peru. He's one of those people you just mentioned, you know, that the world has finished with."

"A hippie?" Larry looked surprised.

"No, a radical, actually an old-fashioned communist. I guess night has fallen for them too."

He nodded, the look of disapproval that had come into his eyes at the mention of the word "communist" growing stronger by the second. "Why would you want to see him again—someone who's so wrong about everything?"

"Because he's my father," she toyed with the spoon in her teacup, "and maybe he isn't so wrong about everything."

Her companion guffawed.

"At least not the way things have been in Peru," she hastened to add. "He's been fighting multinational corporations there for decades. They really do appalling things. The way All American Amalgamated exploits tin miners is dreadful."

"Listen to yourself," the scientologist said, raising his fingers to make quote marks, "'exploit,' 'multinationals'—it's all so old."

"And scientology's new?"

"Scientology's right."

"Well, I'm not good at this kind of argument."

"You don't have to be. Come to one of our meetings."

"Maybe," she rose. "I better look like I'm working."

"Take this," he handed her a copy of *Dianetics: The Modern Science of Mental Health*.

"You think I need psychiatric help?"

"No, no definitely not psychiatric. The psychiatrists are out to enslave us all. But read it. Also this was just published," he handed her another book, *Battlefield Earth*.

"Science fiction?" She was surprised.

"More than science fiction. L. Ron Hubbard's a scientific genius, you know."

"Oh."

"Disguised as sci-fi, this book tells you what's really going on, who intends to enslave us and how."

"You mean besides the psychiatrists?"

He nodded vigorously.

"I don't have a lot of spare time for pleasure reading."

"This is not pleasure reading."

"I have less time for unpleasant reading."

"This is essential, vital—it will open your eyes."

"Oh, they're not open already?"

"Definitely not."

"Ta, ta."

"See you later," and he sat, sipping his iced tea, as the uneasy waitress backed away, looking for somewhere to put the two volumes and the pamphlet.

"Scientology—you go in for that crap?" Asked Danny, the cook, wiping the sweat off his forehead with a brown, equally sweaty arm.

"No, yes. I mean you have to have an open mind, don't you?"

"No, I don't. That L. Ron Hubbard's the biggest con artist since the guru Maharaji."

"I remember him."

"The fat kid from India, who took all the premis money. All those crazy rich white people from the suburbs just went ape over him. L. Ron Hubbard's even worse. He's got that snake oil down to a science."

"That's why they call it scientology, I guess."

"You got it. Here, pass me them books."

She did and he promptly dumped them in the trash. "The pamphlet too." That followed the books. "Don't waste your time on that claptrap," the cook went on. "Next thing you know, they'll be into you for your money, and you ain't got enough of that."

"How do you know?"

"If you did, would you be working at the Veggie Garden? I know I wouldn't."

Meanwhile the rather solemn Larry Lawless, unaware that his offerings had been unceremoniously disposed of, paid his tab and stepped outside the restaurant into a cool, foggy, April morning. Lost in thoughts of intergalactic warfare and humanity's struggle to overcome its status as a slave race, he fished in the pockets of his khaki pants for his keys, unlocked his Ford Escort and slid into the driver's seat. As he maneuvered the car out of the parking space, he made a mental note to phone Eileen in a week to check on the progress of her reading assignment. She seemed so lost, stranded in the present with habits and views at least a decade out of date, yes, she was good material for a new recruit. He had been like that himself, he mused, thinking back to his high school graduation, the nervous breakdown that preceded it and his announcement to his mother, prone in a lounger beside their backyard pool in upper middle class Narberth, Pennsylvania, surrounded by blue hydrangeas, red, purple and pink azaleas and yellow forsythia bushes, that he could not go to college, simply could not face it, because he did not fit in, there or anywhere. Sylvia Lawless had sat up straight, the straps of her mauve one-piece bathing suit dangling like two decorative loops beside her upper arms: "But you have to go to college. No one in our family has ever *not* gone to college."

"Wake up, Mom. It's me, Larry. I can't do it."

"But don't you want to leave home and be with friends who are your age—"

"Of course, but I can't."

"And choose a career?"

"No."

"You don't want to go into dentistry anymore?"

"I can't face it."

"What about something else? You could be a photographer."

"I can't even work the Polaroid. And I never, never wanted to be a dentist."

"But your father said you did."

"That was his fantasy and yours. I don't want to train for anything. I don't want to be anything. The thought of a career makes me sick."

"You need psychiatric help, Larry."

"Do you even care who you're talking to?"

"It's because I care that I'm saying—get help."

"I'm not going to Oberlin, Mom."

"Well, thank God we didn't pay all the tuition yet. Martin!" She shouted for her husband, half hidden by bushes across the yard, as he clipped a hedge. He continued clipping. "Martin!" She bellowed, noting with satisfaction that she had a very loud, powerful voice when she wanted.

"You don't need to wake up the neighborhood," her spouse grumbled, ambling toward the sparkling pool and attired, from head to toe, in L.L. Bean splendor.

"Larry doesn't want to go to college."

"What's this?" Martin glanced at his son, his blue eyes blinking in bewilderment behind his somewhat fogged glasses.

"I can't do it."

"Why not? I did it. I went to Bard. If you think Oberlin's going to be bad, you should have been to Bard. I was the only student on the G. I. Bill, the only one who had even heard of the G. I. Bill or the army, for that matter. They were all too busy playing their ukuleles."

"Their what?" His wife raised her sunglasses, pushing back her perfectly auburn tinted mane.

"It's a stringed instrument that has—"

"What's this got to do with Larry?" She snapped, lighting a cigarette.

"And I'm not going into dentistry."

"But Sylvia said you were."

"I did not. Martin, I need a drink. Get me a scotch and soda on the rocks."

"It's only one p.m."

"And my only son is dropping out of college before he begins."

"You have a daughter."

"What's that supposed to mean?"

"He's not your only child."

"He's my only son," she resumed flipping through the glossy pages of *Vogue*.

"Would you mind not talking about me in the third person? I'm right here."

"Who said that?" Sylvia demanded.

Larry rolled his eyes.

"You said a rum and Coke?"

"No, you nincompoop," she snapped her magazine shut, "a scotch and soda."

"No need to get cranky."

"Larry's dropping out of college. If I don't need to be cranky now, when do I need to be cranky?"

"Never," her son said. "It's too unpleasant."

"You're going to Dr. Goldenstock."

"I am not."

"Larry, you need a shrink."

"Dr. Goldenstock? In Ardmore?" Her husband asked. "Isn't he the one that hollers at his patients?"

"No, that's Dr. Finklestein in Bala Cynwyd."

"Goldenstock…Goldenstock…Oh!" Martin exclaimed brightly. "He's the one that falls asleep, told me at a cocktail party that I could not imagine how excruciatingly boring it was to listen to forty-five year olds yammering on all day about the trauma of their toilet training."

"That was Dr. Shapinsky from Bryn Mawr. No. He's going to Goldenstock, who neither sleeps nor hollers. Goldenstock's the best."

"All five of Goldenstock's children are the wildest hippies on the Main Line," their son asserted, "and one daughter, Eloise, crashed their sports-car into a mailbox. I am not going to Dr. Goldenstock."

"Go into the house, Martin," Sylvia enunciated as if she were speaking to a mental defective. "Call Herman Goldenstock and make me a scotch and soda."

Her husband, evidently distracted by the antics of two gray squirrels in a nearby maple, murmured absentmindedly, "call Finklestein, one Manhattan, coming up."

"Oh, God help me!" She exclaimed, throwing herself back upon her lounge chair in despair. "Do I have to do everything myself?"

"You know," Martin said, "none of this would have happened if that Naomi Lichter hadn't gallivanted off with some other boy."

"I got over her in the sixth grade," Larry clarified.

"They why aren't you going to Antioch?"

"Antioch?" Sylvia sat up in shock, as though she had just encountered something alarmingly distasteful.

"Because I never applied to Antioch," Larry answered.

"I don't believe you said that," Sylvia growled, simmering with rage. "You can't even keep straight which college your only son is not going to."

"Since he's not going, what does it matter?" Martin mused again, this time casting a furtive and rather admiring glance at his son. "I wish I'd had the nerve not to go to Bard."

"Then you wouldn't have met me."

"And I wouldn't exist," Larry said. "That would have been much better."

"Sounds like you need Shapinsky."

"What, so he can get another nap and charge us seventy-five dollars for it?" Sylvia snapped. "Call Goldenstock! And get me that scotch and soda!"

"Eloise was high on pot at the time," Larry continued.

"What time?" Martin wanted to know.

"When she crashed the car into the mailbox."

"Not a very good advertisement for Goldenstock's parenting ability—pot and crashing sports cars," his father said mildly.

"It didn't stop her from going to Cornell, I notice," Sylvia replied grouchily, stubbing out her cigarette in an ashtray. "All his kids go to Ivy league schools—Brown, Penn."

"Penn's a second rate school," Martin averred.

"What would you know about it?"

"Goldenstock told me, at the Sheehan's cocktail party. Said he's on some board there at the medical school, can barely keep his eyes open, it's so stultifying."

"Great, now we've got another psychiatrist falling asleep."

"But that was because of these mediocre Penn professors. He said they all get their ideas out of *Reader's Digest*."

"I doubt that. Where's my drink?"

Martin ambled into the house, whence soon emanated a loud crash. Sylvia sat up alertly on her lounge chair. He appeared at the glass sliding doors, waving and calling: "Nothing, nothing, just tipped over the ice bucket. The ice is fine."

"Well thank goodness for that," Sylvia rolled her eyes. "We wouldn't want anything to happen to the ice. His only son is cracking up, and he's worried about ice cubes."

"I can hear you," that young man said, seated now at a table beneath its large, two-toned umbrella.

"You never remember anything I say anyway."

"You have a point."

Her husband reappeared, carrying a glass in one hand and a slip of paper in the other. He handed the glass to his spouse.

"Where's the soda?" She asked after sipping it.

"I thought you said scotch on the rocks."

Sylvia tilted the glass, decanting half the scotch into a flowerbed. "Go back and put in some soda."

Martin retreated like a knight of old, chastised by his fair lady. A moment later, yet another thunderous crash could be heard in the large, many-windowed house. He poked his head out the door.

"I know," Sylvia bellowed. "The ice."

He nodded.

"And it's all right."

He nodded again.

"How would the ice not be all right?" Larry asked.

"It might get a crack and need a shrink," Sylvia answered.

"I am not going to Dr. Goldenstock."

Her husband made his entrance, handed the beverage to his wife and hung there, awaiting her response as she sipped. She nodded approvingly, and he visibly relaxed.

"If you go to Dr. Goldenstock—" She spoke while sipping.

Martin proffered the slip of paper. "I made an appointment for Monday at four thirty."

"I'm not going."

"Then you can skip dinner at aunt Harriet's tomorrow night."

"I'll consider it," Larry quickly rejoined. "But just for one visit."

"That's what they all say," Sylvia remarked.

"Then twenty years and a hundred thousand dollars later, someone's father is still paying the psychiatrist's bills," Martin said morosely.

"If you don't want to pay, I don't have to go."

"And do what?" His mother demanded. "Loaf around the rest of the spring and summer, then not go to Oberlin in the fall? You're going to be awfully bored when your friends all leave for college."

"I don't have any friends."

"What about Barry?"

"I can't wait till he leaves."

"Neither can I," Martin spoke rather contemplatively. "For some reason that kid always gets on my nerves."

"He's a neurotic," thus Larry.

"Look who's talking," thus Sylvia

"And he comes by almost every day. Why do you suppose he does that?" Martin asked. "Nobody here gives him any encouragement."

"He likes Una."

"Una went to college a year ago."

"He likes the memory of her," Larry explained. "He said I remind him of her."

"Uh-oh. Next thing you know, he'll be after you."

"No, he'll be after Una. He's going to Bennington."

"But she's transferring out of there."

"He doesn't know that."

"He'll be very disappointed when he finds out."

"No, he'll probably transfer too."

"To Sarah Lawrence, like her?"

Larry nodded.

"You know, Martin," Sylvia lit another cigarette, "I believe that was the longest, most sustained and focused conversation I've heard from you in two decades."

"Something about that kid Barry makes me think."

"What about?"

"How to get away, elsewhere, where he's not."

"Well, you don't need to worry today," Larry said. "He left this morning."

"Thank goodness. You know I never did care for Una's friends either," Martin retrieved the clippers from over by the diving board where he had left them.

"I believe the feeling was reciprocated," Sylvia remarked.

"Snotty, artsy fartsy types."

"Sounds like this whole family," Larry said. "You'll never get me to go to Oberlin."

"Don't be too sure," Sylvia smiled. "I got you to go to Goldenstock."

"I haven't gone yet."

A few days later, Larry parked his father's BMW under the porte-cochere of Dr. Goldenstock's enormous Tudor style house. The psychiatrist appeared on the porch, waving at him.

"Park in the back," he called, "otherwise one of my kids is liable to crash into you. My son was in an accident yesterday. Hit a public bus."

"Blotto, no doubt," Larry muttered to himself, then steered the car into the back, parking it between a Buick and a Ford station-wagon, behind a badly smashed Volvo.

"Don't park behind the Volvo," the doctor called again, this time from the back porch. "My wife is taking it out in a little while. It has a dent."

"Looks totaled to me," Larry muttered again and moved the BMW. Unfortunately he overshot the edge of the parking area, and the BMW rolled down a little hill, coming to rest in a flower garden.

Dr. Goldenstock emerged from the porch, portly, white-haired, in a dark suit, smoking a cigar and looking remarkably like Sigmund Freud. "The Volvo got scratched. My daughter was driving it over spring break. A professor from Temple rear-ended her. The moron couldn't see straight, and you can bet he can't teach either. You seem to have gotten stuck in the daffodils. Jeanie won't like that."

Larry, who had stepped out of the BMW, surveyed his vehicle's predicament. "I could back it up, but I'd never get it up that slope again."

"Hmm," puff, puff on the cigar. "No, I don't' suppose you could. You're the one with the career problem."

"I don't want a career."

"Well, I won't charge you for this, but take my advice, don't drive a cab."

"I won't."

"Or a bus."

"That either."

"If you drove a bus, my son might hit you."

"It's a possibility."

"Or worse, you might ride the bus into my backyard, ruining this entire flower bed and the next one. I'd never hear the end of it from Jeanie."

"Should we call a tow truck?"

"Now there's an idea," puff, puff on the cigar. "The last time this happened, we didn't call a tow truck."

"This happened before?"

"Hugh Sheehan—you know the Sheehans—was turning around here one night, when my daughter was backing the Volvo out. She accidentally rammed him and bloop!"

"Bloop?"

"Bloop. Over the hill and into the flowerbed. It's a miracle those things grow."

"But you didn't call a tow truck."

"It never occurred to us."

"Oh."

"Hugh drove his Mercedes across the yard, like so," Dr. Goldenstock pointed, "then around between the side of the house and the hedge, then across the front yard, then back into the driveway." Puff, puff, "worked like a charm. To think those idiots at Penn didn't give him tenure—a man who can drive like that! Well, he's better off at Haverford."

"I think we should call a tow truck."

"I'm not calling any tow truck. Bunch of thieves. Here, give me those keys." With that, Dr. Goldenstock lowered himself into the driver's seat, moved it back, adjusted the mirrors, and with the cigar clenched between his teeth, started the engine. He removed the cigar and rolled down the window. "Now the trick is not to go over any more daffodils. You just crushed a few—maybe Jeanie won't notice." With that, the BMW charged over the rest of the flowerbed. "Oops," said the doctor. "I thought I was in reverse. Well, the die is cast. Here goes." Whereupon the BMW labored out of the daffodils, across the lawn and disappeared around the side of the house. A moment later Dr. Goldenstock returned on foot, disappointed and incongruous on the lawn in his suit, and waving at Larry. "It didn't work," he called.

"Uh-oh," Larry muttered.

"I got stuck on the side of the house. I'm going in to make a call."

"A tow truck?"

"No. Hugh Sheehan."

The Haverford professor was tall, lanky, red-haired, freckled and smoked a pipe, emitting such quantities of smoke that, when combined with the psychiatrist's cigar, it nearly asphyxiated the would-be patient. The trio conferred in serious tones over the BMW, stuck in a ditch, Larry coughing furiously.

"You and Lawless here could push," the professor suggested, "and I'll guide her out of the hole, thataway."

"But the hedge," puff, puff.

"I think we need a tow truck."

"The hedge will have to go," the professor said. "It's the price you pay."

"For what?" Puff, puff.

"Incompetent driving."

"At least I didn't hit the house."

"You may yet."

"Or a bus, like my son."

"Or my car, like your daughter."

"By the way, where did you park?"

"Under the porte-cochere," Professor Sheehan said. "After my last experience in your back yard, you can be damn sure I wasn't parking there. So I'm in front."

"That was a bad idea," Dr. Goldenstock averred, as, at that very moment, came a tremendous crash from the vicinity of the porte-cochere.

"My Saab!" Professor Sheehan cried.

"My Mercedes!" Dr. Goldenstock groaned.

"I think we should call a tow truck."

Dr. Goldenstock's daughter Eloise appeared, looked at the trapped BMW and asked: "Who was the idiot who parked under the porte-cochere?"

"I am the idiot who parked there," Hugh Sheehan spoke with great dignity, "and I am obviously a complete and utter imbecile for thinking I could park anywhere on this property without having my car rammed and smashed."

"You can't see what's under it when you come up the driveway," Eloise explained.

"Under what?"

"The porte-cochere. All that wisteria impedes the view."

"Jeanie won't let me cut the wisteria," puff, puff on the cigar.

"But you have no such excuse for this BMW in the ditch," she continued. "Whatever retard did this, could obviously see exactly where he was going."

"That retard would be your father," Hugh said.

"Well, I can't be held responsible for the actions of morons," she said and walked away. Hugh followed her.

"Hello Hugh?" Puff, puff.

"Gotta check on the damage to my car."

"Imbeciles," Eloise breathed.

"I think we should call a tow truck," Larry repeated.

"My, my, tenacious," puff, puff, "aren't we?"

"Well, this doesn't seem to be going too well."

"You have a point," and Dr. Goldenstock ambled off after Professor Sheehan. Larry followed. The foursome gathered around the wreckage: the Saab's rear had buckled, as had the hood of the Mercedes.

"Exactly how fast were you going?" The professor asked.

"That's irrelevant," Eloise dismissed his question with a haughty gesture.

"And where were you looking?"

"In the rearview mirror, I believe."

"Why?"

"Why? Because my mascara ran, that's why."

"I think my hour's up," Larry said. "I guess that's seventy five dollars?"

"It's on the house," Dr. Goldenstock genially enlightened him. "However, when you come back, if you drive into my flowerbeds again, I may have to charge you. Just look at the disastrous chain of events your inept driving has set in motion."

"I'd say we have more than one inept driver in this group," puff, puff on the pipe.

"To say nothing of someone who doesn't have the vaguest idea where he's supposed to park," Eloise added.

"Evidently nowhere near a vehicle with a Goldenstock behind the wheel."

"Let's keep this civil," Dr. Goldenstock suggested. "Eloise, you're grounded."

"You can't ground me. I'm going back to Cornell tomorrow."

"Oh, well, you can't take a car."

"I should say not," Hugh said. "I wouldn't even let her ride a bus."

"That's my son who's got problems with buses."

"I don't think I want to know about that," Hugh puffed on his pipe.

An hour later a tow truck removed the Lawless' BMW from the ditch on the side of the house.

"Excuse me, sir," Dr. Goldenstock addressed the tower, "you left tread-marks on my front lawn."

"You don't want marks on your lawn, don't drive your car in the hedge. Marks, now I've heard everything." But evidently he hadn't, for Dr. Goldenstock wanted his company to pay for new turf. "Mister—" the tower began.

"Doctor, actually. Dr. Goldenstock."

"Dr. Goldenstock, I been on your property twenty minutes. I seen three wrecked cars and a BMW in a ditch. You're lucky I'm not charging you for the marks. And if you want me to tow that Mercedes and the Saab, forget it. The bumpers are locked."

"How could the bumpers be locked?" Hugh demanded. "I never heard of such a thing."

"Neither did I. But it sure looks like it."

"How could it happen?"

"Ask whoever was driving the Mercedes."

"How am I supposed to know?" Eloise snapped, when summoned from the powder room, where she had been perfecting her mascara. "That Saab never should have been there."

"Well, this has certainly been an experience," Larry said, opening the door of the successfully towed BMW, now safely parked at the end of the driveway. "Let's hope my next appointment is less eventful."

"Could you bicycle over?" Dr. Goldenstock asked hopefully and then, when Larry frowned: "I'd rather you didn't' drive. Maybe my son Isaac could pick you up."

"I'd turn that offer down, if I were you," Hugh Sheehan remarked.

"I'll take a taxi," Larry said. "Ta, ta."

"Ta, ta, till Thursday."

"How did it go?" Sylvia demanded, sitting up on her lounger by the pool. "You know, it looks like rain."

"A two-car pile-up in the driveway and the BMW landed in a ditch. All very therapeutic."

"My goodness. I didn't realize your problems could cause such drama."

"We didn't discuss my 'problems,'" and Larry made quote marks with his fingers.

"Then what am I paying for?"

"Nothing, this session, or I should say experience, was gratis."

"Oh, well, I thoroughly approve of that. As long as it's gratis, go every day."

"And I don't have problems. What I don't have is ambition or any desire to have a career. I don't fit into the world, and I don't want to."

"Tell Dr. Goldenstock, not me."

"If I can extricate him from his various automotive difficulties, I will."

"Sometimes you really are odd," Sylvia said, lighting a cigarette. "Martin!" she hollered. Martin, still in a gray Brooks Brothers suit from work, ambled out toward the pool, a martini in one hand, clippers in the other.

"What are you going to do," she demanded, "trim the martini?"

"I'm ignoring that remark. You called?"

"Larry's first session with Dr. Goldenstock was on the house."

"Which house?"

"His, you idiot. Whose house would it be on besides his?"

"Ours."

"Nope," she exhaled a long stream of smoke, "completely free."

"Well, well, this is good news. Let's hope it continues this way."

"It won't, unless, maybe, I drive over his daffodils again."

"How peculiar," Sylvia said.

"Then by all means drive over the daffodils."

"I can't. He forbade me to bring the BMW. I have to take a taxi over next time." Sylvia sat up sharply. "What, precisely, does all this have to do with getting you to go to Oberlin in the fall?"

"I'm never going to Oberlin. I'd rather join a cult."

"Well, I have to change," Martin said. "I'm not finished with that hedge yet."

"Do the bushes by the pond while you're at it."

"Maybe scientology."

"Isn't that science and astrology mixed together?" Martin asked absentmindedly, wandering back toward the house, as he sipped his martini.

"Sounds good to me," Larry said.

"Hogwash," Sylvia said. "Scientology's hogwash."

On Thursday Larry took a taxi from Narberth to Ardmore. Dr. Goldenstock greeted him on the immense front porch. "Well, this is certainly civilized compared to the last time," the psychiatrist beamed, clapping his hands together once and rubbing them. He led Larry into his office, a high-ceilinged, dark, mahogany paneled affair with thick red Persian carpets, pre-Colombian art in every cranny and behind glass cases, somber furniture, all in dark browns and ochres, and overall imparting the impression to Larry that he had entered a mausoleum. One wall contained the complete works of Sigmund Freud in black bookcases with glass covers. Larry felt quite distinctly that he had nothing weighty enough to say, or anything to say that might be deserving of his august and rather overwhelming surroundings. He cleared his throat several times and said nothing.

"Your mother, Lydia,"

"Sylvia," Larry corrected.

"Sylvia tells me you don't want to go to college next fall."

"Ever."

Dr. Goldenstock's bushy eyebrows went up.

"I want to join a cult, like scientology."

"Why?"

"Because I can't think of anything else to do."

"So you don't really want to join a cult."

"I don't?"

"No. Besides L. Ron Hubbard's a quack. He thinks psychiatrists are evil. Next thing you know they'll be putting him on the board at Penn. Now there's a school you don't want to go to."

"But one of your children goes there."

"Really? Oh yes, you're right."

"I think dianetics might be for me. I was reading up on it in the bookstore yesterday."

"Hmm."

"My mother disapproves, calls it hogwash."

"That doubtless increases its appeal."

"Well…yes."

"Did it ever occur to you she might be right?"

"No. That thought never crossed my mind. Frankly, it's impossible."

"I felt the same way about my mother. But in my case, unlike yours, I was right."

"Maybe I should be a psychiatrist."

"There you go."

Later, after the taxi had pulled up to the Goldenstock's palatial residence, and the young patient was safely ensconced inside, sure to make his escape, he called out to the doctor on the porch. "I really don't think I need to come back."

Dr. Goldenstock came down the stairs and leaned into the open cab window. "You're going to do it, aren't you?"

"What?"

"Join that scientology club."

"Cult."

"Cult."

"Yes, how did you know?"

"I had a hunch. Just like I had a hunch one of my children would take up something idiotic called macrame. Tell your mother, we parents are helpless."

"Hopeless is more like it."

"That too."

Thus had ended Larry's encounter with psychotherapy on the threshold of his induction to the mysteries of the scientological faith. As he left Eileen in Berkeley, and drove his Ford south toward Menlo Park, he thought how much she reminded him of himself, eleven years earlier. "Stalled," he said out loud. "She's stalled, lost and doesn't know what to do." And though there was more than a trace of smugness in this analysis, a self-satisfaction rooted in his own ever-present belief that he had found all the answers, there also lurked a genuine wish to be helpful, the glimmer of a hope that he could do some good for this unaccountably bereft human being. Already he could envision her life, her emotional quandary transformed by exposure to the transcendent truths revealed by L. Ron Hubbard, who had, he thought, rescued him from the wreckage of his aimless, desultory, affluent upbringing in Narberth. Olga had insisted he get career training, so he had received his BA in accounting from a state school in California. She had a degree in business management. Together they donated a hefty sum each month to the church of scientology. So did their three housemates, and all five did so with great satisfaction and gratitude for the genius of their leader.

Since it was a Saturday, he descried his wife's slight form, bent over her bank of colorful petunias, busy weeding, as he parked the car in the driveway. He paused to contemplate the scene with a contentment unmarred by the slightest recognition that it very much resembled what he had grown up with and fled with such abandon, so long ago. At the sound of the Ford, she looked up, pushed back a strand of light blond hair and waved a trowel at him. "Poor Eileen Meer," she said after he had described his visit to the Veggie Garden.

"She's one of those left-over sixties hippies," he explained, "except that it's 1981, and she can't make sense of the world."

"Was she always this beautiful?"

"More so. Now she looks…older."

"I wonder why she didn't get married, like us."

"She's adrift. She used a phrase, I had too, but she made it hers. She asked—regarding her father, who, by the way, is still a communist,"

"Good grief."

"She asked if 'night had fallen' for him. I said yes. What I didn't want to add, though, was that without scientology, night has fallen for her."

"As surely as it will fall this evening."

They gazed at each other, his hazel eyes, her blue ones, in perfect agreement about what lit their lives and without even a palpitation of the faintest doubt about it, doubts that might leave room for the shadows, uncertainties born of shadows, and that most special knowledge born of uncertainty that they so abhorred. "We have the answers," he said quietly, "she doesn't. She'll come to see that."

"It's been three years," Naomi said into the phone. "You think Larry would realize that he's not going to recruit you, because you're not scientology material."

"I don't even work at the Veggie Garden anymore," Eileen replied, "and I just lost my apartment, because they're jacking up the rent, and he thinks I have money to donate to Scientology? It's just weird."

"Come visit me in New York over the winter holidays. Snow will be here and you can see my new one-bedroom apartment on the Upper West Side."

"Is it anything like that dump on Essex Street?"

"Much better," her friend chuckled. "Come visit."

"I can't really," Eileen evasively let the remark hang.

"What'll you do?"

"Well, I've got the sedan. I may head to Santa Fe, camp out or live out of the car for a while."

"Live out of the car?!"

"Not everyone's a reporter at *The Daily News*."

After vigorous, failed efforts to persuade her friend to move in with an acquaintance in Oakland or relocate to New York, Naomi hung up the phone. Then she dialed her son's number, as she did every night.

"We're taking a week off and driving to Wichita to see Harry," he announced, then deflected his mother's complaints about truancy with the words, "I'm almost sixteen now and almost finished high school. I can miss a week." Then his father picked up the phone, and she complained to him, to no avail. "We're leaving tomorrow morning, early. I like to rise early on Saturdays."

"Is Snow still going off into the woods by himself for days at a time?" She asked, worried.

"He's fine. He takes his tent and checks on all his traps. He fishes, hunts and sometimes I go with him. It's all familiar territory."

"I don't like it."

"He's fine," the father repeated. "Sometimes he brings food. Other times—well, he knows exactly what plants, roots and berries he can eat. Sometimes he even makes a soup from boiled bark. I've had it. It's pretty good. He's the most independent kid I've ever known. It's phenomenal."

"But you said he encountered a bear."

"Yeah, well that's not half as dangerous as that Wall Street shark you were dating."

"I wasn't, wouldn't dream of, dating him. He was an acquaintance, a friend of Sonya's."

"That Sonya's somewhere to the right of the John Birch Society."

"Her family was dispossessed by the Soviets."

"I sympathize, but then…I don't. She's too reactionary, even for me."

"You'd have to go to the Soviet Union to understand how that could happen to a person."

"Excuses, excuses. I just hope you don't let Shane know you're hanging around with stockbrokers."

"I am not."

"Because he'll slit your throat," Jack paused to light a cigarette. "They're coming out here, in a month. Snow's crazy about them both."

"I don't know if I like how you're raising my boy."

"Now you disapprove of Betsy and Shane?"

"Not at all, but why's Snow crazy about them?"

"He thinks this capitalist system stinks."

"Uh-oh."

"Yup. Last time we visited the windy city, he spent days with Shane, just soaking up the stuff like a sponge, till he turned completely red."

"He better go to college."

"Fat chance," the father exhaled cigarette smoke loudly. "Shane convinced him it was a waste of time. That's why I'm taking him to Wichita. Let Harry talk some sense into him. Harry considers himself a walking advertisement for a college education—or rather a byword, such as 'look what happened to my lousy life, cause all I ever did was graduate high school,' alternating with the most inane car dealer boosterism. It's tons of fun to be around."

"You think that'll knock some sense into Snow?"

"If that doesn't, nothing will. I'm telling you, Harry's spiel is well nigh intolerable, and I intend to expose Snow to it for a full seven days."

"Maybe Snow should move to New York with me."

"He hates New York, hates civilization, hates capitalism—"

"Oh brother."

"You get the picture."

"He'll never fit in anywhere."

"That would appear to be his intention."

She paused, beaten down by the conviction that had she remained in Laramie, she would have softened this man's influence on her son, who would, then, have turned out differently.

"It's not your fault or mine," he went on, as if aware of her thoughts. "He's just made this way. He probably gets it from his biological father, who, you tell me, disappeared on the road years ago. These things are often genetic, like Tommy and my father, which, by the way, is another tack I intend to take. Tommy's coming to stay with us in mid-January—"

"Oh, no, no, no," she began.

"Wait, listen. I intend to use this visit as another opportunity to pound home the lesson that higher education and a stable income are the way to go."

"It could backfire, like your stay at Shane's."

"Nah. Tommy's condition is pretty damn frightening at this point. It's a miracle he's still alive." Jack paused to recollect the shambling wreck, who had shown up the previous spring at his laboratory at the university. At that time, although utterly identical in appearance to his father, Tommy at least still had his mind intact. The chemistry professor had quickly donned his leather jacket, leading his brother out of the building to his Oldsmobile in a campus parking lot. "Why the fuck do you live this way?" Jack had shouted, the minute the car was on the highway that snaked through high, dark timber toward the cabin.

"Don't get upset, Jack."

"You're gonna die if you keep this up—you know that? I told you six months ago, I could get you a job as security at the university—"

His younger brother guffawed, his long, filthy blond hair with a thistle in it, glinting gold in the sun.

"Or you could go live with Ethan, up in Sioux Falls. He's willing to take you in."

"I don't want charity."

"You *need* charity. But if you really think you don't, take the security job."

"Me—security? I'm what they got security against."

"You haven't been stealing again?"

"A man's gotta live, Jack."

"Shit!" Jack hollered, pounding the steering wheel.

"It's okay, Jack. I don't mind the time in the joint. Not in the winter. It's warm and the food's damn good."

At the cabin, the destitute man showered and donned some of his brother's clothes. He downed two cans of Campbell's chicken noodle soup and the better part of a loaf of bread with butter.

"Now I'm taking you to that barber in Tower Oaks Bend. After that you stay with me and Snow. But if you start in with the glories of the hobo life, I'm kicking you out. That boy doesn't need to hear your nonsense."

"The kid's made for life on the road, Jack."

"He better not be. And you fucking better not encourage him."

"Watch your language."

"Watch your lies."

"They ain't lies."

"Aren't! And yes they are. Life as a bum isn't worth shit. I'd rather be dead. So if you want to follow in Dad's footsteps, be my guest, but you're not dragging my son down along with you."

"It's in his bones, Jack. He's made that way."

"I don't want to hear it," the father hollered, his fist raised.

"Okay, okay. Let's go to the barber."

"I can't cut this," the barber said. "It's too matted."

"Then shave it off," Jack said savagely.

"He'll look like a Marine."

"He would've been better off a Marine."

"Lot's of vets are homeless," Tommy put in.

"What you want to be homeless for?" The barber kindly asked. "Live with your brother Jack here and that kid Snow. Though whoever heard of naming a boy Snow, I confess, I can't imagine."

"She was a hippie at the time."

"So what's your name?"

"Tommy."

"Tommy Diamond. I could tell right off you were Jack's brother. You look just like him, only Jack's…neater."

"There's a euphemism for ya," the younger brother chuckled.

"He does look like a Marine," Jack surveyed his brother's buzz cut.

"Now what'll keep me warm in winter?" Tommy wailed.

"The indoors," Jack said. "Try that."

Over dinner that evening, the boy, taller than his mother or father, lean and eagle-eyed, sporting a bruised cheekbone, explained that he had been in a fight.

"Keep that up," Jack munched his broccoli, "and I'll ship you off to your mother. You know what she'll do—get money from her parents and put you in private school."

"He swung at me first," the boy, fifteen and looking very angry now, cut his roast chicken savagely. It did not comply, so he reached over, yanked off a drumstick and chewed on that.

"Yeah?" Jack asked. "Why'd he swing at you?"

"I said something."

"What?"

"I can't repeat it," the boy pointed the drumstick at his father. "The guy's a jerk, a first-class asshole. He gets on my nerves."

"You suspended?" Munch, munch on the broccoli.

"No, detention on Wednesday."

"That's your seventh detention in five months."

"Can I help it if the school is populated with dingbats who think their monosyllabic insults are pearls of wisdom?"

"What'd he say to you?"

"Some garbage about my name. What else? Boy, Mom really saddled me with a turkey. Snow. Who names their son Snow?"

"Shut up. You mom loves you."

"Yeah, from New York."

"Maybe it's better that way," the visitor put in. "If she was here, how do you think she'd feel about all these fights and detentions?"

The other two stopped chewing and stared at him with open mouths.

"Mr. Model Citizen," Snow said.

"The king, absolute *king* of high school detentions," Jack guffawed.

Their guest seemed vaguely pleased and embarrassed by this appellation. "I had my share," he modestly averred.

"Yeah, like twice a week," his brother went on, "every week starting in ninth grade. It's a miracle they didn't kick you out."

"I was a straight A student," Tommy told Snow.

"Piffle," Jack snorted.

"In the first semester of ninth grade," the visitor clarified. "After that it was downhill. I got in all kinds of trouble, Snow, the kind of garbage you want to avoid—drinking, drugs, fighting. It was a disaster. And now look at me—nearly destroyed by living all these years on the street. I shoulda gone to college."

The boy, head down, as if in contemplation of an undeniable truth, did not detect Tommy's wink at Jack. Then he looked up. "Yeah? What college should you have gone to, Tommy?"

"UCSD. The students have it so good there. It's like paradise. They live like kings, in sumptuous dorms, and they study at the beach, then they graduate and get jobs running corporations in gleaming skyscrapers with carpets so soft you could sleep on them," he paused, his eyes misted over at this fantasy, then resumed: "UCSD, San Diego. Heaven on earth. I shoulda gone to college there. I could have become a resident and then it would have been dirt cheap. But I was hard-headed, which is another word for stupid."

The boy glanced at his father. "Did you pay him to say that?"

"You could do worse than UC San Diego," munch, munch on the broccoli.

"I hate the beach."

"But those gleaming corporations," thus Tommy.

"Capitalist thieves, who deserve to have their throats cut in their sleep like Shane said."

"Boy, was that trip to Chicago a mistake," more munching on the broccoli.

"Think about life in a place that never gets cold," his uncle went on.

"My name's *Snow!*" The boy cried. "I don't belong in the tropics. I belong in Canada."

"University of Toronto's top notch," more munching, "But you might not have the grades. However, I have a buddy—"

"I'm not interested in cities. Cities are full of people. People make me sick. I'm talking about the Canadian wilderness."

The two men looked at each other.

"Now see here," the visitor cleared his throat, putting down his forkful of chicken. "I lived in the wilderness, on my own, with no help from anybody, and let me tell you, it's no picnic,"

"If I wanted a picnic, I'd go to UCSC."

"You better wise up, boy. It is damn cold in the Montana forest in winter. I got first-hand experience. And there are so many bugs in spring, they could eat you alive, just make your life a holy hell. Now my brother here has tried to reason with you and that's fine, but I'm telling you, if you just take off and hit the road, when you got a mother who's a reporter in New York City and a father who's a professor at the University of Wyoming, then you are one thing."

"What?"

"A first-class idiot."

The boy rose. "I don't have to take this."

"Oh yes you do," his uncle roared.

Jack stood up, separating them. "Let's be reasonable. Tommy knows what it's like to live with no visible means of support. Since you, Snow, obviously consider that an attractive career option, then I suggest you listen to him. He's going to be with us for a while—"

"Oh, brother," Snow muttered.

"So you should listen to what he has to say. At least *listen*," his father emphasized.

"Don't be a knucklehead," Tommy said.

"He sounds like my counselor."

"Now there's a good job," Tommy exclaimed.

The boy rolled his eyes. "Talk about making suicide look appealing!"

That Friday after school, the wandering uncle found his nephew stuffing a backpack.

"Where ya going?"

"Into the woods for a few days. I need to think."

"Got a tent?"

"Yep. And a sleeping bag and some food."

"Bugs are fierce this time of year."

"I've done it before."

"Glad to see that shiner's about gone and that you didn't get any new ones."

"Yeah well, I've been thinking about what you and Dad say. I decided to cut back on the detentions."

"Good move. Oh," the man watched Snow grab his fishing rod. "You didn't tell me you're going fishing. I love fishing."

"Me too—alone. See ya," and the boy tromped out of the cabin, around the back and along a path through the pines that, narrow to begin with, soon became nearly nonexistent. There were no sounds, except for the occasional birds chirping, and the sun, high and clear, promised good weather for the weekend. He glided silently through the forest. After two hours, his path began to slope downhill, not much, certainly not enough to affect a hiker's legs and then, after another hour, he came upon the river, gurgling musically, with lily pads bobbing by the shore. He tramped through the reeds, until he found his small canoe, overturned as he had left it, tied to a log. He flipped it and stored his fishing gear inside, then walked along the water's edge until he found a little way through to a clearing, with a fire pit he had made long ago, and he pitched his tent. He started a fire, heated a can of beans and Chef Boyardee ravioli and, with the fiery sun low over the river, shooting out tongues of orange flame that rippled over the depthless water, he drew out his copy of *War and Peace* and read by the dying light. His mother had raved about this book and, as he read about Prince Andre lying wounded on the battlefield, he briefly regretted that there was no war at that time for him to fight in, which led to thoughts about his uncle Ethan and his tales of hideous carnage in the steaming jungles of Vietnam, so different from Tolstoy's account. Darkness came on fast. As the shadows lengthened out toward the river and the mauve sky sank into banks of brown clouds, then dusk became the black of night, he decided not to stay up reading but to sleep. He lay down and was out instantly in a damp, dreamless and salving oblivion.

He rose just after dawn, ate a canned spaghetti breakfast, then tromped through thin mist to his slightly battered canoe. Soon he had drifted out midstream, the dark water purling past his boat, buzzed by the occasional, iridescent dragonfly, a fringe of cattails swaying along shore, their tops unready for eating, while he fished, gazed now and then at the indefinite, silvery haze of sky and guzzled a warm soda. He got lucky that day, catching two trout and assorted other species, most of which he threw back. But he cleaned, filleted, cooked and ate the trout for lunch, then passed the late, sun-filled afternoon checking his traps in the forest. They were empty. But something, he noted at one of them, had eaten his bait without getting caught. So he squatted down and searched for tracks. "Wily coyote," he said aloud after a few minutes. "I don't want to catch you anyway."

Sunday he fished again, then packed up his camp and tramped back home. As he rounded the cabin, he saw his father, standing out front in his lumberjack shirt and jeans, waiting for him. "Your mother called. She's frantic, says if I let you wander off in the woods again, she'll go to a court for custody—then it's Manhattan for you, buddy boy."

"She's a party pooper."

"She has a point."

"You never disapproved before."

"You always got your homework done first."

"I don't have much, just a little trigonometry, which, you know, I'm good at."

"Well you better cancel your solo camping expeditions for the next couple of months or there could be real trouble. What did you catch?"

"A couple of trout."

The man rubbed his chin. "Not bad. Maybe the three of us should go down to the river next weekend."

"Tommy has to promise to stay off the sauce," the teenager said rather sharply. "I don't want some drunk scaring off all the animals and fish and probably flipping the canoe in the water."

At that, the deep seriousness of an old, painful recollection flickered like a living wound in the blue of his father's eyes. The older man averted his glance, and gazed off into the silence and shade of the forest, thinking of that other fatal day of woodland silence, of remoteness and inaccessibility to any human help. "No. There won't be any booze. Not anywhere near the river."

Overall, the uncle's visit helped sway the boy in the right direction, Jack thought, though he retained his worrisome, asocial aimlessness. Since he had never remarried and had few friends outside his chemistry department, over the years the boy had come to mean much, very much to him. He regarded him completely as his own child and fretted that his own sarcastic aloofness and lack of interest in other people had, as his ex-wife also secretly believed, pushed Snow onto his solitary path. If only this teenager had some friends and an academic interest that he might dream of pursuing in college. But he had neither and did not seem to miss them. In moments of paternal fear, as he thought of his own father, his wayward brother and what Naomi had told him of Ron Swurl, an abyss opened before him, in which he saw the boy on the road, his thumb out, his few possessions loose in his backpack and it was a road along which stark portents rose one after another that this was his irrevocable fate. He did not tell his erstwhile spouse. He had raised Snow. If the boy's destiny was drifting destitution, then he believed he was to blame.

There were many other moments, however, when he stood in utter solidarity with his son's aversion to the social world, thinking that human society was largely "made up of assholes," as Ethan had put it and that he wanted nothing other than his paying job, his interest in chemistry and his cabin in the middle of nowhere. He could not imagine glad-handing all day, like his brother the car salesman, "smiling at idiots and kissing the asses of a bunch of sons of bitches," as Ethan, yet again, had described it, Ethan, who, of course, had to do some of that, being a contractor in a town, not a hermit like Jack, but not as much as the oldest, whose boundless geniality and depths of forgiveness of others' failings dumbfounded his brothers. Sometimes it even dumbfounded Harry himself, who would then lament how his lack of college had constricted his prospects, but his bitterness never went much further. Yes, Harry was the one the boy should spend time with. Maybe, the father thought, a sabbatical in Wichita, the fall of the boy's senior year; he could work on publishing his papers and Snow could complete a semester of high school in Kansas.

"That's a recipe for disaster," Tommy averred.

"Why not, when he sees Harry, what a great guy he is—"

"And how that great guy has to grovel all day long for his dinner? Yeah, he'll be real impressed with that."

"It might teach him a good lesson, about going to college, so you don't have to grovel so much. And on the other hand, Harry's open, happy, forthright, and optimistic. He's done well, and he doesn't have a side to him. He's living proof that you can have a position in the world and thrive. So either way he looks at it, the kid gets a good lesson."

"Harry runs a car dealership, for Christ sake."

"Since when are you a snob?"

The homeless man snorted in derision. "You couldn't pay me to set foot in a dealership, no less run one. And I'll bet you don't have to go very far deep down to see that you feel the same way."

"It's not my cup of tea," his brother mildly commented.

"A cup of tea that would make you throw up."

"Perhaps."

"The kid likes rocks," Tommy said.

"What?"

"You heard me."

"What good is that?"

"Ever hear of geology? Ever hear that your university, where he could go for free since you teach there, has a great geology department?"

"How'd you know that?"

The youngest brother tapped an ear. "I listen, pay attention. I retain a few things. Not a lot. Not as much as you, maybe, but enough. Couldn't he," Tommy went on, wheedlingly, "couldn't he take a college level intro course in geology in the fall of his senior year?"

The father was startled. "That is a *very* good idea."

"I am available for thank-yous, IOUs, or any form, preferably alcoholic, that your gratitude might take."

"It's an even better idea that going to Wichita that fall."

"Way better, 'cause unlike Wichita, it might actually work."

Jack chose an abbreviated trip to Kansas and sounded the boy out about a university class.

"I'm not that good a student."

"But I could pull strings. There's an introduction to geology course that you could take fall senior year. Local high school students have enrolled in courses in the university before."

"Yeah, but they usually have things like straight As, 800s on their SATs, great teacher recommendations and no history of serial detentions. Geeze, I can't even think of a teacher that likes me enough to recommend me for the school play, no less a university course."

"The school play?"

"*Guys and Dolls*. I wanted to be one of the guys."

Jack was astounded.

"But only star students with backing from a teacher got to try out."

The question of the university geology course was temporarily abandoned. But it resurfaced on the ride to Wichita, on the flat, desolate, wintry whites and browns of the great plains; the boy, who had been gazing out the window of the Oldsmobile, turned despairingly to his father, his expression somehow mirroring the cold emptiness of the season, "give it up, Dad."

"What? We weren't talking."

"Geology."

"Whoa, Snow. That's a conversation we let lapse six months ago."

"Well," the young man said stubbornly, his face suddenly hard and set, "this is the conclusion. It won't work. I'm not university material, and I don't want to be."

After an apprehensive pause, the father plowed on grimly: "Harry never went to college. Wait till you see him, then tell me what you think about striking out on your own after high school." The car suddenly shot forward on the smooth, empty highway.

"Slow down, Dad."

"It's the mid-1980s," Jack growled. "Everybody goes to college. I could see if it was the late sixties or early seventies, when everybody was quote turning on, tuning in and dropping out, unquote, but we live in the age of the yuppie, Snow, a barren, cutthroat age. You will be at such a disadvantage—"

"Shh," the boy said. "I'm looking at the scenery."

"There is no scenery. There's just flat nothing, not a soul on this plain as far as the eye can see. Is that what you want—nobody, nothing?" The car accelerated again.

"What're you doing—getting ready to launch this Oldsmobile to the moon?" The boy demanded.

"If that would get you to go to college, then yes."

"Did Ronald Reagan go to college?"

"That idiot? Yes. Are you asking 'cause now you want to be president?"

Snow chuckled. "First thing I'd do is disband the military."

"Then you'd get assassinated."

"Before that, I'd nationalize the banks."

"Then you'd really get assassinated."

"I guess I wouldn't make such a great president."

"Pick something modest and attainable. Be a geologist."

"I do like rocks. They don't talk or think they're the greatest thing on earth, God's gift to the universe. They don't brag about themselves and their rank in the world. They just peacefully, wordlessly exist."

"Sounds like you want to be a rock, not just study them."

"I think you've got it."

"What?"

"My ambition in life."

"That's just dandy," his father lit a cigarette.

"When are you going to quit that filthy habit?"

"When you go to college."

"Give it up when I say I'll go."

Jack nodded.

"Okay, I'll go."

"I don't believe you."

"That wasn't part of the deal."

Jack said nothing, but continued smoking. "So you'll get to see your Mom's new apartment over Christmas," he said at length. "Let's hope it's better than the last one."

"I liked the one on Essex Street."

"That pit."

"Don't knock the urban frontier."

"I don't mind the frontier. It's all the ruffians that inhabit it that bother me."

"They only got burglarized twice."

"And assaulted, and pick-pocketed, and every night the cops descended on the neighborhood, sirens blaring."

"Boris said there was a gang problem."

"Now there's someone who's committed to a cause."

"Don't start, because I'm not going to be a social worker. Boris is okay, but I loathe social workers on principle. They bear a terrifying resemblance to the most repulsive creature on earth, the school counselor."

"Mrs. Thwaite is all right."

"She is a moron."

"She agreed with everything I said."

"And she then proceeded to do the opposite."

"That was a bit of a problem," his father said absently, guzzling now on a soda.

"She couldn't' even get to step A, namely, register me for the courses I wanted."

"She has a lot of students to take care of."

"She has a lot of hot air, all of it to do with her son, the fabulous CEO of the adult diaper corporation in New York State."

"That was bizarre."

"Downright disturbing. Every time I tried to get her to pre-register me for a class I had to hear about incontinence in the elderly."

"It's a big problem, apparently."

"Yeah, well, it's not my problem. I'm fifteen."

"Almost sixteen."

"That still puts me at least six decades away from having to wear a diaper."

"Maybe she does."

"I wish you hadn't said that."

"Just a thought."

"Well, keep it to yourself. I have to meet with this woman."

"So do I, given all your detentions, the number of which, by the way, I wish you'd reduce. I would think the chance of not having to hobnob with Mrs. Thwaite on a regular basis would be a great motivation to shape up."

"Yeah, but all the other idiots who are quote teaching me unquote are a great motivation to act up. Besides I reduced the detentions for a while."

"You should pity mental defectives."

"Look, I don't mind retards, I just don't like them telling me what to do, like Mr. Berly, my shop teacher. The guy's all thumbs. He's a menace. He should not be allowed within twenty yards of a power tool, but I have to risk my neck, literally, every other day, as he waves that drill around. It's goddamn terrifying. Everyone in the class just sort of cowers when he approaches, waving that drill—and don't get me started on him and that nail gun. We're lucky there haven't been any deaths in that class."

The Oldsmobile sped over the plains, with the boy's fulminations about his teachers filling the warm interior. By the time they arrived in Wichita, Jack felt as though he had relived high school. It was not a pleasant feeling.

Harry had a large, three story, brick house that he shared now with his much enfeebled mother, who seemed unable to remember who Snow was, alternately mistaking him for Jack's biological son, hence her grandson, or for Tommy, many years younger.

"But he doesn't look like Tommy," she complained.

"That's because he's not. He's Snow."

"It's snowing? I don't think so."

"No, Snow."

"That's what I said."

"That's his name."

"What a peculiar name. Why did you ever pick Snow?"

"I didn't."

"Well, who did?"

"His mother."

"But aren't I his mother?"

Jack shook his head.

"Oh dear, you've lost me."

"Don't worry, Ma," Harry smiled, patting her shoulder. "Jack lost all of us with this snow business."

"Sometimes I like my name."

"I didn't name him," Jack cried.

"How about dinner?" Harry clapped his hands together and rubbed them. "I made a roast beef."

"It isn't done enough," his brother criticized.

"And Mom made her famous scalloped potatoes."

"Oh," Jack said in dull disappointment, then in a whisper to Harry, "you know I can't stand those. That and macaroni and cheese. If I ever eat either again, I'm liable to croak."

"Not tonight, please," his brother muttered back. "It would upset her. She'd think the rare roast beef killed you, and I'd never hear the end of it."

The next day Harry took Snow to the car dealership. "See?" He said, flinging himself happily into his large, padded, leather, swivel chair. "I got the best office in the place. That's because I run the whole shebang."

"Dad told me."

"And this is where you could be year after next, once you graduate."

"What a thought."

"Yes. If you want to take a year off before college, what could be better than coming to live with me and working here? I guarantee you'll make plenty of money," Harry beamed at him jovially.

"Just what I want."

"Do you? Because it doesn't sound from your tone that you've got the fire for it. What do you like, Snow?"

"Doing nothing."

"Hmm. Anything else?"

"Going deep into the wilderness, where there's not a soul around, and living in a tent, eating fish, roots and berries and not talking to another human being for a long time."

"Well, those skills won't get you very far here."

"I suppose not."

An awkward silence ensued.

"There was something else I liked. It kind of surprised me,"

"Yes," his uncle replied absent-mindedly, flipping through some papers on his large, sparkling clean desk.

"A place my Mom lived in Manhattan, on the Lower East Side. Objectively it was a dump."

"Objectively," Harry repeated, staring out the open office door onto the dealership floor. "Hey, that Cadillac needs a shine."

"But I loved the neighborhood. You could get lost there. I guess it was the anonymity and the utter lack of pretension—"

"The anonymity? Where'd you say this was?"

"Essex Street in Manhattan."

"Oh well, Manhattan's famous for its anonymity. But the big apple's not for me. No, no. A fellow could go broke there in no time. You said you liked upper Fifth Avenue?"

"No. Essex Street."

"Never heard of it, but I'm sure it's swanky. That Manhattan's a playground for the rich."

"Not all of it. Not the part I like."

"And what would that be?"

The boy gazed in despair at the distracted adult across the desk from him. "Never mind."

"Now where were we?" His uncle was lifting books now, looking for a paper. "There you are," he flourished the paper he had just found in triumph. "Oh yes, Snow," and he winked at the boy. "You enjoyed that Park Avenue didn't you?"

"Never been there."

"No? You gotta see it, the way it stretches north from the Pan Am building, all those gleaming glass skyscrapers and then the ritzy residential apartment buildings."

"I think I'm going to throw up."

Harry looked concerned. "Something you ate? I told Jack those peppers were old. But he insisted on putting them in the omelet. Still, he didn't use a lot of them. You shouldn't be nauseous."

A man appeared in the doorway. "Johnson," Harry barked, "See to it that Caddy gets a shine. There are some smudges so big I can see 'em from here. Oh, and get me your Pepto Bismol. The kid here is feeling sick. I can't imagine why."

That winter holiday week Naomi took the train to the plane to meet her son at JFK airport. Never had she been prouder than when the tall, handsome sixteen-year-old boy, clad in jeans and a warm coat, strode up to her at the gate with news of an unexpected academic award. He had no luggage aside from his back pack— "I wanted to bring my hunting rifle, but Dad dissuaded me"—so they skipped the baggage claim and went out into the slowly falling snow, thence to the subway train back to Manhattan.

"Is it always so ugly?" He asked, gazing out the subway car window at the cold, gray outskirts of the city.

"I don't find it ugly," she replied.

"Mutatis mutandi," he murmured.

"Jack says you may take that geology course."

"Yeah well, anything to get out of a year in Wichita, living with Harry and working at the dealership."

"That bad?"

"Don't get me wrong. He's a great guy. I just have absolutely nothing in common with him, but, in his presence an odd powerlessness comes over me. He dragged me to church."

"You let him?"

"I couldn't say no. He's like, hypnotic or something. It's horrible. I was ready to vomit the whole time. And those lectures about God! They were unbearable. How could Dad stand it, growing up with him?"

"He said the same thing you did, about knuckling under to Harry's will."

"Give me vagrant Tommy with his half-hearted attempts at tough love any day."

They stopped at a tavern on upper Broadway for dinner, where the young man noted the gray in the hair at his mother's temples. But in the restaurant's dimness, as they ate their chili, he could not discern any crow's feet or wrinkles.

"I'll be gray by the time I'm forty," she explained. "It's hereditary."

"I saw a silver fox once, a real one, by the river."

"Oh, was that when you were tramping off on your own, into the woods?"

He decided not to enlighten her that such jaunts had never ceased. "Those expeditions," he slurped his chili, "were a good bit less dangerous than exploring your old neighborhood on the Lower East Side, which, by the way, I loved. I want to see the world, Mom, not just the wilderness."

Mollified, she inquired about his father.

"Lonely," came the immediate reply and with it, though not visible in the shadows, his mother reddened with guilt. He was lonely because of her, had never remarried because of her. He had raised her boy, out of spite at first, to demonstrate who in their small family took their responsibilities seriously. She pictured him clattering around the cabin alone at night, beer bottle in hand, distracted now and then by the blurred, gray light of the television. And then, she was lonely too. Life as a divorcee in Manhattan was frighteningly solitary. She routinely worked late, in part to avoid the empty apartment that awaited her, and looked avidly forward to her weekend telephone conversations with her mother, when she could hear news of her sisters and brothers and voyeuristically participate in their lives—their marriages, children, careers and homes. She had some friends, but mostly she just worked. That, it seemed, was to be her life.

"But he doesn't see it that way," the boy went on. "If he did, he wouldn't have broken off with Marlene."

"Marlene?" She sat up straight, guilt vanishing into thin air like smoke. "Who's Marlene?"

"His girlfriend this past year, an assistant professor of English. For a while I was afraid she was going to move in with us."

"If she did, you could have come here."

"Well she didn't, and she won't. Dad scared her off real good. He has a rather sarcastic way about him, as you have noted."

The yellows and ambers of the bottles above the bar glimmered merrily in the mirror and in the gloom, inviting her to soften the sharp edge of marital failure with a drink. She ordered a beer. "I don't have many happy memories of Jack," she remarked sadly.

"Most people don't. He's a hermit like his other brother."

"Brothers," she corrected.

"I'm excluding Tommy. Tommy's interested in the world, at least in the people who live on the street. I have the most in common with Tommy."

"I hope not," she decanted the beer from bottle to glass. "Look at you—handsome, strong, tall, academic awards, young. You don't even wear glasses. You've got the world ahead of you. What could you possibly have in common with Tommy?"

"I guess I have more in common with your old friend Shane."

"Now there are two stellar role models," and she rolled her eyes.

"I think so."

"Don't be odd, Snow."

"You were."

"I outgrew it."

"And look at you now. You were happier before."

"We live in a dark time. That's why I'm glum. This Ronald Reagan is terrible, and the entire consensus that's been accepted since FDR about the relation of people to their government has been thrown out the window. There will come a time when they'll do away with welfare. They're deregulating everything. And this arms race with the Soviets is madness. I've been to the USSR. Those people were paranoid to begin with, and now they've got a good reason to be—an American president who believes in Armageddon."

"That's not why you're sad."

"No?"

"You're sad because the world of your youth just disappeared. Everybody scattered. Not everybody made it. The party's over."

"We thought it would go on forever."

"Well it didn't. Welcome to the dark times."

"Let's just hope this loony president doesn't irradiate us all, though if he did, maybe I'd finally get some sleep."

"Insomnia again?"

"I don't know…yes, and it's torture. Here, sweetie," and she poured some of her beer into his now empty soda glass. She did not want the talk to continue on its current trajectory, because that would only lead to complaints and more sodden complaints. So they sat quietly, sipping their drinks, glancing curiously at the other patrons. Then she paid, and they trudged out into the still lightly falling snow and up darkly luminous Broadway to Ninety Fifth Street, where they turned and walked down to the corner of Riverside Drive.

"A doorman!" The boy exclaimed. "I'm impressed."

They rode the elevator up to the seventh floor, where she undid her abode's various locks, then ushered her son into her spacious, one-bedroom apartment. He noted the parquet floors, the over-flowing bookcases, the plants crowding the windows, the not particularly stylish but comfortable furniture, the copies of Daumier prints on the wall, courtesy of Morris, and the many framed photographs of himself, from birth to age sixteen, that decorated a shelf above her desk. He walked over to study the prints.

"If you're so smart, how come you ain't rich? That's what Morris said to me on my last visit to Philadelphia," she remarked.

Her son frowned, thus markedly resembling Ronald Swurl. "He seems to be given to cracks like that."

His mother opened the roll-out bed from the couch, freshly made up for him, and he flung himself down on it. "So who's the girl?" She asked.

"I knew you'd get around to that. Her name's Lin. We've only been going out for about two months, though that's kind of a problem, since there's nowhere to go in the wilds of Wyoming. She thinks it's peculiar you didn't get custody of me."

"Tell her to mind her own business."

"She doesn't do that. She says what she thinks,"

"I guess she's a good influence. You seem much less taciturn."

"She wants my opinion on everything. It's exhausting."

Still chatting about the loquacity of girlfriends and their demands for same from their beaux, she flipped on the TV for the evening news. The mayor of New York, interviewed about the problem of crime in the city, gave a prescription that essentially gutted the Bill of Rights. The two viewers guffawed. "What a jerk!" The boy exclaimed. "Even I know from my stupid civics class you have to follow the rules of search and seizure. There's something called the Fourth Amendment."

"Yeah, but there's also a mayor of the big apple, and he has no use for that particular amendment."

"Or any of the others from the sound of it. Sheesh, I thought our local politicians out in Wyoming were a bunch of ignoramuses. But he's got them beat, hands down." Her son paused to guzzle another beer his mother had permitted him. "Does he always go on like this?"

"Twenty-four hours a day. Mayor motor mouth, Mister law and order."

"Put it on the public cable channel. The one that says here in the guide shows the City Council. I want to see how they compare to the mayor."

"You'd see more sense and decorum if we went to the Central Park zoo."

"Nah," her son said, after observing the antics of the council members for a few moments. "Your mayor's way more entertaining."

"He's a pernicious virus in the body politic."

"He's a fucking riot."

"We're invited to dinner tomorrow night at Mike Dellico's, after you see my office on East Forty-Second Street."

"Is it in a high rise?"

"Of course my office's in a high rise. This apartment building is a high rise."

"Is your office higher?"

"Naturally."

"Skyscrapers make me nervous. I'm afraid the uncontrollable urge to smash a window and jump may overcome me."

"I'll keep you away from the windows."

But Snow was not comfortable in the newsroom. Shyness overcame him, and he soon lapsed into monosyllables. The reporters and editors he met all seemed like fine people, but he clearly felt awkward and out of place. He took his mother's keys and announced that he intended to walk back to her apartment.

"It's over fifty blocks," she warned. "And it's cold. You might want to take the subway."

He did not mind the cold, however, and was in no mood for being packed in an aluminum train car with scores of strangers. He walked. He had to admit, ambling up a snow-decorated Central Park West, that this city had its beauties. He also liked the way strangers left him alone, unlike small town Wyoming, where everyone was so annoyingly friendly and made him feel like a boor, as he searched desperately for a means to escape pleasantries. The bigness of the city did not intimidate him, the anonymity appealed to him, and so he began, on this return journey, to fit it in his mind among places he rather liked and would care to explore again, which included Chicago and San Francisco, and the open road between those places, with its promise of the unknown. True, one had to make small talk with drivers when one hitchhiked, but somehow that did not bother him. Besides, many of his rides had come from truckers, who, he had noted, were not particularly demanding conversationally, tended not to get offended when the chit chat lapsed into silence, and indeed, often regarded this development as he did—with relief. He went west on Seventy-Second Street, stopping to marvel through the plate glass at the bright interior of a Viennese café and bakery, Éclair's, bustling with patrons, whose older, European style aroused his curiosity. Rubbing his benumbed fingers, he trudged through the slush back to his mother's apartment, where he lay down on the sofa bed and went to sleep.

That evening, Boris, Mike—now finally married to Natalie—and the other guest, Ian Donohue, whom he had met several times before, all greeted him with an enthusiasm that he believed far exceeded the merits of his modest self. Indeed all this adult attention, his mother's boasts about his academic award, the questions about college, made him want to scamper back down the stairs and disappear into the dark, semi-criminality of Seward Park across the street. Ian, still Naomi's editor—indeed it was he who had hired her at the metropolitan tabloid—was the only one who seemed even remotely aware of his discomfiture. "Boy, when I was your age, you never would have caught me at one of these confabs if I could help it, surrounded by friends of my parents," he paused to drink his beer, then elaborated: "But then, you never met the friends of my parents, so it's hard for you to appreciate my frame of mind."

"Old leftists," Naomi broke in for a second, then returned to her discussion with Boris.

"Communists," the editor clarified, "unswervable, rock-solid supporters of Joe Stalin. And I, as a teenager, was flirting with being something more like a social democrat. I couldn't open my mouth without getting torn to shreds, usually by my father. And then of course, many of these people had relocated to Co-op City. So I had to hear all about the wonders of life in Co-op City. Which I knew was a crock. And I was very eager to contradict them, lest my parents take it into their heads, as they did periodically, to move there. But you can't contradict your parents' friends about how wonderful their new homes are without being rude, so there I was, listening to this hogwash about paradise in Co-op City and watching my happy life on Kossuth Avenue swirl down the drain. It was a horrible experience and scarred me permanently. I'm surprised you're taking it as well as you are. Smoke?"

"He's not allowed," Naomi popped back into their conversation then out of it again.

"Well, I guess that takes care of that," Ian said. "What do you do in your spare time—since we know you don't smoke."

"Hide from people in the wilds of Wyoming."

"Hard to make a living that way."

"Well, I'm still in high school."

"Ever think of relocating to Manhattan?"

"Never."

"I guess not, since you don't like people. I was like that in high school. So I spent all my time exploring the Bronx, going to little known spots like City Island or riding the elevated train all over the place. I started in seventh grade, when my father was still a motorman in the subway system—later he got a desk job—but he'd had a hard time with promotions, due to a dustup in the McCarthy era over his political views. That takes me back to elementary school and playing hooky to ride the trains with him. Now that was paradise—not some phony Co-op City you can't even get to by subway. I guess I kind of felt about Co-op City the way you feel about New York—"

"Suicidal?"

"Bingo. But that's common in high school. Certain kinds of changes, like moving, look terrifying."

"I wouldn't mind changing all my teachers."

"That's a given. There can be no question that there exists among the ranks of public high school teachers a species of lout so nauseating that it is extremely difficult to tolerate five minutes of exposure to—no less the required sixty minutes of your average class. If you are unlucky enough to land in one of these quote people's unquote classrooms, you have to transfer immediately. You explain to your counselor that you would be happy to take a course from an alligator, but that you cannot tolerate this so-called person and certainly cannot be held responsible for your actions if contact persists. The oath of irresponsibility for one's actions always gets a counselor's attention, and with the prospect of lawsuits looming in their otherwise feeble imaginations, your transfer will be assured."

"I'll have to try that. Unfortunately my counselor doesn't have an imagination."

"Is it a he or a she?"

"It's a cretin."

"I ask, because with a she, you can try to pull the heartstrings."
"Ha!"

"I said try. I didn't say you'd succeed."

"What's this about your counselor?" Naomi asked, holding out her glass to Mike for more red wine.

"She's a cretin."

"Oh dear, that doesn't sound good."

"Sounds about average for high school, to me," her editor commented.

"Can't you switch? Oh, thanks, Mike."

"Only if I'd alter the first letter of my last name. That's how they're assigned."

"Jack should talk to her."

"He did."

"And?"

"He got a pitch about buying stock in an adult diaper corporation."

Ian sputtered his beer back into his glass. "Now that's a new one."

"How peculiar. I hope she doesn't try to get you into an adult diaper."

"Oh, I'm sure that's coming."

"Because you're not even an adult yet."

"And with her as an example, I don't want to become one."

"That's excessive."

"That's the truth."

"My, my," Ian murmured. "High school really never changes. Plus ca change…"

"I don't speak French," Snow said dully. "Languages are not my forte."

"Just because you had to repeat Spanish," his mother began.

"It was the easiest class in the entire school. I flunked. I don't have an ear for languages."

"You just have problems with the conversational aspect."

"But that's what it was—a language conversation class."

"Oh."

Six months after returning to Wyoming, the young man and his girlfriend broke up. He took it very hard. Distracted, withdrawn, reluctant to look anyone in the eye, he alternately fled into the woods or moped around the cabin. Preparing to enter his senior year, he had become more isolated, silent and asocial than ever.

"Get a new girlfriend, then you'll feel better," his father advised.

"Yeah, it'll be great getting dumped a second time."

"Always looking on the dark side."

"What other side is there?"

He made no college applications and, after graduation, spent his summer hitchhiking around Wyoming and camping in the woods. At one point, he was gone for three weeks. Upon his return, he and his father had an extremely animated dispute. "You always, always tell me when you're going," Jack hollered. "I had no idea where you were or when you'd come back." Finally, one warm August morning, with the daisies blooming outside the cabin, the young man knocked on the door to his father's room. Jack opened it and saw his son in jeans, a T-shirt and a jacket, with his back pack, sleeping bag and tent. "So you're going again," the father said, each word dropping with a hard, lifeless thud.

Snow nodded, then spoke almost sadly: "And to be honest, I don't know when I'll be back. I'm going to see the world."

"There are other ways—"

"Not for me." The words froze in the air, as if written there in the ice particles of a finality and a truth that the father could not gainsay and that seemed to imprison him there in the doorway with their fatality that deprived him even of the impulse to fight. And then his son turned and strode off down the dirt road, through the trees, in the direction of the highway.

That night Jack phoned his ex-wife, who, at first preoccupied with her own predicament—she was two months pregnant by a writer she had been dating and had decided, again and not very pragmatically, to have the child whether they married or not—did not grasp the seriousness of his words. "But he's gone off before," she protested, the truth beginning to sift down through layers of distraction, money worries and the ever-present, subliminal feminine panic at the prospect of looming single parenthood.

"No, not like this. Frankly I don't know if we'll ever see him again."

For her the world went dark. She hung up the phone and, convulsed by huge, bone-rattling sobs, collapsed into a chair.

Some months before these events, Ian travelled to San Francisco on business. He had previously met Eileen and in fact knew all about the ruckus in the press over the communist infiltration of the Port Authority so many years earlier, which had caused her father to flee to Latin America. Indeed friends of his parents had been intimately involved in the matter. So when Naomi, worried about her childhood friend, asked him to check up on her, he happily agreed, his mind full of memories of beautiful dark eyes and hair and a lovely, pale oval face with a melancholy cast. Thus on a crisp spring morning, he found himself in a small apartment building in Oakland, ringing a buzzer next to the name Meer.

"Actually I just got evicted," Eileen said, pouring him a cup of black coffee. "I have to leave at the end of the month. They raised the rent. This is the fourth time in recent years. Rents in the Bay Area just go up and up."

"You should see Manhattan!" He replied. "They're going through the roof." He looked around the large, bright living room, the sheet music on stands, the oboe, flute, recorders, guitars and other instruments. "Where will you go?"

"I could always live out of my car."

"In the city? That's none too safe."

"I'd head down to Monterrey. My job ended a week ago, but I don't get unemployment, because I was technically a free-lance contractor. So…not too many options."

"Hey, I can't let a fellow red diaper baby fall through the cracks. Come to New York. I'll help you get a job. I know lots of people in studio music recording."

"There's Natalie, Mike's wife, who's a graphic artist. She said her employer needed an administrative assistant."

"And you wouldn't even have to live in their neighborhood."

"No? My impression was it was the cheapest in Manhattan."

"Cheap is a euphemism."

"Well, it's a little run-down."

"It was run-down when they originally built it, in the nineteenth century. It's never been anything else."

"I thought you liked it."

"To visit. Not to live."

"Boris' ambition is to move into a townhouse on Forsythe Street, around the corner."

"Boris needs a therapist."

"I saw them. They had a kind of faded elegance."

Ian rolled his eyes.

"Boris said some are inhabited by urban pioneers."

"Urban lunatics," the editor lit a cigarette, "and I might add that he's been talking like that for the better part of a decade. I haven't seen him act on this quote ambition unquote."

"It couldn't be worse than where he is now."

"That's what you think. Where he is now is two steps from the subway, convenient for making a quick getaway. In his dream apartment, he'd be marooned in the slums. Forsythe Street. Give me a break."

"I could afford Forsythe Street."

"But could you afford being a crime victim?"

"Where I live now is not exactly sheltered."

"I noticed that," he paused pensively, smoking. "What about Peru?"

"My father's life is too much of a roller coaster ride. Everything for him depends on the government. He's in, then he's out, then he's in—"

"As is so often the case for your average Soviet agent."

"In the late sixties he got All American Amalgamated kicked out of Peru. Now they're back."

"I did a story on them. They were involved in a superfund clean-up site in New York State. Seems they weren't doing what they were supposed to."

"They never do. They're a very sleazy corporation. You know, they're opening a new office in New York. That could be a hook for a story on the junta-mob-corporate web."

"When are they opening it?" He asked, very alert now.

"In the next month, and my father says they're involved with several Latin American juntas, even to the point of advising death squads, which is what they've done in Chile and Argentina."

"Would your father consent to be interviewed?"

"On background, maybe. But I know someone who might be easier to contact—Morris Lichter."

"If he's still there, and even if, he's just a public relations guy and knows nothing, from what I understand, about their foreign operations. I need someone in the guts of the company."

"For that you have to go to Houston."

"Advising death squads," Ian mused. "Boy, if I could back that up…"

"And I mean *advising*, like picking targets, supplying lists, and then the people just vanish."

"New York Company Gives Hit Lists To Death Squads—not a bad headline. This could be good."

"Then you'd have to go into witness protection."

"Like Jorge Ramirez, and the other drug lord witnesses."

"You know Jorge? I dated him years ago, in Boston."

"Now you may have to go into witness protection. Everyone else he's ever associated with has." Ian sipped his coffee. "Can you call your father, now, and have him talk to me?"

"He thinks my phone's tapped. And we have an arrangement. I call him at a pay phone in Lima."

"When?"

"Tomorrow, in fact. If you want to come with me to a phone booth, be my guest."

The next day, under thick, dark, storm clouds and in a persistently annoying drizzle, Ian crowded into a telephone booth with Eileen. After she and her father exchanged pleasantries, he took the receiver, with a gruff, "Hello, Mr. Rathman," and explained his interest in All American Amalgamated.

"It's not so much what they're doing here in Peru, though that's bad enough. There was just a massacre the other day, men women and children, who sided with the Maoists against the military, and though corporate involvement was less than usual, they support this murderous military. They keep it in power. But the things occurring in Chile are just plain atrocities, and All American is involved there up to its scaly neck. Yes, I'll give you names, dates and names of disappeared activists, but if you ever reveal my name, those storm troopers will kick down my door and shoot me so fast, I won't have a minute to think. You got that, comrade?"

"I'm going to need some corroboration," the editor said after scribbling furiously for a few moments. His source gave him some other names and arranged another paid telephone booth conversation with a Chilean expatriate. "Lastly, you might want to call Chester Swurl in Houston. He'll deny everything, but then again, the man's so brazenly evil, who knows, he might take credit for wiping out undesirables."

When he returned to his hotel, the editor phoned Morris Lichter.

"Oh, you're Naomi's friend, that half-tile reporter."

Ian chuckled. "Unless I'm mistaken, Naomi's a half-tile too."

"As far as I'm concerned, she's one hundred percent Jewish." Then he made clear that everything was off the record. "Now you wanted to know about Amalgamated, well, I left there ages ago. I do PR for Jones, Stine and Walker now, the big drug company in Philly."

"Boy, you sure can pick 'em."

"What's that supposed to mean?"

"They're getting a little bad publicity at the moment."

"That'll blow over. But if you want the goods on Amalgamated, you'll have to go to Houston—better start making arrangements with witness protection today."

"Do I detect a hint of criticism of your alma mater?"

"Look, it doesn't take a genius to figure out how they deal with people who stand in their way. I hope you don't put Naomi on this story, because I'll get her off by screaming conflict of interest. I'm not about to have my daughter's body turning up in the East River."

"You know nothing about Amalgamated's ties to Chilean death squads?"

"On background, I'll confirm for you that they may exist. But I can't help you with details, because I don't know and I don't want to know. Unlike some people, I intend to live to a ripe old age." And Morris hung up the phone.

Ian phoned Eileen: "Come live in New York."

"I'll think about it."

"You're going to wind up living out of that car, if you don't get out of here. But if you do, you have my number in New York. Call me any time."

"Thank you for being so helpful."

"Don't thank me. I have ill-disguised ulterior motives."

They both laughed, then he resumed: "But seriously, call my friend at that studio music firm in San Francisco. She may be able to give you work."

When she hung up, Eileen went to the window and glanced down at her old car, parked beside the curb. The sun shone blindingly off the roof, and she noted the neighborhood teenagers, leaning up against the back, so she went downstairs and shooed them away. She climbed in and drove out of the city and down to Menlo Park, where she parked in front of Larry Lawless' trim, two-story house with the screened in porch. Unfortunately, as she pulled around the semi-circular driveway, she hit a lamp, staked into a bed of purple impatience. It was clear, south of the city, not a drop of rain in the sky, so she was not surprised to see Larry, with the characteristic look of alertness in his hazel eyes contradicted by a rather lost expression on his face, rounding the house, trowel in hand. "Oh dear, you've hit one of the lights," he said.

She poked her head out the driver's window. "Are they expensive to replace?"

"Not very. It's just a hassle. Oh," he said, extracting it from the ground and holding it up for her to see, "the stake's just bent. I can fix that."

While he struggled with the light, his visitor stepped out of the vehicle and came around the front of it toward him. "It won't work," she said. "I'll never be able to believe all this scientology stuff."

"It doesn't matter," he said simply, "at least we became friends. You're my only friend who isn't into it, which is nice. I like a little contact with the outside world."

"Yoo-hoo! Is that Eileen?" It was Sylvia Lawless, stepping off the front porch and waving, Martin in tow, as he carried two martinis, one in each hand.

"But not as much as I've been getting this week," Larry muttered.

"We've heard so much about you," Sylvia enthused, approaching, her hand outstretched. She and Eileen shook, Martin making a self-deprecating nod of the head, as if to indicate that he would shake hands if he could, but clearly had both full. "You're the one who does *not* go to the church of astrology," Sylvia said.

"Scientology, mother."

"But Larry here tells me you read that awful book on dianetics and mental health. My God, I had to have a psychiatric session with Dr. Goldenstock after one chapter. Poor man, you wouldn't believe what he pays in auto insurance. His rates are through the roof, which is no surprise, since he always has about five cars parked in back of the house, two of them smashed by that dyslexic daughter of his who lives at home—Edie, I think her name is."

"Edie is not dyslexic," her son corrected. "She's just a dangerous driver."

"It's not surprising, considering she's off her rocker. Can you imagine, she graduated from the University of Chicago and cracked up. And I thought I had it bad," Sylvia said.

"When did you crack up?" Martin demanded. "I mean I always knew, but—"

"No, no. I meant in the wayward children department."

"Thank you, mother." Larry spoke through clenched teeth.

"Well, you're pretty far into your second decade with this cult stuff. Don't you think it's time to give it up? Come home. Bring Olga—"

"That's big of you."

"If she drops it too. And see Dr. Goldenstock. What a marvelous man, except, I must say, I wouldn't want to get in a car with him or his children. Especially that lunatic Edie. I saw her back his Mercedes into a hedge on the side of the house."

"Oh," Larry mused, replanting the light in the flowerbed, "are they still doing that?"

"What?"

"Driving into the hedge on the side of the house?"

"I should say so. Every time I went for a session, there was some car or other stuck in that hedge."

"I was friends with Edie in elementary school," Eileen said. "She was in my class."

"Was she crazy then?"

"No, she was quiet, shy and a model student."

"Well, she's a fruitcake now."

"Exactly what evidence do you have of this," Larry demanded, "aside from her backing into the hedge, which, as far as I can tell, every member of the Goldenstock family does on a regular basis."

"Everybody says she's nuts."

"Maybe she just wants to live at home. Maybe she doesn't like the world."

"Your sister says she's a ferocious insomniac, doesn't sleep for months at a time."

"My sister lives in Oregon!" He cried. "How would she know about Edie Goldenstock's sleep habits in Ardmore, Pennsylvania?"

"No need to work yourself into a lather," Sylvia said.

"Here," Martin gallantly offered, "have my martini. Good for the nerves."

"Not at one o'clock in the afternoon, thank you," his son replied.

"Why not? I started drinking at eleven," he turned to smile at Eileen. "Family visits, you know, require a little alcohol to help them go right."

Larry rolled his eyes. "They require leaving when you said you would, in order to go right."

"Now, now," Sylvia smiled. "We've decided to stay another three days. We like Menlo Park. We may move here."

"And I'll be such a psycho, I'll make Edie Goldenstock look like the perfect picture of sanity."

"So there. You agree she's a lunatic."

"I did not," Larry nearly hollered. "It was for rhetorical purposes."

"I've never seen you so worked up, Larry," Eileen said soothingly.

"He's not like this all the time?" Sylvia asked, adjusting her sunglasses atop her auburn mane.

"Only when you're here," Larry said.

"Dr. Goldenstock says you're getting your revenge on us."

414

"Oh, how?"

"With your astrology."

"Astrology?! Now who exactly is getting revenge on whom?" Larry demanded.

"He makes no sense," Sylvia commented to her husband, finally taking the proffered martini and sipping it. "You need to resolve your Oedipal conflicts."

"He didn't say that to me when I last saw him."

"That was in 1971. They got worse."

"How would he know?" Larry asked, running his fingers through his short, light brown hair in a way that somehow emphasized the expression of despair on his face.

"He's an excellent psychoanalyst."

"Him and Dr. Shapinsky," Martin irrelevantly put in.

"Shapinsky's the one who falls asleep on his patients," Sylvia corrected, "or is that Finklestein? I forget."

"Forgetting is good," Larry remarked, heading now toward the screen porch. "I've almost managed to completely forget my childhood. It's been hard work. Now there's nothing but scientology. And you want me to return to the Main Line, ugh, and to Dr. Goldenstock, so I can explore feelings I had when I was five, feelings, I'll have you know, that I have done my best to submerge in oblivion. Olga!" He hollered into the house, holding the screen door for Eileen, who was mounting the steps with his parents right behind, "stay upstairs. They didn't go."

"Oh, let her come down," Sylvia admonished him, seating herself next to her husband on the glider. "I love this porch."

"She knows when she's not wanted."

"If we move here, we should get a house with a porch like this."

Eileen sat in a wicker chair.

"She knows you blame her for scientology," their son pursued, also sitting in a wicker chair.

"Then we could visit Larry every day."

"God forbid."

"And I was very impressed with that supermarket."

"What—you thought California doesn't have supermarkets like the East Coast?" Larry demanded.

"But what will I do without Dr. Goldenstock?" Sylvia asked her husband.

"Stay in Narberth," her son advised. "In fact, return this afternoon and see him. Give him my regards."

"I'm not so crazy about California," Martin averred, "flaky, too flaky for me."

"Well of course it's flaky. Larry lives here. And look at him with his science and astrology."

"I can hear you."

"And Reagan came from California," Martin continued. "I voted against him, twice. A lot of good that did. Bad enough I have to see him on television, now you want me to move out here, where I'd constantly be reminded of him."

Larry put his head in his hands.

"What would remind you of him? I think you've lost me there," Sylvia said.

"Kind of lost myself. I guess it's that Manhattan I had at eleven."

"And the other one at twelve thirty," Larry said, his head still in his hands, "and the martini you're guzzling now."

"Well, it's Saturday. Nope. I'm definitely not up for a trip to the airport."

"Oh that was settled a while ago. We're staying with our darling boy till Tuesday."

"Aargh."

"And we'd love to get your view on this, this—"

"Scientology?" Eileen asked.

"Yes," Sylvia beamed at her. "Your view. You're so helpful, dear. Do you live in Menlo Park too?"

Eileen shook her head.

"Where then?"

"My car, very soon."

"You're going camping?"

"No, I'm going homeless."

"You're welcome to stay with us," Larry said.

"Homeless!" Sylvia exclaimed. "But how could you be homeless? You went to that nice private school with Larry, and you certainly look presentable."

"I lost my job, my apartment,"

"Damn that Reagan," thus Martin.

"He didn't fire her," Larry said.

"He's responsible for all these homeless people. You see them everywhere."

"You do?" Sylvia asked.

"I'm looking at one right now."

"Oh. I guess you are. Well, she's the first I've ever seen."

"Nonsense, Sylvia. Think Vine Street in Philadelphia."

"But I never go there. It's too depressing," Sylvia gave a little start, as though a shocking thought had just occurred to her. "You're not moving to Vine Street, are you Eileen?"

"No, just south along the coast. I'll find some park somewhere."

"Nonsense," Larry said. "Stay here."

"But she's not a scientologist," standing in the door was Olga, slight, blond and severe, a flower-print apron over her jeans and white blouse and a spatula in her hand.

"She could join," Larry ventured and looked at Eileen questioningly.

"I'm afraid not," Eileen replied.

"Good for you," thus Sylvia.

Eileen arranged to leave the possessions she cared most about in Larry's basement, then, in a daze, she drove home. She did not call Ian, her father or anyone. She skipped dinner, downed three beers and went to bed.

On Monday, she did not phone Ian's friend, the studio music engineer. Instead she gathered up her instruments and sheet music, loaded them into her car and drove back to Menlo Park. Larry was at work, but his wife, terse and tight-lipped and far from welcoming, held the door for her, as she transported these objects to the basement.

"Is it dry down here?" Eileen asked.

"It's completely remodeled. You can see that."

"But sometimes—"

"No, we have no problems with the damp."

"I really appreciate—"

"Thank Larry. It was his idea."

"I hope it's not an imposition."

"Excuse me? I've got his parents here. They hate me. They blame me for his religious beliefs. And Sylvia Lawless is doing everything she can to persuade Larry to leave me."

"It'll never work. You know that."

"It's just that it's a hard time for me to be rescuing his friends, especially someone who referred to *Battlefield Earth* as trash."

"Oh," Eileen dimly recollected making that literary evaluation to Larry, but she had forgotten that it had also been in Olga's presence. She slunk out.

For the rest of the month, the dazed musician felt as though she were moving through molasses, or worse, as if some blunt, nameless and never-before encountered force stopped her at every turn, so puissant it literally caused her fingers to drop the Help Wanted section of the newspaper, made her forget what she was doing, and generally operated like an implacable enemy in command of every detail of her life and one that was knowingly, purposefully causing her to deteriorate with the object of obliterating her entirely. Reading an account of the Nazi murder of mental patients, she opened her eyes to the bizarre and frightening apercu that the hatred behind such acts was still loose in the world. The supreme contempt with which TV characters uttered the word "psycho" or "weirdo" or "sicko" seemed directed at her personally. She had abandoned actively looking for work, but now she did not even bother to glance at the classifieds. She did not clean her apartment; she bathed less, slept more and vaguely noted that her thoughts seemed somewhat disordered. Every time the notion that "I must get myself together and look for work," briefly lit the shadows that had enveloped her mind, she would turn this way and that, wondering how, and "who would want to employ me?" She kept her vehicle, however, in excellent condition, as if in preparation for the inevitable. And the inevitable came, because, as she told herself, she had done nothing to stop it. But after a month living in her car outside Monterrey, she decided the time had come to take matters into her own hands—no more excuses, no more lethargy, no more pain. She walked into a hardware store, bought a garden hose, drove to what she considered a secluded spot, duct-taped one end of the hose into the tailpipe and ran the other through the driver's window. Before she expired, however, a passing squad car spotted her, illegally parked at a worksite.

Olga picked up the insistently ringing telephone. A policeman explained that he had found one Eileen Meer, a homeless, attempted suicide by carbon monoxide poisoning, with the phone number of Larry Lawless on a piece of note-paper in her purse. The young wife grimaced as if she had just come into contact with something unclean and there was a flash, a bad, bad flash in her eyes.

"Larry's at work, but I'm his wife, and I know Eileen very well."

"Is she in her right mind? Because we are considering a court-mandated institutionalization."

"No. She is not in her right mind. She's crazy. And I will be happy to drive down and give you a statement to that effect. She belongs in an institution."

Ron Swurl had lived in the San Francisco area for many years; he had lived in Haight Ashbury during its heyday and then long into its ugly decline. He lived cheaply in towns outside the city, and settled for a long time in Oakland, where he shared an apartment with three people he scarcely knew and worked as a custodian in a hospital. His panhandling days were over. He joined Alcoholics Anonymous. But he still sank at times into pitch black despair and then would drink and commiserate with his roommate Carl, who drove a city bus, over his wasted life. He was careful, however, never to show up for work drunk. His memories of his bedraggled and desperate years on the street, of begging for change, sleeping on park benches, shaving in the men's room at the bus station, showering at the YMCA, lunching at a soup kitchen, applying for jobs, occasionally snagging one only to lose it later for showing up high or inebriated—these memories of destitution, etched clearly and indelibly into his mind, made him a model custodian, never late, never loud, never looped. He thought little about the past, his friends from Philadelphia or his family there, though he occasionally did encounter Eileen on the street or the bus. So it was with some unpleasant surprise that, one bright clear afternoon, when facing a four-day weekend in which he had decided to prowl around San Francisco, while ambling in the financial district, he should come face to face with none other than his older brother Chester. Though older, grayer, heavier, that impressive corporate baron still would have been recognizable to his destroyed younger brother anywhere. The thick snub nose was ruddier than ever and immediately made Ron long to have a beer with lunch. As for the corporate bigwig himself, he was shocked to see that his younger brother had not changed in the least and that, except for his rather shabby attire—which could be quickly cleaned up—he could be made to look quite presentable.

"You cut your hair," Chester said, without even the trace of a greeting.

"Nice to see you too."

"Well, it's been how many years—ten, fifteen? You been in touch with Mom?"

"Well," the custodian evasively drawled and glanced up at a pigeon, wheeling in an arc against the azure strip of sky between two glass and steel towers.

"Me neither," the older one said. "I leave that to my sisters."

"Let's hope they don't leave it to us."

"I live in Houston now."

"Still with Dad and All American?"

"You bet. We made a killing in zinc and tin out of the Andean countries, so we're not about to stop that, no matter what you read in the paper about a bunch of angry campesinos. We'll be suing that Houston paper for libel, if they don't watch out."

"Still spoiling for a fight, eh Chester?"

"Gotta fight to keep what's mine," and he winked horribly at his brother. "You should come out to Houston for a visit."

"When? I work."

"You're not at work now, are you? I'm heading to the airport. Come with me. I'll have you back in time for work Monday morning."

"Actually, I have Monday off."

"Great. Then I'll put you on a plane Monday night."

"Hmm…I've never been to Houston."

"Come on!" And he clapped the back of the poor, reluctant man's shoulder. "The old man would love to see you. You always were his favorite."

"Really? I haven't heard a word from him in fifteen years. My impression from Roz was he was too busy with his Mexican heiress to give a thought even to Howard, who, if I may correct you, really was his favorite."

"That woman's long gone. He remarried."

"Who's the lucky bride?"

"Delia. She was his secretary. But don't worry, Dad's smart, signed a pre-nup."

The younger brother rolled his eyes, but the older did not notice. He was flagging town a taxi. To Ron's protestations that he had not even packed anything, Chester replied that he would buy him new clothes. "Those look kind of seedy anyway," he said, fingering the frayed lapel of Ron's jacket. Shortly and in somewhat of a daze, the custodian found himself selecting a lunch entrée on a United flight, direct to Houston.

"So where do you work?" the businessman asked, munching on smoked almonds and stretching his legs rather thoughtlessly into the aisle. A flight attendant politely requested he move them.

"I'm a hospital custodian."

"Oh, no, no, no. We're going to fix that," Chester said. "How does something with vice president in the title sound to you?"

"God awful. Look, I'm just coming out for a visit, to see you and Dad. I'm not interested in giving hit lists to death squads."

"So you read that pack of lies?"

His brother nodded and cast him a dark, brooding glance.

420

"You know it originally ran in a big Manhattan daily paper" Chester said, "under the byline of one Ian Donohue. Then the AP picked it up. Boy, are we going to sue his ass."

"Well, you'd better leave it at that. This ain't Santiago. You can't have him abducted in the night."

"Pack of lies," munch, munch on the almonds.

"Looked like he did his homework, to me."

"Is it Amalgamated's fault these puny countries are riddled with communists?"

"Trade unionists—that's what I read."

"They're all a pack of Reds, and they've infiltrated everything, the government, the press. When that happens, you can't stick to the democratic niceties."

"I can't? I certainly can. If it was up to me, those paramilitary death squads would all be cooling their heels in prison."

"Spoken like a blissfully ignorant American. See Ron, I've been down there, even had a meeting with Pinochet. Nothing, nothing's going to shut down our mines. That happened in Peru, with that leftist coup, but it's never, never happening again, no matter what some Ian Donohue writes in some New York newspaper. That's one reporter's gonna get a subpoena—"

"I doubt it. My guess is he got his facts right, your suit will get thrown out and the judge may even get mad at your frivolous litigation."

"Frivolous!"

"Hey, what am I doing? Why am I on a plane to Houston?" Ron sat up, looking around, as if he had awakened from a trance.

"To see the family, little brother and," munch, munch, "to improve your career prospects."

"How did I get into this? I must have lost my mind."

"By Tuesday, you could be running operations in Peru."

"By Tuesday I'll be back on my shift, mopping up blood and vomit in the emergency room. It's a lot cleaner work than what you're proposing."

"Eat you beef bourguignon."

"Looks like crap."

"Well, it was frozen. What do you expect?"

The plane landed smoothly, to the young derelict's dismay—he had started to hope that a crash might exempt him from the upcoming meeting with his horrendous father and his murderous underlings. For that was how Ron now regarded the managerial ranks of Amalgamated. He had read Ian's story—reprinted via the AP in *The San Francisco Chronicle*—quite closely and decided that it had the harsh, jarring ring of truth, that the company he had detested in the late 1960s and early 1970s had graduated from mere brutal exploitation of indigenous miners, to giving lists of opponents to blood-thirsty executioners, who carried out these murders then hid the bodies in mass graves. It was as if, he thought, the European fascism of the 1930s had transplanted itself in the Americas. Wreck that he was, he acutely knew evil when he saw it, and always had, which, in turn, was, he thought, partly why he was such a wreck.

As he rose to exit, he turned to his brother. "I'm not leaving this airport till you purchase me a return ticket on Monday."

"Whoa, Ron. Let's wait and see how things go."

"No. I will not leave unless you buy that ticket. And if you refuse, I will start to panhandle in the airport, doubtless get arrested and then get the name Ronald Swurl rather ignominiously in the news."

This gave the ever-up-and-coming company man some pause. He agreed to purchase the ticket.

Once that transaction was complete and the younger of the two had his return ticket safely in his pocket, they went in search of his brother's car. Chester spotted it in the garage, and soon Ron found himself ensconced in a gleaming, black BMW, zooming into downtown Houston. The executive parked his vehicle in a reserved spot in front of a brutalist skyscraper with the words "All American Amalgamated" emblazoned across the front.

"I think this is a bad dream," the custodian muttered, slamming the car door shut, then gazing at the open, bluff, genial face of his brother with its freckles and blue eyes slightly unfocussed from afternoon alcohol, so blithely, even self-righteously capable of thoughtless wickedness, muttered again, "make that a nightmare."

"You'll have to stop that mumbling to yourself. It makes a very bad impression, as if you're not executive material."

"I do it all the time."

"We may have to hire you a personal coach."

"You may have to hire me a taxi, back to the airport, tonight."

"Tonight? That ticket I bough you is for Monday. Come on Ronnie," and Chester patted him on the back. "You can do this. Think positive." And they crossed the plaza, entered the gleaming, marble-floored lobby and rode the elevator to the top level. "Never do anything on a whim," Ron said.

"Is that a motto of yours?"

"No. It's a lesson I learned today."

Ron Swurl senior's opulent office was immense, with a view on two sides of the city and the clouded, opalescent, early evening sky. The president and CEO of the corporation, cut from the exact same mold, physically and morally, as his aggressive, ambitious underling and son, looking older but still ruddy and hale, rose upon catching sight of his two guests.

"Surprise!" Chester exclaimed.

"I don't believe it," the older man gasped. "Eight years ago Roz told me she thought you were dead."

"Eight years ago I was. How's Roz?"

"We haven't spoken."

"In eight years!" Chester guffawed, slapping his thigh with his hand.

His father ignored this outburst. "The marriage to that guy in Brazil didn't work out. He was a loser. I had warned her. When we talked, she had just moved back from Sao Paolo. She wanted money for your mother and was none too polite about it."

"It's hard to mind your manners when your mother's living on a shoe string and doesn't have enough to eat," Ron replied.

Evidently in the habit of not deigning to reply to anything he found remotely offensive, the old tycoon said nothing, just lit a Marlboro and offered one to each of his sons. Both accepted and seated themselves in the black leather armchairs facing the elegant desk, which, Chester informed Ron, had cost many thousands of dollars.

"Howard was the only one of you who was ever pleasant to talk to. Never a sharp word from Howard," their father paused to smoke his cigarette, then turned to Chester. "Did you meet with those investors?"

"All taken care of."

"This flap in the press didn't cause any trouble?"

"No. But my advice would be to keep General Sanchez off the premises until this whole thing dies down."

"Who's General Sanchez?" Ron Junior asked.

"Well, speak of the devil!" His father cried, for the door had opened and in had stepped a short, very well-groomed, dark-haired man in a dark suit, wearing sunglasses. "General Sanchez, meet my son Ron Junior."

Afraid that he was going to be required to shake the hand of someone he strongly suspected was a war criminal, said young man waved nervously from his seat. Meanwhile, the general, none too favorably impressed by the latter's threadbare attire, did not advance.

"Sunglasses Jose? At dusk?" Chester asked.

"I prefer to travel here as discreetly as possible."

"There's no problem for you in Houston, you can be sure of that."

"There were demonstrators downstairs this morning, from a group called CISPES."

"Well, they're barking up the wrong tree," Ron Senior said. "You're from Chile, not Central America."

"You forget, I came here directly from El Salvador, where I was advising the military. I'll keep my sunglasses on, gracias."

Ron Senior, who had started scowling at the mention of demonstrators, looked sharply at Chester. "CISPES—they bothered us the last time the general came here. Isn't security your department?"

"Among many others, Dad, but I'm sure they didn't get in the building."

"One followed me into the lobby, shouting 'murderer,'" the general enlightened him.

"Geeze Chester! And the board met here today. Imagine what they must have thought."

"I doubt they were frightened by a bunch of scruffy students."

"There were priests," the general continued, still not advancing into the room and evidently uncertain whether to speak frankly in front of Ron Junior.

"Priests!" The father exclaimed. "That looks terrible."

"And TV cameras," the general went on. "I refused to give any of them my name."

"I'm on it, Dad," Chester rose and left the room.

"Well it's about goddamn time," his father barked.

"I had my secretary do some research. I got the names of the people involved in this CISPES," the general volunteered.

"No, no. We don't do things like that here, General Sanchez. You leave these loud-mouthed protestors to us."

"Some have come, not so long ago, directly from El Salvador. They have families back there."

The young visitor in the expensive chair felt a chill creep up his spine and seemed to see the room fill with a diseased and unrefreshing light. He realized that his hands, gripping the leather armrests, were sweating. And then, to his horror, at the center of that terrible and sickening light, he saw his father wink at the general.

"I need a drink," he said after a moment, and then, following his father's glance to the bottles of liquor arrayed on a mahogany sideboard, said, "In a bar."

"There's a bar called Friday's right down the street," his father said.

Ron Junior rose and, still chilled and sweating at the same time, passed through what had become for him an unspeakable and nauseating atmosphere and left the office. On the next floor, Chester stepped into the elevator. "That General Sanchez is scary," the younger brother involuntarily blurted out.

"Oh, he's one tough cookie, but he has to be. It's a dirty war against all those leftists in Latin America." Chester exited the elevator on the next floor. His brother rode the rest of the way down alone and in a daze. He found Friday's and skipped the bar, walking directly to a telephone booth in back. He dialed information, then a number in New York City.

"Ian Donohue here."

"Yes, I can't give you my name, but I read your story, and I'm in Houston now, and a certain General Jose Sanchez from Chile is in the offices of Amalgamated's top management."

"*The* General Sanchez?"

"Who's *the* general?"

"Oh, he's an infamous killer—from Chile, but he also advises the military in El Salvador."

"That's the one. Apparently there were protestors at Amalgamated's headquarters today. Sanchez brags that he didn't give the news his name and then said he's done research on the people who were here. I think he intends to retaliate against their families in El Salvador."

"What groups were protesting?"

"Something called CISPES. He says he had his secretary research them."

"And he's there right now…what's your name?"

"I can't give you that, but I think the protestors recognized him. If you could find out who was here this morning, then you'd have an eye-witness besides me. And they might give you their names."

"How can I get back in touch with you?"

"You can't. But I'll call you again if I learn more." Then he went to the bar and drank a Tequila. Fortified, he had a beer. Then he had a Margarita. By the time his older brother extracted him from this lively drinking establishment, he had had another Tequila and another beer and could not pay. Chester put the money on the bar in annoyance. "You're going to make a great impression on Dad's wife. You're plastered."

"Just so long as the generalissimo isn't coming to dinner."

"He's busy."

"He's got blood on his hands."

"Half of Latin America has blood on their hands. Those leftist degenerates deserve what they get. They're subhuman, I don't care who screams to the press about their human rights. Wake up, Ronnie. It's a dog eat dog world."

"How could you do business with him?"

"To make money, that's how," the businessman snapped, then, "bartender, get me a Tequila. You're driving me to drink little brother."

"Better than murder."

"Cut it out about that," Chester said savagely, and for once his genial, easy-going, ordinary guy façade seemed to have cracked. "Without people like General Sanchez, we have to contend with a hostile population, with miners who want raises, with fanatical socialists who think we're raping their country and shouldn't be there. Without him, and lots of people like him, we can't do business."

"So he does your dirty work?"

"So? At least we don't have to do it, because without him, we would. We'd have to hire—"

"Thugs, right? You'd have to hire thugs, murderers and thugs."

"You're blasted out of your mind. I'm not even taking you to dinner."

"Where are you taking me?"

"To my house. You're going to bed, sleep off this booze, sleep of this goody two shoes crap. Come on." And he hustled his brother out of the bar and back into his sleek, black BMW.

The drove out of the city and into a posh, flat suburb of enormous houses at the ends of long, perfectly paved asphalt drives. Chester's mansion was white, though how he perceived even this, drunk and in the dark, Ron could not later say. He collapsed on an evidently expensive living room couch that looked, the inebriated custodian thought, like it belonged in a hotel lobby.

"No he can't come meet Delia," Chester spoke into the phone. "He's got himself completely ripped. I don't know what; he drank a few Tequilas—"

"Some Margaritas!"

"Some Margaritas, some beers. He's not presentable. But don't worry, he'll be here another two nights."

The younger brother groaned piteously at this prospect.

"Oh, now he's trying to talk." Chester put his hand over the receiver, "what is it?" He asked.

Ron groaned again.

"He's incoherent. He can't even talk. Yup. See ya."

426

A little while later, the corporate [illegible] to get him upstairs in a bed. But the sno[illegible] forth from the couch, as Ron did not stir. In [illegible] Budweiser from the fridge and sat in an armchair, [illegible] on the matching ottoman, sipped his beer and co[illegible] form of battered humanity defacing his perfect deco[illegible] that so obviously wounded human being repulsed him. "[illegible] softly, lighting a cigarette. "Making your living as a custodia[n], [illegible] father's a multimillionaire. You fucking idiot." The bluff genial[ity, illegible] the most notable quality in his face, had vanished completely, repla[ced] [illegible] something alien, hard and never on public display. His features were t[ight] and sharply immobilized with a cold anger and pride, frozen in a haughty pallid marble of dislike and disdain. "So what if the old man's a pain? I put up with it, and I get rewarded. I don't climb on my high horse about a bunch of murdered peasants like you. What are they to me? Nobodies. Why should I care about them? Nothings. They're in the way. I got my money to make. Look at this house, you moron! You think I got it worrying about Sanchez's or anybody else's bloody hands? I wouldn't have it without the likes of him. They damn near nationalized the mines in Peru. If they'd done that, we'd be out of business. Me, my house and my bank account—that's what I care about, and someday the old bastard will die, and because he's an old bastard, one who holds grudges, he won't leave his money to you or to Roz. He'll leave it to me and to Howard. He always favored Howard, and so Howard doesn't have to kiss his ass. That little idiot has something, some kind of angel looking out for him. But far as I can tell, I don't, so I've got to brown-nose, and I'll get paid for it when he kicks the bucket. I'll also rise in the company. And the worst of it for you, Ronnie, is that I didn't have to be a genius to figure all this out. I just had to look out for myself. If you were looking out for yourself, you wouldn't have gotten plastered instead of meeting your stepmother. Personally, I can't stand the old bag, but when the CEO invites me to dinner, I don't get so drunk I can't go. You jerk. You pathetic drunk with your useless, out-dated principles." He paused to inhale his cigarette smoke. "But I suppose it's for the best that I got reminded of this side of you. Otherwise I might have really made an effort to get you in at Amalgamated. And then what—have you act like this? It could have reflected badly on me. It could have damaged me. And we aren't having that—Oh, no. I stick my neck out for no one, not even my hopeless little brother, who will die without a penny, thanking who knows what—God? Don't make me laugh—that at least he didn't compromise some idiotic sense of good and evil that did nothing but stand in his way. Right and wrong! Money says what's right and wrong. But my little brother doesn't acknowledge that, so he'd have been better off never having been born."

...he empty beer can, pitched it into the hall trash, ...watch television.

...younger brother boarded his flight back to San Francisco ...was evident despite his drunken swagger. Friday had been ...had been instead the resumption of a habit he thought he ...but that now roared back, like engines out of hell, breaking ...When he was unable to show up for work Tuesday or Wednesday, ...to admit that his weekend sojourn had opened a Pandora's box. ...end of two months he was jobless and sleeping in the park. His ...mmates, sick of the booze and frightened by his vaguely minatory manner of demanding money for it, had resolved not to take him back under any circumstances. By the end of autumn, the lost soul considered his fate sealed. "But at least some good came of it," he said aloud, scanning a headline in the *Chronicle*: "Link Between Amalgamated and Death Squad General Confirmed." Then he folded the newspaper, mumbled blearily and, he felt, uselessly to himself, "God works in strange ways," but then heard the very alert correction in his heart, "He works through people," raised his head, as if sloughing off some unbidden and momentary oppression, and trudged off toward the park, hoping for a late morning nap on a bench.

Sunlight shot through the branches and leaves, shining like emeralds, of the trees overhanging the narrow, deserted, scantily paved road that wound through the low hills, past an occasional clearing for a farmhouse, log-house or trailer. It was a bright, painfully clear, sunny autumn day. The maroon Buick sped through the silent woods, with a whoosh of rubber on asphalt and an occasional rumble, where the tires hit gravel. The road curved around a large pond, large enough for the ripples in the breeze to glitter like diamonds, as the green frogs, floating on silky lily pads in toward shore croaked melodiously, oblivious to the Buick, as the deer at the water's edge raised his antlers inquisitively, while the doe, perhaps secure in the belief that her mate would protect her, kept drinking and did not raise her velvet eyes. The car plunged back into the foliage, gliding up and down hills, stopping once for a raccoon that tiptoed across the road, unaware that the driver had spared its life. Soon the road began a steep upward incline, then leveled off, then up again, while to the left, golden fields appeared where the forest had been beaten back, fields that sloped down, affording a view of the low green and purple hills all around. Soon an uneven stone wall, constructed of granite boulders wrenched out of the ground, loosely set on top of each other with no mortar, appeared on the left, presumably to pen the kine that no longer pastured there. The wall stretched unbroken along the roadside, until a trim, two-story farmhouse with bright blue shutters and a blue door came into view. There a break in the wall opened up for the drive that led up to this house, with its wrap-around porch and view of the hills and valleys from all sides save the one facing the road. On the lawn, surrounding this farmhouse stood a mighty oak at one end and a dark, melancholy hemlock at the other, "Mr. and Mrs.," as the owners of the house were wont to joke. Beneath the porch, ringing the house, was a flower garden in which Black Eyed Susans bloomed, while the hollyhocks on the corners drooped and wilted, their summer gone by. The wicker furniture on the porch, the glider, the discrete stacks of books here and there, the red Retriever asleep with its head on its paws, the brown and yellow cat prowling in the flowers, leaping futilely at white cabbage butterflies and the calico cat asleep on the woman's lap, the woman herself, seated before a typewriter, in jeans and a pink T-shirt, her long blond hair loose in the breeze, the regular clacking of the machine, audible even down at the start of the driveway, all betokened solitude and peace, refuge from a noisy, hostile world of planes, bombs, superhighways and cities—all of that was gone, could not penetrate the splendor and isolation of this corner of western Massachusetts. Alderway turned off the Buick's engine, but did not get out of the car. Instead he sat, rubbing his upper lip, where his moustache no longer was, indeed had not been for many years, and watched Ingrid type.

When they had first moved to Amherst, more than ten years earlier, they had built a log house deep in the forest, with him teaching her as they worked and his wife catching on quickly. They lived there for five years, constantly sprucing it up, so that when Ingrid said she wanted a view— "Who wants a view?" He had demanded, "a view of what? I like being surrounded by trees." "A view of hills, fields, the sky, space," she had replied—they were able to sell it for good money and put a down-payment on the blue and white farmhouse with the view. It had a shed off to the side, which he rescued from his spouse's plans to scrap by remodeling it into a tool shed/workshop. But as things developed, he did not enjoy the solitude of his shed, finding that he preferred weeding in the flower garden with his wife or the vegetable garden in the field, also with her. They grew string beans, zucchini, winter squash, radishes, lettuce, tomatoes, corn, spinach, every kind of herb, including small quantities of marijuana, which neither any longer smoked or ingested in any manner, but which, she said, they had to grow on principle, since it should not be illegal. Two apple trees grew in the field—though Alderway said he was giving a prize to the first person who found an apple without a worm in it—and there were raspberry, blackberry and blueberry bushes at the tree-line along the field's far end. Despite his wife's stern disapproval, he went hunting with buddies from his work in the state trooper hierarchy and noted with some triumph that her criticism did not extend to turning down the venison, once it was cooked.

At her job, as an assistant professor of comparative literature at the state university, it was regarded as charmingly eccentric that she was married to a policeman. This, however, had its disadvantages.

"If that Professor Pitter calls me one more time to fix his parking tickets, I cannot be responsible for my actions," Alderway had announced one evening over dinner.

"He's a harmless oddball."

"He's a pest. And I'm not a traffic cop, nor a corrupt traffic cop. Will you kindly make that clear to him?"

"I've tried, but he's rather dense."

"How does he get so many parking tickets? I've lived here ten years, and I've never even seen a parking ticket."

"That's because all the cops are terrified of you. Your reputation preceded you."

"How come Professor Pitter's not terrified of me?"

"He's an idiot, okay?"

"Of course he's an idiot. No normal person could get that many parking tickets if they tried."

"I think he parked in front of the firehouse once, you know, where the fire trucks exit."

"Why am I not surprised?"

"Then there was a fire, and the trucks couldn't get out," Ingrid chewed her venison thoughtfully. "It's gamey," she said.

"What, Pitter's parking?"

"No, the venison."

"Of course it's gamey. It's called wild game."

"Takes some getting used to."

"Well, I notice you're doing a pretty good job of that."

"I may join PETA."

"Who? What?"

"People for the Ethical Treatment of Animals."

"Uh-oh, I don't like where this is going."

"Yup, and then I'll have to confiscate your gun."

"Good luck."

"My, my. Touchy tonight, aren't we?"

"It's that imbecile Professor Pitter. What's he teach anyway?"

"The semiotics and deconstruction of literary texts from eighteenth century France."

Alderway stared.

"I kid you not."

"Translate," he demanded.

"Bullshit," she explained. "It's basically bullshit." She paused, chewing more thoughtfully, "definitely gamey."

"What? The semiotics and deconstruction of literary texts from eighteenth century France as taught by Professor Pitter?"

"That poor moron. It's not his fault he's a quack. You see, he believes all this mumbo jumbo because it comes straight from the horse's mouth."

"The horse's behind is more like it. Who's the horse?"

"A French intellectual named Jacques Derrida, a phenomenal charlatan. He's quoted in every literature department in the western world. It's pathetic. The man single-handedly destroyed literary criticism in Europe and the United States and in the process ruined the lives of the Professor Pitters of this world, who are basically modest little drones, whose imaginations caught fire once from some novel they read and now, ten years later, they're wrestling with semiotics, which they can't understand because it's a fraud. But the term fraud, you see, is not in their vocabulary, so they have absolutely no idea what's been done to them and live in terror that some student or faculty member is going to find out that they basically don't know what they're talking about, teaching or reading."

"Sounds like someone should expose this Derrida."

"Someone is working on it."

"From a feminist perspective, of course."

"Of course."

"When you're done, you should give it to Professor Pitter, for his criticisms. That might give him a jolt."

"A jolt? It might send him into cardiac arrest. Who knows, he might abandon his car in the middle of an intersection and wander off into the woods, leaving it to collect a dozen parking tickets and get towed."

"Then he'd be after me about the towing fees. On second thought, don't give your article to him to read. Oh, look out the window—a wild turkey. Where's my rifle?"

"You are not shooting that bird during dinner. Besides it's probably gamey."

"Undoubtedly the very definition of gamey. But still good to eat."

"PETA. I'm definitely joining PETA."

"Join anything you like, but you're not getting me to give up my gun."

"Guns, plural."

"True, I have more than one. What do you want? I'm a cop. Besides, I don't like the idea of you out here alone and defenseless two days a week."

"I'm not defenseless."

"Oh, you're going to stop an intruder with your judo?"

"I sure as hell am not going to do it with your rifle."

"You just need a little target practice."

"You saw me. I couldn't hit the broad side of a barn."

"That was fairly terrifying last time we tried in the field. Maybe I should take you to the range."

"What? So I can get lucky and actually hit a person? Are you nuts?"

"You know, they razz me at work about my wife, the egghead professor. They'd be merciless if they saw how you shoot."

"Then why take me to the range? That'll be putting my quote shooting skills unquote on display."

"Eat your venison."

"I'm becoming a vegetarian."

"Well I'm not."

"Then you can cook your meat for yourself."

"I already do. And last time I checked I do most of the cooking," he said rather emphatically.

"Oh yes. You have a point."

"Not that I'm complaining."

"You don't like my cooking?"

"Don't get me wrong."

"I remember what you said about my oatmeal."

"Uh oh."

"That you had never tasted anything quite as lacking in any flavor whatsoever."

"That was ten years ago."

"I have a long memory."

"And a thin skin."

"Cooking is not my forte."

Alderway rolled his eyes.

"Criticism—that's my forte."

"Just leave the cooking to me, please," he said.

"And poetry."

"Of a wonderfully graphic and violent nature."

"Pitter called it castrating," she complained.

"Oh pooh. What would he know? He doesn't have any balls to begin with. All he's got are parking tickets, and some French charlatan enmeshed in some unpronounceable fraud."

"Semiotics."

"Semiotics. That's a good one. I'll have to run it by the guys at work, see if any of them ever heard of it. I'll tell them it's the latest academic scam. Maybe then they'll put me on the case. I'll present your paper and voila."

"You don't speak French."

"But I know voila. I'll get promoted, you'll get famous, and Pitter can give up this deconstruction crap once and for all and devote himself to the pursuit of legal parking spaces."

"And learning how to park."

"That's a problem too?"

"You should see him in that Saab. What a fiasco. The man cannot parallel park, even a little car like that. I can't imagine what would happen if he had a Lincoln town car."

"Probably never teach again, he'd be so busy trying to back into a space, thus sparing countless students his Derrida nonsense," Alderway paused to chew. "But honestly, you need some target practice."

"Nonsense."

"Ingrid, you're the wife of the man who sent up half the Boston mafia."

"That was over ten years ago."

"You think you have a long memory? Think mobster with a grudge. Said mobster gets paroled after ten years. He's got contacts with corrupt cops. How long before he finds us? And we're not just talking about one mafioso. We're talking about thirteen—the bums I arrested and everyone they turned states' evidence against."

"They're terrified of you. They think you're insane. Sometimes *I* think you're insane."

"Well I definitely will be if they come after you. If they so much as touch a hair on your head, I can't be held responsible for the mayhem that may cause me to release—with multiple semi-automatic weapons."

"All right, I'll get some target practice. Anything to stave off a murderous rampage."

So he took her to the range, with chaos the predictable result—policemen ducking for cover and bullets flying everywhere except at the targets. Ingrid was banned. So he led her out into the field, with the tall grass up to their knees, the goldenrod and Indian paintbrush swaying in the gentle wind, hung a huge, pink, plastic bucket from a low branch down by the fringe of trees, stood behind her and tried to help direct her aim. It was hopeless. Sometimes, he noted in despair, she even shot straight into the sky. "You think mobsters fly?" He demanded. "You think one's going to zoom in the second story window on wings like a turkey buzzard?"

"I thought if I aimed higher—"

"At the moon?"

"There's no moon. It's one p.m."

"Try again."

"Not if you're going to criticize."

"It's nothing personal. It's self-defense."

"How is it self-defense?"

"If I tell you what not to do, there is a chance, albeit a slim one, you may not do it."

"Okay, I won't aim high."

The next shot went into the ground, some yards away.

"Yikes," Alderway said.

"I did what you said."

"Then I'll keep my mouth shut." But of course he could not, so that session, like every session, ended with mutual recriminations and lots of wasted ammunition. After two weeks, there was not so much as a mark on the big pink pail.

"I don't think we're making progress," he said one afternoon.

"Maybe you're not a good teacher."

"Maybe I've taught dozens of cops how to shoot. Maybe I even taught my friend Maury, who was so near-sighted that even with glasses he was almost legally blind. If Maury can hit a target, how come all you can hit are the trees?" A sudden light flashed in his eyes.

"I prefer judo."

"Ingrid, did it ever occur to you, you might be near-sighted?"

"Baloney."

"We're going to the ophthalmologist."

"There's nothing wrong with my vision. You're just compensating for your lousy teaching skills."

Ingrid had an astigmatism.

"My goodness," she exclaimed. "I never knew."

Alderway rolled his eyes.

"How could you not know?" The ophthalmologist demanded.

"I just thought the world looked like an impressionist painting. Put those lenses on me again."

"All those years you've been walking around blind as a bat," the ophthalmologist mused.

"Well not that bad," Ingrid said.

He removed the lenses. "Young lady, how did you ever get a driver's license?"

"Maybe it wasn't always this bad?" She asked.

"This explains a lot," Alderway said.

"Like what?" She demanded.

"Some of your more terrifying vehicular maneuvers and why you never seem to recognize me from a distance."

"You're lucky she recognizes you standing next to her," the ophthalmologist said. "It's a miracle she recognizes herself in the bathroom mirror in the morning."

After that Ingrid was a much better shot.

As he sat in the Buick that brilliantly clear autumn afternoon and listened to her type, she seemed poised in a flood of golden light, like some rare bird in a purling pool at dawn. She did not look up. She was so absorbed in her work, doubtless demolishing the deconstructive techniques of Jacques Derrida, that she had not heard the car, nor noticed the way Rover raised his auburn head, shining red like flame in that same light, gazing expectantly with dark, eager, glistening eyes at Alderway, who could not stop gazing at the woman motionless in the vitreous light, thinking how he had noticed some silver hairs in her part that morning and projecting forward to a future in which they were both gray, both had lines in their faces, lines that testified to the life they had lived together, to their love and to the incontrovertible fact that there was no one else who walked the earth for either one of them, not a soul who mattered as much as they did to each other and to his worry and relief that she could shoot now, that she could destroy his enemies if she had to, because they might come and then, at that possibility, all his muscles clenched and he remembered those men in the courtroom and his promise to himself to blast them between the eyes if they ever harmed or attempted to harm the woman he loved. Twice a week, it was only twice, her days off, he rode up here after work with a slight clutch of apprehension in his throat, a feeling that settled over him when he left her on those mornings, only relieved when he phoned her to chat at lunch and then again, right before he left to come home. But always, on the way back through the woods, he began to imagine the worst, always he approached the lovely old farmhouse with the apprehension of her blood and death, and always he sat and watched her type, thanking God or fate, he was not sure which, perhaps in the absence of either it was just dumb luck, for sparing her from the cruelty of his demons.

She glanced up and waved when she heard the car door slam.

"It needs a wash," she called.

"What?"

"Your Buick. You park under that elm, so it's covered with bird shit."

"They'd find it wherever I parked," he approached and scratched the back of the dog's head. "They regard it as their personal latrine. And if I did get it washed, every bird on this hill would send out the alarm: 'Time to crap on the car! Time to crap on the car! Quick, he just got it cleaned! Let's go crap on the car!'"

"Nonsense. I'll wash it."

"Oh, this I'd like to see. Miss Lazybones is actually going to bestir herself and do something physical."

"We made love this morning. That was physical."

"That doesn't count. Besides I did all the work."

She threw a cushion at him.

"I am going to wash it, you'll see."

"When?" He asked, looking at his watch, "because if it's any time before the millennium, I'd like to know."

"Soon."

"But what I really don't understand is why they don't crap on your VW." And he turned to regard Ingrid's Bug, sparkling red and immaculate. "Hey, it's not where it was this morning. Did you go out?"

"Yes, mister police detective."

"I can't help it. I noticed it was moved."

"I went to the office briefly, found out some very startling news and then returned."

"What?" He demanded apprehensively, sitting in a wicker chair across from her.

"For the past two months, since the beginning of fall semester, the African studies department has had a visiting lecturer—"

"Oh," he yawned, relieved that no member of a mafia family had accosted her on campus and delivered a death threat.

"Someone you know very well, who's living with her husband and his best friend, who you also know very well, in Amherst." She paused to stack her papers neatly, then resumed: "And they're leaving in two weeks, emigrating to Ghana, in fact. So if you want to say hello, you better hurry up."

"Ghana? I don't know anyone going to Ghana."

"What about Tiwana and Jeremiah Allenhurst?"

Alderway sat up straight. "Uh, somehow I don't think they'd want to see me."

"Oh, they'd love to. They say bygones are bygones."

"And they've got Olushola in tow."

"As always."

"The last thing he said to me, personally, before the trials, was that I was one sick white motherfucker. We were in an ambulance. I had shot him. He had shot me."

"Water under the bridge."

"I don't think he wants to see me, Ingrid."

"He thinks it would be peachy."

"He said that."

"Not exactly," she qualified.

"Oh. You didn't talk to him. Tiwana said that."

"Yes. But honestly—so you shot him. These things happen. People move on."

"And he shot me."

"Like I said, move one."

"I have no intention of moving on. He shot me."

"They're really completely different."

"Did they have personality transplants? Because that's what it would take for me to be civil to them."

"Why? What did Tiwana ever do to you?"

"She was an uncooperative witness."

"That was the prosecution's problem, not yours."

"It was a headache, a many months-long headache. You would think she would have been grateful we were trying to put away some racist, very armed and very dangerous Italian and Irish criminals."

"She was looking at jail time."

"Which she whittled down to time off for good behavior, by driving us crazy."

"She drove a good bargain. You can't fault her for that."

"Always looking out for herself."

"Who else should she be looking out for?" Ingrid snapped.

"Her husband, for one, because he received multiple death threats from these creeps, who, had they walked, would have been sure to carry them out."

"I always wondered why they targeted Jeremiah and not Tiwana."

"The code of honor."

"What code of honor."

"She's a woman."

"What? Those revolting sexists."

"You would have preferred she take a bullet to the back of the head?"

"She was just as dangerous as Olushola or Jeremiah."

"I always said so. That's why I pushed for twenty-five to life."

"I don't know why she wants to see you. She must be a masochist."

Alderway rolled his eyes. "Not that sharp cookie," he said. "She's after something, something she needs the Massachusetts state police for."

"Oh nonsense. She just wants to say good-bye."

"I said good-bye. I told her she should be going to prison, not walking, and that if it was ever in my power, if I ever had the opportunity again, I would put her behind bars for as long as possible."

"Well, how could she be satisfied with such a charming adieu?"

"So she's gone from buying machine guns from mobsters to teaching in the state university system. There must be a violation in that somewhere. I'll have to look into it."

"Don't you dare. They leave for Ghana in two weeks."

"Lucky Ghana. Well, you tell them good-bye and don't write. I'm sure I'll read about them in the newspapers, when they pull off a coup d'état and install a radical left-wing government."

"I think they have peaceful intentions."

"That'll be the day."

"Olushola said he just didn't like living around so many white people anymore."

"You talked to him? Does he know you're my wife?"

"I think he was fuzzy on that."

"If I were you, I'd leave things that way."

Two days later Alderway stopped by campus to drop off his wife's lunch, which she had, not for the first time, forgotten. He immediately bumped into Professor Pitter.

"Lieutenant Alderway! What a pleasant surprise. I was just thinking of you."

"Not in connection with a parking ticket, I hope."

"As a matter of fact, yes. You see I somehow pulled into a no standing zone, and raced into a building, Oh just for a second—"

"How long a second?" Alderway growled.

"Well, maybe a minute."

Alderway raised an eyebrow.

"Perhaps I was in there for a half an hour. But it was very important. I had to pick up the latest volume of Derrida,"

"Oh, the quack."

"What quack?"

"Nothing."

"It's funny you should say quack, because there's a letter in *The Boston Globe* book review section signed by someone with a very unusual name that makes exactly that allegation. Do you think the name could be an alias?"

Alderway grunted.

"I mean, I could understand why someone would want to conceal his identity—making such shocking allegations. Why, if it was an academic, it could ruin his career."

"Or hers."

"Yes of course, I shouldn't assume that only a man would go out on a limb like that."

"Well, see you. Don't go out on any limbs."

"Oh, I'd never do that. But what about my parking ticket?"

"Regard it as a sacrifice, in the course of your service to society."

"What service?"

"Good question. I know—fetching the volume of Derrida to cram the brains of young students with his incomprehensible semiotics."

"I hadn't looked on that as a service to society. How novel."

"Think how many English majors you'll be dispatching straight into law school, where they can corrupt the world so much more effectively than had they gone for their PhDs in literature."

"I'm afraid you've lost me."

"Good. Ta, ta."

"But the ticket."

"My advice would be to pay it."

"Not contest it?"

"No. When you ask the judge to fix it for you, he's liable to take that the wrong way. On second thought, yes, contest it. Gotta run."

"Thanks for the advice, lieutenant."

Alderway saluted him and hurried away. He opened the door to his wife's office to see Olushola, sitting in her desk chair. "Shit," Olushola said. "Today is not my day."

"What have you done with my wife?"

"Someone was psycho enough to *marry* you?"

"Listen you little creep—"

"I knew I should have stayed in bed."

"If you've harmed a hair on Ingrid's head, so much as a hair—"

"Ingrid? She always seems so rational. But evidently she married you. Clearly there's a screw loose somewhere," then he looked up at the irate husband, jaw clenched, fists clenched, eyes blazing, "make that all the screws loose."

Alderway lunged, throwing Olushola up against an over-filled bookcase. Tomes tumbled to the floor. "How'd you get out of prison?"

"I am a private citizen. I have served my time and paid my debt to this sick, racist society. Now I suggest you unhand me before I call the police."

"That would be me."

"Are you going to shoot me again?"

"I'm considering it. What have you done with Ingrid?"

"I believe she went to the ladies room."

"Nothing like a happy reunion," that woman said, stepping lightly into her office. Her husband released her guest.

"You married him?" Her visitor was incredulous. "What were you thinking?"

"Hey, she didn't consult you, all right?" Alderway demanded.

"You can be damn sure she didn't consult me. Had she done so, she would not be wearing that ring right now. I've got the scars from a bullet wound, a bullet that came from your gun, to testify to the fact that that man," he pointed at Alderway, "is an unhinged, dangerous, trigger-happy pothead, given to shooting the prosecution's star witness."

"Yeah, well, that star witness would have been a fugitive in Ghana if I hadn't shot him."

"He's not going to follow you," Ingrid placated.

"I don't want him in my business. I don't want him knowing where I live or who I associate with—"

"I wonder why," Alderway said.

"Look, I am done with all that revolution stuff. I'm retiring to a nice, fairly prosperous African country, where no psychopathic white policemen can follow me around, set me up, shoot me and generally try to drive me insane."

"It wasn't policemen who were your problem, buddy."

"I am *not* your buddy. Let's get that straight."

"It was the mob."

"Yes, and now, thanks to you, I am a marked man."

"Well you have my word I won't inform the mafia you've moved to Ghana. But frankly, if they didn't kill you in prison, you're probably safe."

"Thanks for the reassurance, but I got out five years ago, and I been in hiding ever since. I can't take it anymore."

"You should have gone into witness protection, like they offered you."

"Yeah, and start life over in a studio apartment in Watts—because that's what they offer black people, Alderway. It's no spacious ranch in Idaho like you get if you're white."

"The program has its inequities."

"Like every other program run by this—"

"This?"

"I was going to says something intemperate. I am holding my tongue."

"Keep holding it."

"And I thought the five of us might go out for dinner," Ingrid sighed.

Alderway rolled his eyes.

"Even if he keeps his hands visible at all times," Olushola said, "so I'm sure he won't shoot me again, there is no way I ever break bread with that, that…person."

"And there's no way I'd break bread with anyone who'd break bread with you."

"Aren't we adult?" Ingrid asked. "Let's just try not to have another brawl," and she bent over to pick up the books that had fallen to the floor. Neither man moved to help her. "I'm so glad you two clean up behind yourselves and wouldn't dream of making some luckless woman do it for you."

"His hands," Olushola said. "I have to be able to see his hands at all times."

"Oh shut up," Alderway said, but still did not move to pick up a book. "You shot me too."

"I cannot wait to get to Ghana."

"I cannot wait for you to go."

"Oh goody. You two agree on something. Can you close your mouths now and help me clean up this mess?"

"Ahem," Alderway said, and looking the visitor in the eye, gestured at the books.

"You first," Olushola replied.

Keeping his eyes fixed on his adversary, the policeman began restoring the books to the shelf. After a moment, Olushola helped as well.

"Just like two grownups," Ingrid muttered.

"Don't thank me for your lunch," her husband said, pointing to the brown paper bag he had deposited on her desk.

"I'm hungry," Olushola said.

"Yeah, well, it's not for you."

"Ham and cheese, how nice," Ingrid commented.

"I ran into Pitter."

"Pitter?" Olushola asked.

"Mind your own business."

"It's just an odd name. Make's you think of pitter patter."

"He's not even a man, he's a rabbit," Alderway continued, opening his wife's can of Coca Cola and sipping it. "A rabbit who can't park."

"More tickets?" Ingrid asked.

Her husband nodded. "I told him to contest them. Hopefully he'll offend the judge and get thrown in jail."

"Remind me not to come to you for legal advice," Olushola remarked.

"Now there's a thought," Alderway paused, a copy of Boccaccio's *Decameron* in one hand. "Maybe I could trick you into a parole violation."

"Parole? What parole? You're looking at a free man, Alderway."

"And woman," came a voice in the doorway. Alderway turned to see the rather short form, the straight dark hair, dark glasses and flamboyant magenta blouse and purple slacks of Tiwana Allenhurst, holding a plastic cup and straw.

"Geeze. Today's my lucky day," he breathed.

"Oh, it's not so bad, lieutenant. Ingrid tells me you're a lieutenant now. I have no hard feelings toward you, even though you went out of your way to try to get me locked up for twenty-five years. And even if I did, I'm leaving for lovely Ghana in two weeks, and we will never have to look at each other's miserable faces again." She sipped on her straw.

"What's that?" Olushola demanded, pointing at the cup.

"None of your business," she replied.

"I'm thirsty."

"It's wheat grass juice. Get your own."

"I hate wheat grass. Why couldn't you get a soda, like a normal person?"

"Because I don't want to share with you."

"Well, I'm glad to see nothing has changed between you two," Alderway remarked. "Because if it had, it might rock my conception of the universe."

"Your conception of the universe is a narrow, pig-headed, violent—"

"Look who's talking."

"Good guy, bad guy, primitive view that I won't even dignify with the term conception," Tiwana concluded and then, to Olushola, "and no, I cannot give you change for the soda machine downstairs."

"I knew I should have stayed in bed this morning."

"Why?" She demanded, "So you can set the world's record for lazing around the house, mooching off your friends and generally taking advantage of the good will, kindness and generosity of man who has ten times the intellect, ten times the breadth of spirit and ten times the courage of anyone in this room."

"Oh, and who's that?" Alderway demanded.

"My husband, Jeremiah."

"Oh, please," Olushola caviled. "He makes me reimburse him for my share of the newspaper he buys in the morning. He's a cheapskate, a tight-wad and a teetotaler."

"I heard that, Shola," came a deep voice behind Tiwana.

"I don't care if you heard it. What do I have to reimburse you seventeen cents for every morning over breakfast? It's petty, man. After I took the fall for you."

"Took the fall?" Jeremiah demanded. "I was across the country, in Chicago, wounded, you may recall, and healing from those wounds."

"I am not getting into this," Shola said.

"You sure better not," Tiwana replied, "'cause you would lose."

"I can just see that airplane ride to Ghana right now," Alderway said. "The pilot may crash it in the ocean, just to shut you three up."

"Well at least you won't be on it. That's something to be thankful for," Tiwana replied. "Ingrid, how did you marry him?"

"She fell madly in love with me."

"She sure must've been mad. I'm sure she couldn't do it sane. You should come with us to Ghana, Ingrid. It would be a lot safer. This man you married is hated, loathed, detested, despised by the entire Boston underworld. There are more thugs than you can count—"

"Thirteen, to be exact," Alderway said. "Let's not exaggerate."

"Waiting to get out of the joint and just plug this man between the eyes. They are seething with fury and fantasies of revenge—"

"You don't know that."

"Yes I do, because they came after Jeremiah and then they came after me. And on their list, compared to you, I'm small potatoes."

"I keep tabs on them," Alderway said.

"What are you going to do? Hunt them down as they get paroled?"

"Maybe. It depends how they behave."

"How they behave?" Tiwana laughed. "And if they act up, what are you going to do—send them to the principal's office?"

"Maybe I'll plug them between the eyes."

"I told you he was crazy," Olushola said. "I wish we were leaving today. I don't like it. I am sick and tired of being surrounded and hounded by sociopathic white people. I want to go to Africa."

"Maybe I've got me a machine gun," Alderway continued, "and I'm just waiting for one of those jerks to try something."

"Today," Olushola repeated. "What do we have to wait two weeks for?"

"You really are nuts," Tiwana said to Alderway.

"Yeah, and they know it," Jeremiah put in, stroking his goatee thoughtfully. "They may not come for him after all. They may be idiots, but they're pretty good at assessing risks. They probably figured we were easy marks, that it was unlikely we'd have any AK-47s under our pillows. But Alderway here—they've got to assume he's armed to the teeth. And they know he's homicidal."

"Change that goddamned plane ticket," Olushola cried. "Change it today!"

"Oh, stop your whining," Jeremiah snapped.

"Excuse me, am I interrupting something?" It was Professor Pitter, parking ticket in hand. "I found it, lieutenant."

"Great," Alderway rolled his eyes again.

"Perhaps I can leave it with you?"

"If then you'll leave, yes."

"Oh, so sorry to interrupt," and the semiotician tip-toed away.

Ingrid gave Tiwana a hug. "I'll miss you, even if my husband won't."

"We still have two weeks. Let's have lunch."

"Are you nuts?" Alderway demanded, after the trio had departed. "You heard Jeremiah—they came for them."

"Who came for whom?" His wife asked vaguely.

"Those killers they helped me put away. Spending time with the Allenhursts could be dangerous."

"If I worried about that, would I ever have married you?"

Two weeks later, after this trio had departed for Ghana, Alderway steered his Buick up the back road at dusk. He parked as always at the end of the drive, and as he gazed at Ingrid in profile, typing on the porch, the night creeping toward her from the woods beyond and shadow already enveloping him in the car, a sudden, faint glimmer of hope sparked within him. "The world is dark," he said aloud, "but I have a light." He stepped out of the car and walked up toward the porch and the regular tap tap of the typewriter. "It is you," he said to Ingrid.

He stood with his thumb out in the blistering heat for over an hour, before a trucker took pity on him. At first he did not think the tractor-trailer would stop, but then he heard the brakes and the crunch of gravel as it pulled onto the shoulder. He ran and climbed up into the cab, with profuse thanks.

"A man could roast out there," said the driver, a medium height, medium build fellow with red hair and alert blue eyes. "And you look about half cooked. Here, I bought this soda a while back and didn't open it. You like ginger ale? Go on, you can have it."

"Thanks," he said, guzzling.

"This stretch of road is mighty impressive. I notice they keep the highways out here in the west in good shape. Not like Maryland, where I'm from. Holy cow, what a disaster the roads are there, and the street lights—don't get me started. Texas, now there's a state knows how to deal with lights, paving, entrance and exit ramps, signage, you name it. I'd never want to live there, just too conservative for me, but I got to hand it to them, they got highway transportation down pat. Our geniuses in the DOT in Maryland could learn a lot from them. Ever been to Maryland?"

"Never, nor D.C."

"Pothole capital of the nation, not D.C., Maryland." The driver fell silent for a moment, then began whistling.

"You been driving this rig a long time?"

The red-haired man nodded. "I'm a trucker and a teamster from way back. It's a great union. Got a terrible press, though. Half the country, when they hear the word teamster, they think of Jimmy Hoffa and the mob. What they never hear about are the decent wages, the health benefits and the retirement. I wouldn't do this job if I wasn't a teamster. I'd go back to the mines and, Sheesh, that's sayin' something, 'cause those West Virginia mines are so dangerous—well, don't get me started. They got some union, though. And they'll need it, with this President Reagan union busting and firing workers at the drop of a hat. That business with the air-traffic controllers—I may never get over it." The man rambled on for forty minutes, obviously delighted to have an audience. Then he pulled out an enormous bag of pretzels, saying, "Go on, have some. I'm happy to share. I got pretzels coming out of my ears."

They traversed pine covered mountains and lush valleys and saw little traffic. Huge piles of purple clouds drifted across the sky, the sun blazed down, and the man informed him sorrowfully that he would not be heading down into Utah, so they stopped at a gas station, and he gathered his things.

"It's been great talking to you," the driver said, holding out his hand. "My name's Jones, Clarence Jones." They shook hands.

"Snow. Snow Lichter."

"Where ya headed, Snow?"

"I'm not really sure. The West Coast, San Francisco. I was there once. I really liked it. I've heard San Diego's nice too."

"Oh San Diego's great. I told my wife Jessie, if we ever get our hands on some money, we'll relocate there. La Jolla is fantastic, the beach, the city, nothing like it on the East Coast, except maybe parts of Florida. But Florida's not for me—too many hurricanes."

"You prefer earthquakes."

"Point well taken, Snow. Hey, if you don't mind my asking, how'd you come by that name?"

"My mother was a hippie who loved the snow, and I was born in a snowstorm. As for the Lichter—her father's family emigrated from Odessa, but before that they lived in Germany, around Berlin."

"That's some sojourn. You mother can't be too happy with you hitch-hiking all over the country out in the wilds of Wyoming on your own."

"No, I suppose she's not."

"I mean, you don't look older than seventeen."

"Got it right exactly."

"She's probably worried sick."

"I hope not. I'm not doing this to worry anybody. In fact, I don't want anyone even to think about me. I just want to vanish."

Clarence looked at him gravely.

"That's not the way it sounds," the young man hastened to explain. "I've got to do what I've got to do. I want to see the world. I just don't want it to bother or be a burden to anyone."

"What about…your father?" The trucker asked diffidently and tentatively.

"The man who raised me—"

"Oh, your father didn't."

"No, as far as I know, he was not a great guy."

"That's not your fault."

"I know, but it's kind of a curse. My mother said he lived his life like he was under some kind of shadow. Sometimes I think that shadow looms over me, too."

"But the man who raised you—"

"He's terrific. But I have to see the world, and I sure am not going to do that living in a cabin in Tower Oaks Bend, Wyoming."

"I guess you didn't want to go to college."

"I don't have the grades, and it's not for me. Look, it was a triumph I graduated high school."

"I know what that's like," Clarence laughed, then paused and gazed out the windshield for a moment. He turned to Snow as if he were about to go on, then thought better of it and merely sadly said: "Well, good luck, Snow."

He hoisted his pack onto his back and, observing that it was late, tramped off into the woods. Soon he had his tent up, a fire going to heat his can of beans and enough pretzels, courtesy of Clarence, to keep hunger away for days. Now that the effort of conversing with another human being had subsided, his mind sank into a daze. He had no plan and no idea how to get one. "Maybe after I sleep, something will come to me," he said aloud, noting with relief that neither the trees nor the rocks nor the vines had any reply to make to that.

When he woke, he remembered that two days ago he had had the forethought to empty his bank account. So he broke camp, walked back to the gas station, got directions to a diner down the road and hitched a ride there. He ate scrambled eggs, bacon and toast and downed a cup of coffee and orange juice. Somehow, he struck up a conversation with a truck driver who had to get to Salt Lake City quickly. He was happy to take the boy along.

He did not care for Salt Lake City and got out of it as fast as he got into it, by means of a ride from what he realized was a real, bona fide lady of the night, all the way to Las Vegas.

"Take my advice, Snow," she said, letting him off on the strip, "don't stick around here. It's not for you."

A week later, early November now, he was in San Francisco, grimy, unwashed, unshaven, still in a daze. After a night in a men's shelter in the mission district, he found himself downtown, near Union Square at twilight, contemplating a nap on a park bench in the gathering gloom. But there were too many bums, and besides, he had read an article about wildlife in British Columbia and about the beauties of Vancouver. He would go there. He asked directions to the bus station and exited the park in the dimness, nearing a snoring derelict on the corner. It was Ronald Swurl, who had spread a newspaper over his chest, the plainly visible headline blaring "CEO Swurl Ousted Amid Death Squad Allegations." The blondish man lying under that headline looked, Snow thought, strangely happy, blessed even, and seemed to be smiling, as though in his inner world he was free of evil and did not fear the shadow of death. He stepped over the prone vagrant, who did not even notice, then traversed the deep shade, from which now, at last and so fortunately and unexpectedly, ideas seemed to be coming to him, and finally walked out into the crosswalk. Amid the roar of traffic, the distant honking of car horns and the slow subsiding of the evening rush, his thoughts began to coalesce. He would go north. He would try Vancouver— at the next corner he stopped and, looking back, again gazed through the shadows at the man asleep under the newspapers, who seemed suddenly to him to be the burdened, uncomplaining form of a certain portion of humanity broken by circumstances and perhaps something else, yes north, into Canada, perhaps his destiny lay there.

About the Author

Eve Ottenberg has published eight other novels and a collection of short stories. Her criticism, journalism and short fiction have appeared in many newspapers, magazines and literary journals, including *The New York Times Book Review*, *The New York Times Magazine*, *Vanity Fair*, *The New Yorker* In Brief section, *The Washington Post*, *The Philadelphia Inquirer*, *The Baltimore Sun*, *In These Times*, *The Washington City Paper*, *The Nation* and *USA Today*, and she has written a political column for *The Village Voice*.

Other books by Eve Ottenberg, from most recent to oldest:

Dark Is the Night

The Walkout

What They Didn't Know, Stories and Essays

Suburbia

Reluctant Reaper

Dead in Iraq

The Unblemished Darlings

Glum and Mighty Pagans

The Widow's Opera